Slave Girl of Gor

Gorean Saga

Slave Girl of Gor

John Norman

OPEN ROAD

INTEGRATED MEDIA

NEW YORK

Copyright © 1977 by John Norman

978-1-4976-4867-8

This edition published in 2014 by Open Road Integrated Media, Inc.
345 Hudson Street
New York, NY 10014
www.openroadmedia.com

Slave Girl of Gor

One

The Collar

I lay in the warm grass. I could feel it, the warm, individual green blades, separate, gentle, on my left cheek; I could feel them on my body, my stomach and thighs. I stretched my body, my toes. I was sleepy. I did not wish to awaken. The sun was warm on my back, even hot, almost uncomfortable. I snuggled deeper into the grass. My left hand was extended. My fingers touched the warm dirt between the grass blades. My eyes were closed. I resisted the coming of consciousness. I did not wish to emerge from bed. Consciousness seemed to come slowly, dimly. I did not wish to emerge from bed. I wished to prolong the warmth, the pleasantness. I moved my head, slightly. My neck seemed to wear a weight; I heard the soft clink, a tiny stirring, of heavy links of metal.

I did not understand this.

I moved my head again, sleepily, eyes closed, to its original position. Again I felt the weight, circular, heavy, on my neck; again I heard the small sound, the stirring, simple and matter of fact, of heavy metal links.

I opened my eyes, part way, keeping them half shut against the light. I saw the grass, green and close, each blade seeming wide, blurred in its nearness. My fingers dug into the warm earth. I closed my eyes. I began to sweat. I must emerge from bed. I must snatch breakfast, hurry to class. It must be late. I must hurry.

I remembered the cloth slipped over my mouth and nose, the fumes, the strength of the man who had held me. I had squirmed, but had been held in his grip, helpless. I was terrified. I had tried not to breathe. I had struggled, but futilely. I was terrified. I had not known a man could be so strong. He was patient, unhurried, waiting for me

3

to breathe. I tried not to breathe. Then, lungs gasping, helpless, had at last inhaled, deeply, desperately, taking the sharp, strangling fumes deep into my body. In an instant, choking in the horrid, obdurate fumes, unable to expel them, unable to evade them, sickened, I had lost consciousness.

I lay in the warm grass. I could feel it on my body. I must emerge from bed. I must snatch breakfast, and hurry to class. Surely it must be late. I must hurry.

I opened my eyes, seeing the grass blades not inches from my face, wide, blurred. I opened my mouth, delicately, and felt the grass brush my lips. I bit into a blade and felt the juice of the grass, on my tongue.

I closed my eyes. I must awaken. I remembered the cloth, the strength of the man, the fumes.

My fingers dug deeply into the dirt. I clawed at it. I felt the dirt beneath my fingernails. I lifted my head, and rolled screaming, awakening, tangled in the chain, in the grass. I sat bolt upright. I realized to my astonishment and horror that I was nude, literally, totally nude, stark naked. My neck wore its encircling weight; the heavy chain, attached to the collar, dropped between my breasts and over my left thigh.

"No! No!" I cried. "No!"

I leaped to my feet screaming. The chain's weight depended from the collar, heavily, gracefully. I felt the collar pulled down, against my collarbone. The chain passed now between my legs, behind the left calf, then lifting. I jerked wildly at it. I tried to thrust the collar up, over my head. I turned it, again tried to thrust it up, over my head. I scraped my throat, hurting it. My chin was forced up; I saw the bright sky, blue with its startlingly white clouds. But I could not slip the collar. It fitted me closely. Only my small finger could I thrust between its weight and my neck. I moaned. The collar could not be slipped. It had not been made to be slipped. Irrationally, madly, nothing in my consciousness but my fear and the chain, I turned to flee, and fell, hurting my legs, tangled in the chain. I, on my knees, seized the chain, pulled at it, weeping. I tried to back away, on my knees; my head was pulled cruelly forward. I held the chain. It was some ten feet long. It extended to a heavy ring and plate fastened in a great granite rock, irregular, but some twelve feet in width and depth, some ten feet in height. The plate, with its ring, was attached near the center of the rock, low, about a foot above the grass. The rock had apparently been drilled and the plate fastened with four linear bolts. They may have passed through the entire width of the rock and been clinched on the other side. I did not know. On my knees I pulled at the chain. I wept. I cried out. I pulled again at the chain. I hurt my hands; it moved not a quarter of an inch. I was fastened to the rock.

I rose moaning to my feet, my hands on the chain. I looked about myself. The rock was prominent. There was none like it in view. I stood on a rolling plain, grassy and gentle, widely sweeping, trackless. I saw nothing but the grass, it moving in the soft, unhurried wind, the distant horizon, the unusually white clouds and blue sky. I was alone. The sun was warm. Behind me was the rock. I felt the wind on my body, but not directly, as the plate in the stone was on the sheltered side of the rock. I wondered if the wind was a prevailing one. I wondered if the plate and chain were so situated in order that the chain's prisoner, such as I found myself to be, be protected from the wind. I shuddered.

I stood alone. I was naked. I, small, white, was chained by the neck to that great rock on the seemingly endless plain.

I breathed deeply. Never in my life had I breathed such air. Though my head was chained I threw it back. I closed my eyes. I drank the atmosphere into my lungs. Those who have never breathed such air cannot know the sensations which I then felt. In so simple a thing as the air I breathed I rejoiced. It was clean and clear; it was fresh, almost alive, almost sparkling with the exhilaration of swift, abundant, pristine oxygen. It was like the air of a new world, one yet innocent of the toxins of man's majority, the unquestioned gifts, ambiguous, poisoned, of civilization and technology. My body became vital and alive. So simply did a proper oxygenation of my system work its almost immediate effect in my feeling and awareness. Those who have never breathed the air of a clean world cannot understand my words. And perhaps those who have breathed only such an atmosphere may, too, tragically, fail to comprehend. Until one has breathed such air can one know the glory of being alive?

But I was lonely, and frightened.

It was a strange world on which I stood, wide and unfamiliar, open, bright and clean. I looked out upon the vast fields of grass. I had never smelled grass before. It was so fresh, so beautiful. My senses were alive. In this atmosphere, my blood charged with oxygen, I found that I could detect odors which had eluded me before; it was as though an entire new dimension of experience had suddenly opened to me; yet I suppose it was only that here, in this place, my body did not have reason to fight its world, shutting it out, forcing it from consciousness in order not to be distracted or sickened; here there was an atmosphere which was unsoiled, undefiled, one in which the human could be a part of nature, not a rampart raised against her, not a defensive sojourner treading at night, stepping softly, scarcely daring to breathe, through the country of enemies. My vision, too, in this pure air, was keener. I could see farther and with greater detail than had been possible before in the clouded, contaminated atmosphere in which I had been raised. How far away now seemed the familiar pollutions of the gray world I remembered. On certain days there I had thought the air clean, and had delighted in its freshness. How little I had known. How foolish I had been. It had been only less murky, less dismal, only a sign of what a world might be. My hearing, too, seemed acute. The wind brushed the grass, moving in it, stirring the gleaming leaves. Colors, too, seemed richer, deeper, more vivid. The grass was richly green, alive, vast; the sky was blue, deeply blue, far deeper than I had known a sky could be; the clouds were sharp and white, protean and billowing, transforming themselves in the pressures of their heights and the winds which sped them; they moved at different heights at different speeds; they were like great white birds, stately and majestic, turning, floating in the rivers of wind. I felt the breezes of the field on my exposed body; I trembled; every bit of me seemed alive.

I was frightened.

I looked at the sun. I looked away, down, then across the fields.

I was aware now, as I had not been before, or so clearly, of the difference in the feel of my body and its movements. There seemed a subtle difference in my body weight, my movements. I thrust this comprehension from my mind. I could not admit it. I literally forced it from consciousness. But it returned, persistent. It could not be denied. "No!" I cried. But I knew it was true. I tried to thrust from my mind what must be, what had to be, the explanation of this unusual phenomenon. "No!" I cried. "It cannot be! No! No!"

Numbly I lifted the chain which hung from the collar fastened on my neck. I looked at it, disbelievingly. The links were close-set, heavy, of some primitive, simple black iron. It did not seem an attractive chain, or an expensive one. But I was held by it. I felt the collar with my fingers. I could not see it, but it seemed formed, too, of heavy iron; it seemed simple, practical, not ostentatious; it gripped my throat rather closely; I supposed it was black in color, matching the chain; it had a heavy hinge on one side; the chain, by a link, opened and closed, was fastened to a loop; the loop was fastened about a staple, which, it seemed, was a part of the collar itself; the hinge was under my right ear; the chain hung from its loop and staple under my chin; on the left, under my left ear, as I could tell by feeling it with my finger, there was a large lock, with its opening for the insertion of a heavy key. The collar, then, fastened with a lock; it had not been hammered about my neck. I wondered who held the key to that collar.

I turned about and looked at the great rock, the granite, streaked with feldspar.

I must try to awaken, I told myself. I must awaken. I laughed bitterly. I must be dreaming I told myself.

Again the difference in the feeling of my body, its weight, its movements, intruded itself into my consciousness. "No!" I cried. Then I went to the granite, and looked at the heavy plate and ring bolted into the stone. A link of my chain had been opened, and then closed, about that ring. The chain was some ten feet in length. I idly coiled it at the foot of the ring. "No!" I cried. I must awaken, I told myself. Surely it must be nearly time to arouse myself, to hurry to breakfast, to hurry to class. There is no other explanation, I told myself. I am dreaming. Then I feared I might be insane. No, I told myself. I am dreaming. It is such a strange dream, so real. But it is a dream. It must be. It must be. It is a dream. All a dream!

Then to my misery I remembered the man, being seized from behind, not able even to see him, my struggles, being held so helplessly, the cloth over my mouth and nose, his waiting for me to breathe, at last my gasping helplessly for breath, the terrible fumes, nothing else to breathe, nothing else, which could not be tolerated by consciousness, nothing else to breathe, and then my loss of consciousness. That, I knew, had been no dream.

I struck my fists until they bled on the granite rock streaked with feldspar.

Then I turned and walked from the rock, some five feet, and looked out over the vast grassy fields.

"Oh, no," I wept.

The full consciousness of my waking state, and my awareness of truth, welled up within me. It flooded my consciousness, overwhelmingly, irrefutably.

I knew then what must be the explanation for the difference in the feelings in my body, the explanation for the sense of subtle kinesthetic differences in my movements. I stood not on Earth. The gravity was not that of Earth. It was on another world I stood, an unknown world. It was a bright, beautiful world, but it was not Earth. It was not the world I knew. It was not my home. I had been brought here; no one had consulted my will; I had been brought here; my will had been nothing.

I stood alone there, naked, defenseless, before the great rock, looking over the fields.

I was lonely, and frightened, and I wore a chain on my neck.

Suddenly I cried out with misery and put my face in my hands. Then it seemed the earth spun beneath me and darkness swept about me, rushing in upon me and I lost consciousness.

Two

The Retinue

I felt myself being rolled roughly on my back. "Veck, Kajira," said a voice, harshly. "Veck, Kajira." It was not a patient voice. I looked up, startled, frightened. I cried out with pain. A metal point jabbed into my body, at the juncture between my left hip and lower abdomen. The point lifted, and the shaft of the spear turned; he struck me on the right thigh, hard, with the butt of the spear. My hand went before my mouth; his foot, in a high, strapped sandal, heavy, almost an open boot, kicked my hand away. He was bearded. I lay between his legs. I looked up at him in terror.

He was not alone. There was another man a bit behind him. Both wore tunics, red; each, at his left hip, had slung a blade and scabbard; each, at his belt, carried an ornamented knife; the man behind him who stood over me had slung over his back a shield, of layers of leather and brass, and carried a spear, beneath the blade of which was slung a helmet with a plume of dark, swirling hair; he wore a cord of teeth, from some carnivore, about his neck. The man who stood over me had put his helmet and shield to one side; the helmets of both would cover the entire head and most of the face; the helmets were cut and opened in such a way as to suggest a "Y." The hair of both men was long; the hair of the man behind was tied back with a narrow piece of folded cloth.

I slipped from between the feet of the man who loomed above me, moving back. I had never seen such men. I felt so vulnerable. They were mighty, and like animals. I crouched, backing away. The chain hung from my collar, heavy. I stopped. I turned, and tried to hide myself, as I could, with my hands. I dared not even speak.

One of the men barked a command at me. He moved his hand,

angrily. I removed my hands from my body. I turned, still crouching. I understood that they would look upon me.

How dared they!

I was angry!

But I dared not cover myself. It was not permitted.

Then I was afraid, not angry, but afraid, very afraid.

Could I, here, in this place, I wondered, be such that men might so look upon me?

I gathered that I might indeed, here, in this place, be such that I might be so looked upon.

The bearded man approached me. I dared not meet his eyes. I could not understand such men. My world had not prepared me to believe that such men could exist. He stood closer to me than would have a man of my world. Each in my world, it seemed, carried about with him a bubble of space, a perimeter, a wall, an invisible shield, an unconsciously acculturated, socially sanctioned remoteness, a barrier decreed by convention and conditioning. Behind this invisible wall, within this personal, privately owned space, we lived. It separated us from others; it kept us persons. In my particular Earth culture, this circle of inviolate, privately owned space had a radius of some two to three feet. Closer than this we did not, commonly, in my culture, approach one another. But this man stood close to me. He stood within my space. Suddenly I realized that my space did not exist on this world. I began to tremble with terror. So small a thing it seems, perhaps, that this convention should on this world not be acknowledged or respected, indeed, that, at least in my case, it did not exist, but it is not, truly, a small thing; no, to me the crumbling of this artifice, this protective device, this convention, was catastrophic; it is difficult to convey my sense of loss, of helplessness; on this world my space did not exist.

I saw the black leather strap, wide, shiny, across his body, from which depended the blade slung at his left hip. Behind it I saw the coarsely woven, thick red fibers at his tunic. I knew that were he to seize me in his arms and crush me to his chest, with what strength must be his, that the mark of the strap, the coarse fibers, would be imprinted on my breasts.

I felt the point of his dagger beneath my chin. It hurt. It thrust up. I cried out, rising almost to my toes. I then stood straight before them. I stood straighter than I had ever stood in my life.

The man then stepped back, and he, and the other, inspected me, completely, walking about me. They discussed me, candidly. I could not understand their speech. My chin was very high, as the point of the dagger had left it. I trembled. I heard the small movement of the chain in the collar loop. I wondered what could be the status of women on this world, on a world where there were such men.

It took the men some minutes to complete their examination. They did not hurry.

The two men now stood before me, one a bit behind the other, looking at me.

I felt the collar, weighted by the chain, pull down against my collarbone; the chain hung between my breasts; I felt its heavy links on my body. I stood very still.

"Please," I whispered, not moving my position.

The bearded man approached me. Suddenly he struck me with his right hand, a swift, savage, open-handed slap. I was hurled stumbling, spinning, to the end of the chain, which caught me, cruelly, at the neck, jerking me to the ground. My lip and the side of my mouth were cut. My head seemed to explode. I tasted blood.

The man barked a command. In panic and misery, in a movement of collar and chain, I fled again to my place and again stood before them, so straight, my chin again high, precisely as I had been before.

I wondered what could be the status of women on this world, on a world where there were such men.

He did not strike me again. I had placated him by my obedience.

He spoke to me again. I looked into his eyes. For a moment our eyes met.

I knelt.

Was it unaccountable that I knelt? No, it was what was to have been done.

How naturally, how fearfully, I had knelt! How necessary, how appropriate, it had been!

And I realized then that they had expected me to kneel, and had not given the possibility of my failing to do so a moment's thought.

But it seems I was not doing so correctly.

To my terror I found myself being regarded with irritation. Was I stupid? Did I not know how to kneel? Or perhaps I was merely ignorant? Certainly I wanted to please them. They must understand that!

The other man thrust my body down on my heels, so that I knelt back on my heels. He took my hands and placed them on my thighs. I looked up at them.

I am a brunet, with very dark brown hair. My eyes, too, are dark brown. I am lightly complexioned. I am some five feet five inches in height and weigh about one hundred and twenty pounds. I am thought to be not amply but excitingly figured.

The men looked down upon me. At that time my hair was cut short. I felt the side of the point of the bearded man's spear under my chin, and I lifted my chin, so that my head was high.

My name was Judy Thornton. I was an English major and poetess.

I knelt before barbarians, nude and chained.

I was terribly frightened.

I knelt exactly as they had placed me, scarcely daring to breathe. I feared to move in the slightest. I did not wish to be again struck, or to irritate or offend them in the least. I did not know what they might do, these mighty and terrible men, so unpredictable, so uncompromising and primitive, so different from the men of Earth, if they were not completely and fully, and absolutely, pleased with me. I determined to give them no cause for anger. I determined that they would have my absolute obedience. Thus I knelt not moving before them. I felt the wind move the hair on the back of my neck.

The men continued to regard me. This frightened me. I did not move at all. I remained, of course, as they had placed me. I looked straight ahead, not even daring to meet their eyes. I was terrified lest, inadvertently, I might do something to displease them. I moved no muscle. I knelt back on my heels, my back straight, my hands on my thighs, my chin up. My knees were pressed closely, defensively, together.

The man said something. I could not understand.

Then, with the butt of his spear, roughly, to my horror, he thrust apart my knees.

I was Judy Thornton. I was an English major and poetess.

I could not help but moan, the position was so elegant and helpless.

I knelt before them in what I would later learn was the position of the Gorean pleasure slave.

Satisfied then, the beasts turned from me. I did not move. They busied themselves in the vicinity of the rock. It seemed they searched for something.

Once the bearded fellow returned to stand near me. He said something. It was a question. He repeated it. I stared ahead, terrified. My eyes filled with tears. "I do not know," I whispered. "I do not understand. I do not know what you want."

He turned away, and again gave himself to his search. After a time, angry, he returned to regard me. His fellow, too, was with him. "Bina?" he said, very clearly. "Bina, Kajira. Var Bina, Kajira?"

"I do not know what you want," I whispered. "I do not understand you."

I gathered they must be asking after whatever it was they sought. They had covered the area thoroughly, even turning aside long grass with the blades of their spears.

They had not found it.

"Var Bina, Kajira?" repeated the bearded man.

I knelt as they had placed me, the chain hanging, heavy, from my collar.

"I do not know," I whispered.

Suddenly, savagely, he struck me across the mouth with the back of his right hand. I flew to the left, to the grass. The blow was vicious. It hurt me more than had the first. I could not believe its force, its ruthlessness, its swiftness. I could scarcely see; I fought blackness and pain and seething light; I was on my hands and knees in the grass, my head down; I tasted blood; the collar hurt my neck; I spit blood into the grass; he had struck me; did he not know I was a woman! He jerked me by the collar and chain to his knees; he thrust both hands into my hair. "Var Bina, Kajira!" he cried. "Var Bina!" "I do not understand you!" I cried. "Oh!" I screamed with misery. With both hands he shook my head viciously. I could not believe the pain. My small hands were helpless on his wrists. "Var Bina!" he demanded. "Please, please!" I wept.

He threw me down, with a rattle of chain, to his feet. I lay there on my side, terrified. He unlooped the shoulder belt from him and cast it, with the scabbard and blade, to one side. Then he swiftly loosened the belt at his waist. He slipped it free from the sheath and dagger, and doubled it. He struck it once in the palm of his hand. I turned my head away from him, fearfully, so that I could not see him. I lay before him, turned away from him, on the grass. Then I heard it whistle through the air. I cried out with pain. Again and again, viciously, he struck me. Once he stopped. "Var Bina, Kajira?" he asked. "Please don't hurt me," I begged. Again he struck, and again and again. I writhed before him, lashed, squirming on my belly in the grass, weeping, clutching at the grass. In the pain I could scarcely comprehend it. I was being beaten! Did he not know I was a girl! "Please don't hit me," I cried. "Please!" I covered my head with my hands. I lay with my head down. I shuddered with each blow. I would do anything if he would stop! But I did not know what he wanted!

Then he stopped, angrily. I did not even lift my head, but lay, weeping, my hands still over my head, the chain running between my legs, and under my body, to the collar.

I heard him replace the sheath and dagger on his belt, and put on the belt. I heard him lift the shoulder belt and regird himself with the blade. I did not look up, but lay weeping, chained, trembling. I would do anything he wanted, anything.

One of the men spoke to me, and prodded me with the butt of his spear.

I rose to my hands and knees. I felt the chain on my collar. Again I was prodded with the butt of his spear.

Red-eyed, my cheeks and body stained with tears, in pain, my back and sides, and legs, stinging, I adjusted the chain and knelt again as I had originally. There was blood at my mouth. Little had changed. I knelt precisely as I had before. Little had changed, save that I had been struck and beaten.

The two men conferred. Then, to my horror, the bearded one approached me. He crouched before me. He took from his dagger sheath the steel blade, narrow, about seven inches long, double-edged, evenly sharpened. He held this up before my face. He did not speak. The other man crouched down behind me. With his left hand, fastened in my hair, he drew my head back; with his right hand he thrust up, high on my neck, under my chin, the heavy iron collar I wore. It hurt. My jugular vein was, held as I was, prominent and, beneath the clasping, circular iron, prominent and exposed.

"No," I begged. "No!"

I gathered that I was of no use to these men. I felt the delicate, razor-sharp edge of the dagger on my throat.

"Var Bina, Kajira?" queried the man. "Var Bina?"

"Please!" I wept, whispering. "Please!" I would have done anything. I would have done anything. I would have told them anything, done anything, but I knew nothing. I could not give them what information they desired.

"Don't kill me," I begged. "I will do anything you want! Keep me! Keep me for yourselves! Keep me as your captive, your prisoner! Keep me as anything you want! Am I not beautiful? Could I not serve you? Could I not please you?" Then, suddenly, from deep within me, welling up, from somewhere so deep within me that I did not know I contained such depths, flooding from me, startling me, horrifying me with my own wickedness, I cried out, "Do not kill me! I am willing even to be your slave! Yes! Yes! I am willing even to be your slave. Your slave! Do not kill me! I will be your slave! Let me be your slave! I beg to be your slave!"

I shook with the horror, the scandal, the wickedness, of what I had said. But then, boldly, desperately, determinedly, resolutely, repudiating nothing, I whispered, clearly and firmly, my head back, held back, his hand in my hair, "Do not kill me, please. Yes, I will be even your slave. Yes, I, Judy Thornton, will be your slave. I, Judy Thornton, beg to be your slave. Please. Please, let me be a slave!" I tried to smile. "Make me your slave," I whispered, "—Masters!" How startled I was that I had called them Masters, and yet, how natural, it seemed, for I was a girl, suitable prey for such as they, a natural quarry and prey for such as they, and they, as I sensed, were the natural masters, by the dark laws of biology, of such as I.

"Please, Masters," I whispered.

"Var Bina, Kajira?" queried the man.

I moaned with misery. I did not know but they, rich and powerful masters, had access to many women as beautiful, or more beautiful, than I. On Earth I had been noted as a beauty, an unusual, even ravishingly beautiful girl, but on Gor, as I would come to understand, I, and others like me, could be acquired and disposed of for a handful of copper tarsks. There was little special about us. In many houses we would be kept with the kettles, as scullery and kitchen girls. I had been the most beautiful girl in the junior class at my elite girls' college. In all the school, there had been only one more lovely than I, or so some said, the lovely Elicia Nevins, who was in anthropology, in the senior class. How I had hated her. What rivals we had been!

15

I felt the edge of the dagger anchor itself in the outer layer of skin on my throat, preparing for its slash. I felt the man's hand and arm, through the steel of the dagger, flex for the movement of his arm. My throat was to be cut.

But the blade paused. It withdrew from my throat. The bearded man was looking outward, away from me, over the field. Then I, too, heard it. It was a man singing, boldly, a melodic, repetitious song.

Angrily the bearded man stood up, sheathed the dagger, took up his shield, his spear. His fellow, the other man, already accoutered, even to the helmet, watched the man approach. He balanced his spear in his right hand. The bearded man did not yet don his helmet, but stood near it.

I went to my hands and knees in the grass. I could scarcely move. I threw up in the grass. I pulled at the collar and chain, futilely. If only I could have run, or crawled away. But I was fastened in place.

Numbly I lifted my head. The other fellow was approaching at an even, unhurried pace. He seemed good-humored. He sang in a rich voice, a simple song, as though to content himself in long treks. His hair was black and shaggy. He, too, was clad in scarlet, as were the other two men. He was similarly accoutered, with short sword, slung at the left hip, with a shoulder belt; a belt at his waist with a sheathed knife; heavy sandals, almost boots. He carried a spear over his left shoulder, balanced by his left hand; from the spear depended a shield, behind the left shoulder, and a helmet; about his right shoulder was slung a pouch, which I gathered must have contained supplies; a bota of liquid, water I assumed, was fastened at his belt, on the left, behind the point at which the scabbard depended from the shoulder belt. He strode singing, smiling, through the tall grass. He seemed similarly garbed to the other men, wearing a similar tunic, but they reacted to him in a way that indicated they were not pleased that he had now appeared. His tunic was cut slightly differently from theirs; there was a mark at the left shoulder, which theirs did not bear. These differences were subtle to me, but to those who could read them perhaps acutely significant. I pulled at the chain. No one paid me attention. Had I been free I might have slipped away. I moaned to myself. I must wait.

The approaching man stopped singing about twenty yards from us, and stood grinning in the grass. He held the spear, with its dependent articles, in his left hand now, and raised his right in a cheerful fashion, palm inward, facing the body. "Tal, Rarii!" said he, calling out, grinning.

"Tal, Rarius," said the bearded man.

The newcomer slipped the bota from his belt, and discarded, too, the pouch he carried.

The bearded man waved his arm angrily, and spoke harshly. He was ordering the newcomer away. He pointed to his fellow and himself. They were two. The newcomer grinned and slipped the spear to the ground, loosening the helmet and shield.

The bearded man placed his helmet over his head, it muchly concealing his features.

Carrying the shield on his left arm, carrying the spear lightly in his right hand, the helmet hanging, too, by its straps, from his right hand, the newcomer approached casually.

Again the bearded man waved him away. Again he spoke harshly. The newcomer grinned.

They spoke together, the three of them. I could understand nothing. The newcomer spoke evenly; once he slapped his thigh in laughter. The two other men spoke more angrily. One, he who was not bearded, shook his spear.

The newcomer did not pay him attention. He looked beyond the men, to me.

I then became aware, as I had not been before, in my fear, of a strange emotional and physiological response of which I had been the victim moments before, when I had begged mighty men to enslave me. My feelings had been flooded not only with terror but, mixed with them, with the feelings of terror, had been a strange, almost hysterical release of tension, of bottled-up emotion. I had said things which I had never dreamed could come from me, and they could not now be unsaid. I realized I had begged to be a slave. Of course I had been terrified, but I felt, in my deepest heart, that I had not said what I had said merely to try and save my life. Of course I had been desperate to save my life. Of course I would have said anything! But it was the way I had felt when I had said it that now so shook me, so profoundly, to the quick. Mingled with the terror there had been a release of suppressed instincts, a joy in confession, a rapture of openness, of authenticity and honesty. That I had been terrified, and desperate to buy my life at any cost, had been the occasion, and an adequate justification, of my utterance, doubtless, but this terror could not explain the wild, uncontrollable acknowledgment, the shattering of inhibitions which I had felt, the torrential rapture, the abandonment, the capitulation to myself and my instincts which had, though blurred and mixed with the terror, so shaken and thrilled me. The terror was unimportant. It had been nothing more than an occasion, not even necessary. What was important had been the way I had felt when I had begged those mighty men to be my masters. It was as though, in asking for chains of iron, I had cast off thousands of invisible chains, which had held me from myself. Chains of iron I thought might hold me to my own truths, not permitting me to strive for what, in the heart of me, I did not wish, for what I was not. I wondered then what was the nature of women. I knew then that, before, in the emotions that had flooded me I had not been only terrified. I had felt liberty and release, and joy. Oddly, too, in those moments, besides my terror, I had been aroused. Never before in my life had I been so erotically charged, so aroused, as when I had begged those mighty men to enslave me. I now looked at the newcomer, who was regarding me. I shuddered. I, nude and chained, felt my body suddenly soaked with the heat of desire. Perhaps he had read the bodies of many women. He grinned at me. Beneath the bold appraisal of my bared beauty I reddened, angrily. I put down my head. I was furious. What did he think I was. A chained slave girl, whose beauty might belong to him who was the most strong, or most powerful, to him with the swiftest sword, or to the highest bidder?

He pointed to me. He spoke. The bearded man again spoke harshly, waving his arm, ordering the newcomer away. The newcomer laughed. The bearded man said something, gesturing to me. The tone of his voice was disparaging. I felt angry. The newcomer looked more closely at me. He spoke to me, calling across the grass. The word he spoke I had heard before. The other man had said it to me after I had been beaten, when he had prodded me with the spear, before I had again knelt, though then struck and beaten, before the men, shortly before the dagger had been put to my throat. Tossing my head I knelt, the chain dangling from my collar before my body, to the grass. I knelt back on my heels, my back very straight, my hands on my thighs, my head high, looking straight ahead. I thrust my shoulders back, my breasts forward. I did not neglect the placement of my knees; I opened them as widely as I could, as I knew the men wanted. I knelt before them again in that most elegant and helpless position in which men may place a woman, that position I was later to learn was that of the Gorean pleasure slave.

The newcomer now spoke decisively. The bearded man and the other retorted angrily. The newcomer, as I saw out of the corner of my eye, was pointing to me. He was grinning. I trembled and shuddered. He was demanding me! He was telling them to give me to him! The bold beast! How I hated him, and how pleased I was! The men laughed. I was frightened. They were two, and he one! He should flee! He should run for his life! I knelt, chained.

"Kajira canjellne!" said the newcomer. Though he indicated me peremptorily with his spear, it was at the two other men that he looked. He did not now take his eyes from them.

The bearded man looked angry. "Kajira canjellne," he acknowledged. "Kajira canjellne," said the other man, too, soberly.

The newcomer then moved back a few paces. He crouched down. He picked up a stalk of grass, and began to chew on it.

The bearded man approached me. From within his tunic he drew forth two lengths of slender, braided black leather, each about eighteen inches long. He crouched behind me. He jerked my wrists behind my back, crossed them, and bound them, tightly. He then crossed my ankles, and, too, bound them, tightly, as well. I could feel the braided leather, deep in my wrists and ankles. I winced, helpless. Then, holding me by the hair with his left hand, from behind, I felt a heavy key, which he must have removed from his tunic, thrust deeply into the large collar lock, below my left ear. The heavy collar, with its lock, pushed into the left side of my neck. The key turned. I heard the bolt click back. It made a heavy sound. It must have been a thick, heavy bolt. He dropped the key to the grass and, with both hands, jerking it, opened the collar. He dropped it, with the depending chain, to the grass. I was freed of the collar! I looked at the collar. It was the first time I had seen it. As I had surmised, it matched the chain. It was heavy, circular, of black iron, hinged, efficient, practical, frightening. It bore a staple and stout loop. One link of the chain was fastened about the loop. The loop was circular, and about two and one half inches in width.

I was free of the collar! But I was bound helplessly. I pulled futilely at my bonds.

The bearded man lifted me lightly in his arms. My weight was as if nothing to him. He faced the stranger, who still crouched a few yards away.

"Kajira canjellne?" asked the bearded man. It was as though he were giving the stranger an opportunity to withdraw. Perhaps a mistake had been made? Perhaps there had been a misunderstanding?

The stranger, crouching in the grass, his shield beside him, the butt of the spear in the grass, the weapon upright, its point against the sky, nodded. There had been no mistake. "Kajira canjellne," he said, simply.

The other man angrily went to a place in the grass, to one side. There, angrily, with the blade of his spear, he traced and dug a circle in the earth. It was some ten feet in diameter. The bearded man then threw me over his shoulder, and carried me to the circle. I was hurled to its center. I lay on my side, bound.

The men spoke together, as though clarifying arrangements. They did not speak long.

I struggled to my knees. I knelt in the circle.

The stranger, now, stood. He donned his helmet. He slipped his shield on his arm, adjusting straps. He slid the short blade at his left hip some inches from the sheath, and slipped it back in, lifting and dropping it in the sheath. It was loose. He took his spear in his right hand. It had a long, heavy shaft, some two inches in width, some seven feet in length; the head of the weapon, including its socket and penetrating rivets, was some twenty inches in length; the killing edges of the blade began about two inches from the bottom of the socket, which reinforced the blade, tapering with the blade, double-edged, to within eight inches of its point; the blade was bronze; it was broad at the bottom, tapering to its point; given the stoutness of the weapon, the lesser gravity of this world, and the strength of the man who wielded it, I suspected it would have considerable penetrating power; I doubted that the shields they carried, though stout, could turn its full stroke, if taken frontally; I had little doubt such a weapon might thrust a quarter of its length through the body of a man, and perhaps half its length or more through the slighter, softer body of a mere girl; I looked upon the spear; it was so mighty; I feared it.

The two men who were my captors conferred briefly among themselves. He who was not the bearded man then stepped forward, his shield on his arm, his spear in hand. He stood separated from the stranger by some forty feet.

I observed them. They stood, not moving, each clad in scarlet, each helmeted, each similarly armed. They stood in the grass. Neither looked at me. I was forgotten. I knelt in the circle. I tried to free myself. I could not. I knelt in the circle.

The wind moved the grass. The clouds shifted in the blue sky.

For a long time, neither man moved. Then, suddenly, the stranger, laughing, lifted his spear and struck its butt into the ground. "Kajira canjellne!" he laughed.

I could not believe it. He seemed elated. He was pleased with the prospect of war. How terrible he was! How proud, how magnificent he seemed! I thought I knew then, with horror, the nature of men.

"Kajira canjellne!" said the other man.

Warily they began to circle one another.

I waited, kneeling, frightened, nude and bound, in the circle. I watched the men warily circling one another. I pulled at my bonds. I was helpless.

Suddenly, as though by common accord, each crying out, each uttering a savage cry, they hurled themselves at one another.

It was the ritual of the spear casting.

The spear of him who was one of my captors seemed to leap upward and away, caroming from the oblique, lifted surface of the stranger's shield. The spear, caroming from the shield, flew more than a hundred feet away, dropping in the grass, where it stood fixed, remote and useless, the butt of its shaft pointing to the sky. The stranger's spear had penetrated the shield of he who was one of my captors, and the stranger, bracing the shaft between his arm and body, had lifted his opponent's shield and turned, throwing it and his opponent, who had not the time to slip from the shield straps, to the ground at his feet. The stranger's blade, now, loosed from its sheath, under the opponent's helmet, lay at his throat.

But the stranger did not strike. He severed the shield straps of the opponent's shield, freeing his arm from them. He stepped back. He cast his own shield aside, into the grass.

He stood waiting, blade drawn.

The other man got his legs under him and leaped to his feet. He was enraged. The blade in his sheath leaped forth. He charged the other, the stranger, and swiftly did the two engage.

I knelt terrified. I shuddered with horror. They were not human, as I understood human beings. They were warriors and beasts.

I cried out with fear.

I had always had a fear of steel blades, even knives. Now I knelt bound and nude, helpless, utterly exposed and vulnerable, in the vicinity of fierce men, skilled and strong, who with intent and menace, with edged, bared steel, addressed themselves to the savageries of war.

They fought.

I watched, wide-eyed, bound. Furious, sharp, was the precision of their combat.

They were not feet from me.

I moaned.

Backward and forward, swiftly, did they move in their grim contest.

I wondered at what manner of men they might be, surely like none I had hitherto known. Why did they not flee in terror from such blades? Why did they not flee? But they met one another, and did battle. How I feared, and still fear, such men! How could a woman but kneel trembling before such a man?

One man wheeled back, grunting, turning, and fell to his knees in the grass, and then fell, turning, to his side, lying upon his shoulder, doubled, hunched in pain, bleeding, his hands at his belly, his blade lost in the grass.

The stranger stepped back from him, his blade bloody. He stood regarding the other man, the bearded man.

The bearded man lifted his shield and raised his spear. "Kajira canjellne!" he said.

"Kajira canjellne," said the stranger. He went to extricate his spear from the penetrated shield of the man with whom, but moments before, he had shared the sport of war. The fallen foe lay doubled in the grass; his lower lip was bloody; he tore it with his teeth, holding it, that, in his pain, he might make no sound. His hands were clutched in the scarlet of his wet tunic, bunching it, at the half-severed belt. The grass was bloody about him.

The stranger bent to lift the penetrated shield, that he might remove from it his bronze-headed weapon.

In that instant the bearded man, crying out savagely, rushed upon him, his spear raised.

Before I could respond in horror or my body move the stranger had reacted, rolling to the side and, in an instant, regaining his feet, assuming an on-guard position. As my cry of misery escaped my lips the thrust of the bearded man's spear had passed to the left of the stranger's helmet. The stranger had not remained at the vicinity of the shield with its penetrating spear, but had abandoned it. For the first time now the stranger did not seem pleased. The bearded man's spear had thrust into the grass. Its head and a foot of its shaft had been driven into the turf. He faced the stranger now, sword drawn. The instant he had missed the thrust he had left the weapon, spinning and unsheathing his sword. The bearded man was white-faced. But the stranger had not rushed upon him. He waited, in the on-guard position. He gestured with his blade, indicating that now they might do battle.

With a cry of rage the bearded man rushed upon him, thrusting with his shield, his sword flat and low. The stranger was not there. Twice more the bearded man charged, and each time the stranger seemed not to be at the point of intended impact. The fourth time the stranger was behind him and on his left. The stranger's sword was at his left armpit. The bearded man stood very still, white-faced. The stranger's sword moved. The stranger stepped back. The bearded man's shield slipped from his arm. The straps which had held the shield to his upper arm had been severed. The shield fell on its edge to the grass, and then tipped and rocked, then was still, large, rounded, concave inner surface tilted, facing the sky. I could see the severed straps.

The two men faced one another.

Then did they engage.

I then realized, as I had not before, the skill of the stranger. Earlier he had matched himself, for a time, evenly with the first opponent. In a swift, though measured fashion, he had exercised himself, sharply and well, respecting his foe, not permitting the foe to understand his full power with the blade, the devastating and subtle skill which now seemed to lend terrible flight to the rapid steel. I saw the wounded man, now on an elbow, watching, with horror. He had not even been slain. Lying in the bloodied grass, he realized he had been permitted to live. It was with humiliating skill that the stranger toyed with the stumbling, white-faced bearded man, he who had, minutes before, been preparing to cut my throat. Bound, kneeling in the circle, it was with sudden, frightening elation that I realized the stranger was the master of the other two. Four times was he within the other's guard, his blade at breast or throat, and did not finish him. He moved the bearded man into a position where his fallen, discarded shield lay behind him. With a cry he forced back the bearded man, who fell, stumbling in the shield, backward, and then lay on the grass before the stranger, the stranger's blade at his throat. The stranger, in contempt, then stepped back. The bearded man scrambled to his feet. The stranger stood back, in the on-guard position.

The bearded man took his blade and hurled it into the grass. It sank to the hilt.

He stood regarding the stranger.

The stranger slipped his own blade back in the sheath. The bearded man loosened his dagger belt, dropping the belt and weapon to the grass. Then he walked, slowly, to his fellow, and similarly removed his dagger belt. The man held his bloodied tunic to his wound, to stanch the flow of blood. The bearded man lifted the other man to his feet, and, together, the bearded man supporting the other, they left the field.

The stranger stood watching them go. He watched them until they disappeared in the distance.

He removed his spear from the shield which it had penetrated. He thrust it, upright, butt down, in the turf. It was like a standard. He sat his shield by it.

Then he turned to face me.

I knelt within the wide circle, torn by the blade of a spear in the turf. I was naked. I was bound helplessly. It was an alien world.

He began to approach me, slowly. I was terrified.

Then he stood before me.

Never had I been so frightened. We were alone, absolutely.

He looked at me. I thrust my head to the grass at his feet. He stood there, not moving. I was terribly conscious, helpless, of his presence. I waited for him to speak, to say something to me. He must understand my terror! Was it not visible in my bound body, my complete vulnerability? I waited for him to speak some gentle word, something kindly, something to reassure me, a thoughtful, soft word to allay my fears. I trembled. He said nothing.

I did not dare raise my head. Why did he not speak to me? Any gentleman, surely, by now, speaking reassuring, soothing words, averting his eyes from my beauty, would have hastened to release me from my predicament.

He removed his helmet. He put it to one side, in the grass.

I felt his hand in my hair, not cruelly, but casually and firmly, as one might fasten one's hand in the mane of a horse. Then I felt my head drawn up and back, and back, until, his right hand on my knee, his left hand in my hair, I knelt bent backward, my head on the ground, my back bent painfully, my eyes looking up, frightened, at the sky. He then examined the bow of my beauty. I am quite vain of my beauty. Then he threw me on my side and stretched me out, to examine its linear aspect. I lay on my right side. He walked about me, and looked at me. He kicked my toes straight, that the line of my body would be more extended. He crouched beside me, then. I felt his hand on my neck. He rubbed his thumb in a scrape the collar had made on my throat when I had foolishly struggled, earlier. It smarted. But the scrape was not deep. He felt my upper arm, and forearm, and my fingers, moving them. He moved his hands on my body, firmly, following its curvatures. He put one hand on my back and another on my side and, for a few moments, holding me thus, felt my breathing. He felt my thigh, and flexed my legs, noting the change in the curve of the calf. It did not seem what a gentleman would do. Never before had a man handled and touched me as he did; no man on Earth, I felt sure, would have so dared to touch a woman. I felt examined—as casually, as clinically, as professionally—as an animal. Did he think I was an animal, a mere pretty animal? Did he not know that I was a person! That I was a person of station and class, that I was an excellent student at an elite girls' college, that I was an English major, that I was a poetess! At one point, turning my head, thrusting two fingers of his left hand and two fingers of his right hand into my mouth, he pulled my mouth open, widely, examining my teeth. This added to the distinct and unwelcome impression that I was being assessed as an animal, assessed as no more than a young, lovely beast. Could that be true? Was that all I was here? Was that all I was, truly, anywhere? I have excellent teeth, white and small and straight. I was pleased about that. I found myself, interestingly, hoping that he would find them acceptable, that he would not be displeased. I had had two cavities. They had been filled. He seemed to have noted this, but, to my relief, had not been much concerned. I suppose this is a small thing, but I did not know their culture. How did I know what these men would take seriously? Might I be beaten or slain for a meaningless blemish? He had seen, as I later learned, women from Earth before. Such tiny things can be used to determine Earth origin. Goreans seldom have cavities. I am not certain what the reasons for this are. In part it is doubtless a matter of a plainer, simpler diet, containing less sugar; in part, I suspect, the culture, too, may have a role to play, as it is a culture in which undue chemical stress, through guilt and worry, is not placed on the system either in the prepubertal or pubertal years. Gorean youth, like the youth of Earth, encounter their difficulties in growing up but the culture, or cultures, have not seen fit to implicitly condition them into regarding the inevitable effects of maturation as either suspect, deplorable or insidious. He then threw me to my other side, and subjected my helpless beauty, on its right, to a similar examination.

I was horrified at the boldness, the frankness, with which he handled me.

Did he think I was an animal! Did he think I was only property?

Then he threw me on my stomach at his feet, and I lay there. My wrists were crossed and bound behind me in slender, braided leather. My ankles, too, were crossed and bound in that simple, secure fastening. I felt the grass under my body; I felt it brush my left side, as the wind moved it. I kept my toes pointed.

He regarded me for some time.

How beautiful I must look to him, I thought. And I had sensed his incredible maleness, the animal maleness of him, so different from the thwarted, crippled sexuality so commended and tragically endemic among the males of Earth. For the first time in my life I felt I understood what might be the meaning of the expression 'male,' and, as I lay before him, too, dimly, it frightening me, what might be the meaning of the expression 'female.' How beautiful I thought I must look to him, lying bound, totally vulnerable, helpless at his feet. How such a sight must stir the splendor of his manhood, to see the female, his, caught, helpless at his feet, his to do with, in lust and pleasure, and joy, as he pleased, helpless to escape him, free for him to work his will upon her!

I felt him turn me. I must resist him! He is a beast! I was sitting now, my face turned to one side, trying to push back, but his left arm, behind my back, held me. I found it futile to struggle. With his right hand he turned my face to face him. He regarded the delicate lineaments of my face. His thumb was at the right side of my jaw, his fingers at the left. I could not move my head. He was darkly complexioned. His face, in a broad, coarse way, was brutally handsome. His eyes were very dark, his hair dark, shaggy, long. He said something to me. I felt his breath on my face. I trembled. I stammered. "Please, please," I said, "I do not speak your language. Please untie me."

He said something again.

"I cannot understand you," I said. "Please untie me."

He stood, and lifted me, by the arms, to my feet. He looked down into my eyes. My head came only to his chest; the width of my body seemed but half the width of that mighty, scarlet-clad chest. His hands were very tight on my arms. My ankles fastened, crossed and bound, I would have fallen had he released me; I could not stand by myself. He said something again, a question. "I cannot understand you," I said. He gave me a sudden shake. I felt my head would leave my body. He repeated his question. "I cannot understand you!" I wept. He shook me again, angrily, but not cruelly. Then he released me. Bound as I was I could do nothing but fall before him, on my knees. I looked up. Never had I felt such strength.

He crouched down before me. He looked at me intently. Once more he spoke to me. I shook my head, miserably. I looked up at him. "I will learn any language you want," I blurted, weeping, "but I cannot, now, speak your tongue."

He seemed satisfied, or resigned, after this outburst, that there was little to be gained in attempting to communicate with me. We could not speak to one another. He rose to his feet and looked about himself. He was not pleased. He was not looking at me. I shrugged, a bit angrily. He could not see me. It was not my fault I could not speak to him! But then, as he looked about the field, and the rock, I, in that large, rude circle torn in the turf, put my head down, alone, miserable.

I was small in the grass, alone. I knelt helpless, an ignorant barbarian girl, naked and bound, who could not even speak to her captor, on a strange world.

In time, after scouting the terrain of the rock, perhaps searching for clues as to my meaning or identity, the tall man in scarlet returned to face me.

It was late afternoon.

I looked up at him, and trembled.

He took me by the hair and threw me to my belly in the grass at his feet. I lay there, helpless.

I heard the sword slip free from his sheath.

"Don't kill me!" I wept. "Please do not kill me!"

I lay there, terrified. I felt the sword, with an easy movement, as though meeting no resistance, sever the binding on my ankles.

He then left me. He fetched the pouch and bota which he had carried, and slung them both, this time, at his belt. He picked up his helmet. He went to the spear thrust in the turf, upright, blade to the sky, and the concave shield at its foot. He slung the shield and helmet over the butt of the spear, suspending them behind his left shoulder, his left arm over and resting on the shaft of the spear, steadying it in place. Then, without looking at me, he left the field.

I watched him go. I struggled to my feet, my hands still bound tightly behind me. I looked about at the field, at the signs of battle, the discarded shields, one deeply punctured and cut, the scattered weapons. I looked at the great rock to which, by the neck, I had been fastened with a heavy chain. I stood in the circle torn in the turf. The wind blew the grass, my hair. The sky was darker now. I gasped. Low on the horizon I saw, rising, three moons. The man was distant now. "Don't leave me," I cried. "Don't leave me here alone!"

I fled from the circle torn in the turf, running after him. "Please stop!" I cried. "Wait! Please, wait!"

Gasping for breath I fled after him, stumbling, sometimes falling. "Please, wait!" I cried.

Once he turned to see me running after him. I stopped, panting. I stood in the grass, some two hundred yards from him. Then he turned again, and continued on his way. Miserable, stumbling, I began running again. He turned again when I was some twenty yards from him. Again I stopped. Under his gaze, for no reason I clearly understood,

I put my head down. He again continued on his way and I again followed him. In a moment or two I had caught up with him, and lagged behind, some ten feet. He stopped, and turned. I stopped, and put my head down. He continued on his way again, and again I followed. Then again, after a few minutes, he stopped. I stopped, too, my head down. This time he approached me, and stood about a yard from me. I stood extremely straight, with my head down. I was terribly conscious of his nearness, my nudity, his eyes upon me. Though I was female of Earth I had some dim inkling of the tumult of joy and pleasure which the sight of a female body could wreak in a man. And I knew that I was very beautiful. He put his fingers and thumb under my chin and lifted my head. I saw his eyes, and looked quickly away, not daring to meet them. To my horror, I wanted him to find me pleasing—and as a female. He regarded me for a minute or two, and then, from his shoulder, unslung the shield, and helmet, from his spear. From his belt he took the pouch and bota. He slung them about my neck. Then, adjusting the straps, he fastened the shield at my back. I staggered under its weight. Then, carrying the helmet by its straps in his left hand and the spear, lightly, in his right, he turned and began to stride again through the grass. Staggering under the weight of the shield, the pouch and bota about my neck, I followed him. Once he turned and, with the spear, indicated the position and distance at which I should follow. These things vary, I learned, from city to city, and depend, also, on such matters as context and conditions. In a market, in the crowding and jostling, for instance, a girl may follow so closely she pressed against the back of his left shoulder. Girls seldom follow behind and on the right. If she is thusly placed it is commonly a sign she is in disfavor. If more than one girl is involved, she who follows most closely on the left is generally taken to be in highest favor; girls compete for this position. In an open area, such as the fields in which we trekked, the girl is placed usually some five or ten feet behind, and on the left. If he must move suddenly she will not, thusly, constitute an impediment to his action.

He again took up his march. Carrying his shield, the pouch and bota, some eight or nine feet behind him, on his left, I followed him. I suppose I should have minded. I knew I was heeling him. How strange it seemed. I understood so little of what had occurred. I had awakened, stripped and chained, on a strange world. Men had come to the rock where I had been fastened. They had had the key to the collar. Doubtless they had come there to fetch me. But who had left me there for them? And what had they wanted of me? They had questioned me, beaten me. The word 'Bina' had often occurred in their demands. "Var Bina!" they had demanded. I, of course, had not understood. Then, angry, they had prepared to cut my throat. I had been rescued by a chance male, armed and skillful, who had happened in the fields at the time. He had been, judging from the reactions of my original captors, completely unexpected, and not welcome. By his own reactions I had gathered he knew nothing of the men he had met there, and had behaved as he might have with any others, similarly of his scarlet-clad, helmeted, armed sort. I had been part of a plan, a design, I suspected, which I did not understand, which had been, by a chance encounter, disrupted. But what did the word 'Bina' mean? There must have been something, I supposed, I was supposed to have, but, as nearly as I could determine, did not have, or something which was supposed to have been with me, but, as far as I could determine, had not been with me. There had been, as far as I could determine, only myself, stripped and chained, and the grass, the rock, and sky. The plan, perhaps, had been disrupted, or had failed, prior even to the arrival of the two men at the rock. I did not know. I understood nothing. But perhaps the plan had not been disrupted. Perhaps, even now, I carried some secret with me, which had been unknown to the two men. Perhaps they had not understood the way in which I was to have been useful. Perhaps their information had been incomplete or incorrect. I suspected I was intended to be instrumental in something I did not understand. I could neither explain nor understand my nature or purpose, if any, on this world. Had I been brought here merely as a naked woman, it seemed pointless to have placed me as I had been placed in the wilderness. Too, it would have been pointless to have questioned me so closely; too, why, if I had been brought to this world for an obvious purpose of men, say, for my beauty, had the men prepared, in their anger, to end my life? Surely it must have been obvious to them that I was eager to do anything they wanted, that I was eager to please them. Had I been brought here merely for my beauty surely they would not have behaved as they had. I shuddered, recalling the feel of the knife at my throat.

Then the stranger had arrived.

"Kajira canjellne!" he had said. I had been released of the chain and collar. A circle had been drawn in the turf. Bound, I had been thrown to it. Kneeling, I had watched men fight. I now, naked and bound, carrying his shield, followed him who had been victorious.

I remembered his might, his insolence, his skill, his power. I admired the width of his shoulders as he walked before me. I remembered the simplicity and audacity with which, after his victory, he had examined me.

I now carried his shield. I walked behind him, and to the left. I suppose I should have minded. I knew, of course, that I was heeling him. I thought about it. Whereas it would have seemed unthinkable on Earth that a man could be so strong, so mighty, that a woman would walk at his heel, here, on this world, it seemed not so impossible or strange at all. There were men here strong enough to put women at their heel. I felt, briefly, profoundly stirred erotically, and, perhaps strangely, marvelously pleased to be a woman. I had never met such men as these, the former two, and he whom I now followed, mightiest among them, who would simply, unthinkingly, put a woman at their heel. I had never known such men. I had not dreamed such men could exist! I had never felt so feminine, so stirred, so alive and real, as in their presence! For the first time in my life I was pleased to be a woman.

Then I castigated myself for my terrible thoughts. Men and women I knew, as I had been taught, were identical. Biology, and a nature, the product of harsh, exacting thousands of generations of evolution, of time, and breeding and animal history, was unimportant. It must be ignored, and dismissed. It did not suggest the correct political conclusions.

I looked up at the three moons.

I did not know what to believe or how to live. But, as I followed the man, trekking through the glorious grass, under the bright, marvelous moons, carrying his shield, literally heeling him, as might have an animal, his captive, nude and bound, I felt, paradoxically, a fantastic sense of freedom, of psychological liberation. I wanted to run to him and put my head against his shoulder.

For hours we trekked the grass.

Sometimes I fell. He did not stop for me. I would struggle to my feet, staggering under the weight of the shield, and run to catch up with him. But then I could go no further. My body was not readied for such treks. I was only a girl of Earth. I fell. My breath was short, my legs weak. I lay in the grass. I could not move my body. I lay on my side, the weight of the shield upon my shoulder. After a time I sensed him standing near me, looking down. I looked up at him. I tried to smile. "I can go no further," I said. Surely he could see my exhaustion, my helplessness. I could not even move. I saw him loosen his belt. I struggled to my feet. He did not look pleased. He would have beaten me! He refastened his belt. He turned away. Again I followed him.

Toward morning we crossed more than one tiny stream. The water was very cold on my ankles and calves. Bordering these streams was brush, and some trees. The fields were broken now, with occasional trees, many of them flat-topped. In what I conjecture would have been an hour or so before dawn he stopped in a thicket of trees, near a small stream. He removed the pouch and bota from my neck, the shield from my back. I fell to the grass between the trees. I moved my wrists a bit, and lost consciousness. In what must have been a moment or two I was shaken awake. A handful of dried meat, cut in small pieces, was thrust in my mouth. Lying on my side I chewed and swallowed it. I had not realized how hungry I was. In a moment, he lifted me to a sitting position and, his left hand behind my back, supporting me, thrust the spike of the bota in my mouth. Eagerly then did I drink. He much watered me. I lay then again on my side. He lifted me in his arms, so lightly that it startled me, and carried me to a tree. As he tethered my right ankle to the tree I, bound as I was, overcome with exhaustion, fell asleep.

It seemed to me that I was in my own bed. I stretched in the pleasant warmth.

Then I awakened suddenly. I was in a thicket, on a strange world. It was warm, and the sun, high, filtered through the branches of the trees. I looked at my wrists. They were now unbound. Each wrist, deeply, wore the circular marks of the leather constraints which, earlier, had confined them. I rubbed my wrists. I looked about myself. My right ankle, by a short length of black leather, was tied to a small, white-barked tree. I rose to my hands and knees, my back to the tree. I was still naked. I then sat with my back against the tree, my legs drawn up, my chin on my knees, my hands about my knees. I watched the man, who was sitting, cross-legged, a few feet away. He was putting a thin coating of oil on the blade of his sword.

He did not look up at me. He seemed totally absorbed in his work. He must have sensed my awakening, my movements, but he did not look at me. I felt angry. I was not used to being ignored, particularly by a male. They had always been eager to be pleasing to me, to do anything I wanted.

I did not realize that on this world it was such as we who must be pleasing to them, who must comply eagerly with whatever their whim might decree.

I watched him.

He was a not unattractive man. I wondered if it would be possible to work out a meaningful relationship with him. He must learn, of course, to respect me as a woman.

He finished with the oil and blade. He wiped the blade with a cloth, leaving on it only a fine, evenly spread coating of oil. He replaced the cloth and the oil, which was in a small vial, in his pouch. He wiped his hands on the grass, and his tunic. He resheathed the sword.

He then looked up at me.

I smiled at him. I wanted to make friends with him. He slapped his right ankle, and pointed to it, and then beckoned me to approach him.

I bent to untie the dark leather which fastened me to the white tree. I first bent to remove the leather from my ankle. But a sharp word from him, and a gesture, indicated to me that I must first remove the tether from about the trunk of the small tree. Doubtless he thought me stupid. Did not any girl know that the last bond to be removed is that on her own body? But I was of Earth and knew nothing of such matters. I struggled, with my small, weak fingers, with the knots. I worked hard, frightened, sweating, that I might be taking too long. But he was patient. He knew the knots he had tied could not be easily undone by one such as I.

Then I approached him, and, with my left hand, handed him the supple tether. He replaced it in his pouch, and indicated that I should position myself before him and to his right. I knelt there, and smiled at him. He spoke sharply, harshly. Immediately I knelt in the position I had learned yesterday, which had been clearly and exactly taught to me, back on heels, back straight, hands on thighs, head up, knees widely opened. He then looked at me, satisfied.

How could I make friends with him, kneeling so? How could I get him to respect me as a person, so desirably and beautifully positioned before him? How could I, so kneeling, so beautiful and small, so exposed and vulnerable, so helpless, so much his, get him to accept me as his equal?

I bent forward and took the piece of meat between my teeth from his hand. He did not allow me to touch it with my hands.

How miserable I felt. On this world I had not yet even been allowed to feed myself!

When I had eaten some meat, he then gave me to drink, again from the bota.

He must learn I am an equal and a person, I resolved. I will show him this.

I broke the position to which he had commanded me. I sat upon the grass before him, my knees drawn up. I smiled. "Sir," said I to him, "I know you cannot understand my language, nor I yours, but, still, perhaps, from my voice, or its tone, you may gather something of my feelings. You saved my life yesterday. You rescued me when I was in great danger. I am very grateful for this."

I thought my head would fly from my neck, with such swift savageness was I struck! The blow was open-handed, taking me on the left side of the face, but it must have been clearly audible for a hundred and fifty yards about; I rolled, stinging, crawling, for more than twenty feet; I threw up in the grass; I couldn't see; blackness, violent, velvet, plunging, deep, lights, stars, seemed to leap and contract and expand and explode in my head; again I shook my head; again I threw up in the grass; then I sank to the side on my stomach.

I heard a word, of command. I recognized it. I had heard it before. Swiftly then did I reassume the position which I had dared to break, and again I knelt, though this time in an agony of terror, before the strange, mighty man, his legs spread, his arms crossed, who stood before me.

Blood ran from my mouth; other blood I swallowed. My vision cleared; I could not believe the pounding of my heart. I had been cuffed. I knelt, terrified. At that time I did not realize how light had been my discipline considering the gravity of my offense. I had both spoken without permission, and broken position without permission. Most simply, I had been displeasing to a free man.

Had I known the world on which I knelt, how I would have rejoiced that I had not been lashed! As I later realized, allowances were being made for me which, had I been more familiar with the world on which I found myself, would not have been made. Later, such allowances would not be, and were not, made.

I knelt before the man. He stood before me, legs spread, arms crossed, looking down at me. Gone from me in that moment, with the blood that ran from my mouth, were my illusions. No longer did I deceive myself that I might be his equal. The farcicality of that illusion was now transparent to me. The pitifulness of that pretense vanished before the simple, incontrovertible biological reality which had been impressed upon me, in the light of his uncompromising masculine dominance which he, in health and power, chose to exercise over me, a female. How beautiful to men must be women, I thought, who are at their feet. I wondered, frightened, if it were at the feet of men, or at least at the feet of such men as this, that women belonged, if that might be the unperverted order of nature. The thought of dominance and submission, pervasive in the animal kingdom, universal among primates, ran through my head. Never before had I so clearly, and profoundly, understood the meaning of those words. I looked up at him. I was frightened. My world, I knew, had chosen to deny and subvert biology. This world, I gathered, had not. Before him I knelt terrified, his.

To my relief he turned from me. Yet I remained immobile, absolutely, fearing to move, as though frozen in that elegant and helpless position, so vulnerable and exposed, which later I learned was the position of the Gorean pleasure slave.

He looked up at the sun.

It was late afternoon. He lay down, to sleep. I did not break position. I had not been given permission. Perhaps he kept me in position to discipline me. I did not know. I was afraid to break position. I told myself, of course, that this was rational, that he might wake and discover me out of position, or that, perhaps, at times, he was not truly asleep, but was, through half-closed eyes, watching me, to see if I, in the slightest, moved. But in my heart I knew I had not broken position because he had not given me permission to do so, because he had not released me from his command. I was terribly afraid of him. I was afraid to break position. I was obeying him.

For more than two hours, I think, I knelt in position. He awakened.

He looked at me, but he did not release me from position. I remained as I was, in that position so symbolic of female subjugation.

It was now in the early evening.

He gathered up the pouch and bota, and slung them at his belt. He slung his sword, in its scabbard, over his shoulder. He donned his helmet. He lifted his shield and spear.

I looked at him. Was I not to bear his burdens? Was I not to carry the pouch and bota? Was I not to bear his shield?

With a snap of his fingers and a movement of his hand he released me from position. Gratefully I moved my body. I stretched. I saw him watching me stretch, catlike. Reddening, I stopped. At a sharp word from him I continued to stretch, luxuriously, brazenly, and fully relished doing so. He watched me as I moved my body, and rubbed my legs, that their full circulation might be restored; they were stiff and cramped, as was the rest of my body, after the fixed position in which I had been kept, as that discipline sequent upon my cuffing. I was aware, though would scarcely admit it to myself, that my movements, as I stretched, and moved my hands upon my legs, were performed rather differently than they would have been had I been alone. I realized, though scarce would admit it to myself, that I was displaying myself as a female before him. He laughed. I blushed, and lay back, angry, on the grass. The body, kept overlong in any position, of course, even the most natural, becomes stiff and cramped. A girl, incidentally, in the position of the Gorean pleasure slave, but who is not being kept in the position as a discipline, in which case she remains rigid, is allowed much subtle latitude, which she exploits, without breaking the position. Sometimes, as she becomes animated, she rises a bit from her heels, sometimes her hands move on her thighs, her shoulders and belly move, her head moves, her eyes are live and vital, she speaks and laughs, and, radiantly, every inch, every bit, of her alive, converses lyrically and delightedly. Any girl knows that an interesting body is a moving body. Even within the apparent restraint of the position of the pleasure slave a girl's body can be a subtle, provocative melody of motion. The interplay between the restraint of the position and her animation gives the position incredible power and beauty. Yes, power. More than one master, I suspect, has been enslaved by the beauty who kneels before him. It is one of the excruciating delights of the mastery to expose oneself fully to, and yet skirt, the dangers of the girl's beauty, to keep oneself strong, to draw the absolute fullness of pleasure from her, and yet to resist her wiles, to get everything from her, and yet to keep her on her knees, fully, perfectly, completely.

I lay back on the grass.

Some girls fight one another with whips to obtain such a master.

I looked up at the sky. It was darker now, through the trees. The man in whose company I was, and in whose power I was, had left the thicket. I did not fear that he would not return. He had not been angry with me. Too, I had seen him look at me, and had heard him laugh.

On Earth, I had found boys of little interest, except for the admiration which they had accorded me. I had held myself, though frequently dating, rather aloof. I did not much care to have boys put their mouths on me. I would brush them back, or thrust them away, appear offended, say "No," firmly to them. They would apologize, stammer, redden. Perhaps I was angry? They were sorry, truly sorry. Perhaps I was angry? Would I forgive them? Could I even consider going out with them again? Perhaps. But what sort of girl did they think I was?

I lay in the grass, and smiled to myself.

I wondered at what sort of girl I was. There had begun to stir in me feelings which I had never felt before. Dimly I had begun to sense how it could be that a woman could give herself totally to a man.

I thought of the stranger. I laughed to myself. He was no boy. With boys I had always felt in command, but with the strange, mighty man in whose power I now was I knew I was not in command. He was in command, completely. At his slightest word I would leap to serve him. How furious, how jealous, would the boys have been had they seen how perfectly the haughty, beautiful girl they could not even interest or impress now responded swiftly, eagerly, even to the snapping of fingers of another, of a true man. How they would have hated and feared him! How they would have envied him his casual sovereignty over the beauty! How perfectly he controlled her, as they could not!

They could not even please her. She feared only she could not please him.

I lay nude on the grass of that strange world, in which I found myself in the power of a man other than I dreamed men could be. I had been aloof, haughty, smug, too good for men. Now I feared only I might insufficiently please one man, him in whose power I was. Feelings stirred in me which I had not felt before. Dimly I had begun to understand how it could be that a woman could give herself, fully, to a male. But I wondered if I would have the opportunity to give myself. I might not be accorded this honor. On this world it seemed men took what they wanted. I might not, on this world, I knew, be extended the courtesy of delicately proffering my virginity as I saw fit, in accord with my will. I smiled. I would not be, I suspected, on this world, permitted to choose upon whom I would bestow it. Perhaps, rather, I supposed, it would be I who would be chosen, and, regardless of my will, it would simply be taken from me.

I sensed the return of the man. I rolled to my elbow, quickly. He was standing nearby.

I looked up at him.

But he did not command me to my back upon the turf; he did not kick apart my legs.

Rather he gestured that I should rise. I did so.

I stood straight before him, as I knew he wished me to do. On Earth never had I stood so straight. On this world I knew it was expected of me. On this world I did not know what I was. But I did know that on this world, whatever it was that I was, I was expected to stand beautifully. I did so. It was part of my obedience.

He did not move, but stood, leaning on his spear. He did not pay me much attention. I was merely there, subject to him, should he speak or gesture.

After a time, he moved about the small clearing and, with his foot, erased the slight signs of our camp, the few small signs of our sojourn in this tiny forest glade. He had made no fires.

Then again he stood near me, leaning on his spear. Again he did not pay me much attention. I stood to one side. I stood straight. I did not, of course, dare to speak, or, in any way, to intrude myself on his attention. I did not wish to be again cuffed or disciplined. I stood there. I stood to one side, unimportant.

I watched him. It was dark now.

My mind raced rapidly. Contrary to yesterday, he had not this day traveled in the light, but had spent the day in this tiny glade, only a few feet wide, concealed by trees about, and, overhead, by their interlacing branches. He had made no fires. He had now, with the coming of darkness, taken up his weapons and erased the small signs of our brief camp. That he had erased the signs of the camp, that he had taken these precautions, suggested to me that we stood now in a region within which there might be those who would be hostile to him, that at our peril we trespassed now in what might be a country of enemies. I shuddered. I looked about myself, with apprehension, at the shadows of the trees and branches. Did they contain enemies, with steel, approaching even now? Might we be set upon, ambushed or attacked? There was a rustle in a thicket of brush, at which the man had been directing his attention. I almost cried out with fear. I sank miserably to my knees. I tried to take his left leg in my hands, to hold him, but, with the butt of his spear, he thrust me back and away. I flew painfully back to the grass. The jabbing blow had not been gentle. I crawled back. I was terrified. I crouched closely behind him, hiding myself behind him, one knee in the grass. I tried to peer about his body. If I had had a weapon, a civilized weapon, even so slight as a small pistol, which I might have grasped, steadying it, with both hands, I might have feared less, but I had nothing, absolutely nothing. I had nothing, and was totally vulnerable. I did not even have a stitch of clothing, a thread, with which to protect my body. My single and only defense was the steel and prowess of the man who stood between me and what, some yards away, rustled in the dark brush. I depended upon him, completely. I needed him. Without him I would have been helpless, utterly. I moaned thinking of how defenseless women must be on this world. I supposed they might carry perhaps a slim blade, manageable to their small strength and weight, a poniard or dagger, but what if an assailant, such as the man in whose power I was, was simply to take it from them? I did not know it at the time but girls such as I was to be were not permitted to carry even so slight a weapon as a woman's dagger. Girls such as I was to be were completely dependent upon the protection of men, and whether they chose to extend it or not. My hand went before my mouth. I saw it, in the darkness, emerging from the brush. I thought, at first, because of its sinuous movement, that it was a great snake, but it was not. I thought, seeing it, holding itself closely to the ground, but yet free of the ground, that it might be a long-bodied lizard. Then, as moonlight fell through the tree branches in a pattern across its snout and neck, I saw not scales, but rippled fur, long and thick. Its eyes caught the light and flashed like burning copper. It snarled. I gasped. It had six legs. It was perhaps twenty feet in length, perhaps eleven hundred pounds in weight. It approached sinuously, hissing. The man spoke soothingly to the beast. His spear faced it. It circled us, and the man turned, always, spear ready, facing it. I kept behind the man. Then the beast disappeared in the shadows. I collapsed at the man's feet, shuddering. He did not admonish me. I was not punished. He had not acted as though he particularly feared the beast. It was not simply that he was brave, and had hunted such animals, but, as I later understood, that he was familiar with the habits of such beasts. The beast had not been hunting us. Commonly such a beast scouts prey, surreptitiously, and then, unless suspecting a trap, as with a tethered victim, perhaps a staked-out girl, used as a lure, makes its swift, unexpected strike, its kill charge. The beast had been on another scent, probably that of tabuk, a small, single-horned antelope-like creature, its common game, and, on its trail, we had constituted only a distraction. Such a beast is a tireless and single-minded hunter. Domesticated, it is often used as a tracker. Once it sets out upon a scent it commonly pursues it unwaveringly. Evolution, in its case, has, among other things, apparently selected for tenacity. This is a useful feature, of course, in tracking. Fortunately ours had not been the first scent that night which the beast, upon emerging from its lair, had taken. Had it been there would have been grim dealings. It is called a sleen.

I had not known such animals could exist. I knelt at the man's feet, the right side of my head to his ankle. How perilous suddenly I realized was the world in which I found myself. I was completely defenseless, helpless. In a world such as this, without a man such as he to protect me, I might be simply hunted down, and torn to pieces by wild beasts. I needed a man such as he to protect me. I looked up at him. He must protect me! I needed his protection. I would pay any price necessary for his protection. In his eyes I saw that he would exact what price he pleased. I put my head down. How I feared a world on which there were such men, and beasts! The name of this world is Gor.

* * * *

He gestured me to my feet and I stood again, straight, frightened, he regarding me. He had already erased the signs of our small camp. This I had taken as evidence that he was ready to soon make his departure from this place. I did not meet his eyes. I did not dare to meet them. In his presence, aside from my fear and vulnerability, I felt, for the first time in my life, certain deep, and overwhelming and indescribable sensations. These sensations, I knew, had something to do with sexuality, his maleness, so strong, so dominant, and my femaleness, so small, so weak, so much at his mercy. I was confused, astonished, troubled. I wanted to please him. Yes! Could it be possible? Can that be imagined in such a situation! That I, an Earth girl, the helpless captive of a brutally handsome, mighty barbarian, wished to please him, and as a woman? Yes, it is true. It is simply true. Hold me in contempt if you must. I do not object. I am not ashamed. I wanted to please the dominant beast. Further, I wanted to please him not simply from fear but also, incredibly perhaps to your mind, out of an inexplicable gratitude for his dominance, which, for no reason I understood, and in spite of my Earth conditioning, I found glorious. I found myself grateful for his strength, and proud for it, though I knew I was the helpless object upon which it would be exercised. I found these sensations deeply disturbing, and profoundly thrilling. I stood straight. I, though a girl of Earth, virginal, well trained and conditioned, intelligent and of good family, wanted to throw myself naked in the grass at the feet of such a man, his.

He lifted his head, and looked away from me, out through the trees.

I was eager to carry his shield, to have its heavy weight placed across my small back, that I might serve him again, as I had before, as his lovely beast of burden, heeling him, but he did not again stagger me beneath that ponderous weight. He stood now, I knew, in a country of enemies. He retained the shield, as he did the spear, the sword.

I wanted to beg him on my knees to rape me.

He turned and left the tiny glade. Swiftly I followed him.

We did not walk far.

As I walked behind him I castigated myself for my weakness in the glade. How I hated myself! How I must improve and strive to be strong. So narrowly had I evaded the loss of my personhood, my self-respect. In the glade, in the darkness, among the trees, so much his, I had almost compromised my identity and integrity! I, a girl of Earth, had wanted to yield to him, a harsh barbarian! Was I not a free individual, a person? Had I no pride? How furious I was with myself. I knew that, in the glade, had he so much as put his hand forth to touch my shoulder, I would have sunk trembling, eager, moaning, helpless, to the grass at his feet. I would have writhed before him for his slightest touch. How relieved I was that I had escaped this degradation. How angry I was. Why had he not taken me in the glade? Had he no regard for my feelings? Had I not been sufficiently pleasing to him?

He turned about, and, with a gesture, cautioned me to immobility and silence.

We stood at the edge of the trees.

Approaching, in the darkness, we saw some twenty torches. I was frightened. I did not know what manner of men these might be.

There were some seventy or eighty individuals in the retinue, which was strung out. The length of their line of march was perhaps some forty or fifty yards, its width some ten yards. Ten men, armed, on each side, flanked the march. These carried the torches. Some five men, armed, preceded the march, some three followed. Some ten or twelve other armed men, here and there, occupied positions in the march. In the march, too, there occurred two platforms and, following, toward the rear, one wagon. The platforms were white, and carried on the shoulders of ten men apiece; the wagon was brown, and was drawn by two large, brown, wide-horned, shaggy, oxlike shambling creatures, conducted by two men. The men who carried the platforms and those who conducted the shambling oxlike creatures were dressed not dissimilarly from the others, those flanking the march and those in and about the march.

The march approached. The man in whose power I was slipped back more deeply among the trees. I, of course, drew back with him. He did not seem disturbed, or surprised, at the line of march. I sensed that he had expected it, that he had, perhaps, been waiting for it, that he had scouted it.

The line of march would take its way rather closely to us. We were concealed in brush, silent.

The line of march approached the trees. I could see that, on the first carried platform, there were some five figures, those of women; on the second there were several chests and boxes, some covered with sheens of glistening material; in the wagon, under a loose canvas, were other boxes, but simpler and grosser in appearance, and poles and tenting materials, and arms and casks of fluid.

We withdrew a bit further into the brush.

The line of march would approach us rather closely. My captor had put aside his shield and spear. He now stood behind me, and slightly to my left. His hands were on my upper arms. We, in the light of the torches, watched the approaching retinue.

I was thrilled, it was so barbaric.

What different humans these were, on this unhurried, stately, barbaric world, so different from that which I knew. I wondered how I had come here, and what I might be doing here.

The vanguard of the torched procession neared us. I could see the weapons of the men. The tunics, scarlet, the helmets and shields, were not cut and formed, and decorated, as were those of the brute who held me by the upper arms.

He did not seem to wish his presence detected.

Suddenly I wanted to cry out. My body had perhaps moved in the slightest tremor. I froze. The blade of his knife was across my throat. His left hand, large and heavy, was firmly fixed across my mouth. I could utter no sound. With the blade at my throat I did not so much as squirm. I remained absolutely still.

Perhaps these men, toward whom he conducted himself as an intruder and enemy, might rescue me! Surely they could be no worse than the brute who held me. He was not a gentleman. Perhaps they were. He had fought with savage steel to possess me; he had candidly, upon his victory, to my horror, appraised my flesh; he had kept me bound for hours; he had made me carry his shield, and heel him like an animal; he had cuffed me, and put me under discipline! He had not treated me as the free and rightful person I was! I had wanted to cry out, to attract the attention of the other men. Perhaps they might rescue me! Perhaps they might return me, somehow, to Earth, or put me in touch with those with whom I might negotiate arrangements for my return to my native world.

I saw the women on the white platform, being carried. How beautifully garbed they were. Obviously these men held women in proper respect, regarding them with rightful reverence, not treating them like animals.

I had decided, swiftly, boldly, to cry out, that I might, by my resolute action, procure my rescue. Perhaps the slightest anticipatory tremor of my decision had coursed through my body. There was a knife at my throat. I did not cry out. Almost instantaneously his hand had closed over my mouth, heavy and firm, and efficient. I was pulled back against his tunic and leather. I could make no sound. I did not even squirm. I could still feel the knife at my throat.

The vanguard of the torched procession passed us.

Over the man's large hand, closing my mouth, making me helpless, I watched the palanquin carrying the women past. On it were five women, girls. Four of these were bare-armed, but garbed in flowing, classic white. Oddly enough, considering the beauty of their raiment, they were bare-footed. They did not wear veils. They were dark-haired and, to my eye, startlingly beautiful. They wore what appeared to be golden circlets about their neck, and a golden bracelet on the left wrist. They knelt, or sat, or reclined about the foot of a white, ornate curule chair set on the platform. In this chair, in graceful lassitude, weary, sat another girl, though one whose features, as she wore sheaths of pinned veils, I could not well remark. I was startled, discerning the volume and splendor of her robes; they were multicolored and brilliant in their sheens and chromatic textures, and so draped and worn that, particularly at the hem, the diverse borders of these various garments seemed to compete with one another to win the observer's accolade as the finest, the most resplendent, of all. About the robes and over the hood and veils of the garmenting were slung medallions and necklaces of wrought gold, pendant with gems. On her hands were white gloves, fastened with hooks of gold. Beneath the final hem of the innermost robe I saw the toes of golden slippers, jeweled, and scarlet-threaded, sparkling in the torchlight. Only in a barbarian world, I thought, could raiment dare be so lavish, so gorgeous, so rich.

Then the palanquin had passed, and more torches, and men. The second palanquin was preciously freighted with chests and boxes, colorful and bound with brass and chains. Some of these were covered over with rich cloths that sparkled under the torchlight.

I supposed that the procession was a wedding procession, and that the second palanquin carried rich gifts, perhaps the bride's dowry, or rich gifts to accompany her, perhaps to be delivered to the groom or his parents.

The wagon which followed late in the procession, that drawn by the conducted, shambling oxlike creatures, carried, I conjectured, the supplies of the retinue. The journey I gathered was long. The bride, and her maids, as I assumed them to be, doubtless had far to travel.

Then the men, the torches, disappeared in the distance, through the trees.

They were gone.

The hand left my mouth. He released me. The knife no longer lay at my throat. My knees felt weak. I almost fell. He resheathed the knife and turned me, by the arms, to face him. He pushed up my chin that I must look at him. I met his eyes, briefly, and put down my head. He knew that I had intended to cry out, to reveal our position. But I had been unable to do so.

I shook with terror, for I feared then he might slay me. I fell to my knees before him, and, though I was an Earth girl, I put down my head and, delicately holding his booted sandals, fearfully, pressed my lips to his feet.

Yes, I kissed his feet, as though I might have been no more than a beautiful, stripped, guilty, frightened slave!

How natural, and necessary, and perfect, in such circumstances, seemed this act of timid abject obeisance!

Would any girl of Earth, I wondered, so in the power of such a man, on such a world, have dared to do otherwise?

He turned about and left the forested area, and I hurried to accompany him.

He had not slain me. He had not tied me to a tree, for sleen to devour. He had not even lashed me to within an inch of my life.

I followed him.

My mind was in tumult. How confused, and shamed, I was at the immediacy, the naturalness, of my act of prostration before him, and yet, on another level, scarcely daring to admit this to myself, I knew that I had, too, perhaps inexplicably, unaccountably, felt enraptured.

I had not known such men could exist.

Then, however, I thought to myself, now I know how to deal with this man. I need only salve his vanity. I need only perform placatory gestures. I thought myself then clever, and he a fool, to be so manipulated by a girl. I did not understand at that time the incredible lenience with which I had been treated, or that the patience of such a man is not inexhaustible. I would be taught these truths shortly.

I was an ignorant and foolish girl. I would learn that ignorance and foolishness are not long tolerated in a girl such as I was to be on Gor.

Three

The Camp

Angrily I tended the brazier, on my knees, fanning the coals. Sparks flew from the iron-banded fire, stinging my body.

Eta strode past me. I hated her. She was dark-haired, incredibly beautiful. Her dark hair swirled behind her to her waist. She had been given clothing. I had not. I envied her the sleeveless body scrap of brown rag, short, high on her thighs, which briefly concealed her. It was fastened with two hooks, which might be swiftly broken and torn away.

A man sat drinking to one side, a strong brew called paga. Spears were stacked to one side, and shields lay about against the sheltering, enclosing cliffs. We were in a wooded canyon, one of many in the area. A small stream, also one of several in the area, ran through the camp. Roughly as we were situated, some two thirds of the camp was closed in by projecting sides of the canyon; roughly, then, about a third of its perimeter was closed by a thick wall of recessed, cut thorn brush, some eight feet high and ten feet thick, a defense against animals. Within the camp itself and about it were several trees, some of them rather large. The camp would not be much visible from the air; similarly it would not be visible from the ground unless one should almost stumble upon it, following this small canyon, rather than various others in the vicinity. My captor and I had arrived at this camp after some four days of trekking. During this time he had not spoken to me, and I had followed him at the position and distance which he had indicated. How relieved I had been that he had not forced his attentions upon me, and used me as a female. And how sullenly and angrily I had followed him, more so each day. Was I not pleasing to him? I knew I had been very fortunate. I had been in his power, completely, and he had not pressed his advantage; he had not exploited his opportunity. How pleased I was! And how furious! How I had begun to hate him! He had not permitted me to feed except when kneeling and from his hand; he watered me similarly, except that, when a stream was encountered, he would sometimes order me to my belly on the pebbles; I would then, his hand in my hair, not using my hands, drink from the water. Was I not in his power, so much so that perhaps I was even, in some sense, a sense I scarcely dared conjecture, "his"? Was I not physically attractive to him? Why had he not forced me to serve him as a woman? He kept me under his dominance, strictly, and then, when I obviously ached for his touch, he would turn away; he would not so much as glance at me. I hated him! I hated him! The last two days of the trek we had traveled much in daylight, and he had permitted me to carry his shield. We had come then, I had gathered, out of overtly hostile territory. That this camp was sheltered and set as it was I took to be a matter of common camp practice among such men as he, and those who served him. Men such as he, in small parties, even in their own countries, seldom made open camps. Why had he not used me? I hated him!

With a piece of stiff leather I fanned the coals in the brazier. An iron protruded from the coals.

Eta passed me again, a haunch of meat upon her shoulder, grease from it in her hair. She was vital, barefoot and tanned. Her body was beautiful in the brief rag she wore. Her only jewelry was a sturdy steel band, looped closely, quite attractively, rather snugly, about her throat. She was a long-legged, sensuous, hot-eyed slut. She was the sort of woman, I supposed, whom the men of Earth, in fear, would not even dare to let enter their dreams. Yet she seemed to fit in well at the feet of the mighty men of Gor who, without thought, would handle her well and get much, and all, from her.

How disgusting she was! I hated her!

I had been in the camp now for better than two days. We had arrived in the late afternoon of the day before yesterday. In the vicinity of the camp, upon our approach to it, my captor had taken his shield from me, which I had been bearing for him. One does not approach a camp, even one's own, unarmed. One does not know what may have transpired in one's absence.

He had left me alone, kneeling, while he had scouted the camp.

Shortly thereafter he had returned, and gestured for me to rise and follow him.

He approached the camp singing, and striking his spear blade on his shield.

Call words were exchanged.

Royally was he greeted by the men of the camp, who rushed forth to welcome him, men among whom I gathered he was chieftain. They shouted, and clasped him, striking him upon the back and laughing. I stood back, frightened of such men. Then a long-legged dream of a girl, Eta, had stood, timidly, near the entrance to the camp, where thorn brush had been wedged aside, during the daylight hours. She had stood there, not daring to approach. Then my captor had indicated that she might enter his presence. Radiantly, joyously, she fled to him, and knelt before him, putting her head to his feet. His shield and spear, and helmet, he handed to another. At a word from him, then, she leapt to her feet and he took her in his arms, as though he might own her, and she kissed him, too, as though she might be owned. Never had I seen human beings kiss like that. It seemed a deeply sensuous complementarity that shook me to the core. It was the kiss of lovers, but more than the kiss of lovers. It was the kiss of a lover who is owned and of one who owns his lover.

Then he laughed, and thrust her to one side. Then all turned to regard me.

How I wished that he had held me and kissed me as he did her. How jealous I was. Then, suddenly, realizing the eyes of all upon me, I was frightened.

The men, and the girl, stood about me. I stood straight. They moved about me. I reddened, assessed. Comments were exchanged. I sensed myself being discussed with open frankness, as might have been an animal. Some of the comments, I sensed, were less than completely flattering. Some, I sensed, were clearly disparaging. Most cruelly I resented the laughter. At that time I had not been brought by strict diet and enforced exercise to optimum measurements. Perhaps, too, at that time, I was not standing as well as I might have. I was standing straight, but perhaps too stiffly, too immobilely, not subtly in movement, in my breathing, the movements of my shoulders, the tiny movements of my head, almost imperceptible, but contributing to the impression of a profoundly alive body, one richly latent with the promise of incredible responsiveness. But mostly I suspect I was found wanting in subtle psychological dimensions, available to the acute observer as a consequence of almost subliminal cues. These matters are conveyed by subtleties of facial expression and physical demeanor. I was a girl raised in a culture predicated on the denial of primate biological realities, a girl from a world in which hypothetically cogent animals denied, denounced and hysterically strove to suppress their own animality, a world in whose social insanity even sexuality had now come to be politically suspect. Most simply, as a normal girl of my world, I had been negatively conditioned with respect to men and sex. In the last few years, an accretion to this form of conditioning, I had been taught that men were my equals, and that men and women were the same. If this were so why then did I feel so small and slight among the Gorean men, and tremble when they put their hands upon me? Among the men of Earth, thoughtful, and cute and kind, I had not felt small and slight, nor did I tremble when they put their hands upon me; I had felt only irritation, and would push them away; I did not dare to push away a Gorean man; I might have been put under discipline; further, I found myself longing, though I did not admit this to myself at the time, to lie lovingly in their arms, theirs. I think the major reason I so failed to impress the men at the camp of my captor was because at that time I had not yet been taught to come alive as a woman. I did not yet know what men were like, or what they could do to me. I did not then know how they in their power could wrench out my insides and bring me to my knees before them. I had not learned their manhood; accordingly I had not yet learned my womanhood. Sexually, I was, like most girls of Earth, negativistic and inert.

Only on Gor, in the presence of my captor, had I, at times, begun to suspect that there was an incredible, glorious world of experience, not forbidden on this planet, to which my nature as a female fully entitled me, could I but dare to be myself. But my fear was groundless. I needed not dare. I needed not decide to become myself. Gorean men do not tolerate pretense and hypocrisy in a girl such as I was to be. Against my will, I would be forced to be what I was.

Much did my captor's men jest with him on the deficiencies of his prize. Laughing, did he strike and kick at them. And the girl, taking his arm, smiling, kissing at him, pulled him away from me. They turned, the entire party, and went into the camp, leaving me outside. I

stood aside, alone. I was furious. I had, in effect, been spurned, rejected. Nothing in my experience had prepared me for this treatment. I
felt the gravel of the canyon under my feet, the sunlight reflected from
the walls. My fists were clenched. Who did these barbarians think they
were? I was the most beautiful girl in the junior class at an elite girls'
college on Earth, perhaps in the college as a whole. The only exception
might perhaps have been the beautiful senior in anthropology, Elicia
Nevins. We had been great rivals. But she had only been an anthropology major, whereas I was an English major, and a poetess. But then I
recalled the beautiful, intelligent-seeming, hot-eyed slut in the brown
rag. In a world where there might be such women, I realized, gasping,
Judy Thornton's beauty and even that of an Elicia Nevins would not
be particularly outstanding. As I would later learn, the value placed
on girls such as we were, a Judy Thornton or an Elicia Nevins, girls
of our quality, would commonly be a tiny sack of copper coins, a few
more, a few less.

I went inside the brush wall, and knelt down. I wanted to be protected and fed. I would do what they wished to pay for my lodging.
Behind me, the thorn brush, so thick and high, by means of hooked
poles, was pulled into place, closing me in the camp with the men,
and the girl.

I had now been in the camp for two days. Angrily I tended the brazier, on my knees, fanning the coals. Sparks scattered about. My body
was stung by them. I used a squarish piece of stiff leather to fan the
coals. From the brazier, protruding, was the handle of an iron.

Many were the menial tasks which I was forced to perform in and
about the camp.

I was not pleased.

I had been forced to build fires and help cook the food. I had been
forced to help serve the food, and to pour wine and paga for the men,
as though I might be a servant. I had been forced to help put food away
afterwards, and clean goblets and utensils, and clear away the litter
and debris of the feeding. I had been forced to sew rent garments, and
once, not satisfied with a seam, Eta had had me rip out the thread and
perform the entire task again, doing it well. To my humiliation, too, I
was taught to wash clothing on rocks, pounding and rinsing, on my

knees, at the edge of the tiny stream which moved through the camp. Outside the camp I was set to picking berries and gathering armloads of wood. Outside the camp I would be accompanied by one of my captor's men. On Earth, I had enjoyed a rather elevated socioeconomic status. In my home we had always had, as long as I could remember, both a maid and a cook. From the age of fifteen I had enjoyed giving them orders, as an equal, but not quite. I was not the sort of girl who was accustomed to perform menial tasks, or be of service to others. That was for women of a rather different class, one beneath mine. But here, in this camp, I was helping Eta to cook, and clean and sew, and performing even more degrading tasks, such as serving men at their meals. That might be all right for Eta. I did not know her class. Judging by her garment it was low. But it was not all right for Judy Thornton. I was a brilliant girl, and I wrote poetry. Sometimes, when no men were about, I would refuse to help Eta. She would then, not speaking, not protesting, but sullenly, perform the task herself. When men were about, I would do what tasks she set me. I was afraid of the men.

There were sixteen men in the camp, including my captor, though seldom, during the day, were there more than four or five within its confines.

My captor himself had set me the work of tending the coals in the brazier, where the iron was heating.

I did not dare disobey him.

I was not surprised that there were coals for the brazier, as, on my first full day in the camp, moving about it, I had discovered that it was well stocked with supplies. It was in the nature of a cache camp, which might be returned to now and again. In a cave in the adjoining cliff there were several boxes. Several were locked, but others were open. There were flasks of wine there, and bottles of the brew called paga; stores of salt, grains, dried meats and vegetables; tunics, cloths and blankets; too, there were tools and utensils, and threads and needles; I found some perfumes and jewelries; I did not dare to bedeck myself with them, though I was curious to do so; they were quite barbaric; the girl, Eta, I noted, wore as her only jewelry a sturdy band on her neck; this suggested to me that one were not simply free to help oneself to such finery; doubtless if the men wished me to wear such jewelries they would throw them to my feet and order me to don them, or perhaps, more frighteningly, they would, with their large hands, put them on my body themselves; I found a chest containing medicines and bandages; too, there were some rolls of furs; a box of leather goods, too, I found, which contained strips of leather, pieces of leather, and straps of various sorts; I found two whips, but I did not understand their function, as the men seemed to have no animals on which to use them; also, though heavy enough, they seemed rather short-bladed for the ponderous beasts I had earlier seen in the retinue, those shambling, oxlike beasts drawing the wagon; their soft leather blades were not more than a yard long; indeed, the blades of one were scarcely wider than a girl's back; there was also a box of chains there; I did not look at them closely; I did not understand their purpose. To one side had lain the sacks of coals and some irons.

I tended the brazier.

It was now late afternoon.

A few yards away, Eta was roasting the haunch of meat on a spit. I could smell the roasting meat.

I was hungry.

In the confines of the camp my captor had continued to restrict my feeding to his degrading handouts, which he would place in my mouth, or make me reach for, kneeling, not using my hands.

How I hated him!

How he kept me on my knees to him. How I hated him! And yet he was the most magnificently attractive man I had ever seen. I hoped he would let me have a scrap of the roast meat. How relieved I had been on the trek that he had not abused me, not used me for his pleasure, as would have been so easy, I, his helpless, naked captive. And yet, too, how angry I had grown, so amorous, so weak, so frustrated. Had I not been, in effect, "his"? Was I not physically attractive to him? I knew now I was no Eta, but surely I was better than nothing. Why had he not taken me, if only, throwing me to the grass, briefly, brutally? He had kept me under his dominance, strictly, and then, when I had obviously ached for his touch, he would turn away, not so much as glancing at me. One night when I had laid near him, bound hand and foot, I had literally whimpered in my need, trying to put my head against him. He had put wadding in my mouth, and lashed it in with binding, gagging me, then pushed me from his side that he might sleep. I slept little that night, rolling and squirming with misery. Two days later, after we had stopped to camp, my need so much upon me, I knelt before him and, tears in my eyes, began kissing at his feet and legs. I lifted my eyes to him, filled with tears. "Rape me," I begged. "Rape me!" And even though we did not know one another's language, there could have been no mistaking the nature of my needs, and the import of my petition. But he had turned away. That night, in my bonds, for hours, I had wept and squirmed. I was then a virgin. I did not even know, fully, then, what a man could do to me. Yet, even then, had I been told how it is that girls of a certain sort, of a sort which I was soon to find myself to be, could sometimes in their need scream and writhe in the grass, could sometimes dance wildly beneath the moons, clawing at them, could sometimes tear their fingernails bloody scratching at the cement of their kennels, could sometimes bruise their bodies hurling them against the bars of their cells or tear their flesh pulling against their shackles to touch a guard, I would have dimly understood. How cruel men are sometimes, not to satisfy such a woman.

But I resolved to resist my captor.

All of the men had, by now, filtered back into the camp. Two men were playing, to one side, a board game, with tall pieces. There were one hundred squares on the board. Some four or five men crouched about, watching the play. Other men sat about. Most talked. Two drank wine together. One man worked on the scabbard of his sword with a small, fine tool. Another man was, slowly and smoothly, sharpening the blade of his spear. My captor, with two lieutenants, sat over a map, drawn with a stick in the earth. They discussed some project, the nature of which I, of course, ignorant of the language, could not understand. Once, one of the lieutenants glanced up, toward me, looking at me; then he returned his attention to the map.

My captor rose to his feet and approached the brazier. I knelt back, on my heels. With a heavy glove, picked up from the grass, he pulled forth the iron and examined it. It was whitish hot. I withdrew from it, leaning back, so intense was its heat. He thrust the iron back in the brazier, deeply, and indicated I should continue my labors, with which directive, of course, I complied.

He returned to his lieutenants. They continued their conversation, their discussion or planning.

Eta hummed and sang as she tended the roasting meat, heavy and hot, dripping fat, hissing, into the fire, on its greenwood spit. Sometimes she glanced over to me. I was not too pleased with the way she smiled at me. She seemed in an unusually good humor, especially considering that I had refused to help her several times this afternoon. The last time she had wanted my help in polishing leather. Of course, I had refused. Such work might be appropriate for a girl such as Eta, but not for the likes of Judy Thornton. I was no cook, no maid, no polisher of a man's leather! I was Judy Thornton. I was not a servant! No, I was the sort of girl who had servants, who gave them their orders, who managed them and supervised them in their duties. I was too good, too fine, to be a servant.

I did not understand the purpose for which the iron was being heated. It was clearly a marking, or branding, iron. Yet there was no animal in the camp to be marked. I had expected one to be brought in, perhaps one which had been somewhere acquired, but none was brought in. I then conjectured that one of the men, perhaps my captor, since it was he who had had me tend the brazier, wished to mark something which he owned, imprinting in it an identificatory design, perhaps a harness or belt, or the leather of a brass-hooped shield. It seemed to me a sensible idea. I had seen the design at the tip of the iron. It was a small flower, stylized; it was circular, about an inch and a half in diameter; it was not unlike a small rose; it was incredibly lovely and delicate. I thought the design was very beautiful; I certainly would not have minded marking something I owned with it. The only reservation I had pertaining to the design was that I thought it might be a bit too delicate and lovely, like a lovely rose, to appropriately mark goods of a gross masculine nature, such as, say, harnesses or shields. It seemed it might, considering its resemblance to a rose, much more appropriately mark something feminine.

The sun was down now and the supper would soon be ready. The coals in the brazier glowed.

There was a white-barked, fallen tree close at hand, within the camp enclosure. It was broken off some four feet from the ground, and the fallen trunk, from that height, inclined downward.

I looked about the camp, at the men, and at Eta. They were rough, strong men, who played cruel games. Yesterday evening I had been forced to aid Eta in serving the men, carrying meat to them in my teeth; later I had moved among them, as they had summoned me, pouring them wine and paga. I must take the goblet, fill it, kiss it delicately and proffer it to the male. After the supper Eta was taken and belled. I shrank back. They wound thongs, more than a yard in length, closely set with small bells, about her tanned ankles. More bells they tied about her wrists. They then took strings of bells and threw them, looped, about her neck. Five men stood in a line, some yards from her, who were to be the contestants. He who was to act as referee then tore away from Eta the brief rag she wore. The men cried out with pleasure, smiting their left shoulders with the palms of their right hands. Eta regarded them, the bells upon her body, and about her neck and breasts, proudly, arrogantly. There was a mark on her left thigh but I could not well see it in the darkness. Then her hands were taken behind her and tied. Opaque cloths were brought and bets were placed. Eta continued to regard the men, haughtily. Then, about her belly, the referee fastened a tight thong. On this thong, at her left hip, was fastened a single bell, larger than the others, and of a different note. It would serve in particular to guide the men. Then, as she stood proudly, a cloth was thrown over her head and tied under her chin. She was hooded. The girl is hooded in order that she not be able to influence the outcome of the sport. Too, I suspect the men enjoy having her hooded that she, in the darkness of the hood, in her helplessness, will not know who it is who seizes her. Gorean men, the beasts, find such things amusing. The five men were then similarly hooded, the opaque cloths thrown over their heads and tied under their chins. Eta, in her hood, stood absolutely still, not causing the rustle of a bell. The five men then, to the amusement of the observers, were led about the camp, and turned muchly about, that they be completely disoriented. The referee then, taking up a switch, went to the vicinity of Eta. I watched from the shadows. I was indignant, and horrified, of course. Too, I was consumed with pity for my poor unfortunate sister. Too, I was curious to see who it would be who would first seize her. Of the five contestants I knew well whom I would have first chosen, had I had a choice in such matters, to get his hands on me, a blond, shaggy haired young giant, with freckled wrists, whose hair clung about his shoulders. To me he was the most attractive man in the camp after my captor. My captor did not join in the game. He was chieftain and leader. It was sport for the lower ranks, something to relieve the tedium of the camp. But my captor watched with interest and pleasure. He lifted paga to his lips. I think, too, he had wagered on the outcome.

The game of Girl Catch is played variously upon Gor; it can be played as informally and simply as it was in the camp of my captor, for the pleasure of his men, or it can be a fairly serious business, closely supervised and regulated in a sophisticated manner, as it is by merchant administrators in the rings outside the perimeters of the Sardar Fairs, where the young men of various cities compete. In one form there a hundred young men and a hundred young women of one city, the women selected for their beauty, enter the ring in competition with a hundred young men and a hundred young women of another city, similarly selected. In this form no hoods are worn. The object of the male is to protect his own women and secure those of the enemy. A girl is caught, stripped, bound hand and foot, and carried to the Girl Pit of the capturing city, into which she is thrown. If she cannot free herself, she is counted as a catch. Her own men may not enter the Girl Pit of the capturing city to free her. Sometimes this game is played with the winning side determined by its catches within a time limit, sometimes, in more brutal versions, by the first city which secures the hundred women of its enemy. A male is disqualified from further participation in the contest if he is forced from the ring. Women from the victorious city who may have been captured are, of course, upon the victory of their city, freed. Women from the conquered city, on the other hand, are not; they are kept; they are turned over to the young males of the capturing city; in the game in which the first hundred captures decides victory this means there is a girl for each participating young man, usually one he himself brought bound to the Girl Pit. Accordingly, particularly in the early phases of the game, the young males often devote their acquisitive attentions to those young women of the enemy city who are the most attractive to them personally, to those they would most enjoy taking home with them at the end of the day. This sport of Girl Catch, interestingly, when matters of honor are not thought to be involved, has been used upon occasion by cities to settle boundary disputes and avert wars.

In the camp of my captor, however the rules were simple. The referee lifted his switch.

He cried out a word, which I would later learn meant "Quarry." It is the signal that the game has begun, that the girl is now available, that she is now at large for capture. At the same time that he had cried out this word he had swung the switch and struck Eta a swift, stinging blow below the small of the back, making her cry out, identifying her original position and, with a jangle of bells, starting her into motion. The men wheeled toward the sound. Eta stopped, frozen. She was crouched over, her hands tied behind her back. Whether the slender, supple disciplinary device would be used often in the game depends much on the skill of the girl player. She must, following the rules, move at least once in every five Ihn, which is a little less than five seconds. If she does not move within five Ihn, perhaps being frightened, or having miscounted, the referee, with the switch, swiftly and exactly identifies her position for the contestants. An instant before the five Ihn were up Eta, jangling with bells, darted off, changing her position. Some of the men cried out angrily, for she had darted, unknowingly, between two of them. The referee cautioned the men sharply. The male contestants must not identify themselves. Such an identification, in that it might affect the girl's behavior, she perhaps desiring capture by a particular male, might unfairly influence the outcome of the game. Needless to say, the girl is expected to be an excellent quarry. If she is a poor quarry, and puts up a disappointing run, and is too soon captured, her wrists are tied over her head and she is lashed. It is seldom necessary to do this, of course. Girls pride themselves on their evasive skills in Girl Catch; they strive with every fiber in their small bodies to be cunning, elusive quarry, not to be easily caught; with delight do they struggle to elude the predator; with relish do they know, belled, their capture and seizure is inevitable.

Eta was skilled in the game. But so, too, were the men. Often I suspected had she been thusly hunted and the men of the camp her hunters.

Twice did the referee, with his switch, incite the beauty to motion.

At last it seemed she knew not which way to turn. The men, silent, were about her.

Blindly, hooded, she fled—into the arms of the young blond giant. With a cry of pleasure he seized her and flung her to the grass, pinned beneath him. She was caught.

The referee called out a word, which I would later learn was "Capture," and slapped the man on the shoulder. The other men stepped back. Then, to my horror, I saw Eta, still hooded and bound, in her bells, ravished in the grass.

When the young man had finished with her he stood up and unknotted the hood from his head, casting it aside. Men lifted cups to him and shouted and pounded him upon the back. He was grinning. He had won. He returned to his place. Moneys were exchanged. Eta lay on her side in the grass.

She seemed small, lying there, hooded and bound, in her bells. By all but me she was forgotten. I felt terribly sorry for my poor sister. And I envied her her ravishment.

In a few moments the referee had returned to her and, by the arms, thrown her again to her feet. She stood unsteadily, trembling, the motion of her body agitating the bells.

He again called the word I was later to learn was "Quarry," and again he put her into motion with the switch. Again the men stalked her. Second place was at stake. She did not run as well this time, but, perhaps because this time there were only four pursuers, performed on the whole commendably. In some two or three minutes she was again taken and, to my horror, was, with pleasure and ruthlessness, again subjected to the indignity of the caught female, her second captor handling her with an audacity and simple physical proprietorship scarcely inferior to that of the first. How sorry I felt for her, and how, secretly, I envied her. I watched while third place and fourth place were won. The fifth man, when he had removed his hood, was the butt of much good-humored laughing and pushing. He, losing out, had not won the right to ravish the belled beauty.

The referee removed the hood from Eta, who threw back her head, shaking her hair, drinking in the night air. Her face was flushed and broken out. It was suffused with pleasure. Oddly, she seemed shy. Her hands were freed. She sat on the grass, removing the bells from her body. She, removing bells from her right ankle, looked over at me.

I looked at her, angrily.

She smiled. She removed the last of the bells. Then she laughed, and came over and kissed me.

I did not even look at her.

Then she went to pick up the brown rag which the referee had removed from her before the start of the sport. She did not try to put the rag on but carried it in her hand, loosely, and went to lie at the feet of my captor. I remembered how she had looked at me. It was the look of a woman who knows herself incredibly desired and beautiful, who was at the mercy of men, and who, because they had wished it, had been put muchly to their pleasure.

I was angry with her. Too, I envied her. Too, she had looked upon me as though I might be a naive girl.

It was dark now.

The white-barked tree, fallen, within the camp enclosure, broken off some four feet from the ground, the trunk then inclining to the ground, was near.

I saw that Eta had finished with the meat. Two men had, by the spit, lifted the hot, impaled roast, and put it on the grass for cutting. I was pleased that supper was near.

I tended the brazier. It glowed in the darkness.

Two men came and stood over me. I looked up, startled. They pulled me up by the arms and took me to the white-barked tree. They threw me on my back, my head down, on the tree. I looked at them, wildly. My hands were tied together before my body and then pulled up and over my head. They were fastened, behind my head, out of my vision, to the tree. My body was stretched out, one leg on each side of the trunk. "What are you doing?" I cried. I felt my body being tightly roped to the tree. I squirmed, my head down, my legs up. "Stop!" I cried. Ropes were placed on my neck and belly, and on each leg, above the knees and at the ankles, and lashed tightly. "Stop," I begged. "Please stop!" I could barely move. The men stepped back; I was fastened to the tree. "Let me go!" I cried. "Please!" I whimpered. "What are you going to do?" I asked. They looked at me. I was helpless. "What are you going to do?" I whimpered.

"Oh, no!" I cried. "No, no, no, no!"

My captor had gone to the brazier and, with the leather glove, and another, too, with two hands, withdrawn the white-hot iron. I felt the heat of it, even feet away. "No!" I screamed. "No!" Two men, large men, strong, held my left thigh immobile.

I looked into the eyes of my captor. "Please, no!" I wept. "Please, no!"

Then, head down, helpless, held, I was branded a Gorean slave girl.

The marking, I suppose, took only a few seconds. That is doubtless true. Objectively I grant you the truth of that. Yet a girl who has been marked finds this obvious truth difficult to accept psychologically.

Perhaps I may be granted that those seconds, those few seconds, seem very long seconds.

For an hour it seemed I felt the iron. It touched me firmly, kissing me, then claiming me.

I screamed, and screamed. I was alone with the pain, the agony, the degradation, the relentless, hissing object, so hurting me, the men. Mercifully they let me scream. It is common to let a girl scream, a Gorean kindness, while she is being marked with a white-hot iron. Afterwards, however, once the iron is pulled out of her body, and she is fully marked, Gorean males are less likely to accord her such consideration for her feelings. They are less likely, then, to be so indulgent with her. This makes sense. Afterwards, she is only a branded girl.

It begins swiftly, almost before you can feel it. I felt the iron touch me and almost instantaneously, crackling, flash through my outer skin and then, firmly, to my horror, enter and lodge itself fixedly in my thigh. It was literally in my body, inflexibly, burning. The pain then began to register on my consciousness. I began screaming. I could not believe what was being done to me, or how much it hurt. Not only could I feel the iron, but I could hear it, hissing and searing in the precise, beautiful wound it was relentlessly burning in my thigh. There was an odor of burning flesh, mine. I smelled burning, as of a kind of meat. It was my own body being marked. I could not move my thigh. I threw back my head and screamed. I felt the iron tight in my body, then, to my horror, pressing in even more deeply. The marking surface of the iron, then, lay hissing, literally submerged, in my flesh. I could not move my thigh in the least. I threw my head from side to side, screaming. The marking surface of the iron is some quarter of an inch in depth. It was within my flesh. It was lodged there, submerged, hissing and burning. Taking its time, not hurrying, it marked me, cleanly and deeply. Then, swiftly, cleanly, it withdrew.

I smelled burned meat, my own. The men released my thigh. I began to choke and sob. Men regarded the mark. My captor was commended on his work. I gathered I had been well marked.

The men then left me and I continued to lie, head down, roped and helpless, on the broken, inclined trunk of the white-barked tree.

I was overwhelmed, psychologically, with what had happened to me. The pain was now less. My thigh still stung, and cruelly, but the pain seemed relatively unimportant now compared to the enormity of the comprehension that shook me to the core. I had been branded. I shuddered in the bonds. I moaned. I wept. My thigh would be sore for days, but that was unimportant, even trivial. What would remain was the mark they had placed in my flesh. That, unlike the pain, would not vanish. I would continue to wear that mark. It would, from now on, identify me as something which I had not been, or had not explicitly been, before, but now was clearly, and for the eyes of all. I lay there. I knew I now was, because of the brand, deeply and profoundly different than I had been before. What could a brand mean? I shuddered. I scarcely dared conjecture the nature of a girl who wore such a mark on her body. She could be only one thing. I forced the thought from my mind. I tried to move my wrists, my head and body, my legs and ankles. I could move them very little. They were helpless in their constraints. Only animals wore brands. I lay there, helpless, miserable. I was Judy Thornton. I was an excellent student at an elite girls' college on Earth. I was the most beautiful girl in the junior class, perhaps in the whole school, unless for my rival, the lovely senior in anthropology, Elicia Nevins. I was an English major, and a poetess! How was it then that I lay bound on a strange world, and bore in my flesh a fresh brand? How Elicia Nevins would have laughed with delight could she have seen me, her lovely, saucy rival, brought so low, even to a brand. I considered Elicia. We had been catty, haughty and smug to one another, competing in our beauty, our honors and popularity. How she would laugh to see me now! I could not even, now, have looked her in the face. The brand had made me different. She did not have a brand. I did. Had she faced me then, and I been unbound, I would have lowered my eyes and head, and, in shame, knelt before her. Had a simple mark on my thigh made me so different? I suspected that it had. I shuddered. I thought of the boys with whom I had gone out on Earth, those immature young men, many of them rich and well-placed socially, whom I had accepted as escorts and dates, often for no better reason than to display my unusual popularity before the other girls in the school. What if they should see me now? Some, I supposed, would have fled in terror, had I, a branded girl, been thrown to their feet. Others, perhaps, stricken and confused, would have blubbered and stammered, looking away, covering me with their coats, speaking tumbled, incoherent, soothing words, solicitous and hypocritical. How many of them, I wondered, would do what they truly wanted, as I had little doubt Gorean men would do? How many of them, I wondered, would simply look down and see me at their feet as what I was, a branded girl? I wondered how many would look down upon me, laugh with pleasure and say, "I have always wanted you, Judy Thornton. Now I am going to have you," and then take me by the arm and throw me to their sheets? Few I suspected. Yet, now, branded, for the first time I was acutely aware of the fantastic strength and size of even such boys, not even men, not even Gorean men, compared to my own diminutive strength and stature. Such matters had not seemed important before; now they seemed extremely important. Before I had been able to put off boys with a glance, a gesture, a sharp word, but what if, now, they should see me as I now was, wearing a brand. Would they simply laugh now at my silly glance, my gesture, my protest. Would they simply laugh, and do what they wanted with me? Or, perhaps, like Gorean men, would they first discipline me, and then perform upon me what actions they chose? With the brand, I knew I was somehow deeply and profoundly different. I lay on the white-barked tree trunk, head down, weeping. The brand has on Gor legal, institutional status; that which it marks it makes an object; its victim has no rights, or appeal, within the law. Yet the most profound consequences of the brand seem to be less social than intensely individual, personal and psychological; the brand, almost instantaneously, transforms the deepest consciousness of a girl; I resolved to fight these feelings, to keep my personhood, even wearing a brand. I lay confined in bonds. I could scarcely move. But I suspected, and truly, that the mightiest bond I wore was not the strict, confining loops on my wrists or belly but the newly incised brand on my body; later, I suspected, even if coils of rope and heavy chains might be heaped upon me, or I should be confined in cells or kennels, the most complete and inescapable shackle placed upon me would nonetheless be always that delicate, feminine design, that small, lovely flower, resembling a rose, burned into the flesh of my upper left thigh.

I heard the sounds of the camp about me. The men were near the fire. The roasted meat was being cut. There was conversation. Eta, long-legged and beautiful, was serving the men. I looked up at the rich Gorean night, beautiful with bright stars. Turning my head I could see the three moons. I felt the smooth, brittle bark of the white-barked tree beneath my back, on the interior of my thighs, tied as I was. I could smell the roast meat, the vegetation about. I heard insects. I tried to move my ankles and wrists. I could move them very little. I had cried a great deal. My cheeks, tear-stained, felt tight under the salty rivulets which had dried upon them. I wondered what could be my status on this world, now that I had been marked. What could be the nature, on a world such as this, of a girl who wore such a mark on her body?

Men from about the fire, including my captor, and Eta, too, approached me.

My captor took my head in his hands, and held it so that I must look up at him. I looked to him for pity. In his eyes there was no pity. I, branded, shuddered in his grasp. "Kajira," said he to me, clearly and simply. "Kajira." Then he released my head. I continued to regard him. "Kajira," he said. I understood that I was to repeat this phrase. "Kajira," I said. I had heard this word several times before on this world. The men who had first come to the rock and chain in the wilderness had used it to me. And, too, there had been the cry of "Kajira canjellne," which had seemed to play some ritualistic role in the fierce contest which had brought me, helpless, into his uncompromising power. "La Kajira," said Eta, indicating herself. She drew up the brief garment she wore, turning to me, exposing her left thigh. It, too, bore a brand. She, too, was truly branded. I now realized that I had seen the mark before, in torchlight and half darkness, yesterday evening, when she had been stripped, hooded and belled, and set as lovely quarry to run for the amusement of the men. I had not even understood it at that time, not well seeing it, as a brand. It had never even entered my mind that it might have been a brand. It had been only a puzzling mark of some sort. I would not have believed, yesterday night, that a woman could have been branded. But now, after my recent experience with the iron, I was prepared to believe the evidence of my senses. Women, on this world, could be branded. Eta and I were, in a profound sense, I realized, now the same; we were both branded women; no longer was I her superior; a mark had been put upon me by a hot iron at the pleasure of men; I was now exactly the same as Eta; whatever she was I, too, I knew, was now that, exactly that, and only that. Her brand, however, was not precisely the same as mine. It was more slender, more vertical, more like a stem with floral, cursive loops, about an inch and a half in height, and a half inch in width; it was, I would later learn, the initial letter in cursive script of the Gorean expression 'Kajira'; my own brand was the "dina"; the dina is a small, lovely, multiply petaled flower, short-stemmed, and blooming in a turf of green leaves, usually on the slopes of hills, in the northern temperate zones of Gor; in its budding, though in few other ways, it resembles a rose; it is an exotic, alien flower; it is also spoken of, in the north, where it grows most frequently, as the slave flower; it was burned into my flesh; in the south, below the Gorean equator, where the flower is much more rare, it is prized more highly; some years ago, it was not even uncommon for lower-caste families in the south to give the name 'Dina' to their daughters; that practice has now largely vanished, with the opening and expansion of greater trade, and cultural exchange, between such cities as Ko-ro-ba and Ar, and the giant of the southern hemisphere, Turia. In the fall of the city of Turia, some years ago, thousands of its citizens had fled, many of them merchants or of merchant families; with the preservation of the city, and the restoration of the Ubarate of Phanius Turmus, many of these families returned; new contacts had been made, new products discovered; even of those Turians who did not return to their native city, many of them, remaining in their new homes, became agents for the distribution of Turian goods, and for the leathers and goods of the Wagon Peoples, channeled through Turia. That in the north the lovely dina was spoken of as the "slave flower" did not escape the notice of the expatriated Turians; in time, in spite of the fact that "Dina" is a lovely name, and the dina a delicate, beautiful flower, it would no longer be used in the southern hemisphere, no more than in the northern, as a name for free women; those free women who bore the name commonly had it changed by law, removed from the lists of their cities and replaced by something less degrading and more suitable. "Dina," in the north, for many years, had been used almost entirely as a slave name. The reason, in the north, that the dina is called the slave flower has been lost in antiquity. One story is that an ancient Ubar of Ar, capturing the daughter of a fleeing, defeated enemy in a field of dinas there enslaved her, stripping her by the sword, ravishing her and putting chains upon her. As he chained her collar to his stirrup, he is said to have looked about the field, and then named her "Dina." But perhaps the dina is spoken of as the slave flower merely because, in the north, it is, though delicate and beautiful, a reasonably common, unimportant flower; it is also easily plucked, being defenseless, and can be easily crushed, overwhelmed and, if one wishes, discarded.

The brand Eta wore was not the "dina"; it was, as I would later learn, the initial letter in cursive script of the Gorean expression 'Kajira'; it, too, however, was, in its delicacy and floral nature, an incredibly beautiful and feminine brand; I recalled that I had thought that the brand I had heated might be too feminine to mark a man's properties, such as a saddle or shield, but that it would be perfect to mark something feminine in nature; now I realized that it marked me; both the brand that I wore and that which Eta wore were incredibly feminine; our femininity, whether we wished it or not, had been deeply, and incontrovertibly, stamped upon us. It was natural, given the fact that the dina is the "slave flower," that eventually enterprising slavers, warriors and merchants, those with an interest in the buying and selling of women, should develop a brand based on the flower. Beyond this, there exists on Gor a variety of brands for women, though the Kajira brand, which Eta wore, is by far the most common. Some merchants invent brands, as the dina was invented, in order to freshen the nature of their merchandise and stimulate sales. Collectors, for example, those who are rich, sometimes collect exotic brands, much as collectors on Earth might collect stamps or coins, populating their pleasure gardens not only with girls who are beautiful but diversely marked. A girl, of course, wants to be bought by a strong master who wants her for herself, muchly desiring and lusting for her, not for her brand. When a girl is bought, of course, it is commonly because the man wants *her, she, the female*, and is willing to put down his hard-earned money for her and her alone, for she is alone; all she brings from the block is herself; she is a slave; she cannot bring wealth, power, or family connections; she comes naked and sold; it is she alone he buys. There are, of course, men who buy for brands. To meet this market various brands are developed and utilized. The "slave flower" brand was a natural development. Unfortunately for these entrepreneurs, their greed and lack of control over the metal shops resulted in the widespread proliferation of the dina brand. As it became more popular, it was becoming, simultaneously, of course, a fairly common brand. Girls branded as I was were already spoken of on Gor, rather disparagingly, as "dinas." Collectors now seldom sought for dinas. This development, though perhaps a disappointment to certain merchants and slavers, was not unwelcome to the girls who bore the brand, though few cared for their feelings. The girl who is bid upon and sold from the block wants to be bought because men have found her desirable, so desirable that they are willing to part with their silver, perhaps even with their very gold, to buy her; how miserable she would be to learn that it is only for her brand that she is valued. There were other brands in my captor's camp. Yet I had been made a "dina." He had not done this for economic reasons. He had "sized me up," my nature and my body. He had decided the dina brand would be, for me, exquisitely "right." Accordingly, he had burned it into my flesh. Now, in my body, deeply, I wore the "slave flower."

Eta bent over me, smiling. She indicated the steel band she wore on her throat. It had writing on it, incised in the steel, in a script I could not recognize. She turned the steel band, not too easily, on her throat. It fitted her closely, as though it might have been measured to her. I gasped. It was literally locked on her throat. I understood then, to my horror, she could not remove it. Eta wore a steel collar!

Eta then faced my captor. "La Kajira," she said, submissively inclining her head to him. Had I been a man I might have been driven wild, I supposed, by the way in which this had been said. Then Eta turned to me, laughing, pointing to my mouth. I did not understand. She pointed to her own mouth, again faced my captor, and again said, "La Kajira," again performing an obeisance before him. Then, smiling, Eta pointed to my mouth. Bound, I looked upward, into the eyes of my captor. "La Kajira," I said to him. Then, weeping, I closed my eyes and turned my head to the side. Bound as I was I could not well incline my head to him, but, instinctively, I had turned my head to the side, exposing my throat vulnerably to him. This had occurred so naturally that I was shaken by it. Then his large hand lay on my throat. I knew he could have crushed it easily. I turned my head under his hand, and again looked up at him. Tears welled hot in my eyes. "La Kajira!" I whispered, and again turned my head to the side. His hand left my throat, and he, and the others, saying nothing more, returned to the fire, to continue their meal.

Again I lay alone on the inclined trunk of the white-barked tree. What could be my status on this world? Only animals were branded. I wore a brand. Only now, for the first time, now that I was branded, did they show any interest in teaching me their language. Before they had not even taught me the words for "Run" and "Fetch." I suspected that I must now, now that I had been branded, address myself with great diligence to the acquisition of their language. I did not think they would now be patient with me. I had been branded. I would have to learn swiftly and well. The first words I had been taught were "Kajira," which my captor had addressed to me, and "La Kajira," which expressions I understood, from Eta's example, I must utter to my captor. I knew then that I was a Kajira, and, too, I gathered that this status, whatever it might be, was one I shared with Eta; she had said "La Kajira" to him in a fashion which clearly suggested that she was acknowledging herself a "Kajira" before him. Both Eta and I wore brands. Eta wore even a collar; I wore no collar, but I knew that if they wished to place one upon me, they, unhesitantly, would do so. Though I wore no collar, I knew I was, should anyone wish, subject to the collar. I knew now I was a Kajira; I knew that I had, too, following Eta's example, acknowledged myself as such to my captor; I had proclaimed myself a Kajira, whatever it might be, before him. What could a Kajira be? I forced from my mind the only possible answer, refusing to admit it to consciousness. Then, overwhelmingly, irresistibly, like a cry of anguish, it welled up within me; I could no longer ignore, suppress or repudiate it; no longer could I, like a foolish girl of Earth, deny and flee my reality; the comprehension, insistent and explosive, overpoweringly, erupted within me; I was naked and bound; I was subject to the collar; I had been branded; I had said "Kajira"; I had said "La Kajira"; these were the first words I had been taught; I knew I was a Kajira; I did not even know if any longer I had a name; I supposed I had not; I supposed now I was only a nameless animal in the power of men; I had been too good, too fine, to be a servant; now I was a Kajira; my thigh stung; I moaned with anguish; I wept; a Kajira, I knew, was not even a servant, could not aspire to be even so much; a Kajira was a slave girl; and the meaning of "La Kajira," which I had uttered to my captor was "I am a slave girl."

I cried out, a long, anguished cry, then knowing myself a slave girl. "Kajira" and "La Kajira" are often the first words a girl of Earth, carried to Gor, must learn. The women of Earth, to the mighty men of Gor, are good for little but slaves.

When I had cried out with anguish, bound on the inclined trunk of the white-barked tree, two men rose from near the fire and, as though they had been waiting for some such cry on my part, evidence that I now, to my horror, understood truly what I was, that I had now, in my own heart, and to my own misery, incontrovertibly acknowledged my new nature, came to the tree and, swiftly, casually, unbound me. They then carried me by the arms and put me to my knees before my captor, who sat, cross-legged, by the fire. I knelt, my head to the grass, a slave girl trembling before him.

In the camp, hitherto, my captor had confined me to degrading handouts, which he would place in my mouth, or make me reach for, kneeling, not using my hands. Eta now came forward. She held two copper bowls of gruel. Next to me, she knelt before my captor; she put one bowl down before me; then, holding the other bowl, she handed it to my captor; one of the men pulled my head up by the hair, so I could see clearly what was being done; my captor took the bowl of gruel from Eta, and then, saying nothing, handed it back to her. Now he, and his men, and Eta, looked at me. I then understood what I must do. I picked up the bowl of gruel, with both hands, and, kneeling, handed it to my captor. He took the bowl. Then he handed it back to me. I might now eat. I knelt, shaken, the bowl of gruel in my hands. The symbolism of the act was not lost upon me. It was from him, he, symbolically, that I received my food. It was he who fed me. It was he upon whom I depended, that I would eat. Did he not choose to feed me, I understood, I would not eat. My head down, following Eta's example, I ate the gruel. We were given no spoons. With our fingers and, like cats, with our tongues, we finished the gruel. It was plain. It was not sugared or salted. It was slave gruel. Some days it was all that would be given to me. A girl does not always, of course, take food in this fashion. Usually she prepares the food and then serves it, after which, if permitted, she eats. Many men permit a girl, for most practical purposes, to eat simultaneously with him, provided he begins first and it does not interfere with her service to him. Thus he gets his girl, fed, more swiftly to the furs. Much depends on the man; the will of the girl counts for nothing. In some dwellings a girl must, before the evening meal, hand her plate to the man; he will then, normally, return it to her; if she has not been completely pleasing to him, on the other hand, she may not be fed that night. Control of a girl's food not only permits the intelligent regulation of her caloric intake but provides an excellent instrument for keeping her in line; control the food, control the girl. Food control, for the man, also has unexpected rewards. Few things so impress a man's dominance on her, or her dependence upon him, than the control of her food. So simple a thing thrills her to the core. It makes her eager to please him as a slave girl. I finished the slave gruel. It was not tasty, but I was grateful for even so simple a provender. I was hungry. I felt starved. Perhaps the brand had made me hungry. Furtively, I looked at the man over the edge of the copper bowl. He seemed so strong, so mighty. The ceremonial taking of food from the hand of the man, as it had been done this evening in the camp, would prove to be somewhat unusual, though it would be reasonably common to be handfed, when it amused him, or thrown scraps of food. Among many men, it might be mentioned, however, the monthly anniversary of a girl's acquisition as a slave would be marked by this, and similar ceremonies. A slave girl is a delight to a man; she is extremely prized and precious; that the day of her acquisition should be celebrated each month with special ceremonies and rites is not surprising. These numerous anniversaries are deliciously celebrated, as they may be with a girl who is only a slave, and seldom forgotten; should such an anniversary be forgotten, should it be such that it is commonly celebrated, the girl redoubles her efforts to please, fearing she is to be soon sold.

I put down the bowl of gruel.

A switch was put in the hands of Eta. She stood over me. I put down my head. She did not strike me. I looked up at her. I realized then that she was first girl in the camp, and that I must obey her, that she had been empowered to set me tasks and duties. Suddenly I feared her. Before I had looked down upon her. Now I trembled. It was she who held the switch over me. Before I had generally obeyed her only when men were present. I had preferred to leave her the work. Now I realized I must, without question, take slave instructions from her and discharge swiftly and well whatever menial duties she might place upon me. I met her eyes. Though I was a delicate girl of Earth, beautiful and sensitive, even one who wrote poetry, I had little doubt she would use the switch, and richly, upon me, did I not work well. I put down my head. I determined to work well. In this camp I, though of Earth, was inferior to her. She could command me. She held the switch. I would obey. She was first girl.

Eta took me to one side and, together, we cleaned the copper bowls in the stream, wiping them dry. We tidied the camp. Men called. Eta hurried to bring them wine and paga. I helped her carry the beverages, and goblets, back to the fire. She began to serve them. I stood back. How beautiful she seemed, those lovely legs in the brief rag, the beauty of her, the firelight on her face, and hair, serving the men; how perfect it seemed to me then, so perfect and natural, that she, so beautiful, served as she did. How grotesque it would have been, had the men served her, or had they all, she, too, served themselves. It was the order of nature, unperverted, which I observed, as she moved about, among those mighty men.

"Kajira!" called a man. I trembled with horror. He had summoned me. I fled to him and knelt before him. Roughly he turned me about and, with a slender strap, tied my hands together behind my back. He then pointed to the meat, and gave me a shove. I fell on my belly, then turned on my side, wildly, to look at him. He pointed to the meat, laughing. How could I, bound, serve him? My captor beckoned to me. I regained my feet with difficulty, with an awkwardness that made the men laugh, and went to my captor, kneeling before him. He cut a small piece of meat and put it between my teeth. It was roast tabuk. He gestured back to the other man with the knife. I went to the other man and knelt before him, the bit of meat clenched between my teeth. The man, sitting cross-legged by the fire, indicated I should approach him, and put the meat in his mouth. Reddening with shame, I did so. I extended my head to him delicately and he, with his mouth, took the meat from between my teeth. The men struck their left shoulders with pleasure. Man after man I so served. I had carried meat before in my mouth, not permitted to touch it, but then I had not been bound, then I had not knelt, then they had not taken it from me in their mouths. I was now serving them, and it was their intention, to their amusement, as only a slave girl would serve men. I was being taught, as they laughed and spoke of me, what I was. The only man I did not so serve was he who cut the meat for me to carry, my captor. He did not cut me a piece of meat to convey in that humble manner to his own mouth. He, of all, I most wished to so serve. I wanted to dare to touch my lips, my mouth, to his, when he took his meat. But he did not have me serve him in this fashion. I wanted to throw my small, naked, bound body into his arms. He frowned. I shrank back.

He indicated I should lie upon my belly before him. I did so. He cut small pieces of meat and threw them to me. Lying on my belly, hands tied behind me, I fed. Tears fell into the grass, as I caught at the meat. I had little doubt I was a slave. The men began to talk. One of the men, at a word from my captor, untied me, and I crept to Eta, outside the circle of firelight, and hid in her arms. Later the men began to tell stories, and then to sing. They called for more wine and paga and Eta, and I, too, now, hastened to serve them. We, two, moved among them. I, too, now served them in the firelight. I would pour the paga, which I carried, into a goblet, kiss it, as was expected, and give it to the man. "Paga!" called my captor. I almost fainted. I went to him and, shaking, poured paga into his goblet; I was terrified that I might spill it; it was not only that I feared, should I spill the beverage, that I might be beaten for my clumsiness; it was even more that I wished to appear graceful and beautiful before him; but I shook, and was awkward; the paga sloshed in the goblet but, as my heart almost stood still, it did not spill; he looked at me; I was a clumsy girl, and a poor slave; I felt so small and unworthy before him; I was not only a girl, small and weak before these mighty men; I was not even a good slave. Trembling, I extended the goblet to him. He did not take it. I shrank back, confused. I did not know what to do. I realized then that I had, in my confusion and distress, forgotten to place my lips upon the goblet in subservience. I quickly pressed my lips to the goblet, kissing it. Then, suddenly, as I was to hand it to him, I boldly, again, lifted the goblet's side to my lips. Holding it in both hands, I kissed it again, lovingly, delicately, fully, lingeringly, my eyes closed. I had never kissed a boy on Earth with the helplessness and passion that I bestowed upon the mere goblet of my Gorean captor. I belonged to him. I was his. I loved him! I felt the metal of the cup beneath my full, pressing lips. I opened my eyes. I proffered, tears in my eyes, the cup of paga to my captor. It was as though, with the cup, I was giving myself to him. Yet I knew I needed not give myself to him, for I was his, and a slave girl; he could take me whenever he wished me. He took the cup from my hands, and dismissed me.

Late that night the men went to their furs and tentings. Eta and I put away the extra food; we cleaned the goblets and cleared the side of the fire of litter and debris. She gave me a thin blanket of coarse cloth; it was rep-cloth; I might huddle in it at night. "Eta!" called a man.

She went to him. She slipped within his bit of tenting, onto his furs. I saw her pull away the rag she wore and I saw him, in the moonlight, enclose her in his arms. I was suddenly frightened. The bit of blanket about my shoulders I went to the cliff wall and looked upward at the sheer cliff above me. It shone in the moonlight. I scratched it with my fingernails. I went to the wall of thorn brush, a small, forlorn, white figure in the night, clutching the bit of rep-cloth blanket about me. The thorn-brush wall was some eight feet high, some ten feet thick. I extended my hand. Miserably I drew it back, bloody. I went back to where Eta had given me the rep-cloth blanket, and lay down on the hard ground. I shuddered, knowing that, as she had been summoned to the tenting of one of the men, so I, too, might be as helplessly summoned. The major duty of a slave girl, I suspected, was not to cook, or sew, or launder, but to give men lengthy, profound and exquisite pleasures, such as only a beautiful female could give a man, to be to him whatever he might wish, and to give to him all that he might command, and, to the extent of her beauty, ingenuity and imagination, a thousand times more.

I began to sweat. I was frightened of the totality and completeness of being a slave girl. I am a girl of Earth, I cried to myself. I am not a slave! I do not want to be a slave! I am a girl of Earth!

"Kajira," I heard.

Terrified, clutching the bit of rep-cloth blanket about my shoulders, I rose to my knees, then to a crouch. My captor stood before his tenting. I could see the furs within. Too, within, a small lamp burned.

I did not wish him to have to speak twice, for fear I might be beaten.

Holding the blanket about me, I went to him. He proffered me a cup and I, with one hand, holding the blanket about me with the other, drank its contents. It was a foul brew, but I downed it. I did not know at the time, but it was slave wine. Men seldom breed upon their slave girls. Female slaves, when bred, are commonly hooded and crossed with a male slave, similarly hooded, the breeding conducted under the supervision of their respective owners; a girl is seldom bred with a slave from her own house; personal relationships between male and female slaves are usually frowned upon; sometimes, however, as a discipline even a high female slave is sometimes thrown to a chain of work slaves for their pleasure. The effect of the slave wine endures several cycles, or moons; it may be counteracted by another drink, a smooth, sweet beverage, which frees the girl's body for the act of the male slave, or, in unusual cases, should she be freed, to the act of the lover; slave girls, incidentally, are almost never freed on Gor; they are too delicious and desirable to free; only a fool, it is commonly said, would free one.

My captor took the cup from me, when I had downed its contents. He threw it aside into the grass. He had not taken his eyes from me. I felt his hands at my shoulders. He parted the blanket, and then, lifting it from me, dropped it to my ankles.

He looked at me. I stood but inches from him. Then he took me by the left arm and thrust me within the low opening to his tenting. One could not stand upright within the tenting, for its ceiling was low. I half knelt, half crouched, on the furs within. There was little comparison between their depth and luxury, and my pitiful rep-cloth blanket. The tenting was striped on the inside; the small lamp was ornate; on the outside, interestingly, the tenting was a dull brown; among brush and trees it would be easy not to notice it, even if it were pitched but a few yards away. He slipped within the tenting, and crouched beside me. He unslung his gear, his sword belt, with weapon and scabbard, and the dagger belt, and, wrapping them in soft leather, put them to one side. He looked at me. I looked down. I felt very small with him. He held the lamp that I might, turning, examine the brand on my thigh; he held my leg with one hand, the thigh, turning it so that I might more clearly see the mark. His hand on my thigh frightened me. It was so strong. I looked at the brand. It was very meticulous, and clean, and deep, and lovely and delicate; it was incredibly feminine; it was as though my femininity had been literally stamped upon my body; it was as though I had been certified a certain sort of thing, which thereafter, no matter what I wished, or what I might be told, I could never deny; never had I felt so soft, so feminine; I wore, burned in my flesh, one of the most beautiful of brands; I wore, incised in my thigh, resembling a small, beautiful rose, the dina, the slave flower. I looked into the eyes of my captor. Never had I felt so weak, so vulnerable, so soft, so helpless, so feminine. There were tears in my eyes. I knew I belonged to the brute, as a slave girl. I saw him put the lamp to one side. I lifted my lips to his. I felt his arms close about me.

With a moan of rapture, eyes closed, I was pressed back into the furs.

I felt my legs being thrust apart.

"I love you," I whispered, helpless in his arms, "—Master."

Four

La Kajira

I awakened at his feet in the Gorean dawn. I put my hands on his calves and ankles, as though holding them, yet so softly that he would not know himself held. I delicately put my lips to his calves, and kissed them. I kissed, too, his ankles and feet, softly, so that he would not know himself kissed, gently, that he might not be awakened, that he might not be angered by the boldness of the slave girl at his feet. Then I lay beside him, joyously happy. I saw the long, horizontal peak of the striped tenting above me, extending on either side from the leather cord that served as its roof tree. The striped sides of the tenting moved slightly in the early morning shiftings of the breeze. The dawn was a soft gray. Outside the tenting I could see dew glistening on the grass. I heard birds, calling to one another. I lay deep in the furs. I rolled to my stomach, my breasts pendant, to look upon the man who owned me. Much in the night had he overwhelmed me. On the interior of my left thigh, reddish brown, dried now, lay a streak of blood, my virgin blood, which never again would I be able to shed. He, as in a primitive rite, I being only a slave, had forced me to taste it. He had taken it on his finger and thrust it roughly in my mouth, smearing it across my lips and tongue and teeth, making me take into my own body the consequences of his victory, my ravishing, my deflowering, and then, as he held my head in his hands, forcing me to look into his eyes, swallow. I would never forget the taste, nor the calm way he looked upon me, as a master. Then, though my body was still sore from his first assault upon me, again he pleasured himself, like a lion, in my vulnerable, raw softness; I was shown no consideration, for I was a slave. I clutched him, loving him. Much service did he get from his girl that night. How excited and obedient I had been, even sore, knowing full well that I would be swiftly and cruelly punished were I not completely pleasing to him. How happy I was, so subservient to him, so much at his mercy. A girl who has not been owned perhaps cannot grasp the feelings of one who is owned, truly owned; but perhaps such a girl, even if only dimly, can sense the joy of the slave girl. I would not have believed it, had I not experienced it.

Gently I lowered my head to the brute and kissed him, softly that I might not awaken my master.

I lay back in the furs, near him, at his feet, in the Gorean dawn.

Once during the night had he laughed, softly, richly, holding me helplessly, cruelly, to him, looking down into my eyes, deeply pleased with his ownership of me. How grateful, and elated, held, I had been!

My master was pleased with his girl!

I listened to the birds outside, in the glistening velvet of the soft dawn.

How far from Earth, with its pollutions, its crowdings, its hypocrisy, seemed this world. I lightly, with my fingertips, touched my brand. I winced. I would not much touch it, for a few days, for I wished its delicacy to heal perfectly. I wanted the brand to be perfect. No girl is so without vanity that she does not want her brand to be perfect. Even lipstick and eye shadow, which a girl may wash off and reapply, a girl wishes to be perfect; how much more so then the brand, which is always worn! The girl wishes a brand of which she can be proud. A good brand adds to a girl's sense of confidence, of comfort and security. Often, a girl's raiment is limited to brand and collar. Accordingly the brand is of considerable importance to her. Also, it is no secret on Gor that a small and beautiful brand, well-placed, considerably enhances a girl's beauty. I tried to resent the brand, but I could not do so. It was too beautiful, and now, too, it was too much a part of me. I kissed my fingertips and, gently, pressed them to the petals of the slave flower which my master, yesterday evening, with a hot iron, against my will, had caused to blossom upon my thigh. I lay there in the fresh dawn. On Earth it then seemed to me that I had been a true slave; and that, on this world, though I wore a brand, I was for the first time in my life truly free. On Earth invisible chains had kept me cruelly apart from myself and my feelings; conditionings and derisions had put walls between me and my heart and emotions; I had been tight, the miserable victim of bonds of my own acceptance; now, for the first time in my life, though I might wear chains, in my heart, my feelings and emotions, I was truly free, truly liberated; I lay there, happy.

I was suddenly frightened. I felt his hand, groping for me. I crawled beside him, and moved my head to where he might touch it, by his thigh. He was asleep. I felt his hands reach into my hair, and fasten themselves in it. He pulled me to his waist. I was a slave girl. "Yes, Master," I whispered.

I felt Eta's switch poking me. "Kajira," she whispered. "Kajira."

I awakened. It was still very early, though lighter now. My master was still asleep. None but Eta was up about the camp.

The dew of dawn was not yet burned off the grass. I crawled from the tenting.

Eta would set me my duties. I, a slave girl, would now be worked. I looked about at the sleeping men, recumbent and somnolent, in their tentings and furs. They were the masters. We women, slave girls, would now ready the camp. There was much to be done. Water must be fetched, wood must be brought from the piles, the morning fires must be made, breakfast must be prepared. When the masters chose to arise, their girls must have all ready for them.

I hummed softly to myself as I worked. Eta, too, seemed pleased. Once she kissed me.

The men were late to arise, and Eta sent me to the stream, with tunics, to wash upon the rocks. I was once startled by the movements of a small amphibian near me. It splashed into the water. The water was clear. I worked swiftly. The air was fresh and beautiful. Soon I smelled the frying of vulo eggs in a large, flat pan, and the unmistakable odor of coffee, or as the Goreans express it, black wine. The beans grow largely on the slopes of the Thentis mountains. The original beans, I suppose, had been brought, like certain other Gorean products, from Earth; it is not impossible, of course, that the opposite is the case, that black wine is native to Gor and that the origin of Earth's coffee beans is Gorean; I regard this as unlikely, however, because black wine is far more common on Earth than on Gor, where it is, except for the city of Thentis, a city famed for her tarn flocks, and her surrounding villages, a somewhat rare and unusual luxury. Had I known more of Gor I would have speculated that my masters might have sworn their swords to the defense of Thentis, that they were of that city, but, as I was later to learn, they were of another city, one called Ar.

When the first man, yawning, sleepy and bleary-eyed, the lazy beast, stumbled to the cooking fire, we were ready for him. Eta and I knelt before him, and put our heads to the dirt at his feet. We were his girls.

Eta piled several of the hot, tiny eggs, earlier kept fresh in cool sand within the cave, on a plate, with heated yellow bread, for him. I, grasping the pot with a rag and both hands, poured him a handled, metal tankard of the steaming black brew, coffee or black wine.

Following Eta's example, to my pleasure, we prepared ourselves plates and cups. We then, while waiting for the men, ate. As long as a male had taken the first bite, the first drink, at the meal, apparently there was little objection to our also partaking. We did so with gusto. Gorean amenities are more carefully observed, usually, at the evening meal, which is more of a gathering and an occasion than the other two or three meals of the day. At an evening meal Eta and I would, under threat of discipline, wait before eating until the master, and each of his men, had begun. We did not, commonly, however, provided it did not interfere with our service, wait until the men had completed their meal before commencing ours. We, thus, finished nearly with them, or a bit before. Thus, after we had cleared goblets, and bowls and dishes, if they were used, we were soon ready, unimpeded, to devote our attentions to the serving of wine and paga, or our bodies for their pleasure, were they desired. To indicate the greater significance of the evening meal, as compared to the other Gorean meals, no slave girl may touch it without first having been given permission, assuming that a free man or woman, even a child, is present. "You may feed, Slave Girl," is a common way in which this permission is given. If the permission is not given, the girl may not eat. Should the master or mistress, or child, forget to give this permission, it is merely the misfortune of the slave girl.

As the men came to breakfast we extended them obeisance and served them.

When my master came to the cooking fire it was with eagerness, such eagerness that the men laughed, that I knelt before him, and put my hair in the dirt between his sandals.

I remembered the night. Well had he taught me the meaning of my brand! I so loved him!

He gestured me to my feet. I sprang up. I stood straight before him, proud in the pleasure I had given him. From the looks of the men I understood that now I stood much differently than I had when I had come to the camp, that the girl who now stood slave within the wall of thorn brush was far more valuable than she who had so recently miserably stood captive beyond its perimeter. The looks of the men told me that I was now more desirable, more beautiful. I know I should have objected to this, that I should have resented it intensely. Yet how fantastically weak and joyous and alive and happy it made me feel!

My master, crouching down, examined the slave flower on my thigh. I did not dare touch him. I trembled. He straightened up. He seemed satisfied, and this much relieved me. I wished him to be pleased, not only with his slave, but with her brand. Eta examined the brand, too, and smiled, and hugged and kissed me. I gathered that the brand was an excellent one. I hugged and kissed her, too, weeping. She permitted me to serve the master, and I did so, delightedly. I watched him like a hawk, that I might anticipate his slightest desire.

One of the men, obviously, as his looks and gesture indicated, asked him about me. My master responded, chewing. They looked at me. I was the object of their discussion. I did not speak Gorean, but I reddened, and put my head down. Gorean masters commonly speak frankly and openly of the qualities of their girls, even before the girls themselves. My features, figure and performances were being candidly discussed and appraised. The sexuality, qualities and capacities, and skills, of a slave girl, not a free woman, are discussed on Gor with the same openness that men on Earth might bring to the discussion of paintings and music, and that Englishmen of the Nineteenth Century might have brought to the discussion of dogs and horses.

I gathered that I, in many ways, left much to be desired. I felt small and helpless.

My master extended to me his metal tankard. Gratefully I filled it again with the steaming black wine.

He was kind. He was permitting me to serve him. I looked at him. Were there to be no secrets between us? Were my defects, my helplessness, and the completeness of my surrender to him, to be broadcast so publicly? In his eyes I read that my questions were out of place. In his eyes I read that I was slave.

I lowered my eyes, and withdrew, the tankard filled, a slave girl.

It was with joy, later in the morning, that I felt, thrown against my body by my master, a bit of brown cloth. It was a sleeveless body scrap, a shred of slave rag. It was a few threads, fit for a bond girl. Yet I welcomed it as I might have a gown, with gloves and pearls, from Paris. Now I might not be so revealed to the men. It was the first clothing I had been given on Gor. Radiant was my gratitude to him, and abundant were the kisses which, in joy, I placed about his legs and feet. Joyfully I drew on the garment, slipping it over my head, and fastened it, more tightly about me, by the two tiny hooks on the left. The slit made the garment, a rather snug one, easier to slip into; the two hooks, when fastened, naturally increased the snugness of the garment, drawing it quite closely about the breasts and hips; deliciously then, from the point of view of a man, the girl's figure is betrayed and accentuated; also, the two hooks do not close the slit on the left completely, but permit men to gaze upon the sweet slave flesh pent, held captive, within; such a garment, of course, when a man grows weary of having his vision obscured, is easily torn away. I turned before my master, proud in my new riches. He indicated to Eta where the garment must be taken in, the hooks placed subtly differently. As it was the garment was too large for me. Eta was a larger woman. It was one of her cast-offs. The garment would be altered, that I would be as well revealed by it as Eta was by hers. The attire of Gorean slave girls is of great importance to their masters. They concern themselves with its tiniest details. The clothing, you see, as well as the girl, belongs to the master; it is natural for him, thus, to take an interest in it; both, in their diverse ways, can be reflections upon him, his taste, his judgment, his discrimination. That a male of Earth may not even know what clothing his wife owns, or what she buys, would be unthinkable to most Goreans, even those who stand in free companionship. To the master it would simply be preposterous. What his girl wears, if she is to wear anything, is of great interest to him. After all, she is not a wife; she is much more important; she is a prized possession. The clothing she wears, any cosmetics or jewelry, or perfume, must be absolutely perfect. He is "in," so to speak, on everything. Should she tie her hair with as little as a new ribbon, it must pass his strict inspection. If it is not "right" for her, she will not be permitted to wear it. That a wife might wear a new dress and her husband not even notice it would be incredible, if not incomprehensible, to any Gorean, whether a proprietor or a companion. In short, Gorean masters concern themselves closely with their girls. Clothing, like other matters, is quite important. It must be perfect for its purpose. Its purpose may be to humiliate or brazenly and publicly display the girl, to discipline her, to keep her humble, to remind her that she is nothing, only a wench in bondage; it may be to reveal her beauty, of which he is proud, for the eyes of all, or for his own pleasure and that of his peers; it may be to reveal his wealth, the value in girl and raiment which he owns; it may be to augment his prestige, or to incite envy in others; it may be to stimulate her with beautiful things; it may be to excite her sexually, and so on. These purposes, of course, are not all incompatible. Clothing, too, it might be mentioned, like food, is a useful instrument in controlling the girl. Few girls, for example, enjoy being sent nude to the market, to do shopping.

My master drew out his knife. I shuddered, but dared not run. I closed my eyes. I felt him cutting at the garment's hem. He made it scandalously short. It had been a garment of Eta's measured high, but to her own longer legs. Now I scarcely dared move in it.

At a gesture from my master I knelt. I did so in the manner in which I had been taught, back on my heels, back straight, hands on thighs, head high, chin up. I did not neglect a further detail. I spread my knees, widely. It was the position, of course, as I would later learn, of the Gorean pleasure slave. I had seen Eta naturally, unconsciously, assume it when she knelt. Such a girl, in kneeling, does not close her knees before a free man. Any slave girl, incidentally, addresses any free man as Master, any free woman as Mistress, though only one, of course, at a given time, is likely to be her true Master or Mistress.

It gave me pleasure to assume this posture before my master, who had full body rights to me; it gave me less pleasure, in the beginning, to assume it before free men generally; yet, eventually, I did it naturally, and pleasurably; it is a position that not only makes the girl more attractive to the man; but, too, subtly, psychologically, by its effect on the girl, by intensifying her sense of openness, vulnerability and exposure, it makes men much more attractive to her, she thus kneeling, and opened, before them; the girl who finds many men attractive is likely to find the master attractive; the girl who finds few men attractive is to that extent the less likely to find the master attractive; the pleasure slave, so submissively and vulnerably positioned, so helpless and opened before men, cannot help herself but become curious and excited, and heated, about them; and in becoming excited and heated by men in general she naturally becomes excited and heated about the master in particular; after all, it is to him that she actually belongs; he is the one who is her master; in a pleasure slave passion is not an accident; inhibitions are simply not permitted; beyond this, instincts are triggered and intelligently released, and then allowed, untrammeled, to take their natural course; biology's dominance/submission equation is genetic; the most perfect satisfaction of that equation for complex, acculturated psychophysical organisms is the institutionalized bondage relation; this exists on Gor, where girls may be the legal slaves of strong men, capable of mastering them. I was such a slave. I had no doubt the man who owned me was capable of mastering me. He had already done so. I was his slave.

How attractive I found men! How I loved, and feared, my master. I wanted to give myself to him constantly.

He gave instructions to Eta, with respect to me. Then he, with his fellows, left the camp. Eta and I were alone. She went and brought pins, tiny scissors, a needle and thread. The alteration of my slave rag was apparently the first order of the day's business. It must match and betray my slave body perfectly. After that we could attend to our less important tasks. I stood and knelt, and stood, and moved, as Eta instructed me. Once I removed the garment and she sewed the hem, where the knife had ripped it. In making the hem, of course, though Eta took it up as little as possible, the garment was further shortened. I reddened. I wondered if there was much to choose from between such a garment and being nude; I supposed the garment gave the men something to tear away. Then I put it back on. Eta repositioned the hooks. I gasped, as she fastened them. Then Eta deftly, here and there, sometimes cutting, and pinning and sewing, fitted the rag to me with candid perfection. This was done on my body, that the fit be flawlessly snug. Eta was a superb seamstress. Only twice, even under these conditions, and given our objectives, did I feel the needle. Then Eta stood back; and then walked about me. She went and fetched a mirror from the cave; it was a large one, and permitted me to see myself. I gasped at the slave girl betrayed in the mirror. I looked at Eta in horror. I had not seen myself before as a slave. I was shocked, and startled. I had not known I could appear such. I could not believe it was I. No, it could not be I! I looked back at the mirror. How beautiful she was, that lovely slave. Could it be I? I looked at Eta. She nodded, and smiled. I looked again at the mirror. I had not known I could be so beautiful! Then I was afraid, for I suspected what such beauty might mean on the world on which I found myself. What man would not simply put a chain on it, or collar it? I stood before the mirror, stunned, looking at the slave girl.

Eta then, to my surprise, with the point of her scissors, ripped the tiny garment a bit under my right breast, that a bit of skin might show, and again at my left hip, a larger rip. These were done in such a way as to make them appear natural, inadvertent rents in the garment. She then, with the point of the scissors, at two points, ripped the hem she had earlier sewn out a bit, that in these two places it might appear the threads had broken; the hem then, in these two places, was irregular on my legs. She then, at another place, cut into the hem, ripping it, and unraveled and tore it a bit, as though it had naturally frayed; some stray threads hung upon my thigh. These were the touches which, to my horror and delight, made the garment of the slave rag exquisitely perfect. I looked at the lovely slave in the mirror. I wondered if the men knew, or suspected, the female cunning that went into the making of a slave rag. She was arming me with beauty. With what else might a slave girl be armed? Eta kissed me, and I kissed her. The ingenuity and care lavished upon the slave rag, seemingly such a pathetic accident of a garment, is a careful secret well kept among slave girls. If the master does not know why the smallest movement of his girl, clad in what he thought was a mere discipline rag, almost drives him out of his wits with pleasure, that is all right. The masters, as we girls sometimes tell one another, do not have to know everything.

I looked at the girl in the mirror. I approached more closely. I lifted the hem of the garment at the left thigh. I almost fainted with the delicate perfection of the brand. It was still red, rough, raw, deep, unhealed, but the form was clearly imprinted, unmistakably, deeply, and beautifully imprinted. On my thigh I wore one of the most beautiful brands, the dina, the slave flower. I tore the garment there, at the left hip, that as I moved, the brand might be glimpsed. Then I knelt before the mirror. Boldly I assumed slave position. I threw my knees apart. I rested my hands on my thighs. I regarded myself in the mirror. I saw a kneeling slave girl there. There was no doubt about it. She was a slave girl. How incredibly beautiful was that poor, lovely slave. She wore a brand. She wore a slave rag. She lacked only a steel collar. That lack, I supposed, could be simply supplied. It is nothing to put a collar on a girl's neck. I lifted my hair up; I lifted my chin, watching in the mirror. I conjectured what a steel collar would look like, fastened on my neck. I did not think I would mind one. It might be rather attractive. Eta's was, terribly so. I hoped, of course, that I might be able to choose whose collar I would wear. But, shuddering, I realized that a girl does not choose whose collar she will wear; rather it is the man who chooses; it is he, and he alone, who places the collar. Suddenly I sensed the misery of being a slave. I might belong to any man! I might belong to any man who might carry me off, or pay my price. I might be abducted or bought, or bestowed, or lost in gambling! I was only an article of property, helpless and beautiful, without control over, no more than a dog or pig, into whose hands I might come. Tears sprang to my eyes. Surely my master would not sell me! Every bit of me would constantly try to please him. I did not want to be sold! What a miserable, beautiful girl I saw in the mirror, the poor slave! How sorry I felt for that beauty. But what man would be so foolish as to sell such a beauty? Or, even to share her with another? Surely such a man would keep such a beauty for himself alone, not sharing her with others. I wiped the tears from my eyes. I studied the girl in the mirror. How beautiful in her bondage she was. I brushed my hair back and, lifting my chin, turned my head. I had seen earrings in the jewelry in the cave, exotic loops, twists of wire and golden pendants; I imagined them upon me, hanging at my cheeks, adornments suitable for me, a barbarian slave girl. My ears had not been pierced but I had little doubt that this operation, if my master wished, would be promptly accomplished upon me. I considered cosmetics and perfumes, such as I had encountered in the cave. And behold, in my imagination, the girl in the mirror was so bedecked. I had seen bracelets, anklets, chains and necklaces, intricately wrought and beautiful, in the cave. I extended my arms and wrists, and one of my legs, considering how they might appear, ponderous with such barbaric glory. But the girl in the mirror wore only a slave rag. I then considered how I might appear, so made up, so perfumed, so adorned, but now in a snatch of brief silk, yellow or scarlet, clinging, diaphanous, fit for a man's pleasure girl.

Eta called to me.

Once again I saw only the plain girl in the mirror, the beauty in a slave rag. No adornments were hers; only some threads of cloth tight on her beauty. She was not an ornamented high slave. She wore only a slave rag. She was a low slave.

I sprang to my feet and hurried to Eta.

She was kneeling down and I knelt across from her. "La Kajira," said Eta, pointing to herself. "Tu Kajira," she said, pointing to me. "La Kajira," I said, pointing to myself. "Tu Kajira," I said, pointing to Eta. I am a slave girl. You are a slave girl.

Eta smiled. She pointed to her brand. "Kan-lara," she said. She pointed to my brand. "Kan-lara Dina," she said. I repeated these words.

"Ko-lar," she said, indicating her collar. "It is the same word in English," I cried. She did not understand my outburst. Gorean, as I would learn, is rich in words borrowed from Earth languages; how rich it is I am not a skilled enough philologist to conjecture. It may well be that almost all Gorean expressions may be traced to one or another Earth language. Yet, the language is fluid, rich and expressive. Borrowed expressions, as in linguistic borrowing generally, take on the coloration of the borrowing language; in time the borrowings become naturalized, so to speak, being fully incorporated into the borrowing language; at this point they are, for all practical purposes, words within the borrowing language. How many, in English, for example, think of expressions such as 'automobile,' 'corral,' and 'lariat' as being foreign words?

"Collar!" I said. Eta frowned. "Ko-lar," she repeated, again indicating the neck band of steel fashioned on her throat. "Ko-lar," I said, carefully following her pronunciation. Eta accepted this.

Eta pulled at the bit of rag she wore. "Ta-Teera," she said. I looked down at the scrap of rag, outrageously brief, so scandalous, so shameful, fit only for a slave girl, which I wore. I smiled. I had been placed in a Ta-Teera. "Ta-Teera," I said. I wore the Ta-Teera.

"Var Ko-lar?" asked Eta. I pointed to the collar on her throat. "Var Ta-Teera?" asked Eta, smiling. I pointed to the brief rag which I wore. Eta seemed pleased. She had laid out a number of articles. My lessons in Gorean had begun.

Suddenly, stammering, I said, "Eta—var—var Bina?"

Eta looked at me, surprised.

I recalled the two men who had come to the chain and rock. "Var Bina? Var Bina, Kajira!" they had demanded. I had not been able to understand, or satisfy them. They had beaten me. Still I had been unable to satisfy them. I could not even understand them. Then they had prepared to cut my throat. The man in the scarlet tunic, from over the fields, had arrived. "Kajira canjellne," he had said. He had fought for me, and won me. He had brought me to his camp, where he had branded me. I was now his slave.

"Var Bina, Eta?" I asked.

Eta lightly lifted herself to her feet and went to the cave. In a few moments, she emerged. She carried, in her hands, several strings of beads, simple necklaces, with small, wooden, colored beads. They were not valuable.

She held the necklaces up for me to see. Then, with her finger, moving them on their string, she indicated the tiny, colored wooden beads. "Da Bina," she said, smiling. Then she lifted a necklace, looking at it. "Bina," she said. I then understood that 'Bina' was the expression for beads, or for a necklace of beads. The necklaces and beads which Eta produced for me were delights of color and appeal; yet they were simple and surely of little value.

I went to the cave, Eta following. I lifted one of the chest's covers. I took from the chest a string of pearls, then one of pieces of gold, then one of rubies. "Bina?" I asked, each time. Eta laughed. "Bana," she said, "Ki Bina. Bana." Then, from another box, Eta produced another necklace, one with cheap glass beads, and another with simple, small wooden beads. She indicated the latter two necklaces. "Bina," she said, pointing to them. Bina, I then understood, were lesser beads, cheap beads, beads of little value, save for their aesthetic charm. Indeed, I would later learn that bina were sometimes spoken of, derisively, as "Kajira bana." The most exact translation of 'bina' would probably be "slave beads." They were valueless, save for being a cheap adornment sometimes permitted embonded wenches.

Eta and I returned to the outside, to continue our lessons.

I still could not understand what had happened at the chain and rock. "Var Bina! Var Bina, Kajira!" they had demanded. The Bina, or Slave Beads, had meant more to them than my life. It was not I who had been important to them there but the beads. When they had clearly understood that I was unable to help them in their quest, they, viewing me then as useless, had prepared to be done with me. I shuddered, remembering the knife at my throat. I had been narrowly saved by the swordsman whose slave I now was. I had thought, before I was clearly apprised of the nature of Bina, cheap slave beads, that perhaps the men had supposed that I was to be chained at the rock, adorned with some rare and valuable necklace, worth perhaps a fortune. Perhaps it had been that which they had wanted. Perhaps then, either I had not been placed so adorned at the rock, contrary to their expectation, or, if I had been, that someone had, in my helpless unconsciousness, arrived earlier and simply removed the necklace, stealing it from my chained body. I might have been left at the rock either because I was chained, and could not be easily removed, or, perhaps, was not wanted. But it seemed unlikely that, if I should have worn such a necklace, it had not been placed on me; and unlikely, too, that someone, in such a wilderness, would come upon me while I there lay chained and remove the necklace. I was thrown into the greatest consternation by my new comprehension of the valuelessness of slave beads. It now made no sense to me whatsoever that the two men, so angrily and fiercely, should have sought for so trivial an object. Of what importance could be a string of slave beads? Why might they have been put on me in the first place? And where, if they had been put on me, had they gone? Who would want them? And why should men come through a wilderness to obtain them? What could be their importance? What could be their secret? I understood nothing.

Eta lifted up a stout whip, with long handle, which might be wielded with two hands, and five dangling, soft, wide lashing surfaces, each about a yard long. "Kurt," she said. I shrank back. "Kurt," I repeated. She lifted up some loops of chain; there were linked ankle rings and linked wrist rings, and a lock collar, all connected by a length of gleaming chain running from the collar. It was rather lovely. It was too small for a man. I knew, however, it would fit me, perfectly, "Sirik," said Eta. "Sirik," I repeated.

Upon command I had slipped from the Ta-Teera.
I stood among the men.

The warrior indicated that I should suck in my gut. I did so, holding my stomach in, tightly. I felt the strap, black, narrow, loop my belly. It was pulled tight, very tight, and cinched. I wore the bell at my left hip. I looked at my master, reproachfully, in anguish. The bells, rows, strung about my neck, and, loosely, too, depending about my breasts, jangled. The sound was horrifying, sensuous. With anger, with misery, I regarded him. The warrior took my hands behind my back and there, with a bit of black leather, fastened them together. The rows of bells on my wrists jangled as my hands were pulled behind my back and fastened there, wrist to wrist, lashed. How could he permit this? Did it mean nothing to him that he had, the preceding night, taken my virginity from me? Did it mean nothing to him that he had, for long hours, pleasured himself with my body? Did it mean nothing to him that he had won me, that I had yielded to him, that I had surrendered myself, totally, to him? That vulnerably I had been fully his? I tried to take a step toward him. The bells on my body, and those tied about my ankles, jangled. I could not move toward him, for the warrior's hand on my arm held me. I looked at my master with anguish. He was sitting cross-legged, some feet away, with others. He had a goblet of paga, which Eta had served to him. Did my master not love me, as I loved him? He, narrow-lidded, looked at me over the rim of the goblet of paga. "Do not do this to me!" I cried to him, helplessly, in English. "I love you!" Surely, though he spoke no English, he could not have mistaken the anguish, the feelings, the deep intent of the helpless girl so shamefully belled and bound before him. "I love you!" I cried. I saw in his eyes that he, as a Gorean master, had no concern for my anguish, my intent and feelings. I shuddered. I was a bond girl. He gave a sign. One of the men nearby readied a large opaque cloth, soft, black, folding it in four pieces, so that, folded, it would be about a yard square. He looked back at me. "I love you," I said. The cloth was thrown over my head and, with some loops of leather cord, four times encircling my neck, tied under my chin. I could not see. I was hooded. I threw back my head in anguish within the hood. "But I love you!" I cried. I stood there, belled and bound, forlorn and hooded. I loved him. But I had seen in his eyes, in the instant that the cloth had been thrown over my head, that to him, my master, I was nothing, only a meaningless slave.

I stood there, head down, miserable, frightened. I heard the men laughing. Five would do contest.

I hated the bells, so many, so tiny, hung about my body, which I could not remove, which would draw them to me. The sound was tiny, rich, and sensuous. They were slave bells. They would draw men to my body. I moved slightly. I felt them stir on my body and on the loops that held them. So slight a movement made them sound! I, miserable, was caught in their lewd, delicious rustle. I suppose the sound of the bells, objectively considered, is rather lovely. Yet theirs was a music of bondage, one which, in its tiny, delicious sounds, rustling, whispered, "Kajira. Kajira." They said, "You are nothing, Girl. You are a belled Kajira. You are nothing, Girl. You exist for the pleasure of men. Please them well, lovely Kajira." I shook my body, trying to throw the bells from me. I could not do so. In their jangling sound, helpless, I was held, betrayed. I could scarcely breathe without stirring the bells. I began to sweat, and fear. It was suddenly like finding oneself caught, imprisoned, hooded, in a net. No move I made was not betrayed by the bells. Most I hated the larger bell, of different note, fastened tightly at my left hip. It was a guide bell. I tried to free my hands. They had been tied by a warrior. I was helpless. I shuddered. And even so slight a movement was betrayed by the bells, indicating the exact position of she who wore them, the slave girl on whose body they were fastened.

The men were ready.

"Please, Master," I cried, bound, closed in the hood, belled, "protect me! I love you! I love you! Keep me for yourself, Master!"

I heard men laughing, talking, bets being made.

The contestants, by now, would have, too, been hooded. But they were not belled. They were not bound.

My cheeks, inside the hood, were stained with tears. The interior of the hood was wet.

I was Judy Thornton, a junior at an elite girls' college, an English major, a poetess, delicate and sensitive!

A man near me called out a word, delightedly, a word I would later learn was "Quarry!" At the same instant I felt the flash of a switch on my body and I, weeping, fled from its sting.

I was a nameless slave girl on an alien world, at the mercy of primitive warriors in a barbarian camp, an object for their sport, a lovely, two-legged plaything, a mere prize, in their cruel games.

The prize stopped, in a jangle of bells, gasping, throwing her head about, as though she might see. She was trapped in the folds of the hood.

I heard a man near me. I did not know if it were the referee or one of the contestants.

I felt the switch touch my body.

I shuddered, with a jangle of bells. But in had been done gently. It was the referee, aiding me, indicating his presence.

I breathed deeply. The bells rustled. I heard another man approaching, doubtless groping. And another to my left.

I was terrified.

Suddenly I heard the hiss of the switch behind me and, almost at the same time, felt the supple disciplinary device, to the amusement of the men, strike me swiftly and hotly below the small of the back. I fled wildly, jangling bells. I was outraged, and humiliated. My eyes were hot with tears. It stung terribly. The switch is often used on a girl when she is guilty of minor indiscretions or tiny misdemeanors. It is thought a fitting instrument for encouraging a beauty to be more careful or zealous in her service. I had delayed in the game for more than five Ihn. It was for that reason that the referee had administered his admonitory stripe. It was the second time in my life I had felt a switch. I did not care to feel one again, particularly when clothed only in slave bells and a hood. The laughter of the men made me angry, but then I cried. Anger in a slave girl was only meaningless pretense. It was not as though she were a free woman whose anger might have significance, might even issue in actions or words, free from the reprisals of discipline. Men are the masters of slave girls, the masters. Anger in a slave girl is futile, meaningless, though sometimes masters encourage it in their girls, to see them flush and assume an interesting demeanor, but it is in the end always insignificant for, in the end, as both the girl and master know, it is the master and not the girl who holds the whip. Thus it is not that slave girls do not become angry. They do. It is only that their anger, as both girl and master know, is meaningless. I cried. The physical effect of the switch on a girl is not negligible, but, I think, its psychological effect, should the blows be placed on a certain portion of her body, thus cruelly humiliating her, may be even more bitter.

Crying, I fled through the camp, stumbling. I heard men falling, stumbling, getting up, pursuing me. I could not free my wrists. Once

I fell into the arms of a man and shrieked with misery. He threw me from him. There was much laughter. He had not even been a contestant. Another time the referee caught me, and then thrust me back against stone, that I might know where I was. He had kept me from striking into the cliff wall behind the camp. I fled again, into the camp. My running was erratic, terribly so. I was confused and miserable. I was terrified of being caught. I, too, did not wish to be again struck with the switch. Another man, not a contestant, caught me and prevented me from plunging into the thick wall of thorn brush, in which I might have been half torn to pieces. There was much laughter. More than once I heard a contestant, yards away, curse. Then I would hear one not a yard or more from me, and I would wheel, and run from him. Once I struck one, and tripped, and fell rolling in a wild jangle of bells. I heard him leap for me. I felt his hand, for an instant, at my right hip. I felt the hand of another touch my left calf. I rolled and crawled free, and darted away. Once I found myself, it seemed, surrounded by stone. Wherever I turned there seemed a cliff before me. I spun, disoriented, terrified. Then I fled back and found myself again somewhere in the center of the camp. Barely had I avoided being cornered against the cliffs. I then began to play more cleverly, more warily. Twice more in the game was I stung with the switch then, once on the left arm, above the elbow, and once, more cruelly, on the right calf, when I, wishing to make no sound, not thinking the referee near me, lingered too long in one position.

Then I fled again, directly, into the arms of a man. I waited for him to free me, to throw me back to the others. But his arms did not free me. "Oh, no!" I wept. His arms tightened about me. I was thrown screaming and squirming to his shoulder, and carried about. There was laughing. I heard the man who held me from the ground being slapped on his back by the referee. I heard the word which, later, I would learn was "Capture." It is a helpless feeling being held on the shoulder of a man, your feet unable to touch the ground; you are unable to obtain the slightest leverage; you are simply his prisoner. I heard shouting, and the pounding of hands on my captor's back. Then he, in his pleasure, one hand on my right ankle and one closed about my left forearm, lifted me bodily above his head, bending my body, displaying me. I heard applause, the pounding of hands on the left shoulder. I heard, too, in the sounds, Eta cry out with pleasure, much delighted. Was she not my sister in bondage? Could she not under-stand my misery? My captor, whoever he was, impatient then to have me, hurled me as though I were nothing to the dirt at his feet. I felt his hands at my ankles. I turned my head to one side, moaning.

I lay bound in the dirt when he had finished with me. He was then unhooded and led away in his triumph to drink the paga of victory.

I lay weeping and miserable in the dirt. When I moved I heard the rustle of the bells, which were slave bells.

In a few moments I felt the hands of the referee close on my arms. He lifted me, and threw me upright, to my feet. Again I heard the word which, later, I would learn was "Quarry"; again I felt the sudden sting of the switch, inciting me to motion; again I ran.

Four times I ran as quarry in the cruel games of that evening.

Four times was I caught and, on my back in the dirt of that barbar-ian camp, rudely ravished by whom I knew not.

When, later, I had been unbound and unhooded by Eta, I had wanted her to take me in her arms, to comfort me, but she had not. She had kissed me, happily, and one by one, removed the loops and ties of bells, lastly removing that which I had worn at my left hip. She then indicated that I should help her with the serving. I looked at her, aghast. How could I now serve? Did she not understand what had been done to me? I was not a Gorean girl. I was an Earth girl. Was it nothing that I had been, regardless of my will, ravished four times, put brutally against my will to the pleasure of strong men? I saw the answer in Eta's eyes, which smiled at me. Yes, it was unimportant. Did I not know I was a slave girl? Had I expected anything else? Had it not pleased me?

I looked sullenly into the dirt. I was an Earth girl, but, too, I was a slave girl.

It was unimportant, I realized then. It had been truly nothing, no more than the serving of wine or the sewing of a garment. I realized then what might, truly, be the import of being a slave girl. Why had my master permitted it? Was I not his slave? Did I mean so little to him? He had taken my virginity; he had taken much pleasure in me; he had won me, forcing from me my total surrender as a slave girl to his power; then he had permitted his men to amuse themselves with me. Did he not love me? I remembered his eyes on me, before the hood had been thrown over my head in preparation for my service in the cruel game. I recalled his eyes. In his eyes I had seen that I was nothing, only a meaningless slave to him.

I poured wine from the flask I bore into the cup, I holding it, of one of the men.

I froze. I saw dirt upon his tunic. Our eyes met. He was, I knew, one of those who had had me. I was now serving him. He regarded me. I extended to him the cup. He did not accept it. Our eyes met. I took the cup and pressed my lips to it. Again I extended the cup to him. Still he regarded me.

I had not been permitted, following the cruel game, to slip the Ta-Teera, my slave rag, again upon my body. My master had said a curt word. I must then remain nude. It is customary, following the game, that the prize remain nude, that the value of her captured beauty remain discernible to all, to the winners for their pleasure, to the loser for his chagrin, to the onlookers for their admiration, and, too, perhaps, to incite them in another contest, at some future date, to vie for its possession.

His eyes were upon me.

Angrily, with helpless anger, the futile, meaningless anger of a slave girl, I again pressed my lips to the cup, this time fully and lingeringly.

Again I extended to him the cup.

This time he took it.

He then, without looking at me further, turned to his cup companion on his left. I hated him. He had ravished me, and now I must serve him, and as a naked slave girl!

Did he not know I was from Earth? Had he not been told? Did he think I was a Gorean girl? Did he think such things were right for me? Had he no concern for my feelings? But he saw me doubtless as no more than a girl with a mark on her thigh. But, indeed, now, what else was I? And I realized now that such things were right for me, exactly right, and that my feelings were no longer of interest or importance; accordingly, no note would be taken of them, and appropriately.

I was deeply troubled.

But I knew now what I had become.

And others, too, of course, I served.

And as obediently, and deferentially.

But this night, I gathered, as I served, was in some way not as other nights.

Something was different.

This night, as usual, of course, we served, Eta and I. This was to be expected. The meaning of our existence, as I had gathered, was to please and serve men. And I would later learn that this was indeed true. That is the purpose of the slave girl, to please and serve men. But this night, we, with our flasks of wine, in our serving, were instructed to remain in the background, in the shadows, to remain back of the circle of the fire, behind the sitting men. When one of the men would lift his cup, I, or Eta, whoever might be closer, would, of course, hurry to serve him. But usually, you see, we served from more closely amongst the men, often even kneeling amongst them.

Men tend to enjoy having their girls close at hand, you see, perhaps unobtrusively to one side, but in a place from which they may be easily summoned, and easily looked upon with pleasure, for the mere sight of a slave girl gives great pleasure to men, who in their way are glorious, dominating beasts.

But this night, we rather, as noted, with our flasks of wine, remained back in the shadows, behind the circle of the fire, behind the sitting men, as we had been instructed.

The men spoke together, earnestly. Matters of importance, I gathered, were being discussed. At such a time men did not wish to be distracted by the bodies of slave girls. We remained in the shadows.

I watched, angrily. My master, with a rock, drew maps in the dirt by the fire. Some of the maps I had seen before. He had drawn them the preceding night for his lieutenants, when they had spoken alone. He spoke swiftly and decisively, sometimes indicating a portion of the terrain by jabbing at it with the rock. Sometimes he pointed to the largest of the three moons above; in a few days it would be full. I stood there, naked, recently ravished, sweat and dirt on my body, and in my hair, in the shadows, ignored, holding the large flask of wine on my left hip, watching. I wondered at what might be the nature of the camp in which I found myself. It did not seem to be a hunting camp, though hunting was done from it. Too, I did not think it was a camp of bandits, for the men in the camp did not seem of the bandit sort; not only did the cut and differing insignia on their tunics suggest a uniform of sorts, but the clear-cut subordination, the obvious organization and discipline which characterized them and their relationships did not suggest outlawry; too, the men seemed handsome, strong, clean-cut, responsible, reliable, disciplined, trained, and efficient; there was none of the laxness and disorder of either men or environment I would have expected in a camp of bandits. I inferred then that I found myself slave in a camp of soldiers of some city or country. The camp, however, situated as it was, did not seem an outpost or guard camp; it did not command terrain; it was not fortified; it was too small for a training camp or a wintering camp; too, because of its size, so small, it did not seem a likely war camp; sixteen men quartered here, with two girls as slaves; here there were no armies, no divisions or regiments. There was nothing here with which to consummate war, to repel or launch invasions, or meet in wide-spread combat on great fields. What then, I asked myself, was the nature of this camp?

One of the men lifted his cup and I hurried to him. I took the cup and filled it. His tunic, too, I noted, was stained with the dust of the camp. I looked at him, angrily over the brim of the cup. Then I pressed my lips to his cup as I must, as a slave girl, and handed it to him. He took it, scarcely noticing me, and returned his attention to the map in the dirt, which was of importance. I wondered if he had had me first, or second, or third or fourth. I wondered which had been he. Each had been different; yet in the arms of each I had been only and fully a slave. I looked at him. He did not know I looked at him. I wondered how many hundreds of slave girls he had had.

I looked carefully, as carefully as I could in the light, at the large, blond, shaggy-haired fellow, whom I found, after my master, the most attractive male in the camp. It had been he who had first taken Eta, when, the night before I was branded, I had watched her perform, bound, belled and hooded, in the same cruel sport in which I this evening had been so humiliatingly victimized, treated as though I might be only a slave.

I, treated as though I might be only a slave!

But did I think I was any longer free?

But, of course, that was what I now was, a slave, only a slave.

How misplaced and foolish then seemed my resentment, my petulance, my pride!

Such luxuries belonged to free women, not to such as I.

Tears of helpless frustration stained my cheeks.

I was no longer free!

I looked at him. There was not a stain of dust on his tunic. I was just as pleased. Had he run, and I known it, I might have endeavored to throw myself into his arms. Surely no one would think less of a slave for that. I smiled to myself. I looked at him. Who knows, I thought, I might even have responded to him. This thought scandalized me, an Earth girl, but then I smiled to myself, and tossed my head. It did not matter. I was an Earth girl, true, but now I was only a slave girl. A slave girl is not only permitted to be responsive to men, but it is obligatory for her. It is a duty which, further, should she shirk, will be enforced upon her. It is not uncommon for a girl who is even trivially displeasing to be whipped. I looked at the large, handsome fellow. I had no honor to protect, no pride to uphold, for I was slave. He was indeed attractive. Too, I certainly would not wish to be whipped. I laughed to myself. For the first time in my life, I, a slave, felt free to be a woman. I then loved my sex.

A man lifted his cup, and I hastened to him, to serve him. I then returned to the shadows. I noted that Eta served wine to the tall, hand-some, blond-haired fellow. I did not mind. I liked Eta, though she was first girl, and over me. I had worked well under her and she had not switched me. I watched my master. With the rock he jabbed down at the map. Men asked questions. He replied. They hung upon his words. I looked about the circle of the fire. What fantastic males these were, so strong, so handsome, so mighty. I felt small and slight, and helpless, before them. And how proud I felt of my master, first among them, he the mightiest and finest of all. Eta remained in the vicinity of the blond, shaggy-haired warrior. I moved more closely to my master. I wished to pour him wine and kiss his cup, should he give his girl the opportunity to do so. I did not understand their conversation, or the nature of the project which they were apparently planning. It was, I gathered, military in nature. Moreover, waiting was involved in it. More than once had a man gazed at the largest moon in the sky. In some days it would be full.

My master flung the rock down at a certain place in the map. It lay there, solid, half buried in the dirt. It was there that something, I gathered, would take place. The men grunted in agreement. There was a stream there, or a confluence of two streams, and, apparently, a woods. The men nodded. My master looked about himself. None asked a further question. They seemed satisfied. Their eyes shone as they looked upon him. How proud I was of my master. How thrilled I was, secretly, in my heart, to be owned by him.

How precious a woman's bondage can be to her! I wondered if free women could understand that. Surely many a slave understands it—richly, deeply, profoundly.

The men rose from the side of the fire and, some talking among themselves, went to their furs and tenting.

My master looked at me. He lifted his cup. I hastened to him, took the cup, and filled it. I pressed my lips long to its side, then humbly proffered it to the magnificent beast whose girl I was. I knelt before him, and in my eyes, doubtless, he could read my need. But he turned away.

Before he had turned away, again I had read in his eyes, as I had before, earlier in the evening, that I was only a meaningless slave to him.

Was I such poor slave stuff, naked, in need, at his feet, that I was to be despised, and rejected?

Then, kneeling in the dirt, all the fury, the humiliation and frustration, of a scorned Earth girl, scorned by a barbarian, welled up within me. I began to choke with rage. I rose to my feet. I thrust the flask of wine I carried into the hands of Eta, who came to comfort me. "Go away!" I cried. Eta took the flask. I would not permit her to kiss me. She said something, softly. "Go away!" I screamed at her. Some of the men turned to look at me. Eta took the flask of wine and, frightened, hurried away. I stood near the fire, which, now, had muchly subsided. My fists were clenched. Tears ran down my cheeks. "I hate you all!" I cried. I ran stumbling to the thin blanket which I had been given the night before. I tore it from the ground and covered myself with it, holding it about my shoulders. I shuddered, head down, clutching the blanket about me, shaking with sobs, near where the blanket had lain. I had been taken, against my will, from Earth. I had been brought to a strange world. I had been branded. I was being kept as a slave. I lifted my head, wildly, looking about the camp, up at the moons, at the cliffs and thorn brush. I looked at the men, some watching me. "I am better than you all," I cried, "though you abuse me! I am of Earth! You are barbarians! I am civilized! You are not! It is you who should bend to me, not I to you! It is I who should command, not you!" Eta ran to me, to urge me to silence. None in the camp save I myself understood my words, but, clearly, they were uttered in wildness, in hysteria, in rage; they were words, clearly, of protest, perhaps even of hysterical rebellion. Eta was clearly frightened. Had I known more of Gor, I, too, might then have been terrified. I knew little then of the world on which I found myself, or of the meaning of the brand on my thigh. My shield then, as before, was simply my ignorance, the ignorance of a foolish girl. I shouted and cried out at them, raging, weeping. Then I saw, before me, my master. He loomed in the darkness. I looked up at him, in rage. My fists clutched the blanket about me. It was he who had won me in the grim contest with steel in the fields; it was he who had brought me naked to his camp; he who had branded me; he by whom my virginity had been ripped from me; he who had, in his tenting, again and again, at length, reduced me to a panting, surrendered object of his pleasure, a vanquished, loving slave girl. "I hate you!" I cried to him, in rage. I clutched the blanket about me. How hard it is for a girl, stripped, to stand before, and conduct herself with dignity before, as an equal, a man who is fully clothed. I clutched the blanket with my fists. I held it tightly about me. It gave me courage. He had made me love him! I loved him! And yet he cared nothing for me! "Don't you understand," I cried, "I love you! I love you! And yet you treat me as nothing! I hate you!" I shook with rage. "I hate you! I hate you!" I cried. After making me love him, he had permitted his men to amuse themselves with me! He had given me to them for their sport! "You gave me to others!" I wept. "I hate you!" I looked at him, wildly. "You do not know who I am," I said. "I am Judy Thornton! I am of Earth! I am not one of your barbarian girls, a slut for your pleasure! I am a refined, civilized young woman! I am better than you are! I am better than you all!"

I saw, in the moonlight, the hand. It was extended toward me, open. "You cannot treat me badly," I said. "You must treat me well." I looked at him, boldly. "I have rights," I said. "I am a free woman."

His hand extended still toward me, open. I did not know the extent of his patience.

I handed him the blanket. I stood then small and naked before him. The moonlight streamed down on the branded slave girl before her master.

He held the blanket, looking down at it. Then he looked at me. I trembled. I knew a girl was to be punished.

He lifted the blanket. In that instant I felt suffused with joy for I felt then that he would, in his kindness, cover me, protecting me from the eyes of his men; perhaps, too, he had been moved by my plight; perhaps he was now sorry for how cruelly he had treated me; perhaps now he would try to make amends; perhaps now I had stirred pity and compassion in his harsh breast; perhaps, too, he was moved now by my love for him and, overwhelmed with gratitude, and tenderness, at the value and immensity of this gift, might be moved to regard me, too, with affection, with love, in turn.

I looked at him with loving eyes. Then he placed the blanket over my head, and, with a length of cord, looping it several times about my throat, tied it tightly under my chin, so that again, as in the cruel game, I was hooded. Then he threw me to his men.

I lay in the blanket, clutching it about me. I was cold, sullen. I could no longer cry. The men, my masters, were asleep. I lay huddled, my knees drawn up.

I did not know what time it was. The moons were still in the sky.

I crawled to my knees, holding the blanket about me. I looked about the still camp.

My body ached.

I moved the blanket, looking down, shifting it that my leg be exposed. I examined my thigh. I looked at the brand which I bore on my body. It was a flower, lovely and delicate. Yet I could not pluck it. I could not remove it. It was imprinted in my flesh. It had been placed there, burned into my thigh, by a hot iron, as I had screamed under the metal's searing print. I regarded it, that graceful floral badge of bondage. It was now a part of my body. I had no doubt that I was more beautiful, branded, than I had been before. The brand, I could see, considerably enhanced my beauty. It is one of the attractive features of a slave girl. But, more beautiful though I might be on its account, it marked me incontrovertibly as a slave. I wished to escape. I looked at the thorn brush. Yet I wore a brand. Could there be a true escape, on a world such as this, for a branded girl? Would that mark not continue to say, to anyone, and all, softly, persistently, each instant, each moment, every hour of the day and night, when anyone might care to glance upon it, "Here is a slave"? Could there be an escape, on a world such as this, for a girl who wore such a mark? If it should be so much as glimpsed, would not such a girl be instantly placed in chains and a collar? Perhaps I might steal clothing, but the brand would still be on my body, marking me. Suppose men, suspicious, would turn me over to free women, that my body might be, without compromise to my dignity lest I be free, examined by them. When they discovered the mark, worn by a girl masquerading as one of their own lofty station, a woman free, would they not in fury, with whips, drive me stripped, begging for mercy, weeping, to the waiting shackles of the men? What escape, what freedom, could there be for a girl who wore a brand? I looked at the brand. Well and deeply it marked me as what I now had no doubt I was, what tonight I had been well taught I was, what I, in truth, incontrovertibly, now was, a slave girl.

The Earth girl, a slave on a barbarian planet, clutched the blanket about her.

I looked up. On the cliff above me, I could see, crouching, the guard. He was not watching me.

I looked at the cliffs, at the thorn brush.

I sat on the ground, the blanket about me. I knew I was a slave girl, legally, irrefutably; the brand told me that; but I wondered on a deeper question, one beyond legalities and institutions; I wondered if I were truly, in my heart, a female slave. This question troubled me deeply. I had, since my branding, experienced profoundly ambivalent feelings on this matter. It was as though I were trying to understand myself, my deepest emotions and needs. At times I had been on the brink of surrendering myself to myself, acknowledging to my horrified conscious mind forbidden truths, long-denied realities, speaking of a venerable, long-suppressed, antique nature, one antedating huts of straw and limestone caves. I did not know what dispositions slept latent in my genetic structures, dispositions inapt and out of place in the artificial world within the strictures of which I had been conditioned. A nature, like the growth of a tree, the shape of a bush, may be clipped and thwarted. The seed poisoned does not grow; the flower immersed in acid does not bloom. I wondered what might be the nature of men, and what might be the nature of women. I know of no test in these matters, unless it be honesty, and what leads to joy.

Perhaps I would not have considered these matters save that I was unable to drive from my mind the recollection of an event which had occurred late in the sordid abuse to which I had been so brutally subjected. I had been thrown to my master's men. One after another had raped and beaten me, and thrown me to the next. I was handed about as an object. Fierce was the discipline to which they subjected me. Though I wept for mercy, and cried out, none gave ear; no consideration nor lenience was shown to the piteous slave girl in their power. Then, strangely, late in this abuse, the event occurred, which even now troubled me. I lay on my back, weeping, my head bound in the blanket, thrashing and squirming, struck, held, unable to withdraw from, helpless to withstand, the plunging discipline of the brute to whom I had been last thrown, and it had occurred. I suddenly felt an indescribable sensation. First, it seemed to me, incredibly, that this was fitting, what was being done to me; I had been proud and vain before men; what did I, truly, expect men, such men, men on a world such as this, to do about that? As his force struck me, I felt, strangely, "Be disciplined, Woman." I was half choked in the hood. Then, to my amazement, I welcomed the abuse I felt. There was, beyond its sense of fittingness, seeing that I, a woman, had displeased strong males, and must thus be punished, a sense of profound complementarity; the abuse, if he chose, was simply his to give, and mine to bear; he was a man, I was a woman; he was dominant; I was not; it was his to rule, mine to submit. I experienced then, degraded and abused though I was, with a flood of elation, primitive organic, animal, primate complementarity, the complementarity of man and woman, the complementarity beyond mythology and rhetoric, the complementarity of he who takes and she who is taken, of he who has, and owns, and of she whom he has, whom he owns, and makes his. With a cry of joy and misery then, from the depths of the hood, rearing from the dirt as I could, I clutched him; I felt my body locked to his; then I felt my body, as though of its own will, suddenly, spasmodically, grasp him; I could not begin to control the reflexes which he had triggered in me; they jolted and exploded in my body; I clutched him, helplessly; I was his.

Men laughed. "Kajira," said one.

Then I was thrown to another.

I sat in the silent camp, wrapped in the thin blanket, thinking. "Kajira," had said one of the men.

I was angry. I could not forgive myself for having yielded to one of the men. I tried to tell myself it had not happened. It could not have happened. Thus, it had not happened. Yet I knew, in truth, it had happened. I had yielded to one of the men. In his arms, I, who was, or had been, Judy Thornton, had yielded to one of the men. An abused slave girl had wept and bucked in the arms of a master. It had been I. How ashamed I was! I asked myself what could it mean? Could the feelings which had overwhelmed me be denied? Could the sensate truth, the splendor of biological submission, so different from the truth of a man, which is that of domination, in whose glory I had been wrapped, be denied? I resolved that I must not permit myself the weakness which would make a mockery of my personhood. I must not again yield to a male. I thought of Elicia Nevins. How she would have laughed had she seen Judy Thornton, her lovely rival, on her back in the dirt, a branded slave girl, squirming in the throes of submission to a male, so shamefully helpless in his arms, uncontrollably, not the mistress of herself, yielding to his manhood.

I knew then I must escape. It would be difficult, for I was branded.

I looked up at the guard. He was not watching. I crept to the cliff wall. I examined it in the moonlight. At no point could I crawl more than a yard up its surface. I scratched my fingernails on the granite.

I turned to the wall of thorn brush. I feared it. It was high and thick.

The guard was not watching. The camp was not his concern. His concern was elsewhere, with possible approaches to the camp, the fields beyond the valleys.

I cried out with misery. I screamed, frightened. The brush sank beneath me. It would not support my weight. My right leg was deep in it, my right arm. I turned my head to the side, keeping my eyes closed. I felt the thorns. They seemed to tear at me. I was half immersed in the brush. I was caught. I dared not move. I began to weep and scream.

My master was first to my side. He was not much pleased. I immediately fell silent.

Another man came, bearing a torch, lit from the stirred ashes of the fire. Some other men arose but then, seeing it was only a slave girl, returned to their furs and tenting. Eta hurried over to me, but a curt word from my master hurried her back to her rest with dispatch.

"I'm caught, Master," I whimpered. Only too obviously had I been trying to escape.

In the torchlight he pulled my head back, by the hair, to clear it of the thorns. He did not want me blinded. I managed, suffering long scratches, to extricate my right arm. He looked at me. I was afraid he was going to leave me as I was. I could not pull my right leg back because of its position in the brush. I had no leverage, as I stood, to lift my leg out. "Please help me, Master," I begged. I had no wish to remain caught in the thorn brush until morning. It was embarrassing, and I was helpless, and it was painful. "Please, Master," I begged, "help me."

He lifted me up, in his arms, in this action freeing my leg, though it was cut and scratched. In the instant I relished being in his arms, held by him. My weight was as nothing to him. I loved the feel of his strong hands on my body, holding me up, lightly, from the earth, which I, thus carried, could not touch unless he permitted it. I, naked, boldly put my head against the shoulder of his tunic. Then he had placed me on my feet.

I did not meet his eyes. I felt small before him. It had been obvious I had been trying to escape. I did not know, at that time, what might be the penalty for a girl who attempts escape and is so unfortunate as, as is nearly always the case, to be recaptured. Slave girls almost never escape. The major reason for this is the steel collar, which, obdurately encircling her neck, read, promptly identifies her master and his city. Almost no one, of course, would think of removing a collar from a girl, unless it would be to replace it with one of his own. This is because she is a slave. Girls may also be hunted down by trained sleen, tireless hunters. If a girl should elude one master, she will, customarily, soon fall to another. A successful escape, infrequent event that it is, seldom amounts, from the girl's point of view, to more than an exchange of collar and chains. Almost any man on Gor will hasten to put his collar on a loose, beautiful female. Where is she to run? What is she to do? All in all, escape is not a reality for female slaves. They are slaves. They will remain slaves. Too, they are branded, which further makes escape, for almost all practical purposes, an impossibility for them. Interestingly, ear piercing, too, can make it difficult for an escaped girl to elude detection. Ear piercing, interestingly, from an Earth point of view, is regarded by most Gorean women, slave and free, as more degrading than the brand. Slave girls native to Gor dread it terribly, perhaps because it is so visible, the piercing of their flesh being so flagrantly erotic; what man would even think of freeing them if they had pierced ears? They beg their masters not to pierce their ears. Their pleas, those of slave girls, are commonly ignored. Their ears are pierced. Afterwards, it might be mentioned, they are usually pleased with the piercing of their ears, and grow quite proud of this erotic dimension added to their beauty; not displeased are they either with the lovely adornments which their master may now order them to fix upon their body; free women, it is no secret, in many respects, envy their enslaved sisters, their beauty, their joy, their attractiveness to men; this may explain why free women are often quite cruel to slave girls; most embonded girls fear greatly that they might be purchased by one of the dreaded free women. I have wondered sometimes if free women on Gor might not be happier if their culture permitted them to be somewhat more like the slave girls they so heartily despise. It seems a small enough thing that a free woman might be culturally permitted to have her ears pierced and, thus, be permitted earrings. Would it make so much difference? But the bonds of culture are strong. On Earth a free woman would not think of having herself branded, though it might improve her beauty; similarly, on Gor, a free woman would not consider having her ears pierced. Among slave girls, however, ear piercing, inflicted upon them by the will of their masters, is becoming widespread on Gor; one might say it is gaining considerable popularity among masters, which accounts, of course, for its growing frequency in the female slave population of the planet; it is a custom which derives, I am told, from the city of Turia, which lies in Gor's southern hemisphere, an important manufacturing and trading center.

A girl with pierced ears is, of course, either a slave or a former slave. If she is a former slave, her papers of manumission had best be in perfect order. More than one freed woman, because of pierced ears, has found herself again on the block, again reduced by strong men to the helpless state of bondage. Such a woman is usually, by intent, sold away from her city, delivered for a pittance to a foreign buyer.

My ears were not pierced, so I needed not fear that the piercing of my ears would betray me to the casual glance of a Gorean male as a slave girl. I was, however, branded. Gorean free women, no more than the free women of Earth, do not wear brands. Only slave girls, on Earth or Gor, are branded. On Earth, where slavery is practiced, commonly only troublesome girls are branded. On Gor, on the other hand, all slave girls are branded.

I did not think I could well escape with my brand. It marked me too well as a slave.

I did not speak to my master. He was, I supposed, considering my punishment, for having attempted to escape.

I did not know at that time what was commonly done to a girl who has attempted to escape, and has been recaptured. It is just as well. Much depends on the master but, commonly, the first time she is recaptured, she is treated with great lenience, as being only a foolish girl. Commonly, she is only tied and lashed. Should she attempt escape a second time, and be recaptured, she is commonly hamstrung, the tendons behind the knees being severed. Almost no girls attempt escape a second time.

I did not know at the time but even the thought of escape was a foolish one.

Many girls, even should they be so fortunate as to reach the walls of their own city, may not be admitted through its gates. Their slavery, even though no fault of their own, has deprived them of all their rights and canceled their citizenship.

"Flee or be chained, Slave," is often said to them. They turn and run weeping from the gates.

Some girls attempt to flee to the greenwood forests of the north. In such forests, in certain territories, there roam bands of free women, the lithe, ferocious Panther Girls of Gor, but these despise and hate women not of their own fierce ilk; in particular do they revile and hold in contempt girls, beauties, who have been slaves to men; should such a girl, fleeing, enter the cool vastness of their green domain, she is commonly hunted down like a tabuk doe and cruelly captured; the forests are not for such as she; she is tethered and bound, and often lashed, then driven by switches helplessly to the shores of Thassa or the banks of the Laurius, and then sold back to men, usually for weapons or candy.

My master, with a spear and a loop of rope, under the torchlight, the torch held by one of his men, opened a passage in the thorn bush. It was some eighteen inches wide.

He pointed to the passage.

The way to flight was open.

I need only run.

I looked at my master in the moonlight. My knees felt that they might give way. I began to tremble.

The way to flight was open.

I looked with dread down the narrow corridor forced between the walls of fierce thorn brush, into the darkness beyond.

I needed only run.

The naked slave girl shook with terror before her master.

Then I knelt before him and pressed my lips to his feet, trembling. "Keep me, Master," I begged. "Keep me!" I looked up at him, clutching his knees, tears in my eyes. "Please, Master," I wept, "let me stay."

I remained kneeling, shuddering, as he turned from me and reclosed, with the spear and rope, the corridor in the thorn brush.

Then again he stood before me, looking down at me. He motioned me to my feet that I should follow him. Humbly, his girl, I followed him through the camp. The other man, too, he holding the torch followed.

We stopped before the rolled furs of one of the warriors. He blinked in the torchlight, and rose to one elbow, looking at us. My master spoke to him, briefly, no more than four or five words. I looked at the man. I knew him well from the camp. I had usually shrunk away from him. He was the least attractive man in the camp.

Why had my master brought me here?

My master said something to me, briefly, and indicated the recumbent warrior. I could not understand the precise meaning of the words addressed to me, but their import, as my heart sank, was clear. I was to please this man, and as a slave girl.

Yesterday night my master had taken my virginity, much pleasured himself with me, and forced my total surrender to him, the surrender of a completely vanquished bond girl. But should I then have inferred that I was a favored girl? That there was something special about me? No. It had been only first rights with me, naturally taken by him, the leader. It had meant nothing. I was only a girl. What had meant so much to me, what had been so momentous to me, had been meaningless to him. It had been only first rights. Doubtless he had taken first rights with countless girls, many of them more beautiful than I. I was truly for the use of all, as much, or more, than the lovely Eta. There was nothing special about Judy

Thornton. She was only a slave girl in the camp. I had not understood that. I had been confused, scandalized, outraged, miserable, when I had been put up as quarry and prize in the cruel game of the evening. I had, at last, afterwards, even cried out my rebellion, my foolish protest. I had been vain and proud. I had thought myself better than what I was. I, an Earth girl, had presumed to scold Gorean men. Then I had been hooded and thrown naked to them for their pleasure. In the course of the savage discipline inflicted upon me, late in its measures, I had, it both thrilling and horrifying me, sensed the ancient primate complementarity of male and female, that in the ancient biological sovereignties of nature, on this world reasserted, I, a female, was simply subordinate to the male. This truth, much fought and feared, long denied, accepted, burst upon me with a blaze of freedom. With hurricane force it blasted away the brittle webs and bars of falsehood. I, though helpless, hooded, in the arms of the beasts who ravished me, had experienced, exhilarated, an incredible sense of freedom, of liberation. It was not the freedom of convention I then felt but the freedom of nature, not the freedom to be what I was not, which had been prescribed to me, but the freedom rather to be what I was, which, for complex social and historical reasons, had been long denied to me; it was not the freedom of political prescription, but the freedom of nature, the freedom of a rock to fall, of a plant to grow, of a flower to bloom, the ecstatic freedom to be what one was. And I had cried out and seized the man. I, hooded, knew nothing of him but his maleness. I cried out and yielded to him. "Kajira," had said someone. How shamed I had been that I had done this. How sullenly I had lain in the camp afterwards. I had resolved to attempt escape.

In the camp, as I had lain there, I had known I was nothing special, that I was only a slave girl, that I must obey the men, and that they would do with me what they wished.

I attempted to escape. But, in a moment, foolishly, painfully, I was enmeshed in the thorn brush, helpless and caught in its cruel compass.

My master had then extricated me from my cruel prison and, with spear and rope, opened a path in the brush, through which I might, did I choose, take flight.

I had wavered, and then, terrified and crushed, had knelt to him. "Keep me, Master," I had begged.

I now stood beside him, the man with the torch standing to one side. I looked down at the man in the furs, looking up at us. To me he was the least attractive man in the camp.

My master had said something to me. Its import was clear. I looked at him. His eyes were hard. I choked back sobs. I knelt beside the man in the furs, who threw back the furs.

My master stood behind me. The other man held the torch. I then, with hands and mouth, fell to kissing and touching the warrior. I pleased him as well as I could, being an ignorant girl, following his directions. At last he took me and threw me to the furs beneath him. I looked up at my master's face. I could see the side of it in the torch-light. The torchlight illuminated me. Then, suddenly, I turned my head to one side, closing my eyes, crying out. I could no longer resist the man. I then, shamed, under the very eyes of my master, yielded to the man.

When he had done with me to his satisfaction, he thrust me from him. My master then ordered me to my feet and he conducted me to where my blanket had been discarded. There, bending over me, he crossed my wrists and, with a narrow strap, tied them together behind my back; he then similarly fastened my ankles. I lay on my side. He threw the thin blanket over me and left me.

Eta crept to my side. I looked at her, dry-eyed. She did not attempt to untie me. The master had decreed bonds for me this night. I would remain bound. I turned away from Eta, lying on my side. She remained near me. Tonight I had run, belled, both quarry and prize, in a cruel game of barbarian men; insolent, I had been thrown to masters, who had impressed their dominance upon me; no longer had I doubt of their dominance, or of my complete subordination to their will; my master had, later, permitted me to run if I chose, to take flight; rather, I had knelt before him naked and begged to be kept; I would be kept, as he made clear to me, only upon his terms, those of my absolute subjection, my abject slavery; the slave girl had been permitted to run, if she chose; not so choosing, she remained in the camp as clearly what she was, total slave.

I wondered why my master had opened the corridor in the thorn brush; did I really mean nothing to him; was it nothing to him whether I remained in the camp, or fled into the darkness, to starve, or be devoured by beasts, or to fall into the hands of others? I suspected that, truly, it did mean little to him. Yet, as I lay there, naked, bound, under the blanket, I reddened. It had been for my benefit, not his, that he had opened the corridor in the brush. He had understood the slave girl better than she had understood herself; he had doubtless had experience with many girls; perhaps he had even owned Earth girls before; it did not seem likely to me that I would have been the only wench of Earth brought to the chains of this world; there had perhaps been many; as I lay there I realized that he had cognized me well, as a master a girl; the corridor had been opened for my benefit, not his; he, with his skill and experience in such matters, had simply and easily read my emotions, my feelings, my nature; they had lain as open to him as my flesh; I had been unable to conceal aught from his discerning eye; he was a master of female psychology; nothing in me had been secret from him; I had been, with ease, "sized up" and understood; I shuddered, thinking how easy this would make me to control, how simple to manipulate and defeat; I was both gratified and frightened that this man understood me; I was gratified because I wanted, deeply, to be understood, and I was frightened, too, because I sensed the power this understanding would give him over me; I had little doubt, too, that he was the sort of man who would exploit this power; he would use it as naturally, as innocently, as savagely, as effectively, as a boar its tusks or a lion its claws; he understood me and owned me; how could I have been more helplessly his?

I clenched the fists of my bound hands.

He had opened the corridor in the brush. He had known I would not run. I had not known I would not run, but he had known. He knew the girl better than she knew herself. He knew she would, when the choice must be made, kneel to him and beg to be kept. It was not he, but she who had not known that she would beg to be kept. That was the point of his small demonstration, that she, not he, learn that she would not run, that she would beg to remain in the camp, that she would sue on her knees to be kept. And what was the lesson to be gathered from that, I asked myself, angrily. I squirmed in the bonds, furious. The lesson seemed a reasonably obvious one, though perhaps one unpleasant for an Earth girl to accept. What did he know about me that I did not know about myself? What did this discerning brute, so much the master of the lovely Judy Thornton, know about her which she herself did not yet know, or admit to herself? "No!" I wept.

I felt Eta's hand, gentle on my head, comforting me. "No," I moaned.
"No."

But I knew that I had made a choice. He had then closed the thorn-
brush corridor.

He had led me to a man, him whom I had found the least attractive
in the camp.

It had then been designated to me that I would please him. Here
there had been no bonds, no hooding. It had been I who must initi-
ate action, I who must perform. I had choked back sobs. My will had
bent helplessly beneath that of my master. I had knelt and, with hands
and mouth, kissing and touching, attempted to please the free man. I
tried to respond to the man's directions. I had done so poorly. I was
an ignorant, clumsy, frightened girl, raw, uncooked "collar meat," as
it is said. But, in time, he had thrown me beneath him and, I think
with pleasure, conducted me through the throes of intimate service. I
had resolved to attempt to resist him. My master observed. I wished
to retain my personhood before my master, that he respect me. But,
in less than a quarter of an hour, I had felt sensations overwhelming
me which I could not resist. There had been tears in my eyes. Then,
though my master observed, I had turned my head to one side, closed
my eyes and cried out, and, unable to help myself, yielded to the man,
Judy Thornton's lovely belly and haunches jolting in helpless slave
orgasm.

I now lay bound, naked under a thin blanket.

Eta sat near me, to comfort me.

No longer did the opportunity to run present itself. The wall of
thorn brush had been closed. Leather confined my body. I was tied
hand and foot. I could not even rise to my feet. I smiled ruefully to
myself.

The slave girl was well secured.

But I was puzzled why I had been bound. Surely it had not been
to prevent my escape. The wall of thorn brush, and the sheer cliffs,
would be more than ample to prevent that. Why then had I been
bound? I supposed, perhaps, it was for purposes of discipline. Binding
is excellent discipline. It is often used on this world for that purpose.
Restraints, their psychological indignity and physical discomfort,
particularly after a time, placed upon a girl by the will of a master, are
among the simplest and most effective instruments of female instruc-

tion; they rank with food and the whip; a girl, under disciplinary binding, once released, is invariably eager to please; she does not wish to
be rebound; the thongs have well apprised her of her place, which is
at her master's feet.

But I did not think I was being disciplined. My master had not
seemed dissatisfied with me.

My performance had not been superb, but surely I had tried hard,
under his will, to be pleasing as a slave girl to the man he had designated.

My master had not seemed angry or irritated. I did not think I was
being disciplined. Why then had I been bound?

I had labored diligently, and without inhibitions, as well as I could,
as a poor, beautiful, commanded slave.

I had done the best I could.

Why then had I been bound?

I had tried to resist the man for several minutes, and had managed
to do so. I had held myself tight and rigid, and had tried to hold in all
feeling. I had not wanted my master to see me squirm as a slave.

I was still deeply ashamed that I had yielded to the man.

Then, as I lay there, bound, with Eta nearby, I asked myself why I
should be ashamed? Was it wrong for a woman to yield helplessly to
a man? Was it wrong for the heart to beat, to breathe, to feel? If the
nature of the man were conquest and victory, what might then be
the nature of the woman; could it be complementary; might it not be
defeat, and delicious surrender and pleasure? I began to sweat in the
bonds. Eta smiled at me. Perhaps an equal must resist a man, but I was
not an equal; I was a slave girl! I belonged to men! I could be a biological woman, as perhaps a free woman could not. I could be a primitive
female, an owned woman, as they could not. I could be a woman, as
they could not. Slavery made me free to be a woman. I reared up, sitting, my hands tied behind me. I could not free myself. Eta held my
shoulders gently. My eyes were wild. I had no choice. I was slave. I
was forced to be a woman.

I cried out with pleasure. Eta cautioned me to silence. I had resisted
the man for several minutes. I had fought not to feel. How foolish I
had been. What pleasure I had lost. I imagined myself then superbly
yielding and kissing and melting in the arms of a master from almost
his first touch, the lengthy, delicious pleasure that I could give him, his

slave, a pleasure, too, which would make me want to scream with the joy of my womanhood.

"Untie me, Eta," I begged. "Untie me!"

She did not understand me.

I turned my back to her, thrusting my bound hands piteously to her. "Untie me!" I begged.

Eta shook her head gently, and held me. I had been tied by the master. I must remain bound.

I shook my head with misery.

I wanted to crawl to the men, to tell them I understood, to beg them to have me, to let me give them pleasure.

I wanted to please them as a slave girl, theirs. My eyes were vulnerable with the helpless lust of a bound girl who would crawl to a man to serve him.

I had not dreamed such an emotion could exist. It was not merely that I was eager to piteously and submissively display my beauty to them, that they might be moved to take it in their arms and vanquish it, but, beyond this, I was overwhelmed by an entire dimension of emotion which might be spoken of, though inadequately, as the desire to yield service and love. I wanted to give, unstintingly, with no thought of return. Always I had been concerned with what I might obtain. Now, for the first time in my life, in my joy and self-acceptance as a female slave, I wanted to give. I wanted to give all of myself, wholeheartedly, to deliver and bestow myself unto them as their girl, who loved them and would do all for them, asking nothing. I wished to be nothing, and to give all.

I wanted to be their slave.

I shook with the selfless ecstasy of the slave girl.

I wanted to crawl to them to tell them that I now understood, and that I was theirs. I wanted to cry out to them, to weep, to kneel to them, to kiss and lick submissively at their bodies in my joy.

"Untie me, Eta!" I wept.

She shook her head.

I knew I had not been as successful as I might have been in pleasing the man to whom my master had earlier commanded me.

I looked at Eta. I looked to the sleeping men. I looked at Eta, again. "Teach me, Eta," I begged, in a desperate whisper, "teach me tomorrow to be pleasing to men. Teach me to be pleasing to men."

Eta could not understand my words, but she could read my eyes, my looks, the movements of my body, my piteous needs. She smiled, nodding. She understood what was occurring in my body. I knew Eta would help me. She knew I was a slave. She would help me to be a better slave. Soon, I knew, when I learned more of the language, and could clearly, or more clearly, express myself, Eta would train me, as she could, in the giving of pleasures to masters. I kissed her.

I struggled with the bonds.

"Please untie me, Eta," I begged, again indicating the bonds. She smiled, and shook her head.

I squirmed in the leather. I now knew why I had been bound. It was to prevent me from crawling to the men as a slave.

I was not to interrupt their rest.

I cried out in anger and misery, confined by the bonds. Eta cautioned me to silence.

The men must not be disturbed.

She then took me by the shoulders, to press me back, softly, to the ground. The thin blanket was about my thighs.

Before she pressed me back, I, resisting, looked at her. "La Kajira," I said.

Eta nodded. "Tu Kajira," she said. Then she indicated herself. "La Kajira," she said. Then she pointed to me. "Tu Kajira," she smiled.

Then she gently pressed me back to the ground and, as I lay on my right shoulder, looking up, covered me with the thin blanket.

I saw the moonlight on her steel collar. I envied her the collar, I, too, wanted to wear a steel collar. It had writing on it. It doubtless identified her master. I, too, wished to wear a collar, which might bear, too, the name of my master.

Eta kissed me and rose to her feet and left.

I lay under the blanket, naked, bound. I rolled to my back. I moved a bit, to find a place where I might lie comfortably. I did not move too much for I did not wish to dislodge the blanket. It would be difficult to replace should it come off in the night. I looked up at the night, the stars, the moons. I saw the cliff. I saw the guard on the height of the cliff. I then rolled to my right shoulder, moving the blanket as little as possible. I regarded the closed wall of thorn brush. I moved somewhat and looked at the furs, and, in some places, the tenting of the men.

I turned my head and looked up at the moons. How wild and white and beautiful they seemed.

Judy Thornton, or she who had once, on a remote and artificial world, been Judy Thornton, looked up at the moons.

I remembered the lovely slave in the Ta-Teera which I had seen in the mirror. She, surely, had not been Judy Thornton.

I was gloriously pleased to be that slave.

I slept out of doors, in a camp of barbaric men. Above me were the bright stars in a black sky, and three moons. I lay under a thin blanket. I was naked. There was a brand on my thigh. I was a bound slave girl.

I was not unhappy.

I looked up at the moons. "La Kajira," I said. "I am a slave girl."

Five

The Raid

"What is your duty?" asked my master.

"Absolute obedience," I replied, in Gorean.

He held the whip to my lips. I pressed my lips to it, and kissed it. "Absolute obedience," I said.

Eta, from behind me, pinned the first of five veils about my face. It was light, and shimmering, of white silk, almost transparent. Then, one after the other, she added the freedom veil, or veil of the citizeness, the pride veil, the house veil, and street veil. Each of these is heavier and more opaque than the one which lies within. The street veil, worn publicly, is extremely bulky, quite heavy and completely opaque; the lineaments of the nose and cheeks are scarcely discernible when it is worn; the house veil is worn indoors when there are those present who are not of the household, as in conversing with or entertaining associates of one's companion. Veils are worn in various numbers and combinations by Gorean free women, this tending to vary by preference and caste. Many low-caste Gorean women own only a single veil which must do for all purposes. Not all high-caste women wear a large number of veils. A free woman, publicly, will commonly wear one or two veils; a frequent combination is the light veil, or last veil, and the house or street veil. Rich, vain women of high caste may wear ostentatiously as many as nine or ten veils. In certain cities, in connection with the free companionship, the betrothed or pledged beauty may wear eight veils, several of which are ritualistically removed during various phases of the ceremony of companionship; the final veils, and robes, of course, are removed in private by the male who, following their removal, arms interlocked with the girl, drinks with her the wine of the companionship, after which he completes

116

the ceremony. This sort of thing, however, varies considerably from city to city. In some cities the girl is unveiled, though not disrobed, of course, during the public ceremony. The friends of the male may then express their pleasure and joy in her beauty, and their celebration of the good fortune of their friend. The veil, it might be noted, is not legally imperative for a free woman; it is rather a matter of modesty and custom. Some low-caste, uncompanioned, free girls do not wear veils. Similarly certain bold free women neglect the veil. Neglect of the veil is not a crime in Gorean cities, though in some it is deemed a brazen and scandalous omission. Slave girls may or may not be veiled, this depending on the will of their master. Most slave girls are not permitted to veil themselves. Indeed, not only are they refused the dignity of the veil, but commonly they are placed in brief, exciting slave livery and may not even bind their hair. Such girls, healthy and vital, their hair unbound, their considerable charms well revealed by the brevity of their costume, are thought by men to constitute one of the more pleasurable aspects of the scenery of a city. Are the slaves of Ar, for example, more beautiful than those of, say, Ko-ro-ba, or Tharna? Men, the beasts, heatedly discuss such questions. In some cities, and among some groups and tribes, it might be mentioned, though this is not common, veils may be for most practical purposes unknown, even among free women. The cities of Gor are numerous and pluralistic. Each has its own history, customs and traditions. On the whole, however, Gorean culture prescribes the veil for free women. Eta fastened the fourth of five veils upon me, the house veil. Though Eta wore only the shameful, scandalous Ta-Teera, she pinned the veils expertly. She, now only a delicious, half-naked slave girl, had once been free. She did her work beautifully.

I felt the street veil fastened upon me. I was veiled as might have been a rich Gorean free woman of high caste, perhaps bound for the song dramas of En'Kara.

"How beautiful," said Eta. She, standing back, observed me. My master's eyes appraised me.

I stood straight. I knew how beautiful I looked, for, once before, some days ago in the camp, I had been so beclothed. I had seen myself, then, in the mirror.

The robes, carefully draped, primarily white, in their richness and sheen, were resplendent; over the veils my eyes would appear very dark. Gloves had been placed upon my hands. On my feet were scarlet slippers.

I knew that I was richly and beautifully bedecked. I knew, too, that I was small, and might be easily thrown to the shoulder of a man.

My master looked at me.

He put his hands on my shoulders.

"Do you dare place your hands on the body of a free woman," I asked him, deferentially adding, "Master?"

He stepped back. He regarded me thoughtfully. "Insolent," said he to himself, as though thinking, "that a mere slave should be placed in such garments."

"Yes, Master," I said.

"Have I ever lashed you?" he asked.

I swallowed hard. "No, Master," I said.

"I should do so, sometime," he said.

"Yes, Master," I said.

"It would scarcely do to run her in the Ta-Teera," said one of his men, standing nearby.

"Doubtless not," said my master, looking at his owned girl. How incredibly, and yet rationally and justifiably, I felt at his mercy. He was my master. He owned me. He could do whatever he wanted with me. He could trade me or sell me, or even slay me upon a whim, should he wish. I was absolutely his, his girl.

"She is beautiful," said Eta.

"She will have to do," said my master.

"They are camped not two pasangs from here," said one of the men.

A black cloak was brought. It was wrapped about me.

"Come, Slave Girl," said my master.

"Yes, Master," I said.

He turned about and, with his weapons, strode from the camp. I followed him, at his heel, where a slave girl belongs.

Eta remained behind.

The other men, the warriors, single file, fell into line behind us, following.

* * * *

"Be silent," said my master.

I did not speak. Together, the men behind us, we observed the camp. There were more wagons in the retinue now. When first I had seen the retinue, several days ago, there had been only one, which had carried supplies.

The largest of the three moons was now full.

The camp lay nestled in a clearing in woods. A stream ran by one perimeter of the camp. This was joined by another stream, some two hundred yards beyond the camp. Guards had been posted.

"Quiet is the night," called one to the other. He was similarly answered.

I knew, by now, a smattering of Gorean. I could understand them. Eta had worked diligently with me. I could now respond swiftly to many commands. I knew the names of many articles. I had acquired some grammar. I was able to formulate simple sentences by myself. My masters could now command me, the barbarian girl, with relative satisfactoriness, in their own tongue, and I, to some extent, the lovely, barbarian slave from Earth, could respond to them in the tongue of my masters, theirs. I now, artlessly, unable to help myself, found myself thinking naturally of Gorean as the language of masters. It is a beautiful, melodious, expressive language. It is also, in the mouths of men, a strong, powerful, uncompromising language. When a girl is commanded in Gorean, she obeys.

I watched the guards, through the trees, make their rounds. There were several tents in the camp. In the center of the camp was a striped tent, almost a pavilion, supported on ten poles. I saw one of the girls, with bare arms, robed in classic white, unveiled, emerge from the central tent and, with a gourd dipper, go to the stream, where she filled the dipper and thence returned to the tent. There was a golden circlet on her throat, and another on her left wrist. One of the men had looked at her as she had walked past him. There was a fire in the tent, and smoke from this fire emerged from a hole at the tent's apex. Within, as they passed between the wall of the tent and the fire, I could see the shadows of one or two other girls. Near the central tent, almost as large, was a brown, turreted tent, with a pennon flying from a central pole. It was, I supposed, the tent of the camp's leader. There were some seventy or eighty men, I had conjectured several days ago, in the retinue. I could now see several sitting around open-air fires. Others were, I supposed, within the tents, perhaps sleeping.

The two palanquins which had been carried, by ten men apiece, were within the camp, turned upside down, to protect them, I supposed, from dew or rain. Beneath the one were several boxes and chests, those containing the riches which it had borne. Added to the one wagon which had been drawn by the shaggy, oxlike creatures were now four other wagons. These wagons, too, apparently, were each drawn by a pair of the oxlike creatures, called bosk. The wagons were now unhitched. Several animals, those called bosk, ten or more, hobbled, browsed among the trees on the other side of the camp.

Eta, though perhaps it was not proper, had much listened to the converse of the men, and, as my Gorean improved, conveyed certain pieces of information to me.

The retinue was the betrothal and dowry retinue of the Lady Sabina of the small merchant polis of Fortress of Saphronicus bound overland for Ti, of the Four Cities of Saleria, of the Salerian Confederation. Ti lies on the Olni, a tributary of the Vosk, north of Tharna. Tharna, sometimes called the City of Silver, is well known for the richness of her silver mines. She is ruled by Lara, a Tatrix. This seems paradoxical, for in Tharna, of the hundreds of known Gorean cities, the position of women is surely among the lowest. The sign of a man of Tharna is two yellow cords carried at the belt, suitable for the binding of the hands and feet of a female. At one time apparently women were dominant in Tharna but this situation, in a revolution of the males, was overturned. Few women in Tharna, even now, years later, are permitted out of the collar.

I looked at the four new wagons which had been added to the retinue. The wagon which I had seen earlier, the supply wagon, was now almost empty, the food supplies perhaps being diminished as the peregrination neared its end, and the poles and tenting, of course, being used in the sheltering for the camp. The other four wagons, however, were fully loaded, largely, it seemed, with produce and coarse goods.

The Lady Sabina, I learned from Eta, was pledged by her father, Kleomenes, a pretentious, but powerful, upstart merchant of Fortress of Saphronicus, to Thandar of Ti, of the Warriors, youngest of the five sons of Ebullius Gaius Cassius, of the Warriors, Administrator of Ti, this done in a Companion Contract, arranged by both Ebullius

Gaius Cassius and Kleomenes, to which had now been set the seals of both Ti and Fortress of Saphronicus. The pledged companions, the Lady Sabina of Fortress of Saphronicus and Thandar of Ti, of the Four Cities of Saleria, of the Salerian Confederation, had, as yet, according to Eta, never laid eyes on one another, the matter of their match having been arranged between their respective fathers, as is not uncommon in Gorean custom. The match had been initiated at the behest of Kleomenes, who was interested in negotiating a commercial and political alliance with the Salerian Confederation. These alliances, of interest to the expanding Salerian Confederation, were not unwelcome. Such alliances, naturally, might presage the entrance of Fortress of Saphronicus into the Confederation, which was becoming a growing power in the north. It seemed not unlikely that the match would ultimately prove profitable and politically expedient for both Fortress of Saphronicus and the Salerian Confederation. In the match, there was much to gain by both parties. The Companion Contract, thus, had been duly negotiated, with the attention of scribes of the law from both Fortress of Saphronicus and the Confederation of Saleria. The Companion Journey, then, when the auspices had been favorable, as they promptly were, these determined by the inspection of the condition and nature of the liver of a sacrificial verr, examined by members of the caste of Initiates, had begun. The journey itself, overland and afoot from Fortress of Saphronicus to Ti, would take several days, but it was ceremonially prolonged in order that the four tributary villages of Fortress of Saphronicus might be visited. It is not unusual for a Gorean city to have several villages in its vicinity, these customarily supplying it with meat and produce. These villages may or may not be tributary to the city. It is common, of course, for a city to protect those villages, whether they are tributary to the city or not, which make use of its market. If a village markets in a given city, that city, by Gorean custom, stands as its shield, a relationship which, of course, works to the advantage of both the villages and city, the city receiving produce in its markets, the villages receiving the protection of the city's soldiers. The policy of Fortress of Saphronicus, extending its hegemony politically over its nearby villages, even to the extent of exacting tribute in kind, is not unprecedented on Gor, but, on the other hand, is not the general rule. Most villages are free villages. The Gorean peasant is a resolute, strong fellow, upright and stubborn, who prides himself on his land and his sovereignty. Also, he is usually the master of the Gorean longbow, in the wake of which liberty is often to be found. He who can bend the longbow, a peasant saying has it, cannot be slave. Women, of course, it might be noted, lack the strength to bend this bow. I suppose if they could bend the bow, the saying would not exist or would be altered. That is the way men are. Goreans enjoy making women slaves. The women, on the whole, interestingly, save some verbally, do not seem to much mind. Interestingly, the longbow is outlawed in the tributary villages of Fortress of Saphronicus. The Betrothal or Companion Journey, ceremonially, included the circuit of the four villages, in each of which a feast was held, and from each of which a wagon of produce was procured, to be added to the dowry riches to be presented to Ebullius Gaius Cassius, father of Thandar of Ti, to be included in the treasury of Ti. I had seen four wagons of produce in the camp, and knew independently from Eta, that the four tributary villages had now been visited. The wagons of produce were not of great value but stood as token of the relation of the villages to Fortress of Saphronicus. Also, of course, visiting the villages presented the opportunity for publicizing the match and, doubtless, unobtrusively, in the feasting and celebration, for gathering the reaction, and general feelings, of the villages. Are they content? Is trouble brewing? Must a leader be deposed, or imprisoned? Must a daughter be taken hostage to the city? Accurate information on the oppressed is essential to the maintenance of the power of the oppressor.

From the striped tent in the center of the camp another girl emerged, clad like the other in the sleeveless gown, a circlet on her throat and left wrist, and made her way toward the supplies wagon. She left the pavilionlike tent sedately but, as soon as she was no longer visible through the opening in the tent she threw back her head, shaking her hair, and then, her gait transformed, sauntered like a she-sleen to the side of the wagon. I gasped. The walk could only have been that of a slave girl. I then realized that the girls in attendance on the veiled woman, who had been seated in the curule chair on the palanquin, were slaves. The circlets on their throats were doubtless collars, and the wristlet each wore was doubtless naught but matching slave jewelry. But they were obviously high slaves, judging by the fineness of their raiment. They were the slave maids of the Lady Sabina, doubtless belonging to her. I wondered how long it had been since one of them had had the hands of a man on her body.

"Quiet is the night," called one of the guards.

"Quiet is the night," was echoed by other guards about the camp.

I looked up at the largest of the three Gorean moons. It was now full.

Tomorrow the retinue would continue on toward Ti, to be met two days from now, outside the city, by a welcoming procession. Or thus it was planned.

I felt my master's hand on my arm. It was not tight, but firm. I was in his power.

I did not understand my role in the events which were transpiring. I was not clear why my master and his men, and myself, scouted this camp, and now remained in its vicinity.

One lunar month from this date, by the phases of the largest moon, after days of preparation, the ceremony of the companionship was scheduled to be consummated in Ti, binding together as companions Thandar of Ti, son of Ebullius Gaius Cassius, Administrator of Ti, and the Lady Sabina, daughter of Kleomenes, high merchant in Fortress of Saphronicus. I hoped, naturally, that they would be happy. I was only a slave, but I did not think myself much less free than the Lady Sabina, whose beauty was being bartered for commercial and political power. I might have to be half naked in a bond girl's Ta-Teera but she, I expected, despite the wealth of her robes and jewels, was in her way as slave as I. Yet I did not feel sorry for her, for I had heard from Eta that she was a pretentious, haughty girl, one bold in speech and cruel to her slave maids. Many of the daughters of merchants are proud sorts, for the merchants themselves, by virtue of their power, tend to vanity and pride, and agitate, justifiably or not, for the inclusion of their caste among the high castes of Gor. Their pampered daughters, protected from work and responsibility, ostentatiously garbed and elaborately educated in caste trivia, tend to be spoiled and soft. Yet I did not wish the Lady Sabina unhappiness. I hoped that she would have a splendid companionship with Thandar of Ti. Too, allaying my commiserations for the girl, for she had had no say in her companionship arrangements, was my understanding, conveyed by Eta, that she looked forward to the match and was much pleased by it. In taking companionship with one of the Warriors she would raise caste, for the

Warriors on Gor are among the high castes, of which there are five, the Initiates, Scribes, Physicians, Builders and Warriors. In many cities only members of the high castes may belong to the city's high council. Most Gorean cities are governed by an executive, the Administrator, in conjunction with the high council. Some cities are governed by a Ubar, who is in effect a military sovereign, sometimes a tyrant, whose word is law. The Ubar's power is limited institutionally only by his capacity to inspire and control those whose steel keeps him upon the throne. Sword loyalty is a bond of fidelity sworn to the Ubar. Gorean warriors seldom break this bond. It is not sworn lightly. It is sworn only to those who are thought fit to be Ubar. When the Ubar is thought to be unfit, it is thought, too, he has dishonored the pledge of sword loyalty. It is not then uncommon for him to die beneath the steel of his outraged men. Only a Ubar, it is said, may sit upon the throne of a Ubar. Only when a true Ubar sits upon the throne is it said the pledge of sword loyalty is binding. It was my hope that the Lady Sabina would be happy. It was said she was much pleased to raise caste and would become, by this match, one of the high ladies of the Salerian Confederation, which was becoming powerful in the north. I did not much think about Thandar of Ti, perhaps because he was a man. I supposed he was not too pleased at being matched with a girl who was not of the five high castes, but surely he could appreciate the commercial and political significance of the match, and would be pleased to serve his city by doing his part. From the point of view of his father the bargain was a good one for Thandar was the youngest and least important of five sons; it was not as if his first or second son had been matched with a merchant's daughter; besides the match was politically and commercially expedient; who knew how ambitious might be the aspirations of Ti, and the Salerian Confederation? Too, from Thandar's point of view, if the match turned out to be a misery he, being a Gorean male of high caste, could content himself with bought women, who would fight one another and beg on their bellies to serve one such as he.

The gowned female slave, the circlet on her throat and wrist, reached into the supply wagon, into a sack, to find a larma. I watched her in the half darkness. I did not think she saw that, behind her, from the pavilionlike tent, the veiled Lady Sabina had emerged and followed her, with two of the other slave maids behind her, one with a switch. The girl at the wagon reached forward, extending her hand into a sack. One of the warriors of the camp was close behind her. I think she must have been aware of his presence but she gave no sign of this awareness. He put his hands on either side of her body, resting them on the wood. She turned, easily, not surprised, between his arms, to face him. She lifted the larma fruit and, her head up, looking at him, bit into it. She regarded him in the half darkness. She chewed at the fruit. He leaned over her. I saw the glint of gold at her throat. Suddenly her arms were about him and he was kissing her, she a slave in his arms in the half darkness. I saw her hand behind his back, the larma fruit, bitten into, still in her hand. "So, Shameless Slave!" cried the Lady Sabina, who had followed the girl, perhaps suspicious of her. The two who had been touching leapt apart, the girl crying out with misery and throwing herself to her knees at the foot of her mistress; the man backed away, angrily, startled.

"Shameless slave slut!" cried the Lady Sabina.

"Have pity, Mistress!" wept the caught slave girl, her head to her mistress' sandals.

"What is going on here?" demanded a man, emerging from the central, dark tent, which I took to be that of the headquarters of the camp. He carried a sword slung over his shoulder, loosely. He wore otherwise only a tunic and the heavy sandals, almost boots, of a soldier.

"Behold," cried the Lady Sabina, indicating the kneeling girl, "a lascivious slave girl!"

The soldier, the leader of the camp, I gathered, was not pleased at having his work or rest interrupted, but was concerned to be deferential.

"I followed her," said the Lady Sabina, "and found her here, shameless in the arms of a soldier, touching, kissing!"

"Pity, Mistress," wept the girl.

"Have I not, Lehna," inquired the Lady Sabina, sternly, "taught you proper deportment? Have I not instructed you in dignity? Is this how you betray my trust?"

"Forgive me, Mistress," wept the girl.

"You are not a paga slut," said the Lady Sabina. "You are the maid of a free woman."

"Yes, Mistress," said the girl.

"Have I not set you always a model of elegance, an example of nobility and self-respect?" asked the Lady Sabina.

"Yes, Mistress," said the girl.

"When you were twelve, my father bought you from the pens in Ar, and gave you to me."

"Yes, Mistress," she said.

"You were treated with great kindness. You were not put in the kitchens. You were not given to tharlarion drivers. You were taken into our own apartments. You were permitted to sleep in my own chamber, at the foot of my couch. You were trained diligently as a lady's maid."

"Yes, Mistress," said the girl.

"Is that not a great honor for a slave slut?"

"Yes, Mistress," said the girl.

"And yet," said the Lady Sabina, sadly, "how have I been repaid?"

The girl dared not answer, but kept her head down, trembling.

"I have been repaid with ingratitude," said the Lady Sabina.

"Oh, no!' cried the girl. "Lehna is grateful! Lehna is grateful to Mistress!"

"Have I not been kind to you?" demanded the Lady Sabina.

"Oh, yes, Mistress," said the girl.

"And yet I find you like a copper-tarsk rent slave in the arms of a retainer!"

"Forgive your girl, Mistress," begged the cringing slave.

"Have I often whipped you?" demanded the Lady Sabina.

"No," cried the girl. "No!"

"Do you think me weak?" inquired the Lady Sabina.

"No, Mistress," said the girl. "Kind, but not weak!"

"Beg," said the Lady Sabina.

"I beg to be whipped," said the girl.

The camp's leader, he with the sword slung over his shoulder, who had come forth from his tent, looked at the soldier in whose arms the girl had been discovered. He indicated the slave girl with his head. "Strip her and tie her," he said.

Angrily the man tore away the girl's gown and, with a bit of binding fiber, tied her on her knees, her wrists crossed and bound behind one of the spokes on the supply wagon.

"You are worthless," said the Lady Sabina to the bound slave. "You should carry paga in a paga tavern."

The slave cried out with misery, to be so demeaned.

A number of men had gathered about, to witness the scene. The captain was clearly irritated. "I shall speak to you later," he said to the soldier, dismissing him. The soldier turned and left.

The Lady Sabina extended her hand to one of the two slave girls who were with her. In her gloved hand was placed the switch the girl had carried for her.

She then approached the bound slave, who trembled. "Have I not always set you an example of nobility, dignity and self-respect?" asked the Lady Sabina.

"Yes, Mistress," said the girl.

"Naughty, naughty, salacious slave!" cried the Lady Sabina, striking her.

The girl cried out with the misery of her switching. I was startled at the fury with which the Lady Sabina struck the bound, collared girl. Richly did she lay the disciplinary device to the back and body of the embonded wench, well punishing her for her lascivious indiscretion. Then, wearied, furious, the Lady Sabina cast aside the switch, turned, and went back to her tent. She was followed by the two girls who had accompanied her, one of whom retrieved the switch. The whipped beauty knelt against the wagon wheel, bound there, shuddering. I saw the gold of her collar beneath her dark hair.

When the Lady Sabina had finished her work and returned to her tent, followed by the two gowned slave girls, the leader of the camp, or captain, angrily, returned, too, to his tent, and the men, who had gathered around, returned to their duties, their rest or recreations.

The girl was left tied at the wheel, whipped.

My master looked upward, at the moons. From through the trees, on the other side of the camp, came what I took to be the sound of a bird, the hook-billed, night-crying fleer, which preys on nocturnal forest urts. The cry was repeated three times.

"Quiet is the night," called one of the camp guards, and this call was echoed by the others.

Again, three times, I heard the cry of the fleer.

My master slipped behind me. He held me, with his left hand. I felt, from the side, his knife slip beneath the veils at my face and throat. Then the knife's edge, I feeling it, thin, obdurate, pressed at my jugular.

"What is the duty of a slave girl?" he asked.

"Absolute obedience, Master," I whispered, frightened. "Absolute obedience." I scarcely dared to whisper, for fear of moving my throat beneath the knife.

I felt the knife leave my throat. I felt the black cloak in which I had been wrapped, concealing the largely white, rich, shimmering raiment in which I had been robed, slipped away.

"Run," said my master, indicating a path through the trees, past the far end of the camp. "And do not let yourself be captured."

He thrust me from him and I, miserable, confused, began to run.

I had gone no more than a dozen steps when I heard one of the guards at the camp cry out, "Halt! Stand! Name! City! Stand!" I did not stop, but pressed on.

"Who is it?" cried a man. "A free woman!" I heard. "Is it the Lady Sabina?" I heard cry. "Stop her!" I heard. "After her!"

I ran, madly.

The men, as I now think of it, must have been as confused as I was. I knew only that I feared them, and had been commanded to run. Too, my master had told me to avoid capture. Ignorant, wild, terrified, I ran.

I stumbled and fell, and scrambled to my feet, and ran again. I heard men crying out, and then, more frighteningly, I heard several leaving the camp, splashing across the stream, crashing through brush behind me. I was now among the trees, out of sight of the camp, but I was being pursued, by how many men I did not know.

They were Gorean men.

I fled in terror.

"Lady Sabina!" I heard. "Stop! Stop!"

As I ran I realized that the probabilities of there being a free woman, robed, in the vicinity of the camp, who was not the Lady Sabina, were extremely low. Perhaps she had fled from the camp? Perhaps, for some reason, she wished to flee the match with Thandar of Ti, whom I understood she had never seen. There must have been men in the camp who, almost immediately, would have verified that the Lady Sabina was still within the camp, but many, having only moments to act, would be unable to make that verification. If the running woman was the Lady Sabina she must be caught for her loss would mean the failure of the alliances pending between the Salerian Confederation and Fortress of Saphronicus. Too, she must be caught swiftly, for the forests at night were dangerous. Sleen might take her or, perhaps, prowling outlaws. Too, in the camp were no hunting sleen. Accordingly, the sooner she could be retaken the better. It was night, and, even in the morning, her trail would be less fresh, less obvious. And, if the woman were not the Lady Sabina she should, anyway, be brought in. Surely a free woman in the midst of the night forest constitutes a mystery which must be solved. Who is she? From whom is she running? Is she alone?

I had no time to think. I was only running.

Too, I believe the men of the camp had little time to ponder their courses of action.

It was natural that many of them should have leapt to my pursuit.

I fled through the thickets. I heard men crashing through the brush behind me. I did not know how many followed. I suspect that of the seventy or eighty men in the camp twenty or more had immediately plunged after me, perhaps even more. Surely, too, attention was drawn to that end of the camp near which I had been first seen. It was there that men would have peered into the darkness, there that they would have been marshaled into more organized defensive groups or more organized search parties.

"Stop!" I heard. "Stand! Stand!"

I ran, stumbling, striking branches and brush away from me. My robes were torn.

The crashing in the brush behind me grew louder.

No more swiftly could I run. It was not merely that I was encumbered by the robes. I knew that I could not, in any case, outrun the men. They were stronger and swifter than I. I was only a girl. Nature, whatever might be her reasons, had not fitted me to outrun males. I was frightened suddenly that it had not been her intention that women escape men. Then I realized how foolish this was, to so personalize nature, to ascribe to the cruel, blind processes of the world deliberate intentions. Rather it had been the selections of nature which had determined this. Women who had escaped men would have been lost to the gene pool. Caught women would have been led back to the caves, to suffer the indignities of impregnation by their captors, being forced to reproduce their kind. Similar considerations may have a bearing on the smaller size and strength of women. Yet matters are far more complicated than these considerations suggest. For, in the intricacies, and interplay of both natural and sexual selection, not merely a swiftness, a size and strength would have been selected for in women but an entire set of genetic dispositions; it seems inconsistent to suppose that evolution would select only for the outside of an animal and not for its inside as well, that only matters such as external configuration would have a bearing on its survival or desirability and not its dispositions to respond in certain ways. Surely the same evolution which has selected for the fangs of the lion and the speed of the gazelle has selected as well for the disposition to hunt and the disposition to flight, that has selected for the strength of the male and the weakness of the female has selected as well for the disposition to conquer and the disposition to surrender. We are, to a large extent, one supposes, the products of environments, but it is well to remember that the maximum, shaping environments in which our nature was stabilized and forged are ancient ones; the sense in which environment determines endowment is the sense in which it determines which endowments are to be perpetuated.

With misery I suddenly realized my genetic heritage was that of a type which could be caught by men.

The hands of a man seized me.

"Hold, Lady," said he.

I gasped, and shook, held in his arms.

"Why have you fled, Lady Sabina?" asked he. "It is dangerous." Then he called out, "I have her."

I tried to escape, but I was held fast.

In a moment several more men were about me. He who had held me then released me. I stood, captured, in their midst. I did not speak. I averted my head.

"Is it the Lady Sabina?" asked a voice.

"Face me," said a voice.

I did not face him, but kept my head averted. I felt hands put on my shoulders.

Firmly I was turned to face the speaker. "Lift your head," he said. "To the moonlight."

I kept my head down, but he, with his hand, lifted my head up, that the moonlight might fall upon my veiled face.

I saw that it was the captain, or camp's leader. Suddenly I realized he should not have pursued me. He should have remained in the camp.

He studied what he could see of my eyes in the uncertain moonlight, shattered through the branches of the forest. He backed away, and studied the robes I wore. Then he said, "Who are you?"

I did not speak. If I had spoken he would instantly have detected my accent, my faltering Gorean, and would have marked me as a barbarian girl.

"You are not the Lady Sabina," he said. "Who are you?"

I kept silent.

"Do you flee an unwanted companionship?" he asked. "Was your retinue ambushed? Do you flee outlaws?"

Again I did not respond.

"Do you flee slavers?" he asked. "We are honest men," he said. "We are not slavers." He regarded me. "You are safe with us," he said.

Moonlight filtered through the branches.

"Who are you?" he said.

I again did not respond. This time he seemed angry.

"Do you choose to be face-stripped before men?" he asked.

I shook my head, negatively.

His hands were at the first veil, the street veil.

"Well?" he asked.

I did not answer.

I felt the veil lifted away from my face. "Remove your gloves," he said.

I slipped the gloves from my hands. He took them and threw them to my feet.

My hands felt the night air.

"Speak," he said.

When I did not respond to him, he pulled away the house veil. The men crowded more closely about. The flesh of my face was now concealed from the direct vision of the strong males by only three veils, the pride veil, the veil of the citizeness and the sheer fifth, or last, veil. Already, in stripping me of the house veil, outrage had been done to me. It was as though the privacy and intimacy of my house had been violated. It was as though they had invaded my house and taken my dress from me, forcing me to stand before them in my slip.

"Who are you?" asked the man again. How could I tell him who I was? My master had not even given me a name.

"The pride veil will be next, if you do not speak," said the man.

I wondered what these men would do with me if they discovered I was not even a free woman. I forced the thought from my mind. Free men do not take it lightly that a Kajira would dare to don the garments of a free woman. This is regarded as an extremely serious offense, fit to be followed by terrible punishments. It can be worth the life of one to do so. I began to tremble.

The pride veil was ripped from me. It was as though my slip had been torn away by the invaders in my house.

The lineaments of my face could now be detected beneath the veil of the citizeness. The last veil, in its sheerness, and transparency, is little more than a token.

"Perhaps now, dear Lady," said the captain, "you will choose to speak, choose to reveal your name and city, and your business in this vicinity so late in the night?"

I dared not speak. I turned my head to the side, with a wild sob, as the veil of the citizeness was torn away. I wore now only the last veil. It was as though in my own home an almost final shield of modesty had been taken from me, leaving me only a bit of wide-strung netting, inviting the ripping hand of a master.

The hand of the man reached to the last veil. His hand hesitated. "Perhaps she is free?" asked one of the men.

"Perhaps," said the captain. He lowered his hand.

"She is quite pretty to be free," observed one of the men. Some assent was given to this.

"Let us hope, for your sake, my dear," said the captain, "that you are free."

I lowered my head.

"Consider yourself my prisoner, Lady," said the man. He felt my forearms, detecting that I was right handed. I felt a loop of leather put about my right wrist and drawn tight. It was a double loop, drawn through itself, and tightened. The other end of the closed loop, about a foot from my hand, was taken in the grasp of a soldier. My captor then turned about and began to return to the camp. He was followed by his men. I was led, wrist-thonged, with them.

I had been captured.

In a few minutes we approached the camp. I was carried across the stream, into the camp area. Many were the torches, much was the confusion we encountered there.

The soldier who carried me put me on my feet. I was then again the prisoner of the wrist thong in his grasp.

A man ran toward us, holding up a torch. "The Lady Sabina," he cried, "she is gone! She has been taken!"

With a cry of rage the leader, or captain, ran toward the tents, his men racing behind him, I struggling and gasping, jerked and dragged by the thong which held me.

Straight to the pavilion of the Lady Sabina sped the captain.

I, on the tether, accompanying the soldier who controlled me, hurried, too, to that pavilion. I was pulled within, on the thong. A man within turned, white-faced, to the captain. "They came," he said. "They took her!"

To one side lay two soldiers, wounded. The maids of the Lady Sabina, who had been with her in the tent, stood terrified to one side. One held her shoulder, where there was a large bruise.

"They were here!" said the soldier, pointing to the shuddering slaves.

"What happened?" demanded the captain.

One of the girls, she with the bruise, spoke. The back of the tent was slashed. "In force they came," she said, "many of them. We tried to defend the mistress. We were buffeted aside. They were men, warriors. We were helpless!" She pointed to the back of the tent. "They entered there, and withdrew similarly, the mistress in their power!"

The application of numbers and power is an element of strategy. The men of my master had been outnumbered, surely, by the many soldiers of the camp, but at the point of attack their numbers were superior, overwhelming. Twenty men may breech a wall held by a hundred men, if the twenty men but attack where the wall is defended by only two. In the confusion, as the attention of men had been directed elsewhere, the forces of my master, though not impressive numerically, had been sharply and irresistibly applied. His stroke, in the context, had not been difficult.

I swallowed hard. I realized I had been only a diversion, a pawn. I felt bitter, and terrified.

"Of what city were they?" demanded the captain of one of his wounded men.

"I do not know," said the man.

I had seen the men of my master removing insignia from their garments before the attack.

"We know their direction of flight," said one of the soldiers. "If we act swiftly, we may mount satisfactory pursuit." "Let us act with dispatch," urged another, "that we may swiftly overtake them."

The captain struck at the heavy pole of the tent with the side of his fist. The pole, though it was deeply anchored, shook in the dirt.

"Arm the men," said he. "Issue bows, light rations. All men. Assembly in ten Ehn."

"Yes, Captain," said a man. Men left the tent. The two wounded men were carried away.

The captain then turned to face me. I shrank back. Some four men besides the captain remained in the tent, one of them he who held my wrist thong.

The captain's hand fixed itself in the sheen of the last veil, the fifth veil. Beneath it my features, frightened, could be seen. It was only a token, but, when it was torn away, even the token would be gone. I would stand before men, face-stripped. It is interesting to me, how I thought of this at the time. Doubtless much depends upon context and is relative to the culture. On Earth, few women veil their face, and yet many will veil their bodies. On Earth body veiling tends to be cultural, and not face veiling. On Gor, for free women, both body veiling and face veiling are cultural, and tend to be widely practiced. I suppose, objectively, there is something more to be said for face veiling than body veiling. Bodies, though differing remarkably, one to the other, tend perhaps to be somewhat more similar than faces. Accordingly, if one should be concerned to protect one's privacy and one's feelings, and such, it seems that the face might preferably be veiled. In the face, surely, it is easier to read emotion and individuality than in a body. Should not the face then, if one is concerned with concealment and privacy, be veiled? Is the face not more personal and revealing than the body? Does it not make sense then to consider it a proper object of concealment in a free person? Is one not entitled, so to speak, to privacy in the matter of one's thoughts and feelings, sometimes so manifest in one's facial expressions? However this may be, there are congruencies and dispositions which seem appropriate in given contexts. Veils seem correct, and right, with the robes of concealment. Too, seeing the lust of men to discern your features, and understanding what face veiling and unveiling means to them, tends to influence one's views of these matters. I was terrified that such men see my face. I did not want my face to be seen by them. In many Gorean cities, only a slave girl goes unveiled.

I felt his hand tighten in the veil. Then he jerked it away. I was face-stripped, completely. I closed my eyes, with shame. I reddened. It was as though the last bit of netting, mockery of modesty though it might be, had been ripped away. My face, my feelings, my emotions, now lay bare to them. My face, though I wore robes of concealment, was as naked as that of a slave girl.

"I wonder if you are free, my beauty," said the captain.

My mouth, now that he had torn away the veil, was fully exposed to his. Nothing now separated his mouth, his tongue, his teeth, from mine. From his point of view I then, though I might be free, might as well have been a slave girl.

I looked at him.

"Release her wrist thong," said he to the soldier who held the thong. He dropped the thong, and it dangled, loosely, from my wrist.

"A wrist thong scarcely comports with the dignity of a free woman," said the captain to me.

He walked about me, as a man walks about a woman. I had the feeling he saw me naked beneath the robes.

"Are you free, my beauty?" he asked. He drew his sword. I shuddered. "Are you free?" he asked. He put the sword at my left ankle, and, curiously, lifted the robes of concealment a bit. "I hope for your sake," said he, "that you are free. If you are not, I will not be much pleased."

I felt the blade on my leg, lifting up the robes further. "Step from your slippers," he said.

I did so, trembling.

I felt the steel on my leg, lifting the robes yet higher. They were above my knee now.

The three slave girls in the tent, gowned, watched with apprehension.

The robes were lifted higher, some inches above my knee.

"If you are free," said the captain, "you are rather pretty to be free."

"Captain," said a voice from outside the tent, "the men are ready."

"I shall join you momentarily," he said.

"Yes, Captain," said the man.

The captain then again turned his attention toward me. He was angry. He spoke softly, but menacingly. "You have made a fool of all of us," he said. "Thus, I hope that you are free." The blade moved a bit higher on the leg. I trembled. "Yet," said he, "the leg is not bad. It is a leg which is pretty enough to be the leg of a slave girl. I wonder if it is the leg of a slave girl." He lifted the robes to my hip. I felt the steel against my hip.

The men in the tent cried out with anger. The slave girls gasped and shrank back.

"It is as I thought," said the captain. He stepped back, but he did not sheath his sword.

"I will give you twenty Ihn," said he, "to remove the clothing of a free woman and to fall naked on your belly before me."

Weeping I tore away the robes, frenziedly, and, stripped, threw myself on my belly naked before him, he a Gorean male, he a master, I a slave girl.

"Standard binding position," he said. I was prone. When a girl is prone, the standard binding position is to cross the wrists behind the back and to cross the ankles. I took this position instantaneously.

That I did this did not cause him any pleasure. No one in the room thought anything of it. I was simply a prone slave girl who had been commanded to standard binding position. No one in the room, including myself, would have expected me to do other than comply. Lack of compliance by a slave girl to a command in the Gorean world is unthinkable. She obeys.

The captain spoke swiftly with two of the men in the room. Then he spoke, too, to one of the slave girls, who, addressed, knelt before him. She left the tent.

I could hear the men outside. There was some rattle of weaponry.

The girl who, earlier, had been tied at the wagon wheel and beaten was brought into the tent. She looked at me and went and lay, miserable, in a corner of the tent. The other girl, too, re-entered the tent.

The captain made ready to depart from the tent, to take command of his men.

I lay there, unbound, but in binding position. I had not moved. I did not wish to be slain.

The captain looked down at me, and then, as though in response to an afterthought, said to one of his men, "Tie her."

The captain's helmet was brought to him. I felt my wrists and ankles being tied. My wrists were tied with the loop of thong which had bound my right wrist previously, when I had been brought to the tent.

The captain turned me over with his foot. Then he knelt on one knee beside me. I felt the point of his sword in my belly. "I will see you later," said he, "pretty little Kajira." I felt the point of the sword push in. I winced. "Speak," said he. "Yes, Master," I wept.

"A barbarian," said one of the men.

"Yes," said the captain, getting up.

"But a pretty one," said one of the men.

The captain regarded me, bound at his feet. "Yes," he said. Then he donned the helmet, turned, and left the tent.

The other slave girls in the tent, save she who had been beaten, who lay miserably in a corner of the tent, looked angrily at me. One rubbed the bruise on her shoulder. "Kajira," she hissed. I turned to my side, in the dirt. I wept. I lay, a captured slave girl, in the tent of enemies.

What would be done with me?

Surely they would not blame me! Surely they would understand that I was only a slave girl! Surely they must understand that I had had to obey my master! Would they so much as give me the opportunity to please them—and as what I was, a slave? Would they find me attractive? Might my beauty, and my zeal to serve them, suffice to divert their wrath? Might they not, in the light of the pleasures which I would be eager to supply them, consider sparing me? If I were sufficiently pleasing, as I would strive to be, might I not be permitted to live? Surely I would beg on my belly to be permitted to please them, to be permitted to provide them with inordinate pleasures, to be permitted to please them as only a slave girl can please a man! They must let me live! Please, I thought, let me live!

I moaned with misery.

Obviously I was nothing to my master!

I had been used to create a diversion, had been employed as a mere pawn. I had been exposed to danger, as though I might have been any slave, any slave at all, even a hated slave. Did my master not love me? Did he not care for me? Did he not reciprocate the feelings which I had for him? I wept, a discarded, abandoned, insignificant slave.

I heard the men leaving the camp. Then the camp was empty, save for the wounded, and the slave girls, of which I was one.

"Dina," said the girl with the bruise to me. She had called me that because of my brand, the Dina, or Slave Flower. Girls who wear the brand are sometimes spoken of as Dinas. As she had said "Dina," it had been a term of abuse. The Dina brand is one of the more frequently found of the specialized brands on Gor. Dinas, such as I was, were relatively common girls.

The camp was now quiet.

The bruised girl came over to me. "Dina!" she said, and kicked me. Then she returned to the other girls.

"Our poor mistress," cried the girl who had kicked me. "Pity her!"

I heard the sounds of the night outside the tent, the insects, the cries of fleers.

Surreptitiously, for I did not wish to be struck or again kicked, I tried to move my wrists and ankles. It was useless. Thongs had been used, not rope; the knots, simple and efficient, had been made by a warrior. With a minimum of means I was held with absolute perfection. A Gorean warrior had bound me.

I heard again, from outside, the cries of the hook-billed fleer.

I reared up.

The slave girls cried out, then were silent. Swords lay at their throats.

My master was in the tent, following his men through the rent silken wall.

One of the men carried a looped coffle chain, with wrist rings.

"Master!" I cried out with elation. I struggled to sit up. He crouched beside me and, with his unsheathed blade, slashed apart the leather which bound me. I flung myself to his feet, pressing my lips to his sandals. "Master!" I wept with joy. He had come back! He had not left me. But he pulled away from my hands and lips at his sandals, and issued orders to his men. The four slave maids crouched terrified, under swords, in the center of the tent, including she who had been beaten. Some men left the tent.

"Kneel to be coffled," said one of the men. The girls knelt, closely, one behind the other. There were six wrist rings on the chain he carried. He placed the girl who had been whipped by the Lady Sabina first in the coffle line. "Left wrist coffle," he said. They lifted their left wrists, frightened. Interestingly, the man snapping the wrist rings on the girls' left wrists did not put the first girl in the first ring, but the second. When the four maids were coffled there was, thus, an empty wrist ring both at the head and the rear of the line. "Stand, Slaves," said the man. "Lower chain." The girls stood. Then, ordered, they lowered their wrists. They were then in line, standing, coffled.

Outside I heard bosk being hitched to wagons. Other bosk I heard being freed and driven into the woods.

I wondered if the camp would be fired. I supposed not, for the glow of the burning silk and canvas in the night sky might too soon apprise the camp's soldiers of what had occurred. An obvious trail had been left for the soldiers to begin to follow; then the men of my master had circled about to return to the camp. The trail would become difficult to detect, then perhaps disappear. The men of the camp had not had trained sleen. While the pursuing soldiers followed a false scent, my master's men returned to their camp, from which, later, in a new direction, they might make their departure. My master prepared to leave the tent. I wanted to run beside him, but he would not permit it. He pushed me back. I must remain within. He left the tent.

The man who had coffled the girls now stood back, looking at them. "May I speak?" begged the first in the line, she who had been earlier whipped. "Yes," he said. "I hate my mistress," she said. "I am ready to love you, Master!" "Do you not enjoy being owned by a woman?" he asked. "I want to love a man," she wept. "Shameless slave," cried the last girl in the line, she who had lamented the fate of her mistress, and who had called me "Dina," and kicked me. "I am a woman and a slave!" cried the first. "I want a man! I need a man!"

"Do not fear, Slave," grinned the man who had locked her in her wrist ring, "you will not be neglected when wench service is wished."

"Thank you, Master," she said, and stood very straight, very proudly.

"Brazen slave," scolded the last girl in the line.

"Comb the hair of the spoiled brat of a merchant, if you wish," said the first. "I will dance naked before a man."

"Slave!" cried the last girl in the line, horrified.

"Yes, slave!" said the first, angrily, proudly.

I heard a wagon being driven from the camp. In it, I suspected, lay the dowry riches of the Lady Sabina of Fortress of Saphronicus. The location of the lady herself I did not know, but I had little doubt she was in a safe place, probably blindfolded, gagged and chained to a tree somewhere. I wondered if she had been permitted to retain her clothing.

"Do you have pretty legs?" asked the man of the second girl in the line.

"Yes, Master," she said, smiling.

"You are aware," he queried, "of the penalties for lying to a free man?"

"Examine them, Master," she said, smiling, boldly. "It will not be necessary to beat me."

The last girl in the line cried out with indignation.

The man, with his knife, cut away much of the long, flowing white gown the girl wore, considerably shortening it, until it was provocatively high, ragged and exciting, on her thighs.

"It will not be necessary to beat you," he acknowledged.

"Thank you, Master," she said.

The last girl in the line snorted angrily, tossing her head in the air.

"Do you have pretty legs?" asked the man of the second gowned girl in the coffle.

"I do not know, Master," she whispered. "I am only a girl's maid."

"Let us see," said the man, and, as he had with the first, transformed the flowing classic, sleeveless garment into a sweet scrap of lovely slave livery.

"May I speak?" asked the second gowned girl.

"Yes," he said.

"Are my legs—pretty?" she asked.

"Yes," he said.

"A girl is pleased," she said. She, too, like the others, stood straight.

"How shameless you are, all of you!" scolded she who was the third of the gowned girls in the line, the last in the line.

"And you?" inquired the man.

"I am a woman's slave," she said proudly. "I am above such things." She did not look at him. "I have dignity," she said.

"But a slave girl is not permitted dignity," he said. Then he said, "We will see your legs." He then, with his knife, shortened her gown, as he had those of the others, until its shreds, too, ragged and exciting, were high on her thighs. She stood before him, her legs, though those of a girl's maid, bared to his eyes.

"Excellent legs," he said.

She shuddered, but I did not think that she was entirely displeased with his appraisal. All women wish to be attractive to men. "I—I want to be a woman's slave," she said, I thought a bit uncertainly.

"Do you fear men so?" he asked.

She did not speak.

"What you want," he pointed out to her, "is not important." He regarded her. "Is it?" he asked.

"No, Master," she said.

He touched her about the throat and chin. "Have you never been curious about the touch of a man?" he asked.

"Come to me," said the first girl. "I will love you like you have never been loved before!"

"He is touching me!" cried the last girl.

"Wanton slave!" laughed the first.

The man then went to the first girl and took her in his arms. She cried out with pleasure and pressed herself to him, melting and yielding to his tunic and leather. He subjected her mouth and lips to a kiss which could have been only the prelude to fierce slave rape.

"I can kiss, too," cried the last girl. "Master! Please, Master!"

"No," moaned the first girl. "She is nothing. Stay with me. I am sensuous. You do not know what it is to have had a slave girl until you have had me!"

I heard a second wagon being driven from the camp. I thought it might be one laden with produce, but, as it later turned out, the treasure freight of the dowry wagon had been divided between two wagons, the dowry wagon itself and another, the produce in the second wagon discarded, to lighten the load and make driving swifter.

My master then re-entered the tent. "Rape her later," he said to the soldier who held the first girl in the coffle in his arms. Reluctantly the soldier put the moaning girl from him.

"Yes, Captain," grinned the soldier.

"When we are to be raped, and must serve you as slaves," begged the first girl, she who had been in his arms, "let me be the first to be raped, the first to serve you as a slave."

"You will not be forgotten, my beautiful little slut," he promised her.

"Thank you, Master," she whispered.

"Do not forget Donna either," said the second girl.

"Nor Chanda," said the third.

"Nor Marla," said the fourth.

"Lehna is first," said the first girl.

The soldier regarded the fourth girl. Under his eyes she stood very straight in the coffle. The wrist ring was closed on her left wrist, inflexibly, fastening her with the other girls.

"Nor Marla?" he asked.

"Nor Marla," she said.

"Are you not a woman's slave?" he asked.

"Save me a place at your feet, Master," she said. "I am a man's slave."

My master walked about the coffled girls. Then he returned to his original place of stand. "Four beauties," said he, "a good catch. We shall have much pleasure with them, and then, should we choose to sell them, we will get a good price."

How right it struck me that he had said this of the beauties, and yet, in its way, how horrifying to me, an Earth girl. Why did these men not hide their dominance; why did they not pretend it did not exist; why did they not suppress it; why did they not thwart and repudiate the birthright of their nature; why did they not make themselves miserable; why did they not torture themselves and diligently cultivate weakness like the men of Earth, shortening their lives and praising themselves for the constriction and mutilation of their instincts? Were they not powerful enough to be manipulated, strong enough to be weak?

"Coffle her," said my master, looking at me.

I stiffened. Surely the coffle was not for me. I was his girl. I was not a new slave. I had served him well.

The soldier whistled, as though he might have been summoning a pet sleen, and lifted an open wrist ring, the last ring on the chain. I ran angrily to the chain.

"We must make haste," said my master.

I felt my wrist taken, and the metal of the wrist ring snap shut upon it. I was coffled.

How angry I was to be chained with the new girls. I felt the chain hanging from my wrist, dangling from the wrist ring of the girl coffled before me. I was furious. I was well fastened. I could not escape.

My master looked down at me.

I lowered my eyes. I wore his chain.

He turned away from the coffle and, moving the slashed silk of the rear wall of the tent with his hand, brushing it to the right, not looking back, disappeared into the darkness.

"Marla was not kind to a poor slave when she was helpless," said Marla, the girl before me. "Marla is terribly sorry. Please forgive Marla."

"What?" I said.

"Marla is sorry, Mistress," she said. "Please forgive Marla." The girl was clearly frightened.

It seemed strange to me, that she had addressed me as Mistress, and her fear. Then I realized the legitimacy of her fear, that of a slave girl. She was the one who had called me "Dina," and who, when I had been bound, had kicked me. Now she was owned by my master, and she was a newer girl than I. She did not yet know the nature of the relationships in which she was now helplessly implicated, relationships which could be every bit as perilous and significant as the physical bond of steel on her wrist. Was I first girl? Was I over her? Did I have switch rights upon her body, as Eta had upon mine? Would I be cruel to her? Would I make her suffer? Would she have to please the masters incredibly, and constantly attend them, that they might perhaps be moved to shield her to some tiny extent from my vengeance? Too, she was coffled before me, and this put her much at my mercy. Chained as she was I might, if I chose, make the march a misery of unexpected blows and torments for her. Her fears, in the light of these considerations, were understandable.

"I forgive you," I told her.

Immediately the girl straightened herself insolently, and dismissed me from her awareness. She had, she assumed then, nothing to fear from me, and I might be contemptuously ignored. This irritated me. Doubtless she considered herself, and quite possibly correctly, my superior in beauty, and thus planned to soon stand higher in the relationships of bondage than I, a lesser girl. Having nothing to fear from me she would freely and opportunistically insinuate herself among the men. Slave girls compete for the attentions of masters. Each strives to be more pleasing to them than the other. The quality of a slave girl's life is commonly a direct function of her pleasingness to her master. Whether she is a treasured love slave or an ignored pot-and-floor wench depends much upon her. Gorean men, unlike the men of Earth, do not bother much with girls that are not pleasing to them. Yet even such may find their utility, and indirectly serve masters, perhaps sweating in the public kitchens of the high cylinders, or laboring, neck-locked, at the looms in the cloth mills, or digging, chained with others, in the sul fields. It is a rare girl who, having tasted the mills or sul fields, does not beg her proprietor to be sold again on the open market, that she may attempt anew, and perhaps more successfully this time, to be pleasing to a man.

I was furious with the posture, so proud and sensual, of the girl before me. I wondered why I had forgiven her. It had seemed the natural thing to do. I had done it, unthinkingly. It was not irrational, of course. For example, she was beautiful, and any dominance which I might have over her might be temporary, and then our relationship might be reversed. What if she much pleased my master one night and he gave her switch rights over me? Also, on another march, it might be I who would be coffled before her, and at her mercy.

Yet I was angry. She now ignored me. Her victory had been cheaply won.

Suddenly, angrily, I kicked her.

She cried out, startled. I stood straight, as though I had done nothing. The soldier with the coffle, who was gathering jewelry into a scarf from various coffers in the tent, pretended that he had not noticed my action. Masters do not much interfere in the squabbles of slaves. Let them impose their own internal order among themselves. On the other hand, they would not approve if one slave injured or marked, or reduced in value, another. That would be serious, and not to be tolerated.

The girl before me now no longer stood proudly and sensually. She was now only a frightened, chained girl, at my mercy. She was coffled before me.

"On the other hand," I said to her, "I may not forgive you either."

"Marla begs forgiveness, Mistress," she whispered.

"I may forgive you and I may not," I said.

"Yes, Mistress," said the girl. She trembled. The chain shook on her wrist. I was pleased. Too, if she feared me, perhaps I could, for a time, frighten her away from my master. She was a lovely female, Marla, and I had little doubt she would be incredibly delicious in the arms of a man. I suppose that I was jealous of her.

The soldier in charge of the coffle slung the scarf, loaded with jewelry from the coffers in the tent, over his shoulder. He grinned at me. I looked down, and smiled.

"We must make haste, Slaves," said he. We readied ourselves. I looked at him. He was not regarding me.

He was Gorean, and a man. It was not that he had dared to be a man. It was rather that he simply was a man.

"Attend me, Coffle," said he, "for bondage march." He held his hand, the visible signal of preparation, poised over his thigh.

We tensed.

But, strangely, though of Earth, I did not object to a world in which men, like larls, were healthy. I wanted them that way, rich and glorious in their power. I sensed, perhaps, my complementarity to them. Only in a world where there were true men could there be true women.

I felt the steel on my wrist, with its chain.

He struck his right thigh with his open hand, suddenly, sharply. We moved out, slave girls, on the left foot, that the pace of the march be uniform.

We were owned.

As I passed the soldier, who stood behind, to follow the coffle, to guard it, I felt weak. I tried to brush my left shoulder against him, but he, with his hand, roughly thrust me to the side. He did not then desire my touch. I and the others must wait, to see if he would permit us to touch him later.

Tears sprang to my eyes. I had wanted to touch him, and had not been permitted to do so. It was his will, the will of the man, which determined matters.

"Har-ta," said he. "Faster." Lehna, who was first girl on the chain, hastened.

Suddenly I was terrified. My will literally meant nothing. Anything might be done to me. The guard had not permitted me to do so much as brush against him. If I could not even placate a man sexually, I was completely without power. Even my attempt to please a man was dependent upon his permission that I should attempt to do so.

I shuddered.

I, hurrying, looked up into the black, starlit Gorean night. I trembled. I, though a girl of Earth, was chained in coffle under three barbaric moons.

"Har-ta," said the soldier.

Again Lehna hastened.

In moments we were leaving the camp, wading the stream. I felt the cold water about my ankles, and then calves; then I felt it over my knees; then I felt it swirling at my thighs; we lifted the chain to hold it out of the water.

"Har-ta," said the soldier, he in whose charge we were.

Again we hurried. One does not dally under the command of a Gorean master.

I felt the pebbles and stones of the bank beneath my feet. The chain pulled forward on my wrist. I looked up at the wild moons.

I was a slave girl.

"Har-ta!" I heard. "Har-ta!"

The chain pulled forward again.

I, hurrying, stumbled behind the others.

I did not know into what bondage I was being led. I knew only that it would be absolute.

Six

Tabuk's Ford

My master extended his cup to me, and I, kneeling, filled it with Sul paga. I pressed my lips to the cup, and handed it to him. My eyes smarted. I almost felt drunk from the fumes.

I withdrew.

Sul paga is, when distilled, though the Sul itself is yellow, as clear as water. The Sul is a tuberous root of the Sul plant; it is a Gorean staple. The still, with its tanks and pipes, lay within the village, that of Tabuk's Ford, in which Thurnus, our host, was caste leader.

"Excellent," said my master, sipping the Sul paga. He could have been commenting only on the potency of the drink, for Sul paga is almost tasteless. One does not guzzle Sul paga. Last night one of the men had held my head back and forced me to swallow a mouthful. In moments things had gone black, and I had fallen unconscious. I had awakened only this morning, ill, miserable, with a splitting headache, chained with the other girls.

"Wine, Slave Girl," said Marla, holding her cup to me.

Angrily I put down the Sul paga and fetched the flask of the Ka-lana of Ar, and filled her cup. She did not look at me, nor thank me, for I was a slave. Was she not, too, a slave? I saw her, in the shreds of her white gown, cuddling with her wine in my master's arms. She had risen swiftly in favor among the masters, displacing even Eta as favorite girl. I had feared, even from the beginning, that she would become excessively popular. My master was, apparently, much taken with her. I hated her. Eta, too, did not regard her with unusual affection.

Marla looked at me, and smiled. "You are a pretty slave," she said.

"Thank you, Mistress," I said, restraining myself. Since she had become first girl in the camp we were all constrained to serve her and

147

address her as Mistress. Even though she was given no jewelry or fine raiment, she was high slave in the camp.

It had been five weeks since the strike on the camp of the Lady Sabina.

Much of this time we had been engaged in a long overland journey.

"Give me of drink," said Thurnus to me.

"Yes, Master," I said. I took the flask of Ka-la-na to him.

Thurnus was a shaggy haired fellow, with yellow hair, big, broad-shouldered, large-handed, clearly in his bones and body of the peasants. He was caste leader in Tabuk's Ford. Tabuk's Ford was a large village, containing some forty families; it was ringed with a palisade, and stood like a hub in the midst of its fields, long, narrow, widening strips, which radiated from it like the spokes in a wheel. Thurnus tilled four of these strips. Tabuk's Ford receives its name from the fact that field tabuk were once accustomed, in their annual migrations, to ford the Verl tributary of the Vosk in its vicinity. The Verl flows northwestward into the Vosk. We had crossed the Vosk, on barges, two weeks ago. The field tabuk now make their crossing some twenty pasangs northwest of Tabuk's Ford, but the village, founded in the area of the original crossing keeps the first name of the locale. Tabuk's Ford is a rich village, but it is best known not for its agricultural bounty, a function of its dark, fertile fields in the southern basin of the Verl, but for its sleen breeding. Thurnus, of the Peasants, of Tabuk's Ford, was one of the best known of the sleen breeders of Gor.

Thurnus looked at me, and grinned. "I said, 'Give me of drink,' small beauty," he said. He emphasized the word 'drink.'

"Forgive me, Master," I said, and, swiftly, turned to put back the Ka-la-na, and fetch the potent Sul paga. As I turned, hurrying, suddenly, frightening me, I realized the Ta-Teera had scarcely concealed me. This frightened me for I had become much aware, in the last few weeks, of the capacity of my beauty to excite men. Eta had told me that I was becoming more beautiful. I did not see how this could be. Yet, apparently, for no reason I clearly understood, I was becoming more provocative and stimulating to men. I suspect this had to do with the gradual loss of layers of constriction and inhibition in my movements and attitudes, and expressions, the sloughing off of modes of impersonality and rigidity in which I had been conditioned since girlhood on Earth. I now related to men in a much more spontaneous and intensely personal way than once I would have dreamed possible. I now saw them as unique, exciting masters, each different and incredibly individual, who might, for a word or gesture, have me; how could I not regard them differently from a free woman; and, too, doubtless, they saw me in a similarly immediate and intensely personal fashion, not as an object shielded, by prejudice and law, and fear and pride, from them, even to touch whom could be a crime, but rather as a slave girl, vulnerable, exposed, at their mercy, unique in her exact helplessness and individuality, the same in some respects as all other bond girls and yet interestingly and profoundly different, too, from all the others. I shared the condition of slavery with other bond wenches, but each of us, of course, as masters know, in the depths and complexity of us, is a surprisingly and uniquely different individual, a latent prize for the chain, an astonishment fascinating to learn and subdue. I suspect the changes in me, at least in part, had to do with two things, the gradual stripping from me of negativistic Earth conditionings and, on the positive side, the Gorean acculturations to which I, a bond girl, was being exposed. I was learning my slavery. Oddly enough, in learning my slavery, I was experiencing an incredible sense of psychological freedom and liberation. I was liberated from political and economic roles of male impersonation and freed to be myself, a woman. The major difference in me, perhaps, however, was not behavioral, social or cultural, but biological. The cultural arrangements, as such arrangements should or may, liberated rather suppressed, constricted or thwarted my inner nature. My inner nature, thus, was permitted to open its petals to the rain and sunlight of a clean, honest, glorious world. I was becoming true to myself. I think that is it. In becoming true to myself, too, I was becoming happy. And, as Eta once told me, it is hard for a woman to be happy and not to be beautiful.

I approached Thurnus with the Sul paga and knelt before him.

But there is danger, too, in the slave girl's beauty, as any delight who wears the brand knows. As I had, naturally, inadvertently, almost in spite of myself, become more desirable and beautiful, the sexual aggressions of men against me, which I, as slave, might not resist, had become more frequent and powerful. Sometimes I was merely taken by the hair and thrown to the grass and raped, or seized by an ankle and thrown over a log, that I might be used for their pleasure, or kicked to my knees before them, that I might intimately please them. I was much at their mercy. They found me desirable. It is dangerous for a girl to be beautiful on Gor, particularly if she is a slave. The more beautiful and vulnerable she is the more likely it is that her beauty will be seized and dominated, and ruthlessly exploited, by masters. Consequently, though I loved my apparently increasing beauty, and desirability, and was incredibly thrilled with it, and my new attractiveness, I was not unaware that it was attended with risks. It was one thing to be raped by my master's men, and quite another to know that the same passions which I aroused in them I would similarly inspire in the breasts of complete strangers. I was not eager to be slave-raped by strangers, which, Eta assured me, was a not uncommon experience for a pretty slave. On the other hand, I feared slave rape less than abduction. I did not want to be carried away. It was one thing for a man to hastily use me and discard me; it was another to bind me and carry me away, to be his own slave. I did not wish to leave my master, whom I loved.

Thurnus held out his cup. I prepared to put Sul paga in the cup. Then he held the cup closer to him. I must needs approach more closely.

Exciting men is a price a girl pays for her beauty. I was more than willing to pay that price. I was joyful to pay that price. Yet I knew that beauty on a world such as Gor was not without its risks. I suddenly wished I wore a name collar, like Eta, that would make it clear to whom I belonged. My master had not even bothered to put a collar on me. I was a collarless slave.

"Come closer, little beauty," said Thurnus.

I crept a bit closer to him, on my knees, with the paga. I wore the scandalously brief, torn, hooked, sleeveless Ta-Teera, which so displayed a girl's charms.

I feared Thurnus. I had seen his eyes on me often.

I poured Sul paga into his goblet, my head bending quite near to him. My hair was longer now than when I had come to Gor. It was still shorter than that of most slave girls. Most slave girls wear their hair long and loose, though sometimes it is held back with a headband or tied behind the head with a string or ribbon, in a ponytail. My hair fell before my shoulders, over the Ta-Teera.

My master, with his lieutenants, sat cross-legged in the large, thatched hut of Thurnus. It was high, and conical, and floored with rough planks, set some six or seven feet on poles above the ground, that it might be drier and protected from common insects and vermin. The entrance was reached by a flight of rough, narrow steps. The entrances to many of the huts in the village, similarly constructed, were reached by ladders. Thurnus was caste leader. In the center of the hut was a large flat, circular piece of metal, on which, on legs, might sit braziers or the small, flattish cooking stoves, using pressed, hardened wood, common in the villages north and west of Ar. About the walls were the belongings of the house, in coffers and bales. Elsewhere about the village were storage huts and animal pens. Mats covered the rough planks. From the walls hung vessels and leathers. A smoke hole in the top of the hut permitted the escape of fumes. The hut, probably because of its construction, was not smoky. Also, though it was windowless and had but one door, it was not, at this time of day, dark. Through the straw of its roof and sides there was a considerable, delicate filtering of sunlight. The hut in the summer is light and airy. The frame of such a hut is constructed of Ka-la-na and Tem wood. The roof is rethatched and the walls rewoven every third or fourth year. In the winters, which are not harsh at this latitude, such huts are covered on the outside with painted canvas or, among the richer peasants, with ornamented, painted bosk hides, protected and glossed with oil. The village of Tabuk's Ford lay some four hundred pasangs from Ar, generally to the north and west. It is some twenty pasangs or so from the "Vosk road." The Vosk road was apparently one of the roads used many years ago by the horde of Pa-Kur, of the Assassins, in its approach to the city of Ar. We had traveled the Vosk road after crossing the Vosk on barges. It is wide, and built like a great wall, sunk in the earth. It is marked with pasang stones. It is, I suppose, given its nature, a military road leading to the north, broad enough to accommodate war tharlarion, treading abreast, and the passage, two or three, side by side, of thousands of supply wagons and siege engines, without unduly, for more than several pasangs, extending and exposing the lines of the march. Such roads permit the swift movement of thousands of men, useful either in the defense of borders, the meeting of armies, or in the expansions of imperialism, the conquests of the weak.

Thurnus looked at me.

"You may kiss my cup, Slave," said he. I pressed my lips to his cup, which he held in his hand. I was weak. I was a girl. I was at the mercy of men.

On the wall of the hut, behind Thurnus, hung the great bow, of supple Ka-la-na. It was tipped with notched bosk horn. It was now unstrung, but the string, of hemp, whipped with silk, lay ready, looped loose upon the broad, curved yellow wood. Near the bow hung a mighty quiver, in which nestled flight and sheaf arrows, and many of each thereof. Such a weapon I could not even bend. It required, too, not simply the strength of a man, but of a man who was unusually strong. Most men, no more than a woman, could use such a fearsome device. It was a common weapon among peasants. It is often called the peasant bow. The other common peasant weapon is the great staff, some six feet in length, some two inches in width. Two such staffs rested to one side, inclining upright against the wall, between a yellow box, about a foot high, and a roll of coarsely woven rep-cloth.

"And do not remove your lips from the cup," said Thurnus, "until given permission."

I kept my lips pressed to the cup, my head bent to the side. A Gorean slave girl dares not disobey.

"Thurnus," said his free companion, a large, heavy woman, in a rep-cloth veil, kneeling to one side. She was squat and heavy. She was not much pleased.

There was a kennel nearby, where Thurnus kept his girls. He did not tend his fields alone.

"Be quiet," said Thurnus, to her, "Woman."

To one side, against the wall of the hut, there rested, on a small table, a piece of plain, irregularly shaped rock, which Thurnus, years earlier, when first he had founded the farm, later to be the community, of Tabuk's Ford, had taken from his own fields. He had, one morning, years ago, bow upon his back and staff in hand, seed at his thigh, after months of wandering, come to a place which had pleased him. It lay in the basin of the Verl. He had been driven from his father's village, for his attendance upon a young free woman of the village. Her brother's arms and legs had he broken. The woman had followed him. She had become his companion. With him, too, had come two young men, and two other women, who saw in him, the young, rawboned giant, the makings of a caste leader. Months had they wandered. Then, following tabuk, in the basin of the Verl, he had come to a place which had pleased him. There the animals had forded the river. He had not followed them further. He had driven the yellow stake of claimancy into the dark soil, near the Verl, and had stood there, his weapons at hand, beside the stake, until the sun had reached the zenith and then, slowly, set. It was then he had reached to his feet and picked up the stone, from his own fields. It now rested in his hut. It was the Home Stone of Thurnus.

"Thurnus," said his companion.

He paid her no attention. It had been many years ago that she had followed him from the village of her father. It had all been many years ago. In the fashion of the peasants he kept her. She had grown slack and fat. She could no longer in honor return to the village of her brother.

I kept my lips pressed to Thurnus's cup. He drew the cup more closely to him. I must needs follow.

I knew he had girls he kept in a kennel.

Thurnus was a strong man, of the sort who must either have many women, or incredibly much from one woman. His companion, I supposed, was no longer attractive to him, or, perhaps, in the prides of her freedom, was too remote to be much in his attention. It is easiest for a man to see a woman who is at his feet, begging to be seen.

"You are a pretty little slave," said Thurnus to me.

I could not speak, for my lips were pressed to his cup.

"What is her name?" asked Thurnus of my master.

"She does not have a name," he responded.

"Oh," said Thurnus. Then he said, "She is a pretty little thing." I felt his hand on my leg.

Angrily, Melina, who was the free companion of Thurnus of Tabuk's Ford, rose to her feet and left the hut.

I shuddered under the intimate touch of Thurnus. I could not withdraw from his caress for my lips must needs remain pressed to his cup.

"Perhaps we should give her a name," suggested Marla.

"Perhaps," said one of the lieutenants, looking at me.

"What do you think of 'Stupid Girl'?" asked Marla.

The men laughed.

"Or 'Clumsy Girl'!" she urged.

"Better," said one of the lieutenants.

How angry I was at Marla, and how jealous of her. She was a saucy slave. Had I so spoken, so freshly and without permission, I might have been whipped.

She was high slave.

"You are right," said my Master. "She is both stupid and clumsy, but she is growing in intelligence, and in beauty and grace."

I flushed with pleasure to hear him say this.

"Let us give her a name more suitable to a slave girl, who, one day, will perhaps be capable of pleasing men."

My lips remained pressed to Thurnus's cup. I could not withdraw from his caress. I began to become aroused. I was a slave. I could not help myself.

Thurnus laughed. He then, with his peasant's humor, suggested two names, both descriptive, both embarrassing.

My thighs moved. How furious I was! I was a slave. I could not help myself.

I was furious, too, at the laughter which greeted Thurnus's proposals. Yet I knew that if I were given either of those intimate, obscene names, I would have to wear it. They would simply be my name.

"Let us think further," chuckled my master. He was Clitus Vitellius, of the caste of warriors, of the city of Ar.

I began to move helplessly under the touch of Thurnus. I could not help myself. I was slave.

My master watched me. "There is something to be said, of course," said he, "for the suggestions of Thurnus."

I moaned with misery.

"But I think," said he, smiling, "we may look further."

I tried to restrain myself, to keep from responding to the touch of Thurnus. I could not do so. I thought of Elicia Nevins, who had been my lovely beauty rival in the college on Earth. How amused the haughty Elicia would have been to see me now, a half naked slave girl, clad in the scandalous Ta-Teera, her lips pressed to a cup, responding so helplessly to a man's touch. How humiliated and embarrassed I was to even think of the proud, serene, contemptuous Elicia in my present predicament. How pleased I was that she could not see her old rival now.

Thurnus moved the cup a bit closer to him, maneuvering me into a yet more helpless position. My hands were clenched on the wrist that held the cup. I felt the cup with my teeth.

"Marla is a pretty name," said my Master. He looked at Marla, in his arms. "Do you not think Marla is a good name for a slave?"

"Oh, yes, Master," she whispered. "Marla is a superb name for a slave." She began to kiss him about the throat and chin.

"Perhaps I should call her 'Marla,'" said he.

I knew that, in an instant, my name might be Marla. I shuddered.

"But we already have one Marla among our girls," smiled my Master, looking down into the beautiful, uplifted dark eyes of the lovely Marla.

"Yes, Master," she whispered.

I did not know what name I would wear.

"If the nameless slave interests you in the least," said my master to Thurnus, indicating me with his head, "you may, of course, do what you wish with her."

I shuddered, a slave girl on Gor.

"But," said Thurnus, laughing, "you have come to examine sleen."

My master shrugged. "That is true," he admitted.

"Let us then waste no more time sporting with slave girls," said Thurnus, "but turn our attention to more serious business." Thurnus looked at me. "You may remove your lips from the cup, Girl," he said.

I withdrew my lips from the cup. He removed his hand from my body, and stood up.

I knelt on the floor. My eyes were wide. My teeth were gritted. I wanted to scratch at the mats on the floor with my fingernails.

My master rose to his feet, and his lieutenants with him. Marla angrily, pouting, put her legs beneath her, and knelt. We were only girls. The men had business. There were more important things for them to attend to than us.

I wanted to roll on the floor and scream.

I looked at the Home Stone in the hut. In this hut, for it was here that his Home Stone resided, Thurnus was sovereign. In this hut, even had he been a lowly man or beggar, he, because of the presence in it of his Home Stone, was Ubar. A palace without a Home Stone is but a hovel; a hovel which contains a Home Stone is a palace.

In this house, this hut, this palace, Thurnus's was the supremacy. Here he might do as he pleased. His rights in this house, his supremacy in this place, was acknowledged by all guests. They shared the hospitality of his Home Stone.

Had Thurnus requested me my master, in such a situation, would have granted me to him immediately. Not to have done so would have been inexcusably rude, a betrayal, a boorish breech of hospitality and good manners.

Yet Thurnus, though I had little doubt he found me of more than casual interest, had not asked for me. I wondered if he had, in his openness with me, been testing my master, to learn him better. Thurnus impressed me as a shrewd man. My master had well respected the house of Thurnus, and his sovereignty within it. Satisfied then with the acknowledgment of this power, which was rightfully his in this house, Thurnus neither put me to his purposes, nor requested of my master his permission to do so, a permission which would have assuredly been promptly and willingly tendered. Having thus certified my master's recognition of his rights, he chose, magnanimously and nobly, as is often done, not to exercise them. I was, after all, my master's property. In this simple manner these two strong men had shown one another, in the Gorean mode, respect.

But Gorean males, I knew, in such situations, not only respected one another, but were often generous with one another.

In the feast to come tonight, Eta had warned me, there would be a general exchange of slave girls, the bond girls of the village being made available to my master's men, and his own girls, among whom I was one, being made available to the young lads of the community. We would be run between the huts within the palisade.

The men prepared to leave the hut.

My master snapped his fingers and Marla sprang to her feet and went out the door of the hut. His lieutenants followed her.

I was on my hands and knees. There were tears in my eyes. I lifted my hand to my master.

"I am afraid I have aroused your slave," said Thurnus, looking back at me.

"Please, Master," I whispered.

"It doesn't matter," he said. Then he turned and went down the stairs. "Let us look at sleen," he said.

Thurnus looked at me. "You are a pretty little slave," he said. Then he, too, turned, and, descending the steps, left the vicinity of the hut.

In the hut, alone, I struck the mats with my fists. In a short time, one of the men of my master entered the hut. He tied my hands behind my back.

"Simmer and cook until the feast, Little Pudding," he said. "You will then be well ready."

Seven

Clitus Vitellius

"Do not run me, Master," wept Slave Beads. "I was once a free woman!"

"To the line," said my master.

Slave Beads stumbled to the long line scratched in the dirt in the village of Tabuk's Ford. She wore the shreds of what had once been the last undergarment beneath her robes of concealment. Its sleeves had been torn away; it had been rent at the side; it had been cut short, and later torn even shorter, until it hung high upon her thighs, exposing even the left hip; at the throat it had been ripped open down to the belly, two inches below the navel. She was barefoot, as is common among slave girls.

"Where will we run?" wailed Slave Beads to me.

"There is nowhere to run," I told her. The village was surrounded by a palisade, the gate of which was barred.

"I do not want to be run as a slave girl," wept Slave Beads. She covered her eyes with her hands.

"Stop blubbering," said Lehna.

"Yes, Mistress," said Slave Beads. She was frightened of Lehna. One of the first things that had been done with her after her branding was to be put in a Sirik and given over to Lehna for a disciplinary switching.

My master, with his men, in a bold coup, had several weeks ago stolen the Lady Sabina of Fortress of Saphronicus from among her retainers, on her journey to be joined in companionship to Thandar of Ti, of Ti, of the Four Cities of Saleria, those comprising the Salerian Confederation. The motivation for this abduction, as well as the motivation for the companionship originally, was apparently political. The companionship was to weld commercial and political relationships between Fortress of Saphronicus and the Salerian Confederation, which was an aggressive and expanding league of cities northeast of the Vosk. The growing power of the Salerian Confederation was not viewed with favor by the city of Ar, which, lying in Gor's northern hemisphere, is the major power between the Vosk and the Cartius, and between the Voltai Range and Thassa, the sea. The Ubar of Ar, whose name is Marlenus, is said to be an ambitious and brilliant man, proud and courageous, and imperialistic. He might view the Salerian Confederation as eventually being capable, if it continued to expand, of posing a threat to Ar, either to its security or to its ambitions. As geopolitical matters now stood a plurality of disunited cities, most of them rather small, lay scattered in the territories north of the Vosk. This created, for a strong state, such as Ar, defensively, a reasonably stable, secure border, and, with respect to her possible ambitions, an attractive, exploitable power vacuum. The growth of the Salerian Confederation, on the other hand, might conceivably alter this situation to the detriment of Ar. If the cities of Saleria should multiply and grow strong, their power might balance or exceed that of great Ar itself. Armies and tarn cavalries might then move south. Already, only some years ago, Ar had tasted the bitterness of enemies within her walls, when, in the political confusion following the temporary loss of her Home Stone and the deposition of her Ubar, Marlenus, there had been a revolt of tributary cities, organized and led by Pa-Kur, Master of the Caste of Assassins. The horde of Pa-Kur, as it is spoken of, had set siege to glorious Ar. Initiates, inept and cowardly, then holding power in Ar, had surrendered the city, an act which to this day in Ar has tended to damage the prestige of that caste. On the day of Ar's surrender itself was she saved, by the uprising of her very citizens, violent in the streets, abetted by the forces of certain cities of the north, notably Ko-ro-ba and Thentis. This is told of in the songs. One of the heroes in the songs is called Tarl of Bristol. Marlenus, too, is a hero in such songs. He later retook the throne of Ar, following upon the forcible, civil overthrew of Cernus of Ar, declared a false Ubar. He sits now upon the throne of Ar. He is sometimes spoken of as the Ubar of Ubars.

Donna, and Chanda, and Marla, too, came to the line in the dirt. Slave Beads stifled a sob.

Marlenus, who has seen his city threatened by a league of cities in the time of Pa-Kur, doubtless views with disfavor the rise of the

Salerian Confederation. To be sure, at this time, it is relatively weak. A Ubar, however, must think ahead. On the other hand, it is commonly suspected that the major threat of the Salerian Confederation is not to Ar's security, but to her ambitions, in the person of Marlenus. The great margin of desolation which once flanked Ar on the north, just south of the Vosk, has not been maintained. It was a long wall of wilderness, an empty, unpopulated, desertlike area without water and beneficent vegetation a thousand pasangs deep. Wells were poisoned and fields burned and salted to prevent the approach of armies from the north. Now, however, in the last years, it has become green. New wells have been dug, peasants have moved into it. This, said to be a plan to bring more arable land under cultivation, is generally viewed as being an opening of this territory to large-scale military passage. It is even being stocked with game and wild bosk. It retains now of its old character only its name, the Margin of Desolation. We had had no difficulty in traversing it, on the great road leading south to Ar. As the Margin of Desolation, no longer an artificially maintained cruel wilderness, has flowered, it has been said the eyes of Ar have been turning north. Indeed, some claim the Salerian Confederation has grown as well as it has because the cities of the north fear the possible imperialism of Ar. Whatever be the truth of these intricate geopolitical matters, it seems clear that Marlenus, for whatever reason, does not see fit to encourage the growth of the Salerian Confederation.

Eta joined us at the line. I looked at Slave Beads. Her cheeks were tear-stained. Like the rest of us she was barefoot. There was dirt about her ankles.

Clitus Vitellius, my master, was a captain of Ar. It had been his charge, I supposed, doubtless placed upon him by Marlenus of Ar, Ubar of that city, to prevent or disrupt the imminent alliance forming between Fortress of Saphronicus and the Confederation of Saleria, an alliance to be confirmed and sealed in the companionship of Thandar of Ti, youngest of the five sons of Ebullius Gaius Cassius, of the Warriors, Administrator of Ti, of the Salerian Confederation, and the Lady Sabina, the daughter of Kleomenes, high merchant of Fortress of Saphronicus.

In a bold coup had my master carried off the merchant's daughter. In a diversion, in which I had figured, he had struck the camp, seized the girl and, apparently, took flight, leaving the beginnings of a trail. In short order the warriors of the retinue had set forth upon this trail, whilst it was still hot and fresh. They safely removed by their own action from the environs of their camp, my master had then returned to the camp, to seize as well the dowry and beauteous maids of the Lady Sabina, Lehna, Donna, Chanda and Marla. We had been coffled by the left wrist and hurried into the night, on the track of the two wagons in which the Lady Sabina's dowry, divided, had been placed. Less than a pasang from the camp we had come to a small tree. The Lady Sabina, in her robes of concealment, stood with her belly to this tree, her wrists fastened about it, locked in the steel of slave bracelets. Her veils lay about her shoulders. Her head was concealed in a slave hood, buckled under her chin. The construction of this hood was such that it served not only as blindfold but gag as well, the wadding being sewn to the inside of the hood, and it being held in place by laces, emerging through eyelets, tying behind the back of the neck. Such hoods are often used in the abduction of women, either slave or free. Their efficiency and convenience mandates their use, regardless of the legal or social status of the girl on whom they are placed. I had noted that her gloves had been pulled down over her fingers, that the steel of the slave bracelets close on the wrist itself. Experienced captors, for greater security, seldom place bonds over clothing. Hose would be removed, or pulled down, for example, before a girl's ankles would be tied. A guard was with the Lady Sabina, to protect her in the event of the arrival of prowling sleen. Her retinue was, even now, hurrying down a false trail in the opposite direction. An open wrist ring stood at the head of our coffle chain, the place in the line before Lehna.

My master had unbuckled and unlaced, and pulled away, the stifling, degrading hood. Beneath it, of course, the Lady Sabina had been face-stripped. She turned her face away, that we be unable to look upon it. My master, to my pleasure, simply took her by the hair and turned her face brazenly to all of us, exposing and baring it to all of us for our full gaze. She twisted but, hurt, could not turn her face away. He held it before us, letting us savor it, for a full Ehn. Then, after an Ehn, he released her hair. She sobbed. She regarded us, angrily. But no longer did she try to hide her face. It was pointless now to do so. My master had not seen fit to tolerate her game of modesty. She had been face-stripped, publicly.

My master stepped to where she might more clearly see him, in the moonlight.

"Who are you!" she said.

He did not respond to her.

"I am the Lady Sabina of Fortress of Saphronicus," she said. "Beware!"

The veils, by a man behind her, were lifted from about her shoulders, and dropped to the ground.

"Return my veils," she said.

The veils lay fallen, gently, upon the ground.

"I am the Lady Sabina of Fortress of Saphronicus," she said.

My master did not speak to her.

"Who are you!" she demanded. "You wear no insignia on your tunics. Who are you?" She pulled at the slave bracelets. The chain scraped at the bark. "Beware my wrath!" she said.

My master gave a sign and a man, from behind, lifting her feet, one by one, slipped her sandals from her. She then stood barefoot, her small feet in the crushed leaves and twigs at the foot of the tree. She shuddered. She was a rich, spoiled girl. I supposed she had never been barefoot out of doors before.

"Who are you?" she whispered. No longer was she arrogant. She was now afraid. Commonly slaves go barefoot.

"Your captor," said my master, speaking to her for the first time.

"I will bring a high ransom," she said.

He put his thumb under her chin, and pushed up her head. She was, the veils gone, a delicately featured, beautiful girl. Her head was up, painfully high, his thumb under her chin. She had a lovely throat. He was perhaps considering in what sort of collar it might look best. Her hair was dark. I could not tell its color in the light. The Lady Sabina, I supposed, was more beautiful than I, but I did not think she was more beautiful than her maids. As a slave, she would be less than they, on most blocks.

"Keep me for ransom, Warrior," she said, frightened. I think she knew her face and throat were being assessed, as might have been those of a slave.

He removed his thumb from under her chin.

"It would be irrational not to keep me for ransom," she said. "My ransom will be far higher than any price you could realize on me in a market."

This was surely true, though it was true, too, she was quite beautiful. "Surely," said she, "you did not attack my retinue merely to carry off a girl to wear your collar."

"No," said my master. "There is, of course, the matter of the treasure dowry."

"Of course," she said. She now breathed more easily. "You are common bandits," she said. Then she said, "You have done well, stout fellows. Your loot is valuable. The dowry is immense and rich. And I, too, in ransom, will bring you much, more even than the dowry you have so boldly taken. But return to me now my veils, and my sandals, too, for my ransom surely will be less if it be understood my modesty has been so grievously compromised. Your boldness, for the honor of my name and the security of your skins, may remain our secret."

"The Lady Sabina is generous," said my master.

"I ask only," said the Lady Sabina, "that you not let me fall into the hands of those of Ar."

"Ah, Lady," said my master, "there, you see, lies your true value."

"What do you mean?" she inquired, apprehensively.

"We have a long trek ahead of us," said my master. "We must move through brush, and woods, and over fields. You must be attired for such a journey in a more practical fashion."

"What are you going to do?" she cried.

He slipped her gloves from her fingers.

"What are you going to do!" she cried.

"We have a long journey ahead of us," he said.

He then, with his knife, to her horror, cut away her cumbersome robes of concealment, until she was clad only in the last of her undergarments. He then ripped the sleeves from the undergarment, and they hung about her wrists, loose, kept from falling by her wrists and the slave bracelets confining her at the tree. "Sleen!" she cried. "Sleen!" He then, too, with his knife, and ripping, in a ragged circle, about her legs, above the knees, shortened the undergarment. Her calves might now be seen. They were pretty. "Sleen!" she cried. He then, upon this outburst, casually ripped away a large piece of the garment, stripping her to the thighs and, on the left side, when he discarded the piece of material, to the hip. Her outburst had earned her only more exposure. She was now as leg stripped or more than Donna, Chanda and Marla. Lehna, who had been stripped for her switching at her mistress's hands in the camp, and I, who had been stripped by the captain at the camp, were nude. The Lady Sabina, I noted, had lovely legs. She seethed at the tree. She pulled at the bracelets, tearing at the bark of the tree.

"I think now," said my master, standing back, regarding the girl, and his work, "that that constitutes a far more practical traveling costume than the robes of concealment for a long, overland journey afoot. Do you not agree, Lady Sabina?"

"My clothing," she said, "return it to me." She tried to be stern.

He, upon this remark, casually, from an inch or so below her left armpit ripped the garment open to an inch or so above her left hip. The line of her left breast, seen from the side, and the sway of her left hip, were lovely.

"Insolent sleen!" she cried. Then she shrank back, in terror. "No!" she said. My master's hands were at the collar of the garment.

"No!" she begged. He ripped it open, to two inches below her navel. She regarded him with horror.

"Do you have any further objections to your traveling costume?" he inquired. His hands were now at the shoulders of the garment, whence it might be simply torn from her.

"No, Captor," she said.

He turned to us, and motioned us forward, the five girls in the coffle. We approached.

"You will note, Lady Sabina," said my master, "that the first wrist ring of the coffle is empty. It has been reserved for you."

He lifted the open wrist ring, on its chain.

"My ransom will be high," she whispered.

One of the men laughed. The girl regarded him, frightened.

"I ask only," she said, "that I not be permitted to fall into the hands of those of Ar."

"May I introduce myself, Lady Sabina?" inquired my master.

"Yes," she said.

He thrust the slave bracelet on her left wrist up. He placed the opened wrist ring about her left wrist, below the left slave bracelet.

"I am Clitus Vitellius," he said.

"No!" she cried.

I gathered from the way in which she had cried out that my master's name was not unknown upon this world.

"Not the captain of Ar!" she moaned.

"There are many captains in Ar, Lady Sabina," smiled my master.

She put her cheek against the bark of the tree. "Few such as Clitus Vitellius," she said.

I felt proud of my master. How marvelous to be the girl of such a man!

My master snapped shut the wrist ring about the left wrist of the Lady Sabina. We were now chained to her, and she to us. She was now of the coffle, as were we.

"What are you going to do with me?" she asked.

"I am going to take you to my secret camp and there, under the iron, brand you a slave girl. You will then be taken to the city of Ar and, from an unimportant block, in a cheap market, sold to the highest bidder."

The girl pressed her cheek against the rough bark of the tree and moaned, and wept, staining the bark with her tears.

At a sign from my master the man who had been her guard freed her of the slave bracelets.

She now led the coffle.

"Am I not to be ransomed?" she said.

"You are too politically valuable to be ransomed," he said.

I recalled that the Lady Sabina was valuable indeed. Her companionship with Thandar of Ti, of the city of Ti, of the Salerian Confederation was to result in an alliance between Fortress of Saphronicus and the Confederation. The companionship, of course, was political. The Lady Sabina and Thandar of Ti, according to Eta, had never seen one another, the companionship being arranged by their parents and the councils of their respective cities. In such a companionship the Lady Sabina would have raised caste, and become one of the high ladies of Ti, and of the Confederation. She had been looking forward, it was well known, with enthusiasm to her attaining this high station.

"Accordingly," said my master, "it is expedient in the affairs of states that you be rendered politically valueless."

The Lady Sabina, at the head of the coffle, moaned.

As a slave she would indeed be politically valueless. She could be exchanged, or bought and sold, for whatever masters might wish. The slave is not a person before Gorean law but a rightless animal.

165

"Do not enslave me, Captain," she said. "Keep me and sell me to the Confederation. Free, returned to them, I will be worth immense riches to you. You and your men, if you return me to the Confederation, will become rich beyond your wildest dreams!"

"Do you ask me, Lady," inquired my master, "to betray Ar?"

She suddenly sank to her knees in terror before him. Would she be instantly slain? "No, Captain," she whispered.

"Considering your future status," said my master, "you may begin now to address free men by the title of 'Master.' The experience and the practice will do you good."

"Yes," she said, "—Master."

"Behind you, Lady Sabina," said my master, "you will note a slave girl, Lehna."

"Yes, Master," she said.

"Earlier this evening," said my master, "you much and richly switched her."

"Yes, Master," said the Lady Sabina.

"Give Lehna a switch," said my master to one of his men. Lehna beamed. She was given a switch.

"Lehna," said my master, "should the Lady Sabina dally or in any way attempt to delay the coffle, it will be your charge to hasten her."

"Yes, Master," said Lehna. I did not envy the Lady Sabina.

"I am sorry I switched you, Lehna," said the Lady Sabina.

Lehna struck her savagely across the back with the switch, and the Lady Sabina, whose thin undergarment shielded her from the blow scarcely at all, cried out with misery. She could not believe the sting of the stripe. It was, I conjectured, the first time in her life she had ever been struck. "Lehna!" she cried.

"Address the girls as Mistress," ordered my master, standing over the kneeling free girl.

"Yes, Master," she said.

Lehna again, savagely, struck the kneeling girl. "Please, do not strike me, Mistress!" wept the Lady Sabina.

My master turned away, to speak to his men. In a few moments he, not looking back, strode away, through the trees, followed by the majority of his men, in single file. One man remained behind, to follow the coffle, some yards to the rear.

"On your feet, Lady Sabina!" cried Lehna.

The Lady Sabina leapt to her feet, with a rustle of chain.

"You will take your first step with your left foot," said Lehna, "upon my signal. Later you will learn to walk gracefully and beautifully in chains. That is too much to expect now from an ignorant girl."

"Yes, Mistress," said the Lady Sabina.

"Are you ready, noble, lofty Lady Sabina?" inquired Lehna.

"I am sorry I switched you, Mistress," said the Lady Sabina.

"Do not fret, my dear," said Lehna. "I will see that you are well repaid."

"Please, Mistress!" cried the Lady Sabina.

"Were you given permission to speak in coffle?" asked Lehna.

"No, Mistress," moaned the Lady Sabina. Lehna then struck her twice, cruelly, with the switch.

"Do you think me weak, Lady Sabina?" inquired Lehna.

"No, no!" wept the Lady Sabina.

Lehna then struck her again. "You are right," she said. "I am not weak."

The Lady Sabina wept.

"Stand straight," said Lehna. "Straighter!" She poked the Lady Sabina with the switch.

The Lady Sabina then, choking back her tears, stood straight in the coffle, the posture accentuating the lovely lines of her chained beauty. I smiled. She stood as straight, as desirably, as beautifully as a slave girl.

"On the left foot, on my signal," said Lehna.

"Yes, Mistress," said the Lady Sabina.

"Now!" said Lehna, crying out, striking her. With a cry of misery the Lady Sabina, moving first on her left foot, stumbled forward. "Faster!" said Lehna, hitting her again. "Yes, Mistress!" cried the Lady Sabina.

We hurried on then, swiftly, through the mixed shadows and moonlit trees, following the men, our masters.

"I do not want to be run for the pleasure of boys," wept Slave Beads.

"Be silent, Slave Girl," snapped Lehna.

"Yes, Mistress," said Slave Beads.

The girls of Clitus Vitellius, I among them, stood at the line scratched in the dirt within the peasant village of Tabuk's Ford, some four hundred pasangs to the north and west of Ar, some twenty pasangs or so, west, from the Vosk road.

The young lads of the peasantry eyed us with pleasure. We were all vital, lithe beauties, and, most excitingly, slaves. It was not everyday that such girls, the girls of a warrior, would be run for their pleasure. Our bondage meant that we must, once captured, be marvels for them.

There was some discussion of the rules of the hunt. Too, bets were being taken. Some of the young men came to the line, to look us over at closer hand.

"Oh," said Slave Beads. One of the lads had put his hand on her leg. "Good stock," said one of the boys. "Yes," agreed another.

Another young lad, strapping, put his hands on me. I tried to pull away a bit, but I did not much resist. I was a slave, and did not wish to be whipped.

On the other side of Donna, Marla stood, her head in the air, seeming not to notice the hands of the boys upon her.

I looked over at Slave Beads. She was crying. Her head was in her hands. Two peasant lads, one standing, one crouching, were, by hand and eye, appraising her flesh. They did this with the same attention and innocence that they would have brought to the examination of any other domestic animal.

The two boys then moved on to me. I closed my eyes. They were not gentle. I was examined with less respect, being a slave, than would have been accorded to a bosk heifer.

I wanted to tear at their eyes with my fingernails. But I did not wish to be whipped, or slain. It is not surprising that the Gorean slave girl is obedient. Those who are not obedient are often destroyed. I was terribly afraid then, that I had even felt a momentary impulse to rebellion. I shook with terror. Did I think I was still on Earth? Did I not know I was now on Gor? I shuddered. Rebellion is not permitted to the Gorean slave girl.

The boys continued to examine me.

Tears formed in my eyes. There is a mock rebellion which is sometimes permitted a slave girl, or even commanded of her, for the master's amusement. I felt a tear on my cheek. "Show rebellion," is a command which a girl must, as any other, obey. Yet it is a terribly cruel command. "Kneel," is the command which, commonly, puts an end to her rebellion. When a girl has been permitted defiance it is then all the sweeter, I gather, to bring her again to her knees before you.

Suffice it to say the girl belongs to her master, completely. I opened my eyes. The young men moved on to Donna.

"You are crying," said Slave Beads to me.

I shook my head, and hair. "It is nothing," I said. I stood on the line. How far I had come from Earth, I thought. I was sensitive, and a poetess. Now I stood on a dirt line in a peasant village on an alien world, no longer the free Judy Thornton but rather now only a nameless, half-naked slave girl, waiting to be run for the pleasure of boys. I understood little of what had happened to me. I did not know how it was that I had come to this world. I did not know, in a sense, who I was or what I was supposed to do.

I smiled to myself. I did know I belonged to Clitus Vitellius, a captain of Ar.

In the belly of me, though I would scarcely admit this to myself, I did not object. He was such a man.

From the line, I glanced back to the open fires, where he sat with men of the village, Thurnus, caste leader, peasant and sleen master, among them.

I shook with pleasure as I stood on the line, and looked at Clitus Vitellius. Within the Ta-Teera my thighs, even looking at him, were hot and damp. He did not notice me, and was talking to Thurnus. He was the sort of man who would set his terms for a woman, even a free woman. No woman, even one who was free, would be permitted to relate to him save on his terms, and on his terms alone. He would not argue, nor would he discuss, nor persuade nor negotiate; to the free woman's horror she would understand that she must, as he saw fit, submit herself as hopelessly and will-lessly as a slave girl for his consideration. He would enter into no relationship except on his own terms. His terms were simple, that the woman be yielded to him, totally, that she be as much his, and as helplessly, though by her own free will, as any slave girl on whom he might choose to fix his collar. He would be, even in a companionship, to the scandal of Ar, master. No woman who failed to meet these understood, publicized and well-known terms would be acceptable.

I looked at my master, sitting cross-legged by the fire, talking with Thurnus.

Yet hundreds of the highborn free women of Ar, many rich, had avidly sought companionship with Clitus Vitellius.

I did not blame them. Had I been a free woman of Ar, I, too, would have sought such companionship. To have such a man as Clitus Vitellius I would have accepted his terms. So, too, I think would have any true woman. Surely it is better to have a true man on any terms than to have half a man, or no man at all. Men are masters; if the man be strong, the woman must submit. Given the opportunity to relate to a true man, few women will settle for less. Indeed, true women, in the belly of them, desire to submit to true men. It is an ancient instinct bred into the bellies of beautiful, feminine women.

"Remove your clothing," would my master say to a high-born free woman, suing to be considered by him in companionship. She would do so, and be assessed. If he was not pleased, he would send her weeping from his presence, clutching the rag of a slave, to don it and return to her dwelling. If he was not displeased he would gesture to the tiles before him where there waited a goblet of slave wine which she, kneeling before him, would eagerly drink. She would serve him that night as a slave. In the morning, she, nude, would prepare and serve to him his breakfast, after which he would make fresh use of her; he would then send her from his presence, first pressing into her hand a coin, usually a copper tarsk or a silver tarsk, commensurate with the quality of her service. Such women went from his quarters proudly, clad in the full regalia of the free woman. They were not discontent. They had been touched by Clitus Vitellius. Some women claimed that they had earned from Clitus Vitellius a tarn disk of gold. Such a coin would buy several girls such as myself. Sometimes a girl, rather than be sent from his presence, would beg to be kept as a collared slave. She would then sign a document of enslavement which, after her signature was affixed, she would be powerless to alter or break, for she would then be only a slave. Clitus Vitellius would commonly keep such a girl for a few days, and then discard her, usually giving her to a friend or selling her. I wondered if such a girl, braceleted, pulled away from him on her leash, regretted her choice. She was then in bondage, subject to chains and the whip, and the will of men. What had she then to look forward to but the degradation of the sales block, being exposed to men as a slave and being vended in a public market; being owned by a succession of hard masters, accustomed to the management of girls such as she; onerous work and strict discipline; and the continuous exploitation of her body and service? Perhaps, for a woman, the thrill of being owned and commanded, of being at the absolute mercy of a powerful man, knowing that she must obey him, and experiencing, if she be fortunate, incredible, helpless, incomparable love, of the sort which can be felt only by a completely rightless woman, fully and absolutely owned by a man, in his total bondage. But such thoughts would not be likely to be prominent in the mind of a leashed girl, helplessly braceleted, being dragged to her first sale.

I looked at my master. How magnificent he was.

His collar, I had heard, was one of the most sought collars in Ar.

When he strode through the streets free women sometimes threw themselves before him, tearing away their veils and robes, begging for his collar.

He was such a man.

One's freedom is small enough price to pay, whisper some highborn women of Ar among themselves, for even ten days in the collar of Clitus Vitellius. The boredoms of freedom are small enough price to pay surely for even a brief sojourn in the arms of such a man, they conjecture.

But such women, I told myself, must be natural slaves, even though they be legally free, as I was not. If they are natural slaves, I asked myself, should they not be made slaves? Why should one who is a natural slave not be a slave? Can it be wrong to enslave a natural slave? Is it not right that natural slaves be enslaved? Is it not what they want? I looked at my master. What woman, I asked, would not be the natural slave of such a man? He was a natural master. Any woman, I suspected, to such a man, would be a natural slave. Almost any woman, I suspected, looking on such a man, would sense herself his natural slave.

That would explain why the women of Ar would twist on their couches like bitches in heat thinking of Clitus Vitellius. In the darkness, remembering him, his stride, his glance, and limbs, they would have intuited him as their master.

"Prepare to run, Slaves!" called a peasant.

I looked at my master. The heat in my thighs made me want to run to him but I dared not leave the line.

Earlier in the afternoon, casually, Thurnus had aroused me, and no one had satisfied me.

I had spent the afternoon in a slave girl's misery.

I wanted to run to my master.

I dared not leave the line.

I looked at my master. I wondered if I, though a girl of Earth, were a natural slave.

How I wanted him to have me.

Clitus Vitellius, in spite of the desires of the women of Ar, had never taken a companion.

I did not think he ever would. He was Clitus Vitellius. He would have slave girls instead.

He would always keep his girls in collars. I loved him!

"When the torch is lowered," called a peasant, lifting up a torch, lit from the fire, "you will run."

"Yes, Master," we said to him.

"The torch will then be placed in the earth," he said. "When it is fixed in the soil, you will have two hundred beats of a slave girl's heart." He pointed to a peasant's slave, who stood nearby. She was a girl of peasant stock, who had been, two years ago, stolen by slavers from a village hundreds of pasangs to the west. Thurnus had purchased her in Ar and brought her on a rope behind his wagon to Tabuk's Ford. She was thick-ankled and blond-haired, a good-looking, wide-hipped, blue-eyed, strapping girl. One of my master's men stood behind her, his left hand on her left arm. His right hand, about her body, was thrust through her brief, woolen tunic. He would count the beats of her heart. She was barefoot. About her throat, looped twice, knotted, was a length of coarse rope. I looked at the rope. It was snug on her throat. It was thus that Thurnus marked his girls. I conjectured that the heart of such a girl would be slow and strong.

"You will then be sought," said the peasant.

Counting the time it would take to fix the torch in the earth and for her heart to beat two hundred times, I conjectured that we would have a lead on our pursuers of some three minutes. I looked at the girl. Her lips were slightly parted. This angered me. She was excited by the hand of my master's man on her flesh. She backed slightly against him. Her heart would now be beating more rapidly. She was, after all, a girl in bondage, like us. Why did they not take a hundred beats of the heart of a standing bosk? Her sexual excitement at the proximity of my master's man might, I now noted, considerably diminish our lead. I decided to count now on a lead of little more than two minutes. Moreover, she was to be his for the night, once he had counted upon her body, using her beating heart as the clock of the evening's sport. It was no wonder that she was excited. This did not seem to me to be fair. But I did not complain. The men decide what is fair or unfair, and will, in any case, do precisely as they please. It is the girl's part to abide by their decision. The men decide; the girl submits. One must be master, one slave.

Eta was to my far right, on the line. Then came Marla, and Donna. I stood on the dirt line between Donna and, to my left, Slave Beads. To her left was Chanda, and on the far left, was Lehna.

"I do not want to be run for peasant boys," said Slave Beads. "I was once free."

"I, too, was once free," I told her.

"You are slave now," said Slave Beads.

"So, too, are you," I snapped.

"Does Slave Beads wish to be switched again?" called Lehna.

"No, Mistress," said Slave Beads, hastily. Slave Beads feared Lehna. For most practical purposes, she had been put in the charge of Lehna almost from the first moments of her capture. She was commonly chained before Lehna in the coffle, and it was under Lehna's supervision that she commonly performed her tasks.

After the capture of the Lady Sabina we had returned to the secret cache camp, to which my master had originally brought me, his barbarian girl. At the cache camp, the first night of our arrival, the Lady Sabina had been stripped and thrown on her back, head down, on the inclining, white-barked tree trunk, to which she had then been, as I had been before her, helplessly roped. When the iron had been pulled from her burned, marked flesh she had been rendered, as was the intention of my master, and those in Ar, politically valueless. She was then only a slave. She was unroped and thrown, a bond girl, to the feet of my master.

"We must name you," he said. "Sabina—Sabina—" said he, as though musing on the thought. "Ah," had he then said, "it seems that you, in your former name, carried already, an excellent slave name."

"Oh, no, no, Master!" she wept.

"Your former name," said he, "was clever. It appears to be the name of a free woman, and yet, within it, in disguise, which we now penetrate, it concealed secretly your true name. Very clever, Slave, but now you are discovered and you will openly wear your true name, that which will perfectly fit you and which I now, in the decree of the master, make yours."

"Please, no, Master!" she wept. "No! Please, no, Master!"

"You are Bina," said he.

She cried out in misery, named.

No longer was there a point in protesting, or begging.

It had been done to her.

That was who she now was. That was now her name. She was now "Bina."

She put her head in her hands, and wept. The expression 'Bina' in Gorean means "slave beads."

"Put Slave Beads in a Sirik," said my master. Swiftly my master's new girl was locked in the light, gleaming Sirik. The collar clasped her throat; a chain dangled from the collar; her small wrists were locked in the slave bracelets fixed on the dangling chain, and the dangling chain, itself, looped down to a short chain and pair of ankle rings, to which it was gracefully fastened at a sliding ring. The ankle rings were then closed about the lovely ankles of Slave Beads, and locked. She was helpless in Sirik. The confinement became her. She was beautiful. I had never worn Sirik.

She knelt before my master, naked, in Sirik. She looked up at him. Her thigh, freshly branded, bore the common slave mark of Gor, the initial letter, in cursive script, of the Gorean expression 'Kajira,' which means Slave Girl. She trembled. She was now no different from thousands of other girls who shared her condition, that of total bondage.

"Greetings, Slave Beads," said my master.

"Greetings, Master," she said, responding to her name, as she must.

My master looked down at her, and smiled. She looked up at him, trembling. He was her master.

"Perhaps you remember, Slave Beads," said my master, "that, on an evening, some days ago, a free woman harshly and at length punished a slave girl."

"You know?" she asked.

"We observed, in scouting the camp," said he. He looked down at the kneeling girl, locked in the Sirik. "The beating was well done," said he.

"Thank you, Master," she whispered.

"The crime of the slave girl, as I recall," said my master, "was to desire the touch of a man."

Lehna stood to one side. She stood straight, as an exciting slave girl.

"Yes, Master," said Slave Beads.

"The free woman," said my master, "was doubtless well within her rights to beat the girl."

"Yes, Master!" said Slave Beads.

"But that free woman," said my master, "has since that time herself fallen slave. Indeed, she is now in this camp."

"Yes, Master," said Slave Beads.

"The slave girl whom she beat is, too, in this camp," said my master.

"Yes, Master," said Slave Beads. She trembled in the Sirik.

"Do you yourself desire the touch of a man?" asked my master.

"Oh, no! No, Master!" cried Slave Beads.

"Ah," said my master, "it seems that in this camp we have a slave girl, too, who is guilty of a crime."

"Who, Master?" asked Slave Beads.

"You," said he.

"Not I!" she cried.

"You," said he.

"What is my crime?" she asked.

"Not to desire the touch of a man," said he.

She looked at him, aghast.

"You see," said he, "in this camp it is a crime for a girl not to desire a man's touch." My master turned to one of his men. "Bring Lehna a switch," he said. He turned again to Slave Beads. "You will be well punished for your crime, Slave Girl," said he.

"I am ready, Master," said Lehna.

"Do not forget this beating," said my master. "You are to desire men. Further, it will be well for you to learn what it is to be a beaten slave girl. What you did to Lehna she will now do to you. Perhaps you will then have a richer understanding of what it was, truly, that you did to her. Perhaps you will regret that you were not a kinder mistress."

"She will regret it, Master," promised Lehna, licking her lips.

"I will now leave you to the tender mercies of Lehna," said my master. "Let us hope that, in the future, your masters and mistresses will be kinder to you than was the Lady Sabina of Fortress of Saphronicus to her slaves."

"Do not leave me with her, Master!" cried Slave Beads. "She will kill me! She will kill me!"

"It is not impossible," said my master. He turned to leave, then turned again to face the kneeling, terrified Slave Beads. "It is my hope, too," said he, "that this beating will prove a useful initiation for you, given your antecedents and nature, into the condition of slavery." He looked at her, sternly. "Yes, Master," she said, looking up at him. "After your beating," he said, "you will be asked again if you desire the touch of men. I trust, then, your answer will be affirmative. If it is not, you will be again beaten, and again, throughout the night."

"My answer will be affirmative, Master," whispered Slave Beads.

My master then turned away from her, and so, too, did we all, leaving her with Lehna.

Later my master took Slave Beads by the hair. "Do you now desire the touch of men?" he asked. "Yes, yes, yes, yes, yes, Master," she wept.

She was then released from the Sirik. "Go to the men," said my master.

"Yes, Master," she said. She crawled to the men, on her hands and knees. She extended her hand to one of them, and looked up at him, with tears in her eyes. "Please touch Slave Beads, Master," she begged.

He took her by the hair and pulled her into the darkness. We did not retire that night until Slave Beads, on her knees, had begged the touch of each of my master's men. He himself was the last to grant her plea. When he had finished with her he put her again in the Sirik and threw her to the wall of the cliff. Eta went to her and, putting a rep-cloth blanket about her, held her and comforted her. "Poor slave," said Eta.

I, and the other girls, went to sleep.

"Run!" cried the man, lowering the torch.

I, and the other girls, sped, scattering, from the dirt line.

Some fifty yards from the line, in the darkness, between the straw huts, on their pilings, I stopped, and, wild, gasping, in the Ta-Teera, looked back.

Already the torch had been fixed in the ground. The slave girl who wore the rope of Thurnus on her throat as a collar leaned back against the man of my master. Her head was back on his shoulder. Her eyes were closed. His hand was tight on her body, counting the beats of her heart. He was calling the count, but I could not hear him.

I looked wildly about, and then ran further through the huts, down the long corridor between them. Then my hands were pressed against the smooth logs of the palisade surrounding the village. I pressed my body and cheek against the wood. I stepped back and, hands on the wood, looked up. The pointed tops of the palings were eight feet over my head. I turned about, my back to the logs, and looked back down the narrow dirt street. I could see the fire in the village's clearing, its light on the faces of the men about it. I saw the boys getting to their feet, eagerly.

"There is no place to hide!" wept Slave Beads, who was near me.

"We are slaves," I snapped at her. "We are meant to be caught."

I saw some of the boys spitting on their hands and wiping them on their thighs. This would improve their grip. The flesh of a girl would be less likely to slip from their hands.

More than one of them I knew wanted me. Bets had been taken on who would bring me as his slave for the night to the ring drawn about the torch, as they had, too, on the other girls. A big red-haired fellow and a smaller dark-haired fellow had bet on which of them would take Slave Beads.

I saw Chanda creeping into a hut.

Slave Beads turned away from me and fled about the interior perimeter of the palisade.

I followed her, and then darted among the huts. I almost died of fear when, suddenly, I heard, not feet from me, a bedlam of vicious snarling. I cried out, my hand before my mouth. Dozens of vicious eyes blazed at me from behind the stout bars of a sleen pen, one of several in the village. Snouts and teeth pressed at the bars. I stumbled back.

I ran again.

I did not see Marla or Eta, nor Lehna. Slave Beads, too, had fled elsewhere.

I did see a white ankle, not covered by a piece of canvas. It was Donna. "You had best cover this ankle, or you will be soon found, Slave Girl," I said, angrily, jerking the canvas over it. Donna shrank even smaller, covered by the canvas. She trembled beneath it, her head down, under her hands. She was slender, small-breasted and lovely-legged. She had dark eyes, dark hair. The name "Donna" is an Earth name, but the girl, as I had determined, was Gorean. Many Gorean names, as words in the Gorean language, apparently have an Earth origin. Her original name had been Tais. She had been a slave since the age of eight, but it had not been until she was seventeen that she had been judged fit for men, and then branded. Donna, in the beginning, had been a block name. Girls are usually sold under a name, it being easier then for the auctioneer to refer to them; too, for some reason, the intensity of the bidding often increases when a named girl is being vended; it makes, I suppose, the buying and selling much more exciting and personal; "See, Generous Buyers, the flesh of Donna! Is Donna not beautiful? Stand straight, Donna. What am I bid, Noble Buyers, for Donna?" The original Donna had perhaps been a girl brought in a chain and collar from Earth. Her name, finding favor with masters, considering it a lovely slave name, would then have been given, from time to time, to other girls, perhaps some Gorean, perhaps some, like herself, of Earth origin. Tais was too fine a name for a slave; accordingly the lovely seventeen-year-old Gorean girl had been sold in Ko-ro-ba under the block name of Donna, a slave name calculated to excite Gorean buyers. Many Earth-girl names, incidentally, on Gor, are regarded as slave names. Gorean males, commonly, regard the women of Earth as fit only to be their slaves. But Donna, though she had been adjudged fit for men and branded, was sold from the block in Ko-ro-ba to a visiting merchant, Kleomenes of Fortress of Saphronicus, who took her with him and gave her to his spoiled daughter, the Lady Sabina, as a woman's slave. Donna had been a virgin until she was raped in the coffle on the first night of the march by two of my master's men. She had been had from time to time since then, but Marla, Eta and, surprisingly, I, had been the most consistently abused of the girls of Clitus Vitellius. The more beautiful I had become the more often I had been raped; and the more I had been raped, the more beautiful I had become. I think that I understood the problem of Donna. She feared men. The slave girl must, surely, if she is rational, fear men, but, too, she must regard them as potentially constituting for her sources of incredible pleasure. Donna's timidity and lingering uncertainty with men, I think, was largely a function of her fear that she might not be capable of giving them pleasure. It is one thing to be thrown down and raped; it is quite another to hear the indolent command, "Please me." The responsibility for pleasure is often placed on the slender, lovely shoulders of the slave girl. It is she, then, who must labor in her bondage to be pleasing. As soon as I had understood that the quality of my life on Gor, given my brand, would depend on my ability to please men I had begged Eta to give me instruction. She had been extremely helpful, teaching me many things I might never have discovered myself. She had actually received some weeks of slave training in the pens of Ar, a tutelage to which Clitus Vitellius in disgust at her ineptness had remanded her; she had attended diligently to her lessons; when she returned to his quarters it had been clear by morning that it would not be necessary to sell her off. She had made an acceptable beginning in learning the arts of the slave girl. These arts, it might be mentioned, are intricate and diverse, and are complex and rich in many modes and dimensions. Most obviously they are domestic, sexual and psychological. Too, they are culinary, kinetic, cosmetic and artistic. Like the painter and the musician the slave girl need never stop growing in her art, which is the creation of beauty and joy for herself and her master. I had swiftly sought slave instruction; Donna had not. Perhaps I was more practical than she. Perhaps, rather, I was simply a slave and she was not. I was of Earth. The men of Gor regard the women of Earth as natural slaves. Perhaps I was a natural slave. That might be the difference between Donna and myself. Yet I suspected that if I were a natural slave so, too, were all women. Donna, I was sure, would learn her slavery. She was beautiful. She would come around. It requires only the right master to bring out the slave in any woman.

I heard a shout from the center of the camp. The hunters were now in pursuit.

"Do not be afraid, Donna," I said to her. "You will not be beaten or much beaten. You will not truly have to serve. These are only peasant boys and will not know one end of a slave girl from the other."

Then I fled from her side, through the spaces between the dark huts.

I hoped that what I had said to Donna was true. I was sure that the peasant boys, indeed, would not know much of the handling of slave girls. Doubtless they would lack the patience and skill to get all from a girl. I did not think, for example, that they would know how to force me into the slave girl's humiliating submission ecstasy. On the other hand, I regarded them with genuine fear. They could well hurt me. I remembered their roughness and the way they had, with brutal exactness, appraised my flesh. I was so much smaller and weaker than they, and their lust would be on them. They could well be terribly brutal with me. I was to them, after all, only an animal. They might hurt me. They might throw me about among them. They might beat me with ropes if I were not pleasing to them.

I heard a young man running by. I shrank back in the shadows, crouching among the pilings of a hut.

I did not want them to catch me. I was locked within the palisade. There was no place to hide!

I heard a girl scream, far to my right. They had taken one of us. I did not know whom.

I did not want a rope put on my throat. I did not want to be dragged to the circle of the torch, a caught girl.

Two young men came by, with torches. I hid back, among the pilings.

Shortly after they had passed, the sleen in a pen, some fifty yards off, began to squeal and hiss. They ran toward the pen. Something had disturbed the sleen. Perhaps it was a girl.

Two more young men were approaching, one holding aloft a torch. Again I shrank back among the pilings, holding my breath. They passed.

I saw them stop beside a hut several yards away. The one lifted the torch. It illuminated what appeared to be a pile of canvas. They stood there, one on each side of the pile, it almost at their feet. Cruelly they stood there, not moving. Donna would know that their footsteps had approached. They had not departed. She must, surely, fearfully suspect that her position was known. Yet she did not know for certain. How miserable she must have felt, huddling beneath the canvas, how tense and terrified, how apprehensive. Cruelly they stood as they were, not moving, for almost a minute. She could hear the crackle of the torch. Did they know where she was? Were they playing with the beauty, tormenting her? Longer yet did they stand there, and then, exchanging glances, one of them, with a sudden, loud cry, pounced on the pile of canvas. Shrieking with misery Donna was lifted, by one ankle and an arm, high into the air, over the head of the boy who had seized her. He held her over his head. She struggled, held from the ground, high, helpless, her lovely limbs without leverage. "Capture!" cried the boy. "Capture!" cried another lad, coming from the direction of the sleen pen, where the sleen, shortly before, had hissed and squealed, revealing their agitation. He held Lehna before him, his left hand on her left arm, his right hand on her right wrist, forcing her right arm high, painfully, behind her back. He pushed her before him, so held. Her "gown," so to speak, had been pulled down about her hips. She grimaced with pain, her head back.

Perhaps a word might be in order pertaining to Lehna's garment, or, as I have suggested, "gown."

It may be recalled that both Lehna and I had been nude in the original coffle conducted from the raided camp. I had been stripped by the soldiers of the camp, and Lehna had been earlier stripped for her beating at the wagon wheel. At the time my master and his men had returned to the camp she had not been permitted to reclothe herself. Permission to clothe oneself, of course, is commonly obtained from a master. "May I clothe myself, Master?" is a question often put to a master in the morning. One does not know but what he might want one nude that day. Accordingly we had both been wrist-locked unclothed in the coffle. I and Eta were now again in our Ta-Teeras. Donna, Chanda and Marla were still in the shreds of their former gowns, shortened and altered, of course, in such a way as to make them acceptable to masters. Slave Beads was clad in what the master had seen fit to leave her of her last, soft, clinging undergarment, which was, frankly, very little. To be sure, she was now a slave, and should be grateful for as little as a thread. Lehna's "gown," then, we might note, was the finest garment of all our garments, as Eta, at the request of the master, had carefully fashioned it of fine silk. To be sure, it was little more than a slave tunic, and did little to conceal her considerable charms. It was the intent of the master, it seems, that her garment or "gown" be considerably and obviously superior in quality, opacity and coverage to the scrap of silk permitted to Slave beads. In this way he made clear the new relationship between the two women. The garment proclaimed Lehna's superiority, and higher status. Not even the favored Marla had such a garment. We all envied Lehna, though, to be sure, on Earth, few women would have dared to appear publicly in such a garment. Even an Earth male, in all his naiveté, might, at least on some level, suspect that no woman could be in such a garment but a female slave.

"Please, Master!" she wept. Lehna was a larger woman than I. She was strong among us girls. Slave Beads lived in terror of her. But in the arms of a male, even a lusty boy, she was slight and helpless, small, to them only another pretty slave girl in their power. I bit my lip. Men were our masters. With the boy who had captured Lehna came four others, two with torches. The boy who had captured Donna had now thrown her, belly down, across his left shoulder. Her head hung down behind his back. His left arm, heavy, brawny, locked her in place. "Let us see your catch," said one of the newly arrived boys. "Tie her ankles," said the lad who held Donna over his shoulder. One of the other boys, who carried a ten-foot length of rope, with one end of the rope, crossed and tied together Donna's ankles, while she was still held on the shoulder of her captor. "Who is your master of the night?" inquired Lehna's captor of Lehna. He thrust her right wrist higher behind her back. "You! You, Master!" she cried. "You are my master of the night!" "Ankle leash her," said the lad who held Lehna. Another lad tied a tether on her left ankle. The ankle leash is cruel. It provides effective control of a girl. There is much that can be done with such a leash, particularly in the control of a skillful master. Most obviously, in an instant the girl may be thrown to his feet in a variety of positions, over which he exercises choice. The lad who had captured Donna, now that her ankles were tied, heaved her with a laugh over his shoulder. She landed in the dirt behind him. She broke her fall, as best she could, with her hands. The long end of the rope which bound her ankles trailed her over his shoulder. Her captor took the end of the rope from the lad who had bound her and, holding it about a foot from her fastened ankles, pulled her feet some six inches into the air. She was lying on her stomach. "There is my catch," he said. Then he said to Donna, "Roll over." She rolled onto her back, her tied feet now held about a foot off the ground by the rope. "There, my friends," beamed her captor, "is my catch!" "A beauty!" said one of the boys. "Yes, a beauty!" said her captor. He was proud of Donna. I did not blame him.

She was indeed beautiful. Donna was a marvelous catch. "I want her!" said one of the lads. "First capture rights are mine," said the lad who had caught Donna, "but I am generous, and will share my prize with all of you!" There was hearty acclaim among the lads upon the receipt of his welcome intelligence. Donna squirmed, but was helpless on her back, her feet bound, held in the air by the captor's tether. "What of my prize?" demanded another lad, he who had caught Lehna by the sleen pen. He now held her ankle leash, and stepped back, bowing and displaying the half-stripped Lehna with an expansive gesture. She, too, I was forced to admit, was a superb prize. Such boys did not have such girls everyday. She was a warrior's belonging. "How can we tell if she is pretty?" asked one of the boys. "Thusly!" said one, tearing away the bit of gown about Lehna's hips. There was laughter. She was very beautiful. "But she is standing!" protested the first lad. "Belly or back?" asked Lehna's captor. "Both!" cried more than one lad. Expertly, with the ankle leash, the lad displayed Lehna's beauty in the luscious modes of horizontality. Some Goreans say that a woman's beauty can only be fairly judged when she lies at a man's feet. More than one of the lads cried out with pleasure and slapped his thigh. Donna then screamed as the boys turned to her. Her gown, too, was torn off. Her ankles were still tied. "To the circle of the torch!" cried a lad. "On your feet, Wench!" said the lad who had captured Lehna. She scrambled to her feet, covered with dirt. "Three have yet to be caught," said a lad. I knew one girl had been caught early; I had heard a scream some time ago; I did not know who she was; now I knew that Lehna and Donna were in the power of the pursuers; if only three remained to be caught, then one other girl, somewhere, had also been captured. I did not know who she was either. "Let us take these to the circle of the torch," said one of the lads, "and bind them securely, then hunt the others." The captors hesitated. "You can put your marks on these in charcoal," said one of the boys, indicating Donna and Lehna. "All right," said one of the captors. "Agreed!" said the other. Lehna was led away on her ankle leash, fastened on her left ankle, and by her right wrist, too, it held in the hand of one of the boys. Donna's captor, to her misery, dragged her behind him through the dirt on the tether which fastened her ankles together. I saw the group, pursuers and fair captives, helpless in their charge, disappear down the street.

I shuddered in the darkness among the pilings. I did not want to be captured.

A bold plan leaped into my mind. I began to move through the darkness. I kept in the shadows. I moved furtively. Sometimes I crawled. As much as I could I kept under the huts, among the pilings. Twice boys with torches passed quite near to me. I shrank back in the shadows. Then I threw myself to my belly. Not more than ten yards away I saw Chanda, wild, running. She was fleeing down a nearby street. There was a rope on one of her wrists. It was a wrist tether rope, knotted about her right wrist, with a handle loop, about a foot long, by which she might be led. I remained still. Behind her, in a few moments, carrying a torch, came two boys. "I was first to see her in the hut," said one. "I was first to put her to the floor and get my rope on her," said the other. The first lad lifted his torch, peering about. "Let us not dispute the matter further," he said. "Let us continue the hunt." "Very well," said the other. Warriors, I thought, would not have lost a girl in such a fashion. Girls do not escape warriors.

I hoped that Chanda would escape.

I continued my journey. I continued to keep largely under huts. Too, I often crawled now. In this way I hoped to be less conspicuous, to be more difficult to detect.

Once I almost cried out with misery, for the path to my desired destination lay across a dark street, down which, a hundred yards or so away, I could see the center of the village, where, about the village fire, were seated several men, villagers and my master, and his men. On my belly I inched across this street and then, gratefully, slipped again into the shadows among and beneath the huts.

For the moment I was again safe.

I darted to my feet and fled deeply into the shadows.

Whereas I feared being seen, or discovered, I did not much fear being trailed for, though slave girls would be barefoot, as I, there would also be in the village the numerous prints of village bond girls, not simply mine, and those of my sisters in bondage. It would be next to impossible, in this populous and much trekked village, particularly in the night, by torchlight, to follow a girl's trail without the use of sleen, which might not, happily for the pursued females, be used in the hunt. If the boys could not find us by themselves they simply could not have us that night for their sport. We would have won our freedom from their aggressions. I determined to escape.

At last, stealthily, now again crawling in the darkness, I reached that position in the village which I had anxiously sought, that portion of the village where my master and his men had made their camp. I crawled among the furs there, in the darkness. Tentings had not been erected.

I heard a girl weeping and stumbling. "Hurry along, female," I heard. "Yes, Master," I heard. I dared not move. I scarcely dared breathe. I lay as small, as tiny, as silent, as still, as I could. Some figures, three of them, were passing me, some yards on my right. Perhaps if they had looked, they might have seen me. When they had passed, I lifted my head, ever so slightly. They had circled our camp area, between it and the edge of the palisade, and were now returning to the center of the village. I looked. Chanda's hands were now bound tightly behind her back, the wrist tether's handle loop having been used for this purpose. She was bent over. She was stumbling. Her gown had been pulled down about her hips. She was weeping. One of the boys' hands was in her hair. She was being hurried along. They were not patient with her. She was being half dragged, not merely perfectly controlled, as is customary, by the cruel grip. I did not envy her. She had irritated them by her earlier escape. Doubtless they would make her pay well for her temerity. Men do not care to be displeased by slave girls. I hoped that she would not be excessively beaten. I saw them take her to the circle of the torch. There they threw her to the dirt, on her belly, and crossed and bound her ankles. She was thus bound hand and foot. They then turned her to her back and marked on her body with some burnt wood from the fire, probably putting their ownership marks on her, marking her as theirs for the night.

When they left she struggled to her left elbow, looking after them. Once she had eluded them. Now, however, she was well tied. She would elude them no more. Rather, while they returned to their hunt, she would remain where she was, tied, awaiting their return, and pleasure.

She had been caught.

I crept into my master's furs. For the first time I now breathed more easily.

I heard two boys calling to one another. "How many of the she-tarsks are still at large?" asked one. "Two," he was answered. I did not know who the other uncaptured beauty might be.

I snuggled down in my master's furs, covering my head. I did not think they would find me there. Who would think a girl bold enough to hide in her master's furs? Too, I did not think the peasant boys would dare to look into the furs of a warrior. Surely they valued their lives. I felt secure. It was probably the only place in the village where I might be safe. I was well pleased with myself. I loved the smell of my master's body, which was in the furs, surrounding me with its excitement. The aura of his ownership enveloped me. I felt warm, and protected, and stimulated as a slave girl, warm in my master's furs. I wished that he, too, were in the furs, that I might perform delicious, servile duties for him, fitting for one who was only a lowly bond girl. I loved him. Was I his slave because I loved him or did I love him because I was his slave? I smiled. I was his slave, totally and complete-ly, whether I loved him or not. That was legal, institutional, on this world. I was his to do with as he pleased, completely. I was without rights; his will determined all. He was everything; I was nothing; he was master; I was slave. I decided that I was both his slave and that I loved him. But I did not think I could have loved him so much had he not been so powerful, and had I not been his slave, so helplessly.

I heard a shout outside, and I lay very still. I heard the boys crying out with triumph, and pleasure. In a few moments, when I dared, I looked out from the furs. They had taken another girl. Did they think she would escape? It was Slave Beads. She was being carried to the cir-cle of the torch. She was carried on the shoulder of a brawny peasant lad. She was roped hand and foot, at the ankles, at the thighs above the knees, her wrists behind her back, and about her upper arms and body. In addition, one lad walked in front with a rope which was tied on her neck, and another walked behind with a rope tied about her left ankle. There were several boys in the group. Several, apparently, had flushed her out and, together, run her down like a startled, confused tabuk hind.

I, now, alone of all the girls, had escaped them. I was proud of my ingenuity and cunning.

For more than an Ahn I lay quiet in the furs. Sometimes the young hunters came near, but they did not molest our camp, nor much penetrate its perimeters. One did walk within two or three yards of me, carrying a torch, but I lay very still. He did not throw aside the furs of my master, nor those of the other men.

I lay warm in the furs, happy. I had escaped from them. There was a possibility, I supposed, that my master would not be pleased that I had hidden in his furs. If this were so, I supposed that I would be tied and lashed. Yet I did not think he would object to my boldness and ingenuity. I knew that my master could see through me, his slave girl, as simply as through glass, but I felt that I, too, in the past weeks, strangely, had become much more aware of him, and much more capable of reading his moods and conjecturing his reactions. Perhaps this was only a slave girl's alertness to the master, an alertness natural enough in a girl who is owned by a man, whose well-being and very life may depend on how well she pleases him; I do not know; that is an alertness which any rational girl strives to cultivate; but I wondered if it might not be more, something more in the nature of a deep, intuitive rapport with another person. I felt that I was coming to know my master. Two days ago I had sensed, watching him, that he desired wine rather than paga. I had gone and fetched wine and knelt before him. "May a girl offer you wine, Master?" I had asked him. He had seemed startled, momentarily. Then he had said, "Yes, Slave," and taken the wine. At times I sensed his eyes on me. Once, in the early morning, when I had lain chained with the other girls, I awakened, but gave no sign that I had awakened. Through half closed eyes I had seen that he stood near me. Yesterday night, he had touched my hair, almost tenderly. Then, as though angry with himself, he slapped me, hard, and sent me to Eta, to be put to work. I was not displeased.

Two days ago I had dared to follow him outside the palisade. I found him sitting alone, on a rock, surveying a grassy field. "Come here, Slave," he said to me. "Yes, Master," I said. I went and knelt near him; later I leaned my head against him, which he permitted. "The grass and sky are beautiful, are they not, Slave?" he asked. "Yes, Master," I had replied. He looked down at me. "You, too," he said, "are beautiful, Slave." "A girl is gratified if she pleases her master," I said. "Why is it," he asked, looking down, "that the women of Earth are fit to be slaves?" "Perhaps," I said, looking up at him, "because the men of Gor are fit to be masters." He then again turned his attention to the contemplation of the grass and sky. He sat still for a long time. Then he stood up, as though shaking his mood from him, as though now he was again separate from nature, alien in its midst, conscious, a man, and I was at his feet, a woman. Then it was we two alone, by the rock, in the grass, he standing, I kneeling. He looked down at me. "The woman of Earth," I said to him, "is ready to serve her Gorean master." Laughing, he crouched down before me and seized me by the shoulders. His strong fingers pressed into my flesh. I was held with great tightness, I was helpless. Doubtless there would be marks there. He then thrust me back, suddenly, with great force, with violence, as a slave, to the grass. The Ta-Teera was torn from me. Well then, to her joy, did he use the Earth woman, his slave.

I felt the furs thrown back.

"I knew that I would find you here," he said.

"I hope that master is not displeased with his girl," I said. Yesterday night, he had touched my hair, almost tenderly. Then, as though angry with himself, he had slapped me, hard, and sent me to Eta, to be put to work. I had not been displeased, though my mouth was bloodied. This morning I had knelt before him. "I beg rape," I had said. He had looked at me, angrily. "Rape her," he had said to a passing soldier. He had then turned angrily away. In the arms of the soldier, I had smiled. I think I had disturbed my master. I think he was fighting his feelings for me, his desire for me. Then I had cried out with unwilling pleasure, and helplessly caught at the soldier with my nails, and the thought of my master had been, against my will, forced from my consciousness as the soldier brought me, twisting and crying out, to obliterating, overwhelming slave orgasm.

"Perhaps I should have you lashed," said my master.

"My master will do with me what he pleases," I said.

He had not been too pleased with the way I had yielded to the soldier. But I had not been able to help myself.

"Slave," had said my master later, standing over me.

"Yes, Master," I had said, looking up at him, shamed, "I am a slave."

He had then turned away again, angrily. He called Marla to him, to serve his pleasure. She hurried to him. Objectively she was more beautiful than I, with her large, dark eyes, her face, her lovely figure; too, she had superb slave reflexes; but she did not, I thought, succeed in making my master forget me. She did, of course, frighten me, for she was a formidable rival. I resented, and hated her. Too, she did not seem to regard me with affection and delight. She had wanted me named "Stupid Girl" or "Clumsy Girl." I did not yet have a name. But, in spite of the fact that my master, currently, seemed to be much taken with Marla, and that she was clearly the preferred bond girl in our camp, I did not feel that she had managed to negate the moments or the tacit understanding which I felt I shared with the man who owned me. I recalled his anger at my helpless yielding to the soldier; I was only a slave; I had not been able to help myself; yet he had been angry; too, he himself had commanded the man to address himself to the work of my rape; yet he had been angry; too, his concern with Marla seemed to me rather sudden and excessive; he seemed to be too obviously unconcerned with me; I smiled to myself; I think he had been jealous; and I think he was using Marla, certainly a delightful diversion, to try and force me from his mind. She was surely more beautiful than I, but in such matters there are rightnesses which are reciprocal and subtle; it is rather like the matching together of pieces in a puzzle, the startling, unexpected fitting together of components, yielding a whole which is, in its wholeness, more precious than the individual pieces or parts could be in isolation; as beautiful and marvelous as Marla was, she was not I; it was that simple, I believe; she was not I; I, not she, I believe, was the one; I had little doubt he was my natural, perfect master; and I think, too, he had begun to fear that I might be his natural, perfect slave; surely he did not want to think of me as more than just another of his girls; yet I had little doubt that I was becoming to him, in spite of his desires, something more than just another lovely wench whose wrist was fastened on his chain.

He stood beside the furs, and slipped aside his tunic. "Remove the Ta-Teera," he said to me. I sat up, unhooked it, and slipped it over my head, putting it to the side. He joined me in the furs, throwing them over us both.

I could hear cries, it seemed from far off, from the circle of the torch, where the peasant boys sported cruelly with their captured beauties.

Then I was in my master's arms. I moaned with pleasure.

I felt my master's eyes upon me.

"Will you turn me over to the peasant boys?" I asked, apprehensive, in the darkness.

I did not want to be roped and dragged, a captured slave, to the circle of the torch. They would be furious that I had eluded them. I did not know what they would do to me.

"No," said he, in the darkness.

"Then," said I, breathing more easily, "I have escaped them."

"But you have not escaped me," he said.

"No, Master," I said, snuggling more closely to him, "I have not escaped you."

"You ran well," he said. "And you are bold. It took boldness, indeed, to hide, unbidden, in the furs of your very master. For such boldness a slave girl might be much beaten."

"Yes, Master," I said.

"But I do not disparage boldness in a slave girl," said he. "A girl who is bold is likely to think of marvels of pleasure for her master which a more timid girl would not dare to even contemplate."

"Yes, Master," I said, frightened.

"Too," said he, "the nature of your flight, and your selection of a refuge, indicates high intelligence."

"Thank you, Master," I said.

I felt his hands on the side of my head.

"You are extremely intelligent," he said, adding, "for a woman, and a slave."

"Thank you, Master," I said. What a beast he was. And yet I sensed that my intelligence was indeed far less than his, and that of most of the Gorean men I had met. Gorean males are unusual in their strength, energy and intelligence.

Sometimes this angered me. Sometimes it pleased me.

I did not feel inferior to most Gorean women I had met, either slave or free. Their intelligence, it seemed to me, compared much more closely, statistically, to that of Earth females. Of my master's girls, I felt that only Eta was my superior.

"I like high intelligence in a slave girl," said my master.

"Thank you, Master," I said.

Then I cried out, and held to him, my lips parted, for he had touched me.

"You leap like a she-tarsk," he said.

I bit my lip.

"That is because you are intelligent," he said. "I suppose you did not know that," he said, "for you are of Earth."

I gasped, and could not speak, for the sensation which he was inducing in me.

"Intelligent bodies," he said, "are far more responsive. Your very intelligence makes you the more helplessly a slave."

I clutched him.

"It pleases me to own intelligent girls, such as you," he said. "Intelligent girls make excellent slaves," he observed.

"Perhaps, Master," I said.

"Do you doubt it?" he asked.

"No, Master!" I said. "No, Master!"

"Good," he said.

"Please, Master," I said. "I cannot resist you!"

"Be silent," he said.

"Yes, Master," I wept.

"It is more pleasurable to control and dominate them than stupid girls," he said. "They are more stimulating to own. They are greater prizes."

"Yes, Master," I said. "Yes, Master!"

"Too," said he, "one profits more from their ownership than from that of a duller girl. They are brighter, more skillful, more imaginative, more inventive. An intelligent girl can do many more things and do them better than a duller girl. She follows commands easily; she learns swiftly. Her performances, in their variety, intricacy and depth, can approach brilliance. She learns well, and continues to learn, in her intelligence and sexuality, how to please a man. Too, in her depths of emotion, feeling and sensation, these associated with her intelligence, she is easier to manipulate and exploit."

"Please, Master," I begged, "take me!"

"Remain immobile," he said. "Do not move so much as a muscle."

I gritted my teeth. "Yes, Master," I whispered. Every bit of me wanted to cry out and explode. I held myself absolutely rigid. I wanted to explode. I was not permitted to move.

"Too," said he, "an intelligent girl, a highly intelligent one, such as yourself, is capable of truly understanding her slavery. A dull girl has no true insight into the bondage relation. She knows she is a slave.

She recognizes the institution, and is cognizant of its legalities. She is familiar with chains, and has worn them; she sees the whip, and has felt it. But does she truly understand her slavery?"

"Forgive me, Master," I said, barely able to speak, "but any woman who is a slave truly understands her slavery."

"Is this true?" he asked.

"In the belly of her," I said, "any woman who is slave knows her slavery. It has naught to do with intelligence, but only with being a slave and a woman. It is an indescribable, helpless feeling in the belly of us, being owned. One need not be intelligent to have this emotion, nor to respond, nor to feel."

"Perhaps," he said.

I wanted to scream. "Please, Master," I said.

"Do not move," said he.

"Yes, Master," I said, obeying.

I held myself rigid. Could the peasant boys have been more cruel?

"You do not think," he asked, "that the dull woman confuses slavery with the chains and the whip?"

"No, Master," I said. I moaned in helplessness. "I am not now chained," I said. "I am not now being whipped. But I could not be more a slave than now if I were chained to a whipping post and the lash being laid upon me. I am owned. I am completely in your power. I dare not even move. I must obey. This could be understood by any woman in my place."

"But perhaps," said he, musing, "your understanding of your slavery, in virtue of your intelligence, your sensitivity, is much more intense, much deeper and richer than would be that of a duller woman?"

"Perhaps, Master," I said. "I do not know!"

"Do you wish to be permitted to move?" he asked.

"Yes," I wept. "Yes! Yes!"

"But you are not yet permitted to move," he said.

"Yes, Master," I sobbed.

"It is pleasant to own a beautiful Earth woman such as you," he said.

"Yes, Master," I said.

"To whom do you belong?" he asked.

"To you! To you, Master!" I said.

"But you are of Earth," he said. "How can you belong to a man?"

"I belong to you, to you, Master!" I said.

"In the past weeks," he said, "you have begun to disturb me."

"Master?" I asked.

"Do not move," he said.

"No, Master," I sobbed.

"I do not understand it," he said. "It is very strange. Today I grew angry with you, and you had merely behaved as a slave."

He referred to my yielding to the soldier in the morning.

"I am a slave, Master," I said. "I could not help myself."

"I know," he said. "Why then should I be angry?"

"I do not know, Master," I said.

He then touched me, and I cried out.

"Do not move," he said.

"Have mercy on your girl, Master!" I begged.

With his touch he had again brought my sensations to the point at which I wanted to shatter and writhe and scream, and yet I must remain at his side, immobile, absolutely motionless.

"You are not important," he said.

"No, Master," I said.

"You are a worthless slave girl," he said.

"Yes, Master," I said.

"You can be bought or sold in any market," he said, "for a handful of copper tarsks."

"Yes, Master," I said.

"Why then," he asked, "do I concern myself with you?"

"I do not know, Master," I said.

"You may move, Slave Girl," he said.

With a wanton cry I pressed myself against him.

"You see," he said, "the women of Earth are natural slaves."

"Yes, Master," I wept.

"You are obviously only a common girl," he said.

"Yes, Master!" I cried softly.

I began to lick at him beneath the chin and kiss him. I clutched at him. I wept and laughed and writhed, holding him.

"Only a common girl," he said. "Only a common slave."

I put my tear-stained cheek against the hardness of his chest, holding him. I could feel the hair on his chest between his body and the softness of my cheek. "Yes, Master," I whispered.

"You do not even have a name," he said.

"No, Master," I said.

"Of what importance is a nameless animal?" he asked.

"None, Master," I said.

"How can you be of interest?" he asked.

"I do not know, Master," I said.

"And yet you are a pretty little animal," he said.

"Thank you, Master," I said.

"I shall conquer you," he said.

"You have conquered me long ago," I said.

"I shall conquer you anew," he said.

"Every time you look upon me, or touch me," I said, "I am conquered anew." I felt his chest beneath my cheek. I held him in the darkness. "I am your conquest, fully and completely, Master," I said. "I am your slave."

"Perhaps my slave should have a name," he said.

"As Master wills," I said.

He took me by the shoulders and lifted and turned me. He put me beneath him. I felt the furs and the ground beneath my back. I felt his arms about me. I moaned as my body received and clasped him.

"Do not move," he said.

"Yes, Master," I said. I wanted to yield.

"I shall name you," he said.

I lay in the darkness, helpless, imprisoned in the strength of his arms, waiting to learn whom I would be.

"The name," he said, "for you are a common girl, and worthless, should be an unimportant name, one plain and simple, one fitting for a valueless girl, an ignorant, branded she-slave such as you."

"Yes, Master," I said.

"You are even a barbarian," he said.

"Yes, Master," I said.

"Some men," he said, "enjoy putting a barbarian girl through her paces."

"Put me through my paces, I beg of you, Master!" I wept.

"Do not move," he cautioned.

"Yes, Master," I wept. I so wanted to yield to him. I was on the brink of yielding, but he would not let me move. It was as though I wanted to burst.

"I myself," he smiled, "enjoy putting any girl, civilized or barbarian, through her paces."

"Yes, Master," I said.

"Did you know," he asked, "that in the throes of slave orgasm there is no difference between a civilized and barbarian girl?"

"No, Master," I said.

"It is interesting," he said. "In slave orgasm they are spasmodically identical."

"We are all women, only women," I said, "in the arms of our masters."

"Doubtless that is it," he mused.

"Permit me to yield!" I begged.

"Do not move," he said.

"Yes, Master," I said, through gritted teeth. I was so much his! Why would he not have me?

"You speak Gorean with an accent," he said.

"Yes, Master," I said. "Forgive me, Master," I begged.

"Do not change," he said. "The accent becomes you. It marks you as different and makes you more interesting."

"Perhaps that is what Master finds interesting about his girl," I said.

"Perhaps," he said. "But I have owned barbarian girls before."

"Other girls from the planet Earth?" I whispered.

"Of course," he said. "Do not move."

"No, Master," I said. Suddenly I resented and hated those other girls from the bottom of my heart. How angry and jealous I was!

"The little slave is angry," he said. "Do not move."

"No, Master," I said.

I lay in the darkness, in his arms, trying not to move.

"What became of the Earth girls whom you owned before me, Master?" I asked.

"Was a slave given permission to speak?" he asked.

"Forgive me, Master," I said. "May a slave speak?"

"Yes," he said.

"You owned other Earth girls," I said. "Where are they?"

"I do not know," he said.

"What did you do with them?" I asked.

"I have had five such women, not including yourself, my dear," he said. "I gave two away, and sold off three."

"*Gave?*" I asked, aghast. "*Sold?*"

"Yes," he said.

"But they were persons," I said.

"No," he said. "They were slaves, like you."

"Are you going to sell me, or give me away?" I asked.

"Perhaps," he said.

I moaned. He could do what he wished, of course.

"Did they love you?" I asked.

"I do not know," he said. "Perhaps. Perhaps, not."

"Did they protest their love to you?" I asked.

"Of course," he said. "That sort of thing is common among slave girls."

"And yet you gave them away, or sold them?"

"Yes."

"How could you do that, Master?" I asked.

"They were only slaves," he said in explanation.

I uttered a cry of anguish. I could be discarded as easily. "You were cruel," I said, "Master."

"How can one be cruel to a slave?" he asked.

"Yes," I said. "How can one be cruel to a slave?"

"You're crying," he said.

"Forgive me, Master," I said.

We lay together in the darkness, I not permitted to move. I heard the peasant boys finishing with my sisters in bondage. Afterwards they would be put in slave hobbles.

"What was your barbarian name?" he asked.

"Judy Thornton," I said, "Master."

"How came you into my possession?" he asked.

"You won me in challenge, Master," I said. "Then you made me your slave."

"Ah, yes," he said. What a beast he was, me so naked, so helpless in his arms.

"Barbarians have such complicated names," he said.

"It is two names, Master," I said. "My first name was Judy, my second name was Thornton."

"Barbarous," he said.

"Yes, Master," I said.

"I do not like those names," he said. "Therefore they will not be yours."

"Yes, Master," I said. I supposed such names did sound unfamiliar, and barbarous, to a Gorean ear.

"What was the name of your barbarian master?" he asked.

"I do not understand, Master," I stammered.

"The barbarian who owned you on Earth," he said. "Perhaps we can use his name."

"But I was not owned on Earth, Master," I said. "I was a free woman."

"Women such as you are permitted to be free on Earth?" he asked.

"Yes, Master," I said.

"Of what sort are the men of Earth?" he asked.

"Of a sort other than Gorean, Master," I said.

"I see," he said. "Are the men happy?" he asked.

"No," I told him.

"Are the women happy?" he asked.

"No," I told him.

"I see," he said.

"Do the men of Earth not find you beautiful and desirable?" he asked.

"They have been weakened," I told him. "I did not know what it was to be desired until I came to this world." I clutched him. "It is only in the arms of true men, such as you, Master," I said, "that I have learned what it is to be a woman."

"You may move," he said.

With a cry I began to respond spasmodically to him.

"Stop," he said.

"Master!" I cried.

"Do not move," he said.

I wept with misery. How cruel could he be. "Yes, Master!" I wept.

He had raised me to the point at which another instant's movement would have precipitated that most incredible and fantastic of sexual experiences to which a human female can attain, that in which she knows herself cognitively and physiologically submitted, fully and completely, absolutely, to a master, the psychological and somatic raptures of submission spasm, the slave orgasm.

"I must drive you from my mind," he said.

I moaned.

"What is your brand?" he asked.

"The Slave Flower, the Dina!" I cried. "The name," he had said, "for you are a common girl, and worthless, should be an unimportant name, one plain and simple, one fitting for a valueless girl, an ignorant, branded she-slave such as you."

"The Dina!" I cried. "The Dina!"

He had begun to have me.

"Permit me to yield! Permit me to yield, Master!" I cried.

"No," he said.

I cried out with misery. I tried to hold myself immobile.

"You are going to be named," he said.

I could not even speak.

I was the only Dina among his girls. It was a common brand. Often girls who wore it were called Dina. For a low, common girl, one not to be distinguished from others, it was a suitable name. It was unimportant. It was simple. It was plain. I was common, and of little value. The name, too, was common, and of little value. It was thus not unfitting for a girl such as I, not unfitting for an ignorant, branded she-slave such as myself.

"You will not forget your name," he said.

"No, Master!" I said. I knew how he would impress my name upon me.

He had told me that I was without value, that I was worthless. I knew I could be bought and sold for a handful of copper tarsks.

I knew what he would name me.

He did not cease to have me.

At length I cried out, agonized. "I must yield, Master! I cannot help myself! I cannot help myself but yield to you!"

"Must you yield," he asked, "even though it might mean your death?"

"Yes, Master!" I cried.

"Then yield, Slave," said he.

With a cry I yielded to him.

"You are Dina," he said, laughing, his voice like a lion. "You are the slave Dina, whom I own." He laughed and cried out with pleasure in his triumph over the slave girl. "Yes, Master!" I cried. "I am Dina! I am Dina!" I clutched him, joyously, his. "Dina loves Master!" I wept. "Dina loves Master!"

* * * *

Later I lay in his arms, an owned slave girl, content beside the mightiness of her master.

How I loved him!

"Strange," he said, looking up at the Gorean stars.

"Master?" I asked.

"You are obviously only a common girl," he said.

"Yes, Master," I said. I began to kiss him gently about the shoulder.

"Only a common girl," he said.

It was true. He was Clitus Vitellius, a Captain, of the city of Ar. I was only Dina.

"Yes, Master," I said.

"I fear that I might begin to care for you," he said.

"If Dina has found favor with her master," I said, "she is pleased."

"I must fight this weakness," he said.

"Whip me," I said.

"No," he said.

"It is not you who are weak, Master," I said. "It is I, Dina, in your arms, who am without strength." I kissed him.

"I am a captain," he said. "I must be strong."

"I am a slave girl," I said. "I must be weak."

"I must be strong," he said.

"You did not seem weak to me, Master," I said, "when you laughed, and took me, and named me Dina. Then you seemed magnificent in your power and pride."

"It was only the conquest of a slave girl," he said.

"Yes, Master," I said, "I am your conquest." It was true. Dina, the Earth girl, she who had once been Judy Thornton, a lovely college student and poetess, was now the enslaved love conquest of Clitus Vitellius of Ar.

"You trouble me," he said, angrily.

"Forgive me, Master," I said.

"I should rid myself of you," he said.

"Permit me to follow at the heels of the least of your soldiers," I said. I truly did not fear that he would rid himself of me. I loved him. I was confident that he, too, in spite of himself, cared for me.

"Master," I said.

"Yes," he said.

"Has Dina pleased you this night?" I asked.

"Yes," he said.

"I want your collar," I said.

There was a long silence. Then he said, "You are an Earth girl. Yet you beg to wear a collar?"

"Yes, Master," I said.

It is said, in a Gorean proverb, that a man, in his heart, desires freedom, and that a woman, in her belly, yearns for love. The collar, in its way, answers both needs. The man is most free, owning the slave. He may do what he wishes with her. The woman, on the other hand, being owned, is institutionally and helplessly subject, in her status as slave, to the submissions of love.

I sensed my master feared his feelings for me. This gave me power over him.

"Dina wants Master's collar," I whispered, kissing at him. The collar would make me the equal of Eta.

"I decide what slaves will wear my collar," he said.

"Yes, Master," I said, chastened. If he saw fit to put me in his collar, he would; if he did not, he would not.

"Does Dina love her master?" he asked.

"Yes, yes, Master!" I whispered. I so loved him!

"Have I given you choice in this?" he asked.

"No, Master," I said. "You have made me love you, helplessly and wholly."

"Your feelings, then," he asked, "have been fully engaged, and you are now mine, at my complete mercy, fully and vulnerably, with no shred of pride or dignity left?"

"Yes, Master," I whispered.

"You acknowledge yourself then hopelessly in love with me, and as a slave girl?"

"Yes, Master," I said.

"Amusing," he said.

"Master?" I asked.

"I, and the men, and other girls," he said, "will leave Tabuk's Ford in the morning. You will remain behind. I am giving you to Thurnus."

Eight

A Girl's Will Means Nothing

I fled for the cage. I must reach it!

I threw myself into the cage on my hands and knees. I turned wildly and seized the bar and flung it down behind me. The snout of the beast thrust viciously part way between the bars. It snarled, and squealed and hissed. I shrank back in the tiny cage. On the other side of the bars of the vertically sliding, lowered gate the blazing eyes of the sleen regarded me. I cried out with misery. Had I run more slowly it would have caught me and torn me to pieces. It turned its head and, with its double row of white fangs, bit at the bars. I heard the scraping of the teeth on the bars; it pulled the cage, moving it, until it caught against the chain and stake which anchored it. Then it moved about the cage on its six legs, its long, furred body angrily rubbing against the bars. It tried to reach me from another side. I knelt head down, shuddering, my hands over my head, in the center of the tiny cage. Once its snout thrust against me, and I whimpered. I smelled its breath, felt the heat of it on my flesh. The bars were wet where it had bit at them; the ground, too, about the cage was wet where the beast's saliva, in its frenzy, its lust for killing, had dampened the clawed dust.

"Back," called Thurnus, coming to the sleen and putting a rope on its neck, dragging it away from the cage. "Gentle! Gentle, Fierce One!" coaxed Thurnus. He thrust his head near the large, brown snout, cooing and clicking, his hands in the rope on its throat. He whispered in its ear. The beast became pacified. Thurnus took a great piece of meat and threw it to the animal, which began to devour it.

"Excellent," said Clitus Vitellius.

I knelt in the slave cage, my hands on its bars.

I had locked myself in the slave cage. When I had flung down the vertically sliding gate behind me, two notched projections, bolts, welded to the flat bar at the gate's bottom had slipped into iron-enclosed spring catches, heavy locks, one on the bottom left, one on the bottle right, the gate being thus secured. I could not open these locks. They responded to a key, slung on the string about the neck of Thurnus. It is necessary to engage the locks not only because the animal follows so closely and the gate must be swiftly lowered, but because if the locks are not engaged, it will thrust its snout beneath the bottom of the gate, between the bottom of the gate and the floor of the cage, and, throwing its head up, fling up the gate, and have access to the cage's occupant. The girl's choices are simple. Either she locks herself in the cage, imprisoning herself helplessly at the pleasure of the cage owner, or the animal destroys her.

I, frightened, watched the sleen tear at the meat.

I knelt in the cage, my fists, white-knuckled, clenched on the bars. The cage is tiny, but stout. I could kneel in it, or crouch, or sit, with my legs drawn up. I could not extend my body, nor stand upright. The roof of the cage was about the height of a man's belt. It is so constructed that it can be linked with other cages, or tiered. Though there is a wooden floor to the cage, the wood is placed over bars. The entire cage, thus, is barred. The bars, and their fastenings, were heavy. The cage in which I had locked myself would hold not only a girl; it would also have easily and efficiently held a strong man. It was, accordingly, an all-purpose slave cage.

I looked up through the bars. Clitus Vitellius did not look at me. Already I had been given to Thurnus.

Thurnus, of Tabuk's Ford, was now my master. I belonged to him. I was now his girl, his slave.

At a word I had changed hands.

It may be so simply done with a slave.

The cage was in a sleen training pit, surrounded by a low, wooden wall and floored with sand. Within the walls were several individuals, my sisters in bondage, those still the property of Clitus Vitellius, one of whom was encaged like myself, Chanda, who was sitting in her cage, wrapping a cloth about her bleeding leg; Thurnus; another of his girls, Sandal Thong; some men assisting Thurnus; and Clitus Vitellius, and some of his men. Within the ring, too, were some eight sleen, tied on short tethers to stakes, at the sides; and a rack of meats, and poles, and ropes and whips, used in the training of the animals. Outside the low walls, several individuals observed the proceedings, the balance of the men of Clitus Vitellius, some villagers, including some peasant boys, and Melina, veiled, the slack, fat companion of the huge Thurnus.

Melina regarded me. I did not meet her eyes, but looked down, into the dust.

I was a pretty slave girl who had been given to her companion. I did not care to meet her eyes. I hoped she would not be cruel to me. But she was of the peasants, and I was only a slave.

I looked across the sand to Chanda. She, too, was locked in a tiny cage. She sat on the boards, hunched over, her legs drawn up, and slowly wrapped a piece of white cloth about her bleeding calf. The blood stained through the cloth. The bit of a garment that she wore had also been torn by the beast who had pursued her. It, too, afterward had been fed. When it had been fed, it had been tethered with the others. The men discussed the animals, and their merits.

I held the bars and, head down, eyes closed, pressed my forehead against the bars. What hope had a girl for escape on a world which contained sleen?

I and Chanda had been used for purposes of demonstration.

Sleen had been dragged to us, to take our scent. We had been held by men while the animals had taken our scent. Then Chanda had been released.

She had been run first. Then I had been released. I had been run shortly after her.

I had run wildly, in misery over having been given away by Clitus Vitellius. I had fully determined, in my hysteria and misery, to escape. What a foolish slave I was!

I had run wildly. I had almost fainted when a brown, sinuous shape sped past me.

I saw it turn Chanda, and, snarling, begin its attack. She fled back toward the training pit. I saw her stumble once, and the beast seize her leg, and she screamed, and then she was again on her feet, running, her hands extended before her. The girl either permits herself to be herded expeditiously, swiftly, or she dies. I turned to flee. I screamed. It was there, in front of me. It lifted its head. I stumbled back, my hand flung before my face. It snarled hideously. Distracted by the first sleen, that in pursuit of Chanda, I had not even seen this sleen, whose brain was alive with my scent, circle me and approach.

"No! No!" I cried. "Go away! Please, go away!"

It crouched there, not five feet from me, its head lifted, hissing, snarling.

"Please, go away!" I wept.

I saw its belly lower itself to the ground, the head still lifted, watching me. Its tail lashed; its eyes blazed. It inched forward. It had two rows of fangs.

I looked to the left and right. It squealed hideously. It came closer.

It was a precisely trained beast, but no training is perfect. It is a balancing of instincts and conditioning. It is never perfect. The beast, at the nearness and intensity of my scent, was becoming uncontrollable. The critical attacking distance for a sleen in the wild is about twenty feet. This distance, in a herd sleen, of course, is much smaller. I could see its excitement mount. The fur about its neck rippled and bristled. Then I saw it gather its four hind legs beneath it.

With a cry of misery I turned and fled. I ran back toward the training pit and the open cage that had been designated for occupancy by the Earth-girl slave.

I ran wildly, helplessly. It ran behind me, snapping and snarling. I felt its breath on my legs. It cut with its teeth at my heels. I gasped. I fought for breath. It drove me faster and faster.

The beast was well trained. It knew well how to herd a slave girl. Doubtless, in its training, and perhaps otherwise, it had herded many girls. I ran before it, in terror, madly, helplessly. I feared I might fall, I feared I might be unable to go on, that I might collapse!

I was mad with terror!

It kept me mercilessly at my limits, not permitting me to think, but only to run, frenziedly, madly, a driven, frightened, herded animal, seeking her cage.

I was at its mercy. It set me the pace which I must make, if I would live.

She who had been Judy Thornton, of Earth, a student, a poetess, had now been much diminished, much reduced.

What was she now?

She was now no more than a running, terrified, herded animal!

I cried out with misery, running.

I was being herded!

It drove me perfectly.

My only hope of survival was to reach the cage, and lock myself within it, where I would await, confined, a lovely animal, the pleasure of a master.

I threw myself into the cage on my hands and knees and, wildly, turned and flung down the gate behind me, it securely locking. The beast tried to reach me, but could not do so. I was safe within the cage, but locked within it, at the mercy of a master. I had been herded.

What hope had a girl for escape on a world which contained sleen? How completely we belonged to our masters!

There are many varieties of sleen, and most varieties can be, to one extent or another, domesticated. The two most common sorts of trained sleen are the smaller, tawny prairie sleen, and the large, brown or black forest sleen, sometimes attaining a length of twenty feet. In the north, I am told the snow sleen has been domesticated. The sleen is a dangerous and fairly common animal on Gor, which has adapted itself to a variety of environments. There is even an aquatic variety, called the sea sleen, which is one of the swiftest and most dreaded beasts in the sea. Sea sleen are found commonly in northern waters. They are common off the coast of Torvaldsland, and further north.

In the wild, the sleen is a burrowing, predominantly nocturnal animal. It is carnivorous. It is a tenacious hunter, and an indefatigable tracker. It will attack almost anything, but its preferred prey is tabuk. It mates once a year in the Gorean spring, and there are usually four young in each litter. The gestation period is some six months. The young are commonly white furred at birth, the fur darkening by the following spring. Snow sleen, however, remain white-pelted throughout their life.

Most domestic sleen are bred. It is difficult to take and tame a wild sleen. Sometimes young sleen, following the killing of the mother, are dug out of a burrow and raised. If they can be taken within the first two months of their life, which seems to be a critical period, before they have tasted blood and meat in the wild, and made their own kills, there is apparently a reasonably good chance that they can be domesticated; otherwise, generally not. Although grown, wild sleen have been caught and domesticated, this is rare. Even a sleen which has been taken young may revert. These reversions can be extremely dangerous. They usually take place, as would be expected, in the spring, during the mating season. Male sleen, in particular, can be extremely restless and vicious during this period. The mating of sleen is interesting. The female, if never before mated, flees and fights the male. But he is larger and stronger. At last he takes her by the throat and throws her upon her back, interestingly, belly to belly, beneath him. His fangs are upon her throat. She is at his mercy. She becomes docile and permits her penetration. Shortly, thereafter, their heat growing, they begin, locked together by legs and teeth, to roll and squeal in their mating frenzy. It is a very fierce and marvelous spectacle. It is not unusual for slave girls, seeing this, to kneel at their master's feet and beg their caress. After the female sleen has been taken thusly once, no longer need she be forced. She follows the male, often rubbing against him, and hunts with him. Sometimes she must be driven away with snarls and bites. Sleen, interestingly, often pair for life. Their rutting, however, is usually confined to the spring. Sometimes slave girls are called she-sleen, but I do not think this expression is completely apt. Sexual congress in the human is not confined to a particular season. We are not she-sleen. The heat of the she-sleen occurs in the spring. We are slave girls. Our masters keep us in heat constantly.

I looked across the sand to Chanda's cage. She had finished wrapping the cloth about her cut calf.

I hoped the wound was not deep. No one seemed to be concerned about her. I gathered that her leg would not be scarred, and that her value would not be lowered. If her leg did scar, with the result that her block value was diminished, it must be recalled that Clitus Vitellius, my former master, had had her for nothing.

Sleen are used for a multitude of purposes on Gor, but most commonly they are used for herding, tracking, guarding and patrolling. The verr and the bosk are the most common animals herded; tabuk and slave girls are the most common animals tracked; the uses to which the sleen is put in guarding and patrolling are innumerable; it is used to secure borders, to prowl walls and protect camps; it may run loose in the streets after curfews; it may lurk in the halls of a great house after dark; it may deter thieves from entering locked shops; it may stand sentry upon wharves and in warehouses; there are many such uses to which the sinuous beasts may be put; an interesting use which might be mentioned is prisoner control; a tiny circle is drawn and the prisoner must kneel, or assume some prescribed position, within it; then, should the prisoner attempt to rise to his feet, leave the circle, or break the position in the slightest, the beast tears him to pieces. Aside from these common uses, sleen are put to other uses, too. In Thentis, for example, sleen are used to smell out contraband, in the form of the unauthorized egress of the beans for black wine from the Thentian territories. They are sometimes, too, used by assassins, though the caste of assassins itself, by their caste codes, precludes their usage; the member of the caste of assassins must make his own kill; it is in their codes. Some sleen are used as bodyguards; others are trained to kill in the arena; others perform in exhibitions and carnivals. There are many uses to which such animals are put. The herding, tracking and control of beautiful slave girls is but one use.

The gate to my cage was unlocked, and flung upward. The sleen outside had been fed and taken, by the men assisting Thurnus, on short ropes, to their cages. The men of Clitus Vitellius had left the sand pit, and the area about it, accompanied by his girls, including Chanda, who, too, had been released. The small crowd which had observed had now dissipated, with the exception of Melina, companion of Thurnus, and two or three peasant boys, who watched me. Sandal Thong, one of the girls of Thurnus, who had assisted in the training pit, had left, too, now, to attend to other duties, including the watering of the sleen. She wore a short slave tunic, white, of the wool of the Hurt, and a rope collar. She was a large, long-armed, freckled girl, of peasant stock. Clitus Vitellius, in the tunic of the warrior, remained in the training pit, to accompany Thurnus back to his hut.

Thurnus tapped on the bars of the cage with a sleen whip. "Come out, little slave," he said.

On my hands and knees I emerged from the cage, head down, crawling out onto the hot sand. It was the first time I had ever been caged. Without thinking I began to rise to my feet. The butt of the sleen whip struck me heavily, driven downward, between the shoulder blades, felling me. I lay in the hot sand, startled. I hurt. I could feel the warm sand, granular, between my fingers, on my thighs. "Master?" I asked, frightened. How had I displeased him?

"Were you given permission to rise, Slave?" he asked.

"No, Master," I said, frightened. "Forgive me." It is common on Gor for a girl emerging from a small cage, on her belly, or her hands and knees, depending on the size of the opening, at the feet of her master to remain, pending her master's instructions, on her belly or hands and knees. I did not know it at the time. I had never been caged before.

I, lying in the sand, was conscious of their feet about me. I did not want to be beaten.

"She is a pretty little thing, is she not?" asked Thurnus. I supposed I did look beautiful, a slave girl, lying at their feet in the warm sand.

"I am pleased that you like her," said Clitus Vitellius.

"I am grateful for the gift," said Thurnus.

"It is nothing," said Clitus Vitellius. "She is only a trifle."

"But a lovely trifle," said Thurnus.

"Perhaps," granted Clitus Vitellius.

"On your hands and knees, Girl," said Thurnus.

I rose to my hands and knees. I felt a length of sleen rope tied on my neck. The other end of the rope was looped several times and the loops loosely knotted about a bar of the sleen cage. The resulting tether was about a foot long.

"Look up at me, Girl," said Thurnus.

I looked up at him.

"You attempted to escape," he said.

"I had no chance to escape, Master," I said. "A sleen was set upon me."

"It is true," said he, "that you had no chance for escape. But you, ignorant girl, did not know that."

I was silent, frightened.

"Did you try to escape?" he asked.

I had tried to escape. "Yes, Master," I whispered.

"Sit with your back against the cage, legs drawn up," he said. I did so, my neck roped to one of the bars. He crouched down, near me.

He drew out a sleen knife.

He felt the back of my legs, with his left hand.

"Pretty legs," he said.

"Thank you, Master," I said.

"Do you know what these muscles are?" he asked, touching the twin cords behind my right knee.

"Tendons, Master," I said.

"Do you know what they are for?" he asked.

"They control the movement of my leg," I said. "Without them I could not walk."

I felt the blade touch the left tendon behind my right knee. If Thurnus were to draw the blade toward him, the tendon would be severed.

He replaced the sleen knife in its sheath.

Then he struck me twice, once striking my head to the right, and, then, with the back of his hand, lashing it to the left.

"That," said Thurnus, "is for having tried to escape."

"Yes, Master," I said.

He then took my legs, drawn up, in his hands, pressing with his thumbs against the inner tendons behind both the left and right knee.

I shrank back, miserable, my head to one side, against the bars.

"Remember, small, luscious, beauty," he said.

I looked at him with horror. "Yes, Master," I said. The memory of the sleen knife was vivid in my mind.

He removed his hands from my legs and I shuddered, uncontrollably.

How foolish I had been!

Had I thought, truly, I might escape? Did I not know that there was no escape for the Gorean slave girl? How merciful Thurnus, my master, had been! He had not hamstrung me, or thrown me as feed to his sleen! He had only struck me, and only twice! I remembered the sleen knife. I did not think he would be so merciful a second time.

I was grateful to my master.

"On your hands and knees, Girl," said Thurnus.

I went to my hands and knees, and he unknotted the loops of sleen rope from the bar of the cage, and threw it loose beside me, in the sand, whence it rose to the bond on my neck.

"Look up at me, Girl," he said.

I looked up at him, the rope on my neck.

"Go to the hut," he said.

"Yes, Master," I said.

They then turned away from me, Thurnus and Clitus Vitellius. "I must leave before noon," Clitus Vitellius was saying. "There are four sleen in which I am interested."

"Let us discuss the matter," Thurnus was saying.

They left the training pit. On my hands and knees, miserable, in the hot sand, the rope on my neck, I looked about the training pit, at the rack of whips and ropes, the sleen tethers, the cages, the wooden barrier about the training area, and then, on my hands and knees, made my way through the sand and out of the training area toward the hut of Thurnus, the rope dragging behind me.

The sun was hot, the sand was hot.

I feared the sleen. They terrified me.

I feared the other slaves, as well, the village slaves. I had seen them about, large, strapping girls, probably of the peasants, doubtless purchased for the performance of hard labor, in their rough, white tunics, with their rope collars. I did not think that I would well fit in with them. I was smaller, weaker, more delicate, sensitive. I was afraid of them, and I did not think they would care much for me. I did not doubt but what they would be cruel to me. And masters, I knew, tended to take little notice of the altercations, or squabbles, of slaves.

And I did not want to be locked up at night, with those other slaves, at their mercy, in a more-than-half-sunken, barred kennel. That is not like lying lovingly in an ankle ring, or collar, at the foot of a beloved master's couch. And what could one hope for? Perhaps at best to be slept at night in a hut, shackled, hand and foot, on a coarse mat?

Surely I did not belong in a peasant village! I was not that sort of slave! Surely I was more the sort who should be an urban slave, lovely in a silken tunic, attracting the attention of strangers in the streets, one perhaps even permitted sandals. Might I not bring a high price in a market?

Too, I had little doubt that if I were so foolish as to attempt escape a second time I would be maimed, if not worse.

No girl could expect a master to be patience with her twice.

There were many fields, too, about the village. They would have to be tended. The days would be long, and the work hard.

How could they expect me to work like the larger, stronger girls? Would I not be overcome with heat and exhaustion in the fields? And would I then be lashed, or worse, for malingering?

I continued toward the hut of Thurnus, my master, on my hands and knees. I, his girl, had not been given permission to rise.

I had begun to understand what it would be to be the girl of a peasant. In the street of the village, I stopped. Feet stood before me. I looked up, miserable, in the dust, the rope hanging from my neck. It was two peasant boys.

"What slave is this?" asked one. He was Bran Loort, leader of the peasant boys, a rugged youth verging into his manhood. He had in him, said some, the makings of a caste leader.

"It is the clever, beautiful slave who eluded us last night in our sport," said his fellow.

"So it is," acknowledged Bran Loort.

"It is said," said the one, "she has been given to Thurnus."

"Then," said Bran Loort, "she will be in the village."

"It seems so," said the other.

"Please, Masters," I said, "do not detain me."

"Let us not detain her," said Bran Loort. They stepped aside, as though I might have been a free woman. Dragging the rope on my neck, on my hands and knees, through the dust of the hot, sunny street, I crawled past them.

How far from me then seemed Judy Thornton, the lovely coed.

I thought of the college boys whom I had despised or tolerated, with whom I had been so haughty. How they would have laughed to have seen me now, on a world where there were true men.

How pleased they would have been to have seen me—*on Gor*!

In the vicinity of Thurnus's hut, at the side of one of the wagons taken in the raid on the camp of the Lady Sabina, being loaded with supplies and gear, was Clitus Vitellius.

I seized at his knees, weeping. "Keep me. Keep me, Master," I begged.

He looked down at me. It was shortly before noon.

I looked up at him, tears in my eyes. "I love you, Master," I wept.

"She does not want to be a peasant's girl," laughed one of the men.

"I love you, Master," I said.

Clitus Vitellius took the rope from the ground, which hung from my throat. He held the rope.

"She does not want to be left in Tabuk's Ford," said one of the men.

"Who can blame her?" asked another.

I looked up at Clitus Vitellius, my hands about his knees, tears in my eyes. He held the rope which was on my neck. "I am your conquered slave," I wept. "Please take me with you."

He put his foot on the rope, pressing it to the ground. Then, beneath his foot, he drew the rope to him. My head was dragged from his knees to the dust at his feet.

I lay before him, helpless.

"You are a slave girl in the village of Tabuk's Ford," he said. Then he threw the rope to the ground and turned away from me.

I scratched in the dust and wept, beside the wheel of the wagon.

Nine

Rain

I cut at the soil with the hoe, chopping and loosening the dirt about the roots of the sul plant.

The sun was high overhead. It was hot. There was a peasant's kerchief on my head.

I worked in my master's fields. I was alone. I wore a peasant's tunic. It was white and sleeveless, of the wool of the Hurt. It came high on my thighs. Thurnus had shortened it. His companion, Melina, had taken the Ta-Teera from me and burned it. "Scandalous slave! Scandalous garment!" she had cried. She had then thrown me a peasant tunic, which had fallen to my knees. Thurnus, wanting to see more of my legs, to her anger, had shortened it with shears.

I straightened my body. My back hurt. I wiped my forehead with the back of my hand.

"You will learn toil, small beauty," he had said when I had knelt before him, among the pilings beneath his hut, my hands tied behind my back, my neck roped to one of the pilings.

I remembered the morning bitterly.

"I am going to Ar with the master," had said Marla, turning before me. "Now who is the most beautiful?" she asked.

"You, Marla," I had said.

"Farewell, Slave," she said, and left me.

I had knelt there beneath the hut of Thurnus, in the Ta-Teera, my hands tied behind my back, my neck roped to one of the pilings.

To another of the pilings four beautiful she-sleen were tethered. They were on short tethers. They were sleek, lovely animals. My master had purchased them. They could not reach me.

Clitus Vitellius and his men milled about.

"I shall miss you," said Eta, kissing me. "I wish you well, Slave," she said.

Lehna, Donna and Chanda came to me, and kissed me, and hugged me. "I wish you well, Slave," they said.

"I wish you well," I said.

Slave Beads stood to one side, looking at me.

"Will you not say farewell to your sister slave?" I asked.

She came to my side, and knelt down beside me. "Yes," she said, tears in her eyes. "We are all slaves," she said. She took me in her arms and kissed me. Slave Beads was no longer the Lady Sabina. She, too, now, was only a slave. "I wish you well, Slave," she said.

"I wish you well, too, Slave," I said to her.

"Coffle line!" snapped a guard.

Swiftly the girls fell into coffle line. I watched them. I wished I were with them.

Each beauty knew her place.

They did not dally forming the line. They did not wish to be whipped.

Marla led the line. What beautiful legs she had! The girls extended their left wrists, for the rings to be locked upon them. They stood straight, their eyes looking ahead, under discipline. Marla's right foot determined the line. Each girl, with the exception of Marla, the line's leader, aligned her right foot with that of the girl before her in the line. Sometimes a coffle line is drawn in the dirt and the right foot of each girl is placed on it vertically, such that the line bisects the ball and heel of each foot.

Clitus Vitellius did not so much as look at me.

The guard, who was the blond soldier, Mirus, whom I found most attractive of the men of Clitus Vitellius, after he himself, unlooped the coffle chain from his shoulder.

The girls stood erect, left arms extended, wrist straight with the arm, their left arms aligned, each at a forty degree angle from her body, right arms at their sides, palms on thighs, ankles closely together, bellies sucked in, chins up.

Marla's wrist was locked in the first wrist ring. She smiled. She was coffled. When the lock snapped on her wrist she placed her chained left wrist at her side, her palm on her left thigh, still looking ahead.

Lehna, who was very beautiful, was the next locked in the coffle. She placed her left wrist at her side, looking ahead.

There are a large variety of coffle arrangements, given mixtures and combinations of materials and bonds, and aesthetic, physical and psychological considerations. Coffle arrangements are seldom random. From the physical point of view, the most common coffles are left-wrist coffles, left-ankle coffles and throat coffles. Left-wrist coffles and throat coffles are useful trekking coffles. The left-ankle coffle and the throat coffle free the hands to carry burdens. Clitus Vitellius still had the wagons stolen from the camp of the Lady Sabina and so his girls did not have to carry the burdens of his camp. Such burdens are often carried by girls in ankle coffle or throat coffle, and are balanced on the head, usually steadied by the right hand.

Donna and Chanda were now added to the coffle. Their left hands, now locked in wrist-rings, lay against their left thighs.

There was another snap of a wrist ring and the chain bore yet another jewel, the lovely, half-stripped Slave Beads.

Last on the chain was Eta. The guard looked at her, and their eyes met, and then he put the chain on her.

I did not know why Eta was last on the chain. I knew the look in the eyes of the guard. He wanted her for his own slave. She looked frightened. He stood behind her for a moment, and she pressed back, putting her head back against his shoulder. Then he moved away from her.

There was a mark on the side of Eta's face, where she had been struck. Perhaps she had not been fully pleasing for an instant to one of the soldiers, or to Clitus Vitellius, and had thus been struck, and put at the rear of the chain. Perhaps she was at the rear of the chain because she was the most beautiful, and her beauty was being saved for last; thus the chain would have begun with the beautiful Marla and then, with a surprise, finished with a girl yet more beautiful than the first. But perhaps she was thought to be ugly for a day or two, until the blow healed, and thus, for ugliness, was put at the back of the line. Or, perhaps it was merely that the last wrist-ring had then been open, I being left in Tabuk's Ford, and thus there was no reason for her any longer to be excluded from the coffle. Thus, she would merely have been placed in the available wrist ring, in my place.

Sometimes masters punish us without explaining the reason. It is then for the slave girl to guess and wonder, and try harder to please. Sometimes, perhaps, there is no reason! We are so much at their mercy!

Beside my knee, in the dirt, there was a pan of water, and one of wet meal.

The last girl, Eta, was now coffled.

"Stand easily, Slaves," said the guard, and walked away.

Marla turned to face me. She lifted her chained left wrist. "I wear the chain of Clitus Vitellius," she said. "You wear the rope of a peasant."

"Yes, Mistress," I said.

She turned away from me.

The men were now hitching the bosk to the wagons taken from the camp of the Lady Sabina.

Two peasant boys stood nearby. They looked at me. I, kneeling, clad in the Ta-Teera, my hands tied behind my back, my neck roped to the piling beneath Thurnus's hut, regarded them.

"Greetings, Slave Girl," they said to me.

"Greetings, Masters," I said to them.

They turned away, grinning, and left the vicinity of the hut.

The first team of bosk was hitched up, two of the great animals, broad, shaggy, with polished horns.

Clitus Vitellius was talking with Thurnus.

"I, and the men, and other girls," he had said, "will leave Tabuk's Ford in the morning. You will remain behind. I am giving you to Thurnus."

I had cried out with misery and horror in his arms. "Master!" I had cried. He had then gagged me. He then tied my hands behind my back, and took me naked and stumbling from his furs. He found an ankle stock of heavy wood near the perimeter of his camp area. He put me on my back. The stock consisted of two heavy, oblong pieces of wood, each about four inches thick, joined together by hinged iron. He flung open the stock. He looked down at me. I half reared up, struggling, to a sitting position, my hands tied behind my back, my eyes wild over the gag. Our eyes met. He then, swiftly, brutally, used me, and I, miserable, helpless, my eyes hot with tears, again could not resist him, and, again, unable to help myself, responded to him, and responded as a slave. He laughed at me derisively and then, crouching beside me, threw my ankles into the stock and closed it, one of the two four-inch blocks of wood on each side of my ankles, and flung the hasp over the staple, which would hold the blocks shut. Then, with a drilled peg and a bit of binding fiber, attached to the stock, he, slipping the fiber through the staple and securing it to the peg, fastened the hasp down. This would hold a bound slave. If my hands had not been tied a padlock would have been used. Tied as I was I was the prisoner of the stock, its weight and constraint. I lay on the ground, twisting, moaning. It seemed my guts had been torn out. I looked up, miserable, at the stars.

Clitus Vitellius then left me, to return to his furs, to sleep.

I cut again at the soil with the hoe, chopping down, loosening the dirt about the roots of the sul plants.

The sun was terribly hot.

On my throat I wore a rope collar. My hands were terribly blistered. It was painful to hold the hoe. My back hurt me. It seemed every muscle in my body ached.

I wanted to throw myself down and weep, but the suls must be hoed.

"You will learn toil, small beauty," Thurnus had told me. I had well learned toil, and misery. It is not easy to be a peasant's girl. It is a hard slavery.

I remembered seeing Clitus Vitellius leave. He had not looked back. I had wanted to call out after him, but I had not dared. I did not wish to be whipped.

It is not easy to be a peasant's girl. It is a hard slavery.

I remembered the sting of the switch across the back of my thighs as Melina had driven me to the kennel.

"I will make you wish you wore a longer tunic, Slave!" she had cried.

I had dropped through the kennel door and, some feet below, struck the straw-strewn floor of the kennel. The kennel was a large cage, a large, altered sleen cage, tipped on its side, barred, sunk mostly into the ground. The cage in its original attitude, when used for sleen, would have been some four feet in height, six feet in width and twelve feet in length. Tipped on its side, to better accommodate humans, it was some six feet in height and four by twelve feet in breadth and length. In this attitude, its original gate replaced with bars, and a new gate fashioned for it, it was entered from the top. Within there was a wooden, round-runged ladder, for climbing out of it. It was sunk some four and a half feet in the ground. Wooden planks, covered with straw, lay over the bars on the bottom. These planks were separated by some two inches apiece, to facilitate drainage. The cage was roofed, too, with planks; these planks were set flush with one another; they were fastened over the top of the bars, including some, sawed, over the upward-opening, barred gate. The gate then resembled a wooden trap, with bars on the bottom. At night a tarpaulin was thrown over the cage roof. Standing in the cage one could look out, one's shoulders being approximately at ground level.

I dropped to the floor of the cage.

I heard the heavy barred gate at the top, over my head, with its attached planks, flung shut. It made a harsh sound of metal and wood. Then I heard the rattle of two heavy padlocks on chains. There were two heavy metal snaps as the door above me was fastened shut.

I looked up. I was locked within.

"Kneel," said a voice.

I knelt. There were four other girls in the cage.

"In the position of the pleasure slave," said one of them.

I complied.

"Let us see your brand," said another.

I turned to the side and drew back the tunic.

"A Dina," said another girl. There were four besides myself in the cage, Thurnus's other girls.

"Did you know," asked one, "that Dinas are suitable to be the slaves of slaves?"

"No," I said, "I did not."

"You were not given permission to cover your brand," said one, sharply.

I drew back my hand. I turned to face them, on my knees. I kept my knees spread, as I had been commanded to assume the position of the pleasure slave. That command had not been rescinded. Before men, of course, I would have knelt naturally in that position. It would not have needed to have been commanded of me. Indeed, I might have been lashed did I not assume it immediately, gracefully, attractively. I had learned what I was. They had left me in little doubt as to the sort of slave I was. Before free women, on the other hand, even a pleasure slave would have been likely to kneel in the position of the tower slave, or woman's slave, knees closed, unless ordered to do otherwise.

The other slaves sat in the cage, on the straw.

I looked at them. They were large, coarse girls, though perhaps not without their charms. Clearly they were field slaves, or kettle slaves, or work slaves.

"Are you a pleasure slave?" asked one, curious.

"Yes!" I said, brazenly.

"Oh?" said one of the girls.

"Men have so regarded me," I said.

"I can see why," said one. "You are a pretty, meaningless little slut."

"What is she good for?" asked another, "save to give pleasure to men?"

"Nothing," said another.

"It is not my fault," I said, "if men see me in terms of the pleasure I can give them."

"And you object?" asked one.

I was silent.

"She is silent!" laughed one of the girls.

"You like being a pleasure slut!" said another.

Again I was silent.

"Of course, she likes it," laughed another. "See her blush!"

"You lick and kiss, and whisper, and squirm well in the furs," said another.

"I am going to ask you a question," said the largest girl, Sandal Thong, who seemed to be first in the cage. "Think carefully before you answer. Do you understand?"

"Yes," I said.

"Yes, what?" asked Sandal Thong.

"Yes, Mistress," I said.

"Are you ready?" she asked.

"Yes, Mistress."

"Keep your knees spread," she said.

"Yes, Mistress," I said.

Reddening, I further widened my knees.

The other girls laughed.

"Think carefully," said Sandal Thong, menacingly. "Are you—*a pleasure slave?*"

I was afraid to answer, but, again, I was even more afraid to remain silent, or to dissemble.

There were four other slaves in the cage, and any one of them could have subdued, bound, and beaten me.

"Speak," said she.

What was I, truly?

All the misery and shame of Earth suddenly swept through me! How unworthy, how contemptible, how despicable, how terrible I was! The negativistic conditioning of a world, of years of pathological conditioning, swept through me, that I might, as intended, be a stranger to myself, that I might be trained to mindlessly, reflexively, behave in accordance with the prescriptions of the inert, the frigid, the ignorant, the unsuspecting, the vain, the ambitious, the manipulative, the biologically disinherited, the organically ill-constituted, that I might be trained to distrust and repudiate my most precious and profound instincts and needs, that I might be taught to fear, hate and loathe my deepest and dearest self, only that I might please those who neither respected me nor cared for me, those who held natural, loving women in contempt, and feared and hated them. And well might they fear and hate them, for such women, natural, loving women, by their very existence are a reproach to them, revealing their pathetic limitations, their linearities and inadequacies.

But surely I who had been Judy Thornton could not be a pleasure slave!

But was I a pleasure slave?

But if so, even then, surely I could not admit that I was so inconsequential and low a thing as that, a pleasure slave!

But even on Earth I had occasionally looked upon my body in the mirror and wondered on what sort of world it might find its meaning.

Then I had been brought to Gor, and had discovered that I was beautiful, truly beautiful, and that such as I might well belong to glorious, male beasts who would relish and treasure us, and master us!

Was I a pleasure slave? Could I be a pleasure slave?

I had been an excellent student at an elite girls' school, an English major, a poetess, and then, inexplicably, for no reason that I understood, I had been brought to Gor, and was soon introduced to my new life, that of a branded slave.

I became aware of men, true men, and their attractiveness, and might. I became aware of how I was seen by them, and the only way I, with my beauty and nature, could be seen by them.

I knew I wanted to love and serve them, and that only in this way could I find my true happiness and fulfillment.

I had been Judy Thornton.

I had tried, on Earth, honestly enough, to fulfill the stereotypes prescribed for me.

Had I not been a "good little girl" of Earth, though they would scarcely, the manipulators and would-be controllers, have used those words? I thought so.

Then I had been brought to Gor.

That had changed many things.

What had she here discovered herself to be, truly, the former Judy Thornton?

"Well?" pressed my interrogator.

Was I a pleasure slave?

Yes, yes, I who had been Judy Thornton was a pleasure slave! Moreover I now realized I had always, even on Earth, though latently, and unfulfilled, been a pleasure slave!

On Gor I had learned myself. On Gor I had found myself!

I was a pleasure slave!

"Speak!" said Sandal Thong.

"Yes!" I said, suddenly, shamelessly, defiantly. "Yes, Mistress! I am a pleasure slave! It is not only what I want to be, but what I am! Yes, Mistress, it is what I am. I am a pleasure slave, a pleasure slave! I should be purchased as such, and sold as such! It is what I am—a pleasure slave, a pleasure slave! I acknowledge this, and rejoice in it! I am a pleasure slave!"

"Yes?" said Sandal Thong.

"Yes, Mistress!" I said.

They were then silent, for a time. I do not think they expected this outburst, this admission, from me.

"Well, little pleasure slave," said Sandal thong, "there is not much silver here to buy you."

They laughed at Sandal Thong' observation.

"No, Mistress," I said.

"You will not find a block here for you to run up on and pose for rich men," said one of the girls.

"I think not," I agreed.

"Too bad," said one.

"Yes, too bad," I said.

"We do not like you," said one of the girls.

"No," said another.

"I did not ask to be here," I said.

"You must be a poor pleasure slave," said one, "or your master would not have given you to Thurnus."

"Perhaps," I said.

Tears sprang to my eyes.

"So you are a pleasure slave?" asked one.

"Yes," I said.

"Here you are not a pleasure slave," said one. "Here you are a work slave!"

"Here you will be worked hard," said another.

I had not asked to be here.

Did they think I wanted to be here?

I straightened my back. They made me angry. I assessed them, obviously to a woman's eyes, though a man might not have noticed, one by one. It is a slight, tacit thing that women understand. I smiled. They were angry.

"Perhaps I will not be worked as hard as you think," I said.

I was clearly their superior in beauty.

"Insolent slave!" cried one. "How haughty you are, Slave Girl!" said another.

I shrugged.

"Do you think you are more beautiful than we?" asked one of them.

"Yes," I told them.

"Do you think you will please the master more than we?" asked another.

"Yes," I told them. "I am clearly more beautiful."

"She-tarsk," said one. "She-sleen!" cried another.

"You will be worked hard!" said another girl.

"We will see to that!" vowed the fourth girl.

"Do you have a comb for my hair?" I asked.

"Do not break the position of the pleasure slave," warned the largest of the girls, she, Sandal Thong, a long-armed, freckled giantess of a peasant wench.

"Very well," I said.

"It becomes you," said Verr Tail, a wide-shouldered, auburn-haired girl.

"Thank you," I said.

I did not wish to be caged with them. I could sense their hostility. Too, they could surely detect that I did not care for them, either. But we were locked in the same small cage.

"Doubtless you will soon become the master's favorite," said Turnip, a dark-haired, wide-faced girl.

"Perhaps," I said, tossing my head.

"Radish is now favorite," said Sandal Thong, indicating a blondish, thick-ankled girl at her left. I recognized her. It was she whose heartbeat had given the time count in the boys' sport of "girl hunt" the preceding night. Last night she had served one of the warriors of Clitus Vitellius. I recalled her pressing back against him, his hand on her heart, his calling the count. I myself had been in the arms of such men many times. They were not peasant boys.

"I was the girl of a warrior," I told them.

"You are very pretty," said Radish. I decided I did not dislike Radish.

"You were poor in the furs," said Sandal Thong. "That is why he gave you away."

"No!" I cried.

"Poor in the furs!" laughed Sandal Thong.

"Why did he give you away?" asked Verr Tail.

"I do not know," I said.

"Poor in the furs!" said Sandal Thong, pointing her finger at me.

"We have few furs in this village," laughed Turnip. "We will see how you roll in the straw!"

"If you are not good," said Verr Tail, "we will soon know. Thurnus will tell everyone whether you are good or not."

"I am good," I told them.

"Why did your master give you away?" asked Turnip.

"It amused him," I said. "He is Clitus Vitellius, a captain. He can have many girls, more beautiful than I. He made me love him, hopelessly and desperately, and then, for his amusement, discarded me. He toyed with me. He used me for the object of his sport. Then, when he had won, fully and completely, he cast me aside, ridding himself of me, giving me away."

"Did you truly love him?" asked Radish.

"Yes," I said.

"What a slave you are!" laughed Sandal Thong.

"He made me love him!" I cried defensively. Yet I knew I would have loved him, even had he not made me love him. Had I had the choice as a free woman I would have chosen to love him; but the choice had not been mine, for I had been a slave; he had overwhelmed me, forcing me to love him, consulting not my will, before I could have chosen to do so; I who had desired to kneel before him of my own free will had been commanded to his sandals as a slave girl.

"You are a fool to have loved your master," said Sandal Thong.

"I love my master," said Radish.

Sandal Thong turned about and struck Radish to the side of the cage. "Slave!" she cried.

"I cannot help it that I love my master!" said Radish.

Sandal Thong spun about, facing me. "Do not break the position of the pleasure slave!" she said.

I held position. "Are you not a slave, too?" I cried.

Sandal Thong stood up. She was a tall girl. She fingered the rope collar on her throat. She stood there in the brief slave tunic, of the wool of the Hurt. It was the only garment she had, as with the rest of us. She was a large girl, heavy-boned, tall, stronger than we, powerful when compared to us, but to a man she, too, would have been slight, at their mercy. "Yes," she said, "I can be beaten, or sold or slain. I can be given as a gift among men. They can put me in chains. They can burn me with irons. They can do with me what they wish." She looked out through the bars of the cage, at ground level. "I must kneel to them. I must be obedient. I must do what I am told." She looked down at me. "Yes," she said, "I, too, am a slave."

"We are all slaves," said Radish.

"I do not want to be a woman!" cried Sandal Thong suddenly, shaking the bars of the cage. She put her face against them, weeping.

"You weep like a woman," I said.

She spun to face me.

"Once," said I, "I did not wish to be a woman. Then I met men such as I had not dreamed could exist. They made me happy to be a woman. Never again would I have wanted to be anything else. My womanhood, though it puts me at the mercy of men, is now exquisitely precious to me. Among such men I would not trade my womanhood for anything in the world. Every girl has a master. It is only, Sandal Thong, that you have not yet met yours."

She looked at me, angrily, the bars in back of her.

"There is some man, Sandal Thong," I said, "whose sandals you would beg to untie with your teeth."

"If Thurnus would so much as look at me," she said, "I would crawl ten pasangs on my belly to lick the dust from his ankles."

"Thurnus, then," I said, "is your master."

"Yes," she said, "Thurnus is my master."

"What is your name?" asked Radish.

"Do you have a name?" had asked Thurnus of me, earlier.

"My former master, Clitus Vitellius, of Ar," I had said, "called me Dina."

"He thought so little of you?" asked Thurnus.

"Yes, Master," I said.

"It is a pretty name," he had said. "It is only that it is common."

"Yes, Master," I had said.

"I name you Dina," he said, putting the name on me, naming his animal. "Who are you?" he asked.

"Dina," I had said, "Master."

"What is your name?" asked Radish.

I smiled. "Dina," I said.

"Many girls with your brand are called Dina," said Turnip.

"I have heard that," I said.

"It is a pretty name," said Verr Tail.

"Thank you," I said.

"It must be nice to have a girl's name," said Turnip.

I did not respond.

"I am Radish," said Radish. "I am Turnip," said Turnip. "I am Verr Tail," said Verr Tail.

Sandal Thong looked at me. "I am Sandal Thong," she said.

"Tal," I said to them.

"Tal," they said to me.

"You are first in the cage?" I asked Sandal Thong.

"Yes," she said.

"It will not be necessary to kick or beat me," I said. "I will obey you."

"We are all women. We are all slaves," said Sandal Thong.

"We are all under the whip," said Turnip.

"I have been hand whipped," I said. "But I have never felt the slave whip."

"Have you been a slave long?" asked Radish.

"No," I said.

"You are very pretty to have been free," said Turnip.

"I lived far away," I said.

"Your accent marks you as barbarian," said Sandal Thong.

"Yes," I said.

"Where did you live?" asked Verr Tail.

"A place called Earth," I said.

"I have never heard of it," said Turnip.

"Is it in the north?" asked Radish.

"It is far away," I said. "Let us not speak of it." How could I speak of Earth to them? I did not want them to think me mad, or a liar. Could they believe a world might exist where men, shouting political slogans, vied with one another to surrender their dominance, hastening gleefully to their own castration? Could such a world be welcomed by any save man-haters, freaks, frustrates and Lesbians, and men who were not men? Truth and political convenience, I thought, do not always coincide.

"Barbarian places are so dull," said Turnip. "Have you never been chained in Ar?"

"No," I said.

"I was sold once in Ar," she said. "It is a marvelous city."

"I am pleased to hear it," I said. Clitus Vitellius, I knew, was of Ar.

"It is strange that you have never felt the slave whip," said Turnip.

I shrugged.

"Perhaps she was too pretty to whip," said Turnip.

"I think it is always the ugly girls who are whipped," said Verr Tail.

"That is not true," said Radish.

"I would suppose," I said, "that any girl, beautiful or not, if she needs a whipping, would be whipped by her master." It surprised me that I, an Earth girl, had said this. Yet, why should a girl who needs a whipping not be whipped, if she has a Gorean master?

"Dina is right," said Radish.

"They whip us," said Sandal Thong, "when it pleases them."

Radish laughed, and slapped her thighs. "Yes," she said, "the beasts! They put us under the leather whenever it pleases them, whether we have done anything or not!"

"Men are the masters," said Turnip. "They do with us what they please."

"This is a peasant village, Dina," said Verr Tail. "If you remain long in the village, you will learn the slave whip well."

I shuddered.

"I have never even really been switched," I said. Eta had never switched me, though she had held switch rights over me, as first girl in the camp. I had been stung twice across the back of the thighs, below the short tunic, by Melina, companion of my master, Thurnus, when she had hurried me to the kennel. It had been terribly humiliating and unpleasant. It was hard to imagine what a true switching would be. I could not even conjecture what it would be to feel the flash of the slave whip on my body.

"Does the whip hurt, Sandal Thong?" I asked.

"Yes," said Sandal Thong.

"Does the whip hurt very much?" I asked.

"Yes," said Sandal Thong.

"You are strong, Sandal Thong," I said, "do you fear the whip?"

"Yes," she said.

"Do you fear the whip very much?" I asked.

"Yes," she said, "I fear the whip very much."

I shuddered. If even the large, strong Sandal Thong so feared the whip, I wondered what it would do to me.

"It is time to sleep now," said Radish.

"I want to be your friend," I said to them. "I want you to like me."

"We like you," said Turnip.

"You may close your knees," said Sandal Thong.

"Thank you," I said, "Mistress."

"You need not call me Mistress," said Sandal Thong.

"Thank you," I said.

"But do not forget I am first girl," she said.

"I will not," I said.

"You are pretty," said Sandal Thong.

"Thank you," I said.

"We are all slaves," said Sandal Thong.

"Yes," I said.

"We must rise early," said Radish. "Let us sleep now."

We lay down in the straw, and were soon asleep. I awakened once, sweating. I had had a strange dream. I had dreamed I knelt naked, in a steel collar, on smooth tiles, in a beautiful room, as though in a palace. Before me had been a low table. On this table had been strands of thread and, in small cups, beads, slave beads, of various colors, red, yellow and purple, and other colors. I understood, somehow, that I must make a necklace. A slave whip had been lifted before me. "What is this?" asked a voice. "A slave whip, Master," I had said. "And what are you?" had inquired the voice. "A slave, Master," I had said. "Do you obey?" asked the voice. "Yes, Master," I had said. The whip then, roughly, had been forced against my face; it pressed against my lips, bruising them; I felt it with my teeth. "Kiss the whip, Slave," said the voice. I had kissed the whip. "Who commands me?" I had asked. It had seemed as though I must ask that. Yet it was not the sort of thing a slave girl would naturally ask. Such an inquiry might be thought to border on insolence. Yet I was not taken by the wrists and thrown flat upon the tiles and whipped. "You are commanded by Belisarius, Slave Girl," was the response. The response, somehow, seemed oddly fitting, expected. Yet I knew no Belisarius. "What is the command of Belisarius, the slave girl's master?" I had asked. "It is simple," said the voice. "Yes, Master," I had said. "Bead a necklace, Slave Girl," said the voice. "Yes, Master," I had said. Then my hands had reached toward the strands of thread on the table, and toward the cups of tiny beads. Then I had awakened. I did not understand the dream. I put down my hand. I was not on smooth tiles. My hand felt straw, and wood, and a steel bar, and the dirt beneath it. The dream was then gone. I lay awake, looking up at the bars and wood above me. The moons were full outside, and I rose to my feet in the straw. I was not in a palace. I was in a cage at Tabuk's Ford. I went to the side of the cage and, over the vertical, banking earth, looked out. My small hands held the bars. The roof of the cage was a few inches above my head. My fists clutched the bars. I had been Judy Thornton. I was caged! I cried out, startled. Bran Loort grinned at me. The other girls turned restlessly, but did not awaken. I shrank back from the bars. I lay down in the straw. He was looking at me. I tried to pull the short woolen tunic more over my legs.

"I am going to be first in Tabuk's Ford," whispered Bran Loort. "When I am first," he said, "Melina will give you to me."

He slipped away from the bars.

I drew up my legs. I huddled in the straw, trembling.

I chopped at the dry earth about the sul plant.

I had been twenty days slave at Tabuk's Ford.

The peasant hoe has a staff some six feet in length. Its head is iron, and heavy, some six inches at the cutting edge, tapering to four inches where it joins the staff. It is fastened to the staff by the staff's fitting through a hollow, ringlike socket at its termination. A wedge was driven between the interior edge of the socket and the staff to tighten the wood in the socket. In some such hoes the socket is drilled and the staff is held in place by means of a pin, usually of wood, sometimes of metal. But even so, as the wood will wear against the socket, a wedge may be used, as well.

I was too small to use such a tool well. I did not make a good peasant's slave.

It is difficult to convey the hardship of slavery in a peasant village, particularly for a slight girl, such as I.

I stood up, straightening my back. It hurt. I shaded my eyes.

On the road from Tabuk's Ford I could see the cart of Tup Ladletender, the itinerant peddler, he between its handles, bent over, drawing it.

I looked at my hands. They were raw and blistered, and dirty. I moved my finger inside the rope collar, moving it out a bit from my neck, wiping sweat and dirt from under it. The rope scratched my neck, but I must wear it. It was token of my slavery.

The day begins early, before dawn, when Melina loosens the padlocks on our cage.

We climb out and kneel before her, our heads to her feet. She holds the switch over us. She is our mistress.

Verr are to be milked, the eggs of vulos gathered, and the sleen must be watered and fed, and their cages cleaned.

In the middle of the morning we return to the hut of Thurnus, where pans of slave gruel have been put out for us, beneath the hut. This gruel must be eaten, and the pans licked clean. In the manner of peasant slave girls we kneel or lie upon our bellies and may not use our hands.

After our meal the true work of our day begins. There is water to be carried, wood to be gathered and fields to be tended. Many and various, and long, are the tasks of a peasant village. Upon slave girls do most of these tasks devolve. We must do them or die. Sometimes the boys surprise us in the fields and tie us together and rape us. It does not matter, for we are only slave girls.

It seemed every bone in my body ached.

Ten days ago Thurnus had used me for plowing. He did not own bosk. Girls are cheaper than bosk.

It was the first time I had felt a whip.

I had been hitched with the other girls, and, together, sweating, we had labored naked in the traces under our master's whip. Slowly, leaning forward, our feet digging into the earth, we had pitted our strength against the restraining band of the harness, and, slowly, the great blade had begun to move through the deep soil, turning it for our master. After a few yards I thought I might die. Who would know if I did not put my full strength upon the trace? It was then that I first felt the whip. It was not the five-bladed slave whip, invented for the full and perfect punishment of an erring slave girl, but only a light, one-bladed bosk whip, little more than a switch of leather, a mere incitement and encouragement to better performance on the part of a slacking plow beast, but it struck my back like a hot snake and a rifle shot. I could not believe what it felt like. It was the first time I had ever been struck with a whip.

"Come, Dina, pull harder," said Thurnus.

"Yes, Master!" I cried, hurling myself against the trace. He had not been angry. My back felt as though it had been lashed with a hot cable.

I could not believe the pain of the whip. I could not even conjecture what it would be to feel a true slave whip on my body. Yet I knew a girl could be subjected to a full and lengthy lashing by the true slave whip for so small a thing as having failed in some way that she might not even understand to be completely pleasing to a master. Indeed, she could be subjected to such a lashing for no other reason than that it pleased the master to do so. I had now, for the first time, the former Judy Thornton, felt a whip. I groaned in misery. I now had a new insight into the condition of my slavery. I would do anything, eagerly, the masters wanted.

But in less than an hour I had collapsed in the traces, unconscious.

I dimly remember Thurnus's hand on the back of my neck and Sandal Thong's saying, "Do not kill her, Thurnus. Can you not see she is only a pretty slave, that she is only for the pleasure of men and not for the fields?"

"We can pull the plow without her, Master," said Turnip.

"We have done it many times before," said Radish.

"Do not break her neck, Master," pleaded Verr Tail.

Thurnus's hand left the back of my neck.

I remember him tying my hands behind my back, and tying my ankles together, and leaving me in a furrow. I then again lost consciousness. That night Thurnus carried me, bound, over his shoulder, back to the village, and threw me down between the pilings of his hut. "What is wrong?" asked Melina. "This one is a weakling," said Thurnus. "I will kill her for you," said Melina. She drew from her coarse robes a short knife. I rose on one elbow, naked and bound, helpless in the dirt at her feet. I regarded her with horror. She approached me with the knife. "Please, no, Mistress!" I wept. "Go into the house, Woman," said Thurnus, angrily. "You are the weakling, Thurnus," snapped Melina. She then put away the knife, and stood up.

"It was a mistake to have followed you," she said.

He looked at her without speaking.

"You could have been a caste leader for a district," she said. "Instead I am only the companion of a village leader. I could have companioned a district leader. You stink of the sleen you train and the girls you own."

There were slaves present, and yet she so spoke.

"You are a weakling and a fool, Thurnus," she said. "I despise you."

"Go into the house, Woman," he said. Angrily Melina turned and climbed the steps into the hut. At the top of the steps she turned. "You do not have much longer to give orders in Tabuk's Ford, Thurnus," she said. Then she disappeared into the hut.

"Untie Dina," said Thurnus, "and take her to the cage."

"Yes, Master," said his girls.

"Poor little Dina," said Thurnus, looking down at me, as the ropes were removed from my small limbs. "You make a very poor she-bosk," he said. Then he grinned. Then he turned away.

I struck angrily down at the ground with the hoe. Of course I made a poor she-bosk! It was not my fault I was not a female bosk, like so many of the lasses of peasant stock. Marla and Chanda and Donna and Slave Beads would have been no better! And I did not think Lehna or Eta would have been much better either! How I would have loved to have seen Marla try to pull the plow! She would have done no better than I! Angrily I hoed the suls. I was healthy and vital, but I was not large, not strong. I could not help that. It was not my fault. I was small, and slight and weak. I could not help that. It was not my fault! I was perhaps beautiful, but beauty availed nothing when one felt the weight of the plow at one's back and knew that behind you the master was lifting his whip. Thurnus was disappointed in my weakness.

I chopped down angrily at the ground with the hoe. It was hard for me even to carry water to the fields, struggling under the great wooden yoke over my shoulders, with its attached buckets. Sometimes I fell, spilling the water. And I was slow. The other girls, who were my friends, did parts of my heavier work and I, in turn, did much of the lighter work which was theirs. Yet I did not like this for it was harder on them. I wanted to do my share. It was only that I was weak, that I was not a good peasant's girl.

Sometimes in the fields I hated Clitus Vitellius. It was he who had left me in a peasant village! He had made me love him, conquering me to the last cell of my body, and had then, laughing, given me to a peasant. He knew the sort of girl I was, delicate and sensitive, slight and beautiful, from Earth, and then he had, to his amusement, put me to harsh, weighty slavery in a peasant village, giving me to Thurnus. I struck down at the suls. How I hated Clitus Vitellius!

I looked up again. The cart of Tup Ladletender, the itinerant ped-dler, was now much farther down the road, on the dirt road leading to the great road, formed of blocks of stone, leading to Ar.

I was thought little of in the village, though my cage sisters were kind to me.

I was not big enough or strong enough to be a good peasant's girl. I hated peasants. What idiots they were! There were better things to do with a beautiful slave girl than hitch her to a plow!

"The village is not a good place for you, Dina," Turnip had once said to me. "You are a city slave. You should be at a man's feet, in the secrecy of his compartments, collared and chained, curled and purring like a content she-sleen."

"Perhaps," I said.

"I would curl and purr at the feet of Thurnus," had said the large Sandal Thong. We had all laughed. But she had not been joking. It seemed strange to me to think of the large Sandal Thong wanting to submit to the domination of a man. Yet she, too, I reminded myself, was a woman.

Because of my slightness of strength Thurnus had had me help him often with the sleen. Some of the animals I grew to know. But, on the whole, I feared the sleen, and they, sensing this, were unusually vicious with me.

"Are you good for nothing?" had asked Thurnus in exasperation. I had backed away from him, in the sand of the training pit where we had been working. The sun had been hot, and the sand was hot. It had not rained in several days. The Sa-Tarna was in danger of drought.

Thurnus took me by the arms and shook me. "You are good for nothing," he said, angrily.

I had shuddered in his touch.

"What is wrong?" he asked.

I averted my eyes, shamed. "Forgive me, Master," I said, "but I have not been touched by a man for several days, and I am slave."

"Ah," he said.

I turned my eyes to him. I looked up at him. He was very large. "Perhaps Master would care to rape his slave?" I said.

"Does the slave beg slave rape?" he asked.

"Yes, Master!" I said suddenly, clutching him. "Yes! Yes!" I could not control myself.

He flung me back in the sand, thrusting up the tunic over my breasts. I lay at the foot of a slave cage. He seized me, and I reached back for the bars of the slave cage, and, holding them, cried out. I twisted and squirmed with the pleasure of his having me. Once I cried out with misery, for I saw Melina watching, from behind the wooden wall. "It is the Mistress, Master," I said. He laughed. "I do what I please with my slave girls," he said. "Let her watch, should she please to do so. Let her find excellent instruction in the behaviors of a hot slave." But Melina, angrily, had left. I then again yielded to the pleasures of him, moaning to the master a slave girl's gratitude. He had deigned to touch me. When he had done with me I knelt at his feet, whimpering. I kissed his feet. "Thank you, Master," I said.

He laughed, and lifted me up, and looked at me, and then, in great humor, flung me to the sand at his feet, from where I looked up at him. "I see, Dina," he laughed, "that you are good for something after all."

I looked down, shyly. "Thank you, Master," I said.

It was now late afternoon.

The cart of Tup Ladletender was now disappearing in the distance, a bit of dust rising behind its wheels.

He had done slave assessment on me this morning.

It was this morning that I had first discovered that I was a whore. But I suppose that every slave girl must be at least a whore, and a marvelous one.

He had not had me, but I had, in his assessment, tried to present myself to him well.

I wondered if I would see him again.

It had begun this way.

"Remain behind, Dina," had said Melina, companion of Thurnus. The other girls had left the village to carry water. Thurnus himself was gone. He would not return until late. He was visiting another village, to buy vulos.

I was frightened of Melina. She was Mistress. Too, once she had prepared to kill me, on the day when I had failed in the plowing. Too, she had seen me in the arms of Thurnus. Yet, she had not of late threatened me. And, I supposed, she was fully aware that Thurnus used all his girls. Radish was used more than I. Surely Melina knew this. Only Sandal Thong was seldom raped.

"Yes, Mistress," I said, apprehensively.

I knew Melina did not like me, but I did not think she hated me more than the other girls. I was certainly not Thurnus's favorite. He preferred larger, wider hipped, larger breasted women than I, more of the sort that Melina might have been at one time, before, in her freedom, she had gone slack and fat.

"Come over here, pretty little bird," had said Melina, gesturing to me. She stood among the pilings of the hut, in the shade. I, the Earthgirl slave, obeyed her. I went to her and, for she was free and I slave, knelt deferentially before her, my head down.

"Remove your tunic, Dina," she said.

"Yes, Mistress," I said. I slipped the short woolen tunic over my head. I was now naked.

"Go to this piling," she said, indicating one of the pilings, "and kneel there, facing it."

I did so.

"Closer," she said. "Put your knees on either side of it, and put your belly against it."

"Yes, Mistress," I said.

"Do you like our village?" she asked.

"Oh, yes, Mistress!" I said.

"Put your arms around the piling," she said, "and cross your wrists, palms up."

I complied.

"Are you happy here?" she asked.

"Oh, yes, Mistress!" I said.

"Would you like to leave our village?" she asked.

"Oh, no, Mistress!" I said. Then I added, hastily, "Unless it be Mistress's will!"

She removed a bit of cord from her robes. I felt my wrists lashed together on the other side of the piling. They were tied very tightly.

"Will that hold you?" she asked.

"Yes, Mistress," I said.

She stepped back from me. She looked at me, and then she went up the stairs into her hut, and, soon, returned, with a coil of rope. She tied one end of the rope on my rope collar and then, pulling my head to the piling, tied the rope there, fastening it about the piling with several loops. The right side of my face was against the piling. I was tied to it, closely, by the neck. The rest of the rope, depending from the piling, she let fall to the dirt.

I looked up at her.

"You are a pretty one," she said.

Because of the rope on my neck I could not stand at the piling. It was clearly the intention of the Mistress that I was to remain on my knees.

"Quite pretty," she said.

"Thank you, Mistress," I said.

I was secured, naked, on my knees, at the piling. I was her prisoner.

"A peddler," she said, "is in the village."

I knew this. His name was Tup Ladletender. Radish had told me this. I had seen his arrival. He drew a handcart. It had long handles, and two large wheels. In the cart were many shelves and racks, on which there was a rich miscellany of cheap goods, and pegs and loops, from which hung many utensils, pans and tools. Drawers in the side of the wagon contained, too, mysteries of goods, such as threads, cloths, scissors, thimbles, buttons and patches, brushes and combs, sugars, herbs, spices, packets of salt, and vials of medicine. No one knew what all might be contained in that unusual cart.

"I am going to fetch him," said Melina, "to take a look at you."

At the piling, my heart leaped. Melina was going to sell me off, I thought, while Thurnus was out of the village.

"Present yourself to him well, you little slut," warned Melina, "or I will switch you to within an inch of your life."

"I will, Mistress!" I promised. Indeed I would! When might come another chance to escape the slavery of the village? I would do anything to escape peasant slavery! Present myself well? Indeed! I would be a wonder to him of obedient, sensuous female flesh! Then suddenly I was afraid. What sort of man was he? Different modalities of wench excite different men. I wanted to be exactly what he wanted. I was desperate to be exactly what he wanted. But what would he want? What a whore you are, I thought to myself. My wrists squirmed in the bonds in which Melina had fastened me. I did not know what he would want! Would he want a quiet, timid girl, one to throw to his feet and abuse? Would he want a lascivious wench, begging to reach him with her tongue? Would he want an angry, defiant girl, to be brought to her knees in docility and surrender? Or would he want, perhaps, a cold girl, haughty, icy with contempt, to be turned into a writhing slave, screaming piteously for his touch? I did not know. One thing I knew was that I would be presented beautifully, physically, to him. Melina had seen to that. She was a clever, shrewd woman. A girl is most beautiful when she is naked, save perhaps for a collar or chain. And I was tied kneeling, in submission position. And my knees were thrust apart by the piling, about which my hands were tied, against which my belly was thrust. This would suggest, perhaps only sub-consciously, my vulnerability, my penetration, and the massiveness and irresistibility of masculine power, to which I, a slave girl, must helplessly submit. Too, my hands, tied as they were, contributed to the carefully calculated effect. When I raised them, tied as I was, the softness of their palms was brought against and about the piling, in an intimate clasp. The piling, thus, would be embraced, and held beautifully. Lastly, there was a rope on my neck, long, a tether. This might easily suggest, again perhaps only on a subconscious level, that I might be removed from the post, have my hands tied behind my back, and be led away, like a tethered tabuk doe, to the master's pleasure. Such a rope might easily be looped on the back of a wagon, and I would follow, naked, barefoot, behind the wagon, in the dust. Melina was clever.

"This is the slave," said Melina.

Startled, suddenly frightened, I clutched the post. It was an invol-untary reaction. But, tied as I was, I could not have helped but seize it beautifully. I then realized Melina had wanted to startle me, from the direction from which she had approached, and the suddenness of her assertion. The man had seen the reaction of a beautiful, startled slave girl, bound at a post. It had been completely natural. Melina had intended that it would be.

I decided that I would be an Earth-girl slave, the desirability of whose flesh was being assessed, tied in a peasant village. I did not know what else to do, and that was what I was. On this world I was a beautiful barbarian and alien, from a world quite different, one which had not prepared me for their world. Perhaps Gorean men might find it of interest to own, and tame and train me. Earth girls, I had heard from Eta, made superb slaves. I supposed it was true.

"How are you, little vulo?" he said.

"Well, Master," I said.

"She is barbarian," he said.

"Oh?" said Melina. She knew I was barbarian.

"Open your mouth," said the man.

I opened my mouth.

"See?" he said to Melina. He had his fingers in my mouth, opening it widely. "There, and there."

I had had two cavities. They had been filled.

Melina peered into my mouth, as it was held open, painfully.

"Physicians can do that," she said.

It is common to publicly examine slaves, their bodies, their teeth, and such. We do not object. We know that we are animals.

He removed his fingers from my mouth.

"Are you from a place called Earth?" asked the man.

"Yes, Master," I said.

"See?" he asked Melina.

"Clever slave," said Melina.

I feared I would be switched.

"There are many ways one can tell," he said. "There is, for example, in many barbarians, this tiny scar on the upper arm."

He indicated a vaccination mark on my upper left arm.

"That is a subtle slave brand, I take it," he said.

"No, Master," I said. "It is called a vaccination mark. On Earth I was free."

"As pretty as you are, you were free?" he asked.

"Yes, Master."

"The men of Earth," said he, "must have very little imagination."

"On Gor," said Melina, "there are many beautiful women who are free."

"Yes," he said, "they have not yet been put in their collars."

This response I could tell did not much please Melina.

"That you were free on Earth," he said to me, "was a mistake, was it not?"

"Yes, Master," I said.

"But you are not free now, are you?" he asked.

"No, Master," I said.

"And you should be a slave, shouldn't you?" he said.

"Yes, Master," I said.

"I am Tupelius Milius Lactantius, of the Lactantii, of the merchants, of Ar," he said to me, "but we fell upon hard times, and I, though only eight at the time, fell as well, it being my duty, caste discipline, family pride and such."

I smiled.

"She smiles well," he said. "In the villages I am known as Tup Ladletender," he said. "What is your name?"

"What do you think of her?" asked Melina.

The man regarded me. "She is obvious collar meat," he said.

I felt shamed at the post. It was obvious to the eyes of a Gorean male that I was a slave. It was only a question as to my price, and to whom I would belong.

"Is she not pretty?" asked Melina.

"In the cities," said he, "such girls are numerous. In Ar alone, each year, thousands of such girls are vended and procured in the slave markets."

I shuddered.

"What is her value?" demanded Melina.

"I could get for her, at best," he conjectured, "only a handful of copper tarsks."

I knew that I was a beautiful slave. What I had not realized was that slave beauty was so plentiful on Gor. Beautiful slaves are not unusual on this world. Beauty in collars was cheap on Gor. Girls more beautiful than I often slaved in the kitchens of great houses or, in state tunics and chains, scrubbed the floors of public buildings at night.

Melina was not pleased.

"Do you not want her?" she asked.

He caressed my flanks, and I held the post. "She is not without interest," he said.

Suddenly, without warning, he touched me, and I cried out, my body thrusting against the post, my hands clutching it, my eyes closed. I could not help myself.

"Ah," he said.

I opened my eyes, startled.

"She is a hot slave," he said. "That is good. That is very good."

"How hot is she?" asked Melina.

Again he touched me, and I cried out, miserable, bound. I could not help myself.

He laughed. "Very hot," he said. He laughed. Then he said, "Steady, little vulo."

"Please, Master, don't!" I begged.

Then I cried out, and began to writhe at the post. My fingernails tore at the wood. "Stop!" I wept. "Please, stop Master!"

He withdrew his hands and I shuddered against the post, fearing only that he might again so touch me.

He stood up.

"How hot is she?" asked Melina.

"She is hot enough to be a paga slut," he said.

"Excellent!" said Melina.

"Yet," said he, "still I think I could get only tarsks for her."

"Why is that?" inquired Melina.

"The wars," he said, "the raids, the falls of cities. There are many beauties, many of them even formerly free, who find themselves upon the block these days, being sold for a pittance of tarsks."

"But are they as hot as this one?" demanded Melina.

"Yes, many of them," he said. "Brand a girl, put her in chains, give her a bit of training, and in a week she is panting, hot and ready for a master."

"So soon?" asked Melina.

"Yes," he said, "take a woman, any woman, not just these Earth girls, who are slave meat, but any woman, even one who is Gorean, and free, and of high caste, even one who is an iceberg, lock a collar on her, which she cannot remove; teach her she is a slave; and she will turn to fire."

Melina laughed. I reddened, bound at the post. How grievously had the women of Earth been slandered! Did they not know I was a woman of Earth? Of course they knew! How casually, how unthinkably, they spoke in the presence of a slave! But I wondered if it were true. If it were true, in Gorean law, it could be no slander.

"Lock a collar on her," said the man, putting his hands about my neck, as though they were a collar. I tensed, my throat collared in his hands. I knew he could crush my throat easily with his Gorean strength, did he choose. I felt very helpless. He removed his hands from my neck and put them in my hair. "No!" I begged. "Hold to the post," he said. "Yes, Master," I wept. He tightened his hands, and pulled my head up and back. "Teach her she is a slave," he said. I cried out as he tightened his hands further in my hair, and pulled my head back further. I held tightly to the post, as commanded, that the rope collar I wore, fastened to the piling, would not pull against my throat. He caused me only enough pain to let me know what he could do to me if he chose. Then he relaxed his grip. Involuntarily I shuddered, gratefully, acknowledging him as male and master. He removed his hands from my hair. I tensed at the post. I felt his hands at my flanks. "And," he said, chuckling, "she will turn to fire." He touched me, and I cried out, tears in my eyes, squirming, thighs grasping the post, turning my head, biting at the wood with my teeth.

"Hot enough to be a paga slut," said Melina.

"Yes," he agreed.

The women of Earth had been pronounced slave meat. I wept. If this were true, it was, in Gorean law, no slander.

I hoped that he would not touch me again.

But I wanted to be touched!

I wanted so much to be touched again!

Oh, please touch me, Master, I thought.

Dina, she who had been Judy Thornton, was so much a slave!

The women of Earth are slave meat, I thought. I am a woman of Earth. I clung to the post, slave meat.

"Pretty slave meat," he said, gently touching my flanks.

I squirmed.

"Disgusting," said Melina.

I wondered if all the women of Earth were slave meat. I knew only that I, undeniably, was such. Perhaps others were not. Let other girls, in their secret heart, ask themselves that question. They need tell no one the answer to that most private and revealing of questions, unless perhaps they meet one before whom they can speak only the truth, their master. Perhaps the matter is hormonal. Perhaps there are hormones which fit a girl for slavery, as there are hormones which fit a man for mastery. I do not know.

Only on Gor had I felt my true femaleness, and that in the presence of Gorean males, who owned or could own me, men capable of owning a woman, as most men of Earth simply are not. My femaleness had been suppressed on Earth, first by my own conditioning, the confused product of centuries of intellectual and social pathology, and, secondly, by the set of societal institutions in which I had grown up and existed, rather than lived, institutions to which sexuality was irrelevant, if not inimical. It is difficult to know what would constitute a good society. Perhaps it would be a necessary condition for such a society that its institutions would be compatible, at least, with the truths of biology. A society which sickens and weakens its members, which cripples them and denies them to themselves, is not obviously superior to a society in which human beings are organic and whole, healthy, and happy and great. The test of a society is perhaps not its conformance or nonconformance to principles but the nature and human prosperity of its members. Let each look about himself and judge for himself the success of his own society. Man lives confused in the ruins of ideologies. Perhaps he will someday emerge from the caves and pens of his past. That would be a beautiful day to see. There would be a sunlit world waiting for him.

There is perhaps little to be said for the Gorean world, but in it men and women are alive.

It is a world which I would not willingly surrender.

It is a very different world from mine; in its way, I suppose it is worse; in its way, I know it is better.

It is its own place, not another's. It is honest and real. In it there is good air.

"Who is your master, little vulo?" asked Tup Ladletender of me.

"My master is Thurnus," I said, "caste leader in Tabuk's Ford, of the caste of peasants, one who makes fields fruitful and is, too, a trainer of sleen." I was proud of Thurnus, who owned me. A peasant who is actively engaged in agricultural pursuits is spoken of as one who makes fields fruitful. Sometimes this expression is applied, too, to peasants who are not actively engaged in such pursuits, as an honorific appellation. Whereas caste membership is commonly connected with the practice of an occupation, such as agriculture, or commerce, or war, there can be, of course, caste members who are not engaged in caste work and individuals who do certain forms of work who are not members of that caste commonly associated with such work. Caste, commonly, though not invariably, is a matter of birth. One may, too, be received into a caste by investment. Normally mating takes place among caste members, but if the mating is of mixed caste, the woman may elect to retain caste, which is commonly done, or be received into the caste of the male companion. Caste membership of the children born of such a union is a function of the caste of the father. Similar considerations, in certain cities, hold of citizenship. Caste is important to Goreans in a way that is difficult for members of a non-caste society to understand. Though there are doubtless difficulties involved with caste structure the caste situation lends an individual identity and pride, allies him with thousands of caste brothers, and provides him with various opportunities and services. Recreation on Gor is often associated with caste, and tournaments and entertainments. Similarly, most public charity on Gor is administered through caste structures. The caste system is not inflexible and there are opportunities for altering caste, but men seldom avail themselves of them; they take great pride in their castes, often comparing others' castes unfavorably to their own; a Gorean's caste, by the time he reaches adulthood, seems to have become a part of his very blood and being; the average Gorean would no more think of altering caste than the average man of Earth would of altering his citizenship, from, say, American to Russian, or French to Chinese. The caste structure, in spite of its many defects, doubtless contributes to the stability of Gorean society, a society in which the individual has a place, in which his work is respected, and in which he can plan intelligently with respect to the future. The clan structures are kinship groups. They function, on the whole, given mating practices, within the caste structure, but they are not identical to it. For example, in a given clan there may be, though often there are not, individuals of different castes. Many Goreans think of the clan as a kinship group within a caste. For most practical purposes they are correct. At least it seldom does much harm to regard the matter in this way. Clans, because of practical limitations on mobility, are usually associated, substantially, with a given city; the caste, on the other hand, is transmunicipal or intermunicipal. These remarks would not be complete without mentioning Home Stones. Perhaps the most significant difference between the man of Earth and the Gorean is that the Gorean has a Home Stone, and the man of Earth does not. It is difficult to make clear to a non-Gorean the significance of the Home Stone, for the non-Gorean has never had a Home Stone, and thus cannot understand its meaning, its reality. I think that I shall not try to make clear what is the significance to a Gorean of the Home Stone. It would be difficult to put into words; indeed, it is perhaps impossible to put into words; I shall not try. I think this is one of the saddest things about the men of Earth, that they have no Home Stone.

"What is your name, little vulo?" asked Tup Ladletender of me.

"My master has been pleased to call me 'Dina,'" I said.

"If your master has been pleased to call you 'Dina,'" said Ladletender, "then you are Dina."

"Oh, yes, Master!" I said, quickly. I had not meant to imply that my name might not be 'Dina.' Melina was glaring at me. "I am Dina," I said swiftly, "only Dina, the girl of my master." Those four letters, in Gorean, as in English, were my complete and only designation. Such matters lie entirely within the determination of the Master.

"Pretty Dina," said Ladletender.

"Thank you, Master," I said.

"Do you want her?" asked Melina.

"She has rough hands," said Ladletender. He pulled my small hands, bound, out from the post, and rubbed his thumbs into my palms. I shuddered. "You have rough hands, Dina," he said.

"I am a peasant's girl, Master," I said. My hands were rough from digging, and washing, and holding tools.

I felt his thumbs rotating slowly in my palms. They pressed in. I thrust myself against the post, eyes closed.

"With lotions," said he, "they may be softened, so that they would be fit to caress men."

"Yes, Master," I said. I shuddered to think what his thumbs might have felt like in my palms, had my palms been slave-girl soft.

"Make an offer for the little she-sleen," said Melina.

Ladletender touched my neck, and put his finger inside the rope collar, and pulled it out a bit from my neck. "You wear a rope collar," he said. "It must be rough and unpleasant."

"What pleases my Master," I said, "pleases me."

"Do you lie to a free man?" he asked.

"Oh, no, Master!" I cried. To be sure, the rope collar was unpleasant, and for that reason I did not like it, but, on the other hand, I, a slave, was naturally desperately eager to please Thurnus, who was my master. It was his will to which mine must conform. It was he whom I must please, fully. There was thus a sense in which what pleased Thurnus pleased me. I was pleased to please him. Did I not please him

I might be summarily slain. I was pleased to please him. To please the master is what most pleases the girl.

"She is trying to be pleasing," said Melina. "Would you not like her naked in your furs? She can be purchased cheaply."

"How cheaply?" he asked.

"Cheaply," she said.

"Does Thurnus know you are selling her off?" he asked.

"It does not matter what Thurnus knows," said Melina. "I am free and companion to Thurnus. I may do what I wish."

"Would you like, pretty Dina," said Ladletender, fingering my neck, "to have a pretty steel collar, perhaps enameled?"

"I have never owned a collar," I said.

"Nor would you then," pointed out Ladletender.

"Yes, Master," I said, humbled.

It was not I who would own a collar, but I, collared, who would be owned. The collar, like myself, would belong to the master. It would be his collar. I would not own it. I would only wear it.

"This rope is rough and coarse," said Ladletender, fingering the rope collar. "Would you not like a smooth steel collar, one slender and gleaming, or perhaps ornamented and cunningly wrought, or enameled, perhaps to match your eyes and hair, one designed in color and workmanship to enhance your style of beauty, one perhaps measured or custom-fitted to the beauty of your own slave throat?"

"Whatever pleases the master," I said. I knew that a steel collar did immeasurably enhance the beauty of a girl. I had much envied Eta her collar, though it had been plain. I had seen few collars on Gor, but I had learned from Eta that there was great variety among them. They ranged from simple bands of iron, hammered about a girl's throat, her head held down on an anvil, to bejeweled, wondrously wrought, close-locking circlets befitting the preferred slave of a Ubar; such collars, whether worn by a kitchen slave or the prize beauty of a Ubar, had two things in common; they cannot be removed by the girl and they mark her as slave. In the matter of collars, as in all things, Goreans commonly exhibit good taste and aesthetic sense. Indeed, good taste and aesthetic sense, abundantly and amply displayed, harmoniously manifested, in such areas as language, architecture, dress, culture and customs, seem innately Gorean. It is a civilization informed by beauty, from the tanning and cut of a workman's sandal to the glazings intermixed and fused, sensitive to light and shadow, and the time of day, which characterize the lofty towers of her beautiful cities. The same attention, of course, which the Gorean bestows upon his own life and world, is naturally bestowed upon his slave girls. They, too, must be perfect. Just as, in our world, it is not uncommon to seek the advice of an interior decorator in obtaining and organizing the appointments of one's own dwelling, so, too, in the Gorean world, it is not uncommon to call in a trainer and beautician to appraise and improve a girl. He considers such matters as her hair, its cut, cosmetics appropriate to her, the proper type of earrings, a variety of collars and slave silks, how she walks, and speaks, and kneels, and so on, and makes his recommendations. Commonly he finds an apparently plain slave, discovers her latencies, and leaves a beauty. An apparently plain girl is a challenge to such a man. They are said to be able to work wonders. They are often employed in slave pens. A common challenge to them is to take an apparently plain free woman, recently enslaved, and transform her into a ravishing, embonded beauty. Half the work, however, some say, is done by the collar. Some say the collar releases the beauty in a woman. Perhaps it is true. I had worn only a rope collar, but yet it seemed to me that it, even in its coarseness, made me more beautiful, more exciting. When Thurnus had tied it on my throat he had shown it to me in one of Melina's mirrors. I had almost fainted at the sight of it, so exciting it had made me appear, so sexually charged it had made me. Seeing my state, he had used me immediately, and I had, my whole body, helplessly, to my amazement, responded instantly to him. He had collared me. I dared not dream what my responsiveness would have been had the collar been not of rope, which I might cut or untie, but of true steel, in which I would be helplessly locked. In a sense I both desired and feared a true collar. Collared, how could I resist any man?

"Make an offer for her," said Melina.

Tup Ladletender rose to his feet and reached into his pouch. "Here, little vulo," he said. He took something from his pouch and thrust it in my mouth, pressing it between my teeth with his thumb, depositing it in the side of my mouth. I was startled, kneeling in the dirt at the post, my hands bound about it. "Thank you, Master," I said. It was a small, hard candy. It was sweet. I closed my eyes. It was the first sweet I had had since I had been brought to Gor. In the plain diet of a slave girl, such things are very precious. Girls would fight and tear at one another for a chocolate. Confections are commonly used by masters as rewards in the training and conditioning of their girls. Beyond this they may continue to function as control devices and incitements. Even a slave girl of many years never loses her taste for a bit of candy, for which she may have to work for hours. It is common to give the girl the candy while she is in a kneeling position, putting it in her mouth for her. On the other hand, in training, candies are commonly thrown to the girls. Sometimes, too, for the amusement of the master, candies will be thrown to the floor among several girls, to observe their struggle to obtain these prizes.

"Make an offer for her," said Melina.

"Why do you want to sell her off?" asked Ladletender.

"Make an offer," said Melina.

"Perhaps," he said, looking at me.

"Is she not pretty?" demanded Melina.

"Yes, she is pretty," he said.

"Imagine her, collared, naked in your furs," said Melina, "rubbing against you, desperate to please you."

"I am a merchant," said Ladletender. "If I buy her, I buy her to sell her for a profit."

"But surely you could richly use her before you sell her," suggested Melina.

Ladletender grinned. "Two copper tarsks," he said.

A strange sensation came over me. I realized a price had been offered for me. It is a very strange feeling. The price, of course, even for an Earth girl such as myself, was not realistic. It was intended only to begin the bargaining. Surely I would be worth at least four or five copper tarsks in any market.

"I will sell her to you for less," said Melina.

Ladletender seemed startled.

I opened my eyes, startled, too.

"I need something from your wagon," she said. She looked at me, narrowly. "Come away from the post," she said to Ladletender. They left me tied at the post. She and Ladletender, who seemed puzzled, went to his wagon, with the two long handles. They conversed there. I could not hear their conversation. I sucked at the candy. It was delicious. I wanted it to last as long as possible. I did move a bit about the post where I might look, as though inadvertently, at the pair of free persons at the wagon. I was curious. I was puzzled. From one of the many drawers in the wagon, Tup Ladletender gave into the keeping of Melina, companion of Thurnus, a tiny packet, such as might contain a medicine or powder. I then turned about at the post, so that they would not know I had observed them, and continued to relish the candy. In a short time Melina returned and untied me from the post, and, to my surprise, removed the long rope, though not the rope collar, from my neck. I had expected to be bound, wrists behind my back, and tethered by the neck of the rear of Ladletender's wagon, to follow him, his slave girl, naked and barefoot from the village.

"Put on your tunic," said Melina to me. "Get a hoe. Go to the sul fields. Hoe suls. Bran Loort will fetch you and bring you back when it is time. Speak to no one."

"Yes, Mistress," I said.

"Hurry," said Melina, looking about.

I donned the brief, woolen slave tunic, slipping it swiftly over my head.

Melina seemed agitated.

"May a slave speak, Mistress?" I asked.

"Yes," she said.

"Have I not been sold, Mistress?" I asked.

"Perhaps, pretty Dina," said Melina, companion to Thurnus. "We shall see."

"Yes, Mistress," I said, puzzled.

"Tomorrow, my pretty little she-sleen," she said, "you will belong either to Tup Ladletender or Bran Loort."

I looked at her, puzzled. "Go," she said. "Hurry! Speak to no one!"

I turned about and, hurrying, went to fetch a tool. The last of the candy dissolved in my mouth. There was no one to speak to.

I chopped at the dry earth about the sul plant.

It had not rained in fifteen days, and it had been dry, too, before that time. The land was in drought.

Tup Ladletender's cart had now disappeared down the road leading from Tabuk's Ford, he between its handles, bent over, drawing it. Left behind now was not even a bit of dust.

It was late afternoon.

I was totally alone in the fields, unprotected.

I did not understand much of what had happened to me. I did not know why I had been brought to Gor. I had awakened naked and chained by the neck. Men had demanded slave beads of me. I had not understood them. They had prepared to kill me. I had been rescued by Clitus Vitellius, who had branded me and made me a slave. He had toyed with me, making me love him helplessly, and had then, for his amusement, given me away! How I hated him! How I loved him! Always I would remember his hands upon me! Always in my heart I would be his slave girl. I wondered if he ever called to mind the girl he had so casually, contemptuously, discarded. Of course not! She was only a slave. And he had his pick of women, even free women, who would wear a collar for his touch. He would not remember me, a slave he once briefly owned and sported with. But I would remember him, always. I loved him. I hated him! Always in my heart I would think of him as my master. I so loved him, and hated him! If only I could have vengeance upon him! How sweet it would be to subject him to the revenge of a scorned slave girl! But what chance had a slave girl for revenge? She was only slave. I cut down at the suls, viciously. I thought of the strange dream I had had, in which I, naked and collared, kneeling on tiles in a beautiful room, as though in a palace, had been strangely commanded to bead a necklace. "Who commands me?" I had asked. "You are commanded by Belisarius, Slave Girl," was the response. The response, somehow, had seemed oddly fitting, expected, though I had known no Belisarius. "What is the command of Belisarius, the slave girl's master?" I had asked. "It is simple," had said the voice. "Yes, Master," I had said. "Bead a necklace, Slave Girl," had said the voice. "Yes, Master," I had said. Then my hands had reached toward the strands of thread on the table, and toward the cups of tiny beads. Then I had awakened. I had not understood the dream. Bran Loort had been near the bars of the cage. He had startled me. "I am going to be first in Tabuk's Ford," whispered Bran Loort. "When I am first," he said, "Melina will give you to me." He had then slipped away from the bars. I had huddled in the straw, trembling. Today, I had thought that I was sold, and perhaps had been, but I did not know. Tup Ladletender, I knew, had left the village without me. I had been sent to the fields. Melina had purchased something from Ladletender, a packet, containing a powder or medicine. I was to say nothing. Bran Loort would fetch me, I had been told. I was to remain in the fields until then. I understood little of this.

I cut down at the suls. I was to say nothing.

I was alone in the fields.

I lifted the heavy hoe, with the stout staff and great metal blade, again and again. It was terribly hot work, and hard. My back hurt. My hands hurt. My muscles ached. I worked hard, very hard, for I was a peasant's girl. Such girls are not treated gently if they do not do full work. I did not wish to be whipped.

The sun was sinking.

My tunic was soaked with sweat. My feet and legs were black with dirt and sweat.

The rope collar clung and scratched about my throat.

I stood upright, in pain. I was too slight a girl for peasant work. I held the hoe, breathing deeply, my head back.

How I had wanted Tup Ladletender to purchase me, to take me from the labors of the fields. I would have been willing to be anything he had wanted at the post, anything to interest him, anything to escape Tabuk's Ford, but he and Melina, in their cleverness, had manipulated me in such a way that I was unable to be anything but what I was, an Earth-girl slave whose passions put her helplessly at the mercy of men. Willing to be a whore, I had been forced to be naturally myself, a slave girl, more helplessly a whore than any whore could be. A slave girl must be at least a whore, and a marvelous one at that. Being a whore is but a small step in the direction of being a slave girl. But I did not care. I would have done anything to escape Tabuk's Ford. A slave girl owns nothing. She has nothing to offer a man but her service and her beauty. She has nothing with which to pay but herself. That is the way men want it.

I was sure that Tup Ladletender had found me appealing. I did not know if he had bought me or not.

I bent again to my arduous labors.

Suddenly I straightened myself. "Bran Loort!" I cried.

He stood a few feet from me, a coil of rope in his hand. My hands clutched the handle of the hoe.

He looked at me.

I flung it down. A girl dares not raise a weapon against a free man. Some girls have been slain, or had their hands cut off, for so much as touching a weapon.

"I have come to fetch you, Dina," he said.

I looked about. There was another peasant lad on my left. He, too, carried rope. I turned quickly. Four others were behind me. Another was on my right. Two others, too, appeared, behind Bran Loort. One of them carried, too, a coil of rope.

There was nowhere to run.

"She is the clever girl who eluded us in girl hunt in the village," said one of the lads.

"Greetings, clever girl," said another.

"Greetings, Master," I said to him.

I extended my wrists, crossed for binding, to Bran Loort. "You are going to take me to my master," I said.

He laughed.

I drew back my wrists. I looked about, fearfully. The boys approached more closely, closing about me.

I spun and ran, but fled into the arms of one of the young males, who roughly threw me back to the center of the circle. I tried again to break the circle and was again caught and flung again to its center. They were now close about me.

I extended my wrists, crossed, to Bran Loort. "Bind me," I said, "and take me to my master."

He smiled.

I trembled, and shrank back before him, almost into the arms of one of his brawny young cohorts.

"Are you going to rape me, Bran Loort?" I asked.

"And more," said he.

"Thurnus will not be pleased," I said.

"Tonight," he said, "you will belong to me."

"I do not understand," I said.

"Tonight," he said, "you will be a feast and a festival to us, Dina."

I trembled.

"Hold her," said Bran Loort.

Two boys held my arms.

"Ankle-leash her, both ankles," he said. This was done. I stood before them, ropes on my ankles.

"Put your arms at your sides," said Bran Loort, "out a bit from your body."

I did so.

I then stood before them, double wrist-leashed, ropes placed knotted on my wrists. The ropes on my wrists and ankles, serving as leashes, were cut from the coils of rope brought to the field. The remainders of the coils swung in the hands of Bran Loort and one of his cohorts. I knew I might be beaten with them.

"You will obey," said Bran Loort.

"Yes, Master," I said.

"Remove your kerchief," he said.

I lifted my leashed wrists and pulled away the kerchief, shaking my head, freeing my hair.

"Pretty," said one of the boys.

"Tear the kerchief," said Bran Loort.

"Please," I said. I did not wish to destroy the kerchief. It, like the girl, Dina, whom I was, belonged to my master. Dina was responsible for it. The master might not be pleased if it were torn or soiled. Dina might be beaten.

"Tear it," said Bran Loort. I, with difficulty, tore the kerchief, the boys amused at my weakness.

"Drop it upon the ground and step upon it, grinding it into the dirt," said Bran Loort.

I did so, with the heel of my leashed foot. I was sure now that I would be beaten upon my return to the village.

I looked at the boys. I realized, suddenly, I had more to fear from them than from the swift switch of an angry Thurnus or Melina. Their eyes terrified me. My limbs were leashed. I stood alone among them, their prisoner.

I knew I must please them.

"Are you docile and cooperative?" asked Bran Loort.

"Yes, Master," I whispered.

"Strip," he said.

"Yes, Master," I said. I reached to pull the coarse, brief tunic over my head. I hoped they would be soon done with me.

But my hands, held by the ropes on my wrists, could not reach the bottom of the tunic. My fingers struggled to reach it, but an inch from its wool, clinging about my thighs. I tried again to seize the tunic but was prohibited by the ropes from doing so. I looked at Bran Loort in alarm, in protest.

"Strip," he said. He swung the coil of rope which he carried, whip-like, easily in his hand. Behind me there was another lad, with such a coil of rope.

Wildly I tried to seize the garment, to pull it over my head, but the boys would not let me touch it. I struggled to get my fingers on the white, coarse wool, but I could not reach it.

"Are you docile and cooperative?" asked Bran Loort.

"Yes, Master!" I cried. "Yes, Master!"

"Strip," he said.

Again I tried to reach the garment but again was not permitted to do so. Then I tried to seize the garment at the neck and tear it away but the boys would not let my hands reach the garment.

"You are a rebellious slave," said Bran Loort.

"No, Master!" I cried.

"Obey then," he said.

I tried again to tear away the garment. Again I was not permitted to do so.

"Rebellious slave," said Bran Loort.

Suddenly the rope, coiled, held by the boy behind me, hissed and cut into the back of my thighs.

"Oh!" I cried.

At the same time Bran Loort himself struck down at me with the rope he carried, striking me across the shoulder and neck.

The boys yanked the ropes on my ankles, and, by their means, and by means of those held by the other two boys, those fastened on my wrists, I was turned and thrown to my stomach, in the dirt, spread-eagled.

Bran Loort and the other lad struck me again and again with the ropes they carried and then I, sobbing, cut by the ropes, marked even through the tunic, was, by the leashes on my limbs pulled to a kneeling position before him, my arms held out from my sides. There was dirt on the side of my face and on my body, blackening and staining the sweat-soaked tunic. I could taste dirt in my mouth.

"Bring her," said Bran Loort.

I was jerked to my feet by the ropes on my wrists and stumbling, dragged among them, was conducted from the sul field. The ruined kerchief, and the hoe, lay behind.

Many are the clever things which may be done to a girl who is, as I was, fully limb-leashed. Much sport had the cruel peasant boys with me. They made me fall when they pleased, and as they pleased; sometimes they threw me forward, sometimes backward; sometimes they carried me, face up or face down, suspended between them; sometimes they dragged me by an ankle or a wrist on my back or stomach, or twisting; sometimes they dragged me or made me walk where they wished, though it might be through rocks or gravel.

I did not know if I could live, so led.

We stopped once. I was still clothed at that time. I was held by the ropes before Bran Loort. I was covered with sweat and dirt; I was gasping; I was trembling, shaken with muscular stress from the cruel march, as well as with fear, knowing myself fully in their hands, not knowing what fate they might choose to inflict upon me. We stood in the vicinity of a thicket of thorn brush, of the sort which is occasionally used to wall camps.

"You are still clothed," said Bran Loort observing me.

"Let me tear away my clothes before you," I begged, "that the beauty of a poor slave girl may be bared to you."

"Do so," he said.

I cried out in anguish. Again the ropes would not let me strip myself.

"You have apparently not yet learned your lesson," he said.

"Please, Master!" I wept.

"Let the thorn brush strip her," said Bran Loort.

"No!" I cried.

By the ropes I was dragged into the midst of tenacious, barbed brush, that thicket of such. I screamed with misery. I begged mercy. I was shown none. The brush tore at my clothing and body. Rudely I was drawn through it. I cried out, throwing my head from side to side. I kept my eyes closed, that I be not blinded. "Please, Masters!" I cried. They did not see fit to show a girl mercy. Bloodied, my body a welter of scratches and linear wounds, I was pulled from the brush. The Earth-girl slave was now naked.

They hit me with the ropes and again we continued our journey. They sang as they conducted me to the place of their feast, on the grass by the stream.

There they held my wrists about a tree and, striking many times, put me under rope-discipline. Held against the tree, feeling its bark with the side of my cheek, weeping, shuddering under the blows of the coiled rope, I wondered what I had done to them that they should be so cruel to me.

They then took me and threw me to the grass on my back. My ankles, by the rope leashes tied on them, held by two boys, were pulled widely apart. Bran Loort looked down upon me.

I realized then that I, a slave girl, had, days ago, eluded them in the game of girl hunt. I had, in that game, by my cleverness, bested them. I did not now feel clever. I would now pay for my cleverness. How foolish of a slave girl to attempt to best a free man. Does she not know she may someday come into his ownership!

I cried out. Bran Loort was the first to have me.

"Come out, Thurnus!" called Bran Loort. "See what I have for you."

I lay at the feet of Bran Loort, my knees drawn up, on my side in the dirt. My hands were tied behind my back. I was naked, and my body was covered with dried blood and dirt. A rope, knotted, ran from my neck to his hand. My cheek was in the dust. I was cold, and my body ached, from the rope beatings and abuse to which it had been subjected. I think I was partly in shock. I could no longer cry. The only flicker of feeling left in me was a fear of free men. I, a slave girl, had once bested free men in the game of girl hunt. I had learned my lesson well. Never again would I try to best free men. They were master. I was slave.

"Come out, Thurnus!" called Bran Loort. "See what I have for you!"

My head jerked as Bran Loort, emphasizing his words, drew on the rope tied on my neck. I put my head down, shoulders trembling.

"Thurnus! Come out!" cried Bran Loort.

I shuddered.

I lay in the dirt before the hut of Thurnus.

It was night now, and men stood about, with torches. There were the eight young men of Bran Loort, and others, too, gathered from the village. The free men and women were there, and some slaves, not yet caged for the night. Sandal Thong was there, and Turnip, and Verr Tail and Radish. Melina had wanted them to see what was to occur. There were no children present. Bran Loort stood forward, his staff in his left hand, my neck rope in his right. His eight young men stood near to him, each with his staff. Ringing us were villagers and slaves. All eyes turned to the doorway of Thurnus's hut. Melina emerged from the hut and descended the stairs to the ground. Thurnus's hut was near the center of the village, near its clearing. I could smell the sleen in the cool, night air. It was chilly.

My back and legs were covered with welts from the rope lashings I had been given. My thighs were sore.

Melina stood at the bottom of the stairs. She, too, turned to face the opening.

I looked at Bran Loort. He looked very splendid, proud and strong, a girl's neck rope in his hand, she, proof of his manhood, at his feet. The staff he held was over six feet in length and some two to three inches in width. "I am going to be first in Tabuk's Ford," had Bran Loort once said to me. I recalled, too, something else he had said. "When I am first," he had said, "Melina will give you to me."

"Come out, Thurnus," called Melina, from the foot of the stairs below the hut.

I looked to the doorway of the hut. It was dark, empty.

The eyes of all looked at the opening to the hut.

Thurnus did not appear.

Men stood about, with torches. It was silent, save for the crackle of the torches. I lay bound. The ropes on my wrists, holding them closely behind my back, were very tight.

I heard a sleen squeal from some eighty yards away, behind the huts, in the cage areas.

There was a change in the breathing of the crowd. Thurnus stood now in the entrance to his hut.

"Greetings, Thurnus," called Bran Loort.

"Greetings, Bran Loort," said Thurnus.

Bran Loort's heavily sandaled foot struck into my belly. I cried out with pain.

"On your knees, Slave Girl," said Bran Loort.

I struggled to my knees. He took up the slack in the neck rope, coiling it, holding my head a foot from his thigh. My vision blurred, and then cleared. I saw Thurnus looking down at me.

He regarded me.

Much and well had the young men of Tabuk's Ford pleasured themselves with the girl from Earth, the former Judy Thornton, now the helpless Gorean slave girl, Dina.

I put my head down, under the gaze of my master. But I was not to be permitted this courtesy. The rope, Bran Loort's fist in it, at my neck, the knot under the left side of my jaw, pulled my head up.

I was to be displayed to Thurnus.

"I have something here of yours," said Bran Loort.

"I see," said Thurnus.

"She is a hot little slave," he said, "juicy and pretty."

"That is known to me," said Thurnus.

"She kneels now at my feet," said Bran Loort.

"I see that, Bran Loort," said Thurnus.

Swiftly Bran Loort then discarded the rope and, with his foot, thrust me to one side. I fell sprawling in the dirt, and turned, lying on one side, to watch.

Bran Loort stood with both hands on his staff, one hand grasped in its center, the other hand, his left, some eighteen inches below the center of the staff. But Thurnus had not moved.

No one stirred in the crowd. I heard the crackle of the torches.

Bran Loort seemed for a moment unsteady. He looked from one of his cohorts to another.

Then he again turned to face Thurnus, who stood, not speaking, at the height of the stairs, some six or seven feet above the level of the ground, in the doorway to his hut.

"I have abused your slave," said Bran Loort.

"That is what slaves are for," said Thurnus.

"We took much pleasure in her!" said Bran Loort, angrily.

"Did you find her pleasing?" asked Thurnus.

"Yes," said Bran Loort. He gripped the long, heavy staff more firmly, standing ready.

"Then," said Thurnus, "it will not be necessary for me to beat or slay her."

Bran Loort looked puzzled.

"Surely you know, Bran Loort," said Thurnus, "it is the duty of a slave girl to be fully and completely pleasing to men. Were she not so she would be subject to severe punishment, including even torture and death, should it be the master's wish."

"We took her without your permission," said Bran Loort.

"In this," said Thurnus, "you have committed a breach of code."

"It does not matter to me," said Bran Loort.

"Neither a plow, nor a bosk, nor a girl may one man take from another, saving with the owner's saying of it," quoted Thurnus.

"I do not care," said Bran Loort.

"What is it, Bran Loort, that separates men from sleen and larls?" asked Thurnus.

"I do not know," said Bran Loort.

"It is the codes," said Thurnus.

"The codes are meaningless noises, taught to boys," said Bran Loort.

"The codes are the wall," said Thurnus.

"I do not understand," said Bran Loort.

"It is the codes which separate men from sleen and larls," said Thurnus. "They are the difference. They are the wall."

"I do not understand," said Bran Loort.

"You have left the shelter of the wall, Bran Loort," said Thurnus.

"Do you threaten me, Thurnus of Tabuk's Ford?" asked Bran Loort.

"You stand now outside the shelter of the wall," said Thurnus.

"I do not fear you!" cried Bran Loort.

"Had you asked of me my permission, Bran Loort," said Thurnus, indicating me with a gesture of his head, "willingly and without thought, gladly, would I have given you temporary master rights over her."

I lay in the dirt, my hands bound behind my back, the rope on my neck, watching. It was true what Thurnus had said. I could have been loaned to Bran Loort, and would have had to serve him as though he were my own master.

"But you did not ask my permission," said Thurnus.

"No," said Bran Loort, angrily, "I did not."

"Before, too, you have done such things, you, and these others, though not to the degree nor with the intent of this day."

It was true. Sometimes the boys had caught us, Thurnus's girls, or those of others, too, and roped us together and raped us in the furrows of the fields, but it had been done in the bullying rowdyism of their youth, having slave girls at their mercy. There had been no intent of insult, or umbrage, in it. It had been the hot, fierce, innocent sport of strong young men, powerful and excited, who held brief-tunicked, branded girls, in rope collars, in their arms, nothing more. Does a slave girl not expect slave rape? Some masters enjoy having their girls raped occasionally; it serves to remind them that they are slaves. This sort of rape is not uncommon in a peasant village. It is usually taken for granted and ignored, save perhaps by the abused girls, but they are only slaves. Indeed, it is sometimes encouraged, to pacify young men whose natural aggressions otherwise might turn aside into destructive channels. It is also regarded, at times, as an aid in helping young males attain their manhood. "If she pleases you, run her down, and take her, son," is a not uncommon piece of paternal advice in a peasant village. I had heard this twice, though it had not been I on whom the young man had been set. Verr Tail had been caught and raped on her back, struggling, in the stream, once, and Radish had been caught and forced to give pleasure between the sleen cages. Each of these young men had walked differently following their conquest. I had shrunk back when they had approached. I knew they were now men, and I was only a slave. These two young men were not among the cohorts of Bran Loort. But what had been done today to me was clearly different in its intent and gravity from the casual, expected, fierce exhibitions of male aggression to which embonded girls such as I must become accustomed.

"I have been patient with you, Bran Loort," said Thurnus.

"We are grateful for your patience," said Bran Loort. He looked about, at his cohorts, grinning. He set his staff, butt down, in the dirt.

I sensed that the codes were to be invoked. What Bran Loort and his fellows had done exceeded the normal rights of custom, the leniencies and tacit permissions of a peasant community; commonly the codes are invisible; they exist not to control human life, but to make it possible. The rapes of Verr Tail and Radish, interestingly, had not counted as code breaches, though in neither case had explicit permission for their conquest been granted by Thurnus; such permission, in such cases, was implicit in the customs of the community; it did not constitute a "taking from" but a brief use of, an "enjoyment of," without the intent to do injury to the honor of the master; "taking from," in the sense of the code is not, strictly, theft, though theft would be "taking from." "Taking from," in the sense of the codes, implies the feature of being done against the presumed will of the master, of infringing his rights, more significantly, of offending his honor. In what Bran Loort had done, insult had been intended. The Gorean peasant, like Goreans in general, has a fierce sense of honor. Bran Loort had known exactly what he had been doing.

"I am disposed to be merciful, Bran Loort," said Thurnus, looking at me. "You may now request my permission for what you have done to this slave."

"But," said Bran Loort, "I do not request your permission."

"I must then call the council," said Thurnus, "that we may consider what is to be done with you."

Bran Loort, throwing his head back, laughed, as did his fellows.

"Why do you laugh, Bran Loort?" inquired Thurnus.

"Only the caste leader may call the council," said Bran Loort. "And I do not choose to summon it into session."

"Are you caste leader in Tabuk's Ford?" asked Thurnus.

"I am," said Bran Loort.

"Who has said this?" inquired Thurnus.

"I have said it," said Bran Loort. And he gestured to his fellows. "We have said it," he added.

There were nine of them, including Bran Loort. They were large, strong young men. "Yes," said more than one of them.

"I am sorry," said Thurnus. "I had thought that you had in you the makings of a caste leader."

"I am caste leader," said Bran Loort.

"In what village is that?" asked Thurnus.

"In Tabuk's Ford," said Bran Loort, angrily.

"Have you conveyed this intelligence to Thurnus of Tabuk's Ford?" inquired Thurnus.

"I do so now," said Bran Loort. "I am first in Tabuk's Ford."

"I speak for Thurnus, caste leader in the village of Tabuk's Ford," said Thurnus. "He speaks it not so."

"I am first here," said Bran Loort.

"In the name of Thurnus, he of the peasants, caste leader of the village of Tabuk's Ford," said Thurnus, "I speak. He, Thurnus, is first."

"I am first!" cried Bran Loort.

"No," said Thurnus.

Bran Loort turned white.

"Will it be the test of five arrows?" asked Thurnus.

In this the villagers, with the exception of the two contestants, leave the village and the gate is closed. Each contestant carries in the village his bow, the great bow, the peasant bow, and five arrows. He who opens the gate to readmit the villagers is caste leader.

"No," said Bran Loort, uneasily. He did not care to face the bow of Thurnus. The skill of Thurnus with the great bow was legendary, even among peasants.

"Then," asked Thurnus, "it will be the test of knives?"

In this the two men leave the village and enter, from opposite sides, a darkened wood. He who returns to the village is caste leader.

"No," said Bran Loort. Few men, I thought, would care to meet Thurnus in the darkness of the woods armed with steel. The peasant is a part of the land. He can be like a rock or a tree. Or the lightning that can strike without warning from the dark sky.

Bran Loort lifted his staff. "I am of the peasants," he said.

"Very well," said Thurnus. "We shall subject this matter to appropriate adjudication. The staff will speak. The wood of our land will decide."

"Good!" said Bran Loort.

I noted that Sandal Thong had slipped from the crowd. None other seemed to note her going.

Slowly, step by step, Thurnus descended the stairs from his hut.

Melina, eyes glittering, stepped back from the foot of the stairs. Men, and villagers all, and slaves, cleared a space near the hut of Thurnus.

"Build up the village fire," said Thurnus. Men hurried to do this. Thurnus opened his tunic, then pulled it down about his waist. He flexed his arms, and hitched up the skirt of the tunic, higher in his belt, until it was high on his thighs. Bran Loort, too, did these things.

Thurnus came to me and lifted me to my feet, his hands on my arms. "Is it because of your beauty, little slave," he asked, "that this has come about?"

I could not answer him, so miserable I was. I could not stand without his holding me.

"No," said Thurnus. "There is more involved here." He turned me about and untied my wrists, and unknotted the rope from my neck, throwing it away.

I stood in my brand and rope collar before him.

I looked up at him. He had been kind to me.

"Gag her and put her in the rape-rack," he said to a man.

I regarded him, startled, as I was dragged from his presence. I would be secured in the rape-rack, the ready spoils for the victor. I did not know why I would be gagged.

The young men of Bran Loort gathered about him, encouraging him. Thurnus stood to one side, not seeming to pay them attention.

With a cry of misery I was thrown onto the beams of the rack. My left ankle was thrust into the semi-circular opening in the lower left ankle beam and the upper left ankle beam, with its matching semi-circular opening, was dropped, and locked, in place. My other ankle was similarly secured in the separate matching beams for the right ankle. The rape-rack at Tabuk's Ford is a specially prepared horizontal stock, cut away in a V-shape at the lower end. My wrists were seized and my hair and I was thrown down on my back, wrists held in place, and my head, too, by my hair, in three semi-circular openings. A single beam, with matching semi-circular openings, on a heavy hinge, closes the stock. It was swung up and then dropped in place, and locked shut. I was now held in the stock, on my back, by my ankles, wrists and neck. I could move very little. I closed my eyes. I opened them to see a man above me. Looking up and back, my head down, I saw a piece of cloth in his hand. It was large. I wept as it was wadded, painfully, in my mouth. He then secured it in place with a narrow piece of folded cloth which slipped deeply between my teeth. He then, with another three scarves, covering the bottom portion of my face, one over the other, completed the task of gagging the slave girl. I could not utter a sound. I did not know why I had been gagged. My neck rested on the back of the semi-circular opening in the lower beam. It was painful. I am Judy Thornton, I tried to tell myself. I am Judy Thornton! I am an Earth girl! This cannot be happening to me! But I knew I was no longer Judy Thornton, and I knew I was no longer of Earth. I knew I was now only Dina, a slave, and was now only of Gor! I was now only Dina, a Gorean slave at the mercy of masters.

I turned my head to the side, to see the combat. I saw Turnip looking at me. Her eyes were frightened. Then she looked away. It could have been she in the stock. Radish was watching Thurnus, frightened. So, too, was Verr Tail. Sandal Thong was nowhere to be seen.

"Are you ready, Thurnus?" asked Bran Loort.

Villagers had cleared a circle. The fire was now high, and one could see well.

"Will you not require a staff?" asked Bran Loort, grinning.

"Perhaps," said Thurnus. He looked at the eight cohorts of Bran Loort. "These fellows, I gather," said Thurnus, "will not enter our competition."

"I am sufficient onto the task of putting a slack, fat fellow such as you under caste discipline," grinned Bran Loort.

"Perhaps," granted Thurnus.

"You will need a staff," pointed out Bran Loort.

"Yes," said Thurnus. He turned to one of Bran Loort's cohorts. "Strike at me," he said.

The young man grinned. He smote down at Thurnus. Thurnus seized the staff and, suddenly, with strength like that of a larl, jerked the young man toward him, at the same time kicking upward savagely, blasting the fellow in the teeth with the heel of his sandal, the young man reeling back, blood spattering from his nose and mouth, clutching at his face, the staff in the hands of Thurnus. There were teeth in the dirt. The young man sat, dazed, on the ground.

"A good staff," said Thurnus, "must be one with which one can thrust," and, saying this, looking at one young man, he drove the staff, like a spear into the ribs of another, "and slice," added Thurnus, who then smote the first fellow, whose attention was now on his struck fellow, along the side of the face. The first fellow fell in the dirt clutching his ribs. I had little doubt that one or more had been broken; the second fellow lay inert in the dirt, blood at the side of his head. "But," said Thurnus, "a good staff must also be strong." The young men stood, tensed, five of them, and Bran Loort. "Come at me," said Thurnus to another of the men. Enraged the fellow charged. Thurnus was behind him and smote down, shattering the heavy staff across the fellow's back. He lay in the dirt, unable to rise. The staff had been more than two inches in diameter. "That staff, you see," said Thurnus, instructing the younger men, "was flawed. It was weak." He gestured to the fellow lying in the dirt, his face contorted with pain, scratching at the dust. "It did not even break his back," said Thurnus. "Such a staff may not be relied upon in combat." He turned to one of the four young men, and Bran Loort. "Give me another staff," he said to one of them. The young man looked at him and, frightened, threw him the staff, not wanting to come close to him. "A better weapon," said Thurnus, hefting the staff. He looked at the fellow who had thrown him the staff. "Come here," he said. Uneasily the lad approached. "The first lesson you must learn," said Thurnus, swiftly jabbing the staff deeply, without warning, into his stomach, "is never to give a weapon to an enemy." The young man, bent over, retched in the dirt. Thurnus smote him sharply on the side of the head, felling him. He then turned to the other three young men, and Bran Loort. "You should keep your guard up," said Thurnus to one of them, who immediately, warily, raised his staff. Thurnus then smote another fellow, at whom he did not appear to be looking, and, before yet another could react, felled him, as well. Thurnus then turned, looking upon these two fellows lying in the dirt. "You, too, of course," he said to them, "should keep your guard up. That is important." This turning of his back doubtless seemed to offer a favorable opportunity to his remaining foes. Surely Thurnus had not forgotten them! I wanted to cry out, to warn him, but I could not do so. I wore a gag of Gor. I could do no more than squirm helplessly in the rack. The other young man, he beside Bran Loort, then suddenly struck at Thurnus, but Thurnus, clearly, as I now understood, had been expecting the blow. He had turned, and parried it, and then slipped behind the other's staff, bringing up the lower end of his own staff. The fellow's face turned white and he sank away. "Aggressiveness is good," said Thurnus, "but beware of the counterstroke." Thurnus looked about himself. Of the nine men only one, Bran Loort, now stood ready. Thurnus grinned. He indicated the young men, strewn about. "These others, I now gather," said Thurnus, "will not enter our competition."

"You are skillful, Thurnus," said Bran Loort. He held his staff ready.

"I am sorry that I must now do this to you, Bran Loort," said Thurnus. "I had thought you had in you the makings of a caste leader."

"I am caste leader here," said Bran Loort.

"You are young, Bran Loort," said Thurnus. "You should have waited. It is not yet your time."

"I am caste leader here," said Bran Loort.

"The caste leader must know many things," said Thurnus. "It takes many years to learn them, the weather, the crops, animals, men. It is not easy to be caste leader."

Thurnus turned away, his head down, to tie his sandal. Bran Loort hesitated only an instant, and then he struck down, the staff stopped, striking across Thurnus's turned shoulder. It had been like striking a rock. Bran Loort stepped back.

"Too, to earn the respect of peasants," said Thurnus, straightening up, retrieving his staff, his sandal tied, "the caste leader should be strong."

Bran Loort was white-faced.

"Now let us fight," said Thurnus.

Swiftly did the two men engage with their quick staves. There was a fierce ringing of wood. Dust flew about their ankles. Blows, numerous and fierce, were struck and parried. Bran Loort was not unskilled, and he was young and strong, but no match was he for the grim and mighty Thurnus, caste leader of Tabuk's Ford, my master. As well might a young larl with spotted coat be matched against a giant, tawny claw Ubar of the Voltai. At last, bloodied and beaten, Bran Loort lay helpless at the feet of Thurnus, caste leader of the village of Tabuk's Ford. He looked up, glazed-eyed. Some five of his cohorts, two of whom had recovered consciousness, seizing their staves, edged nearer.

"Beat him!" cried Bran Loort, pointing out Thurnus.

There was a cry of anger from the onlookers.

The young men raised their staves, together, to charge upon Thurnus, who turned, to accept their challenge.

"Stop!" cried a voice. There were the shrill squeals of sleen. Sandal Thong stood at the edge of the circle, in each fist the leash, a short leash, of a sleen. The animals strained against the leashed collars, trying to creep forward, their eyes blazing, saliva loose and dripping from their jaws, the wet fangs shining in the firelight. "On the first man who moves," cried Sandal Thong, "I shall set a sleen!"

The young men drew back.

Melina cried out with fury.

"Throw down your staves," ordered Thurnus. They, looking at the sleen, threw down their staves.

"She is only a slave!" cried Melina. "How dare you interfere?" she cried to Sandal Thong.

"I freed her this afternoon," laughed Thurnus. I saw no rope collar on her throat. She had removed it when she had stolen away from the circle of the fire.

She stood there, holding the sleen leashes, a proud free woman, in the firelight, though she wore still the rag of a slave.

"On your feet, Bran Loort," said Thurnus.

The young man, unsteadily, stood up. Thurnus, swiftly, tore away the tunic about his waist, and, taking him by the arm, rudely thrust him to the heavy rack, where I lay helplessly secured. "Here is the little slave you find so lovely, Bran Loort," said Thurnus. "She lies before you, helpless." Bran Loort looked at me, miserable. "She is a juicy little beauty, is she not?" asked Thurnus. I recoiled on the beams, so spoken of. "Is she not a pretty little cake?" asked Thurnus. "Yes," whispered Bran Loort. "Take her," said Thurnus. "I give you my permission." Bran Loort looked down. "Go ahead," urged Thurnus. "Take her!" "I cannot," whispered Bran Loort. He was a defeated man.

Bran Loort turned away from the rack and bent down to pick up his tunic. He went to the gate and it was opened for him. He left the village of Tabuk's Ford.

"Follow him, who will," said Thurnus to the young men who had been his cohorts.

But none made to follow their former leader.

"Of what village are you?" asked Thurnus.

"Tabuk's Ford," they said, sullenly.

"And who is caste leader in Tabuk's Ford?" asked Thurnus, sweating, grinning.

"Thurnus," they said.

"Go to your huts," he said. "You are under caste discipline." They withdrew from the circle of the fire. I expected that they would tend his fields for a season.

Melina had withdrawn from the circle of the fire, returning to the hut she shared with Thurnus.

"Let there be made a feast," decreed Thurnus. There was a cheer.

"But first, Thurnus, my love," said Melina, speaking now from the doorway of their hut, "let us drink to the victory of the night."

There was silence.

She carried a metal goblet, and, slowly, in stately fashion, descended the steps to the ground, approaching Thurnus.

She lifted the cup to him. "Drink, noble Thurnus, my love," said she to him. "I bring you the brew of victory."

Suddenly I realized what must be her plan. Melina was a shrewd, clever woman. She had counted on Bran Loort and his young men defeating Thurnus. Yet, in the event they did not manage this, she had purchased a powder from Tup Ladletender, the peddler. Had Bran Loort been victorious she had promised me to him. But, too, I had doubtless been promised to Tup Ladletender, in exchange for the powder, were it successful. In each plan Dina, the slave girl, had been the bauble with which to bring about her will. Had Bran Loort been successful, I would have been his. Ladletender's powder would then be unnecessary, and would be returned to him. If Bran Loort was unsuccessful, then the way would be clear to use Ladletender's powder, and I, of course, Bran Loort defeated, could then be straightforwardly tendered in payment for it. The plans, sharp alternatives, excluded one another; their common element was I, as payment. Melina had planned well.

"Drink, my love," said Melina, lifting the cup to Thurnus. "Drink to your victory, and mine."

Thurnus took the cup.

I tried to cry out, but could not. I struggled in the stock. My eyes were wild over the heavy gagging that had been inflicted upon me.

None looked upon me. I struggled in the stock. I tried to scream. I could utter no sound. I wore a Gorean gag.

"Do not drink it, Master!" I wanted to scream. "It is poisoned! Do not drink! It is poison!"

"Drink, my love," said Melina.

I could utter no sound. I wore a Gorean gag.

Thurnus lifted the cup to his lips. He paused. "Drink," urged Melina.

"It is our common victory," said Thurnus.

"Yes, my love," said Melina.

"Drink first, Companion," said Thurnus.

Melina seemed startled. Then she said, "It is first your victory, then mine, my love."

Thurnus smiled.

"Drink you first, my love," she urged.

"My love," smiled Thurnus, "drink you first."

"First, you," said she.

"Drink," said Thurnus. His voice was not pleasant.

Melina's face went white.

"Drink," said Thurnus.

She reached forth, hands shaking, to take the cup.

"I shall hold the cup," said Thurnus. "Drink."

"No," said she. She put her head down. "It is poison."

Thurnus smiled. Then he put his head back, and drained the cup. Melina looked at him, startled.

"Greetings, Lady," said Tup Ladletender. He had emerged from between the huts.

Thurnus threw away the emptied goblet, into the dirt. "It is a harmless draught," he said. "Tup Ladletender and I, as young men," he said, "have fished and hunted sleen. Once I saved his life. We are brothers by the rite of the claws of sleen." Thurnus lifted his forearm where one might see a jagged scar. Ladletender, too, raised his arm, his sleeve falling back. On his forearm, too, there was such a scar. It had been torn by the claw of a sleen, in the hand of Thurnus; the same claw, in the hand of Ladletender, had marked the arm of Thurnus; their bloods had mingled, though they were of the peasants and merchants. "He now, has, too, saved my life," said Thurnus. "I am pleased to have had the opportunity," said Ladletender.

"You tricked me," said Melina to Ladletender.

He did not respond to her.

Melina looked at Thurnus. She shrank back.

"Better," said Thurnus, "that the draught had been poison, and you had drunk first."

"Oh, no, Thurnus," she whispered. "Please, no!"

"Bring a cage," said Thurnus.

"No!" she cried.

"And a sleen collar," he said.

"No, no!" she cried.

Two men left the group.

"Let me be beaten with flails," she begged. "Set the sleen upon me!"

"Come here, female," said Thurnus.

She stood before him.

"Shave my head and return me in dishonor to my father's village," she begged.

His hands were at the shoulders of her robe. He tore it down, exposing her shoulders.

The shoulders of Melina were bared!

Women gasped and cried out, in protest.

I could see that men were pleased.

Her shoulders were as bared as those of a stripped slave.

The shoulders of a female are apparently exciting to men. This seems to be recognized even on Earth, given, for example, the fact of off-the-shoulder evening gowns. The existence of such gowns, if Goreans were familiar with them, except on slaves, would be taken as more evidence of the fittingness, the naturalness and appropriateness, of enslavement for Earth females. She who wears such a gown begs in her heart to be owned.

"Thurnus," protested Melina.

He held her by the arms, her shoulders bared. He shook her slightly. Her head went back. Her shoulders were wide, and strong, and beautiful. They would take a plow strap well.

Yet every part of a female body is beautiful to a Gorean, a hand, a wrist, an ankle, the back of a knee, the turn of a thigh, the sweet, soft hair, almost invisible and delicate, below and behind the ear. Each part bespeaks the glory and wonder and promise of the whole. I have heard Gorean men cry out with joy at the sight of a woman. There is little on Earth to prepare the poor Earth girl for the lust and desire with which she will find herself viewed on Gor. Initially she is bewildered, stunned and shocked. Then she is thrown on her back, or stomach, or over a saddle or trestle. She finds herself put to frequent and rich usages. She did not know she was so desirable! She makes swift adjustments. She must. It is the Gorean world, a truly man's world, in which she is a woman. The lust of Gorean males has much to do, doubtless, with the robes of concealment worn in most cities by Gorean free women. They would not wish the casual, inadvertent flirtation of an accidentally exposed ankle to lead to their hunt, capture and enslavement. Slave girls on Gor, on the other hand, when permitted clothing, are usually dressed briefly and lightly, that their charms be muchly revealed. Gorean men wish it this way. That, accordingly, is the way it is.

Thurnus's hands were on Melina's upper arms, now bared, her robes pulled down from her shoulders. He looked at her arms. Then he looked at her face.

The cage was brought, a small, sturdy cage, tiny and tight, and a sleen collar.

"Let me be killed, Thurnus," she begged.

Thurnus lifted the sleen collar before her. With her hand she held it from her. "Kill me instead, Thurnus," she begged. "Please."

"Put your hands to your side, woman," said Thurnus.

She did so.

Thurnus then looped the sturdy, leather, metal-embossed sleen collar about her throat. With an awl, brought by a man, he punched two holes, vertically, in the leather strap, and thrust the twin buckle-claws through the holes; he then took the long, loose end of the strap, for the sleen has a large neck, thrust it through the four strap loops, thick and broad, and then, with a knife, cut off the portion of the strap which protruded beyond the last strap loop.

Melina, her shoulders bared, stood before him, wearing a sleen collar. It had, sewn into it, a heavy, dangling ring, to which a sleen leash might be attached.

Instantly she was stripped and thrown to the ground. She looked up in fear at Thurnus.

"Into the cage, Slave," said Thurnus.

"Thurnus!" she cried.

He crouched down and, with the back of his hand, struck her across the mouth, leaving blood across the side of her face.

"Into the cage, Slave," he said.

"Yes—Master," whispered Melina. She crawled into the cage. At a gesture from Thurnus, Sandal Thong, surrendering the sleen leashes to a man, who took the animals from the clearing, came to the cage and, with two hands, flung down the metal gate to the cage, locking her former mistress within.

There was a cheer from those about.

"Let there be a feast!" called Thurnus, caste leader of Tabuk's Ford. "And in the feast fires let an iron be heated for slave branding!"

There was another cheer.

In the tiny cage she who had been Melina crouched down, sleen-collared, her face miserable behind the bars, clutching them with her fists.

She would soon wear the mark of a slave in her flesh.

Men and women hurried about, to prepare the feast. At a gesture from Thurnus Radish, Turnip and Verr Tail ungagged me and freed me from the heavy stock. They helped me from the stock and I, by its head, sank down to the dirt. I could scarcely move. I could still taste the heavy, coarse, sour wadding of the gag in my mouth. I would not have believed so effective a gag was possible. At that time, however, I had not worn more sophisticated devices, equally or more effective, such as the Gorean slave hood with gag-attachment.

Verr was roasted, and puddings made. Sa-Tarna bread was brought forth and heated. Sul paga poured freely.

At the height of the festivities the cage was opened and its occupant, a former free woman, whose name had been Melina, now a naked slave in sleen collar, was ordered forth on her hands and knees. A sleen leash was attached to her collar and she was conducted, crawling, on all fours, as a she-sleen, lashed more than once with the free end of the leash, this hurrying her, to the rape-rack in which I had been earlier confined. Therein she was fastened, the beams locking her ankles and neck, and wrists, in place, and, as her left thigh was held by strong men, branded by the hand of Thurnus, caste leader of the village of Tabuk's Ford. She screamed wildly, branded, and, her thigh released, cleanly marked, moaned and twisted on the wood. Her head was then shaved. Then she wept, her head back, softly moaning, held in place by the heavy beams, forgotten, as men and women returned to their feasting.

At Thurnus's right hand sat Tup Ladletender. On Thurnus's left sat the free woman, Sandal Thong, whom he had earlier this afternoon freed. She, with the two sleen, had boldly aided him in circumventing the concerted attack of Bran Loort's cohorts when they had been individually bested. The feast was served by the village slave girls, Radish, Verr Tail and Turnip among them. I was not forced to serve. I lay near the rack on which the newly branded slave lay secured. After a time she was quiet. I could not conjecture the nature of her thoughts. It did not matter. They could only be those of a slave. She the proud, former mistress, was now no more than I, only another slave, at the full mercy of men.

She was now no more than I, nothing.

I looked upward, and saw dark clouds in the sky, racing across the faces of the moons.

There was a sense of moisture in the air.

This pleased me.

Thurnus, at the feast, stood up. He lifted a goblet of paga. "Tup Ladletender," said he, "by the rite of the claws of sleen, is my brother. I lift my cup to him. Let us drink!" The villagers drank. Tup Ladletender rose to his feet. "You have shared with me tonight your paga and your kettle," said he. "I drink to the hospitality of Tabuk's Ford." There was a cheer. The villagers, and Thurnus, and Ladletender, drank. "And, too, this night," said Ladletender, "I drink to one with whom I do not share caste but that which is stronger than caste, the blood of brotherhood, Thurnus, he of Tabuk's Ford." There was another cheer. The villagers, all, drank. Thurnus stood up again. "I ask this free woman," said he, indicating Sandal Thong, "for whom I muchly care, to accept me in free companionship." There was a great cry of pleasure from the villagers.

"But Thurnus," said she, "as I am now free do I not have the right to refuse?"

"True," said Thurnus, puzzled.

"Then, noble Thurnus," said she, evenly, calmly, "I do refuse. I will not be your companion."

Thurnus lowered the cup of paga. There was silence in the clearing.

Sandal Thong gently lowered herself to the ground, and lay on her belly before Thurnus. She took his right ankle in her hands and, holding it, pressed her lips softly down upon his foot, kissing it. She lifted her head, tears in her eyes. "Let me be instead," she said, "what I want truly to be."

"What is that?" he asked.

She looked up at him, lying at his feet. Her cheeks were tear-stained. Her lips trembled. "—*your slave*," she said.

"I do not understand," he said.

"Be my Master," she said. "I would be your slave!"

"I offer you companionship," he said.

"I beg slavery," she said.

"Why?" he asked.

"I have been in your arms, Thurnus," she said. "In your arms I can be only a slave."

"I do not understand," he said.

"I would dishonor you," she said. "In your arms I can behave only as a slave."

"I see," said he, caste leader of Tabuk's Ford.

"The love I bear you, Thurnus," she said, "is not the love of a free companion, but a hopeless slave girl's love, a love so deep and rich that she who bears it can be only her man's slave."

"Serve me paga," said Thurnus. He handed the goblet to Sandal Thong.

She took it and knelt before him. She held the goblet in two hands, as was proper. She looked up at him. Then she kissed the goblet, almost as though she felt herself unworthy of doing so. Then she put her head down between her lifted, extended arms and, holding the goblet with two hands, proffered it to him.

Though she was free, she served as a slave. Villagers gasped. Free women cried out, scandalized.

There are a number of ritualistic aspects associated with this manner of serving wine. The attitude of kneeling is obvious. Kissing the master's cup is a token of submission, much like kissing his belt, his whip or boots. But, too, it suggests that their lips meet, through metal and wine, or paga, as the case may be. The girl, sensing herself unworthy to feel the kiss of the master, dares at least to kiss lovingly that which his lips will later touch. Then she puts her head down, in submission. Her arms are extended, and her hands are on the cup. This is a beautiful posture in a female, crying out of service, submission and beauty. As her hands are placed so closely together, too, it is reminiscent of her small wrists being linked in slave bracelets. Indeed, wine, or paga, may be so served by a braceleted slave.

Thurnus set aside the cup.

"Have rope brought, and collar me, Thurnus," she said. "I am yours."

"Bring rope," said Thurnus.

Rope was brought.

Thurnus took the rope, and regarded the girl.

She looked up at him.

"Collar me," she said.

"If I collar you," he said, "you are again a slave."

"Collar me, Master," she said.

Thurnus wrapped the rope twice about her throat, and knotted it.

Sandal Thong knelt before him, his slave. He seized her in his mighty arms and crushed her to him, raping her lips with the master's kiss, mighty in its lust and possession of the collared she, and she clutched him, helplessly, crying out. Her head was back, her lips were parted. He had begun to tear the tunic from her with his teeth. "Carry me from the light of the fire, Master," she begged. "But you are a slave," he laughed. He tore the garment from her and threw her between the feast fires. She looked up at him, her eyes wild with the passion-submission of the eager slave girl. "As master wills!" she cried, throwing her head and hair back in the dirt. He leaped to her and, between the feast fires, did lengthy ravishment upon her. Her cries must have carried beyond the palisaded walls.

When he returned to his place at the feast she crawled to his feet, his slave, and lay there, daring sometimes to touch him delicately on the thigh or knee with her fingers.

The feast continued late.

The clouds gathered further in the sky, and I smelled moisture. The moons were darkened by the scudding billows of vapor.

I think that I may have fallen asleep by the rack, from my exhaustion and the pain of the beatings and rapings that I had endured.

But it was still dark when I awakened. I awakened to the clear snap of slave bracelets on my wrists. I looked up. I looked into the eyes of Tup Ladletender. I regarded my wrists. They were confined in inflexible steel. "Get up," said he, "little vulo." I struggled to my feet. I stood there, facing him, in his bracelets. Such devices may be fastened together by as little as one link, or by several links. In these bracelets there were only three links. They were close bracelets. Thus, not only could I not hope to slip them, for such devices are not made to be slipped, but my wrists were fastened closely together. "You are mine now, little vulo," he said.

"Master?" I asked.

"Yes," he said. "You are mine now."

"Yes, Master," I said.

I felt very strange. So simply had I changed hands.

"We must be on our way, shortly," he said.

"Yes, Master," I said.

From the point of simple custody there is usually not much point in braceleting, roping or chaining girls, or such, particularly after they have learned they are slaves, and that there is no escape for them. On the other hand, braceleting, chaining, roping, shackling, blindfolding, gagging, and such, is often done to them. It is a common and familiar part of their life. It is in such ways that their slavery is impressed on them, deeply and ineradicably, in the very depths of their being. They are such that they are subject to such things. It is hard to wear the chains of a man and not know you are his slave. Profoundly, I suppose, these things have to do with nature and her lovely mysteries, encoded genetically into the very heritage of a species, yes, there, a thousand leagues beneath the superficial trivialities of politics and convention, with dominance and submission. In this sense one can understand the ceremony of chains, the rituals of braceleting, the symbolism of the blindfold, the gag, the whip. To be sure we are helpless, in fact, in our ropes and chains, and in our bracelets. And sight is not permitted to us when we are blindfolded, nor is speech permitted us when we are gagged. This power is not only symbolic but real. And the lash, too, is real. Any who have felt it know that. But, too, these things to the slave are enormously stirring and provocative.

How clear they make the complementarities of nature to the slave! They are profoundly sexual, and sensual. Too, in their way, they are profoundly romantic. Not everything romantic, you see, is limited to candy, flowers, wine, and candlelight. To be sure, such things are lovely. They are indeed romantic, very romantic. One remains fond of them. It is true that they are romantic on Earth, but it is not false on Gor either. They can be romantic there, as well, though the context may be different. For example, one might find oneself shackled in the furs, illuminated by candlelight. Goreans, too, are fond of candlelight, and lamplight, and such. A woman is beautiful so illuminated, of course. Do you think Goreans do not know that? Have you not heard of the lamps of love, in the light of which it is common to ravish slaves? And the scent of flowers is surely not unknown in the chambers of love. And is not it likely that it will waft in from the environing gardens? And it is common for the slave to serve her master wine, in the ritual fashion, and then, after he has first sipped, to be herself permitted its delights, though under his supervision. And candy, too, is not unknown on Gor. Perhaps the slave is chained where she cannot reach the candy. It is just out of her reach. But if she performs well, she may hope that her master will permit her to have some. On Gor, if the woman is a slave, she is likely to have to earn her candy, by well pleasing the master, and hope that he will permit her to have some, provided it will not alter her figure from the measurements to which he has decided it will be held.

After all, she belongs to him. She is his property, his animal.

What is it to be owned, to be mastered?

Life, truly lived, becomes a thousand times more exciting, more meaningful, to her. She finds herself in a world whose colors are deeper and richer than she ever knew they could be; she finds she hears sounds she never heard before; she smells smells she has never smelled before; she becomes aware of subtleties of taste which doubtless were there to be experienced, but were never hitherto noticed; and, too, assuredly, in the realm of touch and feeling new worlds, new vistas, are opened for her, to the delicacy of her finger tips, to her body's awareness of pressures, temperatures and textures. These things, the wealth of sensations and realities, bring her alive and stir her belly. They arouse her. She knows she must obey or be punished. The free woman may be coy; she may play her games; she may tease; she may wheedle to be wooed, or coaxed, or cajoled. The master, on the other hand, while perhaps accepting, even enjoying, such amusements with a free woman, for after all he may already have a collar ready for her, does not accept such things in a slave. He does not argue with the slave, nor discuss things with her. He puts her to his feet.

And where else should a slave be? Where else would a slave wish to be?

I looked about. The feast had finished, and most of the villagers had returned to their homes. Some lay about, near the embers of the fires.

We stood near the rack on which the new slave, she who had been the free woman, Melina, lay captive. Thurnus was nearby, and Sandal Thong, and Radish, Verr Tail and Turnip.

"I name you Melina," said Thurnus to the confined slave.

"Yes, Master," she said.

"What is your name?" he said.

"'Melina', Master," she sobbed.

He had much shamed her by giving her in slavery the name she had borne as a free woman. She wore it now as the cognomen of a slave.

"May a slave speak?" she asked.

"Yes," said Thurnus.

"Why have you had my head shaved?" she asked.

"To return you as a shamed slave to the village of your father," said he.

"Please keep me, Master," she said.

"Why?" he asked.

"That I may please you," she whispered.

"Strange words from one such as you," he scoffed.

"I beg to be kept to please my master," she said.

"Have you been bereft of your wits by the brand," inquired Thurnus.

"I only wanted to be the companion of a district leader," she said.

"You are now anyone's slave to whom I give or sell you," he said.

"Yes, Master," she said.

"I did not move to become district leader," said Thurnus, "for it was your urging and intent that I do so. Had I sought the position it would have seemed to all that I did so for your ambition and to avoid the lashing of your tongue."

She squirmed on the rape-rack, confined by the beams, in misery.

"In a man's own hut," said he, "he must be master, even though he has selected out for himself a companion. It is the part of his companion to befriend and aid him, not to insult and drive him."

"I was a poor companion," she whispered. "I will try to be a better slave."

"If I choose to seek the leadership of the district," said Thurnus, "I will do so. If I do not wish to do so, I will not."

"As Master wishes," said Melina, the slave.

"You knew little of the matters of being a companion," said Thurnus.

"I will study more diligently the matters of being a slave," said Melina.

"You will begin in the morning, when you are publicly whipped," he said.

"Yes, Master," she said.

He put his hand on her body.

"At one time you cared for me," she said.

"Yes," he said, "that is true."

"Do you find my body of interest, Master?" she asked.

"Yes," said Thurnus.

"And I am strong," she said. "I can pull a plow by myself."

Thurnus smiled.

"Keep me, Master," she begged.

"Why?" he asked.

"I love you," she said.

"You know the penalties for lying?" he asked.

"I do not lie, Master," she said. "I do love you." One of the penalties which may in a peasant village be inflicted upon a lying slave girl is to throw her alive to hungry sleen. I had little doubt but what Thurnus might do this if he caught one of his girls in a lie.

"How can that be?" asked Thurnus.

"I do not know," she whispered. "It is a strange, helpless feeling. I have lain here in the stocks. I have thought much."

"Tomorrow," said Thurnus, "you will have less time to think, and more time to work."

"Long ago I loved you," she said, "but as a free woman. Then, for years I did not love you, but despised you. Now again, after long years, I feel love for you, only now it is the shameful, helpless love of a bond girl for her master."

"In the morning you will be whipped," said Thurnus.

"Yes, Master," she said. She looked up at him. "You are strong," she said, "and masterful. You are a great man, whether you are a district leader or not. My freedom blinded me to your manhood and your worth. I saw you not for the things you were but for the things you might, enhancing my own person, become. I saw you not as a man but as an instrument of my own perceptions and ambitions. I regret that I did not, in my companionship, relish and celebrate what you were, rather than an image of what you might become. I never truly knew you. I knew only the image of my own invention. I never truly looked at you. Had I done so, I might have seen you."

"You were always a shrewd, clever woman," said Thurnus.

There were tears in her eyes. "I love you," she said.

"I am putting you out into the village as a village slave," he said.

"Yes, Master," she said.

"At night you will be confined in a sleen cage. During the day you will feed on what men will throw you. Each day you will serve a different hut in the village."

"Yes, Master," she said.

He looked down at her.

"May I speak?" she asked.

"Yes," he said.

"May I not, too, sometimes serve my master?" she asked.

"Perhaps," said Thurnus. He made as though to turn away.

"Please, Master," said Melina.

He turned to face her.

"Please touch your slave," she said.

"It is long since you have asked my touch," said Thurnus, regarding her.

"I beg it, Master," she whispered. She lifted her body in the stock. "I beg it!"

"As an abject and meaningless slave?" he asked.

"Yes, Master," she said, "as an abject and meaningless slave—one hoping her master will take pity on her, and touch her."

"Can it be," asked Thurnus, "that the slave, in her sleen collar, is aroused?"

"She desires to please her Master."

"Is she aroused?" inquired Thurnus.

"Yes," she cried, suddenly, half-choking, piteously. "She is aroused! She is aroused! For the first time in years she is aroused!"

Thurnus looked down upon her.

"Piteously aroused!" she whispered.

Thurnus turned away.

"Wait, Master!" she cried. "Please do not leave me! Please do not leave me!"

He turned to look back at her.

"I cannot stand it!" she wept. "I am helpless! I never knew I could feel this way!"

"And what is the nature of your feelings?" he asked.

She knew herself under the gaze of her master.

"Speak," he said.

His voice was not pleasant.

"They are the feelings of a needful slave!" she wept.

"Are you a needful slave?" he asked.

"Yes, Master!"

"So," said he, scornfully, "she who was the proud free woman, Melina, of Tabuk's Ford, is now a needful slave."

"Yes, Master!" she wept.

She lifted her body to him, piteously.

He returned then to her side, then, and regarded her, regarded her as what she now was, a slave, and a piteous slave, and one obviously in the throes of her slave needs.

"Please touch me, my Master! Please touch me. I beg it! I beg it! Please, my Master, please touch your slave!"

Again she lifted her body to him, even more piteously.

We turned away as Thurnus, swiftly and brutally, raped the slave girl in the stock.

When he had finished with her she lay gasping, half shattered in the stock. "Oh, Master!" she cried. "Master," she whispered.

"Be silent, Slave," said Thurnus.

"Yes, Master," she said, and the girl in the sleen collar was silent.

I looked upon her. I suspected that never had Thurnus used her with such authority and force. Years ago, doubtless, she had been loved with the gentle tenderness accorded to free women. This was the first time in her life, I suspected, that she had felt the uncompromising, unbridled lust that may be vented on the helpless body of a female slave. Never before had she had an experience like this. Never before had she been so had. She looked after Thurnus, startled, confused, awe-struck, bewildered, enraptured. I saw she wanted to cry out to him, to beg him to return to her, but she dared not, for she was under discipline. Morning would be time enough for her to be whipped.

Thurnus drew his tunic about him. He looked at me. Under the eyes of a free man, I knelt.

"I have given you to Tup Ladletender," he said.

"Yes, Master," I said.

"He was promised you, in payment for the powder he gave to one in the village," said Thurnus. "The powder was used, though it did not have the effect that one in the village had intended. Accordingly, on behalf of one who was of the village, who can no longer transact the affairs of business, having fallen into the unfortunate state of slavery, I, on behalf of that former person, now one of my beasts, tender you to him in payment for the powder."

"Yes, Master," I said. My fists clenched in the slave bracelets. I was tendered in payment for a small, worthless powder. I grew angry. Surely I was at least a few copper tarsks' worth of slave girl. "But the powder was worthless," I pouted.

"But so, too, are you, pretty little Dina," said Thurnus. He threw back his head and laughed.

"Yes, Master," I said, angrily.

He turned to Sandal Thong. "I pronounce you my preferred slave," said he. "You will sleep in my hut, and tend it."

"A slave is grateful," said she, "Master."

"Too," said he, "you are first girl."

"As Master wishes," she said.

Radish, Verr Tail and Turnip fled to her, hugging her and kissing her. "We are so happy for you," said Turnip.

"I am first girl," said Sandal Thong.

"I am so happy for you," said Radish.

"Fetch a switch," said Sandal Thong.

"Sandal Thong?" asked Radish, stunned.

"Fetch a switch," said Sandal Thong.

"Yes, Mistress," said Radish, hurrying away.

In a few moments Radish returned, carrying a switch, which she placed in the hands of Sandal Thong.

"Kneel," said Sandal Thong to the three girls. They knelt.

"In a straight line, four horts apart, facing the master," she said. She dressed their line. "Straight," she said. She kicked back Radish's knees. "Backs straight, hands on thighs, bellies sucked in, heads high," she said. She tapped Verr Tail on the belly with her switch. Verr Tail sucked her belly in, tight. She tapped Turnip twice under the chin. Turnip lifted her chin. In their eyes I could read their distress. But they knelt beautifully under Sandal Thong's discipline.

Sandal Thong inspected the line.

Something was perhaps not yet just right.

"Ah!" she said suddenly.

It seemed a thought had just come to her.

She scrutinized the girls, and they looked up at her, puzzled.

"Spread your knees, you meaningless sluts!" she snapped. "Now! Instantly! Widely! More widely!"

The girls, in consternation, did so.

"From now on," she said, "you are no longer simple field slaves. You are now also pleasure slaves. You will all be pleasure slaves for the Master! Surely you have learned something from little Dina!"

She again inspected the line.

The girls now knelt in perfection, and as pleasure slaves.

Sandal Thong turned then to Thurnus. "Here are your slaves, Master," she said.

"Excellent," said Thurnus. He looked upon the three girls. They dared not move a muscle. All were positioned with perfection, and unmistakably as pleasure slaves. I had little doubt but that Sandal Thong would richly switch any of them who disobeyed in the least, or gave the least hint of disobedience. Thurnus grinned. He began to suspect the wonders that he would now have from these girls.

Before him, you see, they now knelt as pleasure slaves!

I stood nearby, braceleted.

How I would have loved to provide wonders for Clitus Vitellius!

Every true man, I thought, deserves one or more pleasure slaves.

As a slave myself, of course, I would have preferred to be the only slave of a beloved master.

How the beasts with more than one girl make them compete desperately to please them!

I myself would have wanted to be a thousand slaves to my master, that I alone might please him in a thousand ways, in a thousand modalities, as a thousand girls. I would wish to be such a slave to him, so marvelous a slave, that he would never desire another, that it would never even occur to him to think of another.

"Excellent," said Thurnus. "Excellent."

I had little doubt that Thurnus, for his considerably improved slaves, would soon be the envy of the village. Too, I supposed, shortly, that every embonded wench in the village would discover that she would be subjected to similar delights and disciplines.

This village, I suspected, would become famous for its pleasure slaves.

And I did not doubt but what other villages, too, would be so influenced.

Once a man understands that a woman can be a pleasure slave how will he ever thereafter want her as anything different or see her as anything less?

Sandal Thong then herself knelt before Thurnus, she, too, as a pleasure slave.

The implicit petition of her posture, and its tacit confession of her will and desire, was not lost on her master.

Thurnus gestured to the other slaves.

"You may cage them at your pleasure," he said.

"Yes, Master," said Sandal Thong.

Sandal Thong muchly loved her master.

In her love for Thurnus, clearly, she was determined that he would have the best not only from herself, but from all his girls. Too, I had little doubt but that when it was the turn of the village slave, Melina, to serve the house of Thurnus that she, too, would fall under the same strict discipline. Sandal Thong, switch in hand, would see that Melina served her master to perfection.

"You may rise, Dina," said Tup Ladletender to me.

I rose, standing in close bracelets.

The rope collar of Thurnus was removed from my neck. It was no longer appropriate that I wear it. I had changed hands. I now belonged to another.

"You may bid your former cagemate farewell," said Sandal Thong.

Radish, Verr Tail and Turnip came to me and wished me well, hugging and kissing me. I, too, wished them well.

"Slaves to your cage," said Sandal Thong.

"We must go to our cage," said Radish to me. "I wish you well."

"I, too, wish you well," I said. "I wish you all well."

The three girls hurried to the cage. Sandal Thong, switch in hand, came to me. She hugged and kissed me. "I wish you well, Dina," she said.

"I, too, wish you well, Mistress," I said. I addressed her as mistress, for she was first girl.

Sandal Thong then turned and followed the other girls, to lock them in the cage for the night.

Thurnus came over to me and put his hand on my head, and shook it.

I looked at him, tears in my eyes.

"The village," said he, "is no place for you, little Dina. The days are too long and the work too hard." He looked at me. "You have the body of a pleasure slave," he said. "You belong at the feet of men."

"Yes, Master," I said.

"Come along, Slave," said Tup Ladletender, taking my arm.

He began to lead me away. I stopped, and turned, pulling against his arm.

"I wish you well, Master," I said to Thurnus.

"You cannot even pull a plow," he said.

"I make a very poor she-bosk," I said.

"You are not the she-bosk," he said, "but the meadow." I put my head down, reddening. It was not mine to plow, but to be plowed. "I wish you well, little slave," said Thurnus.

"Thank you, Master," I said.

I felt Tup Ladletender's hand close more firmly on my arm. "Will it be necessary to beat you?" he asked.

"No, Master," I said, frightened, and hurried on beside him, his hand on my arm.

His cart, with the two large wheels, and the two long handles, was near the village gate.

The gate was opened for us by its tender.

I expected to be tied to the back of the wagon, that I might follow in its dust. To my surprise he placed me between the two handles. He removed the slave bracelets, putting them in a drawer in the side of the cart.

"I am too weak to draw the cart, Master," I told him.

He removed two pair of wrist rings and chains from another drawer. He locked one wrist ring from one pair on the left handle, and snapped its matching wrist ring on my left wrist. He then locked one wrist ring from the other pair on the cart's long right handle and snapped its mate about my right wrist. I was chained between the handles. There was about a foot of chain between each wrist ring locked on its handle and its matching ring which clasped my corresponding wrist.

"I cannot draw the cart, Master," I told him.

I cried out as the whip cut my back. I seized the handles and threw my weight against them, bent over, digging with my feet into the dirt.

"I cannot, Master!" I cried.

The whip struck me again.

I cried out with misery and drew the cart.

I pulled Tup Ladletender's cart through the gate and out onto the dusty road leading from Tabuk's Ford.

I felt a drop of rain. Then it began to fall lightly. I looked up. The billowing, scudding clouds were swift in the night. I could see the moons behind them. Then more rain splashed into the dust. I felt it on my hair and naked body. I pulled the cart. Then it began to pour, and

I slipped in the mud. Ladletender helped, pushing, at the wheels and cart. At last we waited, standing in the driving rain. Then he removed me from between the handles, and, together, we sat beneath the cart.

"The drought is broken," said Tup Ladletender to me.

"Yes, Master," I said.

After a time I said, "May I have a candy, Master?" I had not forgotten the candy he had given me beneath the hut of Thurnus. How sweet and good it had been. It had been only a cheap hard candy but such things are rare in the lives of most slave girls. They are very precious.

"Do you want it very much?" asked Tup Ladletender.

"Yes, Master," I said.

He took me in his arms, and thrust me back to the mud between the wheels of the cart.

I looked up at him.

"Earn it," he said.

"Yes, Master," I said, reaching for him.

The rain drove down from the sweet dark sky in torrents. One could scarcely see the trees and road.

Ten

I am an Item of Merchandise

I swam out in the pool to the end of my neck tether, and splashed in the water.

"Clean yourself well, Dina," said Tup Ladletender. "You must be sparkling."

"Yes, Master," I called to him.

I had knelt beside the pool and, the rope on my neck, washed my hair. Then I had been permitted to wash in the pool and cleanse my body. The welts I had received from the beatings of Bran Loort and his bullies had healed. I had only four marks on my body from the animal whip of Tup Ladletender, with which he had encouraged me in my drawing of his cart. These now had almost disappeared. Generally he disciplined me with a cuff of the flat of his hand. I respected him. He managed me well.

I had been his slave for some two weeks.

We had visited various villages, but, on the whole, we had made our way along the road to Ar. He must replenish his stores. I was pleased that he had not sold me to peasants. Another fate, I knew, he had in store for me.

When we had come to the great road I had rejoiced. It is broad, fairly smooth, and built like a wall, sunk in the earth. It is not hard to draw the cart on such a road. My work, thus, was easier. We could see villages here and there more frequently now; too, occasionally there were hostels and taverns on the road. I enjoyed seeing caravans pass, and villagers with their bosk wagons. I feared the great tharlarion of the caravans. Often the animals wore belled harnesses. Once we were passed by a great slave caravan. There were more than four hundred wagons with girls ankle-chained in them. It was a caravan of Mintar, the great merchant. Another time we were passed by a smaller slave caravan. In this caravan, there were few wagons, and those there were showed scarring and marks of fire. Goods and wounded men lay in the wagons. Afoot, between the wagons, walked a chain of forty girls. They were neck chained, and their wrists were fastened behind their backs with slave bracelets. Their heads were down. Many were beautiful.

"What occurred?" asked Tup Ladletender.

"Raiders from Treve," said a man with a bandaged shoulder, in one of the wagons.

The great road to Ar is marked with pasang stones. We had followed the road to within two hundred pasangs of Ar. Then we had left it, and, for two days, followed a side road. The countryside was still relatively populated.

Tup Ladletender's cart was now at the hut of a villager whom he knew.

In the distance, even from the pool, I could see the white, looming walls of the merchant keep, Stones of Turmus, a Turian outpost, licensed for the storage of goods within the realm of Ar. Such outposts are not uncommon on Gor. They are useful in maintaining the security of trade. Their function is not military but commercial. Turia is one of the great trading centers of Gor. It lies far to the south, in the middle latitudes of her southern hemisphere.

"Look, Dina!" said Tup Ladletender, pointing upward.

I looked up and saw, far overhead, some four tarnsmen in flight. They carried the yellow banners of truce.

"They are bound, I wager, for Port Kar," said Tup Ladletender, "whence they will take ship to Cos."

I had heard there was fighting between Ar and Cos, it having to do with the alleged support by Cos accorded to Vosk pirates. The Vosk is a mighty river which flows westward, emptying into a vast rence delta, finding its way eventually to Thassa, the sea. The motivation of the hostilities was apparently mostly economic, having to do with trade monopolies sought by both cities in the territories bordering the Vosk. Ar claimed the southern shore of the Vosk. Cos, and the other major maritime Ubarate, Tyros, on the other hand, had traditionally conducted trade, through overland merchant connections, with these territories. I watched the tarnsmen disappear in the distance. Twice earlier, on the great road to Ar, Tup Ladletender had pointed out tarn-smen in flight, presumably messengers. Marlenus of Ar, and other Ubars, commonly employed such couriers.

The thought of Clitus Vitellius passed through my mind. He had spurned me. How I hated him!

I felt a tug on the neck tether. "I am coming, Master," I called.

I swam in, to the side of the pool. Ladletender handed me a towel. My tether he tied to a tree. I toweled myself.

"You must sparkle, Dina," he said to me.

"Yes, Master," I said. I looked up to the keep of Stones of Turmus in the distance.

I wondered how much I would bring. I had never been sold before.

"Pay attention to your master," said Tup Ladletender.

"Yes, Master," I said.

Tup Ladletender handed me a wide-toothed comb. I began, with long strokes, to straighten my hair. I continued to look at the keep of Stones of Turmus. It was high and formidable. It was within those walls that I would be owned.

We had stayed in a nearby village overnight, in which Ladletender had a friend. His cart was there now. I had not drawn the cart this morning. I must be refreshed.

"Brush your hair," said Ladletender.

"Yes, Master," I said.

After I had finished, Ladletender retrieved the brush and comb, dropping them in his pouch.

He looked me over. I blushed, under Gorean appraisal. I wore only my tether.

"Stand as a slave," he said.

I stood beautifully, back straight, head high, belly sucked in, hip turned. No woman can stand more beautifully than as a Gorean slave girl.

"Excellent," said Ladletender, smacking his lips.

"Master is pleased," I said.

"Yes," he said.

"The slave, too, is then pleased," I said.

"Behold," said he. He drew forth, from a leather bag nearby, a sack, such as vegetables may be carried in. I looked at it. I was puzzled. It was folded; it was small. He removed the tether from my neck. I shook my head and hair, the bond removed.

He gestured to the sack. It had been used to carry vegetables. There was printing on it.

"Put it on," he said.

I opened the sack. In it were cut an opening for the head, and two for the arms. I drew it over my head. It was snug. With binding fiber he cinched it on my body.

He stepped back. "Lovely," he said. It came high on my thighs. There was a casualness about it, a carelessness about the shoulders, with respect to my figure. But the binding fiber, bound twice about my belly, and cinched tight, at my left hip, accentuated my breasts and hips. There was a hint of lusciousness, concealed within so apparently negligent a wrapper. It was well contrived, psychologically, to suggest a cheap, but most tasty slut.

I reddened.

"Here," said Ladletender. He held up a string of slave beads. I smiled. I reached for them. "Not so fast," said he. I put down my hands. He put the beads in his belt. "Turn about," he said. I did so. It is the man on Gor, often, who puts jewelry on the female, bedecking her. It is not uncommon, even, for him, should he have a pierced-ear slave, to fasten her earrings on her. I assumed Tup Ladletender would rope the slave beads on my neck, fastening them behind my neck. They were of wood, and cheap and pretty. I would be pleased to wear a decoration. Once I had nearly had my throat cut for my lack of knowledge of "Bina," or slave beads. I still did not understand why. Too, once I had had a strange dream that dealt with slave beads, a meaningless dream I had not understood, in which I had been asked, strangely, to string such beads. My hands were pulled behind me, and locked in slave bracelets. Then, as I stood helplessly braceleted, Tup Ladletender roped the cheap beads about my neck.

He stepped before me.

"You are beautiful, Dina," said he.

"Thank you, Master," I said.

He then turned away. "Come along," he said.

I stumbled after him, barefoot, wrists braceleted behind my back.

We soon took the road to Stones of Turmus. In an Ahn we had come to the great gate. The high, white walls loomed above me. They were more than eighty feet in height. I felt very small. There were six towers on the walls, two defending the gate, and one at each corner. Suddenly I wanted to turn and flee. But I was braceleted. And nowhere on Gor was there a place for a girl such as I to run. I was slave.

A small panel in a small door built within the great gate slid open.

"Tup Ladletender here," said Ladletender.

"Greetings, Ladletender," said a voice, recognizing him.

"I am vending a girl," said Ladletender, indicating me.

"Welcome, Tup Ladletender," said the voice.

The small door in the great gate opened, and we entered. The small door was then shut behind us.

Eleven

Perfume and Silk

"I will give you four copper tarsks for her," said the captain.

"Ten," said Ladletender.

"Six," said the captain.

"Done," said Ladletender.

My body ached. My wrists were confined in wrist rings fastened to a chain, depending from a ring in the ceiling. My weight was borne mostly by the wrist rings and chain. The tips of my toes barely touched the stone floor.

I was naked. I had been examined thoroughly, in Gorean fashion. I was miserable, and purchased.

I had been unable to resist the captain's touch.

I had struggled, shrieking for mercy, twisting on the chain.

"She needs a bit of taming," said the captain, "but we manage that."

I did not think I needed taming. I was now only too eager to please men, the masters. Too, I had some comprehension as to what my failure to do so might involve. I had learned to obey on Gor.

I hung upon the chain, limp, the steel cutting into my wrists. My eyes were closed. My body ached.

I heard Tup Ladletender paid his money, it being counted out from a small iron chest in the office of the captain.

Then he had left.

"Look at me, Slave," said the captain.

I opened my eyes.

"You are a Turian girl now," he said.

"Yes, Master," I said. I had been sold for six copper tarsks. It was my worth on Gor.

"Are you tame?" he asked.

"Yes, Master," I said.

He went to his desk and, from one of its drawers, drew forth an opened slave collar. It was unlike most of the Gorean collars. It was a Turian collar. Most Gorean collars, decorated or not, are basically a flat, circular band, hinged, which locks snugly about the girl's neck. The Turian collar, on the other hand, fits more loosely and resembles a hinged ring, looped about the throat. A man can get his fingers inside a Turian collar and use it to drag the girl to him. It does not fit loosely enough to permit its being slipped, of course. Gorean collars are not made to be slipped by the girls who wear them.

He threw the collar to his desk. I watched it strike the desk. I had never worn a true collar before. Suddenly I was terrified that it might be put on me. It locked. I would not be able to remove it.

"No, Master," I said, "please do not put a collar on me."

He came to me and, with a key, unlocked the wrist rings. I fell to the stone floor at his feet.

"You do not want to wear a collar?" he asked.

"No, Master," I whispered.

He turned away from me. I half sat, half lay on the stone floor, my legs to the side, the palms of my hands on the stones, my head down. I did not watch him. Tup Ladletender had left. He had taken the bit of sacking I had worn, and the slave beads, and the slave bracelets, which had confined my wrists. All he had left behind was she who had been Judy Thornton, six copper tarsks worth of sold she-slave.

"I will make you beg to wear a collar," said the man.

I turned and looked up, frightened. He loomed over me. He held a slave whip.

"No, Master!" I cried.

Well did he punish me then for my insolence. There was nowhere to crawl or run. He whipped me as a Gorean master. At last I lay blubbering at his feet.

"I think now you are tamed," he said.

"Yes, Master," I sobbed, "yes!"

"Are you tamed?" he asked.

"I am tamed, Master!" I wept. "I am tamed!"

"Do you now beg to wear a collar?" he inquired.

"Yes, Master!" I cried.

"Beg," said he.

"I beg to wear a collar," I wept.

"What collar?" he asked.

"Your collar, Master!" I cried. "Any collar! Any collar, Master!"

He then fastened the collar on my throat. It closed with an efficient metallic snap. I collapsed to the stones.

He turned and left me, placing the slave whip on the wall, where it had hung, convenient to hand. He rang a bell. A door opened, and a soldier, a guard, appeared. "Send for Sucha," said the captain. "There is a new girl."

I lay on the stones. Timidly, when he was not watching, but sitting behind his desk, engaged in work, perhaps entering my acquisition and price in his ledgers, I touched the collar, rounded, steel and gleaming. It was truly locked on my throat. I was collared. Only the brand had made me before feel so much a slave. I wept. I was branded and collared.

I heard the jingle of tiny bells, slave bells.

I became conscious of a woman's feet, bare, near me.

The bells, tiny, in four rows, were thonged about her left ankle. A whip touched me, prodding me, in the back. I shuddered. "Get up, Girl," said a woman's voice. I looked up. She wore a wisp of yellow silk. Her dark hair was bound back with a yellow, silk talmit.

I stood up.

"Stand as a slave," she said.

I stood beautifully.

"A Dina," said the woman.

Her own brand was the customary Kajira brand, the initial letter in cursive Gorean script, about an inch and a half high, and a half inch wide, of the expression "Kajira," the most common Gorean expression for a female slave. It was clearly visible on her thigh. The wisp of silk she wore made no pretense to cover it.

"I am Sucha," said the woman.

"Yes, Mistress," I said.

"Why were you whipped?" asked Sucha.

"I asked not to be put in a collar," I whispered.

"Remove it," she said.

I looked at her puzzled.

"Remove it," said the woman.

I tried to pull the collar from my throat. I jerked it against my neck until I cried. I struggled to force it apart. I turned the collar and, with my fingers, tore at the lock. It remained obdurately, perfectly, inflexibly fastened.

I looked at the woman with agony. "I cannot remove it," I said.

"That is true, Slave Girl," she said. "And do not forget it."

"Yes, Mistress," I said.

"What were you called?" she asked.

"Dina," I said.

Sucha looked at the captain. "It is acceptable," he said.

"For the time then," said Sucha, "until masters wish otherwise, you will remain 'Dina.'"

"Yes, Mistress," I said.

"Follow me, Dina," she said. I followed her. She, too, wore a Turian collar. The girls of the Wagon Peoples, too, I understand, wear such collars.

We walked along a long passage. Then we left that passage, and took others. We passed numerous storerooms, closed by barred gates. At one point, we passed through a heavy iron door, watched by a guard. On the other side of the door, she said, "Precede me, Dina." "Yes, Mistress," I said. I preceded her. We walked along another long passage. It, too, was lined with barred gates, giving access to storerooms.

"You are very beautiful, Mistress," I said, over my shoulder.

"Do you wish to feel my whip?" she asked.

"No, Mistress," I said. I was then silent.

I knew why I was now preceding her. It was fairly common Gorean custom. We must be nearing the slave quarters. If I should now turn and flee, she was behind me, to stop me, with the whip. Sometimes new girls become frightened at the entrance to their slave quarters. There is something fearful about being locked within, as a slave.

"Are you tamed?" I asked her.

There was a pause. Then she said, "Yes."

We walked on.

"We are all tamed girls here," she said. "We have been taught our collars."

"Men can tame us!" I wept.

"Men tame girls or not, as they please," said Sucha. "It is their will which determines the matter. Some men do not tame their girls quickly, in order to tease and play with them longer, but the girl, if she is not a fool, knows to whom it is in the end that she belongs. In the end it is the man who holds the whip. This the girl knows. In the end, when the master wishes, we crawl into his arms, docile and tamed. We are women. We are slaves."

"I hate men!" I cried.

"Speak softly, lest you be whipped," cautioned Sucha.

"Do you not, too, hate men?" I demanded.

"I love them," said Sucha.

I cried out in anger. I turned about. "I am not tamed!" I cried. "I will never be tamed!"

"Tell it to the masters," said Sucha.

I shuddered.

"You are tamed," said Sucha.

"Yes," I said, miserably, "I have been tamed." I had been tamed since the first Gorean male had touched me, long ago, when I had worn a chain and collar in a Gorean field. Something instantly in me had told me who were my masters. And I remembered Clitus Vitellius, and Thurnus, and the captain, strict with me in his office. I touched the Turian collar which I wore, looped and locked about my neck.

"Tamed girl," said Sucha.

"Yes," said the former Judy Thornton, now the slave, Dina, "I am tamed."

I knew I must obey men.

"Here," said Sucha, "is the entrance to the kennels of the female slaves."

I shrank back. The door was small, and thick, and iron, some eighteen inches by eighteen inches square.

"Enter," said Sucha.

She stood behind me with the whip.

I turned the handle on the tiny door and, falling to my belly, squirmed through.

Sucha followed me.

Within we stood up. I gazed about myself with wonder. The room was lofty, and spacious; it contained numerous slender, white pillars, rich hangings; it was tiled in purple, and there was in it a scented pool; the walls were glossy and richly mosaiced with scenes of slave girls at the service of their masters; I uneasily touched the collar at my throat; light filtered down from narrow, barred windows, set high in the glossy, mosaiced walls. Here and there, about the pool, lay indolent girls, not set to work. They regarded me, appraising my face and figure, doubtless comparing it to their own.

"The room is beautiful," I said.

"Kneel," said Sucha.

I knelt.

"You are Dina," she said. "You are slave now within the Keep of Stones of Turmus. This is a merchant keep, under the banner and shield of Turia." That the keep was under the banner of Turia designated it as a Turian keep, distinguishing it in this sense not only from keeps maintained by other cities but more importantly from the "free keeps" maintained by the merchant caste in its own right, keeps without specific municipal affiliations. Similarly, the merchant caste, which is international, so to speak, in its organization, arranges and conducts the four great fairs which occur annually in the vicinity of the Sardar mountains. The merchant caste, too, maintains certain free ports on certain islands and on the coasts of Thassa, such as Teletus and Bazi. Space in a "free keep" is rented on a commercial basis, regardless of municipal affiliation. In a banner keep, or one maintained by a given city, preference, if not exclusive rights, are accorded to the merchants and citizens of the city under whose banner the keep is established and administered. That the keep was also under the shield of Turia meant that it was defended by Turians, that its garrison was Turian. Sometimes a keep will fly a given banner but its garrison will be furnished by the city within whose territory it lies. It is not unknown for a keep to fly the banner of one city and stand behind the shield of another. Both banner and shield of Stones of Turmus, however, were Turian. Stones of Turmus was Turian. "In the garrison there are one hundred men and five officers," said Sucha. "There are twenty men who are ancillary personnel, a physician, porters, scribes and such."

The other girls in the room came casually to where I knelt before Sucha. There were several of them. Most were naked. All wore Turian collars.

"A new silk girl," said one.

I straightened my body. It pleased me that they saw me as a silk girl.

"There are twenty-seven girls in Stones of Turmus," continued Sucha. "We come from nineteen cities. Six of us are bred slaves."

"She is a pretty one," said another girl.

I smiled.

"Teach her she is low girl," said Sucha.

One of the girls seized me from behind by the hair and threw me back to the tiles. I cried out. The other girls then, swiftly, kicked and struck at me. I screamed, twisting. "Enough," called Sucha. The beating had lasted no more than a brief handful of seconds, perhaps no more than five or six seconds. Its purpose was no more than to intimidate me. I looked up, horrified, my head still held down by the hair. My leg was bleeding where I had been bitten.

"Release her," said Sucha. "Kneel, Dina."

My hair released, I knelt.

"You are low girl," said Sucha.

"Yes, Mistress," I said. I was terrified. I did not even dare look into the eyes of the other girls. I could sense their readiness, their eagerness, on the least provocation, to put me under slave-girl discipline.

There was a pounding on bars, from several yards away. I heard a man's voice. It sounded authoritative, especially significant, in such a place. We listened, Sucha carefully, too.

"The girl, Sulda," he called, "is summoned to the couch of Hak Haran."

"Be swift, Sulda," whispered Sucha. "Hak Haran does not like to be kept waiting."

"Yes, Mistress," said a stunning brunet, her face suffused with pleasure, hurrying away from us.

"The girl hears and obeys," called Sucha.

"It is well," said the man.

"I," said another of the girls, "am never summoned except to the couch of Fulmius."

The other girls laughed at her.

"Leave us," said Sucha.

The other girls, some with last looks at me, drifted away.

"They do not like me," I said.

"You are very pretty," said Sucha. "It is natural for them to resent you."

"I thought they were tamed," I said.

"They are tamed to men, who are the masters," said Sucha. "But we are not tamed to one another."

"I do not want to be hurt," I said.

"Remember then," said Sucha, "that you are low girl. Please them. Conduct yourself with care among your sisters in bondage."

"Yes, Mistress," I said.

"Get up. Follow me," said Sucha.

"Yes, Mistress," I said.

I knew that slave girls were often left to impose their own order upon themselves, masters usually not interfering in such matters. The kennel rooms of slave girls could be jungles. Usually the strongest, largest girl, with her cohorts, dominated. Order tended to be imposed by physical means. The head girls, too, their dominance assured, often did not impose a further order among the lesser girls, leaving it to them to determine their own rankings. Squabbles among slave girls can be nasty. In them there is likely to be much screaming and rolling upon the tiles; vicious clawing, biting, kicking and hair pulling tend to figure in such feminine disputations; even more shameful perhaps is the fact that the other girls find such contests amusing and encourage the contestants. Sometimes a strong girl even orders two friends to fight, until one establishes a dominance over the other. "I have been beaten," is the whimpered submission phrase of the loser, clawed and frightened. "Command me, Mistress," she then whispers. She must then serve the victor. If she objects the matter is again subjected to physical adjudication. In a closed set of kennels the order among the girls is usually meticulous and extremely precise. I was low girl.

"Here is your kennel," said Sucha. "You will customarily be locked in here at night, if you are not serving the men."

"Yes, Mistress," I said.

It was a cell alcove, off the large room, with a small, barred gate. It must be entered and left on the hands and knees. A girl, thus, cannot rush from it; too, in leaving it, she is simple to leash. Perhaps most importantly she can enter or leave her "place" only with her head down and on her knees, this involving a tacit, mnemonic psychology, reminding her and impressing upon her that she is a slave. The cell itself was some eight feet deep and four feet wide and four feet high. I could, thus, not stand in the cell. Its furnishings were only a thin, scarlet mattress and a crumpled slave blanket of rep-cloth.

"I trust you find the accommodations satisfactory," she said.

"Yes, Mistress," I smiled. Indeed, it was the most luxurious cage I had seen. It was dry, and there was a mattress. Short of being chained on furs at the foot of a master's couch, what more could a girl desire?

"Follow me," said Sucha.

"Yes, Mistress," I said, following her.

She took me about the pool to another room. In walking about the pool she pointed out the gates of the kennels to me. "This is the rear gate," she said. "It is that through which we entered." It was small and iron. "There is no handle on this side," I said. "No," said Sucha, "it may be opened only from the outside. I recalled the other gate, down the corridor, which had been tended by a guard. "Why then," I asked, "was there a guard down the corridor?" Sucha looked at me. "Did you not see the side gates in the corridor?" she asked. "Yes," I said. "To guard them," said Sucha. "Not us?" I asked. She laughed. "We are the least valuable things in the fortress," she said. "Oh," I said. I continued to follow her, but looked behind me at the small gate. It was stout. It could not be opened from our side. Beyond it, in the corridor, lay storage rooms for truly valuable merchandise, worthy of having a guard posted in the passage. I had passed, earlier, in walking through the corridors, several storage rooms. They had been locked, but not individually guarded. They held less valuable, bulk goods. I was angry that Sucha had said we were the least valuable things in the fortress. But then I remembered I had cost only six copper tarsks.

Sucha walked past a small room, and came to a short corridor, leading from the lofty room. In it was a large, barred gate, with another visible beyond it. It had been on the bars of the innermost gate that the man had pounded when summoning Sulda, the slave, to the couch of the man Hak Haran. But there were now no soldiers, or guards, in sight. Both gates, however, were double locked, with square, heavy locks. Two keys would be required for each. The gates were separated by about twenty feet. An ornate corridor could be seen beyond, with vases and carpeting. I looked at the two heavy locks on the innermost gate.

"They cannot be picked," said Sucha. "They are sleeve locks. The sleeve prevents the direct entry of a wire or pick. Too, within the sleeve there is a plug, a rounded, metal cone, which must be unscrewed before the key can be inserted. A wire or pick could not turn the cone."

"Is there anything," I asked, "in the kennels which might serve as a stout wire or long pick, one of suitable length to even try?"

"No," said Sucha.

I held the bars, dismally.

"You are an imprisoned slave," said Sucha. "Come along."

With one last look at the heavy bars and locks I turned to follow her. She led me to the small room we had passed earlier. It was a preparation room for slave girls. In it were mirrors. In them I saw a lovely dark-haired girl, naked, in a Turian collar, myself, followed by a beautiful woman, dark-haired, in a wisp of yellow silk, carrying a whip.

Sucha indicated one of five small, sunken baths, and oils and towels. She showed me the use of the oils and towels.

"You are an ignorant girl," she said. "You do not even know how to take a bath."

I blushed.

My hair then I washed, and dried, and combed and brushed, taking from it the dust of the road leading to Stones of Turmus, and the sweat of the afternoon and early evening.

"I am hungry," I said.

"Sit on the tiles," she said.

I did so. I sat naked on the tiles.

She threw a linkage of rings and bells to the tiles beside me. "Bell yourself," she said.

"They lock," I said.

"Bell yourself," she said.

I extended my left ankle and, carefully, aligned the four rings. The rings were linked vertically at five places by tiny metal fastenings; each ring, opened, hinged, terminated on one end with a bolt and on the other with a tiny lock; I slipped the small bolts into the four tiny locks; there were four tiny snaps; the rings, linked together, fitted snugly; each ring bore five slave bells.

I looked at the bells. They were locked upon me.

I dared not move my foot, for fear I might cry out for a man.

"Can you dance naked?" asked Sucha.

"I do not know the dances of a slave girl," I whispered. "I cannot dance."

"Do you know the arrangements of pleasure silks?" she asked.

"No, Mistress," I said, putting down my head.

"Do you know the cosmetics and perfumes of a slave girl, and their application?" she asked.

"No, Mistress," I said.

"The jewelries?" she asked.

"No, Mistress," I said.

"Do you know the giving of exquisite pleasures to a man?" she asked.

"I know very little, Mistress," I said. I was afraid to move my ankle, for the bells.

"Are you trained at all?" she asked.

"I know very little, Mistress," I said. "A slave, Eta," I said, "in her kindness, once taught me simple things, that I might not be completely displeasing and would not be too often whipped."

"Who was your last master?" asked Sucha.

"Tup Ladletender," I said, "a peddler."

"Before that?"

"Thurnus of Tabuk's Ford, of the Peasants," I said.

"Before that!" she said.

"Clitus Vitellius, of Ar, of the Warriors," I said.

"Good," said Sucha.

"But I was owned only briefly by him," I said.

"Before that?" she asked.

"Two warriors," I said. "I do not know who they were, only that I was theirs." Sucha did not question this. Often a girl does not find out who a master is. She might be caught in the afternoon, enslaved in the evening and sold in the morning.

"Before that?" asked Sucha.

"I was free," I said.

Sucha looked at me, and laughed. "You?" she queried.

"Yes, Mistress," I said.

Sucha laughed. I blushed, hotly. I gathered that the collar looked natural upon me.

"You know little or nothing of the arts of the female slave," said Sucha. "You seem to know nothing of the movements and glances, the positions, attitudes and postures, the expressions, of a slave girl, let alone the techniques, crafts and subtleties that may determine whether or not men permit you to live."

I looked at her, frightened.

"But you are pretty," she said. "Men are more lenient with a pretty girl. There is hope for you."

"Thank you, Mistress," I whispered.

"Why have you not moved your left ankle?" asked Sucha.

"The bells," I whispered.

"What of them?" asked Sucha.

"They shame me," I said. "They make me feel so much a slave."

"Excellent," said Sucha. Then she snapped, "Rise, Slave Girl!"

I leaped to my feet with a jangle of bells. I was a belled slave.

"Walk to one end of the room and back," said Sucha.

"Please, no Mistress!" I begged. She lifted the whip. I did as she commanded. When I again stood before her she, to my dismay, touched me.

I turned my head away, biting my lip in shame.

"Excellent," she said. "A mere jangle of slave bells and you are ready for the arms of a man."

"Please, Mistress," I begged.

"You are a hot little slut," she said. "Kneel before the mirror."

I did so.

"There are one hundred and eleven basic shades of slave lipstick," said Sucha. "Much depends on the mood of the master."

"Yes, Mistress," I said.

Later many of the other girls joined us in the room of preparation, for they must serve, as I, in the repast of the evening. It is common in a Gorean fortress, if it is not under siege, for the evening to be a time of pleasure for the men.

"In five Ehn," cried a man from outside, "you must be in the hall of the feast."

The girls cried out nervously, making last minute additions or adjustments to their jewelries and silks. Some intently applied cosmetics. Two nearly fought over a small disk of eye shadow, but the whip of Sucha, lowered between them, divided them. Sulda seemed radiant, returned from the couch of Hak Haran. She applied lipstick. The girls smoothed their silks.

I looked at the incredibly lovely girl in the mirror, she bedecked in a rope of red silk, made-up, perfumed, vulnerable, soft, with armlets and bracelets, golden beads intertwined in the Turian collar.

"She is beautiful," I whispered. Sucha had much helped me.

"Rather pretty for a peddler's girl," smiled Sucha.

"I am afraid," I said.

"Do not be afraid," said Sucha.

"What are my duties?" I asked.

"Exquisite beauty and absolute obedience," said Sucha.

I looked at the girl in the mirror. I remembered the words of Thurnus. "You belong at the feet of men," he had said. I looked at the girl in the mirror. Her ankle was belled. She was beautiful. She was a collared, silked, perfumed slave. She was very beautiful. I had no doubt she belonged at the feet of men. She was a slave girl. She was I.

"Exquisite beauty and absolute obedience," said Sucha.

"Yes, Mistress," I said.

I heard the pounding of a metal bar on the inner gate leading to the quarters of the slave girls.

The girls were frightened. Even Sucha seemed frightened. "Hurry," she cried. "Hurry!"

We fled from the room of preparation, to the inner gate. Soon I, and the others, had been ushered through the two gates, and I, with them, found myself beyond the gates, barefoot on the carpeting, between the vases at the ornate walls, being hurried to the pleasure of masters.

Twelve

The Silver Leaf

"Master?" I asked.

I knelt before him, lifting the platter of meats to him.

With a Turian eating prong he forked meat from the platter onto his plate. The girl kneeling beside him lifted wine to him.

I arose and went to kneel before the next man, to offer him viands from the platter I bore.

The sensuous music of Turia filled the room. A girl in yellow silk, belled, danced her beauty among the tables.

I had been more than a month now in the keep of Stones of Turmus.

Often was I kept late to serve the men. I had learned much from Sucha. I was a different girl now from the one who had been sold for six copper tarsks to Borchoff, Captain of the keep of Stones of Turmus. Well could he congratulate himself on his buy.

"What did she cost you?" a lieutenant had asked him.

"Six tarsks of copper," he had said.

"You have an excellent eye for slave flesh," had said the lieutenant.

Borchoff had grinned.

I had hurried away.

"She is paga hot," a soldier had once said. Then he had thrown me to his fellow. I could not help myself. Sometimes I lay awake in my barred alcove, weeping, not wanting to be a slave. "You are a natural slave," Sucha had once said to me. "You were born to the collar." "Yes, Mistress," I had said. I lay sometimes in my small cell, shamed, weeping. Strangely I thought often of Elicia Nevins. I had been her chief competitor in beauty at the exclusive college I had attended on Earth.

How, I thought, she would have laughed at me, and scorned me, to see me now, her former beauty rival, as a slave.

"Meat, Dina!" cried a man.

I swiftly went to him, knelt, and lifted the platter to him. I did not wish to be whipped.

There had been twenty-seven girls in Stones of Turmus before my purchase. Accordingly, upon my purchase, I became the twenty-eighth girl. Sucha, of course, had counted herself among the twenty-seven girls. Certainly her collar was as much upon her as ours were upon us. There were, incidentally, I was pleased to learn, no free women in Stones of Turmus. This made it easier for the slaves. This arrangement was not unusual, of course, for what would a free woman do in such a place? Too, the garrison, the officers and men, were soldiers, warriors, Gorean and virile. Such men need female slaves, and they know well what to do with them.

There were twenty-nine girls now, however, in the keep of Stones of Turmus. The population in the slave quarters had changed somewhat; five girls had been sold to passing Turian merchants, affiliated with the keep, but, similarly, here and there, over the weeks, some six others had been acquired. Thus the stock was kept freshened for the men.

"You will not be sold, Dina," Sucha had said to me. "You are a prize."

"Yes, Mistress," I said.

We girls in the keep were pleasure slaves, but it must be clearly understood, too, that we were the only girls in the keep. Thus, we served, too, as work slaves. Scrubbing must be done, and the sewing, and the washing and ironing of clothes, and the cleaning; too, we aided in the kitchen, usually in the preparing of vegetables and in the scouring of pots and pans; too, water must be carried to the men on the parapets; there was much work of a lowly and servile nature which it fell naturally to us, the girls of the keep, to perform. Yet generally I think we did not have too much to complain of. We were permitted to sleep late in the slave quarters, and manual labors, for most of us, tended to be curtailed in the early afternoon, that we might rest and prepare ourselves for the evening. I think few of us did on the average more than two or three Ahn of light labors on a normal day. We were never under any delusion that our main task was not the delight and pleasure of our masters.

I was no longer low girl in the slave quarters. It was not that I had fought, for there were few girls there whom I suspected could not beat me, but that the matter had been determined by Sucha. She carried the whip. Each new girl, as she was introduced among us, became automatically low girl, the other girls being correspondingly advanced. We obeyed Sucha. She never hesitated to use the whip. We were kept in perfect order. I was not displeased. Had Borchoff not placed the whip in the hands of Sucha, I, for one, would have fared much more poorly in the slave quarters. Slave quarters, as I have mentioned, can become a jungle. This was prevented at Stones of Turmus by the whip of Sucha. I was not the only girl who was not displeased to be protected from intimidation and violence. Sometimes masters, in their cruelty, do not appoint a first girl. Then the slave girls, as best then can, by teeth and nails, must adjudicate their differences and establish a mode of governance for themselves. Sometimes masters do not appoint a first girl in order that the lower ranking girls will strive ever more desperately to please them, to become favorites, and thus to be to some extent more protected. "If you beat me, the master will not be pleased," is not a threat to be taken lightly in the slave quarters, particularly if it is thought to be true. The distant menace of the master's displeasure has its influence and effect, naturally, on the social arrangements of the kennels. Sometimes a girl will pretend to be more favored by the master than she is, for her own prestige, and to win position in the kennels. But it is not hard to know the truth in these matters. Who is most often summoned to his couch?

"Meat, Dina!" cried another man, and I hastened to him, to kneel and serve him. I wore red silk, a golden necklace about my throat, intertwined with my collar, and bells.

I saw Sucha lying soft in the arms of a lieutenant, kissing him. How marvelously she melted in his arms, his.

She was seldom permitted to carry her whip outside the slave quarters, except in conducting a new slave through the corridors and bringing her through the small iron door, as she had me. When she left the slave quarters she normally knelt before a guard and handed him the whip, her authority ended. He would then take the whip and thrust it against her lips, and she would kiss it, after which he would order her to her feet and discard the whip, which she would retrieve on her way back to the slave quarters. Outside the slave quarters we were normally under the governance not of Sucha, but men. We stood under her governance outside the quarters only when she was permitted to retain the whip. I watched her yielding in the arms of the lieutenant, moaning under his touch. She did not now have the whip. She was now, in the hall of Turian pleasures, as it is called, only another slave girl.

"Dina!" called a man.

I was struck by a soldier past whom I hurried. I gathered that the fellow who had called out had called before, and I had not heard him. The soldier had struck me because of my tardiness in responding to he who had summoned me, he who had now again called out. Any free man in such a situation may discipline us. They are all, in a sense, our masters.

Indeed, it is not uncommon, in most cities, for any free person not only to be entitled to, but to be expected to, discipline us if we are in any way displeasing. This helps us to be good slaves. We are slaves—and we are to be full and perfect slaves every Ahn of the day, every day of the week, wherever we are, and certainly not only when we are under the eye of our own master or his agents. On most collars, too, is inscribed not only our own name, but the name of our master. It is easy, thus, for any imperfections or laxities in our service to be brought to his attention. We may be also bound and leashed, and so brought into his presence by a complainant, usually a free woman.

I brushed the silk of the girl who danced between the tables. The music swirled about me.

I knelt before the man who had called.

"Are you deaf?" he asked.

"Forgive a miserable girl, Master," I begged. "I did not hear you."

"Give me meat," he said.

I lifted the platter to him and he thrust the eating prong into a slab of meat, hot with Turian spices. It was the last piece on the platter. He looked at me.

"I will fetch more meat immediately, Master," I said.

"You are the meat I want, Dina," he said.

"It is not yet time to serve the wine," I whispered. This is a common Gorean idiom. I was reminding him, timidly, that the time of general pleasure had not yet arrived. I, and several of the other girls, had not yet been released from our serving duties. There were still courses of the banquet to be served to our masters. In the time of desserts and wines we would crawl to their tables, slave girls.

"Fetch in the prisoner," called Borchoff, captain of the keep of Stones of Turmus.

This afternoon I had been upon the heights of the keep, carrying water to the men on the parapets. I had stood there, looking out over the wall, at the vast fields about. It was more than eighty feet to the ground.

"Is it your intention, Dina," had asked a soldier, coming up behind me, "to dash yourself to the ground?"

"No, Master," I said to him. "I am not a free woman. I am a slave girl." I backed gently against him, and lifted my head, turning it to him. I felt his hands on my arms.

"Attend to your duties, Slave Girl," he said.

"Yes, Master," I said.

I had been summoned more than once to his couch.

I poured him a cup of water from the small verrskin bag over my shoulder.

It was hot on the parapet. The stones were hot to my bare feet. I wore a brief, one-piece, brown work tunic. It was all I wore, with the exception of the collar. We wore such tunics when engaged as work slaves. The tunics of work slaves are usually brown or gray.

I looked above me at the posts mounted on the walls. Between them was slung fine wire, gently bending and swaying in the slow breeze of the hot afternoon. Such wire is tarn wire. It is used to prevent the descent of tarns into the courtyard of a fortress. It is common in Gorean defenses.

I looked again over the wall.

"Master," I asked.

"Yes," he said.

"I see dust there," I said, pointing to the road beneath, winding toward the fortress.

"They have him," said the soldier beside me.

Two tharlarion, ponderous and stately, made their way toward the keep. They were mounted by two warriors, with lances. More warriors, eight men from the keep, followed, bearing spears. Between the tharlarion, fastened by neck chains, running to the stirrups of the two beasts, strode a man. He was dark-haired. He wore chains. His wrists were fastened behind his back.

"Who is it, Master?" I asked.

"We do not know," said the soldier. "But word had come to us that he had been making inquiries concerning the keep, its defenses, and such."

"What is to be done with him?" I asked.

"He has been brought in," said the soldier. "Doubtless he will be branded, and enslaved. I do not envy him."

I watched the man. He walked proudly. I knew there were male slaves on Gor, but I had not seen them. Most Gorean slaves are female. Male captives are commonly killed.

"Bring water to the men, Slave Girl," said the soldier.

"Yes, Master," I said. I took the cup back from the soldier, and hurried on along the parapet, to serve others.

When I was descending the stairs and had come to the courtyard between the walls, the gate had been opened, and the party, with their prisoner, had entered. The gate then closed behind them. Borchoff, captain of the keep, came to inspect the prisoner. I, curious, stood idly by, watching, the emptied water bag over my shoulder, my ankles in the dust of the courtyard.

The man was tanned, dark-haired, very dark-haired, large, strong. He wore chains. His hands were manacled behind him. He stood proudly between the two beasts, bearing easily the weight of the two stirrup chains attached to his capture collar.

It pleased me to see a man captive. He wore heavy iron manacles and could not hurt me. I approached more closely. His guards did not stop me.

"What is your name?" asked Borchoff of the man.

"I do not remember," he said.

He was struck by one of the guards.

"For what purpose," inquired Borchoff, "were you attempting to ascertain the nature of our defenses?"

"It has slipped my mind," said the man.

Again he was struck. He scarcely flinched, though the blows were cruel.

Borchoff turned away from the man, to converse with the lieutenant, one of the men on the tharlarion, pertaining to the details of the prisoner's capture.

I approached the prisoner more closely. None stopped me.

He looked upon me. I blushed hot red. My body was not much concealed in the brief one-piece work tunic, and I wore a collar. Gorean men have a way of looking at a woman which is like stripping them and putting them to their feet. I felt naked. I put my hand to the thin brown cloth, clutching it, as though to close it more, but I only moved it more tightly about me and higher upon my thighs. I felt, under his gaze, that every detail of my body must be clear to him. I shrank back.

Borchoff turned about, briefly. "Taunt him," said he, "Dina."

"I warn you, Captain," said the prisoner. "Do not do to me the insult of the taunting slave girl."

"Taunt him," said Borchoff, to me, then turning away.

The prisoner stiffened in silent rage. Suddenly I felt very powerful. He was helpless. And, too, almost overwhelming me, I felt a sudden fury against men, for what they had done to me, even to the collar and brand. And this man was Gorean, and he had, a moment before, looked upon me as a master upon a slave girl.

"Yes, Master," I said to Borchoff, captain of the keep of Stones of Turmus.

I approached the prisoner, looking up at him. He looked away. "Does Master fear a slave girl?" I asked. I touched him with my finger, idly, and began to slowly, deliberately, insolently, trace patterns, tiny inquisitive, meandering, meaningless patterns, on his shoulder.

"We are not so fearful, Master," I said. "You do not need to fear us."

I stood quite close to him, igniting the male in him. I knew this was what the Captain desired, but it pleased me, too. How often would Dina, a slave, have a man, such a man, so at her mercy?

I could arouse him with impunity, and he could not touch me.

Sometimes, occasionally, when the mood was on me, when it had amused me, I had teased the boys of Earth, seemingly inviting their attentions, and then, when they had responded, as expected, I had feigned astonishment and disgust, rage and scorn, indignation, even horror, that they had been so bold, so offensively rash, and that I had been so woefully misunderstood, so misjudged, and was now so insulted. How they had stammered, and apologized, and groveled, and sought pathetically to ingratiate themselves again in my supposed good graces. It is a simple matter of contradictory signals, honey and gall, luring and stinging, a game, a girl's game, raising hopes, then dashing them. But such things are not part of the life of the slave girl. She obeys, and desperately hopes to be found pleasing.

The man looked away from me, angrily. Muchly was he herewith, by means of a slave girl, insulted by Borchoff, captain of Stones of Turmus.

"Do not be afraid of me, Master," I said. "I am only a slave girl. Does Master fear a slave girl?"

"I think you are a barbarian, and illiterate," he said.

My accent had doubtless betrayed my Earth origin. I was angry. I knew how Gorean men commonly thought of Earth women, on the basis, however, one must acknowledge, of a considerable body of evidence. Earth-girl slaves on Gor, incidentally, are commonly kept illiterate. This was not unusual. Why should a slave be taught to read and write? Indeed, many slaves, particularly those harvested from the lower castes, are illiterate. Many Goreans, particularly of the lower castes, cannot read or write. And certainly the patterns traced on his shoulder had spelled nothing. I could not even write my own name, Dina, in Gorean.

"But I am pretty, am I not?" I said. "And surely, given the lightness and brevity of my tunic, you can conjecture the delights of my figure."

"Beware," said he.

"I am branded," I said. "And I wear a collar before you. I am a slave."

"Beware," he said. "Beware."

"Is Master afraid of Dina?" I asked. "Is Master afraid of a little slave girl?"

I smiled to myself. The only men I knew who would fear a slave girl would be men of Earth. A slave girl would confuse and frighten them. They would not know what to do with one. They would doubtless attempt to indoctrinate her swiftly with masculine values, and turn her into an imitation man. She would then be safe for them. They would doubtless proceed in this matter regardless of her feelings, oblivious of her integrities, for they would not be truly interested in fulfilling her nature, whatever it might be, but in avoiding the responsibilities of their own. Women and men are identical; this is the defensive thesis of weak, fearful men. It is simple. If women are not women, then they need not be men. Why do many men fear manhood? I do not think it would be so terrible.

"You are large and strong, Master," I said to the prisoner. "And you are handsome, too," I said.

He looked away, angrily.

"Why do you not take me in your arms, and kiss me as a slave girl?" I whimpered. "Do you not find me attractive?"

He said nothing.

"Oh," I said, "you wear chains." I kissed at his arm. He was more than ten inches taller than I, and must have weighed twice as much. I was very small next to him.

"Let Dina give you pleasure, Master," I whispered. "Let Dina please you." I bit at his tunic, which was torn, with my teeth. "You should let Dina please you," I said, "for soon you may be branded, and then you will be only a poor little slave like Dina." With my teeth I tore away his upper tunic, stripping him to the waist. He had a mighty chest. I caressed his flanks, and licked and bit at his belly. "Male slaves," I said, "may be slain for so much as touching a slave girl." I looked up at him. "Dina is sorry that you will soon be a slave, Master," I said.

"I will not be a slave," he said. I looked at him, puzzled. Then again he did not look at me.

I took the waist of his tunic in my teeth.

"Do not, Slave Girl," said he.

I shrank back, frightened.

"Run along, Dina," said Borchoff, returning to the prisoner.

"Yes, Master," I said.

I left them, returning to the quarters for female slaves, to swim, and bathe and refresh myself before the duties of the evening.

"Fetch in the prisoner," called Borchoff, rising behind the low table in the hall of Turian pleasures, lifting his goblet.

I knelt near the man to whom I had served meat. The platter was now empty.

The girl in yellow silk had stopped dancing, and the musicians were quiet.

There must have been some fifty men in the hall, and most of the girls.

"Welcome," called Borchoff, as the prisoner was brought in. He wore chains on his ankles, and his hands were locked behind his back in iron manacles. He had been much beaten.

The prisoner was thrown to his knees before Borchoff, captain of the keep of Stones of Turmus.

He was held on his knees by two guards.

"You are guest here," said Borchoff. "Tonight you will feast."

"You are generous, Captain," said the man.

"Tomorrow," said Borchoff, "you will speak beneath our persuasions."

"I do not think so," said the man.

"Our methods are efficient," said Borchoff.

"They have not yet served," said the man.

Borchoff appeared angry.

"But I will speak when it pleases me," said the man.

"We are humbly grateful," said Borchoff.

The prisoner inclined his head.

"You are of the warriors," said Borchoff.

"Perhaps," said the man.

"I like you," said Borchoff. Then he called out, "Sulda, Tupa, Fina, Melpomene, Dina, feast and please our mysterious guest, he who finds it difficult to recall his caste, his name or city."

We fled to the kneeling, chained man, obeying.

"Come nightfall next, we trust," said Borchoff, "his memory will be much improved."

"Is it the nineteenth hour?" asked the prisoner.

"No," said Borchoff.

"I shall speak," said he, "at the nineteenth hour."

"You fear the persuasions of the morrow?" inquired Borchoff.

"No," said the prisoner, "but there is a time and a place for speaking, as there is a time and a place for steel."

"It is a saying of the warriors," said Borchoff.

"Is it?" inquired the man.

Borchoff lifted his cup to him, saluting him. Borchoff, too, was of the warriors.

"It is unfortunate," said Borchoff, "that you fell living into our hands. The tharlarion pens of Turia require slaves for their cleaning."

There was much laughter about the tables at the witticism of Borchoff. I, too, and the other girls, laughed merrily. Much insult had he done to the prisoner, should he be of the warriors. I, and the others, found the thought amusing that the fellow should be enslaved and set to such lowly tasks. He had intimidated me in the courtyard, in spite of the fact that he had been helpless and chained. I thus found the thought of his prospective enslavement and labors particularly delicious. It would serve him so right!

The prisoner did not respond to Borchoff. Borchoff nodded to us, and then drank from his cup.

"Poor Master," I said to the kneeling, chained prisoner. I knelt beside him and took his head in my hands and pressed my lips to his, kissing him. "Poor Master," I said.

He looked at me. "You are the slut of the courtyard," he said.

"Yes, Master," I said.

"It will be pleasant to tag you," he said. I did not understand him.

I, and the other girls, then began to kiss and caress him, to bring him wines and feed him delicacies. Much did we move about him, and serve him.

"It is the time of general pleasure!" called Borchoff.

The men in the room responded eagerly. "Dina!" called the fellow to whom I had earlier served the spiced hot meat.

I kissed the kneeling, chained prisoner swiftly, with the insulting kiss often given by the wives of Earth to their husbands. "Forgive me, Master," I said, "I must now serve another." Then I hurried away.

I heard the prisoner inquire the hour of Borchoff. "It is the eighteenth hour," said Borchoff.

I lay in the arms of the Turian soldier, on the cushions on the tiles of the hall of Turian pleasures. I kissed him. He was the fourth one to whom I had been thrown. "How marvelous you are, Master," I whispered to him. I cuddled up to him, delicately lifting my head. I wanted him to give me a cube of meat, honeyed, from the metal plate which lay near him. I, and the other girls, might not take such food for ourselves. Our hands could be cut off. We are not fed hours before the feast, and, in serving the feast, are not permitted in the least to partake of it. The feast was not ours to eat, but to serve. We were slave girls. We might, however, be fed by the men. If we would eat, we must earn our food. "Please, Master," I wheedled, "feed Dina." He put a cube of meat, boiled in wine, honeyed, in my mouth, thrusting it between my teeth and cheek with his finger. "Thank you, Master," I whispered, kissing him, the meat in my mouth.

I looked up, savoring the meat. I looked across to Sulda. I had fed better than she this evening.

I was well learning, in the keep of Stones of Turmus, how to serve men.

I smiled at Sulda, and she looked at me, angrily. I looked over to the kneeling prisoner, now abandoned. He knelt alone on the tiles, chained. I was surprised to see his eyes upon me. More than once, though, this night, I had noted his eyes upon me. I smiled at him. I pursed my lips and blew a kiss to him, brushing it toward him with my fingers. I was permitted this gesture of insolence. The man with whom I lay laughed. I continued to look at the prisoner. Well had I and the other girls earlier mocked him this night. Well pleased were we with ourselves, and I thought that I had been the best in this work. How dared he adopt the attitude of a master toward me when he was only a chained captive? We had given him of wines, and of delicacies upon which to feast. Often had we spoken to him soothingly as though in deference and pity, as though he might not be kneeling chained in the fortress of enemies; sometimes, too, we had spoken to him in husky whispers, as though he had much aroused our feminine slave bloods; much had we pressed upon him our kisses, our caresses and attentions; well had we teased him, and taunted and humiliated him in his helplessness; slave girls are excellent in such work, and I thought that I had been the best.

He regarded me.

The soldier in whose arms I lay pulled me down and more closely to him. Eagerly I kissed him. I heard the musicians playing the music of Gor. Another soldier seized me by the ankle. "Wait," said the first, his word muffled against the side of my throat, where his mouth and teeth, below my ear, half kissed, half held me. I felt the hand of the first in my collar, behind my neck, pulling the steel up, tight under my chin, that I not be pulled from him. "Hurry with the slave," said the second, his hand on my ankle. "Only if it pleases me," said the first, not releasing my collar. I laughed. Then I cried out, as the first began to make me yield to him.

* * * *

"A little wine for Dina, Master," I begged.

I snuggled closer to him. I, as other girls, had crawled among the tables. Some men are more generous than others. Fina crept close. "Go away!" I ordered her. Angrily, she crept away, to seek another.

"A little wine for Dina, please, Master," I begged. He held back my head by the hair and thrust the rim of the cup against my mouth. I laughed, feeling the wine in my mouth, and spilling at my throat, running under the collar and, beneath the light silk, over my left breast.

The door to the hall suddenly burst open with a crash. Helmeted, armed men thrust their way into the room.

"The tarn wire has been cut!" cried a man. Then he reeled, bloody, from a blade.

Borchoff, drunk, staggered to his feet between the tables. The Turian soldiers looked wildly about. The music had stopped. Outside the hall we could hear fighting and shouting.

"To arms!" cried Borchoff. "Ring the alarm bell!"

More men swept into the room. Turian soldiers ran to the walls, to seize at their weapons. Slave girls screamed.

Then the room was in the control of the strangers. They were fierce, swift men, efficient, terrible. They wore gray helmets, with crests of the hair of larls and sleen. Their leather told me they were tarnsmen.

"The key to these chains," demanded the prisoner, rising to his feet.

Blades were set at the throat of Borchoff. His men were throwing down their weapons. The surprise had been complete. For the music we had heard nothing.

The wire had been cut, with bladed hooks, swung on long lines below tarns, cut, and torn from its posts. The tarnsmen had approached from the dark quadrant, away from the moons, low, not more than a few feet from the ground, hidden by the shadows of the world, and then had, without warning, little more than a quarter of a pasang from the keep, swept into the air, the first wave striking at the wire, the second, third and fourth waves dropping through the cut, billowing wire to the parapets, roofs and courtyard of the keep. Numbers had fought their way almost instantly to the hall. The plan of the fortress seemed well known to them. They moved with dispatch.

Borchoff, angry, now half sober, threw the key to the prisoner's chains to one of the intruders. Swiftly they were unlocked. The man stood proudly, rubbing his wrists.

"Are you the leader of these men?" asked Borchoff.

"Yes," said the man.

"You were apprehended making inquiries," said Borchoff, "into the structure of our fortress and the nature of its defenses."

"The inquiries," said the man, "were completed earlier, and the plans devised. It was then necessary only to let myself fall into your hands."

"You intended your capture?" asked Borchoff.

"Yes," said the man. "I was thus brought into the fortress, where I might make further determinations, of such a nature as to expedite the transactions of my men." He then turned to certain of his lieutenants, issuing orders. The lieutenants, in turn, communicated with their men. Men sped to their work.

"You have been observant," said Borchoff.

"I attempted to improve my time," said the man. He grinned at Borchoff. "And your men, as I anticipated, were most helpful, speaking freely before, and to, one whom they thought destined to the chains of a slave."

Borchoff glared at his men.

The leader of the intruders was handed a pouch, which he slung about his shoulders, and a sword.

"I would continue the conversation, Captain," he said, "but you must understand that we must move with dispatch."

"Of course, Captain," said Borchoff. "We lie within the patrol limits of the tarnsmen of Ar."

"The evening's patrol will be delayed," said the man. "It seems there was a distraction, a burning field some pasangs to the south. It must be investigated and reported."

Borchoff's fists clenched.

"Chain him," said the man, indicating the very chains with which he himself, earlier, had been secured.

The chains were snapped on Borchoff.

"Who are you," demanded Borchoff, in fury, his wrists and ankles confined.

"Is it the nineteenth hour?" asked the man.

"Yes," said Borchoff.

"I am Rask," he said, "of the caste of warriors, of the city of Treve."

The slave girls screamed, and I broke, and fled with them. Behind us we could hear orders being given. The fortress would be sacked.

I fled wildly down a dark passageway. I could hear a man behind me. Then he turned aside, to pursue another girl. The silk was half torn from me.

I tried to tear off the slave bells on my ankle. A girl sped past me, turning into another hallway. I looked wildly about. I saw a steel door. I slipped through. It was not guarded. Beyond the door was a passageway. I ran panting, slave bells jangling on my ankle, down this passageway. Then, opening a door, I saw a new passageway, one in which there burned a lamp, hanging on a chain. I remembered this second passageway. I had been conducted through it on my first day in Stones of Turmus. It was lined with barred gates. I pulled at the barred gates. Then I backed away from them. It would not be wise to hide within, could I even gain admittance. Behind lay treasures. They would be sure to be looted. I must look for the grosser storage places, those in which bulk goods were kept. These places, I remembered, were farther down the passageway, on the other side of a steel door. I fled down the passageway. I came to the heavy steel door. It was not now guarded. I left it ajar. Gate after gate I tried along the passageway below the steel door, those gates giving access to the storage areas for larger, less valuable merchandise, but all were locked. I jerked at the bars. I could not open them. I wept with frustration. I looked wildly back down the passageway, frightened. If anyone should enter the passageway I would be immediately visible, a fleeing, hunted, beautiful, half-silked, belled slave girl. I jerked again at the bars of a gate. I could not hide! There was no place to hide! I spun about, miserably, my back to the bars, moaning. I could feel them against my back. I looked again down the passageway. No one was yet in it. I touched the collar I wore. I clutched the bit of silk which still clung, loose, about my hips. I moaned. I was too beautiful, I knew, to be treated gently by Gorean men. I feared their ropes and whips. I was a slave! Who knew what they would do to me, if they would catch me! I saw then, below me, down the hallway, the door to the office of Borchoff. I ran to the door, pulled it open and entered. On the wall I saw the whip with which I had been disciplined, after some strokes of which I had begged, tamed, sobbing, to wear a collar. I touched the collar at my throat. I shrank back from the sight of the whip. Even the sight of a whip strikes terror into the heart of a slave girl. She knows what it can do to her. She has felt it. One of the most frightening things to a girl about the whip is the knowledge that the Gorean male, if he is not pleased with her, will use it, and without hesitation. I heard shouting from the passageway leading to the other door of Borchoff's office. I heard the striking of swords. I heard a girl scream. I heard a girl crying out piteously, pounding and scratching hysterically at the other side of the door. I hesitated. Then I heard her, an instant later, screaming, being pulled away from the door. "Bind her and take her to the parapets," I heard. "She is your tag," said a voice. "I shall take the next." I heard the girl cry out, in sudden pain. Then, a few moments later, I heard her being dragged away. I heard other voices. Then I moved back toward the door through which I had entered. The handle of the other door was being tried. Then I heard men kicking at the panels. I saw wood breaking in, splintering, and an arm reaching through, to unlatch the door. I turned and fled away, back the way I had come.

I heard men coming into the room which I had left.

Gasping, my bare feet hurting on the stones, I ran back down the passageway.

I darted through the steel door. I spun, running my hands along the door, to find a way to lock it. I cried out with misery. Its five bolts could not be shut. They were controlled by a vertical bar, which slid in brackets. The bar was padlocked back.

I ran again.

I did not know if the men who had entered Borchoff's office were in pursuit of me or not.

I stopped once again, trying to twist the slave bells, one by one, from the five-linked anklet which I wore, with its twenty bells. If I had had a tool to insert in the rings I might have done so. But I had no tool. The task was beyond the strength of my fingers.

I heard men in the passage.

My heart sank. I was still belled.

Then I thought that if I might reach the room of slave-girl preparation I might obtain the key to the bells. The keys were kept in a shallow wooden box in that room, a box the key to which was generally in Sucha's keeping. If the box were not open I might be able to break it, or its small lock, and thus obtain the keys.

I ran back along the passage.

In a few moments I reached the small iron door, through which I had first been introduced into the quarters for slaves.

It opened from this side.

I knelt down and opened the door, peering through. I saw a girl being dragged by the hair from the room, bent over, stumbling and weeping at the side of a warrior. I saw another girl, Melpomene, thrown on her stomach on the tiles beside the pool, a warrior kneeling across her body, tying her hands behind her back. Then he threw her over his shoulder and carried her lightly from the room. Only one other person did I see in the room, red-haired Fina, stripped, lying at the gate to her slave alcove; her left wrist wore a slave bracelet; the matching bracelet was closed, locked, about one of the bars of the alcove. She looked at me, miserably. I could not help her. She would wait for the return of her captor.

I tore bits of slave silk from my garment and wedged them in the two bolt receptacles, that the door not shut behind me.

I hurried to the room of slave girl preparation. It appeared in disarray, ransacked. I gathered girls had been taken there. The box containing the keys had been broken open, perhaps by men, looking for jewelries. Keys were scattered about.

I heard shouting, screaming.

Frenziedly I tried keys in the first of the locks. Outside the door I saw Sulda flee past. I shrank back.

She was taken on the far side of the pool. "Do not tag me," she screamed. Then I heard her cry out. Moments later I saw her, wrists tied behind her, her hair down about her face, being thrust along, stumbling, held by the upper arm, at the side of a warrior.

"Hurry her to the parapet," I heard someone call.

I found the key to the slave bells. I unlocked the first tiny lock, and then the next three. The five-linked, joined circlets, opened. I cast the bells aside.

I then crept from the room of slave girl preparation, and, slipping about the side of the pool, went to the small iron door. I did not exit through it. I heard men on the other side, approaching. I turned again and fled, this time running through the barred gate which leads from the quarters of slaves. I then passed through the second gate. I felt the carpet under my feet.

I must find a place to hide!

I ran lightly down the hall.

Suddenly, ahead, from a side passage, I saw two men emerge. They held a girl, Tupa, between them.

I turned again, to flee back down the hall.

But, behind me, now, came two more men, doubtless those I had heard behind the small iron door, who had then entered the quarters for slaves, examined them, and the room for slave girl preparation, and then emerged through the two gates.

I was trapped in the corridor. I shrank back against the wall.

They approached. "It is the Dina," said one of them.

"Let her go," said the other.

Then the four men joined and went back toward the great hall, taking Tupa with them.

I stood back against the wall, breathing heavily, bewildered, terrified. They had not secured me.

I did not understand this. Did they not want me? Was I not suitable for them?

Was I to be left free?

At the far end of the hall, away from the gates leading to the quarters of slaves, I saw a figure, that of a man, tall, handsome, strong, splendid, with the bearing of one who leads Gorean warriors.

It was he called Rask of Treve. I turned and fled away.

I crouched in the dark passageway, cornered. I saw the tiny lamp approach, from far down the passageway. I felt the walls of the passageway about me.

Behind me there was a barred gate, locked.

The lamp came closer.

There were walls of stone on either side of me.

He lifted the lamp, and the light fell upon me. I knelt. "Be merciful to a poor slave, Master," I whispered.

"Kneel," said he, "with your belly and cheek against the wall, and place your hands behind your back, with your wrists crossed."

I did so. He placed the lamp he carried on a shelf to one side. He placed the sword he carried behind him on the stones of the flooring and crouched behind me. Binding fiber was looped about my wrists and pulled tight; then it was tied; I winced; I was helpless.

"You will not need this," he said.

I felt his hands in the silk I wore.

With a swift movement it was torn away.

He took me by the arms and turned me, sitting me down on the flooring, my knees up, my back against the stone wall.

"Be merciful to a poor slave, please, Master," I whispered. I had muchly taunted him, and muchly had I delighted myself at his expense. Now I wore his binding fiber, and was alone with him, in a dark passageway deep below the keep of Stones of Turmus.

I blinked against the light of the lamp.

He withdrew an object from his pouch, and held it before me.

"Do you know what this is?" he asked.

"No, Master," I said.

It was like a small, veined, metal leaf, narrowly ovate in shape. It had a tiny hole in the wider end, in which, in a tiny loop, there was twisted a small wire.

"It is a marking tag," he said.

"Yes, Master," I said. I had no idea what he was talking about. What would be marked? But I gazed at the object with some apprehension.

On the leaf, indented in, was a sign, and some tiny printing.

"Do you know this sign?" asked the man.

"No, Master," I whispered.

"It is the sign of Treve," he said.

"Yes, Master," I said.

"You are illiterate, are you not?" he said.

"Yes, Master," I said.

"I had thought so," he said.

"Forgive me, Master," I said.

I had not, in the courtyard, of course, acknowledged my illiteracy. Yet he had doubtless surmised it.

"You cannot then read this?" he said, pointing to the printing on the object he held. "Even something this simple?"

"No, Master," I said.

How ignorant, and stupid and foolish I felt!

Of course I could not read Gorean. I had not been taught!

But many slaves, as I have indicated, are illiterate.

Many masters are simply not concerned with whether their girls can read or not. It does not matter to them. They see no point in teaching them. They are domestic animals. "We would not teach a verr or tarsk to read, they might say, so why should we teach a slave to read?" Some masters, on the other hand, make an actual point of seeing to it that their girls are kept illiterate. They want them that way. They think, it seems, that that is simply appropriate for a slave, that she be kept illiterate. Or, perhaps, they think that this makes them easier to control and puts them more at their mercy. Such a view, however, would seem to me incorrect. We are in all ways subject to the complete and perfect control of our masters, and we are totally at their mercy, always, whether we can read or not. Certainly an illiterate master, say, of the tharlarion drivers, may relish having a former high-caste beauty, perhaps of the scribes or builders, educated and literate, cleaning his stalls and, when commanded, crawling to him over the boards on her belly begging his touch. There are no particular regularities involved in these matters and it is not unusual for a literate master to have either literate or illiterate slaves, nor for an illiterate master to have either literate or illiterate slaves. The slaves are slaves, whether literate or not. Some literate masters, of course, relish the ownership and absolute domination of literate girls, preferably former high-caste women, those who are well educated, highly intelligent and gifted. Such girls must be regarded as quite valuable; on the block they commonly bring the highest prices. It is also said they make the best slaves. About that, of course, one does not know. It certainly need not be true. In my view highly intelligent slaves make the best slaves, of course, it being hard to gainsay that, but intelligence, obviously, is not always associated with literacy, and on Gor, quite often, it is not so associated. Intelligence is important in a slave; literacy is not. Had I been sold on Earth, of course, I would have counted as such a girl, a valuable slave, lovely, articulate, literate, highly educated, and such; on Earth, I would doubtless have brought my master a good price; on Gor, however, I was only another piece of illiterate collar meat.

"It is my name," said the man. "Rask."

"Yes, Master," I said.

"It is with these devices," said the man, holding up the tiny leaf, with its wire, sign and printing, "that we of Treve, in our various ventures of raiding, mark our booty."

Suddenly I understood him only too well!

"Please, no, Master!" I cried.

"And you are booty," he said.

"Please, no, Master!" I wept, in misery. "Please, please, no! No! Please, no, Master!"

I shrank back against the wall. He held my left ear lobe, pulling it taut. I cried out, wincing, as the wire pierced the lobe, and then he threaded the wire through and, twisting the ends together, formed a tiny loop, from which the silver leaf dangled. I felt it at my left cheek.

"It will be pleasant to tag you," he had said to me earlier. I had not understood him at the time. I now understood him. I looked at him with horror. I had been tagged.

"You do not now appear so insolent as formerly," he said.

"No, Master," I wept.

He then seized my ankles and pulled me from the wall. I threw my head back, moaning. An ear had been pierced. This, in itself, is little or nothing, but on Gor it is mighty in its portent. The other ear, almost certainly now, to match its mate, would sometime be pierced, and I would then be a "pierced-ear girl," the lowest of female slaves. I had heard another girl crying out earlier, as she had been tagged, although at the time I had not understood what had been done to her. It had not been the pain which had made her cry out so miserably but its meaning. An ear had been pierced.

I looked up at Rask of Treve reproachfully. He laughed. He well understood what he had done to me, and he knew well, too, that I understood.

"Is your vengeance sweet, Master?" I asked him.

"I have not yet begun to take my revenge, pretty little slave," he said. He thrust apart my ankles.

I resolved to resist him. I turned my head to the side, and heard the small sound of the silver leaf, on its tiny loop, fastened in my ear, touch the stones of the flooring of the passage.

But his hands were sure.

"No," I begged, "do not make me yield to you!"

But he did not see fit to show me mercy. I cried out with misery, lost in sensation, lifting my body to him, piteous for his slightest touch.

When he finished with me I lay between his feet, a shattered, yielded slave girl.

He lifted his head. "Smoke," he said.

I, too, smelled smoke.

"The keep is afire," he said. "On your feet, Slave."

I struggled to my feet, bent over.

We journeyed through flaming halls. In a few Ehn we emerged, after climbing stairs, on the roof of one of the buildings, and, thence, by a narrow bridge, crossed to one of the parapets. There there were several tarns, great fierce saddle birds of Gor. I could see fire licking through the roof of one of the buildings. The parapet was crowded. Goods were bound over the saddles of tarns. Strings of plates and vessels were tied at the pommels. Over several of the saddles, bound, belly up, fastened to rings, was a stripped slave. Some were already squirming, being caressed. Other girls stood beside the winged monsters, their hands over their heads, slave braceleted through the stirrups of the beasts. They were fastened one on each side, or, in some cases, two on a side. In this way the weight is balanced. They must cling as they could to the stirrups with their small strength; else, braceleted as they were, they must simply dangle far above the earth, painfully and helplessly, hoping that not a link in the bracelets would fail. Behind some of the beasts there were tarn baskets, on trailing ropes. Girls, too, and various goods, had been thrust in these. I saw Sucha, her hands braceleted over her head, at one of the stirrups. She looked terrified. She cast me a wild glance and pulled futilely at the bracelets, threaded through the stirrup ring. She was beautiful, fastened at the stirrup. In the light of flames, I saw, reflected, the glint of a marking tag, it suspended from its wire, in her left ear. I did not know what fellow had taken her. Surely he was a fortunate fellow and might be well pleased with his catch. She was a prize. Men mounted swiftly to the saddles. Below in the courtyard, chained together, I could see Borchoff, and the soldiers and staff of the keep. There was much smoke about them.

I saw tharlarion, released, in the courtyard. Men struggled not to be trampled. I was pulled along by the arm, by my captor. "Let us hurry, Captain," said one of the men.

"We must move under the cover of darkness," said a lieutenant. "We must be at the merchant rendezvous before dawn."

"To your saddle, Lieutenant," grinned Rask of Treve.

The man grinned, and leapt to the ladder leading to the high saddle of the great beast.

I saw below that the great gate of the keep had been swung open. Tharlarion rushed through.

I was thrust into the hands of a soldier, who conducted me to one of the tarn baskets.

Borchoff, below in the courtyard, looked upward. Rask of Treve lifted his hand to him, in a salute of warriors. The gate had been opened. Borchoff and his men might make their way, though chained, to safety.

Then Rask of Treve looked about himself, making swift inspection of his men and tarns, and their burdens, riches and slave girls.

The soldier lifted me lightly from my feet and thrust me, feet first, through a hatchlike opening, with flat door, in the top of the tarn basket. He pushed my head down, thrusting me down between the other girls. I crouched down, wedged in. I could scarcely squirm. I looked up, seeing the flat door swung shut. In an instant he had tied it closed. I knelt. We could not stand upright. Eight of us were imprisoned in the basket. Our wrists were tied behind our backs. Silk, and gold, too, had been thrust in the basket. I looked about. Scarcely could we move. From the left ears of the other girls, as from mine, there dangled a silver leaf, a tag, which had been placed upon them by the men who had taken them. I wondered who had taken them. I knew who had taken me, who had imperiously thrust the wire of his claiming leaf through the lobe of my left ear, then twisting it shut, tagging me as his property, he, Rask of Treve.

What a fool I had been to taunt him as I had!

Surely I had gone beyond the command Borchoff had imposed upon me.

And how richly he had had his vengeance on me, exacting from me not only the profound and delicious pleasures of a slave girl, which my body had no choice but to deliver to him, but, far beyond this, he had made me piteously cry myself his, had made me yield to him, helplessly, as a devastated, ravished slave!

Well had he had his vengeance!

How thoroughly he had humbled the haughty slave girl, how insolently he had mastered her!

I could see flames through the heavy, woven fibers of the tarn basket. Too, I could catch a glimpse of the moons. It was crowded in the basket. I was wedged in. I struggled a little with my bound wrists but could not free them. The other girls, like myself, were naked. Raiders, I gathered, seldom leave women clothing. Was this to make it difficult to conceal weapons, or to assist in their summary assessments of the catch? Or was it merely because they were raiders and we were woman? To be sure, we were slave girls, animals. Why should animals be permitted clothing? I tried to move a little. I found I could, though with difficulty, do so. Slowly then I made my way, inch by inch, through encumbrances, through the close, flame-lit darkness of the basket, the flickering light from outside oddly in small moving patches illuminating the flesh, the gold, within, to the edge of the basket, so that I might see out more easily through the interstices of the fiber. I wanted to see, though I feared to do so, what was going on, the men who now owned us, their movements, the tarns, the ropes and chains, the slaves bound over saddles, and fastened at stirrups, the flames, the wild, racing, distorted shadows, the parapets and towers of the keep of Stones of Turmus. I reached my goal. The corner of a box hurt my leg. I moved a little. I heard a girl sob. It was crowded in the basket. I could now see outside. Flames were raging. Tarns lifted and spread their wings, uneasily. Sandaled feet hurried by. How magnificent, I thought, were the men! Surely we existed to serve such, hoping only that we might be found sufficiently pleasing. How clearly then did I see the complementarities of men and women! Nothing more was entered into the basket. We would soon depart. I knelt near the side of the basket. The basket had been fastened shut. It was filled with booty. And I knew that I, too, kneeling there in the crowded darkness, as Rask of Treve had called to my attention, was booty, only that, and so, too, of course, were the others. We were all booty, as much as the coins, the plate, the cloth. I thought, oddly, of Earth, and of the rustling of cattle, the stealing of horses. It is not so different, I thought, Indeed, it is the same! We, too, slaves, were properties, animals. We were such that we, too, being animals, could be run off, carried away, driven away, stolen, simply stolen. At that moment, as this comprehension sank in, my entire body shook suddenly with anguish. I think I understood then in yet another dimension what I was, what it was to be such as I, a slave.

I was property. I could be stolen!

I was not being abducted, or kidnapped. No such dignity was mine. Such fates were for persons, not slaves. I was an animal, one being stolen!

I shuddered again, in misery, in anguish. It could not be happening to me!

"What is wrong with you, Dina?" whispered a girl.

"Nothing," I whispered.

"Peek through the fibers, look outside," whispered another girl. "Do not let them see you look. What do you see? What is going on?"

"We are to soon depart," I whispered.

"I am glad to be leaving Stones of Turmus!" whispered another.

"Be quiet!" whispered another.

We had not been given permission to speak. I hoped the masters would not hear us.

"I, too, am pleased," whispered another girl.

We could always be whipped later, I knew.

But it was happening to me!

Of course you can be stolen, foolish Dina, I said to myself. Do you not know by now you are a slave girl?

What do you expect—girl—slave girl!

It can be unsettling, of course, to understand that you can be stolen, that you are the sort of thing which can be subject to theft.

"I hope to come into the keeping of a personal master," said one of the girls.

"I, too," said another.

Foolish girls! Did they not know they were being stolen?

But sometimes, I thought, suddenly, perhaps it is not so bad to be, say, a stolen horse. Who knew to what new stable one might be taken? Perhaps it is not so bad to be a stolen slave, sometimes, I thought. Who knew to what new chains one might be taken?

Was it not even said that occasionally free women, lonely and miserable, their most profound needs unsatisfied, desperate for love, frequented high, lonely bridges at night, putting themselves in peril of capture and enslavement? Surely a slave girl would not dare to do such a thing, for it might displease a feared and hated master. And was it not said, as well, that sometimes the free woman, before daring to embark upon so perilous a venture, would remove her sandals, loosen her hair and don the tunic of a slave, that she might appear the more to the roving tarnsman or raider a man's dream of pleasure, the female slave? But men do not enjoy being tricked. Perhaps, discovering she was free, unbranded, her captor would angrily rectify that omission and soon return her, stripped, bound and helpless, to the very bridge from which she had been captured, that guardsmen might find her there and remand her into custody, that she might become then a despised slave in the very city whose precincts she had sought to flee. But, I wondered, would this truly displease her? To be sure, it is not pleasant to feel the lash. But she would have then at last, in any event, the collar she needed, that circlet necessary to make her whole. But perhaps her captor, if she seemed slave-suitable, and was sufficiently desperate and zealous in her pleadings and prostrations, might be moved to keep her, she weeping and kissing at his feet, petitioning for this privilege.

Much depended on many things.

Perhaps things would be better.

In any event, such things were not within our province to direct, influence or alter. Men would decide what was to be done with us.

We were slaves.

Theft was simply a risk to which we were subject. Surely I should understand that.

"Where are they taking us?" I asked one of the girls.

"We do not know," said one.

"What are they going to do with us?" I asked.

"Surely you know," said another of the girls.

"No," I said.

"What do you think?" she said.

"I do not know," I said.

"What a little fool you are," she said.

"You do not know, truly, what will be done with you?" asked another girl.

"No," I said.

"Then you are indeed a little fool," she said.

What would be done with us?

What would be done with me?

I did not know.

"Ho!" cried Rask of Treve.

I turned my attention back to the tiny interstices in the woven fabric of the basket.

We were ready to take flight!

I was suddenly excited.

I did not know what was to be done with us, other than that it would be what men pleased.

I had never been in tarn flight. I hoped the ropes on the basket would hold.

I thrust my face to the fibers, looking out.

"Ho!" cried the men of Rask of Treve.

The man who had placed me in the basket, and then tied it shut, climbed swiftly to the saddle of his tarn; our trail lines, those attached to the basket in which we were confined, ran to the tarn's stirrups. When the tarn took to flight the basket, following it, would be lifted into the air. He awaited only the command of flight.

"Ho!" cried Rask of Treve. He drew back on the first strap of his tarn's harness.

"Ho!" cried his men.

Rask of Treve's tarn smote the air with its mighty wings. I was frightened. The span of those wings may have been thirty feet or more.

His tarn, screaming, departed the walls of the keep of Stones of Turmus. Those of his men followed him. Even in the shelter of the basket the torrent of air was frightening. If one had stood upon the parapet surely one would have been hurled in its blasts to the court-yard below.

There had been a moment of slack and then the lines on the basket had drawn taut. Our tarnsman drew the basket over the courtyard and, gaining altitude there, then departed the walls of the keep, fol-lowing the others. When the basket dropped from the parapet toward the courtyard we screamed, frightened, but then it swung below the tarn, and we felt ourselves being lifted high into the air, as though toward the moons of Gor themselves.

I wondered how many slave girls, helpless and bound, a tiny silver leaf dangling from their ear, had been carried by the men of Treve in this basket, and how many more in the future would find themselves its captive.

I could see the keep of Stones of Turmus in flames, dropping away below us.

Thirteen

I am Publicly Auctioned

The sheet was ripped from me. I cried out, startled.

"Ascend the block, Slave Girl," said the man.

"Yes, Master," I said. He prodded me with his whip.

I looked at the worn stairs of solid wood, leading in their spiral upward. I glanced down at the other girls, Sulda and Tupa among them, who sat huddled at the foot of the block, clutching their sheets about them. Sucha, and others, had already been sold.

"It cannot be happening to me," I said to myself. "They cannot be going to sell me."

Had I not been of Earth?

I felt the whip push against my back. Slowly I began to ascend the wide, concave stairs, worn by the bare feet of countless slave girls before me.

There were twenty steps to the height of the block.

My hair was longer now, as it had not been cut on Gor, save to trim and shape it. It now fell below my shoulders, and swirled behind me, shaped into the "slave flame."

No longer did I wear the Turian collar; it had been roughly filed from my neck by a male slave, under the whip of his overseer. He had been struck once when he had let his finger touch the side of my neck. I do not know if he did it on purpose or not. No longer did I wear in my left ear the silver leaf, identifying me as a catch of Rask, a warrior and raider of the city of Treve. I had been sold before dawn at a slaver's camp on the outskirts of the city of Ar. I had been thrown naked to the slaver's feet. Swift, expert assessment had been done upon me. I cried out in misery. I brought Rask of Treve, my captor, fifteen copper tarsks. This was not bad for an Earth girl in the current market. This figure had been entered into accounts, on a ledger. On another ledger, one kept by one of Rask's men, this figure was also entered, with a sign following it, indicating him to whose private account the amount was to be credited, he who had taken me, Rask, the warrior of Treve. When the figure pertinent to my sale had been entered in the two ledgers the wire loop, from which dangled the silver leaf, had been cut from my ear. The silver leaf was then returned to him who kept the ledger for Rask of Treve, and he dropped the leaf, with others, into a nearby box. Humiliated, then, I was thrown to the slaver's chain, behind Sulda. A ring lock was placed through the Turian collar, which I wore at the time, and a link in the slaver's chain, and then snapped shut, securing me on the chain by the collar, with the others. The chain was heavy. Tupa was then added to the chain after me. She brought her captor only twelve copper tarsks.

"Hurry, Slave Girl," called the man at the foot of the stairs. I hesitated. About my neck I wore a light chain, locked. From it depended an oval disk. On this disk was a number, my lot number, or sales number. Sucha, who could read, told me it was 128. She had been 124. We were being sold in the auction house of Publius, on Ar's Street of Brands. It is a minor auction house, usually handling lesser, cheaper slaves, usually females, in greater volumes; it lacks the prestige of such houses as that of Claudius and the Curulean; nonetheless, it is not unfrequented and it has a reputation as a place in which, not unoften, bargains may be obtained.

I heard the step of the man on the stairs behind me. I turned about, stricken.

"I am naked," I said. Did he not understand I was of Earth? I had been sold before, but not like this. I was of Earth! Surely they could not truly be going to display me publicly and sell me at auction! I had been sold before, but privately. The thought of my beauty being exposed so publicly, so brazenly, to large numbers of men, buyers, nauseated me. I looked to the height of the block. I thought I might die.

The room was an amphitheater; it was lit by torchlight. I had earlier been exposed in the exhibition cages, that prospective buyers might scan the merchandise at close hand, forming their suppositions as to its value, that their bids later, if they cared to make them, might be shrewd and realistic. In the exhibition cages we were forced to obey the commands of the men outside the cages, moving in certain ways, and such, but they were not permitted to touch us. We were told to smile much in the cages, and be beautiful. I shared my cage with twenty girls, each of us with a chain and disk on our throats. Outside the cage, posted, were our lot numbers, or sales numbers, corresponding with the disk numbers, and a listing of certain of our features, primarily measurements.

I heard the man hurrying up the steps behind me.

I had spent eight days in the slave pens, waiting for the night of the sale. I had been examined medically, in detail, and had had administered to me, while I lay bound, helplessly, a series of painful shots, the purpose of which I did not understand. They were called the stabilization serums. We were also kept under harsh discipline, close confinement and given slave training.

I well recalled the lesson which was constantly enforced upon us: "The master is all. Please him fully."

"What is the meaning of the stabilization serums?" I had asked Sucha.

She had kissed me. "They will keep you much as you are," she said, "young and beautiful."

I had looked at her, startled.

"The masters, and the free, of course, if there is need of it, you must understand, are also afforded the serums of stabilization," she said, adding, smiling, "though they are administered to them, I suppose, with somewhat more respect than they are to a slave."

"If there is need of it?" I asked.

"Yes," she said.

"Do some not require the serums?" I asked.

"Some," said Sucha, "but these individuals are rare, and are the offspring of individuals who have had the serums."

"Why is this?" I asked.

"I do not know," said Sucha. "Men differ."

The matter, I supposed, was a function of genetic subtleties, and the nature of differing gametes. The serums of stabilization effected, it seemed, the genetic codes, perhaps altering or neutralizing certain messages of deterioration, providing, I supposed, processes in which an exchange of materials could take place while tissue and cell patterns remained relatively constant. Aging was a physical process and, as such, was susceptible to alteration by physical means. All physical processes are theoretically reversible. Entropy itself is presumably a moment in a cosmic rhythm. The physicians of Gor, it seemed, had addressed themselves to the conquest of what had hitherto been a universal disease, called on Gor the drying and withering disease, called on Earth, aging. Generations of intensive research and experimentation had taken place. At last a few physicians, drawing upon the accumulated data of hundreds of investigators, had achieved the breakthrough, devising the first primitive stabilization serums, later to be developed and exquisitely refined.

I had stood in the cage, startled, trembling. "Why are serums of such value given to slaves?" I asked.

"Are they of such value?" she asked. "Yes," she said, "I suppose so." She took them for granted, much as the humans of Earth might take for granted routine inoculations. She was unfamiliar with aging. The alternative to the serums was not truly clear to her. "Why should slaves not be given the serums?" she asked. "Do the masters not want their slaves healthy and better able to serve them?"

"It is true," I said, "Sucha." On Earth animals were given inoculations by farmers to protect them from diseases; on Gor it would be a matter of course, provided the serums were readily available, to administer them to slaves.

I stood with Sucha, trembling. I had received a gift which on Earth could not be purchased by the riches of the wealthiest men, a gift which was beyond the reach of Earth's mightiest millionaires, which even the billionaires of my planet could not buy, for it did not exist there.

I was incredibly rich. I looked at the bars of the cage. "But I am caged!" I cried.

"Of course," said Sucha, "you are a slave. Now rest. Tonight you are to be sold."

I felt the hand of the man tight on my arm, beside me on the step.

"I am naked," I said.

"You are a slave," he said.

"Do not show me to the men!" I begged. "I am not as the other girls."

"Ascend the block," said he, "Slave." He thrust me upward. I fell on the stairs. My legs trembled.

I sensed him lift the whip.

"I will cut the flesh from your body with the whip," he said.

"No, Master!" I wept.

"Girl 128," called the auctioneer, from the height of the block. It was an announcement to the crowd.

I looked upward. The auctioneer came to the edge of the block. He smiled down, in a kindly fashion. He extended his hand to me. "Please," he said.

"I am naked," I said.

"Please," he said. He put his hand further toward me.

I lifted my hand to him, and he took me by the hand, helping me to the height of the block.

The block was circular, and some twenty feet in diameter. There was sawdust upon it.

By the hand he led me to the center of the block. "She is reluctant," he said to the crowd, in explanation.

I stood before the men.

"Are you comfortable now, dear lady?" he asked.

"Yes," I said. "Thank you."

Suddenly, angrily, he threw me to the wood at his feet. I heard the hiss of his whip. Five times he lashed me and I screamed, covering my head with my hands. Then I lay trembling, lashed, at his feet.

"She is Girl 128," he said to the crowd. From an assistant he took a board, with rings and papers. He read from that paper which was now first upon the board, others being loose and thrown back.

"128," he said, reading irritably, "is brown haired and brown eyed. She is 51 horts in height. Her weight is 29 stones. Her block measurements, certified, are 22 horts, 16 horts, 22 horts. She will take a number-two wrist ring and a number-two ankle ring. Her collar size is ten horts. She is illiterate, and, for most practical purposes, untrained. She cannot dance. Her brand is the Dina, the slave flower. Her ears are pierced."

There was a ripple of laughter from the men when he mentioned the piercing of my ears. As I lay, lashed, quivering, in misery, on the surface of the block, I realized that that seemingly insignificant little fact, the piercing of the ears, had indeed, as I had been informed, a most significant import on Gor. It made me, in effect, a gutter slave, a low slave, so to speak, one who is helplessly, degradingly arousing.

Why such a little thing is so momentous on Gor I do not know. I only report the fact. On Gor, it seems that only the lowest and most sensuous, the most helpless and vulnerably sexual, of slaves, have their ears pierced. This had been done to me in the pens. The wound in my left ear lobe, from the wire of the marking tag, had been redone, and enlarged, and then its wound was duplicated, with the same needle, in the lobe of my right ear. In the pens, to keep the apertures open, a bit of wire had been twice looped in each lobe. The wires had been removed this afternoon. A woman may wear earrings on the block early in the sale, or even ornate, expensive garments and veils, if one wishes, but before the conclusion of the sale she will be absolutely naked, that the buyers may see her without adornments, without the least enhancement, that they will see her then as she is, simply, in herself. For it is that, of course, that the men are bidding on, the woman herself.

He looked down at me, and kicked me, lightly, with the side of his foot. "Stand, Slave," he said. Swiftly I stood.

No longer was I in doubt as to what was to have been done with us, no longer was I in doubt as to what was to be done with me. We were to be marketed. We were to be sold. It had been a commercial raid, not an insult raid, nor a vengeance raid, in which, say, the free women of one city were taken to be the slaves of those of another city. It was clearly a commercial raid. We were simply to be marketed. Was that not obvious? No wonder the girls had thought me so foolish, so naive, or ignorant, or stupid, in the basket.

But how could I be sold?

They could sell the others, of course, for they were only common slaves. But surely they could not sell me. I had been Judy Thornton, of Earth! It was not my fault that I had been mixed in with the others! Was I not different?

No, I thought to myself, I am not different. I am only another slave on Gor.

I looked about myself, miserably. In the torchlight, I could see, in the rings of the amphitheater, ascending before me and above me, on three sides, the crowd. There were aisles at the side, and two aisles in the tiers, with steps. The tiers were crowded, and, on them, men ate and drank. Here and there, too, robed and veiled, I saw women among them, watching me. One woman sipped wine through her veil, staining it. All were fully clothed, save I, who wore only a light chain, locked, with its attached disk of sale.

"Stand straight," said the auctioneer.

I stood straight. My back hurt terribly from the whipping which he had given me.

"So you see 128," he said. "Are there any bids?"

The crowd was silent.

The auctioneer took my hair in his hand and, cruelly, bent me back, standing. "22 horts," said he, indicating my breasts. "16 horts," said he, slapping me on the belly. "22 horts," said he, reaching across my body and placing his hand on my right hip, indicating the width of my body. These were my block measurements. I knew a master might keep me to such measurements, with the whip, if necessary. "Small," said he, "but sweet, a delicacy, noble sirs, with promise."

"Two tarsks," called a man from the crowd.

"I hear two tarsks," said the auctioneer.

It was true that I was not large, but I did not think I was unusually small. I was, in Earth measurements, some five feet four inches in height and weighed about one hundred and sixteen pounds. My figure though delicate, was in Earth measurements approximately 28-20-28. I had not known my collar size on Earth, for I had not purchased garments with such attention to the neck. On Gor, it was ten horts. Accordingly it must have been, in Earth measurements, in the neighborhood of twelve and one half inches. I have a slender, delicate neck. I do not know what my wrist and ankle measurements would be. I do know I take a number-two wrist ring and a number-two ankle ring. These run in separate series, the ankle rings being larger, of course, than the wrist rings. It is regarded as desirable in a slave that she takes the same number wrist and ankle ring, this suggesting a delicious symmetry. There are four numbers in the series; one is regarded as small, two and three as normal, and four as large. I could not slip a four ankle ring, of course; I could slip a four wrist ring, if it were set at four; most such wrist and ankle rings, however, are adjustable to 1, 2, 3 or 4. Thus, they, like slave bracelets, lock to the perfect holding point on each girl.

The auctioneer stood very near me.

I did not know my wrist or ankle size in Earth measurements, for such measurements are not important for a girl on Earth as they are on Gor, but the interior circumference of the number-two wrist ring is

5 horts and the interior circumference of the number-two ankle ring is 7 horts; thus, my wrist size in Earth measurement must be about six inches and my ankle size must be about eight and one-half inches. In the slave pens, of course, a girl's measurements are taken on a tape measure marked in horts and entered on her sheet of sale.

"She wears the Dina," said the auctioneer, indicating to the crowd my brand, the slave flower. "Would you not like to own this pretty little Dina? Do you have a Dina among your girls?" He twisted my head, held by the hair, from side to side. "And her ears, noble sirs," said he, "are pierced!"

There was a murmur of approval from the crowd.

I might now be put in earrings.

I was a "pierced-ear girl."

"Five tarsks," called a man, a gross, fat man, swathed in robes, sitting in a middle tier to my right. He sipped from a cup.

I shuddered. I could not well see the faces of most of the buyers. It was I, not they, who was well illuminated by the torches.

"Stand straight, suck in your belly, turn your hip out," said the auctioneer to me, under his breath. I complied. My back still burned from his whip. "Note," said the auctioneer, indicating me with his coiled whip, "the turn of her ankle, the sweetness of her thighs, the tightness of her belly, the pleasure of her figure, the delicacy of her throat, awaiting your collar, the delicacy, sensitivity and beauty of her features." He looked to the crowd. "Would you not like her in your compartments?" he inquired. "Would you not like her in a tunic and collar of your choice, on her knees before you? Would you not like the owning of every inch of her, she your slave, yours to command, hers to obey? Would you not like her serving you, responding swiftly and perfectly in all things to the least whim of your will?"

"Six tarsks," called a man.

"Six tarsks," repeated the auctioneer. "Walk, little Dina," said he to me. "And well."

Tears sprang into my eyes; my body burned red with shame.

But I walked, and well. I feared his whip. Men cried out with pleasure at the displayed girl upon the block.

"Note the fluidity and grace of her movements," said the auctioneer, "the sweetness of her figure, the straightness of her back, the proud carriage of her head. For a few copper tarsks you can own her!"

A tear ran down my face, over my left cheek.

"Walk well, little Dina," cautioned the auctioneer. "Yes, Master," I said. I walked, back and forth, turning, red with shame before the buyers.

"Stand proudly, little Dina," said the auctioneer. I stopped, and stood on the block, my head high.

"Buy her and put her to work for you," challenged the auctioneer. "Conceive of her naked in your collar, on her knees, shackled, scrubbing the tiles of your compartments. Consider her cleaning and washing and sewing for you. Consider her shopping for you and cooking! Consider her entertaining and waiting upon your guests! Consider her waiting in the furs for you!"

"Ten tarsks," said a man.

"Ten tarsks," said the auctioneer.

"Eleven," said another man, from the left.

"Eleven," said the auctioneer.

I looked out upon the crowd, the men and women. There must have been some four hundred in the amphitheater. Vendors moved about, among them, proffering light foods and beverages. I lightly fingered the chain and sales disk at my throat. I saw a man buy a roll of meat, wrapped about a sauce. He began to eat, looking at me. Our eyes met. I looked away. Some men conversed among themselves, not noticing me. I hated them! I did not wish to be looked upon, but they did not look upon me!

"Examine this beauty," said the auctioneer, indicating me with his whip. "Consider the perfection of her block measurements. 22 horts, 16 horts, 22 horts!" he cried, jabbing me with the whip.

"Fourteen copper tarsks," called a man.

"Fourteen!" cried the auctioneer. "But can the house let this little beauty slip its collar for a mere fourteen tarsks? Say, no, Noble Sirs!"

"Fifteen," said a man.

"Fifteen," said the auctioneer. I knew I had been sold by Rask of Treve to a slaver for fifteen copper tarsks. The slaver who had purchased me had sold me to the house of Publius for twenty copper tarsks. The auctioneer doubtless knew this; doubtless it was entered on my records.

The auctioneer looked at me. "Girl," said he to me, softly, menacingly, "you will, whether sold or not, spend this night in our pens. Is that clearly understood?"

"Yes, Master," I whispered.

He was not satisfied with the bids. If I did not go for a price which satisfied the house I would spend the night under Gorean slave discipline.

I would doubtless be richly whipped.

"On your belly, little Dina," he said. "Let us interest the buyers."

"Yes, Master," I said.

I fell upon my belly at his feet, awaiting his commands. I looked up, terrified, afraid that he might strike me with the whip. I lay there for a long moment. He did not strike me. The crowd was amused at my terror. "You will be prompt, obedient and beautiful, 128," said the auctioneer to me, softly. "Yes, Master," I said. Then, suddenly, snapping the whip, he said, harshly, "On your back, one knee lifted, the other leg extended, hands over your head, wrists close, as though confined in slave bracelets." I complied. Then he began to put me rapidly through the paces of the exhibited female slave; he held me in each position for the sweet instant that well revealed me, tantalizingly, in that attitude or posture, and then barked forth a new command, to a new position or attitude; the sequence of these moves was not an accident; each move followed easily, sometimes by a roll or turn, from the preceding position; shrewd rhythm and flow, calculated and sensual, physically melodious, characterized the performance humiliatingly inflicted upon me; I must submit to the choreography of slave display; I, who had been Judy Thornton, a girl of Earth, was put through Gorean slave paces; then I lay on my belly at his feet, as I had begun; I was trembling; I was covered with sweat; my hair was loose about my head and eyes; I felt the auctioneer's foot upon my body; I put my head to the block.

"What am I bid?" he called.

"Eighteen tarsks," called a man.

"Eighteen," said the auctioneer. "Nineteen? Do I hear nineteen?"

"Nineteen," called a man.

My tears stained the block. I felt its sawdust with my finger tips. Its sawdust, too, adhered to my body, held by the sweat.

The leather of the auctioneer's whip, loosely coiled, was near my back.

I looked up. There were women in the crowd. Why did they not rise up and cry out in protest at the indignity inflicted upon their sister?

But they looked upon me impassively. I was only a slave.

"Twenty," called a man.

"Twenty," said the auctioneer. He removed his foot from my body and tapped me on the back with the whip. "Kneel," he said.

I knelt on the block, near its front, miserable, in the position of the pleasure slave, the light chain and sales disk on my throat.

"I have a bid of twenty copper tarsks for this lovely little beauty," said the auctioneer. "Do I hear a bid of more?" He looked out, over the crowd.

I knelt very still. I knew the house had paid twenty tarsks for me.

"Twenty-one," called a man.

"Twenty-one," said the auctioneer.

I breathed more easily. The profit was small, but it had been turned upon me.

I was very conscious of the sales disk at my throat; it was on a looped, close-fitting chain; I could not remove the chain; it was locked.

Twenty-one tarsks had been bid upon me.

I would not be a loss to the house of Publius.

It costs only a pittance to maintain and train a girl in the barred, straw-strewn pens of a slaver's house. What is the cost of gruel and a whip?

"I have heard a bid of twenty-one tarsks," called the auctioneer. "Do I hear a bid for more?"

The crowd was silent.

I was suddenly frightened. What if the house were not satisfied with the profit they had turned? Surely it was not much. I hoped they would be satisfied. I had done my best to obey the auctioneer. I did not wish to be whipped.

Gorean males tend not to be lenient with girls who have displeased them.

"Stand, Collar Meat," said the auctioneer.

I stood.

"It seems," said the auctioneer, "that we must let this little beauty go for a mere twenty-one copper tarsks."

"Please do not be angry with me, Master," I begged.

"It is all right, little Dina," he said, with surprising pleasantness, considering how harshly he had managed me upon the block.

I swiftly knelt before him, holding his knees, looking up. "Is Master pleased?" I asked.

"Yes," he said.

"Then Dina will not be whipped?" I asked.

"Of course not," he said. He looked down, pleasantly. "It is not your fault," he said, "that the market is slow."

"Thank you, Master," I said.

"Now, on your feet, little beauty," he said, "and hurry from the block, for we have more animals to sell."

"Yes, Master," I said, swiftly rising to my feet. I turned to descend the block, on the stairs on the opposite side from that from which I had ascended the block.

"One moment, little Dina," he said. "Come here."

"Yes, Master," I said, running lightly to him.

"Place your hands in your hair," he said, "and do not remove them until you are given permission."

"Master?" I asked.

I placed my hands in my hair. He then turned me to face the crowd. His left hand was at the back of my neck. It grasped the chain there. He would hold me in place.

"Behold, Noble Sirs and Ladies," he said.

Suddenly I screamed fighting the looped, heavy coil of the whip.

"Stop! Please stop, Master!" I cried in misery. I dared not remove my hands from my hair. I feared I would, in my helplessness, tear out my own hair. "Please, stop, Master!" I cried out, twisting and squirming, held in place by his hand on my neck. I tried to fight the sensation of the whip.

"Writhe, little Dina," he said, "writhe."

I cried out, begging him to stop.

"Did you truly think," he hissed, "we would take a profit of only a copper tarsk on you? Do you think us fools to buy a girl for twenty and sell her for twenty-one? Do you not think we know our trade, little slut?"

I screamed for mercy.

Then, his demonstration finished, he released my neck. I fell to my knees before him on the block. My head was down. My hands were still in my hair. "You may remove your hands from your hair," he said. I took my hands from my hair and put them over my face, weeping. I shut my knees tightly, trembling, sobbing.

"Forty copper tarsks," I heard call from the floor, "from the Tavern of Two Chains."

"The Pleasure Silk bids fifty tarsks," I heard.

I had been tricked. The auctioneer had caught me by surprise. Without warning I had been forced to reveal myself, despite any pretenses or intentions I might have, as what I had become on Gor, a true slave girl, and reveal myself as such openly, inadvertently, spontaneously, incontrovertibly, helplessly.

"The Jeweled Ankle Ring bids seventy," I heard.

He had handled his work well. He had exacted from the crowd the highest possible price in the given market before he revealed, unexpectedly and to her dismay, the delicious richness and vulnerability of the girl's exploitable latencies, they as much a part of her as her block measurements, and as much for sale. My responsiveness, like my intelligence, my service and my skills, such as they were, came with my price. The Gorean is satisfied only with the whole girl; it is the whole girl that he buys.

"The Perfumed Rope bids eighty copper tarsks," I heard.

I could not believe the bids.

"She is 'paga hot,'" laughed a man.

"True," said another. "I wish I had her in my collar."

On the block I sobbed, kneeling. I could not help that I had responded as I had to the touch of the whip. I could not help it! "The Silver Cage bids eighty-five," I heard. I wept, shuddering. I had been exhibited naked. I was being sold to the highest bidder. And I knew that I was not being sold merely as a beautiful girl, for such a girl might have gone for twenty-one tarsks, but as something more, as a beautiful slave girl.

"I have heard from the agent of the Silver Cage," called the auctioneer, "a bid of eighty-five copper tarsks. Is there another bid?"

"The Belled Collar," I heard, "bids one silver tarsk."

There was silence in the hall.

"There is a bid of one silver tarsk," said the auctioneer. I could tell he was pleased.

I looked down, shuddering, my knees closely together. The recent bids had been by the agents of paga taverns. I had some notion of what it would be to be a paga slave. The belled, silked girls of the taverns were well known in the cities of Gor. Their purpose was to please the customers of their master. They came with the price of a cup of paga.

"The Belled Collar has given us a bid of one silver tarsk," called the auctioneer. "Is there a higher bid?"

I looked up, and, startled, saw the eyes of the various women, over their veils, upon me. The holding of their bodies, and what I could see of their faces, frightened me. I was regarded by them now with unmistakable hostility. It is hard to be naked, as a slave, before a woman. They make you feel doubly naked. I would rather there had been only men in the market. Were the women comparing their beauty with mine, perhaps unfavorably? Were they wondering, perhaps, if they might give a man more pleasure than I? I wondered why now, for the first time, they looked upon me with such resentment, such anger. Before they had only looked upon me as merely another girl slave, to be sold from the block in her turn for a handful of copper tarsks. But now they looked upon me differently. Now they looked upon me with the fury of the free woman for the hot, desirable female slave. Were they jealous? Did they resent the interest of men? Did they wish that it was they upon the block? I did not know. Free women are often cruel to beautiful female slaves. They put us under terrifying discipline. Perhaps they sense in us something of greater interest to men than themselves, something which constitutes to them a threat, something which is subtly competitive, and successfully so, to them. I do not know. Perhaps they fear us, or the slave in themselves. I do not know. Mostly I suspect the women were furious with me because I had been responsive to the touch of the auctioneer's whip. Free women, desiring to yield, pride themselves on their capacity not to yield, to maintain their quality and integrity; slave girls, on the other hand, are not permitted such luxuries; they, whether they desire to yield or not, must yield, and totally; perhaps free women wish they did not have to be free, and could relate in biological naturalness, like the slave girl, to the dominant organism. Perhaps they wish they were slaves. I do not know. One thing is certain, and that is that there is a deep, psychological hostility on the part of the free woman for her sister in bondage, particularly if she be beautiful. Slave girls, accordingly, fear free women; slave girls want to be locked in the collars of men, not women. To make matters worse the women in the tiers, because of the bidding, now saw me, and understood me, as a girl destined for the

taverns, hot, spiced meat, delicious to men, a delectable accompani-
ment, like the music, to the tawny fire of paga. Some of them looked at
their companions, or escorts. Did they wonder if some of them might
now frequent a new paga tavern? I shuddered. I feared the hostility of
the women, for I was a slave.

"Stand, little Dina," said the auctioneer.

I stood.

I brushed back my hair. I choked back my sobs.

I looked out to the crowd, to the men, and the women.

"I have from the tavern of the Belled Collar," said the auctioneer, "a
bid of one silver tarsk. Is there a higher bid?"

Strangely, at that time, I thought of Elicia Nevins, who had been my
rival at the college. How amused she would be, I thought, to see me
being sold naked from a block.

"Sold to the Belled Collar for a silver tarsk!" said the auctioneer.

I had been sold.

He then thrust me toward the stairs and I, stumbling, descended
the stairs, on the side opposite from that from which I had ascended
the block.

"Girl 129!" I heard him call.

At the foot of the block a man from the house took me by the wrist
and pulled me to a chain. Slave bracelets, spaced at regular intervals,
of about four feet each, had already been attached to the chain. He
thrust me behind the last girl on the chain; she was kneeling, braceleted
to the chain, facing away from me; her head was down; I wondered
if she had been sold before; I did not speak to speak to her, of course;
nor did I want to speak to her; what was there to say; and I was miserable; and, too, I was still stung by shame, and my lashing; why had
he beaten me; I was only a slave girl; had I been so displeasing; but,
of course, we may be lashed, for we are slaves; we must be controlled
perfectly, so we are subject to such things; too, of course, even had I
wished to do so, I would not have dared to speak to her; a girl may be
beaten for speaking in coffle; indeed, it is commonly understood that a
girl should request permission to speak before speaking, and not pre-
sume to speak unless that permission has been granted; "May I speak,
Master?" is a simple, familiar, common formula for requesting this
permission; the permission, of course, may not be granted to her; that
is up to the master; I think that there is little that so impresses male

dominance on us as does this requirement that we may not simply speak, but must first obtain his permission to do so; how helpless and vulnerable, and dependent, this makes us feel; the chain was over her left thigh, and against her side; then it went behind her; "Kneel," said the man, my keeper of the moment, he who had conducted me from the foot of the block to my chain-place; I knelt; he fastened my wrists in the next pair of slave bracelets attached to the chain; I then knelt at the chain, secured; he tossed the chain over my left thigh, and drew it against my left side; slavers are fond of such aesthetic uniformities; they display girls well; in time another girl who, too, had been sold, was placed on the chain behind me; and then another, and another, and so on.

We did not speak. We dared not.

I knelt, locked in the bracelets, secured to the chain.

The chain was placed attractively on my body, as it was on that of the others before me, and those behind me.

Men are fond of such touches. We dare not alter them.

We, all of us, were secured with perfection.

I looked down at my imprisoned wrists, locked closely in the slave bracelets, and the chain to which the bracelets were attached.

I was well held.

Such things well convey to a girl her bondage.

We were helpless properties, secured animals, chained. We were held with perfection. It was the will of men, the masters.

There was no escape for us.

We were Gorean slave girls.

This night we would spend in the pens.

In the morning we would be delivered, hooded, bound, to our new masters.

I was a slave girl. I was naked and chained.

I had been sold.

Fourteen

Two Men

"Paga, Master?" I inquired.

He waved me away.

I turned from him with a rustle of bells, looking about me. The girl in the sand was quite good. It was still early in the evening, the sixteenth hour. She scarcely moved, swaying, ankles close, arms over her head, wrists back to back, palms turned out. Yet she subtly danced, controlled by the music of a single flute. Some men watched her. We had five dancers at the Belled Collar. I thought all were fine. The best would perform later in the evening. Four performed a day, and one would rest. I could not dance. There was only one musician at the side of the sand. Others would join him later. Their leader was Andronicus, who played the czethar.

"Paga," called a man.

I hurried to him, carrying the large bronze vessel of paga, on its strap about my shoulder.

I knelt and filled his cup. He did not order me to an alcove. I rose and, carrying the vessel of paga, went to the door of the tavern, to step outside, to taste the air. As a paga girl I came with the purchased cup of fluid, but, of course, I, like the others, was only a lovely option; whether I served in an alcove depended entirely on the whim and appetite of the customer. Many men, naturally, came to the tavern only to meet their friends, to talk and drink. Some nights I had not been used at all. I had been, of course, completely available. As paga girls went I was popular, and my master, Busebius, was not disappointed in me. He had made, I gather, a good buy on me. More than many of the girls had I squirmed in the alcoves, sometimes chained, writhing under the touch of masters, whimpering and crying out the submission I could not help but yield. I knew there were men who came back particularly for me. I had brought business to the tavern. The rules of the tavern with respect to the slave girls were simple. The customer could select any serving slave for his pleasure, providing he had paid the price of the paga; he could pick the girl of his interest, whether she had poured him the paga in question or not; to be sure, the customer usually commanded his paga from the wench who had caught his fancy, if he was planning on using her; if he was not interested in the having of a slave girl he would usually call his paga from the closest wench; each cup of paga entitled him to take one slave to the alcove; thus, theoretically, he might use several in one evening; these arrangements, however, terminated with the dawn, and the closing of the tavern; he might not, so to speak, save his cups for later. Dancers must be separately negotiated for.

I stepped outside the tavern, to drink in the pure air of Gor. We were permitted outside the tavern.

I stood beneath the sign of the Belled Collar, which swung above me, a large collar, from which hung bells.

"Greetings, Teela," said a man, passing by.

"Greetings, Master," I said.

I was Teela, a paga slave of the Belled Collar. That could be read, I understood, on the close-fitting steel collar I wore, a ten-hort collar.

I looked out, over the bridge, to the towers and cylinders beyond, and to the sunset over the walls of Ar. I saw the tracery of the bridges against the sky, the people moving about on them. Far below, in the streets I could see carts and wagons, too, being drawn by tharlarion. I looked up. One or two tarnsmen, on patrol, I saw in the sky. I thought of Clitus Vitellius.

"Greetings, Teela," said the girl who now stood beside me, who had come, like myself, from the tavern. She, like I, wore slave bells on her left ankle, brief, parted yellow silk, the house collar. We stood barefoot on the bridge.

I did not speak to her, but looked away.

"I am sorry I fought you for the candy," she said.

"I won it," I said, angrily.

"Yes, Teela," she said. Then she said, angrily, "It fell closest to me. It should have been mine."

Busebius, our master, sometimes, before ordering us to bathe and prepare ourselves for the floor, scattered a handful of hard candies among us. They were very precious, and, on the tiles of the slave room, we fought for them.

I looked at Bina.

I had leaped for the candy. It had been snatched by her hand. I had torn open her hand and thrust it in my mouth. She had struck me and pulled my hair. Rolling, wildly, screaming, we had bitten, clawed and kicked at one another. Then Busebius had whipped us apart. We had shrunk back from one another, cringing, punished slave girls.

"How foolish you looked," laughed Busebius. We reddened. We were only girls. Did he expect us to fight like men? How small and weak we felt.

"Hurry now to the baths," he said, "and thence to the room of preparation, for you must be soon upon the floor."

"Yes, Master," we had said.

Standing outside the door to the Belled Collar, we stepped back, and knelt.

Bran Loort, who had once been of Tabuk's Ford, carrying a low table, entered the tavern. He performed odd jobs about the tavern in return for his keep and a tarsk a week. We had knelt because he was free. Yet I wondered if in his heart he was free. He seemed a downcast, defeated man. He carried the table past us, which he had taken to the shop of a carver and enameler, to be inlaid with a Kaissa board. He was now returning it to the tavern. He slept in the tavern overnight. He was entitled to the use of the girls of the tavern, as it was his place of employment. Yet he had never used one of us. I feared he could not do so. I recalled he had been defeated by Thurnus and then, stripped, thrust before a rape-rack in the village on which a girl, naked and helpless, awaited him. "I give you my permission," had said Thurnus. Bran Loort had looked down. "Go ahead," had urged Thurnus. "Take her!" "I cannot," had whispered Bran Loort. He had been a defeated man. He had turned away from the rack and bent down to pick up his tunic. He had gone to the gate and it had been opened for him. He had left the village of Tabuk's Ford. He had found his way to Ar. He did small work about the tavern.

Bina and I regained our feet.

"I am sorry I fought you for the candy," she said.

"I am stronger than you," I said. "You should have given it to me."

"No," she said.

I did not speak to her.

"But it is embarrassing to fight before the men as a slave," she said.

"The candy," I said, "belongs to the girl who is strong enough to take it."

"You are the only girl I know here," said Bina. "We were once both the slaves of Clitus Vitellius. We have shared a chain before. I want to be your friend."

"You, too," I said, looking at Bina, Slave Beads, "are the only old friend I have here."

"Let us be friends," she said.

"We are friends," I said.

"Good," she said, hugging me.

I hugged and kissed her.

"But the candy was mine," I said.

"Slave!" she hissed, her eyes flashing.

"Slave!" I cried.

"Hurry inside," said Busebius, standing at the door. "Do you think I bought you to stand outside like fine free ladies and sniff the air!"

"No, Master!" we cried, and hurried within.

"Paga!" called a man. I hurried to him.

It was now the eighteenth hour. The tavern was more crowded. I knelt back against the low wall, my wrists braceleted over and behind my head to Ring 6. A customer had reserved me to himself. I waited while he addressed himself to a game of Kaissa.

I had been longer in the tavern than Bina. I had been twenty days slave here and she had been with us only six. There were twenty-two slaves in the tavern, not counting the dancers, of which there were five.

"Do not run away," had said the man, putting me on my knees and braceleting my hands above and behind my head to the ring.

"No, Master," I had said, through gritted teeth.

I watched him playing Kaissa, completely absorbed in the game. I waited. What was I to be, a dessert, a liqueur? I clenched my fists in the bracelets.

Then I saw that he had brought about capture of Home Stone. They put away the pieces, sliding them into the drawer in the Kaissa table. They then conversed a bit, discussing, it seemed, the game. Then one man left, and he who had reserved me for himself, as though recalling me, took the rental key from his pouch and approached me.

I put my head down.

He unlocked the bracelets.

I looked up at him.

"What is your name?" he asked.

"Teela," I said. I had told him before.

"Go to Alcove Six," he said.

"Yes, Master," I said. "Does Master desire special equipment, or harnesses?"

"Hook bracelets," he said.

"Yes, Master," I said, putting my head down to his feet. He then left me, to return the bracelets and keys to the counter. I rose to my feet and went to the slave room to fetch the hook bracelets, leather cuffs with locks on them, and snaps; they are soft and the snaps, as opposed to the cuffs, require no key; some men enjoy them on their slaves; by means of the snaps the girl may be variously secured by the locked cuffs, her hands being fastened behind her or before her, or perhaps to her collar. I then hurried to the alcove, climbing the ladder.

The master was awaiting me. He put forth his hand and I gave him the hook bracelets. The keys for the hook bracelets are kept at the counter, as are the keys to the steel slave bracelets.

"Remove your silk," he said.

I did so.

"Extend your wrists," he said.

I did so. He fastened the hook bracelets on me. He did not, however, fasten them together.

I knelt before him, on the scarlet furs in the small alcove, in the light of the tiny lamp. I knelt in the position of the pleasure slave, the cuffs locked on me.

"Address yourself to my pleasure," he said.

"Yes, Master," I said, crawling forward, head down, my hair upon his body, to kiss him.

* * * *

352

It was well after the nineteenth hour, and again I was upon the floor.

The tavern was crowded. The music swirled loudly. Our finest dancer, Helen, a slim, blond Earth girl, tantalized the customers of Busebius in her silver chains.

"Paga!" called a man. I hurried to him.

On Gor I had met four Earth girls; all were slaves. Too, I had met several who, though Gorean, bore the names of Earth girls; such names, on Gor, I knew, are regarded as excellent names for slaves.

I knelt and poured the man his paga.

"Paga!" called another. I leaped to my feet, to hurry to him and serve him. Never, it seemed, had we been so crowded. I had not even had time to go to Busebius, behind his counter, to have the hook bracelets removed from my wrists.

I brushed against Bina, she hurrying to serve another of our master's customers.

I heard Helen cry out as silk was torn from her thigh. Still she danced.

A man reached for my ankle. I fled past him.

I hurried to the counter and handed Busebius, who was beaming, the paga vessel and strap. Again it had been emptied.

He dipped the vessel into a great vat of paga and returned it, filled, wet and dripping, to me.

"Paga! Paga!" I heard. I did not even have time to slip the vessel on its strap over my shoulder. Holding its two handles with my hands, I fled back, with a jangle of slave bells, to the floor, to serve.

The door of the paga tavern flew open. The music, for a moment stopped. Helen froze in a motion. Eyes turned toward the door. My heart skipped a beat.

Impressive men stood there, warriors, though not in the garb of Ar.

Their leader, without helmet, but in cloak and medallion, indicated that the music should continue.

The musicians again played, and, again, Helen danced.

The leader of the newcomers removed his gloves, slowly, and thrust them in his belt.

His eyes viewed the slave body of Helen, as a master's eyes look upon the flesh of a property girl.

Busebius, bowing, rushed to him.

The stranger casually looked away from Helen, and she bit her lip, tears in her eyes, no longer under his scrutiny.

He looked upon me, and I straightened my body. He was incredibly strong and handsome. I hoped that I looked my most beautiful.

He turned his attention to Busebius, who was speaking to him.

"Who is it?" I heard a man ask.

Bina stood near to me. She shook. She read the medallion of the stranger.

"See the medallion," said a man.

Busebius conducted the visitors, his honored guests, to a private corner of the tavern from which, on the raised dais there, they might well view the room, the musicians, and the dancer.

"Do you not know them?" asked a man.

"No," said the other.

Beside me, Bina trembled.

"They are the delegation of the Salerian Confederation," said a man.

"Their leader?" asked the other.

"Thandar of Ti," said the first.

I now well understood the agitation of Bina. Thandar of Ti, of the Warriors, of the four cities of the Salerian Confederation, was the fifth son of Ebullius Gaius Cassius, of the Warriors, Administrator of Ti, high officer of the Confederation. At one time a girl, the Lady Sabina, the daughter of a merchant, Kleomenes of Fortress of Saphronicus, high merchant of that city, had been pledged in Companion Contract to this Thandar of Ti. Raiders had struck the companion caravan, acquiring its riches and carrying off the Lady Sabina, and others. To guarantee the frustration of the Companion Contract and to prevent the alliance of Fortress of Saphronicus with the Salerian Confederation, the Lady Sabina had been reduced to slavery. She had been made worthless in the affairs of state. The alliance of Fortress of Saphronicus and the Confederation of Saleria had never taken place. Bad blood now existed between them.

"How beautiful he is," breathed Bina. Never had Thandar of Ti and the Lady Sabina of Fortress of Saphronicus, as far as I knew, looked upon one another. Their companionship had been an intended match of state.

Bina, Slave Beads, gazed upon the powerful, wondrous Thandar of Ti.

"He is handsome," I said.

"My ears are pierced," wept Bina. "My ears are pierced." Never, now, if ever, could she have hoped to be companion to such a man.

Thandar of Ti, and his fellows, some five of them, ordered from Busebius, who stood eagerly about them. They would have more than paga. They would be fed, and have wines.

The presence of the august visitors, except perhaps by the slaves, was forgotten.

Thandar of Ti looked in our direction. We knelt, two beautiful slave girls, lowly pierced-ear girls, paga slaves. It was a great honor for girls such as we that a man such as Thandar of Ti would even deign to cast a glance upon us.

Thandar of Ti looked away.

I smiled to myself at the irony of the situation.

In looking upon one of us, upon one of two lowly, exquisite slaves, he had been looking upon she who had once been the Lady Sabina, of Fortress of Saphronicus, once intended to sit regally at his side, gloriously robed, his free companion.

There were tears in the eyes of Bina.

Thandar of Ti, I noted, was very handsome.

"You have little paga left," I said. "My flask is full. I will serve them."

"More than one must serve them," said Bina. "Please, Teela."

"He is quite handsome," I said. "I will be enough."

"I wish to serve him," said Bina simply.

"I will serve him," I said.

"Do you think he will buy you?" asked Bina.

"I do not know," I said, "perhaps."

I rose lightly to my feet. Bina quickly followed my example.

Busebius hurried toward us. He gestured to us, and to four of the other girls. He gathered us about him. We were excited. "You six will serve," he said, indicating the men on the dais. Two of the girls cried out with pleasure, to be selected. "Go swiftly to the room of preparation," he said. "Garb yourselves as the hunter's catch." I was startled. The guests must be important indeed. We hurried to the room of preparation. Busebius went to give orders to the men in the kitchens.

We must serve the initial wines swiftly, with the matched breads and cheeses.

We tore aside our silks in the room of preparation. We freshened our perfumes and adjusted our make-up. We must be soft, and perfumed and luscious.

Busebius thrust his head into the room of preparation. "Earrings," he said, "jewelry!" Then he disappeared again.

"I do not want to wear earrings," wept one girl.

"Put them on, Slave," I snapped. I did not want to be beaten for one of us who was not pleasing.

I fastened golden loops in my ears, and slung necklaces about my throat. I slipped on an armlet.

Beside me, Bina placed earrings, unprotestingly, on her ears.

"Do you, too, not weep to put on earrings?" I asked her.

"No," she said, "I am a pierced-ear girl." The earrings, I noted, jeweled droplets, were very beautiful upon her.

I reached into a chest for hunters' netting. It is a stout cording, used to net medium-sized game. Its mesh was spaced at some two horts, about two and a half inches.

Cunningly we twisted netting about us, from our throats to our brands, high upon our thighs. We garbed ourselves as "the hunter's catch."

We looked in the mirror. Several of us gasped. Seldom had we seen such exciting girls.

"Hurry!" said Busebius, again appearing at the entry to the room of preparation. We knew then the wines, and the matched breads and cheeses, were ready.

"Teela, wait," said Bina.

The other girls left the room of preparation. "We must hurry," I said.

"I know what you intend, Teela," said Bina. "And it is not proper."

"I do not understand," I said. How could she know what I had in mind.

Bina stood between myself and the door.

"Get out of my way," I said. "Do you want us to be beaten?" I looked at her, angrily. "Do you fear," I asked, "that your Thandar of Ti will find me more pleasing than you?"

"No," she said, "Teela, I do not. I am not a free woman. I do not fear your slave competition. I know that I am beautiful and I can compete with you as a slave girl for any man."

I sniffed.

"But you have more in mind, Teela. I know you. You are not Gorean. You do not understand these things."

I looked at her, in fury.

"Failing to please him more than I, failing to interest him in your purchase," she said, "it is your intention to tell him who I was."

I looked at her, startled. How could she have known my plan?

"You think then he will free me, and free you, for having told him this truth."

I did not speak to her.

She turned her head from side to side. "My ears are pierced, Teela," she said. "You will only do him dishonor if you show him my present state."

"Don't you want to slip your collar?" I asked. I seized the close-circling steel on my throat. "Do you want to wear this?" I cried. "Do you want to be a slave, at the complete mercy of men!"

"I will not do dishonor to Thandar of Ti," she said. "I will serve him, not known to him, lovingly, as only what I am, a lowly paga slave."

"You are mad," I said.

"I am Gorean," she said.

"This decision," I smiled, "we will let Thandar of Ti make. We will let him decide."

"No, Teela," she said. "I have decided it."

"Get out of my way," I said.

"No," she said.

"Look," I said. "Even if he likes me, and buys me, I will tell him who you are, a little sooner or a little later, if only to gain our freedoms."

"I know you would, Teela," said Bina.

"I have your interest, too, at heart," I said.

"I am sure you do," she said. "But you do not understand us. You do not understand Goreans."

"I want to be free," I snapped.

"Look at yourself in the long mirror, Teela," said Bina.

I did so, and saw there a marvelous girl, soft and perfumed, branded; she wore a bit of netting, and jewelry; she wore earrings; she was collared.

"What do you see there?" asked Bina.

"A slave girl," I said.

"Do you think a girl such as you, so soft and beautiful, with your slave reflexes, can ever be anything but a slave on this world."

"No," I said, bitterly.

"And your ears are pierced," she said.

I tossed my head. "I know," I said. That in itself I knew would be enough to keep me a slave on Gor.

I would always be a slave on Gor.

"Abandon then your mad plan to reveal my former identity to Thandar of Ti," said Bina.

"No," I said.

She looked at me, angrily.

"I could win for myself, and you," I said, "if nothing better, an easier slavery."

"No," she said.

"Do you think I want to be only a paga girl?" I asked. "Do you think being a paga girl is an easy slavery for a girl of Earth? I am not as you. I am more sensitive. Do you think I like being at the bidding and mercy of any male who can afford a cup of paga?"

"If you spoke to Thandar of Ti," said Bina, "you would win for us both only a whipping."

"I shall take that chance," I said.

"I am sorry," said Bina. "You shall not."

"Out of my way," I said.

"This is a matter between slaves," she said, "and I have decided it."

"You may think to serve him like a little fool, he not knowing who you are," I said, "but I shall not permit that."

"Hurry! Hurry!" called one of the other girls.

"We must hurry," I cried, miserably.

"It is your intention then," said Bina, "to inform Thandar of Ti of my former identity."

"Yes," I said, "I shall. I will gamble anything for an easier slavery. Now get out of my way."

She did not move, but looked at me, angrily.

"I am stronger than you," I said. "Get out of my way." Surely she remembered how easily I had robbed her of the candy earlier in the afternoon. She was no match for me.

Suddenly I cried out, as she leaped upon me, tearing and scratching. I could scarcely defend myself. She seized me by the hair and threw me headlong across one of the vanity tables before the long mirror. I slid on the table scattering combs and perfume. She was on my back, tearing down the netting, fouling my legs in it. I still wore the hook bracelets. She pulled my wrists behind my back and, swiftly, snapped together the leather cuffs; I twisted on the vanity table, and fell to the floor, my wrists confined by the linked snaps behind my back. "I shall scream!" I cried. Swiftly Bina thrust a scarf in my mouth, wadding it tightly, and fastened it in place with another scarf, pulling the second scarf tight behind my neck, and deeply between my teeth. She then, with the netting, tied together my ankles. She then found another hunter's net, but one which had not been cut. She threw the net over me and, drawing tight its strings, confined me helplessly in it. She then pulled me by the cords to the side of the room. She sat me against the wall and, using the four cords of the net, tying them through a slave ring at the foot of the wall, fastened me, netted, to the wall.

I squirmed in the netting, but could not free myself. I looked at her in fury.

"You are the catch of the huntress," said Bina.

"Bina!" I heard. "Teela!"

"I am coming," cried Bina. "Teela is ill!" She then blew me a kiss, and hurried out of the room.

I struggled, helplessly.

It was the first hour in the morning, of the same night, when Bina returned.

She was radiant.

She removed the netting from me, and the gag from my mouth.

"Thandar of Ti?" I asked.

"He is gone now," she said. She happily undid the netting which confined my ankles.

"You did not tell him?" I asked.

"No," she said. "Of course not."

"You are a fool," I said.

"It was I," she said, "of the six girls whom he chose to pour his paga."

"Six?" I asked.

"When you were taken ill," she laughed, "Busebius sent Helen to serve with us."

"I see," I said. "Would you please unsnap the hook bracelets?"

In an instant, with infuriating ease, she had opened the snaps, freeing my wrists, one from the other. I was furious. It was so simple. She who wears the bracelets, of course, cannot reach the snaps.

"It was I, too," said Bina, dreamily, "whom he took to serve him in the alcove." She closed her eyes, holding herself with her arms. "Oh, how beautiful he is," she said, "and how well I served him." She opened her eyes. "The pleasure he gave me!" she moaned. "I could not believe the pleasure." She looked at me, directly. "How fortunate it is," she said, "that I did not become his companion."

"I do not understand," I said.

"For then, this night, I could not have been his slave," she whispered.

"Oh," I said.

"I shall remember all my life," she said, "the night I was slave to Thandar of Ti."

I looked down. I remembered the joy of once having been the slave of Clitus Vitellius, of having been his to dominate and command.

Then I remembered that I hated him.

"Teela," said a voice, a man's voice, that of Busebius.

"Yes, Master," I said.

"Are you feeling better now?" he asked.

"Yes, Master," I said.

"Why then," he asked, "are you not in your silk and pouring paga?"

I looked at his whip.

"I hurry, Master!" I said, quickly.

"Paga!" called a man, and I, in bells and silk, hurried to him, to pour him drink.

I was barefoot on the tiles. The slave bells, thonged, were tied about my left ankle.

There were fewer now in the tavern, and in another Ahn or two we would close the doors.

Some of the girls, already, had been permitted to retire. I knelt before the man and poured him paga, head down.

The hook bracelets had been removed from my wrists by Busebius, who held their key.

I wore only bells and silk. It was late. The earrings, the necklace, the armlet, I had left in the room of preparation. I was now only a simple paga slave.

Only one other girl was on the floor.

"Paga," said a man's voice. I turned toward him. I saw he sat with a second man.

I knelt before them, head down, and poured the paga into his cup.

"Serve me the paga," said the man.

I put down the paga flask which I carried that I might, unencumbered, assume the position of serving paga, or wine, to a Gorean male.

"First remove the silk," he said.

I did so. He was a customer. I was his to command.

Then I knelt naked before him, head down.

"You may now serve the paga," he said.

"Yes, Master," I said.

I reached to take the cup, in both hands. One kneels, one proffers the cup, head down, with both hands, to the male.

I reached to take the cup.

Suddenly, on my closely placed wrists, as I went to lift the cup, with a startling flash of metal and two swift snaps, slave bracelets locked.

I looked up, startled.

"No!" I cried.

"We have you," he said. I tried to jerk back but his hand, on the chain between the bracelets, held me, my hands confined in his bracelets.

"You have been the object of an intensive and difficult search," said the second voice.

I regarded them, terrified.

"I have sold you for two tarsks to these gentlemen," said Busebius. I felt him remove the thonged slave bells from my left ankle. He placed them on the table. I felt him thrust a key into the small, heavy lock at the back of my collar. He opened it, and placed it, too, on the table.

"She is yours, Masters," he said.

"Oh, no, no!" I begged.

Busebius turned and left the table.

"We have paid two silver tarsks for you," said one of the men. I knelt naked before them, horrified, wearing their bracelets.

"You are now ours," said the other man.

"Do not kill me," I begged.

"Serve us paga," said the first man.

Trembling I, nude, braceleted, head down, arms extended, proffered paga first to one, and then the other. They drank slowly, enjoying their triumph and my misery.

"We must now be on our way," said the first man.

Each took one of my arms, and between them, I half thrust, half dragged, they forced me from the paga tavern.

"Please do not kill me," I begged.

They were the two men whom I had first encountered on Gor, when I had awakened, nude, chained by the neck in the wilderness. They had, at one point, prepared to cut my throat.

"Please do not kill me!" I begged. "Please, Masters, do not kill me!"

Between them, held, braceleted, I was forced from the tavern, and out onto the long bridge, into the Gorean night.

Fifteen

I Am Spoken to by My Mistress

I was thrown to the tiles before the recumbent figure seated on the curule chair.

"This is your mistress," said one of the men, indicating the recumbent figure, with lovely figure, veiled and gowned who sat easily, regally, on the curule chair.

I looked up from my knees, her slave. The bracelets had been removed from me. I had been placed in a brief white house tunic, sleeveless.

I was barefoot. It was all I wore.

"Leave us," said the seated woman. The two men withdrew.

I put my head down to the tiles, alone with my mistress.

"Lift your head, Judy," said the woman.

I looked up, startled.

"Do you not know me, Judy?" asked the woman.

"No, Mistress," I said.

The woman put back her head and laughed merrily.

My mind raced. I could not know her. And yet she spoke as though I should know her. And she had called me Judy. I had not been called Judy since I had left Earth.

"Judy Thornton," laughed the woman. I detected by her laughter that she was young, that she, too, was only a girl, save perhaps that she might be a bit older than I. My mistress was a girl. I was owned by a girl!

"Mistress?" I asked.

"Has slavery been hard for you, lovely Judy?" she asked.

"Oh, yes, Mistress!" I said.

"Would you not like to be free?" she asked.

"Yes, Mistress!" I cried.

Smiling, with a graceful gesture, the woman lifted back her veil, revealing her face.

"Elicia!" I cried. "Elicia Nevins!" I cried, weeping with joy. I threw myself into her arms, sobbing. And she put her arms about me. I could not control my emotions. The ordeal was now over. I shook, half choking, half sobbing. Behind me now was the steel of slave bracelets, the fear of the whip, the misery and degradation of the slave girl. "I love you, Elicia!" I cried. "I love you!" I would now be free. Soon, with Elicia's help, I would be returned safely to Earth. She had rescued me! "I love you, Elicia!" I wept. "I love you! I love you, Elicia!"

The woman thrust me from her, and I, startled, slipped back, losing my footing, to the tiles. I was on my knees.

I looked at her, puzzled.

"It is well," she said, "that a slave girl loves her mistress."

"Please do not joke," I begged.

"Are you not grateful to me?" she asked.

"Yes! Yes!" I cried. "I am grateful, so grateful, to you, Elicia!"

"It is well," she said, "that a slave girl is grateful to her mistress, that she is permitted to live and is not slain."

"Elicia?" I asked.

"Do not rise from your knees," she said, coldly.

"When will I be freed, and returned to Earth?" I asked.

"You always were a stupid little fool," she said. "I wondered what the boys ever saw in you."

"I do not understand," I said.

"That is why you are a slave, and I am free," she said.

"Surely," I whispered, "you do not intend to keep me as a slave. You are of Earth!"

"This is not Earth," she said.

"Oh, please, Elicia!" I said.

"Silence," she said.

I was silent.

"We were great rivals, were we not?" she asked.

"Yes," I said.

"I shall enjoy owning you," she said, "as a serving slave."

"Oh, no, Elicia!" I begged.

"I saw you as a slave even on Earth," she said, coldly. "When I saw you in classes, in the cafeteria, in the library, walking on campus, attending functions, dating, laughing, applauding, lying beside the pool, posing for the boys, cute, pretty, trying to pretend to be more beautiful than I, I saw you as what you truly were and deserved to be, and would someday be—only a lovely little slave.

"Free me," I begged.

She laughed.

"You asked if I wanted to be free," I moaned.

"Do you?" she asked.

"Yes, yes!" I cried.

"That will make the owning of you all the more pleasant," she said. "But you should not be free. You are a natural slave," she said, "like many of the women of Earth."

"You are of Earth!" I cried.

"Yes," she said, "but I am not a natural slave. I am different from the others."

I put down my head.

"Are you familiar with the duties of a serving slave?" she asked.

"Elicia!" I cried.

"Are you?" she asked. "I do not wish to spend a great deal of time training you."

"To some extent," I said, coldly.

"It is all a little thing like you is good for," she said. "I will get much use from you."

"Please, Elicia," I wept, my voice breaking.

"Go into my room," she said, "through the door on your right. On the wall there is an opened slave collar and a slave whip. Bring them."

I went into the beautiful room, lavishly appointed, with chests, mirrors and sunken bath. I found the collar and whip and, barefoot, returned.

I handed her the collar and whip.

"Kneel," she said.

I stepped back, and knelt.

"You were very pretty on the block," she said.

"You saw," I moaned.

"Everything," she said.

I put down my head. She had seen me exhibited naked, and sold. "Why did you not buy me then?" I asked.

"There were excellent reasons not to do so," she said. "It was enough to know your location, and where you could be obtained."

"I do not understand," I said.

"To determine," she said, "that others did not follow you."

"I do not understand," I said.

"The search for you," she said, "was long."

"You have gone to much trouble," I said, "to secure a female serving slave."

"Your name is Judy," she said, naming me.

"Yes, Mistress," I said.

"You understand, of course," she said, "that you bear the name now as a slave name."

"Yes, Mistress," I said. It might be changed, or taken from me, at her whim.

"You will address me," she said, "as Lady Elicia, my mistress, or, as you have done, simply as Mistress, that sort of thing."

"Yes, Lady Elicia, my mistress," I said.

"Excellent, Judy," she said, "you learn swiftly." She leaned back. "Oh, I shall relish owning you," she said. "I shall demean and humiliate you, and work you, and have whatever I wish from you."

"Yes, Lady Elicia, my mistress," I whispered. My former rival now owned me.

She rose easily from the curule chair and stood before me. She held the opened collar before me. It was slender but sturdy, steel, enameled with white, decorated with tiny flowers in pink, a collar suitable for a woman's girl. There was printing in the enamel, tiny, exact.

"See the printing?" she asked.

"Yes, Mistress," I said.

"I know you are illiterate," she said, "so I shall read it to you. It says 'I am Judy. Return me to the Lady Elicia of Six Towers.'" Then she said, "Put down your head, Slave."

I knelt, with my head down. The collar was locked on my throat.

She stepped back. "Judy Thornton," she said, "—collared! Collared at my feet! Mine! Owned!" She turned in the lovely gown she wore, her arms raised, fists clenched, eyes closed. "The triumph! The pleasure of it!" she cried.

"The collar," I whispered, "has my name on it."

"Yes," she said, looking at me. "It has been waiting for you a long time."

"It is a ten-hort collar," I whispered. I could tell by its feel.

"Your size exactly," she laughed.

I wondered when the measurement could have been taken. From what she had said I gathered the collar had not been made recently, that it had not been made following the sale in the house of Publius, in which my various measurements, those of a slave, had been made public.

I looked at her.

"You were measured when you were unconscious," she smiled, "before you left Earth."

"How did I come here?" I asked.

"Unconscious," she said, "naked, in a slave capsule."

I shuddered.

"Do you know," she asked, "who it was who picked you for slavery, who designated you for the collar, from among hundreds of other girls, screened, who might have been taken?"

"No, Mistress," I said.

"It was I," she said.

"But why, Mistress?" I begged.

"Because it pleased me," she said, "and I wanted you for my slave."

I looked at her with horror.

I felt the whip thrust against my mouth.

"Press your lips to the whip," she said.

I did so.

"What is the duty of a slave girl?" she asked.

"Absolute obedience," I whispered.

"Kiss the whip," she said.

I did so.

She then went back to the curule chair and seated herself upon it, regarding me. She held the whip in her right hand, its blades folded in her left.

"I am sure we will get on well, won't we, Judy?" she asked.

"Yes, Lady Elicia, my mistress," I whispered.

She looked at me, intently. "What is it like, truly, to be a slave?" she asked.

"Horrifying, Mistress," I said.

"I mean," she said, "—to be the slave of a—of a man."

"Oh, it is horrifying, Mistress," I said.

"I would have thought," she said, "that you, a girl such as you, not I, might have enjoyed it."

"Oh, no, Mistress," I said. "It is humiliating, degrading and terrible. We must obey them in all things. You cannot conceive of what it means!"

"Are you not what is spoken of as a 'hot' slave?" she asked.

"Oh, no, Mistress!" I protested.

"I saw you on the block," she said.

I put down my head, confused, angry.

"I think you are a little whore," she said, "a little tart. I have always thought so."

"Oh, no, Mistress," I said.

"It is girls such as you, responsive to men," she said, "who demean our sex, who have made it difficult for us on Earth."

"Oh, no, Mistress," I said.

"You insult women, and make us seem slaves!" she said angrily. "I despise your sort. I hold you in contempt."

I shook my head, negatively, tears in my eyes.

"Do you find pleasure in the touch of men?" she asked.

"No, Mistress," I said. "No!"

She looked at me, not speaking. It seemed strange to me, later, that we, together, had spoken so. It was as though each of us desired to appear more frigid and less passionate than the other, as though the restriction or impairment of our natural sexuality were somehow desirable or meritorious. Women of Earth, I knew, sensitive to a heritage of insane values, of antibiological acculturation, sometimes competed with one another in their attempts to appear frigid, a competition which was often carried into the bedrooms of their husbands. Few wives, I knew, would dare to let themselves appear to their husbands as a helpless, lascivious, hot, panting bitch. Slave girls, on the other hand, are given no choice.

"As a free woman," she said, "I have had little opportunity to see a slave girl used."

She looked at me, curious.

"Tellius," she called. "Barus!"

The two men who had caught me entered the room.

The Lady Elicia indicated me to them. "Amuse yourselves with her," she said.

"Have mercy on your slave!" I cried.

By the arms, I was thrown back on the tiles.

I wept, the tunic torn away from me, my body red and helpless, writhing on the tiles.

"Can there be more?" asked the Lady Elicia, amazed.

"She has not yet even experienced the first slave orgasm," said Tellius, crouching beside me, looking up.

I turned my head from side to side, in misery. I looked up at him. I tried to lie still. But my body leaped to his touch. I cried out in misery.

"Is it soon?" she asked.

"Yes," said Tellius, "note her breathing, the mottling of her skin, how she moves, her eyes."

"Oh, please, Mistress, have mercy on me!" I wept. "Do not let them touch me further! Please, please, Mistress!"

Then I threw back my head and screamed. I clutched at Tellius. "You are my master!" I whispered, hoarsely. "You are my master!"

"Do not move," he said.

"Oh, please, Master!" I wept.

"You may now move," he said.

I screamed and clutched at him, eyes closed, clawing at him, trying to bring our bodies closer. Then I threw back my head eyes wild, lips parted, and screamed, delivering my body to my master.

"It is the first of the slave orgasms," said Tellius.

"I love you, Master!" I wept, clutching him. Gone now was the thought of the Lady Elicia. I, a slave girl, was in the arms of a Gorean male. I covered him with kisses and caresses, weeping. "Please touch your slave more, Master," I begged.

"Little whore!" sneered the Lady Elicia.

"Touch me more, Master!" I begged.

"I knew you would be like this, even at the college," she said. "Lovely Judy! A little whore!"

I licked at the hair on the upper arm of Tellius. "Please, Master," I begged him.

"You are lower than a whore," said the Lady Elicia. She looked down at me, in fury. "You are a slave girl!"

"I love you, Master," I whispered to Tellius.

"Finish with her," said the Lady Elicia, rising, angrily, from the curule chair. "And when you are done with her see that she is cleaned and groomed, and presented to me in a fresh tunic."

"Yes, Lady," said Tellius.

The Lady Elicia left the room.

I looked at Tellius with terror. "Please do not finish swiftly with your slave, Master," I begged.

"Do not fear, little slut," he said.

And they did not finish swiftly, but exacted from me the full, ecstatic penalties of my bondage.

When Barus rose from my side, spurning me with his foot, I had been well used.

"Kneel," said the Lady Elicia.

I knelt before her, in fresh tunic, in her bedroom. "You were long," she said.

"Forgive a girl," I said.

"Do you have any doubt," asked the Lady Elicia, "that you are a slave?"

"No, Mistress," I said. I put down my head. I remembered Tellius and Barus.

"Prepare my bath," she said.

I went to draw water from the cistern. Too, I lit the tiny oil fire beneath the tempering vessel, on its iron tripod. One regulates the temperature by mixing warmer and cooler waters. A serving slave must know the exact temperature at which her mistress wishes the water of her bath. The Lady Elicia would tell me once, I knew. After that, if it were not correct, I would be punished. I knew she would have little patience with me. I must serve her perfectly. When the water was ready, I prepared the oils, the towels, and foams of the bath.

"Your bath is ready, Lady Elicia, my mistress," I said, kneeling before her.

"Untie my sandals," she said, sitting on her bed, "and disrobe me."

I obeyed.

"Remove your tunic," she said.

I did so.

"Look now," she said, "in the great mirror. Who is more beautiful?"

I knelt, looking in the mirror. I choked back a tear. I had always thought that perhaps it was I who was the most beautiful but I saw, now that we were naked, that she, my mistress, was more beautiful than I. Elicia Nevins, who had been my beauty rival, I saw, was truly my superior in beauty. I had not known this until now.

"Who is more beautiful?" she asked.

"You, Lady Elicia, my mistress," I said.

"Truly?" she asked, smiling.

"Yes," I said, head down, "Lady Elicia, my mistress."

She walked to the side of the tub.

"Bring me the whip," she said.

I fetched the whip, and handed it to her.

"Judy," she said.

"Yes, Mistress," I said.

"You are now a woman's slave," she said.

"Yes, Mistress," I said.

"You will comport yourself with dignity," she said. "You will not be an embarrassment to me."

"Mistress?" I asked.

Suddenly she struck me with the whip, and I turned, spinning, away, and was struck again, and I fled to the wall, and was struck again, and I knelt at the wall, my face to it, my hands to the wall, and was struck again.

"If you so much as look at a man," she said, "I will whip the flesh from your bones!"

"Yes, Mistress!" I wept.

"Slave girl!" cried the Lady Elicia.

I crouched by the wall, having been whipped. "Yes, Lady Elicia, my mistress," I said.

"Attend me now," she said. "I would bathe."

She entered the water gracefully, her hair bound in a towel, luxuriating in the multicolored foams of beauty. She lifted her limbs, washing herself indolently, beautifully.

I knelt beside the sunken bath, to wait upon her, her slave, should she desire aught.

"What are you thinking, Judy?" she asked.

"If I told Mistress," I said, "she would whip me."

"No," said the Lady Elicia. "What are you thinking?"

"I was thinking," I said, "that a man would love to have his collar on you."

She laughed merrily. "Perhaps," she said. "I am very beautiful."

"Yes, Mistress," I said, "you are one of the most beautiful women I have ever seen."

"Do you think I would bring a high price?" she asked.

"Yes, Mistress," I said.

She laughed.

"Free me, Mistress," I begged, "free me!"

"Do you truly think," she asked, "that you were brought to Gor to be freed and returned to Earth?"

"I do not know why I was brought to Gor," I said.

"I do," she said.

"Merely to be your slave?" I asked.

"It could have been that," she said. "We have our pick."

"But there is more?" I asked.

"Of course," she said. "We needed a girl, one to bear a message. She would be placed in a given location, secured. When it seemed safe, she would be picked up, and transmitted to the proper contact. There she would deliver the message." She looked at me. "Unfortunately," she said, "Tellius and Barus lost you."

"They were going to kill me!" I cried.

"They sought the message in clear form," she said. "They did not, at that time, understand how you carried the message. I do. It is fortunate for us, as well as you, that you were not slain, they thinking you had disposed of the message, cheating us of its contents."

"They wanted slave beads," I said. "I had none."

"Yes," she said.

"I carry no message," I said.

"You do," she said. "But you do not know you carry it."

I did not believe this. But it is not wise to argue with the mistress.

"Could not a man have carried the message?" I asked.

"Slave girls," she said, "attract little attention, save by their flesh and person. They may be bought and sold, and may easily change hands. They are often transported great distances, even hooded. If they are ignorant, they are ideal couriers. They themselves do not even know they carry the message. They cannot even suspect themselves. Why should others, then, seeing only another branded, chained girl, suspect them?"

"You are very clever, Mistress," I said.

"Further," she said, "even should the message fall into the wrong hands, it is concealed, and would not be understood as a message, and even if it were understood as a message, its secret would be kept for it is well enciphered."

"Your security is brilliant, Mistress," I whispered.

She lifted one of her arms, bathing it, letting the water fall from it.

"You are involved in a struggle," I said.

"Yes," she said. "I am an agent of a military and political power, a greater power than you understand exists, one of interplanetary scope. It is called the Kurii. Worlds are locked in war, a fierce, silent war, unknown to you, unknown to millions. At stake are Gor, and Earth."

"In such a war," I said, "communication is important."

"And difficult," she said. "The enemy are not fools."

"Could not radio be used?" I asked. I assumed such devices must be available.

"Signals can be jammed and scrambled," she said. "And it is dangerous to bring such material to the surface of Gor. The enemy swiftly locates and destroys it." She lifted one slim, lovely ankle, observing it, and then dipped it again into the foams of her bath. I thought she would take, like myself, a number-two ankle ring. "As you note," she said, "there is nothing here at Six Towers which suggests that I am not an ordinary woman of Ar."

"What is the message I carry?" I asked.

"I do not know," she said.

"Any girl," I said, "might have carried this message."

"Any piece of suitable slave flesh," said the Lady Elicia.

"Then why was I chosen?" I asked.

She laughed. "At the college," she said, "you competed with me, you challenged me, you dared to set yourself up as a rival to me. It was then that I determined, you lovely, meaningless little fool, that I would have you as my serving slave."

"What is to be done with me?" I asked.

"In the morning," she said, "you will be appropriately identified and transmitted as a naked slave by tarn to the port of Schendi, whence, by slave ship, you will be transported to the island of Cos."

"Identified?" I asked. "Slave ship?"

"A small chemical brand," she said, "which you will wear in your flesh, something by which our agents in Cos will recognize you."

"Chemical brand?" I said.

"It will remain invisible until the proper reagent is applied," she said.

"Can it be removed?" I asked.

"Yes," she said, "but you cannot remove it. It requires the proper combination of chemicals."

"Will it be removed?" I asked.

"Of course," she said, "after it has done its work, identifying you for our agents. It would be foolish to leave it fixed in your body, would it not, to arouse the puzzlement of the curious, perhaps even to identify you as our message girl to the agents of the enemy?"

"Yes, Mistress," I said.

She blew foam from her hand, watching the bubbles drift in the air. "The slave ship," she said, "will not be pleasant."

"What will be done to me in Cos?" I asked.

"You will be placed in the Chatka and Curla, a paga tavern," she said. "And from there our agents will make their contact."

"Will I understand the message?" I asked.

"No," she said. "You will not understand it. You will only deliver it."

"And," I asked, "when the message is delivered?"

"Then," she said, "you will be returned to me."

"And then?" I asked.

"Then," she said, leaning back in the sunken bath, luxuriating in the warm, foamy water, "you will begin your life as my serving slave, Judy."

"Yes, Lady Elicia, my mistress," I said.

Sixteen

A Sail

I screamed wildly in the darkness, jerking back my ankle from the edge of the sturdy mesh about me. My ankles would pull back toward me only some six inches as they were chained. I lay on my back. I clasped my shaven head in my hands. My hands, too, were chained, the two chains running to a heavy ring over and above my head, in the slatted wood of the tier on which I lay. I could lower the heel of my hands only to the side of my neck; but it was enough to cover my ears, when it became necessary to do so. I screamed and thrashed; I could tell my ankle was bleeding, from the feeling of the wound and the wetness about my shin and on the wood. I tried with my right foot to press against the wound, to stanch the flow of blood. I saw the blazing, coppery eyes of the long-haired ship urt on the other side of the mesh. I had let the shin of my left foot rest against the mesh.

"Let me out!" I screamed. "Let me out!"

Sometimes an urt manages to force its way through the mesh, or between one of the vertical cage lids, one at each end of the cage, and the cage. The girl then, chained as she is, is at its mercy.

"Be silent," said a girl's voice, from the next cage. I could not see her, or the others.

"Please, Masters!" I wept. "Let me out! Let me out, Masters!"

"Be silent!" she scolded.

I tried to be silent. I twisted on the slatted wood.

"Please, Master," I had wept. "Put me in a deck cage!" These were small cages, lashed down, sometimes kept on the deck of a crowded slave ship. This ship, a small one, had only twenty such cages, arranged amidships in two rows, back to back, two cages high, five cages long. In harsh weather, and at night, these cages are often covered with tarpaulins; this tends to prevent undue weathering of the cage metal due to salt and moisture. During the day the tarpaulins are usually laid aside, unless they are tied over the cages to discipline the girls. There are two major advantages to having the tarpaulins put aside. First, the sailors may then, for their pleasure, gaze upon the lovely prisoners of the cages; secondly, the girls, when they reach their port of sale, will be tanned perfectly, completely. Any girl on the ship, incidentally, unless she is certified "white silk," a virgin, is free to the sailors for their sport. There were no "white silk" girls on board; we were all "red silk." This was not unusual. There are few virgin slaves. Their virginity usually does not last more than an Ahn beyond their first sale. It is the deck-cage girls who are most often used for the sport of the sailors. In daylight hours their charms are on almost constant display. They are not chained in the hold. They may pose and wheedle, and thrust their arms through the bars to touch the sailors. Also they are more readily available. A cage door need only be opened and the girl pulled to the deck, or thrown across the tarpaulins. "Put me in a deck cage, Master!" I had begged. He had looked down upon me, captain of the ship. "Chain her below," he had said. I had been dragged from his feet.

I screamed again.

"Be silent," said another girl, angrily.

I thrashed on the wood. I could feel the ship lice.

I could not tear at them with my fingernails; I was not chained in such a way as to permit that; this was intentional. I writhed on the slatted wood, screaming.

"Be silent," said the first girl. "It is not the time permitted for screaming!"

"I do not care!" I cried.

I heard a noise. I was frightened.

A hatch was thrown open, and a man descended the stairs into the hold.

Suddenly, in the dim light, falling through the opened hatch, I could see the musty tiers and their helpless, fair occupants.

The man looked about.

"She it was! She it was who screamed!" cried the girl next to me, indicating me with her head.

"No!" I cried. "It was not I!"

"It was she!" cried the first girl.

"Yes, she!" cried several others.

I sensed the man standing behind me, on a ramp. "I was bitten," I said. "I was bitten!" I twisted on the wood, trying to see him. "Have mercy, Master!" I said. "I was bitten!"

"It was not the time permitted for screaming," he said.

"Yes, Master," I said. "Forgive me," I begged, "Master."

There were eight slave platforms in the hold, each with six tiers. These platforms were separated by narrow aisles; also they did not adjoin the sides of the hold, thus allowing a passage between them and the wall of the hold on both the left and right side of the ship. On each tier of each platform there were five girls. There were, thus, two hundred and forty girls in the hold. A cunning mesh and cage arrangement is incorporated into the platforms. The slatted wood of the tiers, on which the girls lay, permits cage mesh to pass unimpeded from the roof of the sixth tier to the bottom of the first tier. The mesh is cleated to the wood of each tier. Each girl, in effect, has her own meshed cage, separate from that of the others. Thus, if an urt manages to enter one area he has at his mercy only one captive, not five. The top of the sixth tier and the bottom slats of the first tier are sheathed in tin, to prevent being gnawed by urts. Mesh, too, heavy and sturdy, closes off the ends of the slave cubicles formed. In the mesh at the ends of the cubicle formed, both the end at the girl's feet and that at her head, there is a tiny gate. The girl may be placed in the cage, or removed from it, from either end. She normally inches her way into the cubicle from the top end and one slaver, from the bottom, secures her ankles in their irons, then shutting that gate, and another secures her wrists in their irons, then shutting that gate. Each girl thus has to herself a small, rectangular cage area, surrounded on four sides by mesh, on the bottom by the slatted wood of the tier, and on the top by the wood of the tier above her, unless she is on the sixth tier, and then she has above her, of course, the ceiling of her cubicle, the bottom of the platform roof. She is chained in such a way as to preclude movement which might tear at the mesh or break it, thus making possible the entry of urts, which might eat at her, lowering her price, and to preclude her tearing hysterically with her hands and fingernails at her own body, bloodying herself, perhaps scarring herself, again lowering her price, in her attempt to obtain relief from the bites and itching consequent upon the infestation and depredation of the numerous, almost constantly active ship lice. The first tier is raised from the floor of the hold by some eighteen inches, providing a crawl space. The open spaces between the tin-sheathed, wood slats on the first tier are covered, from the bottom, by cleated mesh, which prevents urts from entering from the bottom. The crawl space between the floor of the hold and the first tier is cleaned once a day. Each girl, all in all, has a space private to her slavery of some twenty-five inches in width, by some eighteen inches in height, by some six feet five inches in length. In this space she is chained helplessly. Of the six tiers in my platform, I was on the fourth.

I heard the man loosen the small gate behind my head. I did not know why he did this.

"Master?" I asked.

He let the gate then swing down on its hinges, and lie against its bolts.

He did not snap it shut.

"Master?" I asked, frightened.

He turned away. I heard him on the ramp.

"Master!" I screamed, terrified. "I will be silent! I will be silent!" I turned my head wildly, trying to look back. "Please, Master!" I begged. "Please! I will be silent, Master!"

The sharp, furred, cold snout of an urt could now, as the gate lay against its bolts, thrust between the gate and the side of the cage. The animal might now swiftly, furtively, slither into the cage which I, helplessly chained, must then share with it.

"Master!" I screamed. I was terrified of urts. "Master, please," I screamed. "I will be silent! I will be silent!"

I heard him pause on the ramp. He turned and returned to my cage.

"I will be silent, Master," I whispered, terrified. "I will be silent, Master," I whispered. "Please, Master."

He snapped shut the tiny gate, and left. In a few moments the hatch closed and we were again in total darkness. The ship shifted in the water, and I could hear the waves against the hull. In a few minutes, the man gone, I heard the urt, it or another, moving about on the wood between the meshes. I gritted my teeth so that I would not cry out from the misery of the lice. I drew my feet and hands, in their chains, as near the center of my space as I could. I made no sound.

* * * *

The vertical gate of the cage space, that gate behind my head, was thrown open and hooked back. I put my head back.

"Master," I said. But I could not speak for the spike of the bota was thrust between my teeth, and I must drink.

When the spike was withdrawn I again tried to speak. "Master," I begged. But his heavy hand thrust bread in my mouth, crusts of Sa-Tarna bread, wadding it in.

Then he went to the next cage, and the next, similarly watering and feeding their occupants.

I knew he would return, to finish the feeding, with another draft of water, a spoon of salt and a slice of the bitter tospit. Bit by bit, flake by flake, dampened, struggling, trying not to choke, I swallowed the crusts with which my mouth had been crammed.

I heard him again then behind my head. Almost never did I get to see the male at whose mercy I was chained.

The bota's spike was again forced into my mouth. I drank. When the spike was pulled away, I whispered, quickly, "Please, Master, may a slave speak?"

"Yes," he said.

"Remove me from the cage," I begged. "Let me go on deck. I will do anything!"

"You are a slave," he said. "You must do anything anyway."

"Yes, Master," I said, miserably. It was true. A slave had no bargaining power. All that she could possibly give was free to the master at his slightest glance or word.

"Open your mouth," he said.

"Select me out," I begged, "when next a girl is pulled from the cage for the sport of the sailors."

"No, me!" said the girl next to me.

"I am a pleasure slave," I said.

"I, too, Master," said the girl next to me, on my left.

I felt the spoon beside my mouth and I opened my mouth, and the salt was thrown into my mouth.

"You each," he said, "in your turn, will have half an Ahn on the deck."

"Thank you, Master," I said. The slice of tospit was thrust in my mouth. The cage gate behind me was snapped shut. I bit into the tospit. It was bitter, but juicy. It was relished by my body. I made each drop last as long as I could. I had not finished it even when the feeding was done and the hatch closed, shutting us again in the darkness of the hold of the slave ship.

I threw back my head, reveling in the wind and sunlight. I could not believe the freshness of the air, the winds of Thassa, the brightness of the sky.

This morning I had been removed from the cage, a tether put about my left ankle, given a rag and pan, and set to clean the crawl space beneath the slave platforms. Four times had I vomited and fainted but each time, by the tether, I was drawn from beneath the platform and revived, and set again about my work. I was struck twice with the whip. With four other girls, later, with buckets, I emptied the bilge, which lies below and at the center of the floor of the hold, under a removable wooden grille.

We had then been permitted to ascend to the deck, to empty the wastes and seepage. After this we had been permitted to clean ourselves as we could, with sea water and brushes. The deck is kept clean by the girls in the deck cages. The girls in the deck cages are permitted to keep their hair. The hair of the below-deck girls, mercifully, is shaved off; indeed, our body hair, too, was shaved off, completely. These precautions prevent, to a great extent, the nesting of ship lice. After we were cleaned we were leashed and exercised for a few minutes on the deck. Then each of us, for the remainder of our time on deck, the precious half of an Ahn, was chained in a kneeling position, our hands before our bodies.

I had been taken by Tellius, the henchman of the Lady Elicia of Ar, by tarn, to Schendi. This infamous port is the home port of the famed black slavers of Schendi, a league of slavers well known for their cruel depredations on shipping, but it is also a free port, administered by black merchants, and its fine harbor and its inland markets to the north and east attract much commerce. It is thought that an agreement exists between the merchants of Schendi and the members of the league of black slavers, though I know of few who have proclaimed this publicly in Schendi and lived. The evidence, if evidence it is that such an agreement exists, is that the black slavers tend to avoid preying on shipping which plies to and from Schendi. They conduct their work commonly in more northern waters, returning to Schendi as their home port. The ship on which I was carried was the round ship, or cargo ship, Clouds of Telnus, registered in Cos, but with shipping papers clearing it for the waters of Schendi. It was some twenty feet wide at its broadest point and some one hundred and twenty feet in length. It had two masts, with permanent rigging. It was also equipped with oars, but these were primarily used in entering and leaving a harbor. The round ship, as opposed to the long ship, or war ship, relies predominantly upon its sails. The Clouds of Telnus was said to be a medium-class ship. Its deep hold, I gathered, would carry several tons of cargo. I found it a lovely ship, discounting the miseries of its hold, and it was particularly beautiful under sail. The sails, like those of most Gorean ships, were triangular. Telnus, our destination, is the capital city of the island of Cos, one of Gor's two largest maritime ubarates. Cos lies north of Tyros and west of Port Kar, which latter city is located in the Tamber Gulf, which lies just beyond the Vosk's delta. There are four major cities on Cos, Telnus, Selnar, Temos and Jad. Telnus is the largest of these and has the best harbor. The Ubar of Cos is Lurius, from the city of Jad. The capital of Tyros, Gor's other largest maritime ubarate, is Kasra. Its other large city is Tentium. Her Ubar is called Chenbar. He is from Kasra, and is spoken of, I understand, as the Sea Sleen. Some years ago Tyros and Cos joined fleets for war on Port Kar, but in a significant naval battle the two ubarates were defeated. Port Kar lacked the power and shipping to follow up its victory. Tyros and Cos, and Port Kar, remain to this day in a state of war with respect to one another.

The deck was white and smooth to my knees. It had been rubbed with deck stones, and washed down and scrubbed. The deck-cage girls, on their hands and knees, ankles shackled, attended to this work.

I looked out, across the water. The sky was very bright. It was precious being above deck.

"How ugly you are, Below-Deck Girl," said one of the girls in a small deck cage.

I looked at her. She was auburn-haired, and, like all the slave girls on the Clouds of Telnus, whether cage girls or below-deck girls, stripped; girls are not permitted clothing on a slave ship. She was sitting with her knees drawn up in the tiny cage. She could not completely stretch her body.

I did not bother to respond to her. If her hair had been shaven away, she, too, would not be too beautiful. I would have liked to have stood over her, her control slave, whip in hand, when she had scrubbed on the deck. She would not then, I think, have spoken so insolently.

I heard the lookout cry out, from high above on the highest, the second, of the two masts. He spoke of a sail and its location. It could not be seen from the deck. Men ran to the left side of the ship, some climbed one of the two masts. The captain spoke swiftly to his crew.

The two men at the steering oars, one on each side of the ship, at its back, turned the vessel away from the left.

Men rushed to the benches and slid oars through the oar openings in the side of the ship.

Another man began to call to them and their oars, in unison, began to dip and pull.

Men ran here and there about the deck. Some attended to ropes. Some lashed down loose objects on the deck. Weapons were fetched, and sand and water. Hatches were closed, and secured.

I was very excited, but helpless. I could not participate in the least in what might ensue.

I knew the waters of Thassa were plied by many ships, and, among them, were the ships of pirates. Cos and Ar, I had heard, were now at war, the matters having to do with the piracy on the Vosk not having been satisfactorily adjudicated. But Ar had no navy, though it did have a fleet of river ships that patrolled the Vosk. The ship might, of course, be of Port Kar, or of one of the northern ports, or even of Torvaldsland.

I could not free my ankles, wrists and belly of their chains, which kept me, by their arrangement, on my knees. I was frightened. If the ship fell to pirates I, and the other girls, I knew, would fall helplessly to them, too, lovely spoils, naked slave booty, to the victors. I hoped that they would want us. If they did not, we would be thrown overboard. In such circumstances, girls try to be wanted.

"Get those slaves below deck," called an officer.

I and the other four girls, who had been on deck at the same time, were seized by the arms and dragged along the deck. The hatch to the slave hold was opened. To my horror I saw my sisters in bondage tumbled down the ladder. "No!" I cried. Then I, too, was thrown through the hatch, striking the stairs, rolling, chained, tumbling, to the flooring of the hold. I was much bruised. "No!" I heard cry. Then the girls from the deck cages, too, were taken to the hatch and rudely ordered to descend into the hold. "The smell!" screamed one of them, and then she was thrust stumbling, half falling, through the opening. The twenty girls from the deck were then with us. Looking up, we saw the heavy hatch close. The new girls screamed at the darkness. We heard the hatch bolts flung into place, and the two heavy locks snapped shut.

Seventeen

The Leash

The heavy door opened.

Some men were there, one of whom held a tiny lamp.

The room was long, and wide, and low, with many square wooden pillars. The walls and flooring were of stone. I think it may have been beneath a warehouse, near water. I did not know. I had been brought there, bound and gagged, in a closed sack, in a lighter from the pirate ship.

I had been in the room some four days.

The men entered the room.

I did not know where the room was.

I wore the slave oval locked about my belly, and was neck chained.

The slave oval is a hinged iron loop which locks about a girl's waist. Two wrist rings, on sliding loops, are fitted on the oval. It also has a welded ring on the back, through which a slave bolt may be snapped, fastening the girl to a wall or object, or through which a chain might be passed. My wrists were locked in the wrist rings.

I sat on straw, my legs drawn up.

My neck wore an iron collar, with its ring, behind my neck, through which a long chain passed, the chain, too, being held to the wall by its own rings. The chain, with its collars, was more than a hundred feet long. Some forty or fifty girls were chained on my side of the room, and another forty or fifty on the other side of the room. The room was dingy, and smelled of musty straw. The light of the tiny lamp the man carried seemed bright in the room.

"What girls here," asked one of the men, who seemed imposing, in helmet and cloak, with four fellows, of the man with the lamp, a short, fat fellow in the merchants' white and gold, "are from the Clouds of Telnus?"

"None, of course, Noble Sir," said the merchant.

"It is well known," said the tall man, the leader of the others, "that you deal in black-market slaves."

"Not I!" cried the shorter man, the merchant.

The taller man, in the helmet, looked down upon him, menacingly.

"Perhaps the Noble Sirs would like gold," suggested the fat man. "Much gold?"

The taller man extended his hand.

The fat man thrust gold into the other's palm. "That is twice the normal fee," he pointed out.

The tall man dropped the gold into his pouch. "What girls here," he asked, "are from the Clouds of Telnus?"

The fat man shook. "Two," he whispered.

"Show them to me," he said.

The short fat man led the way toward myself and the auburn-haired girl, who had been in a deck cage. We were chained side by side. She wore the normal Kajira brand. I wore the Dina. I felt uneasy, and so, too, doubtless, did she. We could not kneel before the free males for we were in close neck collars, held closely to the wall.

"Were you two from the Clouds of Telnus?" asked the tall man.

"Yes, Master," we said.

The tall man crouched down beside us, irritably. One of the men with him wore the green of the physicians. The tall man looked at us. As naked female slaves we averted our eyes from his. I smelled the straw.

"Wrist-ring key," said the tall man.

The merchant handed him the key that would unlock the wrist rings.

"Leave the lamp and withdraw," said the tall man. The short merchant handed him the lamp and, frightened, left the room.

The men crouched down and crowded about the auburn-haired girl. I heard them unlock one of her wrist rings.

"We are going to test you for pox," he said. The girl groaned. It was my hope that none on board the Clouds of Telnus had carried the pox. It is transmitted by the bites of lice. The pox had appeared in Bazi some four years ago. The port had been closed for two years by the merchants. It had burned itself out moving south and eastward in some eighteen months. Oddly enough some were immune to the pox, and with others it had only a temporary, debilitating effect. With others it was swift, lethal and horrifying. Those who had survived the pox would presumably live to procreate themselves, on the whole presumably transmitting their immunity or relative immunity to their offspring. Slaves who contracted the pox were often summarily slain. It was thought that the slaughter of slaves had had its role to play in the containment of the pox in the vicinity of Bazi.

"It is not she," said the physician. He sounded disappointed. This startled me.

"Am I free of pox, Master?" asked the auburn-haired girl.

"Yes," said the physician, irritably. His irritation made no sense to me.

The tall man then closed the auburn-haired girl's wrist again in its wrist ring. The men crouched down about me. I shrank back against the wall. My left wrist was removed from its wrist ring and the tall man pulled my arm out from my body, turning the wrist, so as to expose the inside of my arm.

I understood then they were not concerned with the pox, which had vanished in the vicinity of Bazi over two years ago.

The physician swabbed a transparent fluid on my arm. Suddenly, startling me, elating the men, there emerged, as though by magic, a tiny, printed sentence, in fine characters, in bright red. It was on the inside of my elbow. I knew what the sentence said, for my mistress, the Lady Elicia of Ar, had told me. It was a simple sentence. It said: "This is she." It had been painted on my arm with a tiny brush, with another transparent fluid. I had seen the wetness on the inside of my arm, on the area where the arm bends, on the inside of the elbow, and then it had dried, disappearing. I was not even sure the writing had remained. But now, under the action of the reagent, the writing had emerged, fine and clear. Then, only a moment or so later, the physician, from another flask, poured some liquid on a rep-cloth swab, and, again as though by magic, erased the writing. The invisible stain was then gone. The original reagent was then again tried, to check the erasure. There was no reaction. The chemical brand, marking me for the agents with whom the Lady Elicia, my mistress, was associated, was gone. The physician then, with the second fluid, again cleaned my arm, removing the residue of the second application of the reagent.

The men looked at one another, and smiled.

My left wrist was again locked in its wrist ring.

"Am I free of the pox, Masters?" I asked.

"Yes," said the physician.

The tall man removed a marking stick from his pouch and, on the interior of the left shoulder, on its softness, of the auburn-haired girl, wrote a word. "Your name is Narla," he said. That was the word, I gathered, which he wrote on her shoulder. "Yes, Master," she said. Then he turned to me and, with the same marking stick, wrote on the interior of my left shoulder. "You are the girl, Yata," he said. "Yes, Master," I said. I gathered it was this name which he had written on my body. The stain of the marking stick would last until it was washed off.

The men then rose to their feet and left the room. They met the merchant by the door.

"There are penalties for this sort of thing," the tall man warned the merchant.

"Please, Masters," whined the merchant.

"Do you have more gold?" asked the tall man.

"Yes, yes, Masters!" cried the merchant.

Then the door closed and, again, we were left in the darkness. I could still feel the press of the marking stick in my flesh. I gathered that a name had been written there, the name "Yata." I was Yata.

"What is your name?" asked the man of the auburn-haired girl.

"Narla," she said, "if it pleases Master."

"It is acceptable," he said.

"What is your name?" asked the man of me.

"Yata," I said, "if it pleases Master."

"It is acceptable," he said.

"I had them from the fine slaver, Alexander of Teletus," said the merchant, "but their papers were lost in transit."

"I will take them both," said the man. He did not much haggle over price. Soon Narla and I, sharing a common neck leash, two collars, with a strap with center grip, stood outside the long, low room, in the corridor. The leash dangled between us, depending from our leather collars. Our hands were braceleted behind our backs.

"Is it a long voyage to Telnus, Master?" I asked.

"You little fool," he said, "you are in Telnus."

"Why have you bought us, Master?" I asked.

"To work in my establishment as paga girls," he said.

Narla groaned.

I smiled. "And what is the name of your establishment, Master, if a girl may ask?"

"It is the finest in all Telnus," he said.

"Yes, Master?' I asked.

"It is called the Chatka and Curla," he said.

"Thank you, Master," I said.

The hood and cloak was then tossed over Narla. The hood was brought about and fastened under her chin, effectively hooding her. She would thus not know from what establishment she had been taken. The lower portion of the cloak was then snapped under her chin, below the leash. The cloak, which was brief, had four circled oval cutouts. It was a tantalizing garment. There was writing on the cloak. I had little doubt but what it advertised the Chatka and Curla. I, too, was then hooded and cloaked. I could see nothing within the hood. I could feel the cloak brief on my thighs. I could sense the air through the cutouts. Then I began to walk, responding to the leash of the master.

I was in Telnus.

Eighteen

The Slave Sack

I moved carefully, the tray over my head, between the tables.

The Chatka and Curla is a large paga tavern. It is built on four levels, a large, open court, wooden floored, an encircling dais, some twenty feet deep, and, over the dais, two encircling balconies, each some ten feet deep.

We were crowded tonight.

The tavern is dimly lit, by wagon lanterns, paneled with red glass, which hang on chains from the ceilings and balconies.

The crowd was boisterous.

I made my way toward the second balcony. I brushed against other girls, and customers, coming and going on the wooden ramps; I managed the tray with care; it is not well to drop a tray; many girls worked at the Chatka and Curla, more than one hundred; I climbed carefully; the ramps have raised, slatted ridges; these are spaced some twenty inches apart, for better footage.

I heard a girl scream in one of the alcoves.

The red cord, or Curla, was knotted about my waist, tightly, the knot, a slip knot which might be loosened with a single tug, over my left hip. Over the Curla in front, slipping under the body and between the legs, and passing over the Curla in the back, was the Chatka, or narrow strip of black leather, some six inches in width, some five feet or so in length; it was drawn tight; when a girl wears the Curla and Chatka, the brand, whether on left or right thigh, is fully visible, for the inspection of masters. I also wore a brief, open, sleeveless vest of black leather, the Kalmak; a patron parted it, holding it open, as I tried to move past him on the ramp; I stood, quietly, stopped helplessly, the tray held over my head; he kissed me twice; "Little beauty," he said;

"A girl would rejoice if she were permitted to please you in an alcove," I said; it was a line taught us, and expected of us, but I uttered it not without some genuine sincerity; he had had me before, several days ago, when first I had been sent out upon the floor of the Chatka and Curla; he well knew how to get much from the helpless beauty of a slave girl; "Later," he said, "Slave"; "Yes, Master," I whispered; I continued on my way; in addition to the Curla, the Chatka and Kalmak, I was belled and collared, in a black, enameled ankle ring, with five, black, enameled bells, on tiny golden chains, and a black, enameled Turian collar, it, too, with five bells, black and enameled, on five tiny golden chains. My hair had begun to grow out, from having been shaved away for the voyage on the slave ship, but it was still quite short; I wore a broad Koora, which, kerchieflike, covered most of my head. When I had come to the Chatka and Curla I, and Narla, too, had been dipped and scrubbed, to clear us of ship lice and the residues of filth accumulated from the voyage and our consequent captivity; the dip was of water saturated with chemicals toxic to ship lice; we did not open our eyes or mouth when held under by the girls cleaning us; they controlled us by a clamp placed on the right ear lobe; later we were permitted to bathe ourselves; few baths in my life had I appreciated more than that one.

"Paga!" cried a man.

"I shall tell a girl, Master," I said, passing him on the first balcony, making my way to the second, which was the fourth level of the tavern.

On the ramp to the high balcony I passed Narla, returning from that level.

"The man at Table Six on the first balcony wants paga," I said, "Slave."

"Fetch it yourself," she said, "Slave."

"I am occupied," I said, "Slave."

"Too bad," she said, "Slave."

"He has a whip," I said, "Slave."

Her face went white. Some patrons bring whips or quirts to the tavern. If they are not pleased, the girls are informed; a slave ring, with thongs, is fixed in the edge of every table; we strive to wait the tables well. I smiled to myself, seeing Narla hurry down the ramp to fetch his paga; on the slave ship she, in her deck cage, had once insulted me, demeaning my beauty and referring to me as a "Below-Deck Girl." It was not my fault that my hair had been shaved off, nor that I was not blond or auburn-haired, like herself. Those hair colors tend to bring higher girl-prices. I thought that I, when my hair was again dark and glossy, would surely be her equal or superior in beauty; and I had little doubt that I could bring a master more pleasure.

I knelt before the table on the second balcony, placing the tray on the floor and quickly, deferentially, placing its contents on the table, the assorted meats and cheese, the sauces and fruits, and wines and nuts.

"Do Masters desire more from Yata, their slave?" I asked.

"Leave, Slave Girl," said the woman's voice, that of a free woman, kneeling in her robes and veil at the table with her escorts, who sat behind it, cross-legged. Free women came sometimes, escorted, to the Chatka and Curla. Her voice had not been pleasant. "Yes, Mistress," I whispered, picking up the tray and, head down, withdrawing. The men I thought, had she not been with them, might indeed have wanted more from Yata, their slave. Often, to the irritation of other patrons, they had kept me at their table, binding my wrists at the slave ring, keeping me for later.

I went to the balcony railing and looked down. I was some twenty-five feet or more above the wooden flooring. Dancers in the Chatka and Curla, and there are several, move between and among the tables; sometimes a dancer, if she is indeed superb, is displayed solo in the center of the scarlet wooden flooring, within the painted, yellow ring of the slave circle.

Men came and went. I stood there, on the high balcony, with the tray beneath my arm.

I had not been contacted. I did not know why this was. For all I knew I was merely another lowly paga girl. I served as the others did, fully, no differently.

I looked about at the decor of the tavern. It suggested the plains of Turia, or the lands of the Wagon Peoples. There were scenes of hunting, of caravan raiding, of girl taming; scenes were fixed there of the great bosk herds and the strings of the wagons of the fierce plains nomads; in one place there was fixed a painting of the walls and towers of Turia, and riders of the Wagon Peoples on hills, looking toward the city. The dress and costume of the paga girls, too, was intended to suggest the common garb worn by the enslaved beauties who well served the mounted, lance-bearing riders of the lofty, silken kaiila. In such a garb a girl was given no place to conceal a weapon and was well displayed, in her captive curves, to the eye of her master.

Below on the first level two men began to shout and fight, squabbling over first master rights to their waitress, Lyrazina, an exquisite little collared blond from Teletus. She crouched, shrinking back, terrified, almost at their feet. Strabo, the floor master, at a sign from Aurelion, the proprietor and master of the Chatka and Curla, hurried to the combative couple, thrusting them apart. They seized at him, and I heard clothing tear. Another man from the tavern, a fellow who did odd jobs about, as Bran Loort did in Ar at the Belled Collar, leaped to the fray. Two more customers joined in.

"Fight!" cried patrons. A girl screamed.

Sometimes I had thought, in the midst of such a diversion, one might flee the tavern. But this was not possible, I had learned, at least not in the Chatka and Curla, for reasons I shall shortly indicate.

Although most taverns are open and a girl might simply slip out the door and run, there is little prospect of her flight's being successful. She wears only a collar and a brand, and a bit of silk, and she flees into a society that will promptly return her to her owner, unless it chooses to keep her for itself.

I wonder if those of Earth, should any of Earth ever read this, can begin to comprehend the categoricality of the bondage in which the Gorean slave girl is held. Perhaps not. Certainly there is little on Earth that will have prepared them to understand the nature of her bondage, its particular reality.

Certainly its nature shook and transformed me, when I first discovered it, what I had become, what I was here. As I became acculturated to Gor, acclimated to her, so to speak, I soon realized the absoluteness of my condition. Indeed, it was quickly taught to me by bonds, and the whip. It does not depend on one's city, or such, or on one's beauty or intelligence, or such. For example, on Earth, in whatever village or hamlet, in whatever country, or continent, in whatever small town or great city, wherever it might be, an animal is an animal; a pig or a dog, for example, is that, simply that, a pig or a dog. So on Gor, where slaves are animals, if one is a slave, one is simply that, a slave.

Can this be made clear, I wonder, to those of Earth?

Categoricality is involved.

The Gorean slave girl is a slave, *a slave;* can you understand that, in its fullness; I wonder; and she will remain a slave, that, *a slave,* unless freed. And that, of course, is fully at the discretion of free persons. And there is a Gorean saying that only a fool frees a slave girl. And I think that that is true. What man, fortunate enough to own a slave, with all the rights and privileges of the mastery, holding all power over a beautiful woman, even as to how she will wear her hair and whether or not she will be clothed, having at his least beck and call her beauty and its services, and having at his disposal the comforts of her devotion and the inordinate, extensive, diverse, inimitable raptures of her pleasures would willingly relinquish such a pleasant state, such unique, matchless joys? A thousand times better to cast diamonds and gold into the sea!

There is no escape for the beauty.

She may run, of course. But she will be caught, sooner or later, by one or another. Even should she attain her own city, she will be kept there as a slave, for she is then a slave, or, more likely, she will be soon sold out of the city, after having been muchly lashed, that she bring no more shame upon it. She is a Gorean slave girl. That is what she now is. There is no escape for her.

Indeed, girls are often sent, unattended, in a brief rep-cloth tunic on errands for their masters. No one thinks twice about this. They return to their masters; there is nowhere else to go; also, interestingly, a girl who is well mastered will often undergo great privations and hardships to return to the brute whom she cannot help loving with every slave inch of her. Slave girls are often hopelessly in love with their masters.

To understand this, perhaps one must first have been a slave. But I do not think so. I think some nonslaves can sense what is involved, what it might be to be such a slave.

Do they squirm in their beds whispering secrets to tear-stained pillows?

The strongest of chains, it is said, is the slave girl's love for her master.

And many slave girls do love their masters, wholly and helplessly. Does not the slave long for her love master, and the master for his love slave?

The love slave does not wish to be freed. Rather she wishes to be totally dominated, owned and mastered, and to be pleasing to her master, and serve lovingly, devotedly and selflessly. Her collar is inordinately precious to her. Does she not sometimes press her finger tips to her lips and then tenderly touch her finger tips to the claiming band locked snugly on her throat? She fears only that she may be sold, or given away.

I could not simply leave the tavern, not even in the tumult and confusion of a diversion.

The Chatka and Curla, you see, did not resemble most paga taverns in their openness. It was not possible there for a girl to even step outside for a breath of air as it is in most taverns. There are double iron gates, and only the free may come and go as they please.

Another deterrent to the escape of slave girls, of course, is the severity of the penalties connected with escape attempts. Whereas the first penalty is commonly only a severe beating, the second one often involves hamstringing, or the cutting of the tendons behind the knees; this cripples the girl and makes her generally useless save as a pathetic example to her sisters in bondage of the foolishness of attempted escape.

I had been made aware of this sort of thing in Tabuk's Ford. I wished that I had been apprised of it earlier.

The most interesting attempted escape which I know of, however, took place in a locked tavern, not unlike the Chatka and Curla. In it, a clever slave girl, taking advantage of just such a diversion as now rocked the Chatka and Curla, neck-thonged a free woman from behind and dragged her, helpless, to an alcove. There, intimidating and overpowering her, she stripped the free woman, and bound and gagged her. Then, in the confusion and noise of the brawl, she, pretending distaste at the activity of the ruffians involved, went to the gate, was released, and made away. She was free only a few hours, however, for, as an unescorted free woman, guardsmen swiftly went to her protection, prepared to help her safely home. In a few moments, they questioning her, it became clear to them that something was amiss. A free woman was found who thrust back her robe and veils. Her ears had been pierced. The free woman, then, as the guardsmen looked away, tore down her robes to the shoulder, revealing the collar, which bore, of course, the name of her master. She was swiftly returned to him for a severe beating. The most interesting portion of this tale deals with the free woman who had been left, stripped, bound and gagged, in the alcove. In leaving the tavern the disguised slave girl, to cover her retreat, placed a discipline sign on the alcove occupied by the helpless free woman. It read "Take me, Masters." Sometimes a girl, as a punishment, is placed helplessly in an alcove, free for the use of all. Several of the men, patrons of the tavern, willing to oblige the tavern's proprietor, entered the alcove and, untying her ankles, well used the helpless free woman, they in the darkness not knowing the loftiness of her condition. This caused a great scandal in Ar. The slave who had so abused her was to be tortured and publicly impaled, but, to the amazement of the citizens of the city, the free woman herself spoke on the slave's behalf, and begged that she be only put lengthily under the leather. It was done in this manner, to satisfy the desires of the free woman; to the astonishment of all in the court, when the chained slave girl crept on her knees, head down, to render gratitude to the free woman, the free woman had knelt beside her and kissed her, and then turned away. Thereafter the free woman had seemed strange and restless. She began to take to walking upon the high bridges. Once, when a tarnsman snapped by, pursued by guardsmen, mounted, too, on tarns, she had torn the veils from her face and, boldly, supplicatingly, had lifted her robes, revealing her left thigh to the hip. The tarnsman, circling about, took mercy upon her and it is said she cried out with joy as his braided leather rope dropped about her and tightened on her body, jerking her, its prisoner, from the high bridge. The tarnsman, with his captive, escaped. He had returned to Ar later, when his city was at peace with Ar. With him was a beautiful slave girl who had once been the free woman of Ar. Much was she abused and spat upon by the free women of Ar in their fury but she did not seem unhappy. She had made her choice. Rendering love and service to a master had not seemed obviously inferior to her to the reduced sexuality and the squabbling competitiveness which had been expected of her as a free woman. Freedom and love are both estimable values. Some women choose freedom; others choose love. Let each make what choice seems best to her.

I felt a knotted, double strand of leather looped about my left wrist and pulled tight.

"Master," I said.

It was the fellow who had earlier opened the Kalmak and kissed me. I was not displeased to see him, nor to be on his thong.

"Come to the alcove," he said. I placed the tray I carried on a rack. The fight continued below. I was pulled by the leather thong on my left wrist toward an alcove in the wall of the level of the high balcony. There was shouting below. Several had now joined the fight. I heard the musicians begin to play, on Aurelion's orders, to attempt to pacify the crowd, to distract it. A dancer, I supposed, had been sent to the center of the floor. Usually such fights are stopped by the separation of the combatants and the awarding to each of a girl for the night. I supposed Lyrazina would be given to one, and an even more exquisite beauty to the other, thus contenting both. But if this strategy was to be successful, it did not seem to be yet successful. I heard glass break below.

"This one," said the man, indicating an alcove.

He released the thong on my wrist and stood behind me. I climbed the five steps into the alcove and crawled within.

It occurred to me that none had noted him conducting me to the alcove. All eyes had been on the fight below.

I crawled to the back of the alcove and, there, turned to face him, he whom I must now, as he chose, please.

He turned his back to me and, with the belts and buckles, closed the leather curtains on the alcove, that we might be closed within, and be undisturbed from the outside.

He gestured that I should remove my garments, and I did so, even to, reading his eyes, the red Koora on my head. He then gestured that I should crawl to him, and kneel, back on my heels, facing away from him. I did so. I felt my wrists, with binding fiber, tied behind my back.

"Master?" I asked.

"Do not face me," he said.

"Yes, Master," I said.

I sensed him remove, with a rustle of leather, an object from his tunic. Suddenly I felt the wadding of the gag of a slave hood thrust in my mouth and, with its straps, secured. It was done swiftly. I could utter no sound. I was gagged. Then the hood itself was pulled up and jerked down, over my head, and buckled under my chin. He threw me forward and I fell on the furs on my right shoulder. He tied together my ankles. I sensed him move aside some furs. Then I felt my body doubled up and my feet slipped inside the mouth of a slave sack. The sack was drawn up, over my body; I sat, doubled up; my head was pushed down a bit; the sack was drawn shut over my head and, with a snap, locked shut.

Then to my wonder I heard him open a door. It must have been behind the hanging at the rear of the alcove. I felt the sack being lifted through the opening, and then it was dragged along a wooden-floored passage; then he threw it lightly to his shoulder, and began to descend short flights of stairs.

Things had gone very smoothly for him. Then I realized that the fight below, probably, had been staged.

I squirmed in the sack but was helpless. He was very strong.

Nineteen

I Bead a Necklace, and Am Then Used for Wench Sport

I was kneeling.

I felt hands untying the binding fiber on my ankles, and at my wrists. The slave hood was unbuckled and pulled up, over and off my head. I could see! Its leather lay against my breasts, held by its attachments to the gag. The gag straps were loosened. A hand extracted the heavy wadding, letting it fall open, to dry. I almost vomited, freed of the gag. Then I put my head back, and breathed deeply. The hood and gag were then pulled away. One of the men put them, with the binding fiber, in his belt. Two other men crouched beside me. Two others stood nearby. The man on my left, in his two hands, took my left wrist; the man on my right, with his two hands, took my right wrist. They stood, throwing me upright to my feet, between them.

I was unclothed, save for the black, enameled, belled collar, and the black, enameled belled ankle ring, as I had been in the alcove of the Chatka and Curla. My face was red from the slave hood. My body was broken out from the moisture and heat of the slave sack.

I stood between the two men, their hands on my wrists. I was in a torchlit anteroom, of large size. A long rug, some forty yards in length, narrow, red, led toward a large pair of white doors, which opened from the center. Two guards, helmeted, with spears, stood at that door. There were shields and crossed spears on either side of the door.

I shrank back, looking at the tall doors.

I felt pressure on my wrists. "Come, Animal," said one of the men. "Yes, Master," I whispered.

By the wrists I was led toward the great door. I was very frightened, for I knew these must be the men associated with the Mistress, Lady

Elicia of Ar. They thought that I bore a message for them, but I did not. They would be disappointed. They would be angry. Gorean males are not patient with displeasing slave girls. I did not wish to be disfigured or tortured, or slain. I was innocent! I would plead my innocence! Perhaps then I would be only whipped.

The doors were swung open by the helmeted guards. I was flung to my knees. "Kiss the floor, Slave," said one of the men.

I did so, my arms held high, straight behind me, thrusting me down. Then again, rudely, I was thrown to my feet and led into the room.

It was a lofty, beautiful room, as though in a palace. It was floored with purple, glossy tiles, broad and shining. There were slender, lofty white pillars, golden hangings. I was led toward a dais on which a large, corpulent man sat, one of enormous weight, reclining on cushions. He wore white robes, stained with wine, swollen with fat, bordered in laced gold. His face was heavy, coarse, pitted where whiskers, one by one, had been pulled from it by tweezers. He was balding, and wore upon his head a crown of grape leaves, from the famed Ta grapes of the terraces of Cos. I sensed in him intelligence, vanity, wealth, cruelty and power.

I saw that at the foot of the dais, before me, before where I now knelt, released by the men who had held me, there was a low table, and, on this table there were strands of thread and, in small cups, beads, wooden slave beads, beads of various colors, of many colors.

I looked down at the low, wooden table, the beads in the tiny cups. I trembled. It seemed I had knelt here before, or somewhere like this, in a dream which had once tormented me in Tabuk's Ford. I wondered if I had ever knelt in such a place as this before, or if it were merely the figment of a slave girl's dream. The dream had seemed real. I wondered if it were in some odd sense a recollection or anticipation. I dismissed such nonsense from my mind. But the similarity of this setting to that of the dream was uncanny and frightening.

A slave whip, by one of the nearby men, was lifted before me. I then was truly frightened, for this, too, had been in the dream.

"What is this?" I knew a voice would ask.

"What is this?" asked the man.

"A slave whip, Master," I said, knowing that I would.

"And what are you?" inquired the voice.

"A slave, Master," I said. I wanted to scream out to them that I knew nothing of their messages or whatever it was they might seek.

I wanted to scream out to them that I was only a miserable slave, and knew nothing. I wanted only a bit of mercy from them.

"Do you obey?" asked the voice.

"Yes, Master," I said.

I trembled. These things had been said, too, in the dream. I did not think the dream was prophetic. Rather I understood now that in some way the dream had recalled to me, or touched upon, a ritual in which I had been rehearsed.

I pulled back my head, fearing the press of the slave whip to my lips.

This puzzled the man, I sensed. But then, as was his part, he thrust the whip against my lips. He did it angrily. He had not been pleased to have been anticipated. The heavy leather of the whip, folded back about its handle, bruised my lips. I tasted a drop of blood. I could feel the whip hard against my teeth, lying across them diagonally.

"Kiss the whip, Slave," said the man.

I kissed the whip.

There was a silence.

"Who commands me?" I asked. I had sudden respect for whoever had devised the ritual we were enacting. My last question was not the sort of question a slave girl, in such a situation, would ask. It was too bold. The master, if he wishes, will inform the girl as to who it is who commands her. If he does not wish to inform her, he does not. The girl needs to know only that she is a slave and that it is hers to obey. Yet the question was not utterly uncontextual. A bystander might simply infer that the girl was new to her collar and did not understand that such a question might bring the whip down upon her. Another subtlety was that the expression 'Master' had not been included in the question.

The gross, corpulent man looked at one of his lieutenants, a helmeted fellow who stood nearby. They exchanged glances.

I had, by this response, identified myself for them. The identification would be confirmed by the next responses.

The corpulent man looked at me, and shifted his weight, rotund, immense and slack, on the cushions.

"You are commanded by Belisarius, Slave Girl," he said. I did not know if 'Belisarius' was his true name, or a code name for the contact.

I knew now, however, incontrovertibly, that this was the contact, this was the specific individual to whom I was expected to communicate the intelligence which I supposedly conveyed.

I wanted to cry out that I knew nothing. The small eyes, deep in the fat of the heavy face, regarded me.

"What is the command of Belisarius, the slave girl's master?" I asked. I could scarcely hear myself speak.

"It is simple," said the voice.

"Yes, Master," I said.

"Bead a necklace, Slave Girl," he said.

"Yes, Master," I said.

A strange state of consciousness seemed suddenly to come over me. I was aware of what I was doing, and yet it seemed as though I behaved in terms of some prearranged pattern.

It was again almost as though I were in a dream.

I reached toward the strands of thread on the table, and toward the cups of tiny beads.

I do not know why I first chose a yellow bead, but I did. And then I chose a blue bead and a red, and then another yellow. I began to bead a necklace.

I knotted the end of the thread on the necklace.

I lifted it to Belisarius. One of his men took it, carefully, and handed it to him. He placed it on the dais before him.

I shook my head. Strangely, as soon as the necklace had been taken from me, my natural state of consciousness returned. The behavior, whatever might have been its import, had been discharged. It was as though I awakened from a dream.

I saw Belisarius looking carefully at the beads before him. I had strung the same order of beads more than once, to complete the necklace. Too, the necklace was long and loose, like most slave necklaces. It would loop at least twice about a girl's throat. It seemed to be indistinguishable from thousands of necklaces which I had seen on the throats of slave girls.

It did not take Belisarius long to regard the necklace.

Suddenly he pounded his heavy fist on the dais with pleasure. "At last!" he said. "At last!"

The men about him did not ask what significance he had found in the necklace, nor did Belisarius explain to them what he had seen in the arrangement of the beads.

I felt a knife at my throat. "Shall we kill her?" asked a man behind me.

"No," said Belisarius. "The message has now been delivered."

"What if she falls into the wrong hands?" asked a man.

"It would not matter," said Belisarius. He looked at me. "Bead the same necklace, Slave Girl," he said.

I trembled. Suddenly I knew I could not. I could not remember the order of the beads.

"I cannot, Master," I said. "Please do not kill me!"

"Even if she could rebead the necklace," said Belisarius, "its message could not be understood, and, even if it could be understood, it would be meaningless to others." He laughed. "And even if its meaning could be understood, it would be too late for the enemy to act. They could then understand only the danger in which they would then stand."

The knife was drawn away from my throat. I almost fainted on the tiles.

Belisarius regarded me. "Besides," said he, "the Lady Elicia wants the pretty little thing for a serving slave."

"The Lady Elicia," said one of the men, "would, I wager, look well naked and in a collar."

The men laughed.

"Perhaps later," said Belisarius, "when she has served her purposes."

The men laughed.

I felt my hands being tied behind my back. The wadding of the gag of the slave hood was rolled and thrust deep in my mouth. The gag straps were drawn back, deeply, between my teeth; I winced; then, behind the back of my neck, they were cinched, tightly.

I looked at Belisarius, bound and gagged before him. "Use her for wench sport," he said, "and then return her to the Chatka and Curla."

The slave hood was pulled up, and opened, and then pulled down and over my head; it was folded and tucked under the chin, taking up its slack, and the leather belt, looped twice about my neck, was drawn through its loops, tightened and buckled shut.

By one ankle I was pulled across the tiles to the side of the room.

Twenty

A Slave Girl's Revenge

I walked in the morning, an Ahn before noon, on the wharves of Telnus. I could see the great gates of the harbor some two pasangs across the water. The harbor was filled with many craft. I avoided the tar on the planks of the wharf. Beneath the planking of the wharves, here and there, I could see water, and small boats tied at pilings. Men came and went, going to and from ships, and disembarking and embarking cargo. I passed the throne of the wharf praetor, he in his robes, with the two scribes, for the settling of disputes which might occur on the quays. Four guardsmen, too, were there.

They grinned at me as I walked past, and I smiled back at them. They were handsome guardsmen, and I was a slave girl.

But I must not annoy them, soliciting their patronage for the tavern, for they were on duty. I had been struck five times across the back of the legs, my wrists held, when I had made this mistake before. The praetor was a sour fellow.

After I had delivered the message to Belisarius, and had served to amuse his men, I had been returned to the Chatka and Curla, still hooded, and bound in the slave sack, as I had been brought from it, by the same men, through the secret door in the rear of the alcove. I had been removed from the sack in the alcove, unbound, unhooded and ungagged. The man who had taken me from the alcove and returned me to it then swiftly used me for his pleasure, and left, through the customary, leather-curtained door. I was left behind in the alcove, naked and had. I put on the garments of the tavern. I looked behind the hanging at the rear of the alcove. There was a stout door there, made of iron. I put my finger tips on it. Timidly, softly I tried the handle. It was now locked. It had been locked, apparently, behind the

403

man who had brought me back into the alcove. There was no key or lock mechanism on my side of the door. It may have been, of course, that the door had been left unlocked originally, and that it had locked automatically, when closed, behind the man when he had re-entered the alcove, returning me to it. I did not know. I did know that it was now locked, and that I could not open it. I let the hanging fall back, concealing the door. Even had I been able to open it, I would not have dared to go through it. Suppose I had been found in an area where I was not supposed to be. I did not know what would be done to me. On the whole surface of the planet there was nowhere to run, nowhere to go. I was a slave girl. I left the alcove, to return to my duties on the floor, those of a paga slave. The man who had taken me from the alcove and returned me to it had not, incidentally, as nearly as I could tell, conducted me to and from the house of Belisarius. I had been carried and transported for a time in a small boat, and, for a time, in a cart. Hooded, and captive in the slave sack, I had no sense of direction and very little of time. I gathered, from what I had heard, that contacts had been made by men wearing masks, who spoke signs and countersigns. I doubted that my original captor himself knew the identity of these other men.

I continued on, down the wharves.

After I had delivered the message I was no longer under the same security which I had earlier experienced at the Chatka and Curla. Sometimes now, like certain other girls, I was permitted to wander forth, before the busy hours of the tavern, to solicit patronage for its proprietor, my master, Aurelion of Cos. I wore the belled collar, and belled ankle ring, of the tavern, and a bit of black silk. On the silk, in yellow, there were words, which Narla had translated for me. "I am Yata. Own me at the Chatka and Curla." I was barefoot. I wore a red kerchief, for my hair had not as yet fully regrown.

"Greetings, Slave," said a man.

"Oh!" I cried, for his hand had suddenly, unexpectedly, thrust upward, beneath my brief silk.

I backed away from him.

I regarded him, uncertainly. I could not feign displeasure, or outrage, of course, for I was a slave. On the other hand, I did not want to encourage him to seize me as I was, on the wharves, and further his explorations.

"I am Yata," I said. "Of the Chatka and Curla."

"I can read," said he.

These things, of course, were sewn into my brief black silk, with yellow thread. I knew that, of course. I felt foolish. What a stupid slave he must have thought me! I was upset, for we are intelligent, almost always, and we wish our intelligence to be recognized by our masters. Indeed, I suspected that intelligence figured into the criteria of acquisition commonly used by slavers. Intelligence, in any event, is almost always prized in a slave. There are simple reasons for that. Intelligent women are more quickly and easily trainable; they learn more quickly; they are quickly apprised, for example, of what the whip can do to them, and so they are almost immediately zealously eager to please; accordingly, they are less likely to be frequently whipped; they tend, too, to have good memories, say, for the master's friends and appointments, and so on; too, they are more aware and sensitive; they learn like dogs to be alert to the master's subtlest moods, and govern themselves accordingly. Too, they are inventive, and imaginative, and this makes them adept in diversifying the repasts they prepare, and the pleasures they provide. Too, sometimes the master wishes to talk about a thousand things, in depth and at length, and what a joy to him it is, it seems, to share these things, a thousand thoughts and observations, and intimacies, with his slave, she perhaps kneeling lovingly before him, naked, his, her hands thonged behind her back. There is little doubt in my view, nor, I suspect, in that of most masters, that intelligent women make the best slaves.

"Can you?" he asked.

"No, Master," I said.

"You leaped quickly under my touch," he said.

"I am a slave, Master," I said.

"And a pretty one," he said.

"Thank you, Master," I said. "I may be had at the Chatka and Curla."

"Of course," he said.

I was pleased to see that he understood my words not as a statement of the obvious, but, rather, as an "advertising girl's" expected hawking of wares, if not as a more personal invitation.

He was handsome and doubtless knew it, the beast, and that I was only a slave girl.

"Are you the best at the Chatka and Curla?" he asked.

"That is for men to decide, Master," I said.

"Are you the most beautiful?"

"I do not know," I said.

"Really?" he asked.

"No," I said. "I am not the most beautiful."

"But you are beautiful?" he said.

"I think so, Master," I said. "It is at least my hope that men will find me pleasing."

"Are you hot?" he asked.

"Hot!" I thought.

I had been Judy Thornton! I had been of Earth!

He regarded me.

"Yes, Master," I said.

He then turned about and continued on his way.

"Try me and see, Master!" I called after him, "At the Chatka and Curla!"

I looked after him.

I was uneasy. His hand had heated me.

What A slave you are, I thought, Yata, or Teela, or Dina, or whatever men will call you! Then I thought, yes, yes, I am a slave! I supposed I had always been a slave, even on Earth. A latent slave, fit for explicit bondage. Then I had been brought to Gor. Here there was nothing latent about my slavery. I had been explicitly collared. Here I was a slave, in full legality.

Is it appropriate that you are a man's slave, I asked myself. Yes, I said to myself. That is what you should be. Do you want to be a man's slave, I asked myself. Is that what you want? Yes, I whispered to myself, that is what I want.

Then I tried to put such thoughts from me.

I then continued again on my way.

I was uneasy, sexually, emotionally, uneasy.

His hand had been strong, provocative. I had no doubt that such hands would be sure, and would quickly bring a slave to such a pitch of need that she would thrash in his arms, and be beside herself in her eagerness to serve.

I saw a sailor, and ran to him, kneeling at his leg, touching it.

"Does Master desire paga?" I asked.

"Begone, Slave," he said.

I drew back, and he strode away, with the rolling gait of his profession.

I looked about, at the boxes and bales on the wharves. I did not bother the men who were busily engaged. Their foremen did not wish them distracted by the presence and banter of a slave girl. More than once they had taken their belt to me, driving me from the vicinity of the men.

I perched on top of a large box on the wharves, holding my legs closely together.

It is not unusual for a slave girl to be demure, and provocatively feminine.

I was calmer now.

My uneasiness, my agitation, at having been touched had now much subsided. To be sure, as little as a touch on my ankle might have returned me acutely to the discomfort of my need. We cannot help reacting to such things. We are sensitized to them.

I enjoyed the smell of the salt water, the sight of the soaring harbor gulls. I wore a collar, and was clad for the pleasure of men. But I was not unhappy.

I had a clear identity. No longer was my life empty. I knew now who I was, and what I was.

When I had first been sent to the wharves, some weeks ago, my wrists had been braceleted behind me, and I had been accompanied by other girls; later I had been permitted to go alone, my wrists still locked behind my back; later I had been permitted to go alone to the wharves in wrist rings and chain, my hands before my body, separated by some twenty inches of light, gleaming chain; there are many things, clever, subtle exciting things a girl may do with such a chain; some of these were shown to me, and others I invented, sharing them with other girls at the tavern; girls struggle to become ever more perfect, and beautiful, in their slavery; girls often share slave secrets; I struggled hard to learn all that I could, to become more pleasing to masters; something in me, you see, was not at all displeased to belong to men; at one time such a thought would have horrified me, and I would have thrust it wildly from my consciousness, not daring to regard it; now I entertained it with a shameless pride; I had become a slave girl. One thing that was shown to me was the slave bridle; the male takes the light chain back between the teeth of the girl and holds it, together, behind her neck, thus, too, pinning her hands there, helplessly; he then controls her by means of the bridle; my own invention was the chain kiss; one clasps the leg with the chain against the interior of the thigh, and then, from the side of the knee, one begins to kiss the leg, one's lips and teeth hot about the chain; the male feels both the chain and her mouth, biting and kissing, climbing the chain; she climbs the chain and descends it, and climbs it again, until he orders her to leave it.

I heard the sounds of chains, and a whip. Below me I saw a line of prisoners, men of Ar who had been captured on the Vosk River in the river fightings. Cos and Ar, I knew, were at war, contesting commerce rights on the western Vosk. There were some twenty of them. They wore rags. Their wrists were manacled behind them. They were in neck coffle. The chain was heavy.

"Hurry, Sleen!" called their whip master. There were four guards with them.

One man fell and the whip master was upon him in an instant. He struggled again to his feet and continued on, in the coffle, trudging along the hot wharf.

They would be taken to a holding area, I knew, and there branded slave. They would then row on the merchant galleys of Cos. Warships commonly have free oarsmen; merchant ships commonly, but not always, use slaves.

Seeing the men, sweaty, chained, under the whip, I was affrighted. It was a grim fate which awaited them, the confinement and pain of the benches, the weight of the long oars, the shackles, the whip, the drum of the hortator, the stench, the black bread and onions of the ponderous galleys.

Then I thought that such a fate was too good for them, for they were of Ar. I remembered Clitus Vitellius, who had sported with me, and then discarded me. I remembered I hated Clitus Vitellius. How I hated him!

But I felt sorry then for the men of Ar.

They were not Clitus Vitellius.

Better it were Clitus Vitellius in their place! But he was a noble captain of Ar, and would not be involved in the insignificant skirmishes on the Vosk.

The prisoners, the men of Ar, disappeared down the wharf. I dropped down from the box on which I had sat.

Aurelion of Cos would not be pleased if I did not bring customers to the Chatka and Curla.

I was not chained now; the last four times I had been permitted to come to the wharves unchained; Aurelion, I think, was pleased with me. Once he had even permitted me to serve his pleasure. How proud I had been, and how envious the other girls had been. I struggled to be fantastic to him. I think he was not displeased. Afterwards he had, before leaving, thrown a candy to the floor before me which I, gratefully, in the manner of the Chatka and Curla, which was necessary, had picked up in my mouth. "Thank you, Master," I had said. The candy was hard and very sweet. I showed it off to the other girls. "I pleased the master," I boasted. "He once gave me five candies," said Narla. "Liar!" I cried. I knew the master had never even called for her. We leaped toward one another. Tima, the first girl, had separated us with a whip.

I looked about the wharves.

A long ship, I could see, was moving into its wharfage, its lateen sail furled on the long, sloping yard. It was a warship of Cos. I saw other girls, from other taverns, running down to its mooring.

Quickly I joined them.

I knelt with them, in a line of some seven or eight girls. We called forth the praises of our respective establishments. But when the men had disembarked, carrying their sea bags and weapons, none had stopped to stand before me.

I rose to my feet, looking about. Some officers, with a few members of the crew, remained on the ship. I turned away.

A sailor passed me. He carried a long bag on his shoulder, tied shut. I saw the bag move. It carried, I conjectured, a bound woman. From the lineaments of the bag, over his shoulder, I gathered she was naked. I wondered if she were slave or free. He boarded one of the numerous ships at the many wharves, going below decks.

Two men passed me, pushing a cart of furs of sea sleen. I could smell spices in a bale near me.

A man walked by carrying a long pole, from which dangled dozens of the eels of Cos.

It was now past noon, and I had not yet conducted a patron to the Chatka and Curla. Soon it would be time for me to report back.

Though I now wore no chains on the wharves I was still, of course, in a sense, chained in my bondage. I was clad as a slave girl, and wore a belled collar, which identified my master, and a belled ankle ring; too, I was branded. Masters take little risk with their girls when they send them to the wharves. They are as slave on the wharves as behind the barred gates. As a pig is a pig, and a dog a dog, so, too, the slave is a slave.

There is no place for her to run; there is no escape for her.

That did not truly displease me, for I had grown content in my collar, but I knew that if I did not report back promptly, when due, I would be beaten. That did not please me, not at all.

Gorean masters, you see, are strict with their girls.

The impossibility of escape for the Gorean slave girl, interestingly, is in its way reassuring to her, and gives her a sense of security. It is one less thing to concern herself with. When a girl grasps that her bondage is categorical, and absolute, she can begin to explore it, and enjoy it. There are freedoms in bondage which the free woman, enslaved by her freedoms, can never suspect. Or perhaps she can, and perhaps that is why they hate us so.

It was now past noon. I was growing apprehensive. I had not yet found a guest for the tables of Aurelion. Girls are not sent to the wharves for the delights of smelling the fresh sea air. They are sent forth half naked in their collars to bring back paying customers.

I parted my silk a bit and ran to kneel before a sailor. I looked up at him. "Own me at the Chatka and Curla, Master," I said. He spurned me from him with his foot, forcing me back to the hot planks of the wharf. I ran to kneel before another. "I am Yata," I said. "Please own me at the Chatka and Curla, Master," I begged.

He, with the back of his hand, struck me from his path, hurling me by the force of the blow to my shoulder on the boards. I tasted blood in my mouth. I knelt on the hot, caulked boards, angrily. He had gone. It had not been necessary to strike me.

I rose to my feet and again looked about. The large, yellow shield on the high pole in the harbor had already been hoisted and fallen, and, near it, the fire of white smoke had been lit. When the shield reaches the top of the pole in the harbor and is permitted to fall it is the tenth hour, the Gorean noon. At the same time the white-smoke fire is lit. At the twentieth hour, the Gorean midnight, a beacon is lit. These things serve to synchronize chronometers in the port, and serve to regulate schedules and the utilization of the tide tables.

I was beginning to feel desperate.

Toward me a couple was moving, a bearded sailor and a red-haired paga girl. I saw by her silk she was from the Cords of Tharna, an establishment competitive with the Chatka and Curla.

I knelt boldly in their path, and looked up at the sailor. "Yata can please you more," I said.

"He is mine!" said the red-haired girl, holding the sailor's arm.

"I am his, should he be pleased to have me," I said. I smiled at the sailor. "Please, Master," I said.

He looked from one of us to the other. I saw we both pleased him. He grinned. "Fight," he said.

With a scream of rage the red-haired girl leaped upon me, clawing and biting, throwing me back to the boards. She was larger and stronger than I.

She could not well get her hands in my hair for, as yet, it was too short. I tore at her hair, rolling with her on the boards, and got my fingers in it but she, with the heels of her two hands, struck back my head. I felt her scratch for my eyes. I screamed as her teeth bit me in the arm. I was then terrified, and tried to defend myself, as she struck me. She crouched beside me, striking down at me with her fists. I rolled over, covering my head. She leaped up. I turned. She kicked at me. I felt her foot strike me in the stomach. I could not breathe. I gasped wildly for air. She threw herself over me and held my head down, locking her right arm about it; she held her legs about my body, preventing me from using my arms; with her left hand she shoved up, as she could, the collar at my throat; then her head was pulled back and away, suddenly, from me; the sailor had her by the hair, kneeling, twisted back; she fought to look at me, held. "La Kajira, Mistress!" I wept. "I am a slave girl, Mistress!" She had clearly won. I was her inferior. I shrank back, fighting for air.

"He is mine!" she hissed.

I put my head down, in defeat.

Then she cried out in pain, as she was flung by the hair to his feet. "You are mine," he said.

"I am yours," she whispered, terrified.

Then he took her by the hair and dragged her to her feet and left, she bent over, held by the hair, running, stumbling, beside him. To me she had been formidable, but to him she was only a wench for his pleasure.

I rose to my feet, shaken. I rearranged my silk. It had not been torn.

I looked after the sailor and the red-haired girl, stumbling beside him, held by the hair. I saw he would use her well, very well. This pleased me.

A male slave, his wrists chained, separated by some eighteen inches of linked metal, pushing a wharf cart passed me. He looked upon me. I was furious! I ran to him, in rage, and slapped him. "Do not look upon me!" I cried in rage. "I am not for the likes of you! You are a slave! A slave!" He pulled back his head, angrily. "Slave!" I screamed. "Slave!" I spun about. I saw one who must be his master, a merchant. I was red with fury. I ran to the merchant and knelt before him. I pointed to the male slave. "He looked upon me!" I cried. "He looked upon me!" "Have you permission to speak?" he asked. "May a girl speak?" I asked, frightened. "Yes," he said. Emboldened then, I pointed again to the male slave. "He dared to look upon me," I said. I knew that male slaves were carefully supervised. I knew it could be quite unpleasant for one of them to be caught looking upon a slave girl. To be caught looking upon a free woman could mean death for them. "He looked upon me," I said, pointing to the male slave. Surely he would be, at the least, whipped for his indiscretion. The beauty of slave girls was for free men, not for the slave likes of such as he.

"You are too good for him?" asked the merchant.

"Yes," I said. I then realized this was not the proper thing to say. But I had said it.

"You are both animals," he said.

"Yes, Master," I said.

"But you are a female," he said.

"Yes, Master," I said.

"And he," he said, "though slave is yet male."

"Yes, Master," I whispered.

"And is not the male animal the master of the female animal?" he asked.

"Yes, Master," I said. I knew that male dominance was pervasive among mammals, and that it was universal among primates. It can be frustrated only by an extensive and complex conditioning program, one adequate, over a period of years, to distort the order of nature.

"Do you find this slave of interest?" asked the master of the male slave.

He shrugged. "She is small," he said.

I looked at him, frightened.

"But she is not without interest," he conceded.

"Do you think you can catch her?" asked the master.

"Of course," said the male slave.

I rose to my feet, frightened. I began to back away.

"She is yours," said the master.

I turned to run. He caught me before a large box, and flung me, face forward, against it. When I recoiled back from the hot wood the chain on his wrists had looped about me, and I was his, held to him by the chain about his wrists.

"It is long since I have had a wench," he said.

He dragged me along beside him, the chain looped about my body, cutting into my waist over the left hip.

"Be merciful to a slave, Master," I begged.

Behind some boxes, on the boards of the wharf, he threw me down, under him.

"Please be kind to a slave, Master," I begged.

He laughed.

The master did not hurry him, but, I think, attended to other matters. The wharf cart had been empty.

When the slave left me I had yielded to him, as though he might have been a free man. I was much shamed.

I lay behind the boxes and looked up at the blue sky. I was miserable. I had been used by a slave. But, too, I was frightened. It was surely past the time when I should have returned to the Chatka and Curla. I did not want to be whipped!

Slowly, painfully, my legs stiff, I climbed to my feet. I rearranged the bit of silk I wore.

I stepped out from behind the boxes. I must hurry back to the Chatka and Curla.

I stopped, startled. Then I shrank back beside the large boxes. He was far off, but I was certain. I began to breathe rapidly. My heart began to pound.

It could not be, but it was.

I did not know what to do. At first I felt, unrestrainable, overwhelming me, an incredible flood of love and elation. I felt the incredible love and joy, the elation, possible only to a slave girl.

He was approaching from down the wharf, carrying a sea bag, in the guise of a sailor.

I wanted to run toward him, crying out, the length of the wharf, and throw myself to his feet, weeping, covering them with kisses.

Then I was frightened that I had made a mistake. It could not be true.

But I watched. I grew more and more sure, and then I was certain. He stopped to buy a cake from a vendor on the wharf. It was he!

It was my master, Clitus Vitellius of Ar!

"Oh, Master," I wanted to cry out, "I love you! I love you, Master!"

Then I saw him glance at a paga girl who posed, turning before him, and spoke to him.

Suddenly I hated her and him!

He dismissed the girl, but I had seen him look upon her, as a warrior, a master.

I hated them both!

It had been Clitus Vitellius of Ar who had first enslaved me. He had marked me with the hot iron, marking my very flesh, branding me a slave girl. He had made me serve him! He had made me love him, and had then, when it pleased him, his sport done, thrown me aside, giving me to peasants!

A bold plan, relentless and terrible, formed in my mind. I breathed deeply, in cold fury, resolved.

He would find that a slave girl's vengeance is not a light thing.

I straightened myself. I parted the silk, lasciviously. I lifted my head, with the small sounds of the bells on the collar.

He was coming toward me now, eating on the bit of cake he had purchased.

I saw he carried no weapons. This pleased me.

I ran toward him, with short steps, and knelt before him. I kissed his feet. At his feet I felt suddenly a wave of love for him, the helpless weakness of a slave girl overcome at her master's feet, but then I caught myself, and every bit of me became cold, and calculating and sensuous. I held the calves of his legs in my hands, and looked up at him.

"Dina," he said.

"My master calls me Yata," I said, "Master."

"Then you are Yata," he smiled.

"Yes, I am Yata," I said. I looked up at him, smiling.

"Are you as innocent and as clumsy as before?" he asked.

"No, Master," I said, putting my head down, beginning to kiss him on the side of the leg, deeply, pulling, sucking, at the hair a tiny bit.

"I see not," he said, laughing.

I looked up. "I have been taught how to please men," I said.

"Of course," he said, "you are a slave girl."

"Yes, Master," I said.

"Are you good?" he asked.

"Some masters have not been fully displeased," I said.

"Do you think you could please me?" he asked.

My heart leaped. I applied myself as subtly and marvelously as I could, touching his leg variously, bringing my mouth slowly, biting and loving, to the side of his knee. "No, Master," I whispered. "Yata could never please a great warrior like you."

He looked about. "Say only 'sailor,'" he said. "Here I am not a Captain of Ar, he Clitus Vitellius, but only a seafarer, a simple oarsman from Tyros, one called Tij Rejar."

I looked up at him. "As master wishes," I said. Then I again applied myself to his legs.

"Master will not cuff me from him, will he?" I begged.

"Clever slut," he said.

He lifted my head and brushed back the kerchief on my head. I reddened.

"I was some weeks ago slave cargo," I said, my head down.

"And pretty slave cargo indeed," he said.

"I am pleased if Master is pleased," I said. I held his legs, my cheek against his thigh. I wanted to cry out that I loved him, but then I checked myself, remembering my project. I knelt at his feet only to bring him low. I did not think it would be difficult if I could get him to the Chatka and Curla.

He would pay! He would pay!

I looked up at him, smiling. "I was once yours," I said, "Master."

He looked down at me, almost tenderly. "Perhaps it was a mistake to have given you away," he smiled.

I caught my breath, but remained firm. I must not relent. I would be remorseless.

How vulnerable in a way I was, in silk and collar at his feet. But I held great power.

"It is strange," I said. "Once you owned me. Now, in faraway Cos, on the wharves, I kneel at your feet in the collar of a paga slave."

"It is a pretty collar," he said.

"Thank you, Master," I said.

"I see by your silk," he said, "that you work in the Chatka and Curla."

"Yes, Master," I said.

"What is your duty there?" he asked.

"To please the customers of my master," I said.

"It is long since I have held your hot little body," he said.

I blushed, though I was a slave girl.

"You are a hot, lovely slave, you know," he said.

"In your arms," I said, "any girl, even the daughter of a Ubar, would find herself only a responding slave." I did not doubt but what this was true. I remembered myself miserable in his arms, writhing with unwanted ecstasy, then, unable to help myself, unable to hold out longer, suddenly surrendering to my enslavement in his arms. Though I had been of Earth he had reduced me to a spasmodic, yielding slave.

"I am thirsty for paga," he said.

"I know a place," I said.

"The Chatka and Curla?" he asked.

"Yes, Master," I said.

"But are there girls there?" he asked.

"Yes, Master," I said.

"Are you one of them?" he asked.

"Yes, Master," I said.

"It is long since I have owned you," he said.

I looked up at him, boldly. "Own me again at the Chatka and Curla," I whispered.

"You are a curvaceous, tempting little slut," said he, "—Yata."

"Does Yata dare to suspect," I asked, "that Master once cared for her a little?"

"Does a slave girl wish to be whipped?" he asked.

"No, Master," I said, head down.

"I have other matters to attend to," he said.

I looked up, frightened. "Please, Master," I begged. "Come with Yata to the Chatka and Curla."

"I am busy," he said.

"But Master thirsts for paga," I said.

He grinned.

"And Yata," I wheeled, "was detained upon the wharves." I remembered the slave who had been set upon me by his master, to discipline me. I had been well ravished, and at length. He had forced me to respond to him, as a slave's slave. It was now well past the time when I should be at the tavern, bathing and preparing for the labors of the evening. "She is late," I said. "If she does not return with a customer, after all this time, her master may not be pleased."

"It is nothing to me," said he, "if a girl is tied at the slave ring and put under the leather."

"Of course not, Master," I said. But then I looked up at him. "But Yata," I said, softly, begging him, supplicating him, "desires to serve Master paga." I knelt before him, on the boards of the wharf, eyes lifted, holding him. "Have me with the cup, Master," I begged. "Please, Master."

He looked down upon me.

"Have pity on a slave, Master," I begged. "Have me with the cup, Master. Please, Master."

He seemed undecided.

"Purchase a cup of paga, Master," I said, "and have me with its price."

He looked down upon me.

"Yata is before Master on her knees," I said. "Yata is on her knees before Master, a slave girl, begging him, begging him!"

He smiled. "Conduct me to your tavern, Slave Girl," he said.

"Thank you, Master!" I breathed. I put down my head, so that he might not see the smile of victory, of triumph, that suffused my features. Submissively, with the sound of bells, those on my collar and ankle ring, I rose lightly to my feet, turned, and, excited, scarcely daring to breathe, barefoot, as a slave girl, led the way toward the Chatka and Curla.

I heard him following me.

* * * *

The double gate, of barred iron, shut behind me.

I turned, suddenly, screaming, pointing to he who had followed me within.

"He is of Ar!" I cried. "He is an enemy! Seize him!"

Clitus Vitellius looked at me, startled.

"Seize him!" I cried. His hand had gone to his left hip but the short sword in its scabbard did not now hang there.

Strabo, assistant to Aurelion of Cos, leaped upon him, and was struck back. Clitus Vitellius looked about himself wildly.

"Seize him!" I cried.

Two of the men who worked within the tavern hurried toward the gate. Men leaped up from tables.

Clitus Vitellius turned to the double gate and tore at the bars, but could not fling them back, for the bolts had slipped into place.

A man leaped on him and he shook him off. He bent to Strabo, to rip the keys from his belt. There were many keys. He cut with the keys, holding their ring, at the face of the second man of the tavern, who fell screaming, bloodied, reeling back. He slashed about him with the keys, long and heavy on their thick ring, some six inches in width. A man leaped at him, low, seizing his legs. Two others leaped bodily upon him. They struggled. Then two others sped to him, and then there was a sword at his chest, where the tunic of the sailor had been torn away. Four men held him, back against the bars of the gate. Aurelion of Cos rushed forward. "What is going on here?" he demanded.

I pointed to the powerful, bloodied captive.

"He is Clitus Vitellius of Ar," I cried. "He is a captain of Ar!"

"A spy!" cried a man.

"Kill the spy!" cried another.

"He says he is Tij Rejar, an oarsman of Tyros, but he is of Ar, of the Warriors! He is Clitus Vitellius! He is of Ar! He is a captain!"

Aurelion looked at me. "It would not be well for you, Slave," said he, "to be mistaken in this matter."

"I am not mistaken, Master," I said.

"Who are you?" asked Aurelion.

Suddenly I was frightened. If his identity were sufficiently well established so as to truly appear an oarsman from Tyros it might not go well for me. I might be boiled alive in the oil of tharlarion. I began to sweat.

"I scorn to conceal my identity from those of Cos," he said. "I am Clitus Vitellius, a captain of Ar."

I laughed with pleasure. "See!" I cried.

"Bring chains," said Aurelion.

Clitus Vitellius looked at me. I shrank back. Chains were placed upon him.

"He is securely manacled," said Strabo, whose face was swollen as a consequence of the blow of Clitus Vitellius.

Ankle chains were then placed, too, upon the warrior of Glorious Ar, and a chain ran, too, from his wrists to the chain on his ankles.

A collar, with two guide chains, one on each side, was fastened on his neck.

"Kill the spy," said a man.

"No," said Aurelion. "We will take him to the magistrates."

The double gate was unlocked by Strabo, who had recovered his keys. Four men made ready to conduct Clitus Vitellius from the tavern.

"It is the heavy galleys for spies," said one man.

"Better to kill him now," said a man.

"No," said Aurelion, "conduct him to the magistrates. They will have much sport with him before he is chained to a bench."

The heavy galleys were round ships, large ships, which usually carried bulk goods, such as lumber and stone. It was usually impractical to employ free oarsmen on such ships.

Clitus Vitellius looked once more upon me. I saw that he was securely chained.

I approached him. "Ho, Clitus Vitellius," I said. "It seems you now wear chains like a slave."

He did not speak to me.

"You will soon be slave in the heavy galleys," I said. I posed before him, as a slave girl, opening my silk. Men laughed. "Look well, Master," I said, "for there are few girls in the rowing holds." I turned before him, and again faced him. "Do not forget Yata, Master," I said. "Remember it was she who put you in chains, who puts you upon the bench of the galleys!"

He regarded me, not speaking.

I went to him and, suddenly, with all my might, slapped him. He scarcely moved.

"The vengeance of a girl," I said, "is not a light thing."

"Neither," said he, looking at me, "is the vengeance of a warrior."

I shrank back, frightened.

"Take him away," said Aurelion.

Clitus Vitellius was conducted from the tavern.

"You did well, Slave Girl," said Aurelion.

"Thank you, Master," I said.

Then, suddenly, I knelt before him.

"What is it?" he asked.

I had rendered great service to the state of Cos.

"Yes?" he said.

Suddenly it had occurred to me that I could become free! When again might such an opportunity present itself? I was from Earth! Surely I was not so contemptible and despicable that I cared to remain a slave! Surely it was wrong that a collar should be on me! Perhaps on others, but not on me! Not on me, surely! Had I not been Judy Thornton, of Earth? Surely I should not be a slave! How could that be? Was I not of Earth? Must I not seize this opportunity to win my freedom! How often might such an opportunity come to a girl? How helpless and vulnerable I was as a slave! Did I not understand that? I viewed the dimensions of my servitude. We were at the mercy of our masters. I shook with the *frissons* of a girl's fear. Did I want truly to be a slave? How could that be? To have no choice but to obey, and serve! Surely that could not be true! I must not let it be true! I must not let it be true! And then I felt, rising within me, the feelings of Earth, so insidious, grievous and ugly, the reflexes, emotions and responses which had been pervasively, subtly engineered into me, to shape me into an ideological product designed to perpetuate a culture at war with nature, a prison of stereotypes alien to a natural world, a culture designed with the success, thriving and welfare in mind only of the those who could profit from the frightened, the shallow, the incomplete, the manipulable, the thwarted, and hating, the ruthless artisans of, and profiteers from, organized pathologies. And as Earth spoke in me, I felt reflexively, dutifully, what I had been told I should feel, what I had been taught I ought to feel, what it had been programmed into me I must feel if I were to satisfy pre-established cultural criteria, if I were to be smiled upon and commended, too, lest I bear the terrible burdens of difference, of ostracization, of isolation and scorn. Surely I must win my freedom! How terrifying to be what I was, a slave! I was in a collar! I was owned! Was this not horrifying, that I might be silked, or stripped, or bound, that I must serve without question, *and in all ways?* They must free me! I must be freed! I must have my freedom! I deserved it! I had done well! Indeed, Aurelion, my very master, had said that, that I had done well! Surely I might now be freed!

"What is it, Yata?" asked Aurelion, proprietor of the Chatka and Curla, my master.

Too, of course, if Clitus Vitellius should somehow regain his freedom, unlikely though that might be, I had little doubt that he would remember the girl who had betrayed him. And I did not doubt but what, as he had said, a warrior's vengeance is not a light thing. If I were free, I might hide, slip away, change identities, be in any one of a thousand cities, be untraceable. As a slave I must await him at the Chatka and Curla, fearing each stranger who might enter, fearing it might be he. Must I await him here, like a silken, caressable verr, unable to flee, observed in the day, chained at night? And if I were sold it might not be hard to track me, from master to master, by means of slave papers, merchants' records, and so on. Goreans tend to keep track of their properties, verr, kaiila, slaves, and such.

"Free me, Master," I begged.

He looked down upon me.

"I have done Cos great service!" I said. "Free me, free me, Master!"

I looked up at him, pleadingly.

"Bring a whip," said Aurelion to Strabo.

"No, please, Master!" I cried.

"You are a slave, Yata," he said. "And you will remain a slave. Do you not think I know women? Do you not think we know women? You should be a slave, and you will remain a slave."

"Master!" I protested.

"And at this point in your bondage," said he, "you are an ignorant, presumptuous slave."

I wept.

"Put her at the slave ring," said Aurelion, "and give her ten lashes, and then throw her a pastry. She has done well."

"I shall, Aurelion," said Strabo.

In moments I knelt at the slave ring, my small wrists crossed and bound to it, the silk pulled away from me, down about my calves. I was struck ten times, and then released. A pastry was thrown to the floor before me. "You did well, Slave Girl," said Strabo. "Thank you, Master," I whispered. I reached for the pastry. The whip stayed my hand. "Forgive me, Master," I said. I put my head down and took the pastry in my mouth.

"Chain her in the kennels," said Aurelion.

On my hands and knees, as a punished slave girl, holding the pastry in my mouth, I crawled from the floor to the kennels, followed by Strabo. There, at the concrete wall, on my blankets, I lay down. The chain and collar was fastened on my neck. Strabo left. I took the pastry in my hands, and began to eat it. What a fool I had been to beg my freedom. I had only to look in a mirror to see that I would never be free on Gor. I lay in the darkness of the long kennel, on my blankets, in my place, chained by the neck. I was a Gorean slave girl. Then I cried out with anguish, weeping, and hurled the pastry from me. I pounded at the concrete beneath the blankets. I wept. I had betrayed Clitus Vitellius, my master!

Strabo, accompanied by Narla, approached me. He poked me with a whip. "Master?" I said, looking up, in misery. "Be quiet, Slave," he said. "Yes, Master," I said. Narla carried a lamp. I blinked against its light. Such a lamp seems dim, nothing, in the daylight, but in the darkness of the unilluminated kennels it seems bright, even painfully so. She was eating the pastry which I had discarded. Strabo unlocked the collar on my neck. "There is a sailor here," said he, "who is drunk, from the Cords of Tharna, who is calling for you."

"Yes, Master," I said.

I recalled the fellow who had had the red-haired girl who had bested me in combat on the wharf. I had said to him that I could please him more than she. He had now, apparently, come to the Chatka and Curla, calling for me.

"Please do not make me serve," I begged.

"Narla," said he, "will help you ready yourself. Be quick."

"Do you want some pastry?" asked Narla holding a piece out to me.

"No," I said. I looked up at Strabo. "I betrayed Clitus Vitellius of Ar," I wept.

"You did well," he said. "Now hurry."

"Please, Master!" I begged.

He struck down with the lash and I cried out in pain. "I hurry!" I wept. "I hurry!"

I fled from the kennel, followed by Narla, to the room of preparation.

I could hear the fellow on the floor calling for me.

Twenty-One

A Convoy Departs
from the Harbor of Telnus;
I Appear on the Cargo Manifest
of One of Its Ships

I scarcely noticed as my wrists were braceleted behind my back. I wore a brief, yellow slave tunic, of closely woven rep-cloth. I stood near the gate of the Chatka and Curla.

"Come, Yata," said Strabo, taking his direction toward the wharves.

I, barefoot, braceleted, head down, followed him.

I knew now that I truly loved Clitus Vitellius of Ar. Yet to my misery I had betrayed him. How I would if I could have undone that deed. How I would if I could have tried to pit my small strength against the heavy oar which he would now draw. I would if I could have changed places with him. Better that I, if I could, be chained to a bench, an oarsman slave, than he. I, a worthless slave girl, in her vanity and pettiness, had laid low not only a warrior, but my own beloved. What mattered it that he cared naught for me, that I was but rude collar meat in his mighty hands? It mattered nothing. I loved him more deeply than I realized one could love. He had stirred such emotion, such rage, such hatred, in me that I would not have believed it possible. I had lived for my vengeance, dreaming of it, and, when I had attained it, I found it only misery and ashes, and unspeakable anguish, for it had cost me my very self, he whom I loved, Clitus Vitellius of the city of Ar.

The men in the tavern, and the girls, too, had been pleased that I had designated Clitus Vitellius. How excited and pleased all had been. "You did well," they assured me. I had been thrown a pastry. But, alone with myself, I wept with misery.

I had not known I could so love. I would have given all, everything, to undo that deed.

He had not treated me well, but it did not matter. He was a free man. I was only a slave. All that mattered was that I loved him.

Yet I had betrayed him.

How small a thing it was that he had sported with me and then, in his simple cruelty, given me to a peasant. Did I not know I was a slave girl? What did I expect? To be treated as a free woman? How vast a thing, how vicious and disproportionate it was that I, a mere slave girl, for so small a fault, if fault it was, had sentenced him to the tortures of the galleys.

I had done well! I cried out in anguish. I loved him. I loved him!

I should have served him in the tavern, and then kissed him farewell, surrendering him to his glory and freedom, I remaining behind, forgotten, a girl whom once he had owned and discarded. I could then have known him free.

Would it not have been enough?

But I had betrayed him, he whom I loved.

Strabo turned and looked at me.

"Forgive me, Master," I said. I had moaned with anguish.

We continued on our way toward the wharves.

The night I had betrayed Clitus Vitellius I had been beaten. I had failed miserably to please the drunken sailor.

Twice later, too, on ensuing nights, I had been beaten. "You seem to be worthless as a paga girl," had said Aurelion of Cos, my master.

"Forgive me, Master," I had said.

"It is perhaps time," said he, "to return you to Ar."

I could now smell fish and salt, for we were quite near the wharves. Between buildings I could see galleys at their moorings. We descended toward the wharves.

I no longer wore the black, enameled, belled collar, and ankle ring, of the Chatka and Curla.

I heard men shouting, and saw them running. There seemed excitement below.

I now wore a ship collar, of locked steel, gray, with its destination tag. The tag, I had been told, read: "Send me to the Lady Elicia of Ar, of Six Towers."

I had betrayed Clitus Vitellius of Ar. I could not have hated him so much had I not loved him so deeply.

I had betrayed him, he whom I loved!

Strabo took me by the arm. This puzzled me, as I was braceleted. He pulled me through the crowd. Men ran here and there. The fire of white smoke had been lit near the shield pole, though it was not yet noon. I heard an alarm bar ringing. On the height of the shield pole there was hoisted a scarlet disk.

"Come," said Strabo, making his way through the crowds, holding my arm.

"Escape!" I heard.

"They have escaped!" cried a man.

"They have escaped!" cried another man.

I saw guardsmen hurrying by, with shields and spears. People stood on roofs.

"Who has escaped?" I cried.

The alarm bar rang steadily. Strabo pulled me through the crowds, and conducted me swiftly toward one of the wharves.

"Who has escaped?" I cried.

"Kneel," he said.

I knelt near the foot of the gangplank, leading to the deck of a ramship, the *Jewel of Jad*. Such ships are sometimes used for merchant service. They carry much less cargo than a round ship, but lean and shallow-drafted, they are much faster.

Strabo conferred quickly with one of the ship's officers, one who held a cargo manifest. Strabo indicated me. The man nodded.

"Stand," said Strabo.

I stood.

He then thrust me up the gangplank, onto the deck of the ship. It was some twenty feet wide.

Strabo gave the ship's officer the key to my collar, and the officer placed it in his pouch.

The officer then gestured to one of the sailors, and indicated me with his head. The man fetched a set of light ship chains. I stood, and felt ankle rings snapped on my ankles, joined by some twelve inches of chain; another chain, attached to this chain, was some three feet in length, and terminated with light manacles. Strabo unbraceleted me, dropping the bracelets and their key back in his pouch. The sailor then, lifting the vertical chain behind me, fastened me in the light manacles. My ankles, then, were chained, and, joined to them by the vertical chain, behind me, were my chained wrists.

"I wish you well, Slave Girl," said Strabo.

"I wish you well, Master," I said. He then left. I saw the gangplank drawn up. From the wharf, moorings were cast off. I saw three sailors, with long poles, edging the ship from the wharf. Oarsmen, free sailors, sat upon the benches. The helmsmen, two of them, were in their places. The oar master stood below the helmsman. On the small, high stern deck, I saw the captain. Slowly, gently, the ship began to move from the wharf. An oar count would not be given until clear of the wharfage. The lateen sail would not be dropped until clear of the harbor gates.

On the wharves men seemed still agitated. I saw more guardsmen. The alarm bar yet rang. White smoke billowed from the platform near the shield pole, from whose height now swung a scarlet disk.

I went to the rail of the ship. The cargo officer was there. Other ships, too, I saw were edging from their wharves. We would sail in convoy.

"Who has escaped, Master?" I asked.

"Have you not heard?" he asked.

"No, Master," I said.

"A chain of twenty men of Ar," he said.

"How could they escape?" I asked. I was sure these must be the same men I had seen some days ago on the wharves, when, later, I had encountered my master, Clitus Vitellius.

"They were freed by an escaped prisoner," he said. "They fought like larls," he said.

"What prisoner freed them?" I asked.

"One called Clitus Vitellius," he said.

I trembled on the deck. I thought I might faint. The joy I felt was incredible.

"They were last seen," said the officer, "heading for a paga tavern, the Chatka and Curla."

I said nothing, but trembled.

"It seems," said he, "a slut there betrayed their leader, Clitus Vitellius." He laughed cruelly. "I would not wish to be she," he said.

"The vengeance of a girl," I had said to Clitus Vitellius, "is not a light thing."

"Neither," had said he, looking at me, "is the vengeance of a warrior."
I had shrunk back, frightened.

"Take him away," had said Aurelion of Cos, my master. He had been conducted from the tavern.

"He is a warrior of Ar," said the ship's officer, standing near me. "I would not wish to be that girl."

I looked at the wharf, which seemed to drift gently away from us.

"Did you know her?" he asked. He knew I had come from the Chatka and Curla.

"Yes, Master," I said. "But he will not find her at the Chatka and Curla. She was sent away."

"Good fortune," said he, "for the treacherous slut."

"Yes, Master," I said.

The bow of the *Jewel of Jad* turned toward the gate of the harbor. There were eyes, two large eyes, one on each side of the bow. They were outlined in black; their interior was blue; their pupils were black. They looked toward the harbor gate. I heard the call of the oar master. "Ready oars!" The oars slid through the thole ports. "Stroke!" he called. The oars, in unison, twenty on each side, dipped into the waters of the harbor, drew and lifted, the water falling from them in bright droplets, splashing back into the harbor.

I was indescribably happy, though, too, I was apprehensive. Clitus Vitellius was free, and had men.

The officer was looking at me. I was chained at his side. "You are the only slave girl on board," he said.

I looked at him, and laughed delightedly. He looked at me, puzzled.

"I will be a wonder to you, Master," I laughed. "I will be a wonder to you!"

He lifted the brief skirt of the yellow slave tunic to my left hip. "You are a Dina," he said.

"Yes, Master," I said.

"I have heard Dinas are good," he said.

"We are fabulous, Master!" I laughed. "We are Slave Flowers."

He laughed at the pun.

"We shall test your boasting later, little Dina," he said.

I tried to press myself against him. I wanted to feel my body in his arms, his. Suddenly, Clitus Vitellius free, and with men, the world seemed open and glorious again. Again, suddenly, I rejoiced in the beauty of men and my slavery to them. Again, almost making me want to cry out with joy, I felt their attractiveness irresistibly and deeply. Again, suddenly, I felt myself helpless and owned by them, loving and helpless to their least touch and command.

I tried to lift my lips to the officer, but he held me from him. "What a slave you are," he laughed.

"Yes, Master," I said.

Again I could not help my responsiveness to men, true men, Gorean men. To an Earth girl, accustomed to the hypocrisy and weakness of the men of Earth, their shame, their inhibitions and pretenses, the Gorean male, in his honesty, his power, his lust, his manhood, is a hurricane of joy. Clitus Vitellius, I knew, had been angry that I could not help but respond to men, scorning me for this rightly, perhaps, as the slave and slut I was, but I did not care. Though any Gorean male might make me, in spite of myself, a panting, orgasmic slave in his arms, I knew it had been only he, Clitus Vitellius, whom I had truly loved, and yet loved. In his arms I had always been the most helpless. He was my love master.

The officer gestured to the sailor who had first chained me, and he approached.

"Though you are the only girl on board," said the officer, "do not think that you will be treated easily."

"No, Master," I said. I knew I was a slave girl.

"Take her below decks," he said, "and chain her by the neck to a ring."

The sailor threw me over his shoulder. I knew I would be kept below decks until late, chained, that my needs might grow even keener and more frustrated.

Then, when I was whimpering, I would be pulled to the deck.

Twenty-Two

What Occurred Southeast of Cos

I walked about the deck of the *Jewel of Jad*. The deck was hot. The sun was bright. I brushed back my hair, which was now about an inch and a half in length, with my two hands and closed my eyes, stretching. I opened my eyes, and looked up at the sky. It was intensely blue, and the clouds were so white it almost hurt my eyes to look upon them. The single lateen sail, stretched from its yard, swelled with a clean, slow wind. I could see other ships to both the left and right, too, with lateen rigging, both ramships and round ships. There were some twenty vessels in the convoy. We were bound for Schendi.

We were two days out of Telnus, and it was the tenth hour. I loved to walk the deck, and feel the wind and the spray. The water was only a yard or so below the railing, as the ship, shallow drafted and freighted, plied the sea, sunlit and sparkling. I looked to the horizon, noting the other ships. They were beautiful with their masts and sails. I understood then how it could be that men might love the sea. Gorean sailors, as the sailors of Earth, speak of her as she.

I fingered the ship's collar on my throat, with its tag. It read, "Send me to the Lady Elicia of Ar, of Six Towers." At Schendi I would be bound and sent by tarn to Ar, there to be returned to the mercies of Elicia Nevins, a former beauty rival from Earth, who would then be again my mistress. I knew she would get much work from me as her serving slave. I touched the ship's collar. It is a hard thing for a girl to belong to a woman. Further, I knew she would wish me to be a demure girl, a fitting serving slave for a lady of wealth and rank, one whose status and image requires that her girls be paragons of shy, perfect obedience, humility and modesty, that they reflect not the least dishonor upon her. If I so much as looked at a man, even a slave, I had no doubt she would tear the flesh from my bones with the delicately beaded, feminine slave whip which, by its slender leather loop, hung upon its peg in her bedroom, where I, her girl, might constantly see it. I had already felt it. It would be torture to belong to her, not only from the shame of being forced to serve her perfectly, but because she would expect me to adopt her values and conform absolutely to them, values which involved her proud, determined independence of men, and her contempt of them. The slave girl must be as the mistress wishes. I had felt the hands of Gorean men, tight and strong, on my slave body. I did not know if I could now live without them.

I resolved to put my mistress from my mind, and live for the moment, for the joy, the men, the ship and the sea.

Near the stern of the ship men who had been trolling a line now began, sweatily, bracing themselves, to draw it in. It pulled back, away from them, powerfully.

I ran to the stern that I might watch. Half out of the water, then returning to it, I saw a great speckled grunt, four-gilled. It dove, and swirled away. Another man came to help with the line. I observed the struggle. One often fishes from the ships on Thassa, and the diet of the sailors consists, in part, of the catch. Part of each catch is commonly saved, to serve as bait for the next.

I cried out with fear. One of the men shouted with anger. Rising from under the grunt swiftly was a long-bodied shark, white, nine-gilled. It tore the grunt from the line and bore it away. Other dorsal fins, of smaller sharks, trailed it, waiting. Sharks, and sometimes marine saurians, sometimes trail the ships, to secure discarded garbage and rob the lines of the fishermen. The convoy, by its size, had doubtless attracted many such monsters. I had seen, yesterday, the long neck of a marine saurian lift from the waters of gleaming Thassa. It had a small head, and rows of small teeth. Its appendages were like broad paddles. Then it had lowered its head and disappeared. Such beasts, in spite of their frightening appearance, are apparently harmless to men. They can take only bits of garbage and small fish. Certain related species thrive on crustaceans found among aquatic flora. Further, such beasts are rare. Some sailors, reportedly, have never seen one. Far more common, and dangerous, are certain fishlike marine saurians, with long, toothed snouts; they are silent and aggressive, and sailors fear them as they do the long-bodied sharks. The sea sleen, vicious, fanged aquatic mammals, apparently related to the land forms of sleen, are the swiftest predators to be found in Thassa; further, they are generally conceded to be the most dangerous; they tend, however, to frequent northern waters. Occasionally they have been found as far south, however, as the shores of Cos and the deep inlets of Tyros.

I walked back toward the bow of the ship.

I reached into a wooden bucket and took a tospit, bit it open and began to suck at the juice. No one stopped me.

Although the cargo officer, my first day on board, had warned me that I would not be treated easily, he had not been as good as his word. I was permitted the freedom of the ship. I was not even chained at night. The men were fond of me, and they treated me well, with the rough camaraderie and friendship that is sometimes accorded an owned girl, one who is common to all, and must obey all. For all the restraints placed upon me I might have been a free woman, save that the distinction between us, apart from my tunic and collar, would have been clear when a man snapped his fingers and pointed to the deck at his feet, or whistled for me in the night, and I must run to him, as might a pet sleen, to serve him. A slave girl, one who truly serves men, has often much freedom. Since they have everything, and anything, they want from her, and she is complete slave, and they total master, there is no struggle between them; she, accordingly, in a strange way, is prized and treasured; how many women of Earth, I wonder, are prized and treasured by their men; one can prize and treasure, of course, only something which one owns; a free person can be respected, and even loved, but cannot stand to another in that unique relationship which is that of prize and treasure; to stand in that relationship a woman must be owned; further, since each man, in his heart, desires a beautiful woman as a slave, he is, when he owns one, at least in this respect, contented, satisfied and pleased; a contented, pleased, satisfied man is a happy man, and a happy man is a kind man, and a generous man; he is jealous only of his prerogatives over the slave; of course, when his heat is upon him, then he becomes less kind and generous, and more the harsh master; she then, to her pleasure, well understands his dominance over her; then her slavery is truly brought home to her; even among free lovers, I have heard, the man, in the fullness of his heat, often laughs at the woman's illusion of freedom and seizes her to him as a slave; how marvelous to the man, then, if she is truly a slave. With what joy may such a woman, in true bondage, be seized and used. Moreover, her bondage, naturally, extends beyond the brief, several hours of pleasure; she simply belongs to him, and must continue to serve him, however he pleases; how exciting it must be for a man to own so delicious a creature as a woman; how utterly marvelous for him! It is more difficult to speak of women. In my heart, I know, there lies a slave girl, once denied, then secretly feared, now openly and joyously recognized, who longs for a master. I do not know if this is true for other women or not. Let them look into their own secret hearts. I do not think the longing of men is an oddity in the genetic history of a species; I think there is a reciprocity which has been intricately evolved; this desire, this longing for a beautiful slave, for a beautiful female, who stands to him as slave to master, which is universal in glandularly normal, strong men does not seem likely to have evolved in isolation; the evolution of the tiger's tooth suggests the presence of game; the evolution of the eye suggests the existence of light; the existence of blood suggests the organism's presence in an environment which supplies water and salt; similarly a man's desire to own a slave suggests that there are slaves to be owned, waiting to be mastered; in the animal kingdom the instinct to dominate and the instinct to submit are functions of one another, each real and deep in the blood of the evolved, complementary beasts; let the woman who desires to kneel naked before her male and put her head to his feet do so; but let her be wary as he cries out with pleasure and seizes her, for she is then a slave.

"Sail!" cried a man. "Sail!" I looked up. He was high above the deck. He stood, barefoot, on the lookout platform, high on the tall, single mast, well above the long yard and the billowing, triangular sail; the lookout platform is a wooden disk, fixed on the mast; his hands were on a ring, also encircling the mast.

"Where away?" called an officer, on the high deck, whipping out a small telescope.

"Schendi half ship!" called the man. The new vessel was abeam on our port side. Sailors of Cos usually refer to the left side of the ship by the port of destination and the right side of the ship by the port of registration; this alters, of course, when the ports of destination and registration are the same; in that case the sailors of Cos customarily refer to the left side of the ship as the "harbor side," the right side of the ship normally continuing to be designated as before, by reference to the port of registration. This sort of thing occasionally presents problems in translation between Gorean and English. For example, an expression in Gorean which might intelligently be translated as "Off the starboard bow," would be more literally translated, for the ship on which we were, as "To the Telnus bow." The exact expressions "port" and "starboard" do not exist in Gorean, though there are, naturally, equivalent expressions. The English expression "starboard" is a contraction of "steering board," and refers to the side of certain ships, particularly northern ships, on which the steering board, or rudder, was to be found. Most Gorean vessels, on the other hand, like many early vessels of Earth, are double ruddered. A reference to the "rudder side" would thus, in Gorean, be generally uninformative. It might be noted, however, if it is of interest, that the swift, square-rigged ships of Torvaldsland are single ruddered, and on the right side. A reference to the "rudder side" or "steering-board," or "steering-oar," side would be readily understood, at least by sailors, if applied to such a ship.

The Captain of the *Jewel of Jad* hurried to the high deck. The officer there on watch handed him the telescope.

"It has two masts, two sails," he said, "and ten oars to a side. It must, thus, be a round ship."

"It flies the flag of Port Kar," said the captain, with pleasure.

"See now," said the officer, pointing.

"I see," said the captain. "She is turning about."

Another officer ascended to the high deck. He, too, bore a glass.

"It is a round ship," said the first officer.

"It is low in the water," said the second officer, he who had just come to the high deck.

"It is heavily freighted," said the first officer.

The captain lowered the glass. He was still looking across the water. He licked his lips.

The *Jewel of Jad* was a long ship, a ramship, though she was now in merchant service.

"She flees," said the first officer. "Let us take her!"

The second officer continued to regard the ship. "She seems long," said he, "for only ten oars to a side."

"She flies the flag of Port Kar," urged the first officer. "Let us take her!"

"We shall take her," said the captain. "Signal our intentions to the flagship. The convoy will lay to."

"Yes, Captain!" said the first officer, and called swiftly to men to run the signal flags of Cos to the mast.

The captain spoke soberly to the helmsmen, and the *Jewel of Jad* turned to pursue the ship of Port Kar.

Men leaped to the benches and our oars slid outboard. The oar master took his place on the steps below the helmdeck. Weapons reposed at the foot of the benches. It would be holiday and carnival. The decks were not cleared. None even noted me, nor, if they did, sent me below. Missile weapons were not readied. Sand was not brought to the decks. They did not even take the time to lower the yard and drop the mast, which is commonly done in such vessels before an engagement. It would be easy work; there would be shares for all.

The captain grinned.

"Stroke!" called the oar master. The *Jewel of Jad*, like a living thing, leaped in pursuit of the fleeing vessel.

Only the second officer, he also with the glass, seemed troubled, observing the fleeing ship with the glass. Then he was ordered to his station.

I stood near the railing, below the steps leading to the helmdeck.

The signal flags of Cos snapped in the wind. Behind us, in the distance, hove to, lay the convoy.

We would rejoin them shortly. I was very excited. Never had I seen a capture at sea. When the Clouds of Telnus had been taken I had been locked below decks, with other slave girls. We had not known to whom we belonged, until the hatch had been opened and we saw strangers.

"Faster!" called the captain.

"Stroke!" called the oar master. "Stroke!"

The convoy fell behind.

"Captain!" called the lookout. "Behold her! Her masts are dropping. She is turning about!"

I could see, from where I stood, the yards lowering, the sails being furled, the masts being unblocked on the other ship. Also, I could see it swing about.

"It is as I feared," cried the second officer, he who had not been sanguine about the vessel's pursuit.

He fled to the high deck.

"Hold!" called the captain. "Hold!" called the oar master. The men looked at him, puzzled.

"See!" said the second officer. "Look!"

"You are to be at your station!" shouted the captain.

"I submit, Sir," said the officer, "you should turn about."

The captain studied the ship in his glass. The second officer, too, observed it.

Round ships, I knew, commonly had two masts, fixed, and permanently rigged.

The ship we now watched had no mast we could see.

"Note the oars, Captain," pressed the second officer. "There are now twenty to a side."

Additional oars had been slid through thole ports.

"That is no round ship, Captain," said the young officer. Its lack of height in the water had not indicated a weight of freighting, buts its design, swift and terrible, like a mighty racing shell. Its oarage had been only half revealed. Now its masts were down. Ramships enter battle under oar power.

"I urge you, Sir," cried the young officer, "turn about or build speed to shear!"

The ship was bearing down upon us, rapidly.

"Turn about or build speed to shear!" cried the young officer.

"See the flag!" cried the first officer, who had been eager to pursue.

Now not only the flag of Port Kar but another flag, too, snapped on its line at the stem castle of the approaching vessel, hurling toward us, like a swift knife, its oars flashing.

It was a broad flag, white, with vertical bars of green. Superimposed upon the bars of green, gigantic, black and horned, it bore the head of a bosk.

"It is the flag of Bosk of Port Kar!" cried the first officer.

"Turn about! Turn about!" screamed the captain.

"We are lost men!" cried a sailor, rising in terror from the bench.

I screamed and saw the new ship, suddenly large, seem to lift itself in the water, and then heard the shattering splintering wreckage of wood and the loud swift swirl of water the ship struck and men screaming and saw the lines loose wild the yard and sail leaning awry the deck shifting and becoming steep and I couldn't stand and I lost my footing stumbling and seized a line, rolling on the deck, it fastened to the mast. The ship seemed then, for a moment, to right itself. The new ship had backed away from us, and seemed turning its prow away. Then the deck of the *Jewel of Jad* began to tilt toward the water, where we had been struck, the water pouring into the hold.

Men leaped from the ship into the water.

The ship then seemed again to right itself, but began to settle. I crouched, terrified, gripping the line by the mast. Suddenly I felt on my feet the cold water of Thassa. The deck was awash. The other ship moved away from us, like a silken sleen.

On the high deck the captain, alone, stood, his hand on the rail.

I looked about. The helmdeck was deserted, the benches empty. I heard a man scream from the water.

Too, from afar, I heard signal horns.

The captain looked down, toward me. "There is no safety here," he said. "Release the line and flee to the water."

I shook my head. "No!" I said. "No!" I was terrified.

Suddenly he looked upon me, as a Gorean master. He began to descend from the high deck, toward me.

"Yes, Master!" I cried. I released the line and fled to the railing, and leaped into the water. I was a slave girl. I feared a Gorean master more than the water.

The water was greenish, and cold. I felt miserable. I went beneath the surface and then emerged.

"Come away from the ship," called a man.

I swam toward him. I was some yards from the sinking vessel when it slipped beneath the water. I was dragged back and submerged, but, in moments, I managed to regain the surface.

I could not see for the salt water in my eyes. It burned in my nostrils for a moment. I spit water out.

A hand seized me and pulled me to a piece of wreckage, some plankings from the ship's side.

"We will be picked up momentarily," said a man. There were some four men on the planking.

I could see other ships from the convoy. There were several about, converging upon us.

"Wait!" said one of the men. "They are turning about!"

"There are other ships!" cried another.

I stood up, unsteadily, on the boards. I could see, to be sure, that several of the convoy ships were turning about. Too, in the distance, between some of them, I could see other ships, approaching.

"The convoy," said one, "is under attack."

I saw the young officer in the water. He was assisting the captain of the *Jewel of Jad*. They found wreckage.

I saw a fin, long and white, suddenly cut the water. A ship passed near us, but it was one which flew the flag of Port Kar, a light galley. It did not pause for us. I saw a trail of smoke looping through the sky as a fire missile was launched from a ship's catapult. Far to our left we saw a galley aflame. It was one of Cos.

Signal horns could be heard.

Two longboats approached, lowered from one of the ships of the convoy. One of them picked up men from the water, and the captain and young officer. The other nosed toward us. The four men boarded the longboat.

I, too, made ready to board the longboat. I was stopped, and thrust back.

"We have no room for a slave," said one of the men.

"Please, Masters!" I begged.

I knelt on the planking. The yellow rep-cloth I wore was wet and thin, and clung close upon me. Gorean slave girls are commonly not permitted brassieres or undergarments.

"Please, Masters!" I begged.

They drew me into the boat.

I knelt between their feet, my head down, making myself small.

In a few moments we drew alongside the mothership and I, and the others, boarded her.

I was taken and put immediately in the hold. "A slave girl!" said a woman's voice. There was a tiny lamp. "Forgive me, Mistress," I said, and knelt. She mounted the stairs. "I will not share the hold with a slave girl!" she cried. "Be silent, Woman!" said an angry man, who was on the deck. She tried to move back the heavy hatch but it had been battened down. She came angrily back down the stairs. I did not dare to look at her. "Forgive me, Mistress," I begged. She paced back and forth. We had both been placed in the hold. We were both women.

I and the free woman, who did not deign to speak to me, remained many hours in the hold, as the fighting and maneuvering continued for several hours, through the afternoon and night. The lamp burned out and we remained in the darkness. Outside and above decks we could hear shouting, and the sound of sprung ropes, as the canisters of flaming pitch were lofted from the deck catapults. Once, late, we were partly sheared, losing several oars on the port side. A few moments later we had been boarded, but the boarders had been repelled.

After the repulsion of the boarders the hatch had been opened, briefly.

"The ship is secure, Lady," had said the captain. "I shall have food brought."

She had ascended the stairs, going to the deck. Behind her, unnoticed, I crept to the height of the stairs.

It was still dark. On deck there were dark lanterns. Sometimes, in the distance, I saw flares lofted from one ship or another, burning upward and then, their silken globelike chutes opening, burning steadily, descending, to settle into the water and be extinguished. Too, there was light on the water, to our left, from flaming ships.

"I will remain no longer in the hold," said the lady to the captain.

"I must insist," said he.

"No," she said.

"You will go below of your own free will," said he, "or I will have you put there, chained to the bottom of the steps."

"You would not dare!" she cried.

"Bring chains," he said.

"I shall comply with your wishes, Captain," she said, angrily, and descended the stairs. I slipped down before her. The hatch was again closed. It was opened in a few moments, and food and drink was brought. She did not share it with me.

I could tell when morning came as I could hear the men above changing the watch.

Then I fell asleep.

I was awakened by the free woman pounding on the hatch, demanding to be released.

That we had not been released led me to believe that there was still danger.

From what I could hear the convoy, as a whole, had maintained good discipline, and given a satisfactory account of itself. We were, apparently, now flanked by several other ships of the convoy.

Then we heard the cry of "Sail! Sail!" Once more the weary men scurried about the decks. We felt the ship shift as oars took the water. We heard the call of the oar master.

"They are coming again!" we heard. "They are coming again!"

We felt the ship come about.

"What happens," asked the free woman of me, "if we, below decks, are rammed?" It was the first time she had spoken to me.

"Perhaps, Mistress," I said, "someone will remember to open the hatch."

"But if not?" she asked.

"Let us hope they will not forget, Mistress," I said.

"We were boarded last night," she said.

"Yes, Mistress," I said.

"If I had fallen into the hands of the enemy," she asked, "what would have been done to me?"

"You would have been declothed, unclothed, Mistress," I said.

"I do not understand," she said.

"Your clothing would have been removed," I said.

"My clothing removed?" she said. "I, disrobed?"

"Yes, Mistress."

"Impossible!"

"I fear not, Mistress," I said. "But forgive me, Mistress. It is difficult for a girl to speak of such things before a free woman. Surely she might find them objectionable."

"No, no," she said. "Speak clearly. This is important. I must understand."

"As Mistress commands," I said. "If the ship is taken, Mistress will be taken with the ship. She will be among its loot, its prizes. The men will help her to understand this by removing her clothing, fully. They would strip Mistress."

"What a vulgar word!"

I was silent. The word did not seem vulgar to me. It seemed to me clear, unambiguous and decisively apt. Considering what was involved and how it would be done, it seemed more straightforward and honest than less candid or more circuitous expressions, enveiling euphemisms. The abruptness and simplicity of its sound suggested the abruptness and simplicity, the rudeness and irresistibility, the meaningfulness and completeness, of the act. Perhaps free women might be disrobed; slaves were stripped. To be sure, if the free woman were captured then she, as a capture, would doubtless not be disrobed, so to speak, but would be stripped, as might be a slave. This might be a useful lesson for her. I almost found myself hoping that my haughty holdmate might find herself stripped. Let her know what it was to be made so before men, to be before males as they, the men, wished her.

I liked the word, and the fact that the free woman might object to it made me, perhaps, like it the more. Certainly it did not dissuade me in the least from my view. It is a good word, an apt word, an excellent word.

Strip.

How excited and thrilled I had been to be stripped by my master, Clitus Vitellius, he tearing away the Ta-Teera, when his need was upon him. How I, his slave, had longed for and welcomed my irresistible and categorical baring at his hands, my stripping!

"Strip me!" she said.

"Yes, Mistress."

"Without my permission?"

"Yes, Mistress," I said.

"I am not a slave!" she said.

"Nonetheless, Mistress, you would be stripped, as clearly and completely stripped as perhaps that which you most despise, say, a vended slave, a property girl on a sales block. They would then have you before them, your captors, precisely as they wanted you, naked—suitably naked."

"Suitably?"

"As loot, and captive, you understand," I said.

"Outrageous!"

"I am sorry, forgive me, Mistress, but you would nonetheless then find yourself before them as I have suggested—precisely as it pleased them for their purposes to have you before them—naked, 'slave naked.'"

"I?" she cried, "I? Slave naked! How dare you use such words of me! As naked as a slave! I? *Slave naked!*"

"Yes, Mistress," I said.

"You have spoken vulgarly before me," she said.

"Forgive me, Mistress!"

"How could I, a free woman, be 'slave naked'?" she cried.

"I fear, Mistress," I said, "as easily as a slave."

"Slut!" she cried.

"Forgive me, Mistress!"

To be sure, each could be as naked as the other. But, as I thought of it, I did not think that the nudity of a free woman and that of a slave were really comparable. Perhaps the free woman could not be truly "slave naked." There are at least three reasons for this. The first is that the slave's limbs and body are likely to be vital and shapely, for she is trained, exercised, dieted and rested, to keep her in prime condition for her master; she is, after all, a lovely animal and thus is subject to a management and care which, while appropriate for an animal, would be unthinkable to impose upon a free woman; too, of course, care is lavished on the condition of her pelt, commonly a wealth of hair, of slave length, and on her skin, which is usually soft and smooth, and often without blemishes; the second reason distinguishing the nudity of a slave from that of a free woman is that the slave, like a dancer, is expected to move gracefully, and is trained to do so; she learns to move sensuously and beautifully; one wonders if some of the secrets of ballet, the turning out of the hip and such, were not brought to Gor at some time or another; to be sure, they may have been discovered independently; the free woman, on the other hand, is usually ignorant of these subtleties, and her movements tend to be comparatively awkward and clumsy, stolid and halting; these differences show up most clearly, of course, when both females are naked, or briefly, lightly clothed; one of the advantages of the robes of concealment on Gor is doubtless to conceal the crudity and ineptness of the movements of the free woman; even when neither woman is obviously moving there is a difference; the slave girl lies beautifully, turns her head in certain ways, may subtly turn a hand in a given way, slightly raise her knee, say, just a little, even use her very breasts and belly in her breathing in such a way as to enhance her attractiveness, and so on; the third major reason for the difference between the nudity of the slave and that of the free woman is perhaps the subtlest of all, and that is that they are "seen" differently. The slave is seen as a slave, and the free woman as a free woman. The slave is seen as a lovely property which may be purchased or stolen, owned and mastered; she has no standing in the eyes of the law; she is rightless and vulnerable; she belongs to the master and must obey and serve him; she exists to please; that is her purpose; she must hope to well fulfill it; she is in great danger if she does not; she lacks the prerogatives and powers of the free woman to tease, insult, torment, humiliate and frustrate as a small, weak, petty, frustrated nature may find gratifying. The free woman may trifle with the feelings of a man; the slave girl may not; rather, she obeys and hopes desperately to please. The very sight of a female slave, particularly as they are likely to be garbed, and must move, would be likely to stun a man of Earth; nothing has prepared him to believe that such women exist; one of the things that would be most likely to startle him, if not trouble him, perhaps cause him initial discomfort until he came to understand it, and reconciled himself to it, and came to relish it, is their profound femininity; they are true women, natural women, not artificially produced, socially engineered artifacts claimed to be "true women," artifacts designed to promote particular political agendas; on Earth, women are supposed to be aggressive, virile, masculine, and such, presumably to forward the power ambitions of unhappy, biologically unsuccessful women, but also, one supposes, to compensate to some extent for the biological vacuum created by the success of negativistic conditioning programs engineered to produce wide-spread male confusion, guilt, self-conflict, self-sacrifice, and devirilization, this useful for the political purposes of particular groups which intend to profit from the reduction of, and possible extirpation, of authentic, rather than surrogate, masculinity. In any event, the Gorean culture is designed to celebrate and enhance nature, not to frustrate her, not to sicken and poison her; in nature there is complementarity; there is dominance and submission; that is in the genes of a thousand species, including our own; if the dice of genetics ever, long ago, rolled the options of equalities and identities it is clear that those numbers did not prove to be winning combinations; genetics suggests; nature selects; and nature, in her impassive, insouciant, ruthless patience, in her merciless indifference, over her thousands of years, did not select for failure; she selected, rather, for complementarity, for dominance and submission, for adaptation, satisfaction, efficiency, health, viability, life, and love. Nature rejected is life denied.

Yes, I thought, they are different, the free woman and the female slave. The female slave is true to her deepest nature; she is exquisitely and vulnerably feminine; she is the most feminine of women; her purpose, destiny and meaning is love; she exists for love.

And so, I thought, it is not strange the free woman and the female slave are seen differently, the one with respect, and commonly with indifference, the other with keen interest; the one with courtesy and esteem, the other with desire and passion; one as a citizen, the other as a delicious animal; one as a civic associate, and the other as a purchasable, inestimably precious sensuous treasure.

"Mistress is right!" I cried. "Even were her clothing taken from her and not so much as a thread left upon her body she could not be 'slave naked. 'She is a free woman. She could not be 'slave naked'! Forgive me, Mistress!"

"So," she screamed. "You think I could not be 'slave naked'! You think then I am less beautiful than a slave!"

"Forgive me, Mistress!" I wept.

"I am beautiful," she cried, "very beautiful!"

"I am sure you are, Mistress!" I cried. For all I knew she would look well on a chain, and, after she had been whipped a little, and had learned a few things, she might look very well there.

Most slave girls, of course, begin as free women. Although there are bred slaves they are, statistically, rare. To be sure, many Goreans believe that all women are bred slaves, slaves that nature has bred for man.

"Would that I had a slave whip!" she cried.

I was pleased, muchly, of course, that she lacked access to this implement.

"You are an insolent slut!" she cried. "And you must be punished!"

"No, Mistress!" I cried in the darkness. "I am not insolent! Forgive me, Mistress!"

"Here, come stand before me, here, in the darkness," she said.

I approached her. She put out her hand, and touched my face, then put her left hand in my hair, to hold me in place. I sensed her pull the glove from her right hand, with her teeth, and then place it in the cincture of her robes.

"Put your arms down at your sides," she said, "and keep them there."

"Yes, Mistress," I said, and closed my eyes, tensed.

She then, several times, with her small, ungloved hand, struck me, slapping me viciously, first on one cheek and then the other. My head moved, and twisted, with the blows, but, held by her hand in my hair, must remain essentially in place. Tears sprang to my eyes. Then, after a time, her hand probably painfully stinging, she desisted. "You may kneel," she said. "Yes, Mistress," I said, at her feet. "You deserved your beating, did you not?" she asked. "Yes, Mistress," I said. "You may then thank me for beating you," she said. "Thank you, Mistress," I said, "for beating me."

"I am a free woman," she said. "That, what you said, that sort of thing, you remember, cannot be done to me."

"Yes, Mistress," I said.

"Can it?" she asked.

"I fear it can, Mistress," I said. "Forgive me, Mistress."

"My freedom, my station," she said, "puts me above the risk of such indignities."

"I fear in that particular Mistress might be surprised," I said.

"But why would they do that?" she asked. "Why would they—men, beasts—*strip me?*"

It was not hard, in the darkness, to detect the curiosity, the suppressed excitement, in her voice, in that question, seemingly so appropriate, so innocent. I gathered that beneath those cumbersome, ornate robes piled and cinched about her, there was a woman.

"May I speak," I asked.

I thought I now understood the fury with which she had struck me, again and again, but moments ago. I had touched in her, however innocently or inadvertently, something in her with which she was familiar, something which terrified her.

"Certainly," she said.

"They would strip you, Mistress," I said, "—to see if you were pleasing."

"Oh!" she cried, angrily.

But surely she had expected that answer.

And I do not think that she was truly displeased.

"And if I were?" she asked.

"Mistress would have been made a slave," I said. "Forgive me, Mistress," I added.

"And if I were not 'pleasing,'" she asked.

"I do not know, Mistress," I said. "The enemy are men of Port Kar. Perhaps you would be thrown to the sharks."

She made a small noise of fear. It pleased me to hear it. I think she understood her womanhood a bit more clearly now than perhaps she had before.

"It is my hope," I said, "that Mistress would be found pleasing."

"I am afraid of being a slave," she said.

"Yes, Mistress," I said.

"I do not know if I would be of interest to men," she said, "—for myself, I mean."

"We must hope that the brutes, the beasts, would find Mistress of interest," I said.

"You are a lovely Kajira," she said. "It is easy to see why men find you of interest."

Her remark startled me, by its unexpectedness. It did not seem to me cruel, sardonic, disparaging. It seemed rather the remark merely of another woman, one frightened, curious, unsure of herself.

"Some men," I said, "seem to have found me of interest. In any event, my collar is well on me."

"I wonder what it is," she said, "—to wear a collar."

"The collar itself," I said, "is light, and pretty, and not at all uncomfortable. Soon one pays no attention to it. One even forgets it is on one. But, of course, it is on one."

There are many sorts of collars; some, for example, are bands of metal, some rings of metal, some chains of metal. All lock, of course, and cannot be removed by the girl. To be sure, there are other collars which might be removed, if given the master's permission, sometimes a leather string, for example, or a bit of ribbon. What is most important, of course, is the meaning of the collar, not its material or whether or not it is locked. Collars, incidentally, are almost always placed upon the slave, or removed from the slave, by the master. The act of either collaring or uncollaring, it is generally understood, is his to perform. The slave without a collar is, of course, no less a slave. But the collar is pretty, and helps her to keep in mind, clearly, her status. Gorean slaves are almost always collared, and wear lock collars. This not only has its profound erotic effect on the slave and others, but it usefully, from the point of view of merchant law, identifies her as a slave. The collar, too, commonly, will contain information as to whom the slave belongs. It may also bear her name, that she wears by the will of her master. Bondage may also be betokened by such devices as bracelets and anklets.

"I do not know if I could be pleasing," she said.

"If Mistress would live," I said, "Mistress must do her best."

"Yes," she whispered.

"Perhaps Mistress, in the secrecy of her own compartments, before her mirrors, has considered her features, and throat and body. Perhaps she has wondered what she would look like—in a collar, or chained."

She made no response to this. We were alone in the darkness. I felt sorry for her, that she should be ignominiously confined in the hold with no more company than a slave girl. But then perhaps she preferred even such company, to the lonely terrors of a dark hold.

One could hear the water about the hull, the creak of the timbers.

Outside, from time to time, from the movement of ships, the cries of men, the hiss of catapults, it was clear that men were still at their games, that war was still afoot on the deep, green precincts of beautiful Thassa, the sea.

How magnificent, but incomprehensible, are our masters!

"You are a barbarian," she said, after a time. "I can tell that from your accent."

"Yes, Mistress," I said.

"But I am Gorean," she said.

"They will chain you as quickly, and as thoughtlessly as I," I said. "What we have in common is that we are both women."

We did not speak then for some time. Occasionally I heard a small sound from her. I thought she was afraid.

The next time food and water was brought, she shared it with me. She let me feed myself, with my own hands.

"Let us not speak further," she said, "of the terrors of bondage."

"As Mistress wishes," I said.

This puzzled me, as we had not been speaking together for some time, about anything.

But in a moment, in the darkness, she spoke again, eagerly.

"Is it so frightful to be a slave?" she asked.

"No, Mistress," I said.

"How can that be?"

"I am a woman," I said.

"I do not understand," she said.

"I wish to relate to strong men," I said, "to masters who will own me, and use me. I respond to male domination. I want it. I need it. I wish to be mastered, to have no choice but to obey, to selflessly love and serve, to give all to the master, and hope to be pleasing."

"But you are subject to the whip!"

"Deliciously so," I said. "We understand its symbolism, but of course, too, its stroke. When I feel the lash of my Master I know that I belong to him. Few things so impress my bondage upon me as his right to lash me, and, of course, the stroke of the proprietary lash itself."

"Does it not hurt?"

"Of course, it hurts," I said.

"Are you frequently whipped?" she asked.

"No," I said. "If the Master is pleased, why should he whip his slave? To be sure, we may occasionally be bound and lashed, lest we forget that we are slaves, to remind us that we are slaves."

"Frightful," she said, but her voice belied her word. It was easy to tell that the slave in her, the slave which was basically and radically she, longed for her master.

I then pitied free women.

"If we are rammed," she said, frightened, in the darkness, "and the men do not remember to open the hatch, or do not have time to do so, what will occur?"

"Sometimes," I said, "the planking is opened widely. Perhaps we could escape."

"It would not be likely that we would be successful," she said.

"No, Mistress," I said.

We heard the count of the oar master increasing. There was not much other noise on deck.

Then we felt the ship, perhaps half of an Ahn later, suddenly veer to one side. We heard some oars snapped.

"I want to know what is going on!" screamed the free woman. She pounded on the closed hatch. None paid her attention.

About a quarter of an Ahn later, suddenly, we heard the screaming of men and, not more than three or four Ihn afterwards, to our horror, the wall of the hull, opening into the hold, with a wrenching sound of rupturing wood, suddenly burst inward, toward us. We could see nothing at first but were struck with a torrent of cold, swirling water. We screamed. Then we could see some light, and the horizon, and the bow of a ship against us, and the curved ram of the predator amongst our planking. The attacker backed his oars and the ram, its work done, splintering more wood, withdrew and settled away from us. The hole in the hull was more than a yard in width. Water flowed through, making it impossible to approach. Suddenly it seemed we were to our waists in water. The ship rocked back and we saw the sky and the water stopped flowing inward, and then it rocked back again, and the water, smoothly, in a broad flow, swirled in.

We climbed the steps of the hold, each screaming.

The hatch was flung up and we saw the sky. An officer stood there, with unsheathed sword.

We climbed to the deck, scrambling, wildly. He seized the free woman by the arm. He pulled her toward a longboat. None paid me attention. The attacking ship had withdrawn, seeking other prey. I saw that there were many ships about. It was early in the morning, apparently. Wisps of fog hung upon the water, and fog was high in the north. Ships engaged. I heard shouting, and, on another ship, the clashing of weapons. Within a hundred yards there may have been as many as four or five ships. Two were aflame. Men began to crowd into the two longboats. One slid, capsizing, into the water. The free woman was handed down into the other. Men fought to right the capsized boat. The stern of the ship began to settle in the water. Men leaped into the water and began to swim toward other ships. I ran to the rail to look after them. I did not see the second ship, from behind me, from amidships, approaching. It was itself a ship of Cos, running, and could not, in the time, given the proximity of the ships, turn sufficiently aside. It, too, struck the ship on which I stood. I screamed, and fell, thrown to the deck. It tilted, and I slipped backward. I scratched at it, as though to climb it toward the bow. Then I caught the railing and, as I felt the ship slipping back into the water, the bow lifting high, I pulled myself over the railing, slipped into the water, and swam from the side of the ship. The mast of the struck ship, lowered, had come loose from its deck lashings, and had plunged through the railing and slipped into the water. It was that mast which I seized, lifting my head and arm above the water. It turned in the water, twisting, and was half submerged when the ship disappeared but, in a moment, it lifted again to the surface. I was not fifty feet from a burning ship. The water was filled with wreckage. I heard signal horns, and saw flags on the signal lines. I saw two men fighting in the water. Then, suddenly, the fog from the north began to move more steadily in about us. The burning ship seemed dim in the gray fog. I heard more signal horns. There was shouting in the water. Then it seemed there were none about me. I cried out. The burning ship sank beneath the water. The horns were now farther off. Men who had been near me in the water seemed now to be gone. I was suddenly alone.

I cried out, helplessly.

Suddenly I screamed with fear as something, long-snouted, with rows of tiny teeth, closed upon my leg. I began to scream with misery trying to hold the mast. It did not tear at, or wrench, my leg. I could not see what it was, but could sense its weight. My hand slipped on the mast. It was drawing me downward, away from the mast. The snout slipped higher on my leg. I struck down at it with my fist. I struck something hard, something heavy and alive. I saw a round eye, lidded and lensed. I screamed wildly. My fingers slipped on the mast. I struck down, striking again and again at the thing. Then, I screaming, crying out with misery, it drew me from the mast and, turning about, twisting under the water, dove downward. I scratched and tore at it, but could not free myself. The cold water swirled about me. I could no longer tell where the surface of the water was. I could not breathe. My blows became weak. Then it seemed, outward from me, in the distance there was a shifting, dull, flickering light. It was the surface. I reached toward it, bent backward. I swallowed water. Something, too, was in the water, moving downward from the surface. Things began to go black. Weakly I tried to push away the jaws that held me, long and narrow, with many fine teeth. I could feel the teeth with my fingers. I could not breathe. I could not fight. There was nothing to breathe. The surface receded. Dimly I was aware of movement near me in the water, something other than the beast that held me. I thrust out my hand, touching nothing. I closed my eyes. I decided that I would breathe. Surely there would be something to breathe. Then the beast, suddenly, startling me, twisted, and swam a tight, angry circle, its long tail thrashing, and then the water seemed suddenly different, somehow more viscous and greasy. The beast thrashed angrily. I felt its grip on my leg loosen. Then, suddenly, it shook spasmodically. I was buffeted away from it. I saw it turn slowly in the dark water, above me, rolling. A tiny fish bit at my leg. Others, darting, pursued the irrationally moving titan that had held me. I felt myself seized by the arm, and pulled toward the light, remote in the cold water. I saw the beast which had gripped me now below me. Swiftly I was drawn toward the surface. Unable to see, my eyes filled with salt water, my head broke the surface and I coughed and gasped. An arm, strong, supported me. I shuddered and lost consciousness.

I think that I was unconscious no more than a few seconds. I awakened being drawn onto a large, jagged, splintered square of wreckage, heavy beamed, like a raft.

I lay on my stomach on the wreckage. Then I lifted myself to my elbows, and threw up into the water, twice. Then again I collapsed.

A few feet from the raft, rolling lifeless in the water, was a grotesque marine saurian, fishlike but reptilian, more than twenty feet in length.

I saw the fins of sharks near it, and saw their snouts pressing it, and then beginning to tear at it.

I was conscious of the feet of a man near me. He stood. There was still fog on Thassa.

He took me by the arms and, turning me roughly, threw me on my back, on the heavy beams of that gigantic, raftlike structure, before him. I wore a bit of wet, yellow rep-cloth; it was thin; it clung about me, revealing me as though I were naked. I lifted one knee; I lay on my back, helpless, at his feet. I opened my eyes.

"Master!" I cried. I struggled to my knees before him, my heart flooded with elation. "I love you!" I cried. I put my head to his feet, covering them with kisses and tears. I shook with emotion. "Master! Master!" I wept. "I love you! I love you!"

He pulled me to my feet. "She-sleen," he said, quietly, and with menace.

He released me. I shrank back from him. "Master?" I said. Then, suddenly, I was terrified. "Oh, no, Master!" I said. "I love you."

He looked to the sharks which moved about the body of the inert, buoyant saurian. Others, too, smaller, restless, white-finned, moved about the raft.

"No, Master," I cried, "I love you! I love you, Master!"

He strode toward me and seized me by the back of my neck and an ankle. He lifted me high over his head.

"No, Master!" I wept.

He strode to the side of the raft.

I could do nothing. He could throw me to the sharks in an instant.

"No," he said, angrily. "This is too easy for a warrior's vengeance." He threw me to his feet on the boards.

He looked about. There was a ring on the wreckage, where it sloped higher out of the water. He dragged me to this ring and tore open my rep-cloth tunic. He knelt across my body and, with strips from the rep-cloth, tied my hands over my head and fastened them to the ring. I lay on my back before him, my head higher than my feet, my body at an angle of some five or ten degrees. With his foot he kicked aside the rep-cloth which he had torn open. In his belt there was a bloodied knife, that with which he had slain the marine saurian.

He drew forth the knife and looked at me.

"I love you, Master," I whispered.

"I shall cut you to bits," he said, "and throw you, little by little, to the sharks."

He could do with me what he chose. I was his.

He drew back the knife, the blade in his hand, behind his head. I closed my eyes.

It struck in the wood, sinking four inches deep, beside me. I opened my eyes. I shuddered.

He was looking down at me. "I have you now," he said.

"Yes, Master," I said.

He dropped to one knee, crouching beside me. He jerked the tag on my collar. He read it aloud, "Send me to the Lady Elicia of Ar, of Six Towers." He laughed.

"You, a lady's serving slave," he grinned.

Then he lifted my flanks from the wood, and then thrust me back, holding me to the wood. I closed my eyes, almost fainting from his touch.

He released me. He stood up, looking down at me.

"I love you, Master," I said.

He kicked me, viciously, and I cried out. "Lying slave girl!" he said.

He crouched again beside me and jerked the knife free from the wood. I felt its point at my throat.

Then he thrust the knife again into the wood, a foot from me. He looked down at me. "No," he said, "the sharks, the knife, are too good for you."

I felt his left hand at my throat. He could crush it easily.

I shuddered.

Then his hand moved from my throat to touch my right breast, musingly. "No," he said, "the sharks, the knife, are too good for you."

"Have pity on a poor slave," I begged. But I saw in his eyes that he would have no pity on me.

I felt his right hand on my body.

"I have pursued you," he said. "Those at the Chatka and Curla were kind enough to tell me that you had been shipped on the *Jewel of Jad*. We seized a small, oared galley. We joined with those of Port Kar. In the engagement I sought you. It was not easy. Captives were persuaded to speak. Survivors from the *Jewel of Jad* were picked up by the ramship, *Luciana of Telnus*. We sought her. We found her. But she was struck, and sinking. Her decks were awash. She was abandoned. We saw one boat fleeing from her in which was a free woman. No sign of a slave there! Others of her crew, and survivors, were in the water, making for Cosian vessels. No sign of a slave then in the water either did I detect. Our own small galley had been rammed, and was shipping water. She, too, in moments would sink. I climbed to the deck of our quarry, she whom we had sought, the *Luciana of Telnus*, forcing aside my alarmed men, but moments before she went under. Perhaps they had discovered the nature of the slave I sought and had left her behind, as garbage, to go down with the ship! But I wanted her! It was important for me to have her! She was worthless garbage but I wanted her alive, to get my hands on her pretty little body, to have her at my feet, to settle my score with her. Better for her for her sake to have gone down with the ship, but I would not allow that possible. That must not be! Surely the Priest-Kings would not permit that! Surely they would see to it that she was delivered rather into my hands, for my vengeance. Only in such a way could the claims of justice be satisfied! I must find the slut! By all the rights of Gor, for what she had done, she was mine! Mine! She was owed to me. But on the flooded decks, as my men called out for me to return, I, to my fury, found no sign of her, no sign of the cringing, treacherous little slave slut from the Chatka and Curla in Telnus. I must search further! I returned to my own galley. She, too, was foundering, and would soon sink. I was furious! Where was the slave? Might she be in the water? Many ships were about. Had she been picked up? That must not be! She must be here, somewhere! Surely none who knew her, and what she was, who knew her true nature, would deign to fish such garbage out of the water! Unless to deliver her, to her horror, to me for my vengeance! Our own galley was subsiding. My men, on my command, swam to a ship of Port Kar. Not I, however. I remained on our galley, its deck pitching and awash. This vantage was precarious and transient, dangerous, yes, but from it, it seemed the presence of the slut, were she about, might be the more easily discovered. I could not see her! Surely I was not to be denied her! Despite the pleas of my men from the water, begging me to join them in seeking safety, I continued to scrutinize the turbulent waters, the debris, some flaming, the pitching wreckage, port and starboard, fore and aft. Thus I continued my hunt. As the galley suddenly rolled and sank, I dove into the water. I did not rest. I continued my hunt."

He looked down upon me.

"Yes," said he, "I continued my hunt."

He looked down upon me, his capture, fastened supine, helplessly, to the ring before him.

"I yet did hunt for you."

"Your hunt has been successful, Master," I said. "You have caught me."

"Yes," he said, "the vicious, little lying slave, the little she-sleen and collared traitress, is now caught." He looked down at me. "She lies now before me, naked and bound, at my mercy."

"Yes, Master," I said.

"Slut," said he.

"Yes, Master," I said.

He turned my head from side to side. "Even your ears are pierced," he said.

"Yes, Master," I said. There were tears in my eyes.

"The vengeance of a warrior," said he, "you will learn, little slut of a slave, is not a light thing."

"I am yours, Master," I said. I looked up at him, in the fog. I felt the raftlike structure shifting beneath us. I was bound at his mercy, my bit of tunic torn aside, on a particle of wreckage on a great sea. "I am yours, Master," I whispered. "Do with me as you will."

His left hand held me. His right hand moved at my body. His teeth and lips pressed suddenly, savagely, against the side of my throat, over the collar.

"I love you, Clitus Vitellius!" I cried.

He struck me, savagely, for I, a slave, had spoken his name.

Then he continued his depredations on my body. In moments, to the sky and sea, and to his manhood, helplessly, I cried myself his.

Twenty-Three

The Raft

I lay in the arms of Clitus Vitellius, my master, under the bright stars of Gor, under the white moons and the black sky, on the rough wood, in the midst of that great, lonely sea. I heard the water lap at the wreckage on which we lay. He had freed me of the ring, that my hands, under his directives, might pleasure him.

I put my head on the leanness of his belly, and my arms about him. He held my head in his hands. He lay upon his back.

"Do not think you are my love slave," said he. "You are only a lying slave, my prisoner, a captured traitress I will have my way with."

"I know, Master," I said, pressing my lips to him. He had been very cruel to me. He had punished me much.

"If I were you," said he, "I would be terrified."

I kissed him.

"You do not seem to be terrified," he said.

"I have always feared you, Master," I said, "your temper, your strength, your will. But I love you, too."

He seized me by the arms and flung me to my back on the wood. He looked down upon me, holding me. He was very rough.

"Lying slave!" he said.

I looked up at him. "It is true," I said, "Master."

"You love any man," he said.

"I wear a collar," I said.

He laughed.

"I am a girl of Earth," I said. "I cannot help myself in the arms of a Gorean male. But it is you, Master, whom I most love, whom I truly love."

"You seek to escape punishment," he said.

"No, Master," I said. "Punish me." I felt his hands on my arms, so tight. He had terrible strength. I felt weak.

"I own you," he said.

"Yes, Master," I said.

"You will not," said he, "with your smiles and pretty noises evade my vengeance." He struck me, cruelly.

"No, Master," I said.

He stood up, angrily on the wreckage. He stepped away from me, looking out to sea. I remained as I was. Then he turned about, regarding me.

"I lie at your mercy, Master," I said. "Avenge yourself."

He drew forth the knife at his belt.

Then angrily he thrust it again in its sheath. He turned away.

I smiled, and climbed to my knees and stretched. "A girl is hungry," I said.

He remained, looking out to sea.

"It is strange," he said.

"What is strange, Master?" I asked.

"Be silent," said he to me, "Slave."

"Yes, Master," I said. He would not speak to me of his thoughts.

"Can it be, Clitus Vitellius?" he asked himself, aloud. He turned about, angrily, and looked at me.

"I betrayed you, Master," I said, "because I so much loved you. Had I not loved you so much I could not have so much hated you. I had lived for the moment when I might avenge myself upon you, and when it presented itself, I performed delicious but unspeakable treachery. When they took you away I felt anguish, and a grief I cannot describe to you. I cried out and wept with misery. I had betrayed he whom I loved. Life then to me was but stones and ashes. Better that it had been I who had been betrayed. When I learned of your escape elation and joy flooded me. It was enough to know you lived and were free."

"Traitress," said he.

"I am here," I said. "Do with me what you want." He regarded me with fury, but then he looked away again. After a time, he turned again to face me. "It is near dawn," he said. "I am weary. It is time to bind you for the night."

"Please do not bind me, Master," I said. I rose to my feet, and brushed back my hair. I smiled at him. "I promise I will not run away, Master," I said.

I stood on the shifting piece of wreckage.

"I am well aware of the penalties for a runaway slave girl," I said.

"Lie down by the ring," he said, "and be silent."

"Yes, Master," I said.

I lay down near the ring.

"On your side," he said.

I complied. He was the master. I felt my wrists taken behind my back, crossed and tied together, tightly.

I wanted so much to find some way to convince him of my love for him. I wanted him to know, truly, how I loved him. After that he could do what he wanted with me.

He took two pieces of my tunic, twisting them together. He then thrust them about the collar I wore, between the metal and my neck. He then, by means of this improvised rope, tied my collar close to the iron ring on the wreckage, no more than an inch from it. He then removed the knife from his sheath, plunged it into the wood a few feet from him, and lay down. In a moment he had turned away from me, and was asleep.

I could understand his anger with me, a warrior's fury. But his distrust hurt me most.

I could move my head but little. I was tied by my collar close to the ring. I could not free my hands. They had been tied by a warrior.

I wanted to be his love slave. Instead I was his prisoner, a girl who had betrayed him, now caught by him, a captive slave and traitress, one who now lay helpless, bound, within the full compass of the displeasure and vengeance of her betrayed master, who was a warrior of Gor.

I knew he had not yet worked his vengeance upon me. I struggled, helplessly. For the first time I became terribly afraid. It became cold upon the raft.

Twenty-Four

I Am Chained
in the Hold of a Galley

"Awaken, Slave," said Clitus Vitellius. He kicked me. I awakened. I recalled, looking up at him, bound, I was the girl who had betrayed him. He freed my collar of the ring and took the rope of twisted cloth, from my torn tunic, which had tied me at the ring, and crossed my ankles, and bound them together. The last bit of rep-cloth tunic, which still clung about me, he tore away, and threw it into the sea. I sat up on the wreckage, naked, my hands tied behind my back, my ankles crossed and secured.

A ship was approaching, a medium-class galley, with twenty oars to a side, dipping unhurriedly. The lateen sail was slackened. Clitus Vitellius stood on the wreckage, waiting.

At the mast line snapped two flags, that of Port Kar and another, that with vertical green bars over a white field, superimposed on which was the head of a gigantic bosk. It had been identified to me earlier, in a conversation of officers on the *Jewel of Jad*. It was the flag of Bosk of Port Kar.

The galley swung about and eased to the side of the wreckage. A large man, broad-shouldered, yet lithe, with large hands, a broad face, grayish blue eyes and unruly, shaggy, windswept reddish hair, stood at the rail. There was something like an animal about him, indefinable, unpredictable, tenacious, intelligent, cruel. To look at him one knew, though it was the deck of a galley he bestrode, that he was of the warriors. I would have feared being owned by him. His eyes, appraising me, made me conscious of my slavery.

Clitus Vitellius lifted his hand, in a salute of warriors. The man returned the salute.

"I am Clitus Vitellius of Ar," he said. "Am I your prisoner?"

"We have little quarrel with those of Ar," said the man. "You have little shipping."

Clitus Vitellius laughed.

"Clitus Vitellius of Ar, and his men," said the man, "by accounts rendered to me by Samos of Port Kar, of the Council of Captains, participated creditably in the action of the day before yesterday on behalf of the Jewel of Thassa."

Port Kar is sometimes spoken of by her citizens as the Jewel of Thassa. Other men speak of her differently, rather as a den of thieves and cutthroats, a lair of pirates. The city is under the governance of a Council of Captains.

"We did the small things we could," said Clitus Vitellius. "Cos, as you know, wars with Ar." Then Clitus Vitellius looked to the man on the ship. "My men?" he asked.

"Sound and hale," said the man, "on the ship of Samos, the *Thassa Ubara*."

"Excellent," said Clitus Vitellius.

"Your vessel," said the man, grinning, "appears seaworthy but has clumsy lines."

"I request passage for two," said Clitus Vitellius, "myself and," indicating me, "this slave."

The man on the ship looked at me. "You have a beauty there," he said.

This appraisal much pleased me. I basked in the favor of a free man. The fellow obviously had taste, excellent taste in women, I thought, and I trusted my master was impressed with this independent evaluation. Perhaps I was pleased too obviously, to the irritation of my master.

But we like to be admired and praised. We are women. What woman is not pleased to know she is of interest to men? What woman is not pleased to realize, even shyly, that her beauty may have unsettled a fellow, even dazzled or astonished him, bewildered him, or awed him? Are we supposed to be upset that a fellow may turn about, perhaps disbelievingly, perhaps startled, to see more of us; perhaps we are to him, somehow, in our tunic and collar, the most beautiful woman he has ever seen? That our slave fascinations and vulnerabilities might have an effect on a male is nothing that we are likely to find objectionable. We do not mind being beautiful. And it pleases us to know that we are seen as valuable, as graceful and attractive, to many men, and to know that our master may be thought a lucky fellow that his collar is on our neck. And surely many men must wonder what it would be like for us to be at their feet, instead. Are we for sale? We are desired. No matter what the masters say, I am sure we are the most precious of their belongings. Why else would they keep us in the custody they do?

Clitus Vitellius shrugged. "There are thousands better," he said.

"Of course," said the other, unnecessarily, I thought.

I turned my head to the side.

"But she is a sleek little animal, with good lines," said the other.

"I suppose so," said Clitus Vitellius.

How they speak of us, I thought!

"But she *is* a beauty," said the other.

"Perhaps," acknowledged Clitus Vitellius.

So! So, even my master, it seemed, was willing to acknowledge that I was a beauty! But what sort of beauty? I had no doubt now about the matter. Oh, I was sure that they were both excellent judges of women, yes, but of what sort of women, I asked myself, women stripped or lightly clad, women in collars or chains! And in what sort of venues had this superb taste in women been developed and honed? In the streets of Ar, seeing girls on leashes or cuffed to rings, in the branding camps of the Vosk, in coffles descending gangplanks in Schendi, on ropes being driven naked to the Sardar Fairs? Perhaps in paga taverns, in the alcoves or in the dancing circles, in brothels, in slave markets? I was being compared with others as flesh, as meat, as an animal, as stock! To be sure, to be regarded as a beauty among slaves is a high compliment to a girl. Most Gorean slaves are beautiful, you see. Indeed, that is why they are made slaves. Men, you see, are interested in beautiful slaves. Who would want an ugly slave? They may remain free. Who would want them? Many free women, captured and stripped, assessed, not found sufficiently attractive, are permitted to return naked to their cities, rejected. Those rejected must surely have mixed feelings about this matter, about their rejection, and their being cast back to freedom, unwanted, just as those in their chains, too, must have mixed feelings, looking at the shackles on their fair limbs. They have been prized, and will be kept. They are beautiful enough to be slaves. "Slave beautiful," in Gorean, as men use the term, is a term expressing superlative regard; it means that the woman is lovely enough, beautiful enough, desirable enough, exciting enough, to be a slave. The beauty is, therefore, the prime target of the slaver's noose, his girl traps, nets, and such. To be sure, interestingly, many women become beautiful in bondage, as their inhibitions are shed, as their emotions are freed, as they learn themselves, as they learn service, as they discover ecstasies beyond the comprehension of the free woman, as they find happiness and love.

I have no doubt that the slavers sometimes make their assessments with such things in mind. I think they are skilled in reading women. It is, after all, their business.

Too, of course, though these things are trivial compared to the emotional transformation wrought by bondage, the slave can always be trimmed, if one wishes, by diet and exercise; or fattened a little, if that is wished, to bring her to more appealing block measurements; be taught that a slatternly appearance is no longer allowed, that she must now keep herself well-groomed, fresh and clean, and so on. Too, of course, she will learn to kneel, to move, and to serve, in many ways; too, she will learn the nature of slave garments, and how to drape and wear them, when she is permitted clothing; she will learn to apply the cosmetics, perfumes and jewelry of a slave, and so on. If her master can afford it, and is interested, or if a slaver thinks she is worth the investment, she may even be sent to a school for training in the arts expected of a proficient female slave, both domestic and intimate. Indeed, any girl processed through a slaver's house is likely to receive some such training. It improves her price. The major transformation in the girl of course goes far beyond the trivialities and mechanics, the externals, so to speak, of such matters as grooming, adornment, training and such, however lovely and important they may be; it is the internal transformation which is most important, and that is wrought within her by the magic of bondage itself; she now understands that she, in her collar, is now for the first time in her life truly free, truly free as a woman, that she may no longer imprison and starve herself; she may no longer deny and repudiate herself; no longer can she conceal the basic she of her; she now understands that she is a slave, owned by a strong man who will see that she well serves him, and this liberates her femininity, frees in her the ancient, biological woman, the slave of her master, and enflames her sexuality.

Free, she was slave; slave, she is free.

Interesting how it is, that the woman is most free when least free.

Perhaps lastly it might be mentioned that Gorean taste in women, while extensive and diverse, as is manifested by the goods offered in the markets, tends on the whole to run to the natural woman, favoring on the whole the configurations, heights, weights, and such, of the normal female. Many women on Earth who have been subtly led to hold themselves in contempt, by advertising and such, for their failure to embody certain currently fashionable stereotypes of female beauty, to seek which could actually jeopardize their health, would find, perhaps to their misery and terror, that they were of great interest to powerful, lustful, domineering Gorean males. Natural men, they tend to be attracted to natural women. That makes sense, I suppose.

"There is something you should know about her," said Clitus Vitellius.

"What is that?" asked the man.

"She is a traitress," said Clitus Vitellius.

"Ah!" said the man, surprised.

It pleased me that the stranger had not anticipated this intelligence. Indeed, he seemed skeptical. My mien, I gathered, whether it was too feminine, too fearful, or too loving, did not suggest that of a traitress. Yet I had, I knew, in fact, in a terrible moment, betrayed my beloved master.

"Yes," said Clitus Vitellius.

"And it is a civic matter, and you have been authorized to apprehend her and bring her before a slave praetor?"

Slaves, as animals, lack standing before the law. Accordingly, under normal circumstances, they are not permitted in Gorean courts. They may, however, figure as exhibits, for example, as samples of contested or stolen goods. They may also, occasionally, though seldom, be utilized to obtain testimony. This testimony is invariably extracted under torture. The slave, accordingly, has little inclination to enter a Gorean court. Such things are for free persons. She is normally more than content to remain outside, chained to a stanchion or ring, hopefully in the shade. In some cities, however, there is a slave praetor, who will make inquiries where the doings of slaves may be involved, and will be in charge of resolving squabbles, for example, in the market, assigning punishments for offenses, and so on, functions commonly thought beneath the attention of the civic judiciary. Any free citizen may remand a slave to the attention of the slave praetor. Perhaps she has been insufficiently deferent to a free person? It is not likely to go easily with her. Sometimes a girl, who may have been spoiled by an indulgent master, does not find the slave praetor so forgiving or tolerant. We fear the slave praetor and do not care to go before him.

"No," said Clitus Vitellius.

"She betrayed a gate, a position, a detachment, a military secret?" inquired the man.

From the look on his face I was glad that I had not done any of these things.

"No," said Clitus Vitellius. "It is a personal matter."

"She betrayed a particular person?"

"Yes," said Clitus Vitellius.

"And whom did she betray?" inquired the man.

"Me," said Clitus Vitellius.

"And she is now yours, helpless, naked and bound, at your feet," said the man.

"Yes," said Clitus Vitellius.

"Excellent," said the man.

I did not know what would be done with me. I squirmed a little in my bonds. I could not begin to free myself. I did know that the vengeance of a warrior was not a light thing. Could my master not understand that I loved him?

Clitus Vitellius looked down upon me, with fury, with contempt.

"She is garbage, garbage," said Clitus Vitellius.

The man regarded me. Under his gaze I, though a slave, reddened. When I dared to lift my head and look again at him, his gaze was still upon me. I looked away, quickly. I trembled. His gaze was that of a master, a master of women.

"She is, at least, an interesting and well formed bit of garbage," he said.

"Perhaps," said Clitus Vitellius.

I tossed my head. I was not garbage!

"In Port Kar," said the man, "we often think of, and refer to, unfortunately and disreputably, of course, free women as garbage, for they are good for very little."

"I like that," said Clitus Vitellius.

I was not sure just how to think about that. I certainly had no great affection for free women. I knew they hated me. I was frightened of them. They could hurt me, terribly. The slave, of course, was good for a great deal. Men saw to that. We had better be.

"But this one," said Clitus Vitellius, kicking me, as I gasped and recoiled, "is not free."

"I can see that," said the fellow. "She has the lines of a slave."

I pulled against my bonds. I was sure I would be bruised.

"But I assure you, she is nonetheless garbage," said Clitus Vitellius.

"We have a saying in Port Kar, a saying pertaining to free women," said the man. "It is this: 'Garbage collared ceases to be garbage.'"

"I see," said Clitus Vitellius, approvingly.

"After it is collared," said the man, "it is reformed. It is scrubbed clean and put under discipline. It is taught how to please men. It is then, at last, good for something."

"Excellent," said Clitus Vitellius.

The fellow then looked at me. "Do you desire to please your master?" he asked.

"Oh, yes, yes, yes, Master!" I cried.

"Look at her," he said to Clitus Vitellius. "Consider her lines. Is she not a trim little ship? Whatever her flaws and faults may be, she is not garbage." The fellow then looked at me. "Are you garbage?" he asked.

"If my Master says I am garbage, then I am garbage," I said.

"What are you?" asked the man.

I put down my head. "I am garbage, Master," I said. And how true then that seemed to me, for I had betrayed my master, I who was unworthy to kiss his sandals, who had no right to aspire to the collar of such a man.

"Well," said the man, "if garbage, at least lovely garbage."

"Thank you, Master," I whispered.

"She is worthless," said Clitus Vitellius.

"I will give you a silver tarsk for her," said the man.

"Please do not sell me, Master!" I cried.

Clitus Vitellius turned about and cuffed me, angrily. I was struck to my side, near the ring.

"Were you given permission to speak?" he asked.

"No, Master!" I said. "Forgive me, Master." How foolish I had been! I lay on my side. I had spoken without permission. I must be silent, while men discussed whether or not I was to be sold.

"She is not for sale," said Clitus Vitellius, angrily.

I saw the stranger smile. He had not been interested in buying me, though he seemingly recognized I might plausibly be a silver-tarsk girl, which was flattering. It had been a test.

"The slut is not worth a copper tarsk-bit," said Clitus Vitellius, angrily, defensively. "You do not know that, but I do. But she is not for sale. No! She betrayed me. You must understand that. I hunted her, and I have caught her. I loathe her. She is worthless. But I want her where she is, at my feet, as she is, guilty, waiting and helpless. She knows I will show her no mercy. She knows I will have my vengeance. Let her tremble! She will pay. She will pay dearly."

"I do not envy her," smiled the stranger.

"May I speak, Master?" I said.

"No," said Clitus Vitellius.

"It seems you hate the slave," said the stranger.

"Yes, with virulence," snarled Clitus Vitellius.

"May I speak to your slave?" asked the stranger.

"Certainly," said Clitus Vitellius.

"It seems your master hates you," he said.

"Yes, Master," I said.

"Do you hate your Master?" he asked.

"No!" I cried. "I love him! I love him!"

"She is a superb actress," said Clitus Vitellius.

"No, Master!" I wept.

"Did you betray your Master?" he asked.

"Yes, Master," I said.

"What then should be done with you?"

"Whatever Masters will," I said.

"I do not think she is likely to betray you again," said the man.

"It is hard for a woman to betray a man when she is at his feet, naked and bound," said Clitus Vitellius.

"I think you love your Master," said the stranger.

"Oh, yes, Master!" I cried. "Yes, yes, Master!"

I was grateful to the stranger. I hoped that he might sway my master. I hoped that I might be permitted to live, and be given an opportunity to atone for the grievous wrong I had done my master. I wanted to serve him, and love him, and give him pleasure, and pleasure, and pleasure! I wanted only the opportunity to prove to Clitus Vitellius my love!

I was sure the stranger saw my love for my master, even if my master did not!

How complete, and helpless, and profound, is the love of a slave girl for her master!

And he can discard her, as he wishes.

"She is a traitress, a traitress," said Clitus Vitellius.

"Doubtless you will discipline her well," said the man.

"It is my intention," said Clitus Vitellius.

I put down my head.

"I grant you passage," smiled the man on the ship.

I felt myself taken and lifted, bound, to a sailor, who lifted me over the rail. He put me by the mast, kneeling, bound.

In a moment, Clitus Vitellius, aided by the hand of the man who had spoken to us, leaped aboard.

"Bring her about," called the man to his helmsmen.

"Left oars!" called the oar master. "Stroke!"

Slowly the galley began to swing about.

The man who had welcomed us aboard, permitting us passage, looked down at me. I looked up at him, naked and bound.

"In courtesy," said Clitus Vitellius, "I grant you and your men slave rights upon this woman. But beyond this, I reserve her to myself. If you wish her beyond my permissions, we must do contest."

"You wish to keep her for your discipline?" asked the man.

"Yes," said Clitus Vitellius.

The man crouched beside me. He thrust open my mouth, holding it with two hands. "Barbarian," he said.

"Yes," said Clitus Vitellius.

The master, a free male, permitted me to close my mouth. He took the tag on my collar in his fingers. He scraped salt from it.

"I was being sent to the Lady Elicia of Ar," I said, "my mistress."

"You should belong to a man," said the man.

"Yes, Master," I said.

"You seem interested in the slave," said Clitus Vitellius, puzzled.

"You are an enslaved Earth girl," said the man to me.

"Yes, Master," I said.

"You were sent once," he asked, "to a paga tavern on Cos, called the Chatka and Curla?"

"Yes, Master," I said.

I felt his hands, hard on my arms. "Excellent," he said. He looked at me, and I felt terror. "I shall now ask you a simple question," he said, "and you will answer it immediately and truthfully, if you would live for another five Ihn."

Two sailors seized Clitus Vitellius, who struggled. I looked at him, wildly.

"Have you heard of one called Belisarius?" asked the man.

"Yes, Master," I whispered. "I brought him a message."

"What message?" he asked.

"I do not know!" I cried.

He stood up. "We shall have the message," he said.

"I do not know what it is!" I cried.

"Release me!" demanded Clitus Vitellius.

"Thurnock," said the man. "Take the slave below. Put her in Sirik. Chain her in the hold."

A large man, blond-haired, powerful, threw me to his shoulder. "Master!" I cried to Clitus Vitellius.

I heard him struggling.

"Release me!" cried Clitus Vitellius.

"I would speak with you upon the high deck," said the man to Clitus Vitellius, "and I would speak with you alone."

"I do not understand," said Clitus Vitellius.

"Release him," said the man. The sailors released Clitus Vitellius.

"Come with me to the high deck," said the man. He turned, and led the way. Clitus Vitellius followed him, angrily.

The large man descended a short flight of stairs, leading downward from an opened hatch.

The ceiling of the hold was low, and, at the bottom, the man bent over, and carried me in his arms. In the hold there were many supplies, and weapons, and riches. The convoy had been broken and it had scattered. Many ships had been taken. Much loot lay in the hold. This ship alone, I gathered, carried the ransom of a dozen Ubars.

The man lay me on my side on the boards of the hold. Against the wall of the hold there were five girls, illuminated in the light of a tiny ship's lantern. They were stripped. Each was chained by the left ankle to a common ring.

The man brought a Sirik, and locked it on my throat, and about my wrists and ankles. Then, with another chain, looping it through the Sirik chain which fell from my Sirik collar to my braceleted wrists and confined ankles, he secured me to a heavy ring, passing one end of the looped chain through the ring and then, with a heavy padlock, closing the open end of the loop. Only then did he untie the bonds on my wrists and ankles. When I was freed of those bonds I was chained in Sirik, fastened at the ring. I was secured much more heavily than the others.

"The men," said one of the women, "were taken from the boat and chained, and put in a round ship."

"What men?" I asked her, puzzled.

"The men who were with me in the longboat," she said. "Do you not remember me?"

"No," I said.

"We were together," she said, "on the *Luciana of Telnus*."

"You are the free woman!" I exclaimed.

She laughed ruefully and lifted with her small hand the chain which held her fair ankle. She indicated the other girls beside her. "We were all free," she said.

"Rejoice," said I, "that men found you pleasing."

The girls shuddered.

"They are going to take us to Port Kar and sell us," said one.

"What is it like, being a slave?" asked one of the girls.

I looked at her beauty, and laughed. "You will find out," I said, "—Slave."

She shrank back, frightened, against the wall of the hold.

"What ship is this?" I asked.

"It is the Dorna," said one of the girls.

"And who is its captain?" I asked, referring to the man who had spoken with us, the lean, strong, reddish-haired man, so like an animal, clearly of the warriors.

He frightened me.

"That is Bosk, of Port Kar," said one of the girls.

"He, himself," whispered another.

Above us the hatch was closed. I heard it lock. I looked upward. I was in Sirik, fastened to a ring, chained in the hold of the Dorna, the ship of the dreaded pirate and slaver, Bosk of Port Kar.

I lay down on the planking of the hold, naked in my chains.

"We shall have the message," he had said.

But I did not know what the message was.

"We shall have the message," he had said.

I did not know what the message was. When I failed to give it to him I did not know what would be done to me.

These were days of war. I had been an unwitting message girl for one side. I had now fallen into the hands of the other side.

I looked at the other girls. How I envied them. They would be branded and made simple slave girls.

They need only obey and be dreams of pleasure to men.

I felt the planking of the hold with my body. The chains were tight on me. I did not know what would be done with me.

Twenty-Five

The Message

I lifted the strung beads to the square-jawed man with short, closely cropped white hair. His face was wind-burned and, in each ear, there was a small golden ring. To one side, cross-legged, sat he who was Bosk of Port Kar. Near him, intent, watchful, was Clitus Vitellius. Beside the man before me, the man with white, short-cropped hair, who was Samos of Port Kar, chief among the captains of the Council of Captains of Port Kar, was a slender, gray-eyed man, clad in the green of the caste of physicians. He was Iskander, said once to have been of Turia, the master of many medicines and one reputed to be knowledgeable in certain intricacies of the mind.

I knelt back on my heels. There were two other slave girls in the room, in slave silk, collared, kneeling to one side, waiting to serve the men, should they desire aught. I was naked, as I had been when I had strung beads for he called Belisarius in a house in Cos.

Samos put the beads before him on a tiny table. He looked at them, puzzled.

"Is this all?" he asked.

"Yes, Master," I said.

Iskander, of the physicians, had given me of a strange draft, which I, slave, must needs drink.

"This will relax you," he had said, "and induce an unusual state of consciousness. As I speak to you your memory will be unusually clear. You will recall tiny details with precision. Further, you will become responsive to my suggestions."

I do not know what the drug was but it seemed truly effective. Slowly, under its influence, and the soothing, but authoritative voice of Iskander, I, responsive to his suggestions, obedient to his commands, began to speak of the house of Belisarius and what had occurred there. I might, in my normal waking state, have recalled much of what had occurred there, even to the words spoken, but, in the unusual state of consciousness which Iskander, by means of his drug and his suggestions, had induced in me even the most trivial details, little things which a waking consciousness would naturally and peremptorily suppress as meaningless, unimportant, were recalled with a lucid, patient fidelity. Notes had been taken by a thin, blond slave girl in a brief, blue tunic, named Luma. Her tunic suggested that she might once have been of the scribes. Her legs were pretty. She knelt close to Bosk of Port Kar.

"What does it matter," Samos had asked Iskander, "whether a word is spoken before or after another?"

"It may matter much," said Iskander. "It is like the mechanism of the crossbow, the key to a lock. All must be in order; each element must be in place, else the quarrel will not loosen, else the lock will not open."

"This seems strange to me," said Samos.

"It is strange to you because it is unfamiliar to you," said Iskander, "but in itself it is no more strange than the mechanism of the crossbow, the mechanism of the lock. What we must do is reconstruct the mechanism, which, in this case is a verbal structure, a dialogue, which will release, or trigger, the salient behavior, the stringing of the beads."

"Could she not simply be commanded to recount the order of the beads?" inquired Bosk of Port Kar.

I could not do so.

"No," said Iskander, "she cannot do so, or can only do so imperfectly."

"Why?" asked Samos. "Is the drug not sufficient?"

"The girl has been carefully prepared," said Iskander. "She is under powerful counter-suggestion in that particular. We might, in time, break through it, but we have no assurance that we would not tap a false memory, set within her mind to deceive or mislead us. What I would suspect we would encounter would be overlays of memories, the true with the false. Our best mode of procedure appears to be to reconstruct the trigger behavior."

"You suspect then," asked Bosk, "that several arrangement orders of beads might be in her memory?"

"Yes," said Iskander, "each of which, I suspect, would be correlated with a different message."

"We would, thus," said Bosk, "not know which of the messages was the true message."

"Precisely," said Iskander. "But we do know the trigger sequence will release the crucial message."

"Otherwise," said Bosk, "the intended recipient of the message would also not know which message was the one intended for communication."

"Correct," said Iskander.

"Proceed then," said Samos, "in your attempts to reconstruct the trigger, or the key, in this matter."

Iskander had then continued his questioning of me.

I lifted the strung beads to the square-jawed man with short, closely cropped white hair, Samos, of Port Kar.

I knelt back on my heels.

Samos put the beads on the small table before him.

"Is this all?" he asked.

"Yes, Master," I said.

"It is meaningless," he said.

"It is the necklace," said Iskander. "I have done what I can. Should it bear an import, it is up to others to detect it."

"Give me the necklace," said Bosk of Port Kar.

Samos handed it to him.

The pirate regarded it. "Note," said he, "the frequency of yellow beads. Each third bead is yellow."

"Yes," said Samos.

"Why should that be?" smiled Bosk.

"I do not know," said Samos.

"From the fact that each third bead is yellow," said Bosk, "we may infer that the units of import consist of pairs of beads, separated by the yellow beads. Note that this pair consists of a red bead followed by a blue bead, and this other pair by an orange bead followed by a red bead. There are several such combinations. We might suppose that, say, a red bead followed by a blue bead correlates with one alphabetic character."

"What if the order were reversed?" asked Samos.

"Doubtless, if that combination were used, it would correlate with a different character," said Bosk.

"We do not have the key to the cipher," said Iskander.

"We can try all combinations!" cried Samos, pounding the table.

"We may suppose," said Bosk, "as a working hypothesis, that the message is in Gorean. As far as we know, Belisarius, whom we know only by name, and it may be a code name, is Gorean."

"Yes?" said Samos.

"See," said Bosk, who was examining the necklace, "the most frequent combination of colors is blue and red."

"So?" asked Samos.

"In Gorean," said Bosk, "the most frequently occurring letter is Eta. We might then begin by supposing that the combination of blue and red signifies an Eta."

"I see," said Samos.

"The next most frequently occurring letters in Gorean," said Bosk, "are Tau, Al-Ka, Omnion and Nu. Following these in frequency of occurrence are Ar, Ina, Shu and Homan, and so on."

"How is this known?" asked Samos.

"It is based upon letter counts," said Bosk, "over thousands of words in varieties of manuscripts."

"These matters have been determined by scribes?" asked Samos.

"Yes," said Bosk.

"Why should they be interested in such things?"

"Such studies were conducted originally, at least publicly, as opposed to the presumed secret studies of cryptographers, in connection with the Sardar Fairs," said Bosk, "at meetings of Scribes concerned to standardize and simplify the cursive alphabet. Also, it was thought to have consequences for improved pedagogy, in teaching children to first recognize the most commonly occurring letters."

"I was taught the alphabet beginning with Al-Ka," smiled Samos.

"As was I," said Bosk. "Perhaps we should first have been taught Eta."

"That is not the tradition!" said Samos.

"True," admitted Bosk. "And these innovative scribes have had little success with their proposed reforms. Yet, from their labors, various interesting facts have emerged. For example, we have learned not only the order of frequency of occurrence of letters but, as would be expected, rough percentages of occurrence as well. Eta, for example, occurs two hundred times more frequently in the language than

Altron. Over forty percent of the language consists of the first five letters I mentioned, Eta, Tau, Al-Ka, Omnion and Nu."

"That seems impossible," said Samos.

"It is true," said Bosk. "Further, over sixty percent of the language consists of those five letters plus Ar, Ina, Shu and Homan."

"We could still try all possible combinations," said Samos.

"True," said Bosk, "and, in a short message, which this appears to be, we might produce several intelligible possibilities. Short messages, particularly those which do not reflect statistical letter frequencies, can be extremely difficult to decipher, even when the cipher used is rudimentary."

"Rudimentary?" asked Samos.

"There are many varieties of cipher," said Bosk, "both of the substitution and transposition type. I suspect we have before us, in this necklace, a simple substitution cipher."

"Why?" asked Samos.

"It was interpreted almost instantly by the man called Belisarius," said Bosk. "A more complicated cipher, indexed to key words or key numbers, would presumably have required a wheel or table for its interpretation."

"Can all codes be broken?" asked Samos.

"Do not confuse a code with a cipher," said Bosk. "In a code, a given character, or set of characters, will commonly correlate with a word, as opposed to a letter. Codes require code books. Codes, in effect, cannot be broken. If the code book can be captured, of course, the code is useless. Codes are vulnerable in one way, ciphers in another."

"Do you feel the enemy would risk a code book, or code device, on Gor?" asked Samos.

Bosk smiled. "It seems unlikely," he said.

"Are there unbreakable ciphers?" asked Samos.

"Yes," said Bosk, "both from a practical and theoretical point of view. From the practical point of view, if a cipher is used briefly and for a given short message, it may be impossible to break. There is just not enough material to work with. From the theoretical point of view, the unique-sequence cipher cannot be broken. It utilizes key words or numbers, but each message is further altered in a prearranged, random manner. Each message is thus unique, but decipherable in its position in the sequence of messages. Both sender and receiver know, for example, that message six will be randomized in manner six, and so on."

"This is complex," said Samos.

"It requires that both sender and receiver have the deciphering tables at hand," said Bosk. "Thus, although it is more convenient than a code book, it shares some of the vulnerability of the code book."

Samos looked down at the necklace on the table before him. "Why should this be a simple substitution cipher?" he asked.

"I think that it is," said Bosk, "from the ease with which Belisarius read the message. Also I find it not implausible that it should be a simple substitution cipher because of the simplicity and convenience of such a cipher."

"Is it as secure?" asked Samos.

"The security of this cipher," smiled Bosk, "lies not in itself, as a cipher, but rather, as is common, that it is not understood as a cipher. It is not, for example, a strange message written upon a scrap of paper, calling attention to itself as a secret communication, challenging the curious to its unraveling, but apparently only an innocent necklace, beaded with wood, common, vulgar and cheap, fit only for the throat of a lowly female slave."

Samos lifted the necklace. I did not know what secret it contained.

"Further," said he who was called Bosk of Port Kar, "the slave herself did not understand the nature of her role in these matters. She did not, for a long time, even understand that she bore the message. Great security was achieved, too, in the manner of releasing the behavior of stringing the beads and in the counter-suggestion that she be unable to recall the order of the beads without the appropriate trigger structure being reconstructed." Bosk smiled. "Add to this," said he, "the convenience of a simple substitution cipher, the absence of the necessity for a code book, the lack of need for cipher wheels or deciphering tables, and you have an arrangement of circumstances which maximizes not only security but, under the appropriate conditions, ease of communication."

"Worthy of the enemy," said Samos.

"I think so," said Bosk.

"Could we not seize this Belisarius?" asked Samos.

"We do not know where he is," said Bosk. He looked at Iskander, of the Physicians. "If we should be able to seize him who is spoken of as Belisarius, do you think we could derive the cipher key from him?"

"Perhaps," said Iskander, "but I suspect that a spoken word, uttered by Belisarius himself, would, by suggestion, remove the cipher key from his mind."

"Could the enemy be so subtle?" asked Samos.

Iskander, of the Physicians, pointed to me. "I think so," said he. "You see what their power is in such matters."

I looked down.

"Could we, by the use of drugs, obtain it?" asked Samos.

"Perhaps," said Iskander, "but presumably we would encounter numerous keys. Who knows?"

Samos looked at Bosk. "Can you read the cipher?" he asked.

"I do not know," said Bosk. "See the repetitions of the beads. There are several repetitions, to compose the entire necklace. The message itself is thus short."

"It may be impossible to read?" asked Samos.

"Yes," said Bosk.

Samos looked at me. "I wonder," said he, "why, when finished with this wench, they did not cut her throat?"

I shuddered.

"They apparently feared little," said Bosk. "Their security, they deemed, was impregnable."

"May I speak, Masters?" I asked.

"Yes," said Samos.

"Belisarius," said I, "said that others would not understand the message, even if they might read it, that it would be meaningless to them."

Samos looked to Bosk. "Captain," said he, "begin work."

"I shall, Captain," smiled Bosk. He turned to the slave girl, Luma. "Copy down," said he, "on your paper the order of the beads, in widely spaced rows. Give me then your marking stick and your paper."

"Yes, Master," she said.

In moments her quick hands had accomplished this business and she surrendered to Bosk of Port Kar both the paper and the marking stick.

"We shall begin," said Bosk, "by supposing that the sequence of blue and red corresponds to Eta. The next most common sequence is orange and red. We shall, tentatively, suppose that corresponds to Tau."

I leaned back on my heels, and watched. No one spoke. Samos and Clitus Vitellius were intent. Bosk worked swiftly, but, upon occasion, he seemed angry. More than once, for certain letters, he altered his initial hypothesis of correspondence, substituting another, and sometimes yet another and another.

At last he laid down the marking stick, and, ruefully, viewed the paper before him.

"I have the message," he said, soberly.

Samos turned to the two slave girls who knelt to one side. "Begone, Slaves," he said. Swiftly, in their silk, they fled from the room, commanded by a man.

Bosk looked to Luma. "Yes, Master," she whispered. She, too, rose to her feet and, in her brief, blue tunic, hurried from the room. Under the command of masters, slave girls do not dally.

"Would you wish me to withdraw?" inquired Clitus Vitellius.

Samos looked at Bosk of Port Kar. Then Samos said, "Remain, if you would, Clitus Vitellius, Captain of Ar."

Clitus Vitellius nodded.

I knelt as before, a naked, captive slave.

Bosk looked angrily at the words on the paper before him. "It makes no sense," said he.

"What is the message?" asked Samos.

He called Bosk of Port Kar read from the paper before him: "Half-Ear Arrives," he said. Then he added, "It is meaningless."

"No," whispered Samos, his face white. "It is not meaningless."

"What is the meaning?" asked Bosk of Port Kar.

"When did you give this message, Slave Girl?" demanded Samos of me.

"In the last passage hand, Master," I said.

"I took her from two men near the country of the Salerian Confederation," said Clitus Vitellius, "in the early spring."

Since that time I had been the slave of Clitus Vitellius, of Thurnus of Tabuk's Ford, of the Keep of Stones of Turmus, and of the Belled Collar. I had been owned, too, by Elicia Nevins and had labored, too, in the Chatka and Curla.

"It is too late," said Samos, miserably.

"In what way?" asked Bosk of Port Kar.

"Doubtless Half-Ear, even now, is upon the surface of Gor," said Samos, grimly.

"Who is Half-Ear?" asked Bosk of Port Kar.

"We do not know his true Kur name," said Samos. "He is only known upon Gor as Half-Ear."

"Who is he?" asked Bosk of Port Kar.

"He is a great war general of the Kurii," said Samos.

"Is his arrival on Gor significant?" asked Bosk of Port Kar.

"He has doubtless come to Gor to take charge of the operations of Kurii upon this world."

I did not understand this talk of Kur and Kurii. They were, I gathered, the enemy.

"That he should come to Gor at this time is significant?" asked Bosk.

"I fear terribly so," said Samos. He seemed shaken. This surprised me, for he seemed generally so stern and strong. It must be a dire intelligence indeed conveyed by the simple message, to disturb to such an extent so mighty a man.

"What does it mean?" pressed Bosk of Port Kar.

"It means, I fear," said Samos, "the invasion is imminent."

"Invasion?" asked Clitus Vitellius.

"There are enemies," said Samos.

"Of Ar?" asked Clitus Vitellius, angrily.

"Of Ar, and of Port Kar, and of Cos and Tharna, and of a world," said Samos.

"Half-Ear," said Bosk of Port Kar, musingly. "I should like to meet him."

"I, too!" cried Clitus Vitellius.

"I know something of him," said Samos of Port Kar. "I do not think I would care to make his acquaintance."

"We must locate him!" said Bosk of Port Kar.

"We have no way to do so," said Samos. "We have no way to do so." Samos looked down at the necklace, which lay again now upon the table before him. "We know only," said he, dismally, "that somewhere upon Gor Half-Ear is among us."

I could hear the oil crackling in the bowl of the tiny lamp on its stand near us.

Samos looked at me, absently. Then he said to the guards behind me, "Take her to the pens and chain her heavily."

Twenty-Six

I Return to Ar; What Was Done to Elicia Nevins, My Mistress

"Your bath is ready, Mistress," I said, kneeling, head down, in brief white slave tunic, before the Lady Elicia of Ar, of Six Towers.

When a girl is tunicked it is all she wears, other than her collar. The tunic was of rep cloth, crisp, starched, pressed, pleated, and brightly white. It was, I suppose, all things considered, tasteful, modest and demure, suitable for a woman's slave. Surely to some extent its stiffness concealed my lineaments, a feature which commended itself to my Mistress, particularly when I was out of the house. On the other hand, it was clearly a slave garment; it was short, sleeveless, and without a nether closure. The Lady Elicia enjoyed having me so before her. In this way she sought to shame me. It was her decision, of course, as to what I would be permitted to wear, and even, of course, if I were to be permitted clothing. The Lady Elicia had no intention of letting the former Judy Thornton, her formal rival at the college, lose sight of the fact that she was now a slave. I was in no doubt about this on Gor, of course. On the other hand, I did not object to a slave tunic, as I was a slave. It was appropriate that I be so clad. Too, I relished its freedom, and its attractiveness, and its meaning. Thus, I was pleased to be tunicked. Yet I would have preferred to have been tunicked for the pleasure of men, perhaps in a scrap of clinging silk, or in a bit of soft, clinging, colored rep cloth, rather than in starched, white rep cloth for the gloating contempt of a free woman.

She seated herself on her great couch, and extended her feet, one after the other, to me. I, kneeling, removed her sandals, kissing each and laying it aside. She stood up and I, rising and standing behind her, lifted away her robe. I kissed it, and put it upon the couch.

She smiled, approvingly. "Perhaps I shall yet make a serving slave of you, Judy," she said.

"It is my hope that I will be pleasing to my mistress," I said. She gestured and I brought the towel, kissing it, which I then wrapped about her head, that her hair not be dampened.

She then went to the edge of the sunken bath, and slipped her toe within the water, and then stepped down into the bath and reclined, leaning back. "Excellent, Judy," she said.

"Thank you, Lady Elicia, my Mistress," I said. I had well judged the temperature of the water, mixing the water from the cistern with other water, heated in the tempering vessel on its iron tripod. The temperature was acceptable. I would not be whipped.

I served her as she wished, with absolute perfection. I glanced at the beaded, feminine slave whip, hanging by its loop upon the wall. I had no wish to feel it.

I looked at the mistress luxuriating in her warm bath, beautiful in the multicolored foams of beauty.

I was Judy, her house and serving slave. I kept her compartments, dusting and cleaning. I cooked and washed. I did all trivial, unpleasant and servile work for her. It was a great convenience to her to own me. Often she would send me shopping, my hands braceleted behind my back, a leather capsule, a cylinder, tied about my neck, containing her order and coins. The merchant would then fill her order, tie the merchandise about my neck, put the change in the leather capsule, close it and, sometimes with a friendly slap, dismissing me, reminding me that I was pretty, regardless of being a woman's slave, send me back to my mistress. At other times my mistress would shop and I would follow her, deferentially, to carry her purchases, eyes cast down, lest I should be caught so much as looking upon a man. A handsome male slave had once smiled at me and I, inadvertently, had reddened and basked in his pleasure. I had been turned about and marched home, to be put under the whip. The Lady Elicia, as I soon discovered, and had earlier suspected, despised and hated men. Yet, too, she found them, somehow, intensely fascinating and intriguing. Often she asked me questions which a slave girl might respond to intimately and easily if asked by another slave girl, but which were difficult to respond to if asked by a free woman. She would ask questions about the tethering and chaining of slaves, and their feelings, and what men made them do and how they were expected to speak and behave. She wanted to know intimate details of such things as what it was like to be a peasant's girl and what men exacted of girls in a paga tavern. I tried to answer her honestly. She would profess rage and indignation. "Yes, Mistress," I would murmur, putting my head down. "How pleased you must be, Judy," she sometimes said, "to have been rescued from all that, to be a woman's slave." "Oh, yes, Mistress," I would say. How could I tell her the joys of a slave girl, obeying the uncompromising, dominant male and writhing in his arms?

She lifted one fair limb, her left arm, from the foam, and washed it slowly with her right hand, regarding it approvingly.

Like many frigid women she was incredibly vain of her beauty. Did she not understand that it, and she, were biologically meaningless, if not seized in the arms of a master?

"How rude and despicable men are, Judy," she said.

"Yes, Mistress," I said.

Often, in the bath, for some reason, she would speak of men and her contempt for them.

"Today," she said, "in the market, I saw a man beating a slave girl, tied to a ring. It was terrible."

"Yes, Mistress," I said. I wondered what the girl had done. I supposed she had been displeasing. I had not accompanied her today to the market. I had been left at home, chained to the ring at the foot of her couch.

"Afterwards," she said, "the miserable girl covered his feet with kisses."

"Terrible, Mistress," I said. I supposed the girl was attempting to placate her master, and express her gratitude, her joy, at his reassertion of his dominance over her.

"Yes, terrible!" said the Lady Elicia of Ar, my mistress, of Six Towers.

"Too," she said, "my errand took me, inadvertently, near the Street of Brands."

"Oh, Mistress?" I asked. Sometimes, when she went on errands, I did not accompany her.

"There," she said, "I saw a chain of girls, stripped, in the open, men looking upon them. Disgusting!"

"Yes, Mistress," I agreed.

She lifted one leg, her right, gracefully from the water. Foam and water fell from it. Her toes were pointed. Her leg was shapely.

"Do you think I am beautiful, Judy?" she asked.

"Yes, Mistress," I said. She often asked me this.

"Truly?" she asked.

"Yes, Mistress," I said. It was indeed true. My mistress was an incredibly beautiful young woman. She was clearly more beautiful than I.

"Do you think that men might find me pleasing?" she asked.

"Yes, Mistress," I said.

"Do you think," she laughed, as though jesting, "that I would bring a high price?"

"Yes, Mistress," I said. She had asked me this sort of thing before. I had answered her truthfully before, and I answered her truthfully now. I wondered at her curiosity concerning such matters. I had no doubt that Elicia Nevins, on the block, naked, under the auctioneer's whip, would sell for at least a piece of gold.

She finished washing her legs, one after the other, dreamily.

I heard the small noise that I had been waiting for, for several days.

She reclined in the tub, easing her lovely body gently lower in the water, closing her eyes. The water, the multicolored foams of beauty, were about her chin. Then she lifted herself a little in the tub, the water and foam about her shoulders. She opened her eyes and looked up at the ceiling.

"What is it like being a man's slave?" she asked.

"Mistress will soon know," I said.

She turned about and then, suddenly, first seeing him, cried out, startled.

"Who are you!" she cried.

"Are you the lady Elicia of Ar, of Six Towers?" he asked.

"I am she!" she cried.

"I charge you," said he, "in the name of the Priest-Kings of Gor, with being an agent of Kurii, and as such subject to the penalties connected therewith."

"I do not understand a word you are saying," she cried.

He drew forth from his tunic a folded yellow paper, closed with a seal and ribbon. I saw, on the yellow paper, stamped upon it, in black ink, large, the common Kajira mark of Gor. "I have here," he said, "a bill of enslavement, signed by Samos of Port Kar. Examine it. I trust you will find that all is in order." He threw the paper to the tiles.

"No!" she cried, frightened, trying to cover herself. Then she cried out, "Tellius! Barus!"

"Your minions," said the man, "will be of little service. It is understood they are of Cos. They are already in the custody of the magistrates of Ar."

"Tellius! Barus!" she screamed.

"You are quite alone, Lady Elicia," he said. "There are none to hear your screams."

He was tall and strong, clad in a warrior's scarlet. At his belt there was a long leash, looped.

"Emerge from your bath," said he, "and prepare to accept slave bonds."

"No!" she cried. Then she cried out to me, "Run, Judy! Fetch help!"

"Do not," said the man.

"Yes, Master," I said. I looked at the Lady Elicia. "Forgive me, Mistress," I said. "I am a slave girl who has been commanded by a man." I knelt to one side.

"Bitch! Bitch!" she cried.

"Yes, Lady Elicia, my Mistress," I said.

She spun in the tub, agonized, covering herself, to face the tall guest.

"There is some mistake!" she cried. "Leave me! You intrude in a lady's compartments!"

"Emerge from your bath," said he, "to accept the bonds of a slave."

"Never!" she cried.

"Are you a virgin?" he asked.

"Yes," she said, angrily.

"If I must fetch you in the water," he said, "you will be taken in the water."

"Bring me my robe," she said.

He went to the robe on the couch, but, instead of handing it to her, he examined it, lifting it to the light. In one sleeve, in a tiny, narrow sheath, he found a needle, which he held up. Then he approached the bath. She shrank back, frightened. He washed the needle, dried it on a towel and replaced it in the sheath. I had not known the sheath and needle were there, so cunningly had they been concealed in the weaving.

He looked at her.

I had little doubt the needle had been poisoned, probably with Kanda.

"You have disarmed me, Warrior," she said. "Will you now, please, hand me my robe."

He threw the robe to the side of the room. She looked at it, crumpled at the side of the room.

"Please," she said. "I am rich. I can give you much gold."

"Stand in the bath," he said. "I would see your hands above your head."

"You intrude upon my privacy!" she cried.

"Soon," he said, "you will have no right to privacy."

"My modesty!" she cried.

"When you are a slave," he said, "you will not be permitted modesty." This was true.

"Have mercy, Warrior!" she cried.

"Obey, or be lashed," he said.

Elicia Nevins stood in the tub, and lifted her hands over her head, in an attitude of surrender.

The guest regarded her, casually, openly, at length, with the appraisal of a master.

She shook with fear, seen by a Gorean warrior.

The warrior then went to the side of the tub, crouching near what had been the side to her right. She stepped back in the water, away from him. He brushed back the foam. Carefully he examined the wall of the tub. In moments he had retrieved the tiny dagger which lay there, in its small compartment, concealed behind a tile. He cleaned the poison from the side of the dagger, dried it with a towel, as he had the needle, and then threw it to the side of the room, where lay her robe, which he had earlier discarded. I had not known of the existence of either the compartment or the small, poisoned weapon which it concealed.

Elicia stood in the water, on the far side of the large, sunken tub, her hands lifted.

"Free me!" she said. "I will pay you much."

He regarded her.

"I will give you enough to buy ten slave girls in my stead!" she said.

"But they would not be Elicia Nevins," he said.

She shook her head, haughtily. She still wore the colorful towel about her head.

"Would you care to examine the bill of enslavement?" he asked.

"If I may," she said.

"Step forth," he said, "keeping your hands lifted."

She did so, and went to stand near the paper on the floor, her hands lifted.

"You will make a lovely slave," he said. Then he said, "You may lower your hands, and kneel." The woman always examines the papers of enslavement on her knees. "Slave Girl," said the man, speaking to me, "remove the towel from about her head and permit her to dry her hands upon it."

"Yes, Master," I said.

I removed it carefully, lest it contain a needle or other device of which I might be unaware. The lovely cascade of dark hair which was Elicia's fell down her back. "Yes," said the man, "a lovely slave." Elicia dried her hands and, miserably, broke the ribbon and seal and examined the paper.

"You are literate?" inquired the man.

"Yes," she said, acidly.

"Do you understand the document?" he asked.

"Yes," she said. "It is an order of enslavement."

"You understand further, of course," said he, "that under Gorean merchant law, which is the only law commonly acknowledged binding between cities, that you stand under separate permissions of enslavement. First, were you of Ar, it would be my right, could I be successful, to make of you a slave, for we share no Home Stone. Secondly, though you speak of yourself as the Lady Elicia of Ar, of Six Towers, you are, in actuality, Miss Elicia Nevins of the planet Earth. You are an Earth girl and thus stand within a general permission of enslavement, fair beauty quarry to any Gorean male whatsoever."

Earth girls had no Home Stones. No legalities, thus, were contravened in capturing them and making of them abject slave girls.

"The first to capture you owns you," he said. "Prepare to be leashed as a slave." He unlooped the long leash at his belt, with its slip ring and snap lock.

"Wait," she said, extending her hand.

"Yes?" he said.

"Beware of leashing me in this city," she said. "I am truly of Ar!"

"Describe to me," said he, "the Home Stone of Ar."

She looked down, confused. She could not do so.

Young men and women of the city, when coming of age, participate in a ceremony which involves the swearing of oaths, and the sharing of bread, fire and salt. In this ceremony the Home Stone of the city is held by each young person and kissed. Only then are the laurel wreath and the mantle of citizenship conferred. This is a moment no young person of Ar forgets. The youth of Earth have no Home Stone. Citizenship, interestingly, in most Gorean cities is conferred only upon the coming of age, and only after certain examinations are passed. Further, the youth of Gor, in most cities, must be vouched for by citizens of the city, not related in blood to him, and be questioned before a committee of citizens, intent upon determining his worthiness or lack thereof to take the Home Stone of the city as his own. Citizenship in most Gorean communities is not something accrued in virtue of the accident of birth but earned by virtue of intent and application. The sharing of a Home Stone is no light thing in a Gorean city.

"You claim to be of Ar," said he. "Yet you cannot describe her Home Stone. Explain to me then in precise detail the ceremony of citizenship, or, perhaps, the performances enacted upon the Planting Feast."

"I cannot," she stammered.

"Shall I have you taken before the magistrates of Ar," he inquired, "to substantiate your claim of citizenship?"

"No," she said, "no!" She looked at him, terrified. To claim a Home Stone as one's own when it is not is a serious offense among Goreans. Elicia Nevins shuddered. She had no wish to be impaled upon the walls of Ar.

"Mercy, Warrior!" she begged.

"Are you of Ar?" he asked.

"No," she said, "I am not of Ar."

"Read further in the bill of enslavement," said he.

Her hands shaking she read further.

"Sex?" he asked.

"Female," she read.

"Origin?" he asked.

"The planet Earth," she read.

"Name?"

"Elicia Nevins," she read. The document designated her by her own name. She trembled. The document shook in her hand.

"Is that your name?" he asked.

She looked at me, and then she looked again at the warrior. "Yes," she said, "it is my name."

"You are Elicia Nevins?" he asked.

"Yes," she said, "I am Elicia Nevins."

"Fate?" he asked.

"Slavery," she read. She handed him the document with trembling hands.

"Prepare to be leashed," he said.

He looked aside, casually, as he returned the bill of enslavement to his tunic. In this moment Elicia, springing to her feet, ran to the side of the room and picked up the small dagger. I cried out. She whirled, holding the dagger. He closed his tunic, the bill of enslavement concealed within it. He looked at her, unmoved.

I do not think Elicia realized at this time that he had already begun her training.

"Get out!" she cried. "I have a knife! I will kill you! Get out!"

"You have finished your bath," he said, "and are fresh and ready. Adorn yourself now with cosmetics and scents."

"Get out!" she screamed.

"You seem slow to obey," he remarked.

She looked wildly about her, toward the open door leading from the chamber of her bath and couch.

"There is no escape," he said. "The outer door is secured with a small chain."

She fled through the door and ran to the outer door. We followed her, watching. We were then in the room containing the curule chair, the room in which she had first interviewed me, her new slave girl.

She pulled at the chain on the door, looped in rings, holding the bolt in place, and cut at the door with the knife, hysterically. Then she turned again, wildly, gasping, her hair about her face, viewing us. She fled then again into the chamber she had so recently vacated, and shut the door, throwing its bolts in place.

The warrior rose from the curule chair, in which he had taken his place, and went to the door. I stood back, startled. He kicked it twice, splintering it back, until it hung wildly open, on one hinge. The side of the door and the door frame had been splintered loose. With one foot he then brushed the door back. Within the room, miserable, brandishing her knife, stood Elicia.

"Stay away!" she screamed.

He entered the room, and faced her. I, too, slipped into the room, remaining much behind him.

"You have not yet complied with my command to adorn yourself with cosmetics and scents," he observed. "Are you disobeying?"

"Get out!" she screamed.

"Apparently you require discipline," he said.

"Get out!" she screamed. "Get out!"

He approached her swiftly. She struck down at him, and he took her wrist and, turning her body, suddenly, savagely, thrust her wrist behind her and forced it up high against her back. She screamed with pain. She was high on her toes. His left hand was on her left arm, holding her; his right hand held her right wrist, small, high behind her back. The knife clattered harmlessly on the tiles. With his right foot, he swept it to one side. He held her still for a moment. Her head was back. Her eyes were shut. Her teeth were clenched. Then, with his left foot, he kicked her feet from beneath her and she knelt at his feet, head down, her arm twisted high behind her, the wrist now bent, held between two of his fingers. She knelt near the bath. "You require discipline," he said.

"Please," she wept.

He released her wrist and arm, and taking her by the hair, thrust her on her stomach on the tiles, at the edge of the bath, her head over the water.

"I will buy my freedom!" she cried. "Let me pay you!"

He thrust her head under the water, under the foams of beauty. After a time he pulled her up, sputtering.

"I do not want to be a slave," she gasped, water running from her head.

Again he submerged her head, holding it under the water. After a time, a longer time, he again pulled her head up, freeing it of the water. She gasped. She spit water. She coughed. Water streamed from her head. Her eyes were blinded by water and foam.

"I do not want to be a slave!" she cried. "I do not want to be a slave!"

Again he thrust her head beneath the water. I feared he might drown her.

Again he pulled her head, by the hair, from the water. "I will obey, Master," she gasped.

He kept her on her stomach by the bath and slipped the leather loop of the leash over her head. Quickly his large, efficient hands shortened the loop, sliding the slip ring to a snug fit, then securing it in place, preventing its backward movement, with the snap lock. The leash could then tighten, functioning as a locked choke leash, but could not loosen.

Elicia Nevins turned to her side, unbelievingly. She touched the leather. She had been leashed. She looked up at the warrior. "Master?" she asked.

"Soon," he said.

"Whose leash do I wear?" she asked.

"That of Bosk of Port Kar," he said.

"Not he!" she cried. I gathered she had heard of her enemy.

"He," said Bosk of Port Kar.

She trembled, leashed. I did not think hers would be an easy slavery. I did not envy her. The name of Bosk of Port Kar was dreaded among women on Gor.

He pulled her to her knees by the leash. She looked up at him.

He gestured to me. "Where is the key to her collar?" he asked.

"In the yellow drawer, in the vanity," she said, hastily, "beneath silk."

"Fetch it," said Bosk of Port Kar to me.

I fled to the drawer and found the key. I did not dally to obey. He had spoken to me in the voice of the Gorean master.

He indicated that I should press the key into the hands of Elicia and kneel with my back to her. I did so. "Remove the collar," said he to Elicia. Fumbling, she opened my collar and pulled it away, putting it and the key on the tiles. "Say, 'I no longer own you'," commanded the warrior. "I no longer own you," whispered Elicia, to me, frightened. I sprang to my feet, and turned to face her. She shrank back, leashed.

My fists were clenched. She looked up at me. It was sweet to me to see her on her knees, leashed. "Kneel," said Bosk of Port Kar to me. "Yes, Master," I said. I was still a slave. Elicia and I knelt near to one another.

He stood near Elicia, and looked down upon her. Her lip trembled. "You are an agent of Kurii," he said, "and are a valuable as well as beautiful catch."

"Will I be taken to Port Kar to be interrogated?" she asked.

"Yes," he said.

"I will be cooperative," she said. "I will speak all I know." She had no desire to be put under the tortures of Port Kar.

"Of course," he said.

He glanced outside the long, high window in her compartments, out upon the towers of Ar. It was still bright. The blue sky was intense among and over the lofty towers of the city.

"It is early afternoon," she said. "It will be difficult to take me from the city by day." That was true. Tarnsmen, periodic and aflight, patrolled the city. "Doubtless," she said, "you are awaiting the fall of darkness."

"That is true," said he, "Prisoner."

She looked up at him, his leather on her throat.

"Do not fear," said he, "we will find a way to while away the time."

"How am I to be taken from the city?" she asked.

"Bound, naked, belly up," said he, "across the saddle of a tarn."

"Scarcely the way to transport a free woman," she said.

"By nightfall," said he, "you will be fit cargo for such mode of transport."

She shuddered.

"Go to the vanity," he said, "and kneel before it." She did this. He then, crouching behind her, crossed her ankles and, with the long, loose end of the leash, tied them together. The leash then ran from her throat back to her ankles. Her hands were free.

"Apply cosmetics and scents," said he. "You are to be absolutely beautiful," he said.

She reached, miserably, for the tiny boxes and brushes.

"Go into the outer room," he said to me. "Among my things you will find an iron. Prepare a brazier and heat the iron. You will find there, too, earrings and a saddle needle. Bring them."

"Yes, Master," I said.

It was in the late afternoon that I, holding its handles with quilted cloths, slid the brazier into the chamber of the couch and bath. I had not done this earlier in order that the room not be made uncomfortably hot. "How beautiful you are, Mistress," I said, startled. She sat at the foot of the couch, her knees drawn up and together, on furs thrown to the tiles from its surface. She no longer wore the leash. Her ankles were tied and her hands were tied behind her. She was made up beautifully for her branding. Her left ankle, I noted, on a chain of some five feet in length, was fastened to the slave ring at the couch's foot. On many nights I had slept there chained. It had been Bosk's decision that she would be branded at the slave ring of her own couch.

"Judy," she wept, "what is he going to do?"

"He is going to brand you," I said.

"No!" she said.

"You were not forced to come to Gor," I said.

She struggled in the bonds. Bosk of Port Kar, with the quilted cloth, drew forth the iron, and thrust it back. It would soon be ready.

"You are a beast and a barbarian!" she cried to him, drawing back. Then she could move no further back against the stone couch. She could draw her feet up no further.

He took her and threw her to her right side, wedging her in the corner formed by the tiles and the foot of the stone couch. With the leash he tied her thighs tightly together, leaving between the tight, confining leather strips an open space, a small, lovely territory, for the passage of the iron. He gestured that I slide the brazier near to him, and I did so. He indicated that I should give him the quilted cloth with which he might seize the iron, and I did so.

"Help me, Judy!" wept Elicia.

"You were not forced to come to Gor, Mistress," I told her. She lay on her right side, bound, thrust against the foot of the couch. Wadded furs helped to hold her in place. Her thighs had been tied for the iron. Bosk's weight, too, pressed upon her. She shut her eyes.

I looked outside, at the clouds, the blue sky of the late afternoon. It was sunny. The towers were beautiful. I saw some small birds in flight.

I closed my eyes when she screamed. I listened to the iron, patient, performing its identificatory work. I smelled the branding. Bosk did not hurry. He did his work upon her well.

I again opened my eyes. The sky was lovely and blue outside of the window. More birds flew by.

I heard the girl sobbing. There was a new slave girl on Gor.

I looked upon her. She looked at me, tears in her eyes. She had been marked incontrovertibly, and well.

"I am a slave," she said.

"Yes," I said.

"Remove the brazier and iron," said Bosk of Port Kar. "Set the iron to cool."

"Yes, Master," I said.

With the quilted cloths I took the brazier from the room, and the iron, too. Outside, in the outer room, I put the iron aside, on the tiles, near his belongings. It would cool.

When I returned to the chamber of the bath and couch he had sat the new slave up, against the couch. He, with a saddle needle, was piercing her left ear lobe. I saw the needle run through and a tiny spot of blood. He had already pierced her right ear lobe. Then he took the earrings I had brought, golden loops, an inch in diameter, and fastened them in her ears. He then gave me the saddle needle to clean and replace in his gear, which I did.

When again I returned to the chamber of the bath and couch he had freed her of her bonds, with the exception of the chain on her left ankle, which fastened her to the slave ring at the foot of the couch.

She lay on the deep furs at the foot of the couch, chained by the ankle, branded, in earrings.

She looked up at me.

"Greetings, Slave," I said.

"Greetings, Mistress," she said.

"Bring wine," said Bosk of Port Kar to me. "I will be served by the slave."

"Yes, Master," I said. I fetched wine, and placed it on the tiles, within reach of the girl.

"Does she not even know how to kneel?" he asked.

Quickly I instructed the girl in the position of the pleasure slave, kneeling, back on heels, back straight, head high, hands on thighs, knees wide.

"What shall we call her?" he asked me.

"Whatever Master wishes," I said.

He saw the discarded collar, inscribed "I am Judy. Return me to the Lady Elicia of Ar, of Six Towers."

He opened the collar. He approached her. "Perhaps," said he, "we shall call you 'Judy.'"

She shook with misery. "Please," she begged, "Master." How offended and miserable she would be, the proud, former Elicia Nevins, to be forced to wear my name, I of whom she had been so contemptuous.

"What think you?" asked the free man of me, grinning.

"I think, Master," I said, "that the name is not truly fitting for this slave, given her nature and appearance."

There is often a fittingness sought between name and slave. It did seem to me that 'Judy' was not the proper name for the newly enslaved beauty who knelt before us. It was not merely my desire that she not be given a name which I had worn when free.

"True," said Bosk of Port Kar, commending me on my view of the matter.

The girl breathed more easily.

"Bring from my belongings the open slave collar there to be found," said Bosk of Port Kar to me.

"Yes, Master," I said, and hurried to comply. From his belongings I fetched the collar.

He took the collar from me. It was simple, and steel, straightforward and secure.

"Read it," said he to her.

"I am the slave Elicia," she read. "I belong to Bosk of Port Kar."

She looked at him with horror. She would wear her own name as a slave name.

"Submit," he said.

She looked at me, wildly, piteously. I aided her. I showed her how to kneel back on her heels, her arms extended to him, wrists crossed, her head down, between her arms. "Say, 'I submit,'" I said. "I submit," she said. He bound her wrists, tightly, before her body. "Look up," I told her. She looked up. He collared her. I was very pleased to see her in the collar of Bosk of Port Kar.

Bosk then left the room, I heard him, too, leave the outer room. I heard him outside, moving to the roof. Doubtless he, a warrior, was checking the avenue of his egress. I did not know if the tarn would be waiting on the roof, or would be summoned from the roof, by tarn whistle.

I looked at the new slave girl. She knelt, miserable, collared, branded, her wrists bound before her body, on the thick furs at the foot of the couch.

She looked at the surface of the couch. She would not dare to ascend to it, unless ordered there by a master. Her place, unless commanded otherwise, was at the foot of the couch, at the slave ring. I, a slave, had spent nights at that slave ring, at the foot of my mistress's couch. Now, she who had been Elicia Nevins of Earth, who had been my mistress, knelt there, no more than a lowly slave herself.

She looked at me, disbelievingly. "We are both slave girls," she said.

"Yes," I said.

"I have been branded," she said. "My ears are pierced. I wear a collar!"

"That is true, Elicia," I said. I had used her slave name. She understood this.

I looked at her. "Your collar is very becoming," I said.

"Is it?" she asked.

"Yes," I said.

"It is a common collar," she said.

"It is still very beautiful on you," I said.

"Truly?' she asked.

"Yes," I said.

"Is it more beautiful because it is locked?" she asked.

"Yes," I said. I did not doubt but what that was true. That the collar was locked did not simply mean that she could not remove it, a fact which played its important role in guaranteeing slave recognition and identification, but, perhaps even more importantly, was momentous in its significance of bondage. A brand might be concealed by clothing, even the brief garb commonly allotted a female slave, but the collar, consistently and openly, proclaimed her girl property. The collar, stressing her vulnerability as a slave, is sexually exciting to the girl who wears it, and to the men who look upon it. Perhaps that is why free women do not wear collars. The steel on her lovely throat, lost beneath her hair, glinting beneath it, contrasting so with her delicious softness, is sexually and aesthetically maddening. No girl is so beautiful, I suspect, as she who wears a Gorean slave collar.

Elicia looked at herself in the mirror across the room. She lifted her head, and turned it to one side. "It is not unattractive," she said.

"No," I said. "It is extremely exciting and attractive."

She looked at me, frightened. "What will men think?" she asked.

"That you are a slave," I said. I shrugged.

She shook with fear. Then again, she regarded herself in the mirror, turning.

"Is my brand pretty?" she asked.

"Why do you ask?" I asked.

"I was only curious," she said.

"Oh," I said.

"Is it?" she asked.

"You were a student of anthropology," I said. "You can look upon the institution of slavery dispassionately and objectively, as an interesting cultural phenomenon, characterizing certain civilizations."

"I am a slave!" she cried. "Do you not understand what that means!" She struggled with the bonds on her wrists.

"I understand very well what it means," I assured her. I thought of Clitus Vitellius. "Where is your coolness?" I inquired. "Where is your objectivity?"

"I am owned," she said.

"Yes," I said.

"I did not know it could feel like this," she said. She looked at me, wide-eyed. "It is indescribable," she said.

"You are now experiencing a cultural institution from within," I said. "So, too, one who is a master experiences it from within."

She shuddered as she thought how a master must look upon her, with what desire and power.

"In the past," I said, "you have had some verbal acquaintance with cultural institutions. Now, perhaps for the first time, you have some inkling of what it is to understand one."

She looked at me with fear.

"Do not be afraid, Elicia," I said. "You need only learn how to please men immensely." I laughed.

"I do not even like men!" she cried.

"It does not matter," I said. "The earrings are pretty," I said.

She rose to her feet, the chain on her ankle, and turned her head back and forth.

"They are pretty," she said.

"Yes," I said.

"I never wore earrings," she said, "for they were too feminine."

"You are very feminine, Elicia," I said to her. "You should not have fought your femininity."

She looked angrily at me.

"Your days of fighting your femininity are at an end," I told her. "Men will not permit it. They will force you to yield to your femininity."

"To be feminine is to be less than a man!" she said.

"Whatever it is," I said, "it is what you are."

"Is it what I am?" she asked.

"Yes," I said.

"Judy," she said.

I did not answer her.

"Mistress," she begged.

"Yes," I said.

"Is my brand pretty?"

I laughed. "Yes," I said. "It is deep and clean, and it marks you well."

"The beast put the iron well to my body," she said, angrily. I could also detect a bit of pride in her voice.

"Yes," I said, "he did indeed."

"I wonder if I am the first woman he has ever branded," she said.

"He is a warrior," I said.

"Oh," she said, subdued. Then again she regarded the brand. "It is deep and clean," she said, "and it marks my body well as that of a slave, but Mistress, is it pretty, is it attractive?"

"What do you think?" I asked.

She looked at me in anguish. Then she said, "I think it is beautiful."

"I do, too," I said. "It is a perfectly beautiful brand. Many girls will envy you such a lovely brand."

She looked at me, gratefully. The brand with which she had been marked was the common slave brand for the Gorean female; incised deeply in her thigh, about an inch and a half in height and a half inch in width, was the initial letter, in cursive script, lovely, of the expression 'Kajira,' the most common expression in Gorean for a female slave. It was indeed a most beautiful brand. More than half of the branded beauties of Gor, I conjecture, wear that brand.

"Look into the mirror," I said.

She did so.

"What do you see?" I asked.

"A slave," she said. She smiled, shyly, lowering her head. It seemed an uncharacteristic gesture for she who had been Elicia Nevins. I smiled.

"But a slave who has much to learn," I said.

She looked at me, questioningly.

"Do you not hear the step of your master, descending the stairs outside the compartments?" I asked.

She listened. "Yes," she said.

"You will learn to listen for that step," I told her.

She looked at me, frightened.

"Is that how you will receive your master," I asked, "standing, like a free woman?"

Swiftly she knelt, in the position of the pleasure slave. "I do not know how to please men," she wept.

"You will be taught," I assured her. "Lift your head a little higher." She did so.

I looked upon her.

I do not know why it is, but the condition of slavery makes a woman very beautiful. It removes inhibitions to the manifestation of her femininity and her deepest needs.

Bosk entered the room. He stopped for a moment, almost startled, then grinned. He saw a slave knelt at the foot of the couch.

"All is in readiness," he said to us. "I shall gag and saddle-bind the slave at midnight," he said, looking at Elicia. "Then," said he, "I will take flight from Ar."

"Master must be wary of the patrols," I said.

"I have counted from the roof," he said. "They are not randomizing their flights."

"I see, Master," I said. Bosk was thorough. He left little to chance. Yet there would be risk. Yet I feared little for him. I did not think I would care to pursue him on tarnback, were I a mounted guardsman of Ar.

He looked down at Elicia. She knelt in the position of the pleasure slave. Her wrists were bound before her body. Her left ankle was chained to the slave ring. "A lovely slave," he said.

"It is not yet midnight, Master," she said.

He untied her wrists. "Serve me wine, Slave," he said. I gasped.

She lifted the vessel of wine I had earlier brought and filled the goblet.

"No," I whispered to her, and then instructed her how to serve him.

"Wine, Master?" she asked.

"Yes, Slave," he said.

Then she knelt before him, back on her heels, head down, lifting the goblet to him, proffering it to the master with both hands.

He took the goblet from her and, regarding her, drank. I could see he was well pleased with his new acquisition, the lovely beauty, Elicia.

"Bring a pan, and pour wine into it," said he to me, "and give it to the animal."

"Yes, Master," I said.

I found a pan and poured wine into it, shallowly, and put it on the tiles before Elicia who, frightened, putting her head down, drank from it. She lifted her head. "You have made me drink like a she-sleen," she said.

"You are a slave," he said.

"Yes, Master," she said. He was teaching her her slavery.

"Now," said he, "you will serve me the second wine."

Elicia turned to me, frightened. She knew the second wine which was commanded of her. It was the wine of her slavery. Then she looked to Bosk, terrified.

"I shall withdraw, Master," I said.

"I do not know how to please a man, Master," said Elicia.

I saw this did not please Bosk.

"I do not know how, really, Master," she wept. "Forgive a slave, please!"

"Fetch the whip," said Bosk to me.

I went to fetch the whip.

"I will try, Master!" cried Elicia. Then she looked wildly at me. "Please, Mistress," she begged, "help me! Please help me, Mistress!"

"Does a slave wish assistance?" I asked.

"The slave, Elicia," she said, "begs the aid of Mistress."

I looked to Bosk of Port Kar. "Instruct her," he smiled, "with the whip."

I touched her on the neck with the whip. "Put your head down, Slave," I said. She did so. "Although you are only a slave your master is permitting you to serve him," I said. "This is a great honor." She seemed startled. Then it became clear to her that this was, for her, a slave, an honor. "You have a treasured opportunity," I pointed out, "to serve the master." "Yes, Mistress," she said. "A man such as Bosk of Port Kar," I said, "has many women. Will he keep you for himself, or will he throw you to his men, or sell you or discard you?" She trembled. "If you are not pleasing," I said, "you may be slain." She shuddered. "I will try to be pleasing," she stammered. "Do you wish to serve your master?" I asked. "Yes," she said, "yes, Mistress!"

I pointed to the feet of Bosk. "Hold his feet," I said. "Remove his sandals with your teeth."

She did so.

"Begin now," I said, "to lick and kiss, very slowly and lovingly, the soft flesh just below the inside of the left ankle."

She did so. "Desire to please the master as a slave girl," I said.

"I do," she suddenly said, throatily.

I laughed, and stepped back. She seemed startled. She looked up. There were tears in her eyes. "No!" she said, suddenly. "I did not mean that!"

Bosk laughed and slipped to the furs beside her and threw her on her back. She looked up at him, terrified. "I shall have her instructed in long lovings at my leisure," said Bosk to me. "Obviously she is an ignorant slave."

Elicia squirmed on the furs, the Earth girl in her suddenly fighting to retain her self-image.

"No," she wept. "I am not a slave! I am not a slave!"

Bosk kissed her on the throat, and she closed her eyes. I saw her small hands seize at him.

"I am not a slave," she said to him, her eyes open, sternly.

"Touch her," laughed Bosk to me. "Feel the helpless oil and heat of her."

She cried out in misery.

"Naughty, naughty, Elicia!" I laughed.

She looked at me, in fury.

"You are a slave, Elicia!" I laughed delightedly. I was very pleased to have learned this.

She threw back her head, wildly, twisting it from side to side. Bosk had touched her.

I saw her eyes, wild, trying to retain the image of the Earth girl. Then, suddenly, I saw that she was becoming sensuous, uncontrollable, appetitious. She was fighting the Gorean slave girl in herself. In the arms of a man such as Bosk of Port Kar I did not think her struggle would be successful. He toyed with her resistance, sometimes permitting it to become stronger, sometimes even letting her think she might be able to withstand him, but then again he would begin to induce in her, subtly, the surrender spasms of the female slave. She well knew he was playing with her. "Beast," she wept, "how long will you sport with me?" Many times he brought her to the verge of surrender, teeth clenched, eyes shut, and then let her subside, retaining yet, to her cruel disappointment, a shred of her Earth-girl dignity. "I do not want to be a slave," she would cry. But I could see that her eyes, and her body, locked in his arms, were begging him to complete her conquest. How small she seemed in his arms. "You squirm as a slave girl, Elicia," I observed. "No!" she would cry, in her collar. She tried to hold herself still, rigid, but, when he chose, could not do so. "At his least touch, Elicia," I pointed out to her, "you leap as a slave." "No," she would cry. "No!" But it was clear to me that she wanted him to make her a slave girl. She wanted to be his slave girl. "I will show you," she said to me, "how a woman can resist a man." Then he had rolled away from her, turning his back to her. "I am weary," he said. "I would sleep." I suddenly saw, to my amusement, fear, and keen disappointment, registered on the countenance of the beautiful Elicia. "Master?" she said. She turned to him. She touched him on the shoulder. "Please, Master," she said. "What is it?" he asked. Elicia swallowed hard. I was present. "Please do not stop touching your slave, Master," she said. I laughed, but Elicia was not deterred. "Why?" he asked. "Because I am your slave," she said, acknowledging herself his. I smiled gently, but Elicia did not notice. I saw that she was truly his slave. I felt great happiness for her. "Does the slave Elicia beg the touch of her master?" he asked. "The slave Elicia," she said, "piteously and humbly begs with all her heart the touch of her master, Bosk of Port Kar." He rolled over and seized her. "You are a slave, Elicia," I said to her. "Yes," she said, "I am a slave." Then she cried out to Bosk of Port Kar, "The slave is yours. Take her, Master!" Quietly I withdrew.

* * * *

502

Gently, with his foot, Bosk of Port Kar awakened me. I had lain asleep at the foot of the curule chair in the outer room.

"It is nearly midnight," he said to me. "I must be away."

"Yes, Master," I said, rubbing my eyes.

Elicia knelt behind him. Her hands were tied behind her back.

He would take her to the roof and tie her over the saddle of his tarn, carrying her away to Port Kar.

I looked at her.

Her dark hair was loose about her shoulders. I could see the gold of the earrings almost hidden in the hair, the steel collar on her throat. There is something vulnerable, sensuous and soft about a female slave. She was beautiful in her bondage.

"May a slave speak?" she asked.

"Yes," he said.

She looked up at him, his slave. "I know," she said, "that I am to be taken to Port Kar and will there be assiduously interrogated."

"Yes," he said.

"I will speak all I know," she said.

"That is true, Slave," he said.

"But then?" she begged. "What then, when I am emptied of information and can be of no further use to you in your strategies? What then will be done with me? Will I then be bound and thrown to the urts in your canals?"

"Perhaps," he said.

"Is there no hope for my life?" she asked.

"Yes," he said. "You are beautiful," he said to her, in explanation.

"I will try to be pleasing," she said. She pressed her lips to his thigh. She had been well conquered.

I had little doubt the beautiful Elicia, even when rendered valueless in the conflicts of worlds, would be kept for the pleasures of men; again I looked upon her; no longer was she a high agent of a mysterious power of interplanetary proportions; she was now only a lovely, bound Gorean slave girl.

"On your feet, Slave," said Bosk of Port Kar to Elicia.

She rose lightly to her feet.

In his hand he had the gag he would fix upon her before taking her to the roof.

"Please, Master," she begged. "A moment, please, Master."

He stepped back.

Elicia approached me, her hands tied behind her, the collar on her throat. "We are both now slaves," she said, "Judy."

"Yes," I said, "Elicia."

"The college seems far away now," she said.

"Yes," I smiled.

"I love you, Judy," she said, suddenly.

"I love you, too, Elicia," I said. I embraced her, holding her, her arms bound behind her. We kissed.

"I wish you well," she said, "Slave."

"I wish you well, too, Slave," I said.

Then, from behind, Bosk of Port Kar thrust the wadding in her mouth and secured it in place. She faced me, gagged.

Bosk of Port Kar then tied my wrists behind my back. He then gagged me, as he had Elicia. "Your throat," he said, "is for the collar of another." I could not question him, for I had been gagged. He then said to me, "Kneel," and I knelt. "Cross your ankles," he said. I did so. Then, with the loose end of the fiber which bound my wrists, he tied my crossed ankles together, fastening them, thus, to my wrists. Some six inches of strap separated my bound wrists and bound ankles. He then, not speaking further, freed the door of its control chain, slung his gear about his shoulder and, taking Elicia by the arm, conducted her through the portal. I heard them climbing the stairs to the roof.

I knelt alone on the tiles before the opened door. It was after midnight. I was a gagged and bound slave.

In time I heard steps approaching, climbing stairs to the level of the compartments.

My heart leaped. I knew the step.

Clitus Vitellius stepped into the threshold. He looked at me, troubled. I wanted to cry out my love for him, the helpless, vulnerable love of a female slave.

He looked down at me, angrily. I did not understand his anger.

He untied my ankles and I lay before him on the tiles. I wanted to tell him how much I loved him. I could not do so. I was gagged. Angrily he crouched down and, by an ankle, drew me to him, half under him. With his hands he thrust up the brief skirting I had been permitted as a female slave, and, ruthlessly, used me. I threw back my head, reveling in his touch. Swiftly he finished with me and, cutting a length from the loose end of the strap which bound my wrists, rebound my ankles. My wrists and ankles were no longer bound to one another. I looked at him. There were tears in my eyes. I loved him. I wanted to tell him of my love. I wanted to tell him how much I loved him. He did not remove the gag. He did not permit me to speak. He threw me to his shoulder and carried me from the compartments.

Twenty-Seven

I Kneel in the Yellow Circle

I lay at his feet, like a pet she-sleen, he, Clitus Vitellius, in his compartments, sitting in a curule chair. His hands were on the arms of the chair. He stared moodily out the window, at the towers of Ar.

I rose to kneel before him. "Master," I said. I did not think I could dissuade him. I wore a brief street tunic, his collar.

I put my head upon his knee. I felt his hand in my hair. There was a tear in my eye.

"You trouble me," he said.

"I am sorry," I said, "if I have displeased you."

"I do not understand the feeling I have toward you," he said. He held my head between his hands, and looked down at me. "You are a mere slave," he said.

"Yes, Master," I said.

He thrust me from him, to the floor. I looked up at him.

"And you are of Earth," he said, "only a wench of Earth, collared and enslaved."

"Yes, Master," I said, softly.

He stood, angrily. He had, in the past days, treated me with great brutality.

"I fear you," he said, suddenly.

I was startled.

"I fear myself," he said, angrily. "I fear you, and myself," he said. He glared down at me.

I shrank back from him, for I was a slave.

"You make me weak," he said, angrily. "I am a warrior of Ar."

"A slave laughs at her master's weakness," I shouted, angrily.

"Fetch the whip!" he cried in fury.

I ran to the whip and brought it to him, kneeling before him, thrusting it into his hands. I looked up at him, angrily. His hand seized my tunic at the neck and shoulder and prepared to tear it from me, that I might be hurled to the floor at his feet, to be put writhing beneath the sharp discipline of his domination. His hand was on my tunic, the whip was uplifted. Then he released my tunic and threw the whip from him. He held my head between his hands. "Oh," he said, "you are an interesting and clever slave! That is one of the reasons you are so dangerous, Dina. You are so clever, so intelligent."

"Whip me," I begged.

"No," he said, angrily.

"Does Master care for Dina?" I asked.

"How could I, Clitus Vitellius, a captain of Ar, care for a slave?" he demanded.

"Forgive a girl, Master," I said.

"Should I free you?" he asked.

"No, Master," I said. "I could not then help myself. I would oppose my will to yours. I would strive against you."

"Do not fear," he said to me. "I am Clitus Vitellius, of Ar. I do not free slaves."

On the way to the Curulean we stopped at the Belled Collar. There Clitus Vitellius untied my hands, that I might, as though I were still a paga girl there, serve him.

"Will you not force me to the alcove?" I asked him.

"She-sleen," he smiled, sipping his paga.

I saw Slave Beads serving men. It was early afternoon.

"I was quite good as a paga girl," I said.

"I do not doubt it," he said.

Various of the girls whom I remembered, and Slave Beads in particular, had, with the permission of Busebius, the tavern master, spoken with me and kissed me. I think several of them envied me my master, but I informed them that I was being taken to the Curulean, there to be sold.

"Do you need a slave girl, Master," asked Helen, the Earth-girl dancer at the Belled Collar. She put out her hand, timidly, to touch his knee. "Buy me," she whispered. "I will serve you well." He cuffed her sharply back, bringing blood to her mouth. She looked up, frightened, from the floor. "Dance for us, Earth wench," he said. Her accent had betrayed her. "Yes, Master," she said. Before the table, to the music of some four musicians, Helen, commanded, danced before a Gorean master. There were tears in her eyes. Then he dismissed her, and she fled away. I was not displeased.

I saw Bran Loort entering the tavern with a basket of vegetables. He saw me, and looked away. He went to the kitchens. He did small work at the tavern.

"Where is Marla, Master?" I asked. I had regarded her as my greatest rival where Clitus Vitellius had been concerned.

"I sold her to a slaver," said he, "who specializes in the training of dancing girls."

I remembered Marla's long dark hair, her beautiful face, her stunning figure. She would look well, belled, in the dancing sand, I thought. She would be a marvelous dancer.

"I gave Eta," said Clitus Vitellius, "to the guard, Mirus."

"I am pleased, Master," I said. I remembered the young, blond giant, Mirus, how he had put her on the coffle in Tabuk's Ford. I had seen they had been intensely attracted to one another. Now he owned her. I thought Eta would be extremely happy. I was much pleased for her. Mirus, I had thought, had been the most attractive of the men of Clitus Vitellius, saving himself, of course.

"Slave Beads, as you know," said Clitus Vitellius, "is now owned by Busebius."

"Yes, Master," I said.

"Lehna, and Donna and Chanda," said Clitus Vitellius, "I gave to two of my men, Lehna to one, and Donna and Chanda to the other, for good service in war."

I nodded. It is not unusual among warriors to bestow beautiful slave girls as rewards for good service or valor. Slave girls make lovely gifts.

"Are we to leave soon for the Curulean, Master?" I asked.

"Yes," he said. "But first I am awaiting the arrival of a friend."

"May I ask whom, Master?" I asked.

"Only if you wish to be whipped," he said.

I was silent.

"But you know him," said Clitus Vitellius.

I looked at Clitus Vitellius, curious. But I did not ask. I did not wish to be whipped, certainly not before the other girls. There are diverse philosophies of discipline. Some masters believe a girl should be whipped only privately. Others believe she should be whipped whenever and wherever she deserves it, immediately, while her offense, such as it is, is fresh in her mind. Clitus Vitellius, perhaps wisely, believed it depended upon the girl and the context. Sometimes punishment is much more effective when a girl must wait for it. Generally a girl is not whipped before another girl who is owned by the same master. They only know, when the door is closed, that their sister in bondage is to be whipped. That is enough for them. I had little doubt, however, that Clitus Vitellius, in the present context, would hesitate to whip me in the Belled Collar itself. He knew I would not care to be exposed and publicly put under the leather here where I had worked, and certainly not before the girls I knew. To be whipped with Helen watching, for example, would be almost unspeakable agony. I was very quiet.

Soon I heard a roisterous peasant singing. Thurnus, whatever might have been his virtues, was not skilled in melody. "It is Thurnus!" I laughed. "Yes," Clitus Vitellius. "Do not give me to him again!" I begged. "Do not fear, little slave," said Clitus Vitellius. He leaped to his feet and he and Thurnus, who was carrying his great staff, met, embracing, among the tables.

In moments they had come to our table. Thurnus was already drunk, I thought. It seemed strange to me that they had met here, though I knew that they were friends. Thurnus, clearly, was in Ar on some business. "Greetings, little Dina," he roared. "Greetings, Master," I said.

He looked powerful and hardy, and was much pleased with himself. I knew the drought had been broken. The fields, I suspected, were doing well.

I wondered on what business it was that he had come to Ar. It was in the Fall now.

I noted Bran Loort peering out from the kitchens, but he then withdrew, his face in misery. He dared not be seen in this place, performing the chores of a churl. He had been of the peasants. I recalled the dishonor and agony in which Bran Loort had been banished from Tabuk's Ford. Rather than permit himself to be seen in tavern work by Thurnus, Caste Leader of Tabuk's Ford, I thought he might choose death.

I looked to Slave Beads. She was busily engaged in serving Thandar of Ti, of the Salerian Confederation, and four of his men. When in Ar, negotiating commercial arrangements between Ar and the Confederation, it seemed he regularly patronized the Belled Collar. There was a girl there to whom he had taken a liking. Her name was Slave Beads.

"Sul paga!" cried Thurnus, pounding on the small table with his great staff.

"Be quiet," said a fellow at a nearby table. He was drinking with some five companions.

"Sul paga!" shouted Thurnus, pounding on the table.

"Be silent!" said some fellow at another table.

"Sul paga! Sul paga!" cried Thurnus. The great staff banged on the table.

Busebius rushed to the table. "Master," said he, "we have many pagas, those of Ar and Tyros, and Ko-ro-ba, and Helmutsport, and Anango, and Tharna!"

"Sul paga!" shouted Thurnus. Several men about, at various tables, regarded him, most unpleasantly. I had worked in the Belled Collar, and, later, in the Chatka and Curla, in Cos. It did not require a great deal of experience to sense that Thurnus must soon be quiet or there would be trouble.

The pagas mentioned by Busebius were all, of course, Sa-Tarna pagas, of various sorts and localities, varying largely in the blend.

"Sul paga!" demanded Thurnus. Sul paga, as anyone knew, is seldom available outside of a peasant village, where it is brewed. Sul paga would slow a tharlarion. To stay on your feet after a mouthful of Sul paga it is said one must be of the peasants, and then for several generations. And even then, it is said, it is difficult to manage. There is a joke about the baby of a peasant father being born drunk nine months later.

"Sul paga!" shouted Thurnus.

"Silence!" cried a brawny fellow, some two tables away.

"Please, Master," said Busebius, "we do not have Sul paga here."

Thurnus rose to his feet, his face a maze of conflicting emotions, disbelief and incredulity chief among them.

"Sit down!" cried one critic.

"Eject him," cried another.

"No Sul paga?" said Thurnus.

"No, Master," said Busebius.

"Then I shall sing," said Thurnus.

I thought this a splendid threat.

Thurnus, as good as his word, broke into wondrous song. At this point, unable to help himself, one of the fellows at another table leaped bodily upon Thurnus and began to pummel him. He was joined shortly in this endeavor by several others. Clitus Vitellius, to my surprise, slipped to one side. I crawled between the legs of fighting men. I saw some two men fly off their feet, held up toward the ceiling by Thurnus. Their heads made a dull sound as they were struck together. A slave girl screamed. Then I saw Thurnus go down under a pile of attackers. A blur, brown and huge, leaped past me. I covered my head and backed away. I saw Bran Loort seize a man by the collar and loft him into the air, the fellow flying backward, then falling, crashing, skidding across two tables. "I am done for," cried Thurnus, from somewhere under the pile. But I saw his hand reach out and seize a paga cup which he drained while men fought over him, struggling to pound upon him, largely striking one another. "Do not fear, Caste Leader!" cried Bran Loort. He hurled another fellow away, headfirst into a wall. He seized two by the collars, pounding their heads together. I winced at the sound. He spun another man about and the fellow had little time to register the large hamlike fist which rearranged his features. I saw two teeth fly out of the mouth of the next man struck. Bran Loort fought like a madman. "Do not fear, Caste Leader!" he cried. "I am here!" Thurnus, by this time, had extricated himself from beneath the pile of bodies and stood to one side, a goblet of paga in his hand. "He fights well," said Thurnus to Clitus Vitellius. "Yes," said Clitus Vitellius, moving his head to one side to avoid a flying bottle. Then we saw Bran Loort backed against the wall, with what must have been twenty angry men of Ar encircling him. He looked wildly about himself. He saw Thurnus. "There are only twenty!" called Thurnus. "And you are of the peasants!" He flung his staff to Bran Loort, who caught it. Out stabbed the staff. A man screamed. About swung the staff and men tried to struggle backward. The staff whirled about, almost invisible, a branch lashed in a hurricane. I saw teeth flying, and blood, and a jaw broken. One man howled with misery, a shin shattered. More than one, I think, must have received a broken leg. The staff punched out, thrusting into another man's stomach. It lashed to the side and I heard ribs crack. Men crept to the side to out-flank the young peasant. Thurnus broke a table over the head of one. Busebius was weeping. "Stop, stop, Masters!" he cried. Then Thurnus and Bran Loort were fighting back to back, the goblet of Thurnus left in the hands of Clitus Vitellius. Bran Loort held the staff and, behind him, using half of the broken table, Thurnus protected him, fending blows and thrusting out, now and again, with the shattered table. At last he split the remainder of the table over the head of a brute who staggered back. Then Thurnus and Bran Loort, the wall at their back, stood side by side.

I heard a sword leave its sheath. Then I heard six swords more leap from the sheaths. I was frightened.

"No," said Thandar of Ti, standing on a table. He had drawn his own blade. Then, so, too, one after the other, did the four men with him. All were of the warriors.

The men of Ar looked angrily at Thandar of Ti and his men.

"No," said Thandar of Ti, again.

The sword, too, of Clitus Vitellius, my master, the captain of Ar, had left its sheath. He had placed Thurnus's paga on a nearby table. He stood between Thurnus and Bran Loort, and the men threatening them.

"I must agree with my fellow of the warriors," said Clitus Vitellius. "It is not proper that you should attack with steel those who defend themselves with wood."

"What he says is true," said a man. "We are of Ar!" He resheathed his blade.

"Free paga for all!" cried Thandar of Ti.

"And I," called Clitus Vitellius, "will fee the second round of cups!"

"Cheers for the peasants!" cried a man, with bloody face.

"Cheers for the peasants!" they cried. Then they surrounded Thurnus and Bran Loort, pounding them on the back.

"I shall not sing," promised Thurnus.

"Bring paga!" cried Busebius to the girls, who had drawn back, frightened. With a scurrying flight of bells they hurried to their work.

"And what are you doing here, miserable Bran Loort?" demanded Thurnus.

Bran Loort put down his head. "I have taken service here," he said. "I am shamed that you should find me here."

"Rightfully so," roared Thurnus. He had retrieved his goblet now, handed to him by Clitus Vitellius, and, throwing his head back, splashed its contents down his throat.

"What are you doing here?" asked Bran Loort. "Is it not time to harvest the Sa-Tarna?"

"I thought you might have forgotten," said Thurnus.

"No," said Bran Loort.

Thurnus regarded the young man. "It is certainly a great surprise to me," he said, "to find you here. But, as it turned out, it was fortunate."

"I am pleased," said Bran Loort, "if I could be of service."

"An amazing coincidence," marveled Thurnus. Clitus Vitellius smiled.

"Yes," admitted Bran Loort, puzzled.

"More paga!" called Thurnus. A girl filled his cup. Swiftly again the contents vanished.

"But what are you doing here?" asked Bran Loort, suddenly, shrewdly. "It is time to harvest the Sa-Tarna."

"I am looking for men," he said, "to aid in the harvest."

"I am strong," said Bran Loort. There were tears in his eyes.

"Good," said Thurnus. Bran Loort embraced him, weeping. "Drink a cup of paga," said Thurnus. "Then we must go. The Sa-Tarna grows impatient."

Bran Loort cried out with joy and whirled about, arms uplifted, like a child running and turning in the sun. He seized a cup and tore a vessel of paga from a startled girl and filled it himself. He threw his head back and drained the cup and flung it away.

"He has much to learn," said Thurnus, "but someday he will be a caste leader. He will have, too, his own Home Stone."

"I am pleased," said Clitus Vitellius, "to have been of service."

Thurnus grasped his hand. "My thanks, Warrior!" said he.

Bran Loort looked at me. "I am so happy!" he cried. "You are so beautiful, Dina! So beautiful!"

"I am pleased if Master is pleased," I said. I was very happy for Bran Loort.

Bran Loort looked to Clitus Vitellius and the warrior smiled, and lifted his hand.

"Oh," I cried. Bran Loort seized me by the hair, which was now long enough to permit a master to grasp it.

"Come, Slave Beauty!" he cried and, bending me over, my hands trying to grasp his wrist, ran me, stumbling, to the nearest alcove. He did not even draw the curtain. I turned. I shrank back, my back against the rear wall of the alcove. I drew up my legs.

"How beautiful you are, Dina!" he cried. "How beautiful you are! I am so happy, and you are so beautiful! You are so beautiful!"

"Remove quickly your garment," he said, happily, "or I will tear it from your body!"

I undid the five buttons, red, which ran from the throat of the garment to the waist. Buttons, interestingly, were a relatively recent innovation in some Gorean slavewear. They are not used on the garments of free persons. Most Gorean garments do not have buttons, but are slipped on, or held with brooches or pins. Hooks, however, are used with some frequency. Buttons, interestingly, are regarded as rather sensuous on Gor. Buttons, obviously, may be unbuttoned, or cut away with a knife, thus revealing the slave. Many masters do not permit a girl to button her tunic in the privacy of their compartments. When a slave opens the door of the master's compartment and kneels, head down, say, to admit a visitor, her garment may have been closed only an instant before. This is also true of a hooked slave garment. Slaves, too, may be kept nude in the compartments. These, before answering the door, will usually don a light tunic, slipping it over their heads or wrapping it about their shoulders. When one sees the slave one does not know if, a moment before, she has been beautifully naked in her slavery or if, when the door closes, she has again, behind the door, stripped herself for her master's pleasure. I undid, too, the red, rep-cloth sash of the tunic. The buttons and sash on the tunic were red. The tunic itself, sleeveless, was white.

White, on Gor, when worn by a female slave, tends to suggest a "white-silk girl," that is a slave who has not yet been "opened for the uses of men." It is also not an uncommon color for a woman's slave. When Clitus Vitellius had come to the compartments of the former Lady Elicia of Six Towers to fetch a slave she, bound hand and foot, had been in white. The accents of red on my tunic, of course, the buttons and sash, made it clear that I was not a "white-silk girl." Too, I think that no Gorean male who laid eyes upon me would have taken me for such a girl. We muchly yearn for, and covet, and hunger for, and desperately need, and are excruciatingly miserable without, the touches and caresses, the attentions, of masters. The "slave fires," as it is said, have been lit in our bellies. These put us beggingly at the mercy of the brutes, our masters. Accordingly, our body language, our glances, the tones of our voice, make it evident, at least to a Gorean, one aware of such things, of our desires, and needs. There are many ways of conveying these needs, other than a glance, a seemingly inadvertent touch, and such, many of which are more or less stylized, and some of which involve clearly established conventions. One might, for example, linger, almost imperceptibly, in the placing of a plate of food before the master, that he may see our wrists in proximity, almost as though they might be braceleted; one might boldly, if fearfully, kneel a little more closely than is customary; one might, while kneeling, turn the palms of the hands subtly upward, revealing their vulnerable, concave softness, and such. Other ways of drawing oneself to the attention of the master are more culturally explicit, and in accord with recognized conventions; of these other ways some are verbal, and others behavioral. For example, there are numerous verbal formulas which may be used, ranging from such things as "May my Master's slave serve him wine?" or "May my Master's slave light the lamp of love?" to such things as "I beg use, Master" and "Please, my Master, rape your slave." Similarly, a slave's needs may also be expressed nonverbally, but again, of course, in this case, utilizing obvious conventions. For example, one might tie the bondage knot in one's hair, or, even more simply, kneel, head down, at the foot of the master's couch, by his slave ring. Subtleties, stylized modalities, and recourses to accepted conventions may, of course, be combined. Much depends on the girl and the master. It is not unknown for a red-silk girl to crawl naked to a master and cover his feet with kisses, begging that he, though free, have mercy upon her, she only a slave, and deign to caress her. Our needs, of course, give our masters much power over us.

Sometimes, when a mix of slaves is serving, the distinction between white silk and red silk is marked by a ribbon tied about the collar, white for the white-silk girl and red for the red-silk girl. This can be helpful if the guests become careless or rowdy. It is still not unknown, of course, for a white-silk slave, late in the evening, to be seized and dragged down among the feasting cushions, there to be subjected to an abrupt, brutal, unanticipated slave use. It is common, of course, for a master to have virginity rights to his slave, if she is white-silk. After all, he owns her. To be sure, there are few white-silk slaves, and a "white silker" is not likely to long remain such. Virginity is a very uncommon property among Gorean slave girls. Sometimes a stranger can tell a red-silk girl by simply looking at her. She is likely to look away from him in such a way, with a timidity and shyness, that informs him she is well aware of what he can do with her. And, of course, it is only the red-silk girl who has a clear conception of what that is, the ecstasies which he may, if he wishes. enforce upon her, the rapturous yieldings which he may derive, she willing or no, from her lengthily, vulnerably exploited flesh, and such. Gorean slave girls, incidentally, it might be mentioned, though it is perhaps unnecessary to do so, while sexually needful, and often pathetically so, are not sexually aggressive; that would be absurd; they are too feminine, and too vulnerable; too, they do not wish to be beaten; they are the aggressed-upon. They may, of course, plead, and lick and kiss, and beg for attention, and such. I have never seen, incidentally, an example of sexual aggression on the part of a woman on Gor, either slave or free. One supposes, if it were to be encountered, most men would not really understand it; I think they would be puzzled or repulsed. Is the woman trying to be a man? But she is not a man. At the least I suspect that it would be regarded as peculiar and tasteless. The true woman, whether slave or free, carries on her campaigns more subtly and effectively. I do not know if this is because we are stealthier and more cunning, or simply because otherwise we would be an object of ridicule and a laughing stock to Gorean males. The average Gorean male would presumably regard a sexually aggressive woman as mentally deranged, and perhaps in a rather unpleasant way. These strictures, of course, do not deny us our weapons, or our power. Certainly we lure, we display, we entrance, we seduce. The slave does not demand, she begs; the slave is not the possessor but the possessed; she, in her smallness, her softness, her loveliness, is the quarry; she it is who is sought; it is she who surrenders, she who is vulnerably, helplessly ravished; it is she who must submit, she who will be helplessly conquered and owned; she is the slave, not the master. This is as it should be, and, shortly after coming to Gor, this is brought home to her, clearly; on

Gor she finds herself restored to the antique rights of her biological heritage, and meaning; she learns complementarity; she learns about dominance and submission, and that she is not dominant; at last, in the order of an ancient and profound nature; she becomes, perhaps for the first time in her life, a woman; she discovers herself, and, discovering herself, she comes to rejoice in the subtleties and depths of her own nature; she comes at last to understand, accept, and love what she is. How precious and glorious it is, she learns, to be a woman! And how joyfully and wondrously different it is from a man! At last she becomes true to herself and in this truth she rids herself of miseries, anxieties, conflicts, and fears; she is no longer a politically engineered social artifact, but a woman, honestly and deeply a woman, a woman in the order of nature; she is thus now enabled for the first time in her life to find happiness, and if fortune and the market be with her, to give and receive love.

The tunic I wore then was substantially white. It was also, for a slave tunic, rather long, coming to just above the knees. These things, I am certain, were no accident. Indeed, he, my master, had kept me generally in plain colors, usually gray or white rep cloth, and in tunics that were, for such wear, rather modest, rather than blatantly, boastfully exhibitory, as is often the case with Gorean masters who are proud of their girls and wish to show them off. Perhaps he wanted to try to think of me more as a woman's slave than a man's slave, or as more of a tower slave than a pleasure slave, so he would be the less attracted to me. I do not know. But I am sure he was trying, in one way or another, to counter, reduce or diminish my appeal to him, which was apparently excruciating. I am sure he wished, insofar as he could, to distance himself from me, and my attractions, at least to him. I found this sometimes amusing, in its way, but, too, irritating, and keenly frustrating. A girl, after all, wishes to be a dream of pleasure to her master, and will commonly, and usually very subtly, go to great lengths to achieve this object. I, his slave, wore, of course, what he gave me to wear. I was not even permitted to beg alternatives to the somewhat plain, certainly limited, doubtlessly calculated, wardrobe allotted to me. That had been made clear to me some days ago with a cuffing. I was to be silent and wear what I was given. He would not even tunic me himself. He would turn his back when I clothed myself, as I must do, according to his dictates. He would not even position me, kneeling me down, facing away from him, and, with comb and brush, groom me. Masters often enjoy grooming their slaves, much as they do their sleen or kaiila. He did not even sleep me naked at his slave ring, but chained me, tunicked, in an adjoining room. I do not think he would have boasted of that to his fellows in the Towers of Warriors! I think, you see, all in all, he did not trust himself to see me about his compartments, or at his feet, subdued and begging, naked, say, or in a bit of red or yellow slave silk. Indeed, I was not to approach him too closely, save when necessary in my serving. I was to avoid eye contact. He did not permit me to tie his sandals, or to bathe him. I was to stay much of the time out of his sight, kneeling, for example, behind him. But surely he knew I was there. And my presence, unseen, may have been for that very reason more subtly, more insistently, obtrusive. I realized that I was agonizingly attractive to him, despite his hatred of me, as he was to me. His various stratagems, I fear, failed him. Often he would at last cry out in rage and seize me and hurl me to the furs, his, venting all his wildness, his hatred, his lust, his power, his ruthlessness, his desire, on me, his fascinating, helpless, troublesome belonging. And I could be only his helpless, loving, ecstatic slave, writhing in his arms, in the arms of my owner, and rape master.

I slipped the tunic over my head and, hastily, cast it aside. I now faced Bran Loort clad only in the collar of my master and my brand.

"You are beautiful, Dina!" he cried.

"Please do not hurt me," I begged.

Joyfully he seized my ankles and dragged me to him, and then, with a peasant's roughness, thrust them widely apart.

"Please, Master," I begged.

"I am so happy," he cried. "And you, Dina, pretty little slave, are so beautiful!"

"Oh!" I cried. "Oh!" And I seized him. I threw my head back. I think that Bran Loort, overcome in his joy, had little time or patience for either his own pleasure or mine.

"Oh!" I cried.

Then he was finished with me and I was shaking. He covered me with kisses.

"I am so happy!" he cried. He then crouched beside me, and kissed me again. "The Sa-Tarna must be harvested," he said.

"Yes, Master," I said.

"I wish you well, Dina," he said.

"I wish you well, Master," I said.

He then leapt from the alcove to find Thurnus. They left the tavern together. I was left lying on the furs. After a few minutes, I pulled my garment over my head, buttoned it and retied the sash. I went to kneel behind Clitus Vitellius. He was drinking with Thandar of Ti, and his four men. They were being served by Slave Beads.

"The Salerian Confederation," Clitus Vitellius was saying, "is a threat to the security of Ar."

"Correct," said Thandar of Ti.

"You seem distracted," said Clitus Vitellius, who apparently wished to discuss politics.

Thandar of Ti was watching Slave Beads who, head down, was pouring him drink.

"A pretty little slave," said Clitus Vitellius.

"Yes," said Thandar of Ti. He reached forth and, gently, touched Slave Beads about the throat, as she poured the drink. She blushed, and trembled, head down. "Kneel before the table, Slave," he said to her. She did so, putting the paga vessel to one side. She knelt in the position of the pleasure slave. She was briefly silked, perfumed, collared and belled. I had learned earlier, in speaking with the girls, that Thandar of Ti, when in Ar, came often to the Belled Collar. I had little doubt that the small beauty, Slave Beads, was the reason. "Do you think I should buy her?" asked Thandar of Ti of Clitus Vitellius, as he regarded the lineaments and beauty of the girl. Slave Beads shook with emotion. She almost broke the position of the pleasure slave. "She is a beauty," said Clitus Vitellius. "If she pleases you, make an offer to Busebius."

"Busebius!" called Thandar of Ti.

I thought Slave Beads might faint.

"I have taken a fancy," said Thandar of Ti to Busebius, who had hurried to the table, "to this little slut of a slave," indicating Slave Beads. "I will give you a silver tarsk for her."

"Master is generous," said Busebius, "to offer so much for so miserable a girl."

"Then it is done?" asked Thandar of Ti.

"Five tarsks," said Busebius.

"'Scoundrel!" said Thandar of Ti. "I will give you two."

"Now done!" laughed Busebius. He was pleased. He had made a profit on Slave Beads whom he had had, I understood, for less than one silver tarsk in the market, and had yet retained the good will of Thandar of Ti, a valued customer.

Slave Beads slipped to the floor in a faint. She was still unconscious when Busebius removed his bells, and collar and silk from her, leaving her naked, save for her brand, lying on the tiles beside the table. She had not yet regained consciousness when Thandar of Ti placed his slave bracelets on her, braceleting her small wrists before her body.

In a few moments she regained consciousness, opening her eyes, discovering herself nude beside the table, in his bracelets. "Am I yours, Master?" she asked, lifting her braceleted wrists to him. "Yes, Slave," he said. She knelt before him, reaching out to him, weeping with joy. She looked to me once, that I might not reveal what had once been her identity. She had once been the Lady Sabina of Fortress of Saphronicus, the daughter of Kleomenes, of Fortress of Saphronicus, promised in Companion Contract, in a proposed political alliance intended to further the fortunes of Fortress of Saphronicus and the Salerian Confederation, to the fifth son of the warrior, Ebullius Gaius Cassius, the Administrator of Ti, Thandar of Ti, also of the warriors.

He rose to his feet. She looked up at him. Thandar of Ti, her master, regarded her. She had once been promised to him in Companion Contract, as a Free Companion; now he had purchased her as a slave.

"I love you, Master," she said.

"Let us return to the inn," said one of the men. "I think we have a slave here who is eager to serve her master."

"Rise, Slave," said Thandar of Ti.

She did so, standing before him, her wrists braceleted before her body.

"Lovely," he said.

"Thank you, Master," she said.

He examined her thigh. "A fine brand," he said. He brushed back her hair and turned her head from side to side, holding her chin in his hand. "Pierced ears," he said. "Excellent." He stepped back, admiring her as superb slave flesh.

"A good buy," said one of his men.

"Yes," he said.

He looked down into her eyes. "I think I shall call you 'Sabina,'" he said.

She started. "Master?" she asked. She looked at me. But I was confused. I had not spoken her secret to anyone.

"Is it not a lovely name for a slave?" he asked.

"Yes, Master," she said. "It is a lovely name for a slave."

"You little she-sleen," he laughed, seizing her by the arms, "do you not think I know who you once were?"

"Master?" she asked.

"You were once Sabina, the daughter of Kleomenes," he laughed, "once promised to me in Companion Contract."

She looked at him, wildly.

"Now, of course, you are only a slave," he said.

"Yes, Master," she said.

"When the Companionship was under consideration by the Council of the Confederation," he said, "I slipped away, on tarn, to Fortress of Saphronicus. I spied on you, to see if you pleased me."

"Pleased!" she cried. It is beneath the dignity of a free woman to please a man. Slave girls please men.

"Yes," he said.

"It must have been difficult," she said, "for you to tell, I clothed in the robes of concealment, if I pleased you."

"You recall your quarters," he asked, "and the window, high in the wall."

"Yes," she said.

"It may be reached by a rope, from the roof," he said.

She gasped.

"You were quite beautiful in your bath," he said.

She looked down, confused, blushing.

"Is a slave modest?" he asked.

"No, Master," she said. Then she looked up at him, shyly. "Did you find me pleasing, truly?" she asked.

"Yes, quite," he said. "The girl, Marla, too, and the others," he said, "were also quite beautiful."

"Yes," she said. "My serving slaves were beautiful." She looked up at him. "Were they more beautiful than I?" she asked.

"Not to me," he said.

"I am pleased," she said.

"You can well understand my dilemma," he said. "Seeing you I wanted you. You were one of those women who is so feminine and attractive that a man finds it difficult to think of you in terms other than jealous ownership. I wanted to own you. I wanted you at my feet naked, in my collar. Yet you were intended to be my companion. How could one relate to a girl as feminine and beautiful as you, I ask you, other than as a master to a slave?"

"I do not know," she said.

"Besides," he said, "you were only of the merchants. It is unseemly for a Warrior to take as a companion the daughter of a merchant. I detest the politics which seemed to make such a match expedient. Surely I was not consulted in the negotiations."

"No, Master," she said. "Nor was I," she added, pointing this out.

"But you are a woman," he said.

"That is true," she said.

"The daughters of merchants," he said, "are fit only to be the slaves of Warriors."

"Oh, Master?" she asked, archly.

"Yes," he said, evenly, regarding her.

"Yes, Master," she said, dropping her eyes.

"Besides," he said, "you, free, were an arrogant she-sleen. You needed enslaving, collaring and whipping."

"Yes, Master," she said, frightened.

"I resolved to refuse the companionship," said Thandar of Ti. "I resolved to flee the city." He grinned. "As it turned out," he said, "that was not necessary."

"How did master find me?" she asked.

"There is a fellowship among Warriors," he said. Clitus Vitellius smiled.

"Thank you, Master," said Slave Beads, now Sabina, to Clitus Vitellius.

He nodded, accepting her thanks.

Sabina, the slave, turned again to face Thandar of Ti, looking up at him. "You have found me," she said. "You own me." There were tears in her eyes. "I had hoped," she said, "that my identity might have remained unknown to you."

"Why?" he asked, puzzled.

She looked down, confused. She shook her head.

"Why?" he asked.

"Must I speak?" she asked.

"You are a slave," he said angrily. "Speak."

She looked up at him, boldly, tears in her eyes. "Because," she said, "I wanted you to keep me as a slave!" She looked down again, confused. "I sense," she said, "that you are my true master, and I am your true slave."

The men looked at one another, cognizing well the confession of the small, beautiful slave.

"Too," she said, "I did not wish my fate, known, to dishonor you."

"That the flank of a merchant's daughter has met the iron cannot dishonor me," said Thandar of Ti.

"I see that it cannot," she said, a bit angrily. But it was true. What is it on Gor that a girl is caught and branded, and made a slave?

"But now, in honor, knowing my fate," she said, "you must free me."

"Oh?" he said.

"Yes," she said. "You will now free me, and once again the plans of Fortress of Saphronicus and the Salerian Confederation will proceed as before. I, freed, will be repledged to you in Companionship. Matters then, regardless of our wishes, will be as they were before."

Thandar of Ti laughed. Clitus Vitellius smiled.

"Master?" she asked.

How beautiful she looked, naked before him, in his bracelets.

"A fine brand," said Thandar of Ti, surveying her thigh.

"Now that you know who I am," she said, "you must free me."

He turned her head from side to side. "And pierced ears," he said.

"Surely you are going to free me," she said.

"You are the daughter of a merchant," he said. "The daughters of merchants are fit only to be the slaves of warriors."

"You are going to free me!" she cried.

"Kneel to be collared," he said.

"Master!" she cried.

"Bring a whip," he said to one of his men.

Swiftly she knelt. The whip would not be necessary. Sabina, the slave, looked up at Thandar of Ti, astonishment in her eyes, and wonder and love. She knew then the nature of the man, and his strength, who owned her.

"Bring the collar," said Thandar of Ti to one of his men.

The collar, from his belongings, was brought.

"I have found a slave who pleases me," he said. "I am collaring her."

He cared naught for the politics of cities, nor did he fear the wrath of states. He was a warrior.

He stepped behind the girl and, in the manner of Ti and certain other cities, thrust down her head and held ready the opened collar.

"Submit," he said.

"I submit myself, totally, Master," she said.

Roughly he shut the collar, enclosing her lovely throat in the obdurate band of slave steel. He then, with his foot, spurned her to the floor.

"Throw me among your women, Master," she begged.

"I shall," he said. He then turned away and strode from the tavern.

But I had little doubt the lovely Sabina would be his preferred slave.

One of Thandar of Ti's men sought out Busebius, and made settlement of the bill.

"He is keeping me as a slave," said Sabina to me, elatedly. "How strong and marvelous he is! I fear only I will not be able to love him enough!"

I kissed her. It is difficult for a girl not to esteem a man who does as he pleases, even though it is to her that it be done. A woman admires strength, especially if it is used to dominate and control her. It is, it seems, for men to command and women to obey, for men to dominate and women to submit, for men to claim and for women to yield. It is, it seems, the way of primate nature. Its test is enactment; its proof is joy; its evidence is love. If we have lost this, we have lost part of ourselves.

"I wish you well," cried Sabina. "I wish you all well!"

"I wish you well!" I cried.

The others, too, paga girls in the tavern, wished her well.

Thandar of Ti's men went to the portal of the tavern. One of them turned about. "Will it be necessary to leash you, Slave?" he asked.

"No, Master!" cried Sabina, and hurried to follow them. We watched them leave the tavern.

"It is time," said Clitus Vitellius, "for us to be on our way to the Curulean."

I reached out, timidly, to touch him. "Please, Master," I begged.

He looked at me, almost tenderly. I thought him sad. "Very well," he said.

He indicated that I should precede him to one of the alcoves.

I entered the alcove, and slipped away the tunic. He closed the curtain behind us.

"Many times," I said, lightly, "I pleased the customers of Busebius in this very alcove."

He took me in his arms. It startled me, for he touched me gently.

"I shall miss you, Dina," he said.

"There are many girls," I said.

"Yes," he said, "there are many girls."

"You will soon forget me," I said.

He brushed my hair with his hand. "Your hair," he said, "will be too short, I wager, until the spring."

"Doubtless," I said, "it will lower my price."

He kissed me.

"Will you come to see me in the exhibition cages?" I asked. In most markets girls are displayed publicly in exhibition cages prior to their sale. This is almost always the case in the Curulean.

"No," he said.

"Oh," I said.

He kissed me, again, softly, tenderly.

"Keep me!" I begged suddenly.

"No," he said.

I tried not to cry.

"It is strange," he said, "I have faced wild sleen and the steel of fierce enemies. I am a warrior, and am high among warriors. Yet you, a mere girl, would conquer me with a smile and a tear."

"No, Master," I said.

"Surely you must understand," he said.

"A slave girl requires no explanation," I said. "It is hers only to obey."

"You see," he said, angrily, "You make me weak!"

"Then conquer me," I said.

"You are different from all the others!" he said, angrily.

"Yet I am only a slave," I said. "Treat me as such!"

"You should be tied at the slave ring and whipped," he said.

"Tie me at the ring," I said. "Whip me!"

"A warrior," he said, "must be hard and fierce."

"Be hard and fierce with me," I said.

"You want to be conquered and enslaved, don't you, you slut?" he said.

"Yes," I said. "I am a woman."

He sat up beside me. "How you must despise my weakness," he said.

"Yes," I said, angrily. "I despise your weakness."

He looked at me, in fury.

"I love you," I said.

He slapped aside my head, bringing blood to my mouth. "Lying slave," he said.

Then he seized me, and well vented his anger upon me. I was well used.

When he had finished with me, he said, "Get up. We must go to the Curulean."

I slipped the tunic on, and sashed it, and, one by one, by the five buttons, closed it. I wished he had torn it open and would march me through the streets as an exposed slave, that other girls might see the strength of the man who owned me.

We left the tavern and made our way to the Curulean, to a back entrance.

I looked at the stout iron door, behind which I would be sold.

"We must enter," he said to me.

"Do with me what you want," I said to him.

"I am," he said.

"Are you?" I asked.

"Yes," he said.

I looked up at him.

"I am a warrior," he said. "I cannot be weak."

"You are weak now," I said.

"No," he said.

"I despise your weakness," I said.

"How am I weak?" he asked.

"You do not want to sell me," I said. "Yet you are doing so."

"I do want to sell you," he said.

"Look at me," I said.

He regarded me.

"What do you see?" I asked.

"A slave girl," he said.

"What now," I asked, "do you truly want to do with me?"

"Sell you," he said.

"No," I said. "You want me in your compartments. You want me at your feet. You want me in your collar. You want not to sell me, but to master me, to own me."

"I want many things from you," he said.

"Then command them, take them," I challenged. "Did you trace me to Ar, and follow me to Cos, to sell me?"

He looked angry.

"No," I said. "You wanted me slave, naked on your chain."

"Yes!" he said, angrily. "I wanted you a naked slave on my chain, mine!"

"Strip me!" I cried. "Chain me!"

"No," he said.

I subsided. "Sell me," I said wearily. "The decision is yours. I am slave."

He pounded on the iron door.

"I had thought Clitus Vitellius strong," I said. "I had thought him of the Warriors. I had thought he had the power to do as he wills with a woman. I see now he is too weak to do with a woman what truly he wants, what pleases him."

He struck again on the iron door.

"He is weak," I said. "A slave despises him."

"Do not make me angry," he said.

I looked away. I had nothing to fear from him.

I heard feet approaching the iron door, from the other side. A small, lateral panel in the door, about eye level, slid back. "Your business?" inquired a voice.

"The vending of a girl," said Clitus Vitellius.

The panel slid shut. A moment later the door swung open. "Enter, Master," said a man.

We entered and found a large room, floored with cement. A yellow circle, in outline, narrow-bordered, the border some six inches in width, the circle itself some ten feet in width, was painted on the cement. A man, at a small, four-legged table, sat to one side. "Remove her tunic and collar," he said. Clitus Vitellius did so. We did not speak.

"Kneel in the circle, Slave," said the man at the table. The fellow who had opened the door stood to one side. A coiled, rawhide rope, on a clip, hung from his belt. I went to the circle and knelt in its center, on the cement. The man with the rope entered the circle and loosed the rope from his belt. He tied it about my neck. The knot was at the side, under my left ear. He backed away, giving me some five feet of slack. The remainder of the rope he held, in long, loose loops, in his right hand. I knew it would serve to whip me, if necessary.

I would be put through slave paces.

"Give me whatever you think she is worth," he said, "and send the coins to the compartments of Clitus Vitellius, in the Towers of Warriors."

"Yes, Master," said the man at the table.

Clitus Vitellius turned about and left the Curulean.

I knelt alone in the yellow circle on the cement.

I felt the rope on my throat pull taut. I sensed the swinging loops of leather near me.

The man rose from behind the table and came to the circle. He looked down at me. "Well now, little beauty," he said, "let us see what you can do."

"Yes, Master," I said.

Twenty-Eight

What Occurred at the Curulean

The first time that one is sold it is the hardest. Yet it is, I suppose, never easy. The hardest part is perhaps not knowing who it is, amongst those many faces in the darkness, who will buy you. You are illuminated, exhibited, forced to perform. At your side is the auctioneer with his whip. You perform, and perform well. Do not think you would not. You feel the wood of the block with your feet, and the sawdust upon it. The block itself is smooth. Many girls have been sold here before. You are not special, you are only another slave, a bit more or less pleasing than others. You feel the sawdust with your feet. On Gor, animals are commonly sold on blocks which are strewn with sawdust. The slave girl is an animal. You lift your head under the torchlight. You hear the first bid. It is hard not to tremble. You have been bid upon. From the voice you try to guess the nature of the master. Then there is another bid. You smile, you turn, you walk, you lift your arms, you kneel, you lie upon your back at the auctioneer's feet, your knee lifted, your arms over your head as though braceleted, you roll to your stomach, you look up at him, over your shoulder; you respond to him, instantly, setting forth for the view of the buyers subtle and provocative positions and attitudes, displaying yourself as you must, fully, and as a slave. You are sweating. Sawdust clings to your body. It clings in your hair. If you falter, or are in the least displeasing, the auctioneer's whip will sharply instruct you in your error. At last, breathing heavily, you stand there, naked. Perhaps you have been struck.

The last bid is taken. It is accepted. The auctioneer's fist closes. You have been sold.

* * * *

Many girls dream of being sold in the Curulean. Its great block is perhaps the most famous in Ar. It is also the largest. It is semicircular and some forty feet in width. It is painted for the most part in blue and yellow, the colors of the slavers, and ornately carved, with many intricate patterns and projections. It is perhaps fifteen feet high. An interesting feature of the block is that about it, on the semicircular side, facing the crowd, tall and serene, carved in white-painted wood, evenly spaced, are the figures of nine slave girls. They represent, supposedly, the first nine girls taken, thousands of years ago, by the men of a small village, called Ar. In the carving it may be seen that the throats of the girls are encircled by ropelike collars, presumably woven of some vegetable substance. It is said that at that time the men of Ar were not familiar with the working of iron. It is also said the girls were forced to breed mighty sons for their captors.

"You, Slave!" said the man.

"Yes, Master!" I said, looking up in the collar, with its two chains, one on each side, which fastened me to the girl on my left and right.

We were in the tunnel leading to the block. Another tunnel left the block.

"Are you familiar with the choreography of your display?" he asked.

"Yes, Master," I said. I had been well rehearsed. Little occurs by accident on the block of the Curulean.

He then went to the next girl, she on my left, farther down the tunnel toward the pens. He addressed to her the same question. She, too, wore a collar, with two chains. It fastened her, on her right, to me, and, on her left, to another girl. "Yes, Master!" she assured him. He then went to the next girl in the line, farthest from the block. Each collar opens, and the chains may be attached or removed. This provides great flexibility. There were one hundred and twenty girls in the line. It would take some five or six Ahn to sell us, if the bidding was brisk. On a slow night it could take as much as eight Ahn, the sales extending into the early morning hours. Some girls sell quickly, and others slowly. When it takes longer to sell a girl it usually means that she is less interesting to the buyers, and that the bids are slow, or that she, an unusual beauty, is being more elaborately displayed, with the object in mind of intensifying and driving up the eventual bids.

"Yes, Master!" said the girl some two girls below me on the chain, responding to the question of the slaver's man. We would all be ready. We would all do our best, or be punished terribly.

I looked to the girl on my right, and to the one on my left. How beautiful they were. We had all had Gorean slave cosmetics applied to us. Let the men beware. We had all been exposed in the exhibition cages earlier, stark, save for perfume. It was at that time that the buyers had had their opportunity to view us objectively. It was their responsibility now, in the bidding, to be on their guard.

I sensed a tremor, sudden, subtle, in the chain. I leaned forward, looking down the line. The whisper was sped rapidly down the chain. "The bidding has begun," said the whisper.

"I'm frightened," said a girl.

"All Ar bids at the Curulean," said another.

I could hear nothing. But I knew the first girl had now ascended the block.

I sat back on the long wooden bench. It was some eight inches in width. It was set against the right side of the tunnel, as one would look toward the opening at the foot of the block. It ran almost the length of the tunnel. The bench is at the right side of the tunnel as the slavers' men are mostly right-handed. Thus, if a lash is used, the girl will be more conveniently directed toward the end of the tunnel near the foot of the block, toward her sale, rather than away from it. It is, of course, seldom necessary to use the lash in the tunnel. Indeed, it is seldom necessary, in general, to use the lash on a slave girl. We have felt it. We know what it can do to us. I pulled the wide bands of green silk about me, more closely. They would resemble, initially, a gown, but they were not truly a gown. They would be unlooped and lifted away, bit by bit, beginning about the head and the feet, gradually, cunningly, revealing me. Toward the end I would be spun almost free of them and then, in the end, I would be ordered, exposed save for the final silk, concealing my breasts and thighs, to lie supine at the auctioneer's feet. He would then stand over me, the two bands extending from me, ribbonlike, in his grasp, taking more bids. When the crowd, fierce in its impatience, demanded it, he would, shrugging, roll me free of them, in two turns, I finishing, lying on my back again, knee lifted, hands over and behind my head, the backs of my hands on the block, the palms exposed, like the rest of me, helplessly. I would lie there, a resigned slave girl, awaiting her rape-taming. Presumably the bids then would much increase. I was to follow the commands of the auctioneer from that point. Presumably he would order me to my feet and, sensing the crowd, playing it with skill, put me through what slave paces seemed suitable.

"Move down one space," said the slaver's man.

We did so.

The girl to my right wore a demure, brief house tunic, of the sort worn by a house slave. She would be presented to the crowd as though, since childhood, she had been owned by a quiet, respectable family which, lately, because of financial difficulties had been forced to sell her. She would be reputed to know little of the lust of men or the duties of a pleasure slave. Still, it would be suggested, a master might teach her. This story was not entirely a fabrication. It would not be said, however, that she was an appetitious girl who had welcomed her sale, or that she hungered for a man. She hoped to be bought by a man of modest means. She wanted to be the only girl in his compartments. I thought she would make a wonderful slave. The girl on my left, who would be sold after me, would be presented quite differently. She was clad in a bit of virginal white fluff, from her shoulders to thighs. The contrast between her dark hair, and her naked arms and legs, and the bit of white fluff about her, was quite striking. She had lovely, slender shoulders and well-curved, slender, trim legs. I thought she would bring a high price. She was the one who had said, "I am frightened." I did not blame her. First, she was a virgin. Secondly, it would terrify almost any lovely girl to be presented in such a costume before Gorean men.

We moved down another place on the bench.

"The sales go rapidly," said a girl farther down, to my left. That was a good sign. For one thing, it meant that the auctioneer would be in a good humor and that, thus, he would probably be less cruel with us on the block. We fear the auctioneer. On the block he is our master. Even when a girl is not sold, if the sales have gone well, she is less likely to be whipped.

"Move," said the slaver's man.

We moved again.

Most girls are sold singly, but sometimes they are sold in groups, in matched pairs or larger sets, usually with a theme, such as blond hair or a given dialect. Sets may also be composed of girls once of complementary castes or those marked with diverse, representative brands. When a girl is enslaved she loses caste, of course, as well as citizenship, rights and personhood; when she is enslaved she becomes an animal, subject to the whips and wills of masters. Most groups, however, are sold for field and kitchen work. The Curulean did not handle such latter groups. We did have two pairs to be sold tonight, one consisting of a singer and her lyre player, and another of identical twins, from the island of Tabor, named for its resemblance to the small Gorean drum of that name.

I could not yet hear the calls of the auctioneer. The occasional response of the crowd, however, carried through the tunnel.

The girl on my left, the slender, virginal girl, in fluff, began to cry. Instantly the slaver's man was upon her, lifting his whip. She shrank back against the cement wall. She must not stain or smear her make-up. Angrily, with a small cloth, he dabbed her face. "Save your tears for the block, sleek little animal," he said. "Yes, Master," she said.

I was Girl 91 on the chain. It was a good position. The sales begin in the early evening and usually, unless there is something special for sale, they begin a bit slowly. Men are, commonly, still entering the market at that point. Often the seats are not entirely filled until the second Ahn of the sale. I was a bit puzzled about the apparent speed of the sales. There was, as far as I knew, nothing special for sale this evening. It was, as far as I knew, a normal night at the market. At any rate, usually, it is not regarded as desirable to be among the first twenty girls on the chain; sometimes these are sold to an almost half-empty house; a reciprocity tends to become involved; the slavers tend to put their least valuable girls up first, because of the smallness of the house in the early market, and many men tend to come later because, normally, the least interesting girls are put up first; this often presents a merchandising dilemma but it was not one which hurt the slavers of the Curulean very much, for their merchandise tends to be generally of high quality and the reputation of their house is such that, even in the early hours of the market, they tend to have a sizable number of bidders on hand. Sometimes an extraordinary girl or girls are marketed almost immediately, to encourage buyers to come early. Although this does tend to bring in larger early crowds the slavers feel that, often, they do not get on these girls what they might have, had their sale taken place later in the evening, in the heat and press of more determined bidding. At any rate, from the girl's point of view, any chain position after forty and before one hundred would be good. The ideal, of course, is to be sold at the height of the sale. With one hundred and twenty girls the most serious bidding would presumably come somewhere between Girl 80 and Girl 95. Late in the sale, of course, it is not uncommon for buyers to be weary and to begin to drift away. These remarks, incidentally, pertain to a normal "long" sale, usually held four times a week at a large house. They are not meant to apply to special sales, private sales, and in-house sales. Sometimes special sales, well-publicized, are held, in which as few as fifteen or twenty girls, of great quality or interest, are sold. All Ar, it is said, tries to fill the house upon such occasions. If a Ubara of a conquered city, for example, were to be sold, it would, customarily, be in such a special sale, unless the victorious Ubar, he who had conquered her city and captured her, chose to have her sold, for his amusement, in a common sale and from an unimportant block. Normally, of course, the conquering Ubar would keep such a regal wench, now collared and debased to slavery, in his own pleasure gardens, as a delicious memento of his victory, and as a woman.

"Stand," said the slaver's man.

My group stood.

"Move to the next position," he said.

We hurried to the next position.

We were now coffled in groups of ten. Early in the sale, for the first twenty girls, the chain had been intact, one chain for us all. With each sale we had moved one position. Each time we had moved one or two positions on the bench we knew that one or two of our sisters had been sold. The psychological effect of this, methodical and relentless, tends to produce anticipation and anxiety, even in an experienced girl. No girl ever grows completely used to being exhibited and sold. Then, after the first twenty girls, when our nerves were keen and taut, we were separated into coffles of ten. We might then seem to relax. But when our nerves had eased and we might seem to breathe a bit more easily, the coffle, as a whole, would be ordered to its feet and moved ten spaces toward the end of the tunnel. The effect of this, being for a time relatively at ease, and then being forced suddenly to move ten times closer to the block tends, suddenly, to whet one's fears and anticipations anew; when one, psychologically, in spite of herself, had begun to feel a little safe one is suddenly hurried even closer to her exhibition and sale, and all it means, the uncertainty, the danger, the not knowing, the being sold, the being owned anew, by someone who can do with you what he pleases.

I could now hear the calls of the auctioneer quite clearly. I could hear individuals, too, in the crowd. A vendor was hawking sherbets.

I was now in the point coffle, that at the end of the tunnel. The sales were doing well.

The girl to my right, she in the house tunic, sat tense beside me. Her fingernails dug into the wood of the bench. Her make-up was inspected and touched up. Then she was removed from the coffle, the collar, and the length of chain on her left, attaching her to me, placed to one side. A man stood near the end of the tunnel, with a tablet and marking stick. He indicated that she should approach him. She did. He inspected her chain number, used in the Curulean as a sales number, which, tiny, was written under her left ear in lipstick. The Curulean does not use sales collars. She was Girl 90.

I heard a roar of approval and I knew the girl on the block had been sold. Another girl, Girl 89, had been waiting at the foot of the block. A man with a whip prodded her to climb to its height. She moved carefully, feeling the stairs, creeping upward. She wore a slave scarf, as a blindfold. It was all she wore. The man with the tablet quickly thrust the girl in the house tunic from the tunnel to the foot of the stairs leading to the block.

"Look at me," said a man.

I sat very still, looking at him. He examined my make-up. Deftly, he improved it.

"You are beautiful," he said.

"Thank you, Master," I whispered.

Another man removed my collar, with the chain that fastened me to the girl on my left, the virginal girl in a bit of white fluff. The man with the tablet indicated that I should stand near him, and I did. From where I stood, at the end of the tunnel, I could see the ceiling of the Curulean, and some of the buyers, crowded in the higher tiers.

Their excitement frightened me. The sales were going too well.

The crowd roared. The girl on the block, naked, was being forced to perform blindfolded before the men.

She screamed with misery when the blindfold was removed, looking out upon buyers.

She was soon sold.

The girl in the house tunic was hurried to the height of the block.

"What have we here?" cried the auctioneer. "Surely there is some mistake. This is only a meaningless little house slave!"

The crowd roared with laughter.

The man with the tablet listened intently. He did not order me immediately to the foot of the stairs, those leading to the surface of the great block at the Curulean.

He glanced back at the slender, frightened girl, in the bit of white fluff, still in chain and collar, on the bench. She looked away from him, frightened, looking straight ahead.

I wished my hair were longer.

I listened to the sale of the girl in the house tunic. It would soon be torn from her.

"Number," said the man with the tablet to me.

I turned, and put my head to the side, that he might read the tiny number printed in lipstick beneath my left ear.

"Ninety-one," he said. He jotted it down on the sales sheets.

I heard the tunic torn from the girl on the block, the roar of the crowd.

She was now being exhibited naked.

The man with the tablet thrust me toward the foot of the block, and I stumbled to the place at the foot of its stairs. I stood, that I not disarrange the bands of silk so cunningly looped about me. The man with the tablet had apparently decided not to alter the order of sales. I think this was wise on his part. The girl in the house tunic, seemingly not yet broken in, not yet humbled and trained to the collar of pleasure, might have whetted the appetite of the buyers for an even more virginal, innocent form of merchandise, but, on the block, as I gathered from the remarks of the auctioneer and the responses of the crowd there was now little illusion left lingering of her formality or restraint, or reluctance; only too clearly, she starved for male domination, was she eager and ready for the slave ring at the foot of a man's couch.

Then she was sold.

I climbed to the height of the block. The block was very large. I had not realized how many were in the crowd. The crowd was silent. This frightened me.

The auctioneer seemed puzzled, too, but only momentarily. "Someone, it seems," he said, "has sent us a gift." He indicated me with the whip. "Its contours," he said, "suggest that it is lovely." He looked out to the crowd. "Shall we see?" he asked.

But the crowd, instead of urging him on, was quiet. His hand shook for a moment. I was frightened. I did not understand the mood of the crowd.

"Let us see," he continued, with feigned humor. He lifted away loops of silk which concealed my head. There was a murmur of admiration from the crowd. I was too vain not to have been pleased. "A lovely face," he said, "feminine, soft, vulnerable, expressive. It would be easy to read in order to control her." He shrugged. "The hair, of course," said he, "is far too short, but I am assured, by officers of the Curulean, that it will grow."

There was no laughter from the crowd.

The auctioneer's hand trembled. He was nervous. I thrust my right leg forward, lifting it, pointing the toes, touching only the toes of my right foot to the floor. My left hip was turned out. I lifted and extended my left arm, wrist bent, palm to the left.

Gracefully then did he unloop, bit by bit, the silk from my left arm.

"A lovely limb," he said.

The crowd seemed quiet, intense, watchful. The auctioneer was clearly disturbed.

"Let us see if there is more of interest here," he said.

I heard an intake of breath from the crowd, but there were no bids.

We did not complete the choreography which had been planned. Much depends upon the crowd. It interacts in the drama of the block in a way that it, or many of its members, fails to understand. The auctioneer, puzzled, finally removed from my person the bands of silk. He did not spin me from them; he did not roll me from them at his feet.

"This is the woman," he said. "What am I bid?"

There was no bid.

"Look!" cried a voice. The crowd turned, and I, and the auctioneer, looked as well. At the height of the center aisle, high, framed in the portal of the market hall, stood a warrior, in full panoply of war. He did not speak. He carried shield and spear. On his left shoulder hung the scabbard of the short sword. He was helmeted.

"Master?" inquired the auctioneer. His voice faltered.

The warrior did not speak.

The auctioneer indicated me, taking his attention from the figure who had recently entered the hall.

"This is the woman," he said, weakly. "What am I bid?"

At this point the helmeted warrior began to descend the aisle. We watched him approach.

In moments he stood, too, on the block, facing the crowd. He struck the butt of his great spear on the heavy wood. "Kajira canjellne!" he said. "Slave girl challenge!" He turned to look at me, and I knelt. I could not speak. I feared I might faint.

He turned again to face the crowd.

"I will have this woman," he said. "For her I will stand against all Ar, and all the world."

"I love you, Clitus Vitellius!" I cried, tears in my eyes.

"You were not given permission to speak!" cried the auctioneer. He lifted his whip to strike me.

But the point of the spear of Clitus Vitellius lay at his throat. "Do not strike her," said Clitus Vitellius.

"Yes, Master," said the auctioneer, white-faced, lowering his arm, frightened, backing away.

Clitus Vitellius turned again to face the crowd of Ar. "Kajira canjellne," he said. "Slave girl challenge."

There was no response from the crowd. Then one man rose to his feet, striking his left shoulder. And then another rose to his feet and did the same, and another and another. Soon the crowd was on its feet, cheering and striking their left shoulders. Clitus Vitellius stood straight on that great platform, his great, circular shield on his left arm, his mighty spear, seven feet in length, headed in tapering bronze, grasped in his right hand. His head was high, his eyes were shrewd and clear, those of a warrior.

"She is yours, Master," said the auctioneer to Clitus Vitellius.

I knelt at his feet, joyfully. He would now free me, and take me as his companion. He put aside his shield and spear, to lift me to my feet as his equal.

"Your whip," said Clitus Vitellius to the auctioneer.

"You did not wish her whipped," he said.

"She is mine to whip," said Clitus Vitellius. The auctioneer placed his whip in the hands of Clitus Vitellius.

"Master?" I said.

"Yes?" he said.

"Are you not going to free me?" I asked.

"Only a fool," he said, "frees a slave girl."

"Master!" I cried.

"Kneel to the whip," he said.

I obeyed. I put my head down, and, beneath my body, crossed my wrists, as though they were bound. My back was bowed, ready for whatever punishment he might see fit to administer to me. I was in consternation. I trembled. Could I be still a slave girl? Could he be serious? Was it his intention to keep me still as a slave?

Surely not. Surely not!

"I would not wish you to take a loss on her," he was saying to the auctioneer. "Here is something which may cover the cost of the miserable little slave."

I heard a pouch, heavy, filled with metal, strike heavily on the smoothed beams of the surface of the block.

"The gratitude of the house, Master!" cried the auctioneer. He untied the strings of the pouch and, crying out with pleasure, spilled coins of gold to the wood. Swiftly he sorted the coins, expertly. "There are a hundred tarn disks of gold here!" he cried.

The crowd roared its approval.

I cried, tears falling to the wood of the block, mixing in the sawdust. It was ten to a hundred times, or more, what I was worth. I saw then the extent of the regard of Clitus Vitellius for me. I wept with joy.

I had not known that a man could desire a woman so much. Yet he kept me as a slave!

Perhaps it is only a slave who can be so bought and sold, and so desired.

Oh, the indescribable, incredible feeling of being owned, literally owned, by a man!

I knelt, a slave ready for punishment.

"Master is far too generous," said the auctioneer. "This is far more than the slave is worth."

"You are right," said Clitus Vitellius.

I shook with fury, but did not break the position.

"Give me the next then, too, on your chain," he said.

"No!" I cried.

He turned to face me, and, again, I swiftly lowered my head. Could he truly mean to keep me as a slave? Could he truly be that strong? I could not believe it.

"Gladly," cried the auctioneer. "Ninety-two," he cried.

The virginal girl, slender, sweetly shouldered, lovely legged, terrified, crept to the surface of the block. The bit of fluff clung about her. It did not much conceal her. Her legs were well exposed to the inspection of masters, and the sweetness of her breasts was evident, it but scarcely concealed in the wafting of insinuative, tantalizing fluff.

The crowd roared its approval, and she shrank back on the block. I wondered what men saw in her. She was herself only a bit of fluff, to rape and serve.

"Come here," said Clitus Vitellius to the girl.

Swiftly she fled to him, to stand before him.

"Position," he snapped.

She dropped to her knees before him, in the position of the pleasure slave.

"Get your back straighter," he said. She did so.

He crouched beside her and, with his belt knife, cut away the strings which held the fluff about her. It floated to the surface of the block, stirring in the slight movements of air.

He regarded the girl. He then looked, too, to me. "I will take both," he said.

"Master!" I cried in protest.

Then he stood over me, with the whip.

I looked up into his eyes. Then I was frightened. I saw that he was a Gorean master. However much he might hold me in regard, however much he might desire me, I saw that I could be to him only a helpless slave girl. Whatever might be his feelings for me I saw that he would have me only at his feet as a slave. I would be uncompromisingly owned. He would have all, fully, from me. I would not be permitted to hold anything back, ever. He would be master, and I slave. No longer did I dare to suggest that I might be freed. No longer did I dare to think it. He was Gorean.

I put my head down, kneeling to the whip.

"Forgive me, Master," I whispered.

"Once this evening," said he, "you, a slave, addressed me by my name, rather than as 'Master.'"

"Forgive me, Master," I said. I trembled. I recalled I had cried out, "I love you, Clitus Vitellius!" How foolish I had been. It was a girl's mistake. It would not go unnoticed.

"Too," he said, "more than once this evening you have spoken without permission."

"Yes, Master," I said.

"Too," said he, "I think you dared to protest this evening my purchase of a girl."

I had indeed done so!

"Do you oppose your will to mine, or question my will in the least?" he asked.

"No, Master," I said.

"Do you think me an easy master?" he asked.

"No, Master," I said.

"Do you beg now to be punished?" he asked.

"Yes, Master," I said. "I beg to be punished."

I saw him grip the slave whip on the long handle with two hands. I put down my head further, I shut my eyes, I tightened my body, I clenched my fists, held crossed, as though bound, beneath my body.

I determined to hold position.

I heard the swift sound of the leather in flight. Never had I heard it approach so swiftly. After the fourth blow I could no longer hold position. "Tie me at the slave ring," I begged. "Put me at a post, Master!" I lay on the block on my stomach, my hands over my head. There was sawdust on my lips and face. I could not, after the second blow, scream. Yet he struck me only ten times. I cried, lying on the block, punished. I felt him thrust a steel collar about my throat, and lock it.

I was collared. He had not been angry with me. He had only been punishing me. I had deserved a whipping. He had given it to me.

Yet it is hard for a girl to grow used to the leather. One can be a slave for years and still fear it. The Gorean master uses it unhesitatingly if we are not pleasing. We know that he will do so. We are pleasing.

Clitus Vitellius had turned to the slender, virginal girl. "Do you wish to be in the least troublesome?" he asked her, lifting the whip, laughing.

"No, Master!" she cried.

He collared her, as he had done me. We both wore his collar. He knelt us together. "I submit, fully, Master," I said. "I submit, fully, Master," said the virginal girl, quickly, following my example.

The slave whip lay to one side.

"We have surely delayed the sales of the Curulean too long," said Clitus Vitellius, to the auctioneer.

The auctioneer bowed, the pouch of gold in his hand.

"Come, Slaves," said Clitus Vitellius to the two of us, naked in his collar.

He lifted his shield and took up his spear, and then descended the steps of the great block. We followed him. He ascended the long aisle leading from the hall. Men cried out his name, and cheered, and smote their left shoulders, as he passed them. He strode as a Warrior. We hurried after him, his slave girls.

"Will he march us through the streets naked?" asked the virginal girl.

"He will do with us as he pleases," I told her. "He is a Warrior."

Twenty-Nine

A Warrior's Vengeance;
The Furs of My Master

We were but four bridges from the Towers of the Warriors when Clitus Vitellius turned suddenly, regarding me. I stopped, suddenly, naked, behind him, where I was heeling him. The virginal girl, too, stopped suddenly. But he did not look at her. He approached me. He stood before me, his shield on his left arm, the mighty spear grasped in his right hand. Immediately I trembled, and knelt, head down.

"Oh!" cried the virginal girl. He, placing the spear and shield to one side, had moved to her and was tying her hands behind her back. He fastened her by the wrists to a ring at the foot of the Four Lamps bridge. Such rings are common in Gorean cities, in public places, and serve the convenience of masters in tethering their slaves. The ring was mounted on a post, about a yard high. She stood at the post, naked, tethered there, her hands fastened behind her back, at the foot of the Four Lamps bridge. I could see the lights of glorious Ar. The light of one lamp was upon her. She was very beautiful. "Master?" she begged.

He took a blunt marking stick from his pouch and wrote Gorean words on her left shoulder.

He then, to her amazement, and mine, removed his collar from her throat.

"Master?" she sobbed.

He replaced the collar and marking stick in his pouch. "Can you read?" he asked her.

"Yes," she said.

"Read then what I have inscribed upon your body," said he.

"I cannot well see it, Master," she said. "But from the feel of it in my flesh, I know what you have written."

"Speak it aloud," said he, "Slave."

"You have written 'Collar me. Own me,'" she said.

"Yes," he said.

"You are leaving me here for the first stranger who passes, Master?" she asked.

"Do you object, Slave?" he asked.

"No, Master!" she said, drawing back. The point of the spear, which Clitus Vitellius had now retrieved, was at her throat.

I then felt the point of the spear in my back. "On your feet, Slave," he said.

Swiftly I rose to my feet.

He then strode past me, and began the crossing of the bridge of Four Lamps. I hastened to follow him, heeling him obediently. I did turn, on the crest of the bridge, to look back at the tethered girl. The area at the foot of the bridge was deserted. It was late. She seemed very much alone there, naked, the light of the lamp on her, tethered, waiting for the first individual who might chance by.

I turned away, hurrying to follow Clitus Vitellius. I remembered the look he had given me when first, moments ago, he had stopped and turned, and approached me. Never had I seen such lust, possessiveness and desire in a man's eyes. I felt weak. I wondered about the service of how many girls I would have to render to him. He had cast aside the virginal girl, arrogantly, in a warrior's gesture, leaving her for whomsoever might find and desire her. Her slave service, and mine, and more, he would now want from me. I did not know if I could be so much a slave to him.

We were but a short way from the Towers of Warriors, on the third of its approaching high bridges, when again Clitus Vitellius turned and faced me.

"I cannot wait," he said to me.

"Yes, Master," I said. We were on a high bridge, one of the highest in all Ar. The lights of the city were strewn beneath us; above us burned the stars of Gor.

He placed his shield upon the bridge, straps down, its convex surface like a bow facing the stars.

He indicated that I should take my position upon it, and I did so, my head down. With the straps, brought about the sides of the great shield he fastened my wrists apart, one on each side, about at shoulder level, at the edges of the shield. I lay over the shield, bound upon it.

"Now I have you where I want you, Dina," said he, "Earth girl."

"Yes, Master," I said.

Swiftly he took me in his arms. I yielded immediately to my master.

"I love you, Master," I said to him.

His hands were upon my shoulders. He dragged me upward to his pressing mouth, pulling me against the wrist straps which held my wrists at the shield's edges. I thought he might tear me from the shield. Then he flung me back, arched across its surface. I felt his lips at my belly and thighs. I could not protect myself from the fierce ardor to which I must submit. Then again I cried out, lost in my slave's love of him, my master.

He unbound my wrists from the shield. He thrust me from its surface. I rolled to my side, on the bridge. I lay quietly on the bridge, in his collar.

"It is getting late," he said. "I must get you to the love furs."

"Yes, Master," I said.

"Get up," he said. He moved his foot against my body.

I tried to get up, but could scarcely stand. I sank to my hands and knees.

He laughed at me.

I sank to my side. I lifted my hand to him.

"Get up, Earth girl," he said.

"I will try, Master," I said.

But again I fell to my knees.

"Do not beat me, Master," I begged. "You have made me so weak."

"I can smell your weakness," he said.

"Yes, Master," I said. I was so overcome by my love for him that I could not stand. I had never known such weakness. I felt I had the strength only to lie vulnerably before him, perhaps holding and kissing him, awaiting him. It is, I suppose, one of nature's utilities, reducing the female's effectiveness in self-defense or flight, putting her all the more at the mercy of the stronger beast.

"I cannot walk, Master," I said. "Let me crawl to your furs."

He slung his shield upon his back, and tied his spear, too, beneath the shield's edge, upon his back.

I felt myself lifted gently into his arms. He carried me, my head against his left shoulder, over the bridge and toward the second bridge, leading to the Towers of the Warriors.

I served him wine.

I was the only girl in his compartments. I well understood the meaning of this. He had chosen the perfection of one man, the complete master, and one woman, the total slave. It is called the perfect bondage, each all and perfect to the other.

It is right for some men, and not for others. Much depends on whether the man has met his perfect slave and the woman her perfect master.

Clitus Vitellius and I, though I would not have dared tell him, were so related. I think he, too, knew this.

When I had served him wine he gave me, too, to drink of the cup. This was, in its way, a great honor, and a token of his recognition as to how I stood to him. I still, of course, did not dare to drink from the same edge of the cup as he, the master.

I put the cup aside.

At his indication I spread the love furs. I did not spread them upon the couch but at its foot. I was slave. Only a small lamp burned in the compartment.

I had lit it earlier.

It was the lamp of love.

I had knelt naked before him, in his collar. I had put my head down to his feet, and had kissed them. "May my Master's slave light the lamp of love?" I had asked.

"Yes," he had said.

At a gesture from Clitus Vitellius I reclined upon the furs, at the foot of the couch.

He slipped away his tunic and crouched beside me. I could see he could scarcely restrain himself from seizing me.

"I'm yours," I told him. I lifted my arms to him. "Take me, Master," I said.

"I care for you," he said.

I regarded him. "Be strong with me, Master," I whispered. "I do not want to challenge you. I do not want to fight you. I want to serve you, and I want to love you. I want to give you all, holding back nothing, ever."

He regarded me.

"Do you not understand, Master?" I asked. "If I had the choice, I would choose not to be free but to be your slave." A woman, I had learned, must choose between freedom and love. Both are estimable virtues. Let each choose which is best for her.

"But I do not give you a choice," he said.

"Of course not, Master," I said. "You are Gorean."

He looked down at the furs.

"Perhaps I will sell you," he said.

"You may do as you wish, Master," I said. I knew I was at his complete mercy, only a bond girl.

He seemed angry.

"Bring me wine, Master," I said.

He looked at me, suddenly.

"A girl is only testing her master," I smiled.

Suddenly he struck me, slapping me cruelly across the mouth. It hurt me. I tasted a bit of blood.

"Do you think," he asked, "that because I care for you I will not be strong with you?"

"No, Master," I said.

I lay in the shadow of the slave ring. A chain and heavy collar lay at the foot of the ring, the chain attached to the ring.

He took the heavy metal collar and closed it about my throat, over and about the lighter collar I wore, confining me at the ring, on the furs at the foot of his couch.

Then he touched me.

"I see you will be strong with me, Master," I said.

"What a fool I am," he said, "to care for a miserable Earth-girl slave."

"I ask only to love and serve you, Master," I said.

"Yet you are attractive," he said.

"A girl is grateful to her master, should he find her pleasing," I said.

"So you would choose to be a slave?" he asked.

"Yes, Master," I said.

"Slut," said he.

"Yes, Master," I said.

"It is I who will decide," he said.

"Yes, Master," I said.

"I decide—" he said.

"Yes, Master," I begged.

"—that you are my slave."

"Yes, Master!" I cried.

Then I writhed in his arms as he took me, exploding in the deepest and most profound ecstasies a female can know, those of the slave orgasm, known only to the owned woman.

"How could I love you so much," he asked, "if I did not truly own you, if you were not fully mine?"

"I do not know, Master," I said. Clitus Vitellius had confessed his love for a slave. I hoped he would not now beat me.

He took me by the hair and thrust my head down to the furs. "A man can truly love only that woman," he said, "who is truly his, who belongs to him. Otherwise he is only a party to a contract."

"A woman," I said, "can love only that man to whom she truly belongs."

"To whom do you truly belong, Slave?" he asked.

"To you, Master," I said.

"You please me, Slave Girl," he said.

"Free me," I said, teasing him.

"Do you wish to feel the whip?" he asked.

"No, Master," I said, quickly, suddenly frightened. I was his. He might do to me what he wanted.

"Beg for your freedom," he said.

"Please free me, Master," I begged.

He laughed. "No," he said. "I do not free you. I will keep you as my slave."

I closed my eyes. I had been Judy Thornton, of Earth. I had been a coed at a small but prestigious college. I had been an English major. I had written poetry. I had been popular on campus. Now I was only a branded slave girl, Dina, helpless in the arms of her master. I thought of Elicia Nevins, who had been my beauty rival at the college. She now, too, wore a collar. I wondered if she were as happy in the arms of her master as I in the arms of mine. She had been an anthropologist. I wondered if now she truly understood, perhaps for the first time, the nature of the institution of slavery. Her master had perhaps taught her. I lay blissfully in the arms of Clitus Vitellius, owned.

I opened my eyes.

"Is a girl not to be permitted sometimes to speak her mind?" I asked.

"Perhaps upon occasion," said Clitus Vitellius, "provided she does so upon her knees and at my feet."

"You are a monster, Master," I said.

Then again I felt his body at mine, and I cried out as my legs were thrust apart.

"You are rough, Master!" I chided. Then, frightened, I said, "Forgive me, Master."

He did not beat me.

I began to respond to him, shuddering under the blows of his manhood, and surrendered myself then, content, to the delicious brutality of my ravishment.

He had many ways of taking me, and I must submit to them all, unquestioningly.

We heard men later upon the bridges outside. It was early morning.

I held Clitus Vitellius. "You are very lustful, Master," I told him.

"I am shamed neither by my health nor vitality," he said. He said this as a Gorean, explaining something to an ignorant Earth-girl slave. "And you," he said, "you must know, are an exquisitely responsive she-sleen. Does that shame you?"

"Not any more, Master," I said.

"It is an indication of your vitality and health, and emotional freedom," he said. "It is a sign that you are vigorous and sound, neither psychologically crippled nor diseased."

I had grown free on Gor, though I wore a collar. Strange, collared, I was free. Uncollared I had been a true slave, a prisoner of a pathological culture, ascetic, mechanistic and twisted.

"Perhaps I am emotionally free," I laughed. "But I scarcely am physically free."

"True," he said. He pulled me by the chain at the back of the collar back to my back on the furs at the foot of his couch.

"You keep me a slave?" I asked.

"Of course," he said.

"I never knew I would meet a man who could lust for me and desire me so much," I said, "that he would keep me as a slave."

"You never knew you would meet a man who would satisfy your deepest needs," he said, "the hidden, profound, scarcely understood, secret needs which you yourself scarcely recognized."

"You are a secret dream, which I scarcely dared dream, come true to me, Master," I said.

"And you to me, Slave," said he.

"Will you truly be hard with me, Master?" I asked.

"Yes," he said.

"Will you truly, though you care for me, keep me as full slave?"

"Yes, Slave," he said.

"Subject even to discipline, if I displease you?" I asked.

"Subject to discipline, at my pleasure, whether you displease me or not," he said.

"My bondage then will be absolute," I said.

"Of course, Slave," he said.

I reached out timidly, to touch him. I kissed him, tenderly, on the shoulder.

"I love you, Master," I said.

"Be silent, Slave," he said, irritably.

"Yes, Master," I said.

He then touched me with sweetness, and tenderness, and I held him closely, but did not speak, lost in his touch, for I, a slave, had been forbidden to speak. He made gentle love to me then, which, I knew, might become abrupt or brutal as he chose. There were a thousand ways to have a slave girl and I did not doubt but what Clitus Vitellius was master of them all. How joyful I was. He was dominant over me. I was subject to him. I was his, completely without qualification. It is impossible for me to express my feelings. Perhaps this is why he had warned me to silence, that I might not try to speak, but would be content to feel what could not, in any language, be spoken. So I did not then try to speak, but, rather, contented myself with turning to the tasks of love.

About the Author

John Norman, born in Chicago, Illinois, in 1931, is the creator of the Gorean Saga, the longest running series of adventure novels in science fiction history. Starting in December 1966 with *Tarnsman of Gor*, the series was put on hold after its twenty-fifth installment, *Magicians of Gor*, in 1988, when DAW refused to publish its successor, *Witness of Gor*. After several unsuccessful attempts to find a trade publishing outlet, the series was brought back into print in 2001. Norman has also produced a separate, three installment science fiction series, the Telnarian Histories, plus two other fiction works (*Ghost Dance* and *Time Slave*), a nonfiction paperback (*Imaginative Sex*), and a collection of thirty short stories, entitled Norman *Invasions*. The *Totems of Abydos* was published in spring 2012.

All of Norman's work is available both in print and as ebooks. The Internet has proven to be a fertile ground for the imagination of Norman's ever-growing fan base, and at Gor Chronicles (www.gorchronicles.com), a website specially created for his tremendous fan following, one may read everything there is to know about this unique fictional culture.

Norman is married and has three children.

OPEN **ROAD**

INTEGRATED MEDIA

Open Road Integrated Media is a digital publisher and multimedia content company. Open Road creates connections between authors and their audiences by marketing its ebooks through a new proprietary online platform, which uses premium video content and social media.

Videos, Archival Documents, and New Releases

Sign up for the Open Road Media newsletter and get news delivered straight to your inbox.

Sign up now at
www.openroadmedia.com/newsletters

CPSIA information can be obtained
at www.ICGtesting.com
Printed in the USA
JSHW021941171121
20545JS00001B/10